He was a slightly fat man with a dishonest smile that pulled the corners of his mouth out half an inch leaving the thick lips tight and his eyes bleak. For a fattish man he had a slow walk. Most fat men are brisk and light on their feet. He wore a gray herringbone suit and a hand-painted tie with part of a diving girl visible on it. His shirt was clean, which comforted me, and his brown loafers, as wrong as the tie for his suit, shone from a recent polishing.

He sidled past me as I held the door between the waiting room and my thinking parlor. Once inside, he took a quick look around. I'd have placed him as a mobster, second grade, if I had been asked. For once I was right. If he carried a gun, it was inside his pants. His coat was too tight to hide the bulge of an underarm holster.

He sat down carefully and I sat opposite and we looked at each other. His face had a sort of foxy eagerness. He was sweating a little. The expression on my face was meant to be interested but not clubby. I reached for a pipe and the leather humidor in which I kept my Pearce's tobacco. I pushed cigarettes at him.

"I don't smoke." He had a rusty voice. I didn't like it any more than I liked his clothes, or his face. While I filled the pipe he reached inside his coat, prowled in a pocket, came out with a bill, glanced at it and dropped it across the desk in front of me. It was a nice bill and clean and new. One thousand dollars.

"Ever save a guy's life?"

—from "Wrong Pigeon" by Raymond Chandler

THE BEST OF MANHUNT 3

FEATURES STORIES BY
RAYMOND CHANDLER,
REX STOUT AND A
NEWLY DISCOVERED
STORY BY GIL BREWER

EDITED BY
JEFF VORZIMMER
INTRODUCTION
BY JEFF VORZIMMER
AND DAVID RACHELS

STARK HOUSE

Stark House Press • Eureka California
www.starkhousepress.com

THE BEST OF MANHUNT 3
Published by Stark House Press
1315 H Street
Eureka, CA 95501
griffinskye3@sbcglobal.net
www.starkhousepress.com

The Best of Manhunt 3 ©2022 by Jeff Vorzimmer
"Who Was Roy Carroll?" ©2022 by Jeff Vorzimmer & David Rachels

"Old Willie," "Services Rendered," "The Faceless Man" and "Throwback," ©1953 Flying Eagle Publications. "Comeback" ©1954 Flying Eagle Publications. "Tin Can" ©1954 Flying Eagle Publications and ©1965 Volitant Publishing Services. "I Didn't See a Thing" and "The Reluctant Client" ©1955 Flying Eagle Publications. "His Own Hand," ©1956 Flying Eagle Publications. Copyright renewed May 16, 1983 Reprinted courtesy of the literary estate of Rex Stout. "Split It Three Ways," "Seven Lousy Bucks" and "The Secret" ©1956 Flying Eagle Publications. "Death Wears a Gray Sweater" ©1956 Flying Eagle Publications. Reprinted courtesy of the literary estate of Gil Brewer. "Joy Ride" ©1957 Mercury Publications. "College Kill," "He's Never Stopped Running," and "Stolen Star" ©1957 Flying Eagle Publications. "Hooked" ©1958 Flying Eagle Publications. Copyright Renewed Nov 7, 1986. Reprinted with permission of the Robert Turner estate. "One Hour Late" and "Down and Out," "Custody," copyright © 1955, 1983 by the Estate of Richard Deming; first appeared in *Manhunt*, December 1955; reprinted by permission of Wildside Press and the Virginia Kidd Agency, Inc. "The Red Herring," copyright © 1963, 1991 by the Estate of Richard Deming; first appeared in *Manhunt*, December 1963; reprinted by permission of Wildside Press and the Virginia Kidd Agency, Inc. ©1959 Flying Eagle Publications. "Wrong Pigeon," (a.k.a., "The Pencil"): a short story by Raymond Chandler. Copyright ©1987, The Estate of Raymond Chandler. Reproduced by permission of the author c/o Rogers, Coleridge & White Ltd. "Hangover" ©1960 Flying Eagle Publications. Copyright renewed Dec 28, 1988. "How Much to Kill?" "Deadly Triangle" and "The Big Haul," ©1960 Flying Eagle Publications. "Eye-Witness" ©1962 Flying Eagle Publications. "Vegas . . . and Run" ©1963 Flying Eagle Publications. "The Grass Cage" ©1964 Flying Eagle Publications. Copyright renewed Feb 4, 1991. Reprinted with Permission of the Alter Estate and the Sternig & Byrne Literary Agency.

ISBN: 979-8-8860-1003-9

Book design by *¡caliente!design*, Austin, Texas

PUBLISHER'S NOTE:
This is a work of fiction. Names, characters, places and incidents are either the products of the author's imagination or used fictionally, and any resemblance to actual persons, living or dead, events or locales, is entirely coincidental. Without limiting the rights under copyright reserved above, no part of this publication may be reproduced, stored, or introduced into a retrieval system or transmitted in any form or by any means (electronic, mechanical, photocopying, recording or otherwise) without the prior written permission of both the copyright owner and the above publisher of the book.

Stark House Press Edition: December 2022

Table of Contents

Introduction	Jeff Vorzimmer & David Rachels	7
Old Willie	William P. McGivern	15
Services Rendered	Jonathan Craig	20
The Faceless Man	Michael Fessier	30
Throwback	Donald Hamilton	40
Comeback	R. Van Taylor	48
Tin Can	B. Traven	55
I Didn't See a Thing	Hal Ellson	65
His Own Hand	Rex Stout	78
The Reluctant Client	Brett Halliday	89
Custody	Richard Deming	98
Split it Three Ways	Walter Kaylin	106
Seven Lousy Bucks	C. L. Sweeney	112
The Secret	Stuart Friedman	118
Death Wears a Gray Sweater	Gil Brewer writing as Roy Carroll	130
Joy Ride	C. B. Gilford	145
College Kill	Jack Q. Lynn	154
He's Never Stopped Running	Aaron Mark Stein	168
Stolen Star	William Campbell Gault	178
Hooked	Robert Turner	195
One Hour Late	William O'Farrell	212
Down and Out	Joe Gores	261
Wrong Pigeon	Raymond Chandler	274
Hangover	Charles Runyon	299
How Much to Kill?	Michael Zuroy	309
Deadly Triangle	Les Collins	320
The Big Haul	Robert Page Jones	327
Eye Witness	Charles Sloan	370
The Red Herring	Richard Deming	395
Vegas . . . and Run	Don Lowry	420
The Grass Cage	Robert Edmond Alter	465

Who Was Roy Carroll?
Jeff Vorzimmer
David Rachels

September 2022

In the heyday of the pulps Roy Carroll was what was called a "house name," a pseudonym used when an author had more than one story in an issue of the magazine. The editor, not wanting an author to appear on the masthead more than once, would use a pseudonym for the additional story, or the "house name," if the author didn't have one of his own. In the case of *Manhunt* that house name was Roy Carroll.

The identity of Roy Carroll has often been assigned to Robert Turner as if it were not a house name but his alone. In large part, this comes from a statement that Turner made in an article on the demise of *Manhunt*, "Requiem for a Magazine" (*The Mystery Lover's Newsletter*, August 1968):

> Several hours later, my agent called and told me that *Manhunt* was buying both stories, would run them both in the same issue; the short-short under the pseudonym of Roy Carrol [sic], which remained my "house name" there when I had more than one story in an issue, for a number of years.

On its surface, this statement is ambiguous. Roy Carroll could have been used not only as Turner's house name but for other writers as well. (The only rule for using house names is that they, too, cannot appear more than once in an issue!) But even if Turner did not mean that the name was exclusively his, he still overstates. A "number of years" implies a number of Turner stories credited to Roy Carroll, but a sidebar to Turner's later article on *Manhunt*, "The Not So Literary Digests" (*Xenophile*, March/April 1978), lists only two Turner stories credited to Roy Carroll: "Shakedown" (April 1953) and "Vacation Nightmare" (December 1956). Furthermore, Turner notes that he used this name "when [he] had more than one story in an issue," but there are four issues of *Manhunt* with stories by Roy Carroll but not Robert Turner: December 1953, May 1955, March 1956, and October 1959. This means, of course, that there is at least one more writer behind the name Roy Carroll. But who?

Gil Brewer was revealed as an additional Roy Carroll after his death in 1983, when his papers were made public. In the late 1950s, Brewer kept a log of his sales, which contained this entry:

(Gil Brewer Collection, American Heritage Center, University of Wyoming)

Brewer writes, "Shot—by-line Roy Carroll / 2 yarns in issue." So that settles that. But if there is one Gil Brewer story as by Roy Carroll, could there be others? Unfortunately, Brewer did not always indicate when stories were published under pseudonyms, nor did he always indicate when a story's title was changed. As a result, there are Brewer stories that have not been located. For example, this 7500-word *Manhunt* story from 1956 is missing from the Stark House volumes collecting Brewer's stories from the 1950s:

4/3   Evil Night   7500   Manhunt 4/25

(Gil Brewer Collection, American Heritage Center, University of Wyoming)

If "Evil Night" did, in fact, appear in *Manhunt*, then its title was changed and Brewer's name was not attached. What story could it be? Is it another Roy Carroll by-line?

Using the database of *Manhunt* stories created for *The Manhunt Companion*, we cross-referenced the authors who appear in the thirteen issues with Roy Carroll stories:

Authors Appearing in Four or More *Manhunt* Issues with Roy Carroll

Author	Number of Appearances
Robert Turner	7
Evan Hunter	6
Jonathan Craig	5
Gil Brewer	5
Richard Deming	4
Hal Ellson	4
Frank Kane	4

Evan Hunter seems an unlikely Roy Carroll because he had three pseudonyms of his own: Richard Marsten, Hunt Collins, and Ed McBain. Hunter often appeared alongside Carroll simply because he published so frequently in *Manhunt*. Richard Deming also had a pseudonym he used for multiple stories in *Manhunt*, Max Franklin, so he seems unlikely as well. This leaves Jonathan Craig and Gil Brewer, along with Robert Turner, as the most likely candidates for unattributed Roy Carroll stories. Of Craig and Brewer, Brewer was the natural candidate to investigate for three reasons: From his sales log, we knew that he had at least one unidentified *Manhunt* story; we already knew of one Brewer story published with the Roy Carroll by-line; and we had an archive of over 5000 e-books that included all of Brewer's known stories from the 1950s (as well as dozens of his later stories and many of his novels).

With all this data at hand and with the advent of inexpensive stylometry software, we thought it possible to identify the authors of the Roy Carroll stories among the 10 or 11 authors of the issues in which they appeared.

Stylometry uses statistical analysis of literary style to identify unknown authors. Stylometry is a fairly new science, dating to the advent of digitized texts, but it has been used to identify anonymous or pseudonymous authors of books such as *Primary Colors*, *The Cuckoo's Calling*, *The Federalist Papers*, and the Richard Bachman novels. Stylometry software compiles information such as lengths of words, sentences, and paragraphs; use of punctuation; word order; and recurring phrases. Stylometry cannot conclusively determine authorship, but it can identify the most likely candidate in a field of several.

Having read Gil Brewer exhaustively, we were already familiar with many of his tics, especially his habit of ending sentences with the word *now* preceded by a comma, as well as his love of the oxymoronic phrases *slimly plump* and *slimly lush*. It turns out that *lush* is one of Brewer's "cinnamon words," so named because of author Ray Bradbury's statistically significant use of *cinnamon* in his writing. Another often-cited cinnamon word is Vladimir Nabokov's *mauve*, which appears in his writing 44 times more frequently than in common usage. (There is even a book on stylometry titled *Nabokov's Favorite Word Is Mauve*.)

Over the last four years, we have used Regular Expressions (Regex), a search language, to compile stylometric search strings for not only Brewer but also many other *Manhunt* authors. Regex can be used to find variations on recurring patterns in an author's writing. Often we'll start with a word such as *slimly* and then build an expression to describe an author's phrasing uniquely so that only phrases from that author's work will be flagged. For example, searching Brewer's writings for *lush* turns up his often-used phrase *slimly lush*, and then a search for *slimly* yields the phrase *slimly plump* as well as the associated adjectives *voluptuous* and *curved*. Now we can use Regex to link these terms together in a search string that looks like this:

\bslim(ly)?\W+(?:\w+\W+){0,4}?(lush|plump|voluptuous|curved)\b

This search yields strings from twelve of Brewer's novels and short stories in our database:

> ...I watched the slimly-curved silken calves scissor...
> ...jouncing, and she was a slimly lush figure of a girl....
> ...She was long, slim, willowy, but plenty lush, too...
> ...her waist quite slim. She was plump in exactly the right...
> ...sheathing her slimly voluptuous body like filmy paint....
> ...Long-legged and slimly lush, with beautiful big ones...
> ...alive between her slimly plump thighs....
> ...smooth flesh. Her body was slim and lush at the same time....

...crossed, and they were slimly plump. Mrs. Loretta Brady was...
...denim shorts above slimly curved legs, an unbuttoned,...
...for now—for now she was slimly lush in her white cotton...
...mouth. She crossed her slimly-plump legs...
...her slim paleness looking somehow over-lush, provocative....
...shorts that bit into her slimly plump thighs, high up...
...most impossibly perfect, slimly lush, long-stemmed...
...the legs long and slimly lush, that taut red rims of...
...holding his hand on her slimly plump thigh. "I want you...
...pink nipples, slim waisted, and white, plump thighs...
...her hips and thighs slimly lush and round, her breasts...
...Impossibly slim waist, with a lush perfection of hip...

Two issues of *Manhunt*, November 1956 and May 1957, include Gil Brewer stories alongside unattributed stories by Roy Carroll. These issues also contain stories by Robert Turner. We began with the Roy Carroll story from November 1956, "Death Wears a Gray Sweater." An initial Regex search of this story flagged several Brewerisms, including his cinnamon words *frill-, nepenthe* and *silvery*, as well as the phrase *said softly*:

> She had on the blue, frilled party dress
> Get him good, now.
> around the side of the house
> the shadowed and silvery bleachers
> Walsh said softly. "You're free, you hear?
> "Get up," Walsh said softly, pleading.

Next we loaded the entirety of the November 1956 issue of *Manhunt* into NeoNeuro's *Author Attribution* software, which uses collation stylometry that focuses on word order of commonly used phrases within sentences and paragraphs. The longest story in the issue, at 15,000 words, is "Manila Mission" by Charles Einstein, so we loaded additional stories by the other known authors in the issue in order to equalize their sample sizes. All of the additional stories came from other issues of *Manhunt* with the exception of two stories from *Alfred Hitchcock's Mystery Magazine*. We then used *Author Attribution*, given the known authors in this issue, to determine who is most likely to have also written "Death Wears a Gray Sweater." Here are the results:

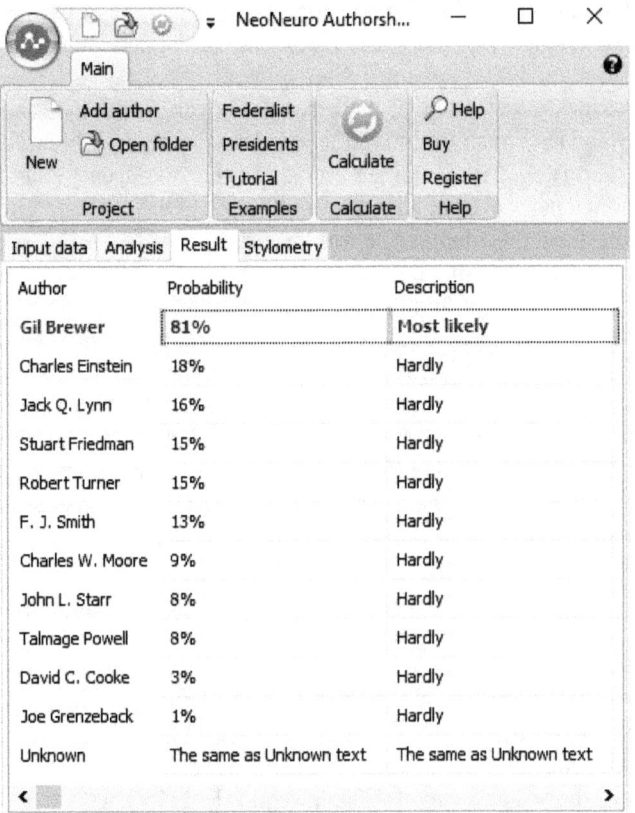

Gil Brewer was not only the most likely author, but none of the other candidates were even close. *Author Attribution* noted multiple phrases that occurred in both the Gil Brewer and Roy Carroll samples, including

> ran around the side of the house
> his face was sheened with sweat
> there was no sign of the
> ordered a bottle of beer
> the sound of the engine
> said his voice was low

Given this evidence, we felt confident that Gil Brewer had written "Death Wears a Gray Sweater," but not confident enough to publish the story as his. Perhaps another trip to the Gil Brewer Collection in Wyoming was in order? Alert to the probability that Brewer had written this story, maybe we would spot evidence previously overlooked? Then something unexpected happened: We were given the opportunity to examine Brewer's "green cards" from the files of the Scott Meredith Literary Agency (SMLA), which someone had rescued from the trash in the mid-1990s when the agency disposed of the cards after entering them into its new computer database. The cards were now in a private collection.

For years we had heard of the green index cards used by SMLA to track manuscripts. Each manuscript had its own card stored in a library-style card catalog, and each card contained everything that the agency might want to know about a particular manuscript. On the front of the card were the author's name; the date the manuscript was received; the title of the manuscript; estimated word count; and the manuscript's submission history. On the back of the card, left side, was a summary of the manuscript along with editorial notes and codes indicating the quality of the work and to whom the manuscript should be pitched (or not pitched). On the back of the card, right side, was listed all sales of the work and the terms. For short stories, this was usually "NASR" for North American Serial Rights, followed by the name of the publisher and the amount of the sale. An interesting detail on Brewer's cards is the notation "Net to Verlaine Brewer," typed on the front of every card with the same electric typewriter. This notation was likely added after Brewer's death in 1983.

As we studied the cards, we saw that, like Gil Brewer with his sales log, SMLA agents were not good about noting whether a story had been published under a different title or a pseudonym. For example, the card for Brewer's "Shot" did not indicate its publication under the name Roy Carroll. But, as with Brewer's log, there were exceptions. When we came to the card for Brewer's "Evil Night," there were handwritten notes that it was published under the name Roy Carroll and that its title had been changed to "Death Wears a Gray Sweater"! The back of the card showed payment of $260, the equivalent of $2,800 today.

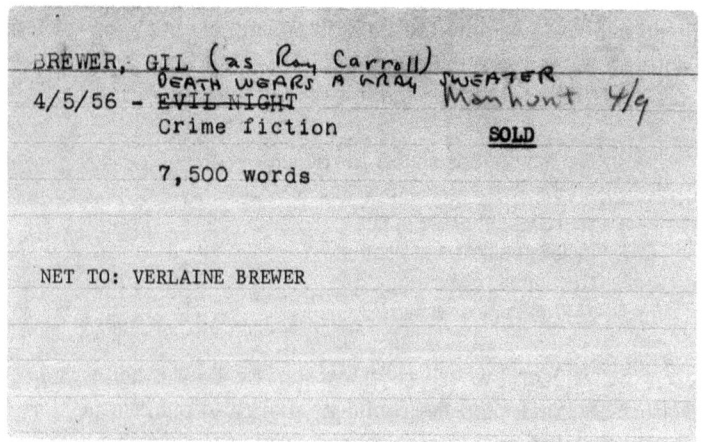

The front of the SMLA green card at 75% of actual size. (Private collection.)

```
    crime fiction - Y            Sold to Manhunt on
    Exciting, but improbable. Father    6-6-56 for
    sees his 11 yr old daughter hit     $260.
    by car, races off after driver.
    Driver's a kid, who realizes he's
    being followed, leads father into
    trap, beats him up. Police pick up
    father, first thinking he was hit-&-
    runner. Father shakes off police,
    goes after kid again. Captures him
    in gin-mill, takes him to stock car
    arena, plans to run him down. Realizes
    his car lights were shining in youth's
    eyes at time of accident, changes mind
    about killing kid. Police arrive & man
    has been saved from murder. jb Manhunt
```

The back of the SMLA green card at 75% of actual size. (Private collection.)

We had a remarkable confirmation. "Death Wears a Gray Sweater" was indeed written by Gil Brewer, and we have included it in this latest anthology of the best stories from *Manhunt*.

Old Willie
William P. McGivern

May 1953

This is a story I've heard told by old-timers around Chicago newspaper offices. They don't insist it's true, of course, since it hangs chiefly on the word of a reporter who was far more at home in speakeasies than he ever was at a typewriter. Still, parts of the tale can't be explained away as the splintered dreams of a drunk. Maybe that's why the old-timers go on telling the story...

It begins in 1927, prohibition-time, when Chicago was run by a band of Sicilian immigrants under the austere leadership of a man named Al Capone. And it also begins when an amiable little man, whom everyone knew only as Old Willie, became interested in a shy Danish girl named Inger Anderson.

Willie was the handy man and janitor around the West Side boarding house where Inger roomed. He was a straight-backed, light-stepping character, with drooping gray mustache and pale blue eyes. He could have been in his middle sixties or seventies—it was hard to say. Everyone at the boarding house liked him because of his obliging, courteous manner, and consistent good humor, but they didn't know very much about him; nor care a great deal.

Old Willie's interest in Inger was purely fatherly, of course. He knew she'd come from a Minnesota village and he felt she needed looking after in the big city. He fussed over her as if she were a baby. Inger was pretty capable despite her shyness, but she was touched by Old Willie's interest in her, and they became good friends.

Inger's ambition was to become a concert singer. She had a pleasant, untrained voice which wouldn't have excited a small-town choirmaster, but she loved to sing and was ready to do almost anything to fulfill her dreams. She signed up for voice lessons in the evenings and found herself a job as a Hotel maid through an employment agency. She was thrilled at her luck in finding work so quickly. What she didn't know was that the employment agency director, spotting her as an earnest but unknowing Minnesota specimen, had assigned her to the hotel which was the Headquarters of the Capone mob—the old Star at Wabash Avenue near Twelfth Street. Considering this, considering that the Star was filled with as choice a collection of gorillas as were ever assembled under one roof, Inger got along okay for the first few weeks. She cleaned rooms, made beds, and kept her eyes cast down when the sharply-dressed torpedoes stared insolently at her lovely, graceful figure and beautiful legs. One of the hoodlums, Blackie Cardina, a Sardinian with alert eyes and a strong, bold jaw, stared longer than any of the others and then grinned.

Old Willie was horrified when Inger told him where she was working. They were talking in the parlor at the time. Inger had just finished her lessons and had been telling Old Willie about the skating and sledding in Minnesota, and about a boy named Lars who wanted to marry her, and then she said something about the Star Hotel.

"Listen, you get out of that place," Old Willie said, shaking his head sternly. "Those are bad men, worse than rattlesnakes, and it's no place for a girl like you."

Inger was amused by Willie's anxiety. She was young and very confident, and the thought that she couldn't look out for herself struck her as funny. After all, she reasoned, she had been at the Star a month and no one had bothered her yet.

About a week after this talk, Inger came home much later than usual and went straight to her room. She didn't come down to eat, and she didn't practice her scales that night. Old Willie, vaguely troubled, tried to find out what was wrong, but she wouldn't open her door, or even talk to him. The next day the landlady brought Inger up some food, and talked to her for an hour or so. When she came out her eyes were red, and that night she glared at all the men boarders as if they were particularly repellent species of vermin.

For a month things went on this way. Inger wasn't working at the Star any more. She stuck close to her room and wouldn't see anyone, not even Old Willie. Then he learned from the landlady that Inger was leaving. She wasn't going home. She was just leaving.

That brought him to a decision. He went up and knocked firmly on the door. "You might as well open up," he said. "I'm sticking here until you do."

There was a wait, and then, in a tired voice, Inger told him to come in. She was in bed looking pale and ill. Old Willie sat beside her and patted her arm with a thin, long-fingered hand.

"You're in trouble, aren't you, Inger?" he said.

She looked away from him, staring out at the bare, black, winter trees.

"Who is it?" Old Willie said. Something had changed in his voice; it was curiously hard, insistent.

"I can't talk about it."

"You've got to, Inger. You got no father or brothers here."

She moaned softly. "They mustn't ever know."

"No need for that. Tell me about it."

Finally she told him, crying openly, her hand clutching his with desperate strength. It was the one they called Blackie, Blackie Cardina. He had followed her into a room, grinning. She had pleaded with him, begged him, and at last she had fought and screamed. But nothing had made any difference to Blackie. He had taken what he wanted . . .

When she finished, Old Willie sighed. "I'll have a talk with him," he said.

"No, no," Inger cried. "They—he'd kill you. You don't know what they're like."

"Now don't worry about me," Old Willie said in a soothing voice. "You try to sleep, and don't be fretting."

And with that he left her. Old Willie went first to his own room and reappeared in a few minutes wearing a long, black frayed overcoat. The landlady met him at the foot of the stairs and asked him where he was going. Old Willie didn't answer. He walked past her, his eyes fixed straight ahead, a tense, angry frown on his old face.

Old Willie reached the Star Hotel a little after noon. He stopped inside the revolving doors, looking like some country bumpkin who'd got into the wrong pew by mistake. And now, right at this point, is where the drunken reporter, Jake Mackey, enters the story in the role of an eye-witness. Jake was at the Star that afternoon, sitting on a sofa and talking to one of Capone's men. Maybe Jake was on a story. Maybe he was just hanging around for a drink. Anyway, he was there, slightly drunker than usual, and he noticed Old Willie immediately, because Old Willie with his drooping mustache and long black overcoat was a sight to catch and hold the eye.

Old Willie stopped a bellboy and asked him where he might find Blackie Cardina. The bellboy jerked his thumb toward a card game at the far end of the lobby. Blackie was there, sitting behind a high stack of chips, a cigar in his strong teeth, and grinning like a wolf because he was winning, and because, at that precise moment of his life, he thought the world was a place that had been kindly provided for him to loot, ravish, and otherwise do with as he pleased.

He glanced up a few seconds later and saw the old man with drooping mustache studying him somberly. Blackie paid no attention to him; he had looked up as he figured the odds against filling a belly straight.

"Okay, I take a card," Blackie said, and snapped his fingers.

"Hold the deal," Old Willie said quietly. "Which of you is a rat called Blackie Cardina?"

Blackie looked up again, seeing Old Willie for sure this time, and his little dark eyes narrowed dangerously. "You aren't funny, old man," he said.

"I ain't trying to be," Old Willie said. "I'm a friend of a girl used to work here. You had your fun with her, you slimy snake-eating bastard, and now you're going to pay for it. I want a thousand dollars from you. That'll help her out some. And you can figure the price cheap."

Blackie got to his feet and it was difficult to judge from his expression whether he would start laughing or cussing. "Look, old man, get out," he said, at last, pointing to the door. "Get out. You hear? I don't want to kick an old man into the street. I'll let you walk, understand." He got madder as he talked, and a flush of color surged up his throat and stained his dark features. "Get out!" he shouted. "Get out, you dirty, rotten old bum. Get out of here!"

"One thousand dollars," Old Willie said, casually unbuttoning his long black overcoat.

The kill look in Blackie's eyes deepened. "Who sent you here? Who are you?" he shouted, and reached for the gun in his shoulder holster. "I'll teach you a lesson, goddamn it."

Old Willie said something then, something which only Jake Mackey seems to have heard, and he said it in a voice that was proud and hard and confident. After that, although it was all part of one, smoothly connected motion, Old Willie yelled, "Draw, you bastard!" and threw himself swiftly to one side in a low, springy crouch.

There was a lot of discussion later as to what exactly happened in the next few seconds. Two facts were incontrovertible: One, Old Willie somehow got a gun into his hand, and, two, Blackie Cardina fell across the card table with a black hole burned neatly into his forehead. No one actually saw Old Willie draw a gun. The onlookers decided later it was probably fastened to a spring arrangement in his holster. Anyway, it got into his hand very fast, and the bullet from it got into Blackie's skull even faster.

Old Willie didn't let things get out of control. With a little wave of his big, old-fashioned revolver he backed Blackie's friends away from the table, and then coolly plucked a wallet from Blackie's hip pocket.

He inspected the contents and stuffed the wallet into a pocket of his overcoat. After that he backed toward the doors, moving easily and lightly, the gun in his hand as steady as something carved from rock.

Jake Mackey said there was something about Old Willie then, something in his eye and manner, that made you want to shrink down in your chair and stay very quiet.

At the doors Old Willie made a short speech. "Sit tight for five minutes. First man don't think that's a good idea is going to get himself killed."

And then he walked out into the street and for five minutes a half-dozen of Al Capone's hoodlums looked uneasily at Blackie's body, and occasionally glanced up at the clock above the lobby desk.

They weren't afraid to go outside, they said later. They weren't afraid of an old man in a tattered overcoat who'd been lucky enough to plug Blackie between the eyes. Still, they didn't go out and they didn't move.

Jake Mackey got on Old Willie's trail right after the five minutes were up, and by checking the cab companies he found a hackie who had picked up an old party answering Willie's description at the intersections of Twelfth Street and Wabash Avenue. This took time, of course; it was late in the afternoon when Jake cautiously approached the boarding house where the cab driver had taken Old Willie and had dropped him.

And by then it was too late. Old Willie had been there, all right, but only long enough to give Inger a roll of money, and then pack up his few things and leave.

He didn't say goodbye to anyone, but simply strolled off down the darkening street, a slender old man with faded blue eyes and a curiously youthful stride. No one watched him leave.

Jake Mackey was fascinated by what he'd seen at the Star Hotel and he hung around Inger to get all the facts she could recall about Old Willie.

She told him how secretive Old Willie had always been, and how he liked to listen to her sing, and so forth, but she couldn't tell him very much more.

He and Inger became good friends in the next week or so, and for a while Jake even thought he was falling in love with her. But nothing came of that. Inger had a miscarriage a week later, and after that packed up and went back to Minnesota.

She married the boy named Lars, and Jake carried the wedding announcement in his wallet, but finally lost it in a bar, the way clippings get lost in bars.

He never did pin down his story. He did a lot of checking on it, and spent a good deal of time in the library, but he never could prove it, and so he never wrote it.

Still, he *knew* that he had missed a great story by a hair's breadth, and in the years that followed he told the story around Chicago bars to anyone who would listen to him.

The thing that convinced him his story was true was the way Old Willie had handled that gun, and what Old Willie had said when Blackie asked him who he was—Blackie had asked him who he was, remember, just before digging for the gun in his shoulder holster. Old Willie's answer had held no significance for the Sicilian immigrants at the card table, but it had raised the hairs on the back of Jake Mackey's neck.

Old Willie had said, in a proud, hard, confident voice, "When I was a kid they called me Billy."

And that's the way the old-timers tell Jake Mackey's story. They don't insist it's true, of course—but they go on telling it.

Services Rendered
Jonathan Craig

May 1953

Detective Lieutenant Henry Callan stood very still in the middle of his cheap hall bedroom, bulky shoulders slumping a little, listening to the early morning sounds in the house around him—a tall, heavily muscled, flat-bellied man with short-cropped graying hair and pale blue eyes with tiny hoods at the corners.

Somebody was running water in the bathroom directly above him, and next door the bed springs had been creaking rhythmically for almost twenty minutes. On the other side, where the landlady lived, a radio announcer interrupted a dance tune to say that the time was seven-twenty.

Callan sighed and lifted his trousers from the back of a chair. Seven-twenty. That gave him another ten minutes before he had to go outside to meet Kimberly. Jesus, that guy Kimberly was hard to take. Ten months on the Force, and already he was bucking for a gold badge.

To hell with Kimberly. And to hell with the Old Man and all the rest of them. He walked back to the bed and reached beneath it for the gin bottle. Thank God he'd saved himself a corner for this morning: his head felt like somebody had worked it over with a billy.

Ten minutes later, when Callan climbed into the front seat of the cruiser with Kimberly, his hangover was fading, but there was still enough of it left to be bothersome.

Kimberly's grinning young face was shaved so closely it was pink. Nodding, he got the cruiser under way, and looked at Callan.

"Looks like another scorcher today, Lieutenant. You can tell already. Worst hot spell we've had in twelve years, the paper says."

"So it's hot," Callan mumbled. "So what?"

Kimberly shrugged. "Where to first? Precinct?"

"No," Callan said. He fished a folded piece of paper from his jacket pocket and glanced at it. "One sixty-seven Beckman Street."

"Who's there?"

"Tommy Hobart's wife."

Kimberly whistled softly. "A real looker, I hear. You ever see her?"

"No."

Kimberly turned right at the next intersection. "How'd you make out with Hobart last night, Lieutenant?"

"No good. We knocked off about midnight, and he hadn't so much as opened his yap." He glanced sharply at Kimberly. "You hear anything around the precinct this morning?"

"Nothing much," Kimberly said. "While I was picking up the car, Sergeant Gault made some crack about Hobart still having lockjaw, but that's all. He must be a pretty tough boy."

"Not so tough. I could put an Irish potato in a sock and find out in five minutes whether or not he killed that florist. If it wasn't for the Old Man screaming like hell, I'd have done it last night."

"The Old Man's pretty tough."

"He used to be, you mean. Not any more. He's soft now, but when he was a rookie cop he used to make an arrest and then hammer the guy on the shinbones with his nightstick, so the guy's legs would be too sore for him to make a break while the Old Man called the wagon."

"Jesus," Kimberly said softly.

Callan stripped the cellophane from a cigar, bit off the end, and worried it around in his mouth without lighting it.

"You figure Hobart did it, Lieutenant?" Kimberly asked.

"Maybe. So far, all we've got is circumstantial crap. Without a confession, the D.A. couldn't even get an indictment. He needs this one bad, and he's putting the heat on the Old Man. So maybe the Old Man'll have to look the other way and let me use that sock after all."

"Jesus," Kimberly said again.

Callan studied him. "You aren't just a little too squeamish for a cop, are you, George?" He laughed softly. "Either Hobart botched a hold-up and killed a fairy florist, or he didn't. Either the D.A. gets a confession and fries Hobart, or he doesn't. What the hell—it's no skin off yours and mine, either way."

Kimberly turned the cruiser into a wide residential street and eased up on the gas pedal. "This is Beckman Street," he said. "One sixty-seven?"

"Yeah. Must be at the end of this block. And listen—I want you to wait outside. You see anybody about to come up the walk, give them the boot. Okay?"

Kimberly nodded, leaning down a little to peer across Callan at the numbers on the houses. "That's it," he said. "Next one to the corner." He braked the cruiser at the curb and sat waiting, his lips tight together, not looking at Callan.

Callan laughed. "You'll get over being squeamish," he said. He opened the door and got out. "This might take a little time, George. It all depends." He slammed the door and walked up the flagstones to the small, freshly painted bungalow.

The woman who opened the screen to Callan's sharp knock was even younger than he had expected her to be. Not more than twenty, he guessed, and maybe not even that. And she was pretty; no question about it. How the hell had a homely jerk like Hobart got himself a kid like this?

Her blue eyes were questioning him.

He waited. Let her sweat a little.

She pushed a loose strand of auburn hair back from her forehead. Even without make-up, Callan noticed, her lips were full and red.

"Police," Callan said.

She drew her thin cotton housecoat more tightly about her and looked past him at the black and white cruiser.

"All right," Callan said. "Do I come in, or do we ring the neighbors in on this?"

She shrugged and opened the screen a little wider. He pushed past her into the living room, picked out the most likely looking chair, and sat down.

He smiled at her. "You're Carol Hobart?" he asked.

She nodded. Her lashes fluttered.

"Lieutenant Callan," he said. He kept his eyes on the jutting swell of her breasts until she colored and looked away from him. "Sit down, Mrs. Hobart. We're going to talk a little."

She sank down on the sofa. "What about Tommy?" she asked.

"What about him?"

"You know he didn't have anything to do with that—that hold-up."

He smiled at her. "I'm a homicide cop, Mrs. Hobart. It's murder we're talking about, not a hold-up."

She shook her head slowly. "Tommy couldn't have done it. He *couldn't* have. Those other detectives kept asking me the same questions over and over again, and I—"

"Sure, sure," Callan said. "You kept telling them Tommy couldn't have done it."

"But he didn't!"

Callan took the unlit cigar from his mouth and slipped it into his jacket pocket. He let his eyes rove down Carol Hobart's body until they came to rest on her ankles.

"Stop it," she said tightly. "Stop staring at me like that."

He was beginning to enjoy Mrs. Hobart. And there was time; as much time as he wanted to take.

"Let's face some hard facts," he said. "Your husband's headed straight for the chair, Mrs. Hobart. I'm in charge of the case now, and I'm going to put him in the hot squat just as sure as hell."

Her hands came up to her throat. "No! God, no!"

"Yeah," he said. "The chair." He watched her carefully. "All the D.A. needs is a confession, and then Tommy gets his head shaved. And you know something, Mrs. Hobart? I'm the guy that's going to get that confession."

"But he didn't *do* it!"

Callan got up and walked to the window and looked out at the cruiser. "Maybe he didn't," he said softly. "But I know ways to make him say he did."

Behind him, he heard her quick intake of breath.

"Yeah." he said. "There are ways, Mrs. Hobart. They aren't pretty, but they work. Every time."

"You—you'd actually do that?" Her voice was scarcely more than a whisper.

Callan folded his arms behind him and watched a woman watering flowers in the yard across the street. A moving van lumbered by, swerved out wide around the police cruiser, and turned the corner.

"It could happen," he told her. "It's happened before—why not this time?" He shrugged. "Of course, it doesn't *have* to happen, Mrs. Hobart. . . ." He turned and stared at her steadily. "What's one more confession to me? My pay stays the same, either way."

She moistened her lips, looking at him without blinking, slender fingers toying nervously with the neckline of her housecoat.

He crossed to her and held her eyes with his until she looked away. "I got nothing to gain by helping the D.A. fry your husband, Mrs. Hobart. Nothing at all. But look at it another way. Suppose I didn't even try to get a confession? Suppose I just told my boss and the D.A. that it was no use, and they let Tommy go?" He could smell her now. It was no perfume, he knew; it was the natural feminine aroma of her young body. He moved a little closer.

"Suppose I work it so Tommy gets off?" he said softly. "What then, Mrs. Hobart?"

She looked up at him with eyes that had grown so dark they were almost black. Her lips spread back from small white teeth and her voice was thick with revulsion. "You animal!" she whispered. "You horrible, filthy animal!"

Callan rubbed his sweating palms along the sides of his trousers. He unbuttoned his jacket and loosened his tie and ran a thick finger along the inside of his shirt collar. "Hot, isn't it?"

Her lips moved, but there was no sound.

"Try to think of it from my viewpoint," Callan said. "There are some things a man has to have. Say I found it right here. Why, then, I'd be grateful. I'd go on downtown and tell the D.A. to call it quits. Tommy'd be home in a couple hours, and he'd never know the difference."

He ran a thumbnail along the line of his jaw and dropped his eyes to her tiny belted waist. "But the cost of living is pretty high these days, Mrs. Hobart. Just one time with you wouldn't be quite enough for me to keep Tommy out of the chair. Naturally, you might see me again now and then. Not often, mind you—but now and then."

He brought his eyes up to her face again, watching her carefully. This was the big moment. This was when they always made up their minds. He flexed his fingers at his sides, and smiled at her, and waited. Jesus, he thought, if this works out it's going to be one hell of a score.

A full minute went by, and another, and still she sat and stared up at him. Occasionally her lips trembled, but there was no other movement. Somewhere nearby a lawnmower started whirring, and a moment later some kids went past the house on roller skates.

Callan sighed. "It's one way or the other, Mrs. Hobart. Either you want Tommy fried, or you don't."

She got to her feet slowly, as if she were very weak and ill, and moved past him toward the rear of the house. He followed her through the dining room to the bedroom. Just inside the door of the bedroom, she paused and turned to face him. Her lips were pale now, and she spoke as if she had scarcely enough strength to articulate the words.

"How do I know you aren't lying? That you won't just . . . just . . ."

"You don't," he said. "It's a gamble, like everything else in this world." He smiled at her, and let the smile widen. "But you're going to be reasonable, Mrs. Hobart, because you know damn well it's the only hope Tommy's got."

Callan waited until the rookie cop had closed and locked the cell door behind him, and then he sat down on the steel mesh cot beside Tommy Hobart.

"Well, Tommy," he said pleasantly, "they tell me you're still being stubborn."

Hobart's thin face was sheened with sweat, and his gray sport shirt was dark with sweat beneath the arms and across his narrow chest. He mopped damp, dark hair away from his forehead and glared at Callan with deep-set eyes that were not quite able to hide their fear.

"So it's your turn again," he said bitterly. "The brainy boys gave up, so now we've got *you* back again."

Callan pursed his lips and stared at the galvanized bucket that served Tommy Hobart as a lavatory. "Yeah," he said, "I can see you're still set on being stubborn."

Hobart's voice was ragged with fatigue. "What do you want me to do? You want me to say I killed a man, and all the time you know goddam well I never even been near him!"

Callan got up and walked to the toilet and flushed it. "You ought to take better care of this place, Tommy," he said. He leaned against the wall and put the dead cigar in his mouth and studied Hobart with tired, hooded eyes. It was past twelve o'clock, and he still hadn't had breakfast, but he felt no desire for food.

I've got to watch it, he thought. I'm as taut as a piano wire. What I need is a good stiff slug of gin.

"How the hell can you hold me at a precinct like this?" Hobart asked. "What kind of slimy deal are you pulling, anyhow? Why can't I see my lawyer again?"

"You saw your lawyer," Callan told him. "But he couldn't get a writ and spring you, could he?" He shook his head sadly. "No, he couldn't do that. He couldn't get to anybody, Tommy, because the D.A. had already got there first."

He watched Hobart's eyes carefully, and suddenly it came to him that Hobart was ready to crack. He'd seen it happen a hundred times before. He knew all the signs, and they were all there, on Hobart's face and in his eyes.

Brother, he thought. How lucky can you get? If I break this kid solo, I can hit the Old Man up for an extra week's leave. He walked to the door and looked both ways along the corridor to make sure there was no one there, and then he leaned up against the wall again.

You've got to bust him up all at once, he thought. Right now he's getting all his guts from thinking of his wife. Make him realize she's been cheating, and he'll bust wide open. Get it in fast, and deep, and break it off in him.

He studied Hobart another moment to make certain the signs were right, and then he said, "That's a real pretty wife you got, Tommy." He made it sound friendly. "Real pretty."

"Leave her out of this, for Christ's sake!"

"I spent a little time with her this morning. Couple hours." He shook his head. "Must be pretty tough for her. Wouldn't you say so?"

Tommy Hobart spat on the floor.

"Heat set a record today," Callan said. "Good day to go swimming. You ever take Carol swimming, Tommy?"

Hobart's eyes narrowed slightly, but he said nothing.

Callan took the cigar from his mouth and looked at it and then slipped it back into his pocket. "I guess you're pretty proud when you take her to the beach, eh, Tommy? I mean, with that body she's got and all."

Hobart started to rise, but Callan put his big hand flat against the younger man's chest and pushed him back down on the cot again.

"You bastard," Hobart said. "Jesus, if I ever get out of here, I'll—"

"Take it easy, son," Callan said. "Don't let me lose my train of thought." He hummed softly a moment, smiling at Hobart.

"You bastard," Hobart said.

"Funny thing, Tommy," Callan said, "but you damned seldom find a woman without a blemish on her somewhere. You ever think about that? Now you take Carol, for instance. Who'd ever figure she had a crescent-shaped birthmark where she's got it. I mean, she'd have to be mother naked before you'd ever guess. Right?"

He watched the things that crawled in Tommy Hobart's eyes, and braced himself. When Hobart came at him, Callan was ready. He caught Hobart's driving fist in the palm of his hand and stabbed the straight, rigid fingers of his other hand into the soft hollow just beneath Hobart's breastbone.

Hobart went down in a whimpering, gagging heap—and only then Callan realized that Hobart had spat in his face. He took out his handkerchief and wiped his cheek and threw the handkerchief in the direction of the toilet.

He watched Hobart being sick on the cement floor. Hobart was ripe now, he knew. He had him sick in every way a man could be sick. All he had to do was start hammering him with the same old question, over and over again.

But even as Callan's mind framed the words, he realized with sickening suddenness that he was cutting his own throat.

It wasn't Tommy Hobart's confession he wanted.

It was Tommy Hobart's wife.

If he got a confession out of Hobart, then he'd have no club to hold over Carol Hobart's head. And without a club, there'd be no more times like this morning.

He ran his tongue across dry lips, breathing heavily, staring down at Tommy Hobart, and then he turned and rattled the bars.

The rookie cop came down the corridor and unlocked the door and stood back to let Callan pass outside. His eyes shuttled from Callan to Hobart and back again. "What happened, Lieutenant?"

"He jumped me," Callan said. "I didn't touch him. He just jumped me for no reason at all."

There was something in the rookie's eyes Callan didn't like; something very close to revulsion. "I'll bet," the rookie said.

Jesus, Callan thought, another squeamish cop. Another George Kimberly. Another jerk with a lot of crap in his head about the way prisoners should be treated. Jesus, it was getting so you couldn't make a move without nine-tenths of the Force ganging up on you and yelping about brutality. To hell with them. To hell with the whole' lily-livered bunch of them.

He smiled at the rookie. "Better straighten him out a little. He looks real sick."

"All right."

"Sir."

"All right, sir."

Callan strode down the corridor, nodded to the desk sergeant, and went down the steps to the street. The cruiser was parked at the curb and Private Kimberly was polishing the windshield. Kimberly glanced up at Callan, and then moved quickly to open the door for him.

"Never mind, George," Callan said. "I won't be needing a car any more this afternoon. I got a couple of things to work out, but I don't need the car."

Kimberly nodded. "Anything you want me to do, Lieutenant?"

"No. Go on in and tell them you can haul somebody else around." He turned and walked slowly toward Locust Street. At the corner he bought a fifth of gin, and then took a cab to his rooming house.

He got a tumbler of luke-warm water from the bathroom, opened the bottle, and sat down on the rumpled bed. He sipped alternately at the gin and the water until he had taken the bottle down a good three inches, and then he put bottle and glass on the floor and lay back on the bed and shut his eyes.

He lay quite still, waiting for the gin to hit him. The house radio. He reached behind his head and rapped on the thin wall, and after a moment the radio was turned down a little.

He listened to the soft throb of the dance music and thought of Carol Hobart. She was really something; no question about it. Jesus, a girl like that could knock a man off his rocker. She could get to be worse than heroin.

Why the hell wasn't that gin taking hold? A slug like he'd had should have grabbed him by now. He sat up suddenly and reached for the bottle. Thank God there was nothing wrong with his stomach. He could tuck a pint away, and the old belly would never holler once.

He tilted the bottle and let the gin run down his throat until he gagged, and then he held the bottle up and looked at it. Damn near half. Should do the trick, if it was ever going to do it.

He finished the water in the tumbler and recapped the bottle and left the room. Maybe if he walked around a while, the exercise and the sun would hurry the gin along. Without exactly the right buzz. Carol Hobart wasn't going to be any good to him. And with that damn husband of hers ready to crack, it had to be this afternoon, or never. Christ, it would be just his luck to have one of the other cops get a paper from Hobart. Maybe Hobart was talking now.

He walked four blocks in the broiling sun before he felt the full effect of the gin. The feeling of urgency left him, and now he began to savor the anticipation of how it would be with Carol. Maybe if he put it *off* another hour, it would be even better. What the hell? Everybody knew that it was always nine-tenths expectation and one-tenth realization. He turned in at the first bar and had two fast gills of gin.

When he stepped out on the street again, he felt right. Exactly right to do justice to Tommy Hobart's wife.

He walked another block to a cab stand and gave the driver the address on Beckman Street. To hell with phoning her first, he thought.

Carol Hobart had changed to high heels and a green silk jersey dress that clung to the swelling curves of her young body so snugly that Callan could see the outlines of her lingerie. She was wearing make-up now, and her thick auburn hair was caught back at the nape of her neck.

She let the screen slam shut behind Callan and stared at him with empty blue eyes.

"I was sort of expecting you," she said tonelessly. "But not so soon."

He let his eyes rove the length of her body, and back again. "Jesus."

"What do you want?"

He smiled at her.

She looked at him steadily, and her expression was exactly the same.

"I was going out," she said. "I have business downtown."

"You've got business right here," Callan said. "Right now."

She moistened her lips. There was something strange about her eyes, Callan noticed. It wasn't fear, and it wasn't revulsion. Maybe she's got used to the idea, he thought. Maybe.

He shrugged. "You know damn well what'll happen."

Her eyes grew cloudy, and then, not looking at him, she moved past him toward the bedroom. He followed her, watching the lithe swing of her hips beneath the jersey.

Callan heeled the door shut behind them and stripped off his jacket and hung it over the back of a chair. Then he unbuckled his shoulder harness with the short-barrelled Detective Special, draped the harness over the jacket, and moved toward Carol Hobart.

"Poor Tommy," he said.

She sprang at him, suddenly, like a tigress. Her fingernails raked across his eyes and down his face deeply.

He yelled and clubbed a fist at her face, and then a hard bare knee blurred upward toward his groin.

Soured gin welled up in his throat, and he fell to his hands and knees in a blinding burst of pain. When, finally, his vision cleared, he looked up into the muzzle of his own revolver.

"You louse," Carol Hobart said.

"God," Callan said. "Don't! For Christ's sake, don't!"

Her eyes were steady now, round and hard and black. She held the gun with one hand, and with the other she reached up and ripped the green dress all the way down to the waist. She caught one of the short, puff sleeves and ripped it loose, and then she tore the narrow belt from her waist.

She drew her lips back from her teeth, and stared at him, and the laugh that came from her mouth was like no laugh Callan had ever heard before.

"They called me," she said. "The police called me. Not ten minutes ago. They said they'd caught the man who killed the florist. Do you hear that, you bastard?"

"God," Callan said.

She moved a step nearer him. "They caught the man, and he admitted it, and now they're going to let Tommy go. I was on my way to him when you came. If you'd come a minute later, I wouldn't have been here at all."

Callan made a desperate lunge for her legs, but she was faster than he was.

She took another step backward, and laughed at him, and then she hooked her fingers in the frothy white material of her brassiere and ripped it apart.

"You know what's going to happen?" she asked. "People are going to think you tried to attack me. They'll see me like this, and you with your face clawed, and they're going to believe everything I tell them. I'm going to scream, so that people will come running. But you'll never see them. Before anyone can get here, you're going to be dead."

Callan shook his head slowly, his eyes pleading with her. "For God's sake," he gasped. "Don't . . ."

"You're never going to do anybody else the way you did Tommy and me! Never!"

Callan tried to speak, but his lips and throat were numb, and the words would not come.

He was still trying to speak when Carol Hobart screamed and pulled the trigger.

The Faceless Man
Michael Fessier
June 1953

At one time if anyone had suggested that the residents of Green Valley could conceivably form themselves into a mob, lusting for the blood of a fellowman, I would have called him insane. Now I know better. Green Valley isn't in the Deep South; it's in a midwestern farming state, which proves that lynching isn't a fault of geography but of humanity, And humanity happens to be a family we all belong to no matter where we live. To those of you who have read about lynchings committed in places far from your homes and who have wondered what sort of a person a lyncher is, I have this to say: A lyncher is neither tall nor short, nor young nor old, nor male nor female, and he is faceless, but, under certain given circumstances and under certain given conditions, he is you and you and you and, yes, he is even me.

The chain of events which led the citizens of Green Valley a long way back down the path of evolution toward their original animal state began during the hot, dry summer when their crops were withering and they were worrying about their mortgages and other debts. Henry Rankins gave them something to talk about other than their troubles by taking Claude Warren, an ex-convict, into his home to live with him and help him run his farm. Claude was hardly more than a kid and his crime had not been committed against us nor among us, but he had served eight months in State's Prison and that was enough to set public opinion against him right from the start.

Perhaps the feeling against Claude might have been passive rather than active if it had not been for Orry Quinn. Orry was the third of Pete Quinn's shiftless sons and he had been employed as a farm hand by Henry Rankins until a week before Claude came along. Henry had fired Orry for general reasons of incompetence and, specifically, for having wandered off one evening to see his girl, leaving the cows in the shed restless and in pain from not having been milked. Any other farmer would have done the same thing under the circumstances and nobody would have been perturbed about Orry's being unemployed, a condition which had grown to be more or less chronic with him anyway, had not Orry seized the opportunity to become a self-constituted martyr to social injustice. He claimed he had performed his labors faithfully and well, only to be removed on a trumped-up charge to make room for a felon, an ex-convict and, for all anybody knew, a potential murderer. This story was accepted at face value by most of the younger and more discontented non-working citizens of the community, and even men of substance and intelligence, who normally wouldn't have accepted Orry's sworn oath as to the date of his birth, began to place credence in it. Green Valley was composed of a close-knit group of families and they believed in taking care of their own. Whether or not they sympathized with Orry, they found it hard to understand why Henry Rankins would have passed up an opportunity to give a native son much needed employment in favor of an outsider who happened, in addition, to be a criminal.

Finally a small delegation called at Henry's farm to seek the answer. They found Henry in a shed cleaning eggs and placing them in cartons. Helping him was Claude Warren. Claude was a husky, clean-cut, towheaded kid not much different than dozens of others in Green Valley, excepting that his skin was pale and there was a half-apologetic look in his eyes.

Henry, a small old man with wrinkled, leathery skin, seemed to know why the delegation was there.

"Would you mind taking a walk, son?" he said to Claude. "I think my good friends and neighbors want to have a talk with me."

Claude nodded, then hurried away, his head hanging as if he, too, knew the reason for the visit. Then Henry faced his friends and neighbors.

"Hello boys!" he said blandly. "How're things? How's crops? Been working hard? Been borrowing money from the bank? How much? Got any insurance in case you kick off and leave your families without support?" As he talked, his eyes seemed to be boring into those of each individual member of the group. "How're you getting along with your wives?" he went on. "Any truth to the rumor that one of you slapped his old lady in front of the kids? And how about your daughters? Do you know where they are of nights and what they do?"

He paused and waited as the others shifted their feet uneasily in the dust, avoided his gaze and remained collectively silent.

"You seem to be very uncommunicative today," Henry finally said. "By the way, boys, is there any little thing I can do for you? Do you, by any chance, want to ask *me* a question?"

They glared sullenly and hatefully at him, then turned in a body and walked back to their cars. By the time they had reached the road they had regained their voices and they were muttering angrily among themselves.

Later on, the same delegation called on Sheriff Ben Hodges. They were thoroughly aroused now and they demanded that the sheriff do something about ridding the county of a known criminal who might at any moment turn out to be a menace to the peace and security of them all. Sheriff Ben was a big man and some of his weight was fat. He was well-disposed and given to indolence, being more inclined to sit in his easy chair and read books than militantly and actively to perform the duties required of his office. He had maintained his job throughout the years by giving the appearance of agreeing with everybody about everything and never taking sides in a public controversy. This time, however, he felt that he had to make a stand.

"Well, now," he said mildly, "as for that kid being a menace, I'm not so sure. You see he's a distant kin of Henry's—son of a cousin on his mother's side, I think—and Henry had him pretty thoroughly investigated before he took him in. Claude lived all his life in the city where they burn coal to make steel and the only patch of green he ever saw was in the public park where the police had signs forbidding him to walk on the grass. One hot evening, when the air was moist and full of smoke and soot, some boys his own age drove by in a car. They had girls with them and they took Claude along for a ride in the country. It turned out that the car had been stolen and Claude was convicted of complicity in the crime." Sheriff Ben spoke as persuasively as he knew how, trying to make them understand so's not to have trouble with them. "I know," he conceded, "that Claude probably had sense enough to realize that those other boys really didn't own that automobile, but, still in all, when a kid's hungry for a breath of country air, he isn't going to be too particular how he gets it, is he?"

The delegation didn't understand and what's more, they didn't believe Sheriff Ben's version of Claude's crime. Rumor had given them an uglier and more interesting version and they preferred to believe that. They resented Sheriff Ben's attempt at cleaning up Claude's character. Claude was a criminal, they said, and, if the sheriff wanted to, he could find some sort of a pretext to run him out of the community. The implication was that, if the sheriff appreciated which side his bread was buttered on, he would do what was required of him. Sheriff Ben understood the implication. He had eaten the public's bread for many years and sometimes it had a bitter taste; it was buttered with humiliation. On this day he had no appetite for it, and he made the political mistake of openly antagonizing a group of representative citizens.

"As for being a criminal," he said, "sometimes that's a state of mind and the result of circumstances. I don't suppose that there's many of us here who, at one time or another, couldn't have been in Claude's shoes. During prohibition, for instance, some of you farmers made hard liquor and some of you merchants sold it. Most of us drank it and I, being sheriff, violated my sworn oath by overlooking it." He stared steadily and defiantly at them. "That isn't all I've overlooked," he said, "and some of you wouldn't like it if I got more specific. In any event there're darned few of us who, according to the strict letter of the law and with a little bad luck, couldn't have a prison or a jail record hanging over us."

He rose and waved a heavy hand in dismissal.

"Come to see me again, gentlemen," he said. "As you know', I am always at your services. But the next time you come to me about that kid, who's working ten hours a day for a chance at a decent way of life, I'd appreciate it kindly if you'd have more to go on than your prejudices."

The delegation clumped angrily out of the office and Sheriff Ben realized that he had seriously jeopardized a job that perhaps he didn't deserve and, with it, the money he didn't at all times earn.

After that the citizens of Green Valley sullenly accepted Claude's presence among them. They didn't offer him any physical harm; no individual would have thought of it, excepting Orry Quinn, and he, being a coward, would not have risked the attempt. They simply ignored Claude and, excepting for Henry Rankins and Sheriff Ben, the kid didn't have a friend or a speaking acquaintance in the community until Laura Hannifer came along. Laura was the only child of one of the oldest families in Green Valley. Her parents had pampered her a great deal and, because she had a will of her own, she was considered arrogant. She had just recently returned home from a visit with relatives in another part of the state, and one day she rode her horse up to Henry Rankins' house and got off and sat on the porch with him.

"Hello, Uncle Hank," she said to Henry, who was no kin of hers, "I just dropped in for a glass of milk and to stick my nose into your business. I understand you're harboring a dangerous criminal hereabouts."

"I sure have," said Henry, grinning at her. "A regular killer-diller."

"Good for you," said Laura. "I've been hearing about him and I understand that the citizens of our community don't like him. Well, anybody these people around here don't like has a long running start toward being my pal. I don't like most of *them*, either."

Then Claude Warren, his face smudged with grease from his working on the tractor, came around the corner of the house and stood staring at Laura as if he'd never seen a girl before. Certainly he'd never seen a girl so healthy and tanned and with such golden hair and with such a friendly look in her eyes.

"Hi, Dirty-face," she said gaily to him. "Come on over and sit a spell." As he stood and goggled at her she laughed at him. "Don't be bashful," she said. "I came over here just to see you. Robbed any interesting banks lately?"

Her grin was so infectious and friendly that he grinned back at her and finally obeyed her command and sat beside her on the porch. Henry departed to get a glass of milk and, when he returned, Laura had already succeeded in thawing Claude out. He was talking to her, a little embarrassed, but with the eagerness of a kid who has long been starved for companionship.

It might have been sympathy and understanding on Laura's part at first, but it soon grew beyond that and presently everybody in Green Valley was discussing the outrageous carryings-on of Laura Hannifer with the ex-convict. The carryings-on weren't very spectacular. After attending a village dance and being frozen cold by the others, Claude and Laura contented themselves with hunting and fishing and riding horses together, and, in order to give Claude time for that, Laura helped him with his chores around Henry's place. The mere fact that Laura kept company with Claude, however, constituted a howling scandal.

Ramsey Hannifer and his wife did their best to break up the affair. At first they pleaded with Laura, and then they threatened all sorts of punishment, but she defied them. She loved Claude, she declared, and she intended to marry him one day. Any interference from them, she told them, would only succeed in hastening the event. They knew her well enough to realize that she meant business. Finally, in the hopes that the whole thing was merely infatuation on Laura's part and that eventually she would come to her senses, they ceased to offer any open opposition to the affair. They had, however, a definite plan of action which they intended to adopt in case the thing went too far.

Other residents of Green Valley did not know of this plan and they were of the opinion that immediate and drastic action should be taken to end what they considered to be an intolerable breach of public morals. There was some talk of forming a citizens' committee to remove Claude forcibly from the community, but it is doubtful if anything would ever have been done about it if, one afternoon, Henry Rankins had not been found dead in a pool of blood on the floor of his barn. Jason Watters, the county tax assessor, who discovered the body, did not bother to investigate the cause of death. He ran from the barn and called for Claude and discovered that Claude was nowhere in sight and that, in addition to this Henry's car was missing. Jason telephoned Sheriff Ben and then proceeded along the road to town, spreading the word that Henry Rankins had been murdered and that Claude Warren had disappeared.

By the time Sheriff Ben arrived at the farm, a dozen cars were parked in front of it and the barn was filled with men who milled in a circle about the body and disturbed or destroyed whatever evidence there might have been. This had not prevented them from forming opinions, however. They had picked up and handled and passed around various instruments, one of which they were certain had been used to crush Henry's skull, and they were in disagreement only as to which was the true weapon. Even if Sheriff Ben had been an expert, which he wasn't, he could not have gained much information from conditions as he found them. He ordered the others out of the barn and then telephoned Doc Doran, the coroner, to come get the body.

By the time Sheriff Ben came out of Henry's house after making the phone call, the crowd in the yard had doubled and they were excitedly discussing a new aspect of the case. Laura Hannifer, it had been learned, had also disappeared. Her worried parents didn't know her whereabouts, but they were afraid that she might have eloped with Claude Warren. This was all the crowd needed to know. They scattered to their cars and the search for Claude and Laura was on.

Sheriff Ben went back to his office and waited. It was not long before Lonnie Hearne, his deputy, assisted by Orry Quinn and another volunteer posseman, came in, dragging Claude and Laura with them. Claude had evidently resisted arrest and he was considerably banged up and bloody about the face. Laura, whose clothes were torn, was breathing fire and defiance and still struggling in the arms of the two possemen.

"Caught 'em with the goods," Lonnie announced proudly. "They were in Henry's car and Claude had a pocketful of money that he didn't earn as no farm hand."

While Lonnie prodded Claude with his revolver, the two kids told their story. They had discovered that Laura's parents had been secretly planning to send her to California to live with relatives, and, aided and abetted by Henry, they had decided to get married. Henry, they claimed, had lent them his car and the money for the elopement and the last they had seen of him he was in good health. They had not known, they declared, that Henry was dead until Lonnie and the others arrested them.

"And that's the truth, so help me," said Claude.

"It's a damn lie and, this time, *nobody's* going to help you," said Lonnie, viciously jamming the revolver against Claude's spine.

"Up until the present moment," said Sheriff Ben, knocking the revolver out of Lonnie's hand, "you're neither judge, jury, nor executioner for this commonwealth, Lonnie. You, Orry, let go of that girl and all of you clear out. I'll take over from now on."

After the others had made a reluctant departure, Sheriff Ben turned to Claude.

"Maybe you're telling the truth," he said. "I don't know. Anyway, I'm going to lock you up until we get a better idea of what the truth is."

Following a struggle with Laura, who insisted on being locked up too, Sheriff Ben succeeded in placing Claude in a cell. Then he sat and talked with Laura until her parents arrived and, after a great deal of difficulty, persuaded her to go home with them.

At first there were only a dozen men in front of the jail. They stood around and talked angrily but without purpose. Orry was one of them. After awhile he detached himself from the group and went into the village where he found a cluster of citizens gathered in front of the hotel discussing the case. He shoved his way into the center of the cluster and soon dominated the conversation by boastfully telling of his part in the capture and subjugation of Claude Warren, the murderer.

"How do you know he's a murderer?" someone asked. "Did he confess?"

"Well," said Orry, hesitating a moment, "not in so many words, but he *practically* did."

Then Orry went about the village and told his story to other groups of eager listeners, embellishing it as he went along. By the time he had reached the end of the main street he had dropped the word *practically* from his narrative. Claude, according to his story now, had *actually* confessed to having beaten Henry Rankins to death for his money. The news swept back up the street and presently even those who had heard Orry's first version of the story, were convinced that Claude had admitted his guilt.

"And what's more," Orry said importantly to a new group of listeners, "they're not going to let him get away with it. There's talk of breaking into the jail and stringing him up."

Soon word flashed through town and into the farming district that a crowd had gathered in front of the country jail for the purpose of lynching Claude Warren. This story in itself created the crowd which previously had not existed. Men, women and children flocked into the square facing the jail and waited expectantly for something to happen. Nothing happened. The crowd had no purpose or direction and they lacked leadership. Each individual member of the throng considered himself not a potential participant in whatever was about to take place, but merely a spectator to what the others were going to do.

An hour passed and it began to grow dark and the crowd grew more and more restless. They were in the mood of an audience that has paid out good money to see a show, the opening curtain of which has been delayed too long. If they had been in a theatre they would have stamped their feet and whistled. As it was they milled about and looked questioningly at one another and began to murmur, at first petulantly and then angrily. Finally, the shrill piping voice of a small boy rose above the murmur: *"We want Claude Warren!"* Others eagerly picked up the cry and, as they began to roar in unison, they ceased to be individuals and became a mob.

Inside his office, Sheriff Ben sat at a desk with three loaded revolvers before him. He opened a box of shells and began to load a shotgun. Lonnie, the deputy, was nervously pacing the floor.

"You're not going to be fool enough to resist them, are you, Ben?" he asked.

"Can you figure out anything else to do?" asked the sheriff.

"It's crazy," said Lonnie. "They'll tear us to pieces. I ain't going to risk my life for no lousy killer. That ain't what I'm being paid for as a deputy."

"And you're not a deputy any more," said Sheriff Ben. He ripped the badge off Lonnie's shirt front, unlocked the door and shoved him out. "Now go howl with the rest of the jackals."

He locked the door again and went back and sat at his desk. He listened to the growing roar from outside and he began to tremble and the palms of his hands were moist. In electing Ben Hodges sheriff, the citizens of Green Valley had not bestowed on him superhuman courage. Sheriff Ben was afraid.

The mob had now achieved purpose and direction and it was not long before they obtained leaders. The people of Green Valley had long looked to certain men for leadership in politics, civic enterprises, and church affairs. It was only natural that, in this current project, they looked to the same men for guidance. And those men, out of long habit, accepted the responsibility. Orders were given and eagerly obeyed and soon a heavy timber had been produced and was aimed as a battering ram at the door of the jail.

"Sheriff Ben," yelled Dolph Hardy, one of the leaders, "we'll give you one last chance to deliver Claude Warren before we come in after him."

There was a moment of waiting and then the door opened and Sheriff Ben appeared. Orry Quinn, who was in the forefront of the mob, yelled an obscenity at him and the Sheriff made a move toward him. Orry scurried back into the crowd.

"If I lay my hands on you, Orry," said the sheriff, "I'll slap your face to pulp." Then he looked over the mob. "I am quite willing, however," he said, "to discuss matters with responsible members of this community."

"Cut out the talk." said Dolph Hardy. "We want Claude Warren."

The mob surged forward but Sheriff Ben held his ground.

"Who said you couldn't have Claude Warren?" He held out his hands placatingly. "Take it easy, boys," he urged. "I'm a reasonable man." As the men in front fell back a little and stared expectantly at him, Sheriff Ben continued to speak in a soothing voice. "The thing is," he said, "I don't want any mob tearing through my jail and ripping things apart. This is your own property and if you destroy it, you'll have to replace it out of your own pockets."

At this there was an angry, impatient murmur from the mob. The sheriff held out his hands for silence.

"I'm not saying you can't have Claude Warren," he declared. "I'll deliver him to whichever one of you wants to come in in an orderly and decent manner to get him." He looked at Dolph Hardy. "How about you, Dolph? You've been hollering your head off for him. Supposing you come in and get him?"

Dolph gave the sheriff a startled look and tried to press himself back into the mob. The others urged him on, however, and finally and reluctantly he came up the steps toward the sheriff. Sheriff Ben shoved him inside and then locked the door.

"There he is," Sheriff Ben said to Dolph, pointing to a corner of the office. "He's all yours."

Dolph turned and faced Claude Warren, who was sitting in a chair, his wrists bound by handcuffs and his face swollen and discolored from the beating administered by his captors. Claude looked up at Dolph and his eyes were alive with hopeless, helpless terror. Dolph stared into those eyes and then his mouth dropped open and he shifted his feet and seemed to be at a loss as to what to do next.

"Funny thing, Dolph," said the sheriff musingly, "but Claude looks a lot like your youngest son, Willie, doesn't he? Same size and age. Want to sock him a couple of times before you deliver him to the mob Dolph? Go right ahead. He can't hit you back, he's handcuffed."

Dolph cringed and turned his face away from the look of animal fear in Claude's eyes.

"Better yet," said Sheriff Ben, placing his hand on Dolph's arm. "Why don't you kill him right here and now, Dolph?"

Dolph stared unbelievingly at Sheriff Ben and began to back toward the door.

"Why not?" asked Sheriff Ben. "You were so all-fired blood-thirsty a while ago. You were willing to *help* kill Claude. Do you mean to say you haven't got the courage to do the job all by yourself? And, look, Dolph, if you do, someday those people out there will be awfully grateful to you. If they kill Claude collectively tonight, someday they're going to have to answer for it individually to whatever God they believe in and, if they happen to believe in hell, why, they're going to have to roast for it. If you take sole responsibility Dolph, think what a terrible load you'll lift from the conscience of your neighbors in Green Valley."

He took Dolph by the elbow and led him over to the desk where the guns were.

"Would you like to shoot him, Dolph?" he asked. "Help yourself. Which do you prefer—a shotgun or a pistol?" As Dolph stared in horror at the array of weapons, Sheriff Ben opened a drawer and picked up a blackjack. "Or maybe you'd rather take this and beat his brains out," he said.

He extended the blackjack toward Dolph and Dolph stepped back, his face beaded with perspiration and his eyes sick with dread.

"Of course," went on Sheriff Ben, "your original intention was to hang him, wasn't it?" He turned and looked about him. "Now, let's see," he said, "where can I find a really good sturdy rope?"

Dolph turned from him and rushed to the door, clawing at the lock with shaking hands. Sheriff Ben unlocked the door for him and shoved him out into the opening in the face of the tensely expectant mob.

"It seems," said Sheriff Ben in a loud voice, "that Dolph doesn't want Claude Warren any more."

Dolph looked over the mob and it seemed that suddenly he hated every individual in it.

"Go home, you fools!" he cried. "He's only a kid!"

And then his large shoulders shook with sobs and he stumbled into the mob, pushing aside or striking at anyone who stood in his way and crying out loudly for all to go home.

The stunned mob milled about uncertainly for awhile, and then the rumor started and swept through the ranks that, in an adjoining county, the real murderer of Henry Rankins had been captured and was being held in jail. The mob became a group of shamefaced individuals and the individuals hurried from the scene as if fleeing from some nameless terror. Soon the square in front of the jail was deserted.

Of course the rumor that had dissipated the mob was as unfounded as the one that had created it, but, later that night, Doc Doran, the coroner, came into the office and found Sheriff Ben sitting at his desk, now cleared of weapons.

"I just finished the autopsy on Henry," Doc announced. "He died of heart failure. He must have been pitching hay up in the loft when the stroke hit him and, in falling, he sustained those head injuries." Doc looked curiously at the sheriff, who seemed not to be listening to him. "Say, what's this I hear about a mob forming in front of this place?"

"They went home," said Sheriff Ben. "Their kids were sleepy."

Sheriff Ben sat slumped over his desk long after the coroner had left. He had, he realized, no more reason to be proud than any member of the recent mob. At first, in his abject fear of personal harm, he had wanted to hand Claude Warren over to the mob. Then he had decided that, no matter what he did, his days as sheriff of Green Valley were ended and his fear had turned into blind, unreasoning hatred and he had felt the urge to turn his guns on the mob and to kill as many of them as possible, not in the interests of justice, but to avenge himself against the others for having placed him in such a predicament. He had been spared having to make a choice between the two alternatives only because, out of his desperation, a third expedient had occurred to him.

That is why I say to you that a lyncher is neither tall nor short, nor young nor old, nor male nor female, and he is faceless, but, under certain circumstances and conditions, he is you and you and you and, yes, even me.

I am Ben Hodges.

Throwback
Donald Hamilton

August 1953

There was a fight in the camp that night. It went the usual way; after three months of this kind of life, George Hardin could have written the script from memory, the firelight, the two men's voices rising suddenly, the girl's half-suppressed scream as she was roughly swept aside. Then the men were flailing at each other in the flickering orange light, then closing in and grappling, tearing up the ground with their feet. There was the usual officious character this time a stranger in a tattered air force uniform who waved everybody back. "Let the boys fight it out," he shouted, "let the best man win!" There was the girl standing back a little watching, her tongue occasionally stealing out to moisten her lips.

Looking up, Hardin saw his wife come around the edge of the light towards him. He tried to catch her eye; failing, he looked back to the straining, panting, sweating men by the fire. They crashed to the ground and rolled almost to the feet of the girl. She stood unmoving, watching them, as if unaware that she could easily be knocked down by their heedless violence and badly hurt. In a world where most of the women along the roads had taken refuge in what durable men's clothes they could find, this girl still wore a wool suit, a sweater, and high-heeled pumps, all hinting vaguely of expensive origin, and all looking about the way you would expect expensive clothes to look after three months of campfires and sleeping in the bushes. But the firelight flattered her, emphasizing the long lines of her body and the strong planes of her face, and almost failing to reveal the uncut, unwashed, uncombed look of her hair and the state of her clothes.

The firelight gleamed on the tip of her tongue as she again moistened her pale lips, long strangers to lipstick. The action gave her a predatory, wanton look as she watched, unmoving, the two men fighting over her. Yet Hardin had a feeling that she was not really concerned over the outcome. He did not think it mattered to her in the least which of the men took her; any more than another snag in her torn sweater would matter, or another stain on her grimy skirt, or another crack in her broken shoes. She did not care, because she was dead. She had died three months ago. Nothing more could happen to her now.

He recognized the look. Right afterwards, it had been understandable; they had all been dazed and unbelieving. He remembered himself and Ellen getting out of the car that morning on the highway, still dressed for the party they had attended at the home of a friend who lived outside of town. The jets had come over when they had been halfway home, the roads had jammed up with traffic within a few minutes, and they had sat in the stalled car all night, the windows up against the fine powdery dust, watching the unimaginable sight of the world being blown to hell. He remembered the little whimpering noise Ellen had made in his arms when the flame had gone up straight ahead of them. Sometimes he still wondered if the kids had been asleep when it hit, or if they had had time to wake up and be frightened, and if Mrs. Strong, the sitter, had been able to calm them. Not that it really mattered.

In the morning they had left the car and gone ahead on foot, neither saying anything about where they were going, but hurrying, breathlessly, along the miles of highway, the stalled cars powdered with dust, the thin sunshine that later turned to rain. There were other people, some standing around, or sitting, dazed and blank; others moving quickly and purposefully like themselves, but with a kind of sleepwalking look about them.

The closer they came to it, the tighter the cars were packed, there had been collisions, bent bumpers, crumpled fenders, once important but now insignificant. In the blast area itself—long before the town was in sight—the going had got progressively worse, with fallen trees and telephone poles and snakelike coils of wire down across the pavement. The very pavement itself had no longer been smooth, as if the earth had moved a little during the night; embankments had run down over the road, bridges had fallen. There had been dead people and injured ones among the living.

Then they had come to the top of the rise above the town, and there had been no need to go further. Beyond there was only dust.

He remembered turning to his wife and looking at her for the first time since the morning, seeing a strange, haggard woman in a torn fur wrap and the remnants of a taffeta evening gown. Then there had been a sound in the air and they had fled together as a flight of jets went over.

He could never remember much about the next few days except that they had hidden in the woods and it had rained most of the time they had been the only people in the world for a while, sharing the warmth of each other's bodies against the cold spring nights in the places where they hid, hearing the planes overhead from time to time. He could not remember anything they had said to each other Then the sun came out and there were no more planes and they left the shelter of the woods and, each shocked at the other's incredible appearance, as if they had not opened their eyes for the days and weeks that had passed, they had stolen soap and food and fresh clothes from a small country store that had already been looted several times. That had been while it was still easy, before the farmers and the scanty population of the untouched small towns had organized against the displaced, hungry hordes from about the destroyed cities. Since then he had twice had to use the revolver which, with a box of cartridges, he had found in the glove compartment of an abandoned car in which they had stayed one rainy night.

It had been another funny war, George Hardin thought, as he watched the two men on the ground pounding at each other with growing weariness, there had been the same year of preliminary skirmishing with the good old-fashioned weapons that just blew cities up a block at a time; for a while it had looked as if nobody would have the nerve to start the ball rolling. But when it started rolling, brother, he told himself, it really rolled. And here these two jackasses, having avoided atomic death by a miracle, were trying to murder each other with their fists. And the girl would give herself numbly to the victor because it did not matter, because she didn't care what happened to her in this nasty world that wouldn't keep her hair in permanents. He had seen the attitude before, and he had no respect for it.

"Who is it?" Ellen asked, reaching him and sitting down beside him. He was always glad to look at her these days, proud of her for managing to keep herself looking clean if not exactly dainty in the overall trousers and the boy's denim shirt they had found for her Some of the other women—and the men, too—had let themselves get pretty unappetizing; it was easy enough to do. But Ellen always looked nice, even at the end of a long day of walking. "Who is it?" she asked. "Anybody we know?"

"One's Jack Dodd," Hardin said. They both knew Jack Dodd, he was by way of being the group bully. He had once made a pass at Ellen, to be discouraged by Hardin's gun. The fact that they were married, which Dodd had claimed not to know, had let the man back down without too much loss of pride. "The other just joined up today with the girl," Hardin said. "I don't know his name." He glanced at his wife. "Where have you been?"

"I want to talk to you, darling. Let's get out of here for a moment."

Hardin glanced at the fighters. "Well, Jack's got him licked, anyway Looks like Miss High-heels has a new protector."

"Mrs. High-heels," Ellen said. "She's wearing a wedding ring."

There was something disturbing about the thought that a few months ago this young girl, now being fought over like a camp floozy, had had a husband, a home, perhaps even children. Hardin put the thought aside; every person you met on the roads these days had a tragedy. Come to that, if he was going to brood on tragedies, he had a perfectly good one of his own. He put this thought quickly aside as well, and followed his wife out of the camp.

Away from the fire, they could see the light of a farm in the distance, up the hill. The camp was down among the trees, between the highway and a creek. Out in the open it was quite bright from a half moon that, getting ready to set, still hung above the horizon. The silence was the thing you noticed, Hardin thought; no traffic on the road, no planes overhead, no radios or television sets playing in the distance.

"Let's not get too far away," he said feeling for the gun in his pocket. "I don't want some farmer to blow my head off with a shotgun. They're getting tougher all the time."

Ellen said, "Do you think we'll ever find a place where they'll leave us alone? I never thought I'd know what it was like to feel like an Okie."

"We'll find some place," he said. "Or make one." They faced each other for a moment; then he took her in his arms and kissed her hard. "Don't go running off like that," he said at last, a little breathlessly "Another couple of minutes and I'd have been chasing around looking for you. Don't get lost, darling. This would be a hell of a world to be alone in."

"George," she said presently, "George, do you really think it's this way all over the world?"

"I don't know Perhaps not. Perhaps it's just such a hell of a big job of rehabilitation that the countries that weren't smashed can't figure out where to start. Or perhaps they simply don't want to."

"What do you mean?"

"When the big boys knock each other out, it gives the little fellows a chance. Why should they rush in to put us back on our feet again? Most of them were never very fond of us, anyway." He stroked her hair gently "It's all right, Ellen. We'll make out."

"We're going to have to," she whispered.

"What do you mean?"

"I saw that doctor, George. He says there's no doubt about it."

He was silent for a moment, taking this in. "Is it is everything all right?"

"Yes," she said. "He didn't think I ought to have any trouble, particularly after having had two normal—" She checked herself; it was something to which they did not refer if they could help it. "In March, he said. And he's writing out exactly what we're to do if . . ." Her breath caught briefly . . . "if there's no doctor handy when the time comes. I'll get it from him in the morning." He could not make out the expression of her face in the moonlight; but he could feel her trembling. "I'm scared, George. Doing it alone . . . it was all made so easy for me, the other times."

"I'm sorry—"

"Don't say that!" she breathed fiercely "Don't ever say that. We wanted it and we're going to have it and to hell with this lousy world. Somebody's got to keep on living. I'm not a bit sorry I'm just scared stiff."

The fight was over when they came back into camp. Somebody told them the stranger had lost and had beat it. Dodd, the victor, was lying back near the bushes, grunting occasionally as the girl, wiping the blood from his face with a wet rag, hit a sore spot. He looked rather exhausted from his victory The girl did not seem to care greatly whether she hurt him or not; and after a while Dodd swore at her, sat up, and used the rag on himself.

The air force officer who had constituted himself referee had got himself an audience, and was holding forth. "I tell you people," he said, "you should have seen it, it was really something. We came in like this at thirty thousand feet . . ." There were the usual gestures; if you tied a fly-boy's hands, Hardin thought, the poor guy would be unable to talk ". . . just like going up in an express elevator, Christ, I thought the old bucket was a goner The instruments went all to hell; I flew her home on the seat of my pants. Hit the coast at Charleston instead of Norfolk where I was heading. No radar, nothing. Christ. But you should have seen that blast, she was a beauty. Hiroshima was a firecracker beside it."

Hardin felt his wife's hand, cold, steal into his own and press it tightly Somebody asked a question.

"Moscow?" The airman laughed. "I wasn't there myself, but I talked to one of the boys. He said that what happened to Moscow shouldn't happen to a Rooshian. Haha. He was a real comic . . . What's the matter?"

The man got slowly to his feet, facing the people who had gradually crowded in around him, as if only now realizing that their faces were hostile. Yet something in his attitude said that he had been through this before. Suddenly there was a big army automatic pistol in his hand.

"Get back there, children. Who do you think you're crowding?"

A middle-aged man said, "That's fine. But where were you boys while my wife and kids were being killed? That's what I want to know."

There was a murmur of approval through the crowd. Somebody cried, "If you were so damn brave, why didn't you stop them?"

"It wasn't my job to stop them," the airman said. "Nobody ever claimed we could stop them. All we said was that we could hit them, and we did." There was something pitiful and savage and lonely about him, Hardin thought, and wondered into how many camps this man had wandered, by how many fires he had told his story in the same challenging fashion, seeking attack so that he could defend himself. "Hypocrites," he said. "You damn hypocrites! We did what you sent us to do, yes, people like you. And now you're squawking because their fliers did the same to you. Did you expect to sit comfortably at your TV sets watching us fight your damn war for you? Well, now you know." He took a step backwards. "Stand back."

Then somebody rose out of the bushes behind him, and Hardin swept his wife to the ground as the pistol in the airman's hand discharged. They were a little back from the fire, and suddenly they were alone. Ellen sat up and shook the hair back from her face. She shivered, and turned away from the knot of people trampling, animal-like, over something on the ground. She buried her face in Hardin's shoulder.

He did not look away. There were certain things to be kept track of, if you wanted to survive along the road, and he wanted to learn who would wind up with the airman's gun, but things were too confused to tell; and suddenly there was more confusion, the bushes crackling and snapping as armed men stepped out of the woods on all aides of the camp.

"All right, you Townies!" a man shouted. "All right, we've had enough of your kind around here. Get on the road and start moving—"

Somebody kicked the fire apart. A revolver went off, answered by the heavy report of a shotgun, and the revolver again, and the shotgun, and something that sounded like a deer rifle; and people were running and crawling through the darkness.

"Come on!" Hardin whispered urgently "Let's get the hell out of here—"

He reached for his wife's shoulder, and suddenly the din and confusion seemed to move to a great distance, as he felt the terrible slackness with which her body yielded to his touch. When he touched her face, his hand came away warm and wet with blood. He picked her up.

"Ellen," he whispered. "*Ellen!*"

Daylight found him crouching in the bushes near the stream. After a while he got up slowly, looked around, and went back to where the camp had been. It was very quiet now The fire was still smoldering. Two bodies lay near it, and various items of personal equipment lay discarded around it. He found a blanket and an army entrenching tool and went back to the edge of the creek, selecting a little rise overlooking a meadow as a suitable place to dig. Then he went back into the bushes with the blanket, wrapped up his burden carefully, and carried it to the grave, filling this and laying the sod back over it with care. He tried to remember a prayer but none would come to him.

He heard a splashing in the creek but did not turn at once, until footsteps stopped behind him. Then he rose to face the newcomers, Jack Dodd and the girl for whom Dodd had fought the previous night. They were both wet to the armpits and muddy to the knees from wading the creek and scrambling up the steep earth bank. The girl carried her high-heeled shoes in her hands; after a moment she leaned down to put them on, making no other effort to pull her wet clothes straight or wring them out; she would dry in time, her attitude said, and who cared, anyway?

"Your wife?" Jack Dodd asked, glancing at the place where the sod had been replaced.

Hardin nodded.

"Hell, that's tough," the other said. Hardin noted that Dodd carried the airman's .45 automatic. "Those damn farmers! Well they'll laugh on the other side of their mouths pretty soon." Dodd glanced at Hardin sharply "Come along. You look like you ought to be handy in a scrap. This ought to be right in your line."

"What?"

"We're sick of being kicked around. A bunch of us is going to raid that farm back there. Raid it and burn it to the ground. Show the bastards they can't kick us around. Just because nobody dropped any bombs on them they think they're God Almighty."

"What will you do after that?"

"Get the hell out, I guess. We just want to give them something to remember us by, for last night, until we get stronger and come back this way . . . You've got a gun, haven't you? That's swell. Look, Hardin, I've got ideas. Get a bunch together—this raiding a farm is nothing, see—get a bunch of tough cookies with guns, like you and me and, hell, we can put the fear of God into these bastards. They'll pay us to lay off. Protection, like. Better than being driven up and down the roads like sheep, eh?" Dodd made a gesture with his big, battered hands. "Hell, I don't like to go in for the rough stuff, but what choice do they give us? It isn't our fault we haven't got a place to stay."

He still could not quite get it into his head that Ellen was dead; but he knew that he was getting very tired of people whose troubles were always somebody else's fault. The guilt for what had happened was everywhere; you might as well take a piece of it and start chewing. You had to get used to the taste.

"Count me out," Hardin said.

"That's a hell of a way to act," Jack Dodd said. "After the way they killed your wife?"

"Let me worry about my wife," Hardin said.

"You'll just leave her lying there dead?" the other man said. "So sorry, Mr. Farmer, my wife got in the way of one of your bullets . . ." Dodd stared at Hardin for a moment, then shrugged. "All right. But if you're that peaceful, you've got no use for a gun, so pass it over I can find a guy who will use it." His voice became harsher "Come on, come on! Listen, Hardin, I haven't forgotten that you slapped my wrist once just for speaking civilly to your wife . . ."

Dodd took a step forward, reaching for the gun in Hardin's fist. Hardin backed away quickly, swinging the gun around and then bringing it hip-high, tilting the muzzle up at Dodd's face.

For an instant, they faced each other, the silence between them as deadly ominous as a primed hand grenade. Their eyes locked, and they each read meaning into the other man's face, each striving to understand that meaning. It was Hardin who grasped it first. His finger tightened on the trigger of his gun. The pistol kicked in his fist, sent a shock rumbling up the length of his arm.

He saw Dodd's face erupt when the bullet took it, and then Dodd pitched forward into the dirt, and the sound of the shot seemed to linger on the air for a long while, long after he had crumpled to the ground, his face holding a look of shocked surprise under the blood.

Hardin looked at the revolver in his hand and frowned; he was getting a little too handy with the thing. That was three times he had used it. He would have to watch that, he reflected, as he picked up the other weapon and felt the dead man for another clip. There was none, but .45 Auto was a common caliber and he had no doubt he would find more shells for it along the road.

Grief struck him suddenly, like the ache of a nagging tooth suddenly flaring into pain. *Where are you going now?* he asked himself. *What are you going to do? You with two guns and nobody, nothing.*

The girl, about whom he had completely forgotten, stirred a little on the spot where she was standing, from which she had not moved. In daylight, her wet and grimy clothes, her streaked face and stringy hair made it almost impossible to recall the hint of beauty that the firelight had suggested the evening before. She looked merely hungry and dirty The wedding ring, and a rather good diamond, gleamed on her hand like a forgotten memory The fact that she had been allowed to retain her rings through all her experiences was, Hardin reflected, a commentary on the situation, it had not taken people long to realize that you could not eat jewelry These days you could carry a bar of gold safely down the highway, but you were very apt to be killed for a can of Spam.

He looked at her for a moment longer. In his mind was something Ellen had said: *Somebody's got to go on living.* After a moment, he put the guns away, one in his pocket and the other under his belt. He did not look at the broken turf by his feet, but turned away.

Somewhere to the south there would be a place where a couple of people could endure the winter to come without freezing to death. After that, who knew?

"Come on," he said irritably over his shoulder, then flushed a little as he saw that the girl was walking right beside him.

Comeback
R. Van Taylor

February 1954

It happened too often to be mere coincidence. The same man each time. He wasn't exactly fat but he was sloppy-looking, like his brown suit and gray hat; and those glasses of his—they left the impression that if he ever removed them his eyes would appear small and weak.

Stevens didn't know how many days the man had been watching him, but it was on Friday that he noticed him for the first time. Around ten-thirty he and a couple of other guys from National Lock had gone down to Harry's for a coffee break. While they sat at the counter Stevens became aware that this man, who sat near the front, was watching him in the long mirror behind the counter. When their eyes met, the man raised his chin slightly as if in greeting. . . .

Saturday, when Stevens got off the bus near his apartment, the man was leaning against the mailbox. He lowered his paper and grinned, displaying tobacco-stained teeth. Stevens ignored him and wormed his way through the kids playing on the sidewalk until his five-year-old son leaped on him and clamped his legs around Stevens' middle, jabbering enthusiastically while Stevens took him inside.

"Daddy!" Billy complained "You're not listening to me!"

Sunday, as they left Mass, the man was standing on the sidewalk outside St. Agnes Church. Stevens tightened his grip on Marge's arm and pulled Billy closer to him. "Let's hurry back home," he said. "It looks like rain."

The sky was dark and the wind whipped in restless gusts. From the east came the faint rumble of thunder.

Then, late Monday afternoon, as Stevens was heading home on the bus, the person beside him got off and another man slid into the seat beside him. Beneath the edge of his paper Stevens noticed the brown trousers. He glanced at the man—the man with the thick glasses which magnified his eyes.

"Hello, Johnny," the man said. "It's been a long time, ain't it? I'd call six years a long time—wouldn't you, Johnny?"

"You must be mistaken," Stevens said.

The man kept looking at him, as if he were trying to read him. "Don't give me that song and dance. I wanna talk to you."

"You've got me confused with someone else," Stevens said. He stood up, forced his way from the seat, shouldered his way to the side door and got off at the next corner. The man did not follow.

Stevens was quiet during supper that evening. Later he went into the living room and stood at the window for a long time. It was a small but comfortable apartment; ground floor and facing the street, in a building that had real marble steps and a wide arched entrance. It was the elite of the not-so-elite McCary Street.

He heard Marge come into the room and sit down. In a few minutes she said, "What's the matter, Fred?"

"I can't figure it out," Stevens said "How come I went to National for a job as soon as I got out of the hospital? How come I knew so much about locks?"

"Fred, please, don't—"

"I've got a right to know! They say I got hit by a hit and run, right out there in front. I don't remember anything about it I wouldn't even have known my name if it hadn't been for the landlady!"

"Don't, Fred," Marge pleaded.

"Why didn't I have any identification on me? What was I doing with this apartment? Why was I carrying over five hundred dollars?"

Marge laid down her magazine and went to him She put her hands high on his arms and turned him around and tried to get him to look at her. He wouldn't.

"I thought we agreed never to talk about this," she said.

"I know, but—"

"Look, you're trembling. You've upset yourself. Oh, darling, darling." She pulled herself to him and held on tightly. "I'm glad it happened the way it did. If it hadn't I would have never met you—I would have never been your nurse. When I fell in love with you I didn't care about your past; I knew that you couldn't remember. But I didn't care. I don't care now."

He squeezed his eyes shut and rubbed his cheek against her silky, golden hair. "Marge, I love you and Billy so much it hurts. You're my whole life now. There never was another life for me."

Then he kissed her as if he'd never be able to kiss her again. "I'm sorry I blew up," he said afterwards, "but it makes a grown man feel kind of silly to be only six years old."

From the bedroom Billy cried out in sudden fright and for a brief moment they both tensed instinctively.

"Another nightmare," Marge said.

Stevens stepped to the bedroom and snapped on the light. Billy was sitting up in his small bed, tears streaming from his eyes and too scared to do anything but sit there and cry. Stevens took his son into his arms.

"It was just a bad dream, Billy," he said. "I know how you feel. . . . I know how you feel."

The following afternoon when Stevens got home he saw Billy on the steps. Someone was sitting there with the little boy, talking to him. Stevens hurried to Billy, jerked him up and told him to go inside. Billy didn't seem to understand his father's abruptness. His eyes clouded as he left.

The man on the steps grinned up at Stevens, but the eyes behind those thick glasses were cold.

"You've got a nice kid there," the man said. "Nice wife, too. You're smart, Johnny—very smart. You act just like any other poor slob. When are you going to start spending the money?"

"What do you want?"

"Just my half. I figure that's a reasonable request, since we were partners."

"I don't know what you're talking about."

The man stood up. His puffy face was so close Stevens could smell him. "You'd better. For six years all I've thought about was finding you. Johnny—the man with the brains; the man who could pull the perfect job; including the perfect double cross."

"You must be crazy," Stevens said.

"Almost, but not quite. What I've gone through would drive anybody nuts. It was like trying to trace a ghost, finding you. To tell you the truth, Johnny, I intended to kill you. But I'm not now because I know you haven't spent the money. You were too smart to do that. The stuff has cooled off by now. I want my half."

"I don't have any money," Stevens said.

"You'd better. My half just comes to around seventy-five G's. Surely your wife and kid is worth that much to you, Johnny."

The man wrote something on the inside cover of a book of matches. He stuffed it into Stevens' shirt pocket. "I know you're going to improve your memory," he said. "I'll give you a couple of days to do it. Call that number. Ask for Smith." Again his mouth twisted into that obscene grin. "That's right—it's not my real name. I'm too smart for that, Johnny. Just like you are."

Marge met Stevens as soon as he entered the apartment. "Billy's crying," she said. "He told me that you scolded him. What—"

"Billy was out on the steps," he said accusingly to Marge.

"Sure he was. He plays out there all the time. Fred, you're white as a sheet. What's the matter?"

"Nothing," Stevens said. "Just keep Billy inside."

While shaving the next morning, Stevens cut his chin badly. The caustic stick burned like the devil when he tried to stop the bleeding. He did a messy job of it. Those hands of his just would not steady down.

Ham and eggs for breakfast. It was a shame to waste them.

"Fred," Marge said worriedly, "are you feeling all right?"

"Sure," he said.

"I think you had a chill in bed at night. You were shaking, hard. Maybe you should stay home today."

"I'll be all right," Stevens said.

The coffee—at least he could get that down.

At his drafting board at National Lock he just couldn't get with it. The points on his pencils kept breaking off. The lines on the paper before him were meaningless. Finally he gave up. He went to see Morgan. Something was the matter with him, he told his boss. Maybe he should go to a doctor. Could he get off?

Sure he could. Take care of himself. Sorry.

But Stevens didn't go to a doctor. He went to see Father Callahan.

"I need your advice, Father," Stevens said to him.

After Stevens had told him about the man. Father Callahan was silent for a moment, then he said, "Fred, there's only one thing for you to do: you must go to the police and tell them this."

Stevens fumbled for a cigaret. His eyes burned and felt strained. His fingers closed on the cigaret and crushed it.

"I can't do it," he said.

"You must."

"I can't, Father! My whole life now is Billy and Marge. If I went to the police and they found out that I had stolen money, I'd have to go to prison. What would that do to Billy and Marge? I don't want to hurt them."

"But this man you tell me about—he might hurt them if you do not."

"There must be some other way. There's got to be."

"There is no other way, Fred Look at it in this light: your wife married you knowing that she knew nothing of your past. She loved you enough that she didn't care about what you had been. She wouldn't care now, even if the worst were discovered. You must believe that."

"But Billy—how about him? He didn't have that choice, Father. What would it do to him if he found out that his dad was a criminal?"

"You must have faith," Father Callahan told him. "Go to the police, my son. Today."

Stevens walked slowly to the park and sat down on a bench. He lit a cigaret, but forgot about it until it burned his fingers and gave him a sudden shock of pain. He got up then and walked until he found a policeman. He asked the cop where the nearest police station was.

It wasn't far away. He could see it now. Two blocks . . . wait for the green light . . . a block . . . half a block . . . his fingers were throbbing from the burn . . . he didn't look back at the police station but just kept on walking, a little faster now.

He turned into a drugstore and went to the phone booth. He took a book of matches from his shirt pocket, read the number on the inside of the cover. He dialed and asked for Smith.

The man suggested a bar and told Stevens where it was. He'd be there at eight. He wouldn't wait any longer than fifteen minutes.

Stevens left the drugstore. Going out the door he bumped into a fat woman who asked him if he was blind or something.

He didn't say he was sorry.

He didn't answer her at all.

He didn't go home that evening. He called Marge and told her that he had to work, that it might be late before he got in.

"Fred, do you have to work tonight, feeling the way you do?"

"Yes. It can't be helped."

"But you sound ill—tense."

"I'll be all right," he said. "Why don't you and Billy go see a picture?"

At eight Stevens entered the bar the man had told him to go to. He went back to the rear booth and sat down.

"Right on time," the man said "You *can* keep a date after all, can't you."

The fellow insisted on having drinks. Stevens didn't want one, but after having it he took another without protesting.

"That's it, Johnny," the man said. "Relax."

"Stop calling me Johnny," Stevens said.

"I used to be scared of you. Johnny. You were a mean sonofabitch. You don't look mean now. Johnny. I ain't scared of you anymore."

"For crissake! Will you tell me—"

"I've been doing a lot of thinking since I talked with you last," the man said. "I got to thinking that maybe you're on the level—that maybe you really don't remember."

"I don't! I swear I don't. That's why I came here tonight. I've got to convince you that I don't."

"Maybe," the man said. "But I didn't stop my thinking there. You see, I found out you had that apartment before you got hit by that cat. Okay, what were you doing with it? I figure you were holding up there. I also figure that someplace in that apartment you hid the dough. That's pretty smart thinking, ain't it? You're not the only one who's got a brain."

Stevens stared into the darkness. "Where did I get the money?"

"We pulled a job up north. A safe isn't all you can crack, Johnny. That poor bastard of a night-watchman, you left his head a pulp. You sure were mean back then. No wonder I was scared of you; no wonder I didn't argue with you when you wanted to split up. You said we'd meet in Chicago and divide the dough. You never did show up. I was scared to hunt you at first. I didn't want my head a bloody mess like that poor—"

"Never mind." The muscles of Stevens' jaws flexed.

"Like I was saying: I figure you hid the money in your apartment, but now you've forgotten about it. So, we go look for it."

"I'll look for it," Stevens said. "When I find it you can have every dollar of it—every goddam cent."

The man laughed. "Huh uh. I'm not giving you a chance to pull another fasty. We'll look for it together."

"We can't do that! My wife and kid—they don't know! I don't want them to ever—"

He looked down at the .38 revolver which had appeared in the man's hand. "I hate to disillusion your wife and kid, but that's the way we're going to do it," the man said.

"Please!" Stevens said. "Give me time. I'll think of something I don't want to hurt Marge and Billy."

"I've waited long enough," the man said. "We do it now. My way."

Stevens' desperation grew. He lunged for the man, swinging wildly, and missed. The man did not miss. He brought the gun up and Stevens felt it come down with a crash on the back of his neck. His head went down; he staggered to the wall and fell against it, upright. For a long minute he knew nothing.

Then a strange wildness came over him, and he pushed himself from the wall and moved quickly forward. He hit the man once and, as he fell, tore the gun free. Bending over the unconscious body, he swung the gun again and again at the man's skull, until it felt soft and blood was coming from the man's ears and nose.

He was dead. Stevens left him there.

Outside, he hailed a cab.

"I want to go to—" He paused, frowning.

"Well?" the cabby said.

"Just a minute," Stevens said. "I'm trying to think."

"Look, mister, don't you know where you want to go?"

"Go to McCary street," Stevens said. "Just keep driving until I tell you to stop."

On McCary, Stevens searched the front of the buildings as they whipped by. Ten blocks . . . twenty . . . thirty . . . then he saw it, not long after they'd passed that big church. He saw the old apartment building with the wide arched door way and the marble steps.

A couple of blocks beyond he told the driver to stop.

He get out of the cab and began walking back down the street. There was no light in the left ground apartment of the building he watched. When he came to the entrance he slipped inside and eased down the dimly lighted hall to a door.

He stood there, listening.

He took some keys from his pocket. The first one did not fit; the second slipped into the lock easily.

He turned the doorknob with a delicate touch and moved inside the dark room, gently closing the door again. He stood there, hardly breathing.

The water faucet in the kitchen was dripping.

He snapped on the lights. The interior of the room brought shock to his face. He flipped off the lights quickly, his hand dropping to the gun in his coat pocket. He stood there for a good five minutes. Then he moved silently through the darkness to the bedroom.

No one there. His shoulders relaxed a bit.

He went to the bathroom, closed the door and turned on the light.

He began unloading the medicine cabinet and when it was empty he took a quarter and removed the screws from the back of it, working silently as possible. Once he froze, his eyes switching to the door The buzzing of the refrigerator stopped and the muted whirr of a motor began.

He removed the medicine cabinet from the wall, exposing the studs Standing to one side of the lavatory, he reached deep down into the wall and took out a bundle made with a towel. He opened it and began stuffing packs of bills inside his shirt.

Suddenly he froze again.

His hand flashed out and hit the switch.

Perspiration rolled into his eyes and stung them.

The moment the bathroom door began to open he grabbed the woman and jerked her inside. She started to scream, but he hit her again and again with the revolver until slipped to the floor limply and he felt the sticky ooze on his hand, the same ooze that matted her golden hair with crimson. He ran, paying no attention to the small figure crying in the corner of the dark bedroom. As he careened from the entrance of the building he thought he heard someone screaming.

It sounded like a kid having a nightmare.

Tin Can
B. Traven

September 1954

The Indian peasant, Eliseo Gallardo, had three pretty daughters of marriageable age, the eldest of whom was sixteen and the youngest thirteen.

One day Eliseo was paid a visit by Natalio Salvatorres, a young bachelor who for several weeks had worked in the nearby bush. From the wages he had made by burning charcoal, Natalio had saved about fifty pesos. But after he had bought a new cotton shirt, cotton pants, bast hat, and paid for his board and lodging, he had little left.

Last Saturday there had been a dance in the village, and it was at this dance that Natalio had seen the three pretty Gallardo girls. However, he had been able to dance only once with each of the girls, because the other young men had always been quicker and more resolute than he. Natalio was a young man who needed time to make up his mind.

He spent all of the next day, Sunday, thinking things over. When, finally, he had arrived at a more definite idea, he spent Monday, Tuesday and Wednesday getting better acquainted with it. On Thursday his idea matured sufficiently so that, by Friday, he knew clearly what he wanted.

It was this which made him go on Saturday to see Eliseo, the father of the three girls.

"Well, young man, which of the three do you want?" Eliseo asked.

"That one," Natalio said, and nodded his head toward Sabina, the daughter who was fourteen and had the prettiest bosom of the three.

"That's what I thought," Eliseo said. "She would suit you very fine. You are not so dumb. By the way—what is your distinguished name?"

After Natalio had given his full name, which he could pronounce but could not write nor spell, the girls' father asked how much money he possessed.

"Twenty pesos," Natalio said. This was twice as much as he really had.

"Then you cannot have Sabina," Señor Gallardo said. "I need a new pair of pants, and my old woman has no shoes of any kind. If you wish to appear so splendid as to ask for Sabina, you can't expect her mother and father to run about in dirty rags. What do you think our standing is in this village, anyway? There must be new pants for me, and there must be at least one pair of white or brown canvas shoes for the woman. Otherwise there is no opening for you in my family. Let me have some of your tobacco."

After the cigarettes had been rolled and lighted, Natalio said, "*Bueno*, don Eliseo. I'll be satisfied with just as fine a girl as that one over there." This time he nodded toward Filomena, the eldest of the three.

"You are smart, *muy listo*, Natalio. Where are you working?"

"I own a burro. And a good young donkey it is, too."

"No horse?"

These questions concerning his financial situation made Natalio quite uneasy. He spit several times upon the earthen floor of the hut before he spoke again.

"I have an uncle who works in a mine up near Parral," he said. "There are more than a hundred mines up there. As soon as I have a woman, I'll be on my way there to work. My uncle will see to it that I find a job. He is very friendly with one of the most important foremen."

"Ah, yes," Eliseo said.

"And what do you think, don Eliseo? One can easily make three pesos a day in those mines."

"Three pesos a day is good money," Eliseo said. "But that pitiful twenty pesos you have right now is not much to boast of. With so little money, we cannot make a wedding."

"Why not?" Natalio asked. "A wedding can't cost that much money. A minister? Well, we surely can't pay him—so we will have to do without the help of the church. And as for the marriage license—we can't pay for that, either, can we?"

"You are right, Natalio," Eliseo said. "There is not enough money in the whole world to pay for such things. And besides, they have little to do with a wedding anyway."

"Very little indeed," Natalio said.

"Of course, we must have at least two musicians for the dance," Eliseo said. "Then we must have three bottles of mescal—or, better still, four bottles. Otherwise the people here in the village might gossip about us. They might say that Filomena was not married to you at all and had only run away with you like a hussy. I tell you, *muchacho,* such things are not done in my family. Not my daughters; no, señor. We are honest folks. Don't ever think one of my daughters would run away with you without my special permission. You might as well wait a thousand years for such a thing to happen in my family. Not with a father like me around. No, señor—not with us."

The two men continued their negotiations for another two hours, during which time they drank many cups of coffee and smoked most of Natalio's tobacco. In the end it was agreed upon that Natalio should return to the bush until such time as he had earned enough to pay for the musicians, the bottles of mescal, two pounds of coffee, six pounds of brown sugar, one pair of light canvas shoes for the mother, and one pair of pants for the father. And in addition, Eliseo pointed out, there should be two pesos for sweet bread to be eaten with the coffee by the women and children who would come to the wedding. In fact, he said, the whole village would be at the wedding, and if a few pesos happened to be left over for unexpected guests from a neighboring village, so much the better for the good reputation of the family.

When the deal was closed, and Natalio had accepted all the conditions proposed by the father, he was told that he would be allowed to lodge and board with the family. He would have to pay for this, of course, but the cost would be one-third less than he was paying now. He was to take up his quarters in a certain corner of the one-room adobe hut, and, as there might be many difficulties and molestations if handled otherwise, Filomena was to be permitted to sleep in the same corner—provided Natalio would buy her a new blanket.

Natalio agreed to this, and hurried to the nearest general store to buy a new blanket with the brightest colors he could find. Then he bought a bottle of mescal to celebrate the deal, and returned to the hut.

All the members of the family, including Filomena herself, had been present during the whole time the two men had been negotiating what, to them, was a straightforward business matter.

After everyone had taken a drink from the bottle of mescal, Filomena was asked by her father if she had something to say.

"I'd like very much to go to Parral," she said.

Natalio was short those ten pesos he had lied into his pocket; and during the eight weeks he worked in the bush his new shirt and pants went to pieces, in spite of the fact that he was very careful with them. He had to buy a new shirt and a new pair of pants for the wedding, and it was because of this that an American farmer, who had a ranch only a few miles from the village, discovered one day that two of his best cows were missing.

The wedding dance was over. Señor Gallardo had been quite drunk. But he had not been too drunk to take great care not to get mud on his new yellow cotton pants. His wife had worn her new brown canvas shoes during only the first hour of the party. She had then wrapped them in paper, replaced them in the cardboard box in which they had been sold and, with pride in being the owner of such a treasure, had hidden them so well that none of her daughters could find them.

Because everything had taken place just the way it had been planned beforehand, Filomena was now Natalio's *esposa*, respected by everybody as a wife whom nobody must covet or try to snatch away.

Natalio loaded his two blankets, a coffee kettle, a small bast bag containing provisions, his machete, his ax, and his Filomena on his burro and started off for the mines.

He had no uncle there. This had been another of his various lies to win the confidence of Filomena's father. Nevertheless, because he was willing to take on any job, no matter how hard it might be, it was less than a week before he found work. He did not make three pesos a day, of course; all he earned was one peso seventy-five.

During his spare time Natalio built a flimsy adobe hut, much like all the others in the village. Here he and Filomena led the life of the average Indian miner and his wife. She cooked his meals, did his laundry, patched his shirt and pants, and warmed up his bed in the cold nights so frequent in mountain regions.

He was very happy, Natalio was; and Filomena, obviously, had no cause for complaint. This status quo might have lasted for a whole lifetime, had it not been for a young miner who discovered in Filomena something special and wonderful—something Natalio would never even have suspected she possessed.

And so it happened that when Natalio came home from work one night, he found no wife in his nest. And as she had taken with her the beautiful blanket, the three muslin dresses, and her comb—all the things he had bought her—he knew she had left for good.

The huts in the village were so carelessly made, and built of such poor material, that there was very little privacy under their roofs. They had no windows, and because of this the doors were always left open until the inhabitants retired for the night.

It was, therefore, not difficult for Natalio to find the hut he was looking for. Through the wall of this particular hut, made of a light network of twigs and sticks, Natalio saw Filomena sitting happily at the side of her newly elected. She and her new man, as Natalio could easily see, were having a much more joyful time than any he had ever had with her. She had never looked at him or caressed him in the way she was now favoring her lover.

There were two other young couples in the hut. And although there was much talk and laughter, Natalio did not hear his name mentioned even once. The way these young people ignored his existence, he might as well have been dead for a long time.

When Natalio had convinced himself that Filomena was now far too happy and too much in love to ever think of returning to his side, he decided to bring this episode of his life to an end. He went to the barn where the explosives were kept, crawled under the sheet-iron wall, and stole some dynamite and a fuse.

Back in his own hut, Natalio worked steadily and patiently. With the cunning of which only an Indian seeking revenge is capable, he constructed a bomb, using as a bomb-case an empty tin can he had found near the general store.

As soon as he finished the bomb, Natalio returned to the hut where he had found Filomena with her lover. The three couples were still there, and even more animated and jolly than before. Filomena's lover was playing a mouth organ, with Filomena cuddled up against him, and by all appearances the three couples intended to keep the party going until the men had to go to work again in the morning.

It was easy for Natalio to throw the lighted bomb through the open door into the hut.

This done, he went back to his own hut and lay down to sleep, content with the knowledge that he had made the most effective bomb of which he was capable. The result was of no special interest to him. Should the bomb go off, as he was sure it would, everything would be all right. On the other hand, if the bomb failed to explode, everything would be all right too. He considered his revenge fully completed with the acts of making the bomb and placing it properly. As to what might happen afterward—he left that to providence. From now on—and for all time to come—Filomena and her new man would be safe from him. For Natalio, this episode was closed forever.

But not for the three couples inside the hut. . . .

In the mining districts, every Indian, man and woman alike, knows what it means to see at one's feet an old tin can to which a smoking fuse is attached.

The occupants of the hut saw the bomb and jumped out of the hut without even taking time for a shout of horror. This took them less than half a second. At once a terrific explosion followed, sending the hut up a hundred feet into the air.

Of the six people who had been inside, five escaped without so much as a scratch. The sixth, the young woman of the couple that owned the hut, was not so fortunate.

This woman had, at the very moment the bomb made its appearance at the party, been busy making fresh coffee in the corner of the hut farthest from the door. She had neither seen the bomb nor noted the rapid and speechless departure of her guests. Consequently she accompanied the hut on its trip upward. And since she had been unable in so short a time to decide which part of the hut she would like best to travel with, she landed at twenty different places in the vicinity.

Two days later a police agent came to the mine to see Natalio and ask him what he might know about the explosion. The agent questioned Natalio at the place where he was working, in an open excavation, but Natalio did not allow himself to be seriously interrupted. Only when he paused to wipe the sweat from his face and roll a cigarette, did he honor the agent with answers to his questions.

"You threw the bomb into the *choza* of Alejo Crespo, didn't you?" the agent asked.

"That's right," Natalio said. "But it's none of your business. It is a purely domestic affair."

"A woman was killed by that bomb."

"I know it. No need to tell me. It is my woman and I can do with her whatever I wish, for she gets from me her meals, and all her clothes, and I have paid for the music at the wedding. There are no debts left. Everything is paid."

Natalio knew what he was talking about. There was no nonsense in what he said, and he was telling nothing but the truth.

"But the trouble is," the agent said, "it wasn't your woman who was killed. It was the Crespo woman."

"So? If it was the Crespo woman that was killed, then I've nothing to do with it whatever. The Crespo woman has never done me any wrong. If she was killed, it was most certainly not my intention. In such a case it was just destiny. I'm not responsible for what destiny may do here in the village. The Crespo woman is a grown-up woman who can look out for herself, and she doesn't need me to protect her. If she'd taken better care of herself, this would not have happened to her. I'm not her guardian, and not her man either, and I don't give a damn for women who don't take care of their health."

Natalio threw his cigarette away, lifted his pickax, and struck furiously at the rocks, indicating he had important work to do and could not waste his time with idle talk which was of no interest to him.

Six weeks later, the case came up for trial. Natalio was charged with murder, though no degree was mentioned. The jury consisted of men from the village. Two were foremen at the mines, one was a carpenter, one a butcher, another a baker, others were storekeepers and saloonkeepers. None of them had even the slightest interest in Natalio's conviction. All of them depended on miners at work, because no money could be made from miners in jail.

Natalio's friends had advised him to keep his mouth shut as much as possible. If he was forced to answer any questions, they told him, he should say absolutely nothing other than, "I don't know."

This advice suited Natalio quite well. He disliked working with his head, and simply answering, "I don't know," required no work at all.

He was not deeply concerned about the outcome of his trial. If he was convicted and had to go to prison—or even if he was sentenced to be shot—it would be all right with him. On the other hand, if he was acquitted, he would go back to his work, which he liked immensely.

He rolled a cigarette, showing no emotion whatever. He cared nothing at all about the preparations going on about him in the crumbling adobe town hall.

Finally, the stage was set. Everybody in the courtroom smoked cigarettes, including the judge, the public prosecutor, the gentlemen of the jury, and the half-dozen or so miners. These visitors had come, not because of any real interest in the trial, but because they were not working, due to injuries received in the mines, and had no other place to while away their time. They would have preferred to hang around the saloons, but they had no money. Some of them had bandages on their face or head, others carried their arms in slings, and one had crutches leaning against his leg.

The public prosecutor stood up. "The defendant has made a full confession," he said. "The police officer who questioned him only two days after the crime was committed is present to be called to the witness stand, should it so please your Honor and the honorable gentlemen of the jury."

The prosecutor was sure he had a clear-cut case and that he would have no trouble getting a conviction. What really did concern him, however, was the chance that he might not be able to catch the train in time to return to town, which would mean spending the night in this miserable, stinking little village.

The men on the jury had begun to dislike the prosecutor. They resented his arrogance and the way he showed how he detested the people of the village, especially the miners, and they had seen how much he hated to have been ordered to a place where he could not walk half a block without losing his shoes in the mud.

Because they wanted to see the overbearing prosecutor miss his train and go home defeated by the men he despised, the jurors insisted on their right to question both defendant and witnesses, if they thought it was necessary in order to clear up the case for their better understanding. If Natalio himself should benefit by this procedure, so much the better. The men on the jury were much impressed by Natalio because he was so calm and stoic.

The judge welcomed these unusual interruptions by the gentlemen of the jury. He had to stay overnight anyway, because he had several other cases to attend to. These interruptions made the trial less dull for him and shortened his day. He was thankful for this, because Natalio's was the only case for the day, and he had nothing to do with his time once it was over. He usually slept the time away in places like this, but he had already slept so much here that he was tired of it.

One of the jurors asked the judge to please ask the defendant if it was true that he had confessed to the murder.

Natalio rose clumsily. "I don't know, señor," he said. He sat down again and replaced his cigarette between his lips.

Another juror asked to see the written statement of Natalie's confession.

The prosecutor jumped to his feet. "This statement, gentlemen of the jury, is written and signed by the police officer, which was necessary because the defendant can neither read nor write. In due time I'll call the officer to testify here in court. The witness is an honorable and reliable police officer with an excellent record and many years of service. We have no reason whatever to question his written and verbal statements, nor the results of his careful investigation of this case." He bent down over his little table and began fingering his papers with obvious uneasiness.

Another member of the jury wanted to know why he and his honorable colleagues should be obliged to believe more in the word of a policeman, who received his salary from the taxpayer's money, than in the word of an honest and sober miner like Natalio, who did not live, and never had lived, on the money of the taxpaying citizens. He said it was well known that Natalio worked hard for his living and that he produced valuable goods for the benefit of the whole nation.

Still another juror asked the defendant to confess right then and there, in the very face of the jury, that he had committed the crime he was charged with.

The judge called upon Natalio. "You heard what the honorable gentleman of the jury wishes to know. Did you kill the Crespo woman?"

Natalio rose only halfway. "I don't know, señor," he said quietly.

The prosecutor jumped to his feet. "But you did throw the bomb, didn't you, Natalio?" he demanded. "Tell us the truth, my man! Lying won't help you. You did throw the bomb!"

With a bored note in his voice, Natalio said, "I don't know nothing." He sat down again and puffed away at his cigarette with signs of an undisturbed conscience.

The prosecutor did not call the policeman, as he had said he was going to do. He knew they would ask the policeman if it was not true that he received his salary from the taxes paid by the citizens. As soon as the policeman admitted it was so, the jury would then ask the prosecutor where *his* salary was coming from. And this, the prosecutor realized, would lead to still another question. The jury would ask, quite seriously, whether—inasmuch as both the policeman and the prosecutor received their salaries from the same source and therefore served the same boss—there might not exist a certain combination with the object of convicting an honest miner for no other purpose than to justify the necessity of their respective offices.

Because he foresaw such a layman's distortion of the facts, the prosecutor decided against calling the policeman to the stand. Instead, he called Filomena, together with the others who were present in the hut when the bomb was thrown. Inasmuch as these witnesses belonged to the mining community, their testimony would be so tight that even the most spiteful members of the jury would have to accept it without question. The prosecutor considered Filomena his star witness. He was sure she would tell the truth, because she certainly knew the bomb had been intended for her, and she would feel much safer knowing that Natalio was in prison for several years.

Filomena and the other witnesses knew perfectly well what the whole community knew; that is, that nobody else but Natalio had been the maker and thrower of the bomb. Natalio had left no one in the village with any doubt as to who it was that knew how to defend his honor and how to punish an unfaithful wife.

But the prosecutor had had but little experience with Indian mining folk such as these, and he by no means fully understood them. He did not know that these mountain people would not, under any circumstances, bear witness against one of their own in a case such as this one. These mountain Indians had their own ideas of right and wrong and justice, just as they had their own attitude toward outside prosecutors and judges, and nothing whatever could have induced them to testify against Natalio.

On the witness stand, the people who had been in the hut declared without wavering that they had not seen the person who threw the bomb. When they were asked by the desperate prosecutor whether they thought Natalio might have done it, they said the bomb might have been thrown by a former lover of the Crespo woman, a man known throughout the state for his jealous nature and hot temper. He was, they said, a man who was ready to do anything if he felt insulted.

Filomena went further still. She said she had known Natalio very well, since she had been his *esposa* for a couple of years, and that she was absolutely sure he would never do such a thing, that he would, in fact, be the last man on earth to do so. She said she was certain Natalio had never had an affair with the Crespo woman, that she could not even imagine he might have wanted to do the Crespo woman any harm. Natalio, she said solemnly, was not of a violent nature, but was, instead, surely the most peaceful man she could think of.

The prosecutor stared at Filomena unbelievingly. "The prosecution rests," he said.

Natalio's attorney, provided by the state, had not said one word so far. Now he rose and said, "The defense rests also!"

The jury retired. Less than an hour later, because they had business to attend to, they returned.

"Not guilty!" the foreman said.

Natalio was set free immediately. Then he and the witnesses, including Filomena and her new man, went to the nearest saloon to celebrate the acquittal with two bottles of mescal. The bottles passed from mouth to mouth, no one bothering with a glass, though now and then one of them would put a pinch of salt between his teeth.

After the bottles were empty, Natalio returned to his job. There were still a few hours of his working day left, and he, honest miner that he was, did not want to miss them.

On the first Saturday night following the trial, Natalio attended a dance in the village. There, dancing with Rudecindo Ortega was a young woman who pleased him greatly. After Natalio had danced with her twice, and discovered that her name was Lolita and that she was neither married to Rudecindo Ortega nor even living with him in his hut, he retired to his own lonely hut for an hour to think things over.

Then, his mind made up, Natalio returned to the woman, reminded her he was a sober man who could stick by his job and earn his money, and asked her to live with him as his wife. She quickly agreed to do so.

Lolita arrived at his hut the next day, bringing with her all her belongings in a sugar sack, which she hung up on a peg. Once settled, she looked around the hut, cleaned the floor, and began to prepare supper.

While the beans were cooking, Natalio walked to the general store to buy his new woman a comb. On his way out of the store, he saw Rudecindo Ortega staring thoughtfully at the pile of rubbish and empty tin cans near the door. He spoke to Rudecindo, but the other man seemed to be brooding about something and did not answer.

When Natalio returned home, he went to the back of the hut, lay down, and stared up at the ceiling.

"You do not seem happy, Natalio," Lolita said. "Why is that?"

"Ah, but you are mistaken," Natalio said. "What man would not be happy with such a treasure?"

Lolita put the steaming beans on the table. Then, as she turned back toward the hearth, she saw lying in the middle of the earthen floor a large tin can to which a smoking fuse was attached.

Natalio saw it too, and in the same instant realized why Rudecindo Ortega had been staring so thoughtfully at the pile of tin cans and rubbish beside the general store.

The woman escaped unhurt. Of Natalio Salvatorres, though, not even so much as a shirt button was ever found for the woman to remember him by.

I Didn't See a Thing
Hal Ellson

March 1955

Moms is in the living room. I hear her making noise cleaning. I can stroll out and she won't know. But I'm heading for the roof again and she don't like that.
Got to play it cool. I wait, sneak to the door when I hear her turn on the radio. I'm closing the door and Moms yells, "Where you going? You fooling around on that roof again?"

I don't answer, don't hear footsteps, I run for the stairs. I'm up them in no time. It's only two flights to the roof.

I look at my coop first thing. It's okay. Nobody busted in. A good day for flying, but I'm on business.

I go down the stairs again. I'm taking my time, making no noise. Halfway down I hear somebody coming up. It's like he's creeping. Yeah, I know who that is.

Bug-Eye. He was born unnatural. I don't have to see him to know him. He walk like a cat. Got a weird head, small, like somebody squeezed it together when he was small. Got a small body, long arms, big eyes popping from his face. He's weird all around. Scares you.

I stop and start down again. He's still moving up, like he don't know I'm coming. I try to pass and he lifts his head, gets in the way. I got to stop. He looks at me with them pop-eyes. I don't say nothing, never say nothing to him.

He don't move so I move. Soon as I do, he blocks the way. But I know him now. I shift the other way, get past and run down. I hear him laugh. He's going on up. Up to the roof landing. He sits up there. It ain't sensible-like. I don't like going up when he's sitting. Yeah, I don't like him, nobody does, but nobody bother him. People in this neighborhood mind their own business.

The hell with him. I'm off to the store. Got business. Silver is jingling in my pocket. I got to get me a good bird from Taffy.

That Taffy-man I don't like, either. He's weird, too, a big fat guy with flabby muscles, but they say he's dangerous. You don't play with him. But he's got birds.

I hit his store, look around. There's plenty of birds, but I don't like them for nothing. This time I want a special bargain.

Taffy don't say nothing. He sits in a rocker in back of the store and pets his cat. He got a big black cat. Them two are like brothers. Everytime you come in you see Taffy petting that cat and smiling to himself like.

There's another guy there, too. A friend of Taffy. That's Mr. Quiet. He don't ever say much. He hangs around, smokes, and watches you like a cop. Snake-eyes he's got, real small, like little marbles. I don't like him for no money.

I walk around the store and don't see nothing but a bunch of clinkers and no-goods. Them birds are almost all bums from the park.

Taffy keeps petting that cat, but I know he's watching me. After a while he says, "What are you having, Dip?"

I'm not having nothing at all, but I make like I'm interested and I point to some Flights. "That one there," I say. "How much?"

"For you, sixty-five cents."

"Keep him," I say.

"That's too much?"

"For what's being offered."

"How much money you got?"

Yeah, that's what he always asks. It's like the National Anthem with him. But I'm not saying.

That made him laugh. "You come into look at them, that's all," he said. "All you kids. You got nothing but holes in your pockets."

I want to tell him he's got a hole in his head from petting that cat. But that's dangerous. He may be grinning but he's a head-buster. I just look at him petting the cat. Then I see that other stud is gone. I hear the door close behind me and I turn. Mr. Quiet is leaving.

When I look back at Taffy he's bent over talking to his cat. The hell with him, I say, and I walk out, hit for home.

2.

Two doors down I see Mr. Quiet. He's got his eye on me like he's waiting. I go to pass and he says, "Hey, Dip."

I don't want to stop, but it's like I got to. "Yeah?" I say.

"You want to buy some real birds?"

I'm suspicious right off, but I smell a deal. "I'm interested," I say.

"How much money you got?"

"That's my business. What kind of birds you got?"

"Good ones. They're a real bargain."

"I didn't know you was in the business."

"I ain't. I fly them. Got too many. I want to get rid of some."

"Then why don't you sell them to Taffy?"

"You know what Taffy offers?"

That sounded reasonable like. Taffy wouldn't give his dying grandmother more than fifteen cents for a pigeon.

"You want to see them?" Mr. Quiet says.

I don't like the sound in his voice, don't like him, but I'm thinking of pigeons, good ones. Maybe he's got real stuff.

I nod and we walk six blocks to his house. It's even worse than the one I live in. The hall stinks, cats is walking around smelling for garbage. We go up creaky old stairs to the roof.

I see his coop. He's got a real setup, plenty of birds, good ones.

"What do you think?" Mr. Quiet says.

I nod my head. There's a bird I like and I point. "How much is that one?"

"You want only one?"

"That's all now."

"No good. It ain't worth the trouble for me. Get some money and drop around again. I'll give you a real bargain."

I expected him to be sore but he wasn't. He just smiled and I told him I'd see about it and left him there.

Going down the stairs I'm mad cause I haven't got money. All the way home I'm kicking myself. Then I see Bug-Eye.

He's standing in the doorway with that look, like he ain't seeing nothing when he's seeing everything in the world. I don't want to pass but I'm hungry. I step up and he blocks the way.

"Where you going?" he says.

I feel like kicking his shins off, but I can't even look in them eyes of his. "Going up," I tell him.

"Wait a minute."

"What for?"

"You want to do me a favor?"

"What kind of favor?"

"Run an errand. You got time?"

I'm not hungry now. I'm mostly scared. Something tells me something is wrong, but I'm thinking of them pigeons I seen on Mr. Quiet's roof.

"Yeah, I got time," I say. "How much do you pay me?"

Bug-Eye is smiling now. "A real slickster," he says. "You'll do all right. Will you settle for five?"

"A stinking nickel?"

He laughed. "Five dollars, slickster."

When he said that my heart stopped. I don't answer.

He was talking, again, giving me directions. I had to see a man, get a package from him and bring it back.

"You got it?" he says.

"Yeah, I understand."

"Okay, start moving."

I'm off like lightning when he calls me back. "Wait a minute," he says, and I come back.

He don't look the same now. There's evil in his eyes. "What do they call you?" he asks.

"Dip."

"All right, Dip. Just so I know how to ask for you. One thing more, you don't say nothing about this to nobody. One word and I'll slice your ears off and fry them."

Yeah, big words, but he means them. I can see it in his eyes. I ain't talking to nobody.

3.

Ten minutes later I reach the place he told me to go to. There's women on the stoop, young ones. They look at me like I'm naked.

I go past and up the stairs. Another one is coming down. She smells pretty. "You looking for somebody?" she asks, and she bugs me with big eyes. They're like black lamps. But her mouth is ugly. I know what she is.

I don't answer. Bug-Eye told me not to. I get to the top floor, see a number, knock on a door.

It's like nobody's there. I don't hear nothing. Then the door opens. I see part of a face, smell something funny. I tell who sent me and the door opens fast. I'm inside in a second. This is a weird cat. A real slim-Jim and he's shaking.

He hands me the package, tells me to put it in my pocket and keep it there. That's all.

I hit for home. I want to run and can't. There's something funny about this package. I want to look at it and can't.

Bug-Eye is waiting at the door. Soon as he sees me he moves. I find him in the vestibule.

"Let's have it," he says.

I take it out and he slaps it away like it's going to bite him. I look at him, waiting for that money. All he does is light a cigarette. Then he smiles and says, "You want something?"

"Yeah, where's my money?"

"Suppose I tell you you ain't getting nothing. What then?"

What could I say to that? I didn't say nothing, not while I'm standing in that vestibule. I got a long face.

Suddenly he laughs at me. "Here," he says, and he slaps a five in my hand. "But you remember to forget." He made a scissors motion with his fingers at my ear.

Yeah, I'm not talking. I don't care about nothing now. I got that five, got them new pigeons.

Soon as I got out the door I legged it back to Mr. Quiet's house. He's sitting out front on a box.

"I want some birds," I tell him right off.

"You got that gold fast," he says, looking at me like I killed somebody for it. "How much you got?"

"Let me see the birds again and I'll let you know."

We went up to the roof and I looked at the pigeons, picked out what I liked, seven of them. I wanted more for that five dollars but I was gone on them birds. I had to have them and that jiving cheapskate knew it. Anyhow, it was good getting rid of that money. It was like getting rid of Bug-Eye. I handed over the five and took the pigeons back to my own roof.

4.

Yeah, it was a big deal. I kept them behind the screen for five days, fed them the best, then let them out.

Right off, they acted funny. They just stood around like they don't mean to do nothing. Next thing I know, they hit off like bullets straight for Mr. Quiet's coop.

Soon as I see that I go see Mr. Quiet. He was sitting on that same box like he's expecting me. I told him what happened and he said, "I don't know nothing about that, kid. I ain't responsible for you losing your birds, and I ain't got them."

"But I seen them fly back," I said.

"You mean you thought you did. They ain't up there. They wouldn't come back."

Yeah, but he was lying. I couldn't do nothing about it so I walked.

Later, I met my friend Jim-Jim. He's got his own birds. When I told him what happened he laughed and said, "Mr. Quiet played you rough. He got them pigeons. It ain't the first time he pulled that one."

"He's going to pay through the nose," I said.

"How?"

"I'm going up on that roof and clip his whole flock."

"You're talking big."

"No. You want to be in on it?"

"Yeah, but what we going to do with all them birds?"

"Sell them. We ask around, or bring them to Taffy."

"Yeah, that's Mr. Quiet's friend. He'll hand your head over to him."

"That greedy cat? When it comes to money, he ain't got no friends."

"You're dead right. Count me in. But we need somebody else."

"Poker will go along on anything," I said.

"Yeah, he's all right."

We looked up Poker and he was all for the job. We set it for that night.

We got sacks from stores. Poker brought his crowbar and we hung around till late, lining up the job.

5.

It was one in the morning when we started out, the streets empty. We cut through a market. The place was full of mean-looking cats. They'd look up and not move.

The big job was getting up to Mr. Quiet's coop. It was no good taking the stairs. We went through a cellar down the block, and came up the back fire escape of Mr. Quiet's house. Me and Poker. Jim-Jim stayed in the yard.

Poker hit the coop with his crowbar and jacked the lock off. Both of us went in with bags. We filled three, tied rope to them and lowered them down to Jim-Jim, then put some birds in our pockets.

Getting down was worse than coming up, and getting out of the yard was real bad. We went through the cellar and waited in the area-way. You could hear cars passing up the avenue, somebody playing a radio in a house close by.

"We better get," Jim-Jim says, "cause if that Mr. Quiet catch us we're dead meat."

We looked out. No cops. Nobody on the block. Next thing we're walking with sacks on our backs, birds stuffed in our pockets.

We're sweating when we get to my house. There's an alley leading to the yard. We took the alley, came out the back and put the birds in an old yard coop for the night. Then we scattered.

Next morning we took off for Taffy's. He's sitting there in his rocker like a man-witch, petting that cat and smiling.

"Where'd you get them?" he says when we show him what we got.

"Brooklyn," I say.

He don't believe that, but who cares? I know he's interested. But he goes on petting that cat like he ain't.

First we try to trade for some good birds of his, but he don't want to. "You got mostly dirty old clinkers," he says, like we don't know nothing.

But that's cause he's got us. We need to get rid of the birds. Yeah, we keep talking and he pets that cat and jives us down to fifteen cents a bird, and busts his heart throwing in some feed.

Next time I see Mr. Quiet he looks at me with needles in his eyes. Yeah, he knows but he don't say nothing. And Taffy won't say nothing, cause he's with us on that deal. Mr. Quiet got to see some other sucker to sell pigeons to.

6.

I got me a big flock now. All good birds. Nobody can fool me no more. I live on the roof. That's what Moms says, and she ain't wrong. It's best of all when you're alone up there and you're watching them birds licking the sky. Damn, they're pretty to watch when they're up. It's like they own the sky. I could build me a coop and live on the roof. If Moms didn't holler so much, maybe I would.

That Bug-Eye is still around. Yeah, I see him all the time in the neighborhood, at the candy store, in front of the pool room. Yeah, he don't buy nothing in the candy store, and he don't shoot pool. What's he hanging around for?

Most of all I meet him at my door, on the stairs, or sitting like an owl on the roof-landing. For a long time it's like he don't know me no more. He don't ask me for favor-errands. But I don't care. I don't want dealings with a cat like that, and none of his weird friends. They're all funny people. Like they're scared. They look through you. Me, I don't have eyes for them.

Like I say, Bug-Eye don't know me any more. Then one day I'm hitting for the roof and he's sitting on the landing. I go to pass and he puts his leg across.

"Where you heading?" he says.

"For the roof."

"Why?"

"I'm going to feed my pigeons."

"You like pigeons?" he says.

"Yeah."

"I guess they're all right. Everybody to his own sins."

He takes his leg away and I go to pass. He stops me again and says, "You ever say anything about that package you run for me?"

"Why should I?" I tell him. "That's my business."

He gave me a toothy old grin. "Fine, chap, fine. I figured you to be a cool kid."

That chap stuff bugged me. I don't like being called that, but I don't say nothing.

Bug-Eye waves his hand. "Okay, you can go," he says. "Keep your nose clean and I can use you sometime."

I start to go and he stops me again. "Wait a minute," he says. "You ever see any strange men around? Anybody asking questions?"

"I see weird people climbing these steps all the time."

He sends me a look, gives me that toothy grin again, and says, "They're friends. I mean flatfoots, the people."

I shook my head.

"Nobody asking about me?"

That Bug-Eye was watching me, watching my brain like he's seeing if I lie. "Nobody," I tell him.

"Okay, that's all."

He let me go. I hit the roof, smell fresh air. It's like I'm leaving evil behind me. I send up my flock and watch them.

It's the greatest, like I'm up there with them. There ain't no Bug-Eye, no evil people, bad-smelling halls, nothing but clean sky.

I'm still watching when Moms opens her mouth. I hear her holler out the window. She figures I'm up here. But I don't answer, don't breathe.

She's shut now, the flock overhead, coming in. I see them Tumblers flip-turn, throw out their wings like brakes. They almost like stop in mid-air, then shoot fast ahead again. I like them Tumbler birds best. They're real acrobats.

Another sweep and they move in like dive-bombers. Bam, they hit the roof. Some go up again. Others stand around on ledges. I whistle them others in the air, wave the bamboo pole. They start gliding down from the sky. Got to get them in. Moms will be calling again. It's time for supper.

7.

Next day I got money and an itch. I go to Taffy's and, like always, he's sitting with his witch-cat, petting it. Mr. Quiet's there too. He looks at me, I look at him, and we look away like neither of us seen nothing.

Taffy is waiting. I jingle money and he's all eyes, waiting.

"Got any good birds?" I ask.

"Nothing but."

"Yeah, nothing but filthy old clinkers." I know that needles him, but he keeps smiling, petting the cat. It's like war between us. You're always trying to swindle him and he swindles you. But sometimes he's got a good bird.

I spot this White Owl, walk away, and come back. You can't show Taffy too much what you like, but he knows. Seems like he reads your mind.

I point at the White Owl cause he looks real good. "How much?" I say.

"That's the best White Owl you ever saw."

"How much?" I say again.

"For you, a dollar."

"Give him to your grandmother," I say, and I walk out hot. Next minute I'm back, cause that bird's in my brain now.

"I'll give you seventy-five cents for him," I say. "No more."

Taffy laughs. "I just wanted to see if you'd come back," he said. "Take him, he's yours. A real bargain."

Yeah, I flew home with him. I know I got something. This bird has good eyes, bright. He's warm in my hand. I feel his heart beating against my palm. Got a big chest, fan-tail, a tuft on his head. It's like a little black skull cap on him. Otherwise he's all white with pink feet and bill.

Got a name for him already. Pinto. Once I'm up on that roof, I throw him in the coop. He flew to the top shelf and looked down. Three boy pigeons look up at him like they mean business. They fly up and peck at him.

Pinto flew to another shelf. Then the leader of the flock gets in on it. He flies up and pecks Pinto on the neck and shoulders.

I'm thinking maybe he ain't got no fight when Pinto dives into him, pecking like sixty. They fall to the floor. The leader flies out the coop into the screen-part. Pinto's after him. Every turn he make, Pinto tails him. They go back in the coop. Pinto knocks him off the shelf. On the floor he pecks him in the eye and that's it. The old leader lays down.

The others fly down, look at him, peck him, like they're waiting a long time for this. He's bleeding on the head and I got to get him out. I put him by himself and they don't bother him after that.

Later, I let him out, and that was it. He flew away and didn't come back till next day.

A sad old pigeon he looked. He hung on the roof and watched but wouldn't come near. I whistled and he'd come and then fly off. Finally he didn't come back at all.

I figured Pinto is the boss now and I take a chance, let him out. I let them all out, but he came first. He looked up like he's wondering about something, then took to the air. Yeah, he puts up speed and the rest take off after him. I thought I was going to lose him. But not Pinto. He's the leader, got his gang now. Zoom! They're making real speed, a wide circle.

Next day I got my Homers up. They always hang together on the same shelf. They bring in other pigeons. I waved the flag, sent the whole flock up. A pigeon is coming from the East Side. The Homers broke from the others and make a bigger circle. They see this East Sider, surround him, fly five blocks, turn and come back, land on the roof.

The East Sider is with them, nervous, ready to fly. He works his way to the screen, flies up and sees the other birds eating. That brings him in. I tiptoe up the ladder, pull the string. The screen door slams down. He turns and runs into the door, then tries to find his way out.

He's all excited, falls down. He can't get out so he settles down. That's when Pinto moves in. Got to show he's boss. He comes out of the coop, looks around, hits that new bird with his wing. He knocks him down, jumps on him, pecks him, then gets a hold and won't let go. Twenty minutes they fight, and the others watch from the shelf. They're like worrying while the fight's going on. Finally Pinto gets his leg and pulls him, hits him from side to side with his bill.

That was all. That new bird limped aside. I put him in the coop and shut the screen.

Yeah, they're like people. One got a piece of corn and the other take it. The strongest gets the most.

Two days later I bought me a girl pigeon and put her in the coop. A Baldy with a tuft and a fantail. Right off, she was Pinto's meat. Another one went after her and Pinto beat him to a frazzle. Then he starts after her.

Damn, she thought she was something. She just keep walking, turn, peck him and walk away. But Pinto got a hard head. He keeps after her all day, his chest big as a balloon, his wings and tail dropped like a fan. He danced like an Indian.

Them two flew away on me and I thought I lost them. They came back two days later, and Mrs. Big ain't so big no more. She don't peck him like at first. Yeah, they was on a honeymoon.

8.

Another day I'm coming from Jim-Jim's roof. I walk up the block and I see this man. He's strange around here. This man is a bull. I smell it. Next thing he stops me.

"Where's Bug-Eye?" he says real quick.

I play dumb as him. "Bug-Eye? Who's that freaky creature?" I say.

"You don't know him? I thought he lived around here."

"There's nobody with that name around here. I'd know."

He looks at me and knows I'm lying. But he can't do nothing. "Okay, thanks," he says and moves off.

I go in the candy store first so he don't know where I live. Get a coke, come back. All the while I'm thinking of what happened. They after Bug-Eye. I knew he was doing evil. All them itchy people he knows is no good. Five dollars for carrying a baby package for him. I wonder what was in it. Yeah, he don't sit on them stairs for nothing. One of these days I'm going to see.

I go up the stairs, leg it for the roof. On the last flight I look up. Two men. Bug-Eye and a conkhead. They jump like it's the cops. Bug-Eye puts something under his jacket.

This is no good, I say to myself. I'm halfway up and I feel like going back.

Bug-Eye calls me. "Where you going?" he says when I reach him.

"To see my pigeons."

"You got to be running up and down these stairs all the time?"

"You own the stairs now?" I say.

That's when he hit me. I don't do nothing, don't say nothing.

"You better find another way up," he says. "You don't and you'll get something you ain't expecting."

That was all. He let me go out on the roof. When I came in again he was gone. So was his friend.

9.

Next evening I took the fire escape to the roof. No use running into that evil Bug-Eye when he might be on the stairs.

Soon as the pigeons see me they get all jumpy. I open the door and let my Homers up after a stray. Moms calls me. She knows I'm on the roof so I come down. Five minutes later I go back up and open the screen for the rest of the flock. Pinto comes out.

He always first. When he don't go up, something's cooking. This time he don't rush out. I watch him and he lifts his head, moves it from side to side. He's seeing something.

I look up and see this bird circling. It's making slow circles and coming down. Pinto is still moving his head from side to side, looking up, following the circles. He steps back and does the same. Next thing he flaps his wings and jumps into the coop. He makes noise and the others follow him on in.

I look up again at that bird. I thought it was a seagull at first. Now I see it's black, with curved wings. That's a hawk, I say.

Damn, three of my Homers are up. They're flying high. Suddenly they split and that hawk breaks from the circle. I see him dive, grab one of them Homers. The other two dove straight down. One almost hit the building. They scramble into the coop like mad.

Fifteen minutes later, Pinto pops from the coop and looks around, up at the sky. He ain't taking no chances on Mr. Hawk. He flies to the roof-edge, looks down, flies to the top of the coop and keeps watching.

At last he takes off. But he's by himself. He makes a few circles, comes back and struts into the coop. Next second they're all coming out. Yeah, he told them Mr. Hawk is gone.

They stay up twenty minutes. I start whistling, waving the flag. Some birds glide in. The flock is moving in a circle. It goes over the avenue, comes back over the roof. The whole pack curves in and down and swoops away from the corner of the building. When they come down, they sit on the television aerials and ledges a while. I let them sit. They're resting.

I give a sharp whistle after a while and they flap up, land on different roofs, then come in.

It's quiet now. Another hour and it'll be dark. I climb up on the coop and light a cigarette. Maybe it's ten minutes later when I stand up. I happen to look down at the skylight. I can see through to the stairs. It's like a deep well.

Next thing I see Bug-Eye. He comes up from the shadows and stops on the landing. His head looks flat from the top. I see him take a cigar box from under that saggy jacket. He sits, takes out a syringe, puts a little water in it, shakes it out.

Two men come up a minute later. They look in a hurry. Bug-Eye ties up their arms, takes a spoon, puts something in it, adds water, lights a match under it. He fills the syringe, sticks them men in their arms.

Two more men come up. Same thing happens. Then they break a pint of whiskey. They drink it and a lady comes up. They all jump.

I see that lady talking to Bug-Eye. He nods his head. She rolls down her stocking and he puts that stuff he cooks in her ankle.

I know what it's all about now. Yeah, Bug-Eye and all them people coming to him. He's like that hawk up in the sky. They come up and he gets them. He's real evil.

It's time to go. I moved. Maybe it was my shadow cause I didn't make no noise. I wasn't breathing, but I see that woman look up. Bug-Eye looks.

I ducked fast, got down off the coop and crossed to the next roof. I hide behind the skylight.

That's when I hear one of them men say, "Somebody's up on that coop."

Bug-Eye answers. He say, "Let me go up there."

Yeah, he went up. The coop is locked. Nobody up there. He comes down. I hear footsteps like they coming close. That's when I get real scared. That Bug-Eye walking around, smelling.

After a while I don't hear him no more. I don't hear nothing but my heart. I wait a minute, then hit the stairs in that next house, run all the way down and come out in the street.

10.

Nothing's happening. There's a stickball game in the street. I see Jim-Jim. He waves and comes over.

"What were you doing in that house?" he asks.

"Nothing," I say. I don't tell him nothing. Nobody's ever going to know.

"You want to get in the game?" Jim-Jim says.

I shake my head. I'm not in the mood. His side flied out and he hit the gutter. I sat on the curb till it got dark, watching my door.

There's no sign of Bug-Eye. I'm scared to go up and scared to stay out. Something's going to happen.

I keep watching that door. The stickball game was long over. The guys drifted down to the corner for sodas. I can hear the jukebox from where I'm sitting, hear voices. They seem so far away.

Got to get up. I waited long enough. Bug-Eye must be gone. I cross the street, open the vestibule door, open the hall door.

There's a dim light burning. I see the stairs. Nothing but shadow at the end of the hall. I'm moving for the stairs when that Bug-Eye comes out of the shadows.

I can't move now. All I see is his eyes at first, nothing else. I'm dead, I say. He's got me. Next thing, he's next to me. He puts a hand on my shoulder.

"Dip, was you on the roof?"

"When?"

"Tonight. About eight-thirty."

I shake my head, feel that hand on me, like it's going to move fast and grab my throat. "No, I was playing stickball," I tell him.

"You sure?"

"Yeah."

"You lying, boy."

"What I got to lie for?"

He smiled then, in a way I don't like. "Since you wasn't up there," he says, "I guess you didn't see nothing."

"What's there to see?"

He's still smiling, like he knows every word out of my mouth is a lie. I'm waiting for him to do something, but I know nobody can help me now. No use calling for Moms. He'll slit me fast. I wait, and after a while that hand of his slides off me like a snake going away.

It feels like ten tons of brick is off me.

Bug-Eye slaps something into my hand. "Here's something for being sure you wasn't up there," he says. Then he makes that motion like with a pair of scissors and goes out the door.

I go upstairs, open my hand on the landing and see green paper-money. A five-spot for seeing nothing, saying nothing.

Yeah, I never told nobody.

His Own Hand
Rex Stout
April 1955

When Alphabet Hicks got home a little before midnight that Thursday evening in October, he found a man waiting for him at the top of the second flight of stairs in the dingy old brick building on East 29th Street.

"Where've you been?" the man demanded, confronting him.

In the dim light from the one little bulb at the end of the narrow hall, Hicks peered at him with yellow-brown cat's eyes. "I don't believe—" he began, and stopped. "Wait a minute. Sure. Sergeant Purley Stebbins, who used to be on Homicide."

"I still am. Let's go in and sit down for a little talk."

"What about?"

"Homicide. Adam Nicoll."

Hicks nodded. "I rather expected one of you, but not a sergeant. I'm flattered. Also I'm tired and sleepy, and if we go in my room I'm stuck with you until you're ready to go, but I'm all for sitting down." He moved to the stairs, descended two steps, and sat on the landing. "What's wrong with this?"

Stebbins suggested a couple of things wrong with it, lost the argument, and propped himself against the newel. He was a big, broad bulk, towering above his target. "Where've you been?" he asked.

"Today and tonight, at Democratic campaign headquarters."

"Doing what?"

"Deciding how to vote. I'm a serious voter. I volunteer for two days' work at Democratic headquarters, and two days at Republican, and then decide. Responsibilities of a citizen."

"Yeah, I know, you're a card. How's the detective work coming?"

"Not coming." Hicks tilted his head back against the plaster to look up at the tower. "Let's get through with me and go on, so I can get to bed. I've never solicited detective work and I never will. The Horley case got me some notoriety, and the Brager thing some more, and a couple of others you know about, and that's all. R. I. Dundee still pays me a hundred dollars a week to think up things for him to worry about in his business, and I spend around ten minutes a day thinking. The rest of the time I look on."

"At what?"

"Life and death." Hicks gestured. "Come on, Sergeant, I'm not worth it. All I have is life, and you've got death on your hands. What do you want to know?"

"How long have you known Paul Griffin?"

"Four years. He came to see me. The publicity I had got had given him the idea I was full of remarkable notions, and he wanted me to hatch plots and stunts for his Kevin Kay. It didn't appeal to me and I turned him down, but he has kept after me and I've seen him off and on—maybe four or five times a year. Does that get us to Tuesday evening?"

"We can go back if we need to. What happened Tuesday?"

"He phoned that afternoon and said he had to see me—that was day before yesterday—and I went up to his apartment on Central Park West. He said he and his associates were in a jam, and lawyers had only made it worse, and they wanted me to meet with them that evening—not the lawyers—and see if I could iron it out. Do I need to tell you what the jam was?"

"We've had it from five angles." Stebbins shifted against the newel. "We want yours."

"I'm tired and sleepy," Hicks objected, "but sooner or later, I guess, so why not sooner? Okay. Griffin first put his Kevin Kay into a couple of novels, that was some twelve years ago, and then movies, and then television. Forty million people think he's a wonderful character, and why should I argue? After Adam Nicoll played the part in eight or nine movies, and on TV for a couple of years, it was another case of Joseph Jefferson and Rip van Winkle, or William Gillette and Sherlock Holmes, you couldn't tell 'em apart, and it was hard to say who it was that had the forty million by the tail. As you know, Sergeant, that's not an angle, it's an open chapter in the history of contemporary American culture."

"Go ahead."

"Of course another element in the chapter, maybe minor and maybe not, is another character who appears in all the Kevin Kay stories, called the Cricket, and in movies and TV Amy Quong has become the Cricket just as Adam Nicoll has become Kevin Kay. For the forty million Amy Quong *is* the Cricket. If you want my angle, one reason I shy off is all the damn K sounds. Not only Kevin Kay, which is more than enough, but the Cricket too. I deplore it."

"Thanks." When Stebbins was sarcastic he growled. "You said you're tired and sleepy."

"I am. Last winter Barry Maddox, the well-known producer, told Griffin he wanted to put a Kevin Kay play on Broadway, and after a lot of palaver Griffin agreed to write one. He finished it in May, and after a series of battles with Maddox about rewrites they were finally ready to start casting in August, two months ago. I can't tell you who it was who first suggested having the part of Kevin Kay played not by Adam Nicoll but by someone else, because I don't know. Anyhow, Griffin and Maddox agreed on it, and the someone else was Ernest Levitan, and Levitan read a script and was engaged for the part. However, they couldn't find anyone around to play the Cricket, or maybe they didn't try. Maddox flew to the Coast and proposed it to Amy Quong, and she jumped at the chance to appear on Broadway, and last week she came East."

Hicks twisted his wrist around to get the light from the one little bulb on his watch. Ten minutes of tomorrow were already gone. "Rumblings had been heard for some time from Adam Nicoll in Beverly Hills, and Sunday, four days ago, he arrived in New York and phoned Griffin from a hotel. He had his wife along. For several years it has been customary for Nicoll and his wife to put up at Griffin's apartment when they come to New York, and Griffin went to the hotel for them and took them to his place. Then the fur began to fly. Nicoll wouldn't stand for Levitan playing Kevin Kay, but he couldn't do it himself, anyhow not this season, because he was scheduled for a Kevin Kay picture to start shooting in December, and also he had his TV contract. Barry Maddox insisted on going ahead with Levitan. Amy Quong wanted to be on Broadway and to hell with everything else. Griffin, who owns the characters and could have Jimmy Durante play Kevin Kay if he wanted to, couldn't tell Nicoll to go climb a tree because of the possible effect on the forty million. That was the jam Griffin told me about Tuesday afternoon."

"And wanted you to iron out."

Hicks nodded. "That evening after dinner."

"And you went. Who was there?"

"Paul Griffin, Barry Maddox, Ernest Levitan, Amy Quong, and Adam Nicoll and his wife. I didn't think there was much chance of ironing it out, but it would be fun to try, and besides, I wanted to meet Amy Quong. I have always wondered if the Oriental slant of my eyes had any genetic basis, and I wanted to see how I reacted to her."

"What was said? By everybody."

"My God," Hicks protested, "have a heart. I was there nearly two hours."

"Yeah." Stebbins shifted position. "Let's go in and sit down."

"Nothing doing." Hicks was firm. "You'd stay all night."

"I haven't got all night. When and how did you hear of Nicoll's death?"

"Early this afternoon at Democratic campaign headquarters. Someone had heard it on the radio."

"Has any of those six people been in touch with you today?"

"No."

"You've heard nothing from any of them, directly or indirectly?"

"Yes. Nothing."

Stebbins shifted again. The newel was not an ideal prop for a prolonged stay. "Nicoll was poisoned with cyanide. At nine o'clock this morning he ate breakfast at Griffin's apartment, alone. His wife and Griffin weren't up yet. Orange juice, toast, and coffee. It wasn't in them, as it stands now. Immediately after breakfast he swallowed a large vitamin capsule, which he always does. In less than ten minutes he was sick. In five more he was in convulsions. By the time a doctor arrived it was too late to pump him, and at ten o'clock he was dead. So it was in the capsule."

"You can't buy cyanide capsules at a corner drugstore."

"No, but you can buy it in a lot of forms for a lot of purposes, for instance a photographers' supply shop. You make a hole in the end of a vitamin capsule with a needle, squeeze out the paste, insert the needle of a hypodermic syringe loaded with hydrocyanic acid, squirt it in, and heat the end of the needle to seal the hole."

"I don't."

"Somebody must have."

"To one of Adam Nicoll's vitamin capsules?"

"Right."

"I saw them Tuesday evening. His wife asked him if he had remembered to take one after dinner, and he said no, and she went and brought the bottle from the dining room and he took one. The bottle had a blue label and the capsule was dark blue. Ernest Levitan asked to see the bottle and passed it on to Barry Maddox, making some crack about getting some since he was going to do Kevin Kay, which didn't help any with the ironing out. Did the capsule this morning come from that bottle?"

"Yes. It was there on the sideboard in the dining room."

"Then that should simplify it. Griffin or Mrs. Nicoll could have had a chance to take one and doctor it and put it back, but surely not Maddox or Levitan or Amy Quong."

Stebbins grunted. "No, but one of them could have bought a bottle of the capsules at any drugstore, and practiced the operation until he got one that looked right, and then all he had to do was sneak it into the bottle. Maddox and Levitan were there again all yesterday after noon, and Amy Quong was there yesterday evening. You haven't been there since Tuesday?"

"Nope. Also I have no hypodermic syringe. Not to mention hydrocyanic acid."

"Yeah. We're on the routine on that, but you know how that is." Stebbins shifted his rump again. "We want a full statement from you about Tuesday evening, and you can make it at the DA's office tomorrow morning at ten o'clock. Right?"

"Right. So now I'll turn in."

"In a minute. You can tell me now anything that anybody said that might help. Anything at all."

"Let's see." Hicks yawned. "They were all more or less on Nicoll's neck, one way or another. His wife kept insisting that he should do Kevin Kay on Broadway himself, and was a little nasty about it, but that's somewhat personal because women who don't care how much they drink annoy me. I gathered that she doesn't like Hollywood. Nicoll said his lawyer had advised him that he had established a property right in common law in the part of Kevin Kay, and if Maddox went ahead and cast Levitan for it he would throw the book at him, including an injunction and a suit for damages. Maddox said he had invested a lot of time and money in the play, and signed up Levitan and the rest of the cast, and contracted for a theater for a December opening, and Nicoll could go choke himself. I suppose Nicoll and Maddox were both somewhat affected by a complication which you probably know about."

Stebbins nodded. "Mrs. Nicoll was formerly Mrs. Maddox. She left him for Nicoll three years ago. Does he still want her back?"

"I don't know."

"Does she want him back?"

"I don't know that either. It didn't come up Tuesday. Paul Griffin said he would have been glad for Nicoll to do Kevin Kay on Broadway if movie and TV commitments hadn't made it impossible. Maddox said he wouldn't. Griffin said he would contract to pay Nicoll the same salary that Levitan would get, during the entire run of the play, and also he would guarantee Maddox against any loss through any kind of action brought by Nicoll, which I thought was damn generous. Nicoll accused Levitan of wanting to horn in on the part, not only for Broadway, but also later for the movies and TV. Levitan said, in a tone meant to leave scars, that that hadn't been in his mind at all, but of course it might work out that way, since it was the finest part in the whole entertainment field and people were already saying that Nicoll was lousing it up and would ruin it for good in another year. Amy Quong said—by the way, I reacted to her normally, a beautiful little creature—she said she loved everybody and everybody was wonderful, and she was sure Adam Nicoll would quit being mad at her because she was going to do the Cricket on Broadway with Ernest Levitan, and he wouldn't do what he had threatened to do, and anyway she didn't care for money so she had turned over all that she had saved to her father and mother. I got the impression that she had saved around two million dollars and it was in good hands."

Hicks got upright and, stepping up to the landing, was on a level with Stebbins. "That's the best I can do, Sergeant." He yawned. "Excuse me. I'll go down in the morning and fill it in. Good night."

Stebbins asked a few more questions, not cordial but not contentious, and tramped down the old wooden stairs. Hicks went along the narrow hall to a door, let himself in with a key, and was in the room he had occupied for more than a decade. Flipping the switch brought light from a lamp on a table by the far wall and a floor lamp off to one side next to a big easy chair. With the bed and dresser and bookshelves, and a few pictures and another chair, the room still looked somehow bare, which was how he liked it. He had hung his topcoat in the closet and started for the bathroom when the phone rang, and he went to the table and got it and said hello.

"That you, Hicks?"

"Right."

"This is Paul Griffin. You've heard about Nicoll?"

"Yes."

"We've had one awful day. Terrible. Will you come up here to my place? Now?"

"What for?"

"We want to ask you what to do. You know about things like that and God knows we don't."

"Ask your lawyer."

"We have. To hell with lawyers, all they do is—Damn it, we want to talk with you!"

"Who does?"

"All of us! We're all here. Amy Quong suggested it, and Maddox—all of us! We need a man with a head on him to tell us what to do in a mess like this. You'll come?"

"Okay. With my head on."

"Right away?"

"Yes."

Hicks hung up, muttered with feeling, "Of all the nerve," went to the bathroom, came out again, and crossed to the closet for his coat.

Even if you are a professional story teller who, by luck or inspiration or both, has created and exploited a pair of gold-mine characters like Kevin Kay and the Cricket, you will do better on the West Side of the park if you want an apartment with a living room you can take walks in and a dining room big enough to feed twenty guests. That was why Paul Griffin's address was the big old stone pile on Central Park West, For a bachelor his tenement on the fifth floor was quite a place. Taking a walk in the living room was not actually practical because of the clutter of chairs, tables, statues on pedestals, couches, cabinets, cushions, and enormous portraits in oil of Kevin Kay and the Cricket on easels but it would have been perfect for a steeplechase.

When Alphabet Hicks was led in and through the clutter by Paul Griffin to where the group was gathered around the fireplace, he stood and looked around at them. They were a dismal sight. Ernest Levitan, sprawled on a couch, might have been cast for a lost soul headed for hell instead of Kevin Kay on Broadway. Cynthia Nicoll, at the end of the couch with a drink in her hand, her corn-silk hair frowzy and her blue eyes puffy, tried to focus on the newcomer and couldn't make it, Amy Quong, a dark compact figurine cross-legged on the rug, was staring at the fire and didn't move. Barry Maddox, the producer, normally big and broad and genial, was a vague, sagging mass propped against the high back of a teakwood chair. Paul Griffin, usually meticulous of manners, collapsed his lanky frame onto a chair while his invited guest still stood.

"So," Hicks remarked, "it's been a hard day."

"Good God," Maddox muttered. "Hard?"

"I think," Levitan said wearily, "I've got the record. Eleven hours straight. I've been questioned by five detectives and two assistant district attorneys. One of the detectives was an inspector. Griffin is the runner-up with four and two. Tomorrow will be another day."

"It hazh been—" Cynthia Nicoll began, stopped, and set her jaw.

"It hazh been what?" Levitan demanded.

She wobbled her head. "We ought to be in bed, resting up for tomorrow," Levitan said tragically. "But Maddox insisted on getting you up here. What for? You tell us."

Barry Maddox grasped the top of the chair back and straightened up a little. "Don't mind him, Mr. Hicks. He's an actor. We all wanted to consult you, knowing of your past exploits. We are under suspicion of murder, and you know what that means. My lawyer has given me certain advice as to what I tell the police, and he has also advised me to have no contact whatever with any of these four people because one of them is a murderer and I might compromise myself. That's not the way I like to act and I want to know what you think of it. Also we want to tell you all about it and ask you if you think the police are justified in limiting their suspicion to us. Why couldn't it have been someone else? Why couldn't the poisoned capsule have been put in the bottle a week ago, out West? Why couldn't Nicoll have killed himself, and did it that way to throw suspicion on someone? We want to ask you, Mr. Hicks. You didn't get us out of our jam Tuesday evening, God knows you didn't, but you impressed us."

Amy Quong had pivoted on the rug to give Hicks her black eyes. "You impressed me here," she hissed, placing the fingertips of both hands delicately between the famous little breasts of the Cricket. "Won't you sit? Near me where I can feel you?" She patted a cushion beside her. "Here?"

As Hicks went and lowered himself onto the big fat cushion, Paul Griffin spoke. "It's worse than a jam now," he said. "It's a calamity. What the devil do we do, just wait until they clamp onto one of us? Damn it, we can't! I know I can't! Of course you probably don't know—ask us anything you want to."

"Don't ask me!" Cynthia Nicoll blurted, and put her glass down.

Hicks felt something on his knee and looked down to see Amy Quong's lovely little dark hand resting there. He sent his eyes around. "As for telling you what to do," he said, "that's a big order and I can't fill it. I was rather expecting you to ask me to find out who killed Adam Nicoll, but that's not it?"

"We couldn't ask you to pass a miracle, could we?" Levitan demanded.

"No, I suppose not, but it's a pity that's not what you want, because I already know who killed Nicoll."

They goggled at him. Ernest Levitan sat up. Amy Quong's fingers on his knee closed into a fist. Barry Maddox said, "That's a good line, Hicks. You ought to use it in a play, end of the second act. See the audience reaction?"

Hicks shook his head. "It's not a line, it's a fact, only I exaggerated a little. I should have said I'm pretty sure I know—say, ten-to-one sure. Get the same effect. Right now one of you is having a hard time with his face, and also inside his skull. Am I bluffing or have I really got something? Wouldn't he—or she, since I mustn't slight the ladies—like to know?"

"We all would." Maddox had released his hold on the back of the chair and quit sagging. "Suppose you tell us."

"It's a good gag," Levitan said, but not wearily.

"Not a gag," Hicks declared. "When I was here Tuesday evening one of you said something that struck me as pretty remarkable, but I skipped it. People do say remarkable things. Today at lunchtime—yesterday now—when someone told me the radio had said that Adam Nicoll had died suddenly and the police were investigating, I wasn't reminded of it because I didn't know enough. But when I got home a couple of hours ago a Homicide detective was there waiting for me, and he told me the details, and naturally I remembered. Among other things he asked me to tell him anything that was said here Tuesday evening that might help him, and I did so, including the remarkable item I have mentioned. If he spotted it he gave no sign. I'm to go down to the District Attorney's office in the morning and make a full statement, and of course that item will be in it, and no doubt sooner or later someone will notice it and come to the same conclusion I did, that the one who said that remarkable thing killed Adam Nicoll. If they miss it I might even call their attention to it, but I wanted to chew on it first, Right after the detective left the phone call came from here, and I chewed on it coming uptown, and decided I might as well spring it."

"I never said a remarkable thing in my life," Levitan asserted.

They looked at him, and then at one another, in tense collective vigilance. "Who said what?" Paul Griffin asked quietly.

Hicks, not wanting the distraction of the soft touch of Amy Quong's little hand, lifted his knee and clasped his fingers on it. "First," he said, "I ought to check a little. After all, a ten-to-one shot is not always a shoo-in, and I could be wrong. For all I know, one or more of you may be already ahead of me. Of course I saw the bottle of capsules here Tuesday evening when the rest of you did, and Nicoll took one. Afterward, as I remember it, Levitan asked to see it and Nicoll handed it to him. Levitan took a look at it and handed it to Maddox, who also gave it a look and then handed it to Mrs. Nicoll, and she put it down on that little table." Hicks pointed. "It was there when I left. Then what happened to it? Of course you've been over all this with the police."

"We certainly have," Griffin said with feeling. "It was there on the table when Levitan and Maddox and Amy left and Adam and Cynthia and I went to bed. When the maid cleaned up in the morning she took it to the dining room and put it on the sideboard. Adam was alone at breakfast, but the maid saw him take a capsule from the bottle and leave it on the sideboard, and as far as anybody knows it was on the sideboard all day Wednesday. After dinner Wednesday, before we came in here for coffee, Adam himself went to the sideboard and got out a capsule, and presumably the bottle was on the sideboard throughout Wednesday night. Next morning after breakfast Adam took another capsule, and that—" Griffin swallowed with apparent difficulty, as if he too were trying to down a capsule. "That was the one."

"And Maddox and Levitan were here all Wednesday afternoon, and Miss Quong that evening. Right?"

"I wasn't in the dining room," Amy Quong declared in her high, thin voice that always had a suggestion of a tinkle.

Hicks nodded. "I know how that is. But you can prove a negative only by proving a positive, and I don't need that. I do need to know whether the police have got a real pointer. That Maddox or Levitan went alone into the dining room for something Wednesday afternoon wouldn't be enough. If one of them was seen with the bottle in his hand I might want to chew some more. If he was seen unscrewing the cap and putting something in, I'll go home and leave it to the law. Is there anything like that?"

"Not on me," Maddox snapped. "I never saw the damn bottle after Tuesday evening."

"Nor me." Levitan was not cocky. "I was in the dining room, certainly. We had lunch there."

Hicks got up and stood with his back to the fire, his hands in his jacket pockets. "Then I'll give it a try. I want you to know that I wouldn't be doing this if I hadn't been asked to come up here. I thought it was nervy to ask me, but maybe not. Who suggested it?"

"I did," Barry Maddox said. "And I think you've done enough stalling."

"Did anyone oppose it?"

"I don't think so. No."

"Even so, it may not have been nerve, merely discretion. I'm not stalling, Mr. Maddox. I'm just making it a little harder for a murderer to hang on after the hard day he's had. I can't indict him, since I have no evidence, but I know him and think I can crack him. If I have this right, and I think I have, it's a strange business. In a way, a man has died by his own hand. In a way, it wasn't Adam Nicoll that was murdered, it was Kevin Kay. Kevin Kay was murdered because there had to be a death before there could be a resurrection. I admit I had—"

"Skip the goddam riddles!" It was Ernest Levitan, not acting. "If you've got no evidence, what have you got?"

"I'm telling you." Hicks' voice sharpened. "I admit I have an advantage on the police, since I was told of the plans for the resurrection long before the death was plotted, and possibly before it was contemplated." His eyes went to Griffin. "You remember, Paul, telling me of the projected play? And later that Levitan would do Kevin Kay in it?"

"Of course." Griffin was undisturbed. "I told several people."

"No doubt. And some of them may have thought as I did. What I thought was that you had been driven to desperation. You had finally found it intolerable that a mere movie actor had usurped the glory and acclaim rightfully due to the creature of your own brain, your Kevin Kay. To millions of people Adam Nicoll was Kevin Kay, the two were indistinguishable, and since for years you had identified yourself with Kevin Kay, that was insufferable. You were in an agony of resentment and rancor. You did your best to conceal it, and it may even be that I was the only one who noted the glint in your eye and the strain in your voice when you spoke Nicoll's name, though I doubt it. You never put it into words. At your trial for the murder of Adam Nicoll, I doubt if a single witness can be produced who will say that he heard you speak spitefully of Nicoll."

"For God's sake." Griffin snorted. "Me on trial? Me?"

"You're already on trial, and you know it. So when Maddox asked you to put Kevin Kay in a play you saw your chance. By putting another actor in the part, the hold of Nicoll on the public mind and heart as the one and only Kevin Kay would be loosened and eventually broken. Two Kevin Kays would be too much for idolatry, and it would all come back to the true Kevin Kay, you. This is not a mere surmise; no other motive could have impelled you to write the play and let Maddox put another actor in the part. You knew it would infuriate Nicoll. You didn't do it for money, because you wouldn't get it anyway; you were already above the eighty-per-cent income-tax bracket. I know you said you wanted Kevin Kay on Broadway, but that wasn't good enough, at least not for me after I had heard you trying to control your voice when you spoke of Adam Nicoll. That's a good idea—clasp your hands to keep them from trembling. But remembering how you felt about Nicoll, you can't keep from trembling inside. You're going to crack, Paul, you're bound to crack. That may sound brutal, but it isn't. I'm deliberately trying to break you down because it will save you harder days than today. If you tell us now where you got the syringe and the poison and the capsules to practice with, it will soon be over. If you don't, if you try to hold on, it may take the police weeks to find out, months even, but sooner or later they'll get it. Do you want to live through those weeks and months? Can't you feel them now?"

"Jesus," Levitan whispered, and asked aloud, "Do you have to? Look at him!"

Amy Quong, on her feet, went to Griffin and put her hand on his shoulder. The Cricket would have done that.

"Go on," Griffin told Hicks in a thin, tight voice. "What did I say Tuesday evening?"

"Not much, but enough for the purpose. In a moment. All that about putting Levitan in the play, I thought all that months ago, and it was nothing in my soup. I wished you luck, but I wasn't surprised when you phoned Tuesday and told me Nicoll had come to New York and fur was flying. After an hour here that evening it looked to me as if you were cornered. If you dropped the play your whole plan was sunk, and if you didn't Nicoll was obviously going to raise a stink that might tie up Kevin Kay for years. When you said you would pay Nicoll the same salary that Levitan would get for the run of the play, and that you would guarantee Maddox against any loss that might result through any action brought by Nicoll, I thought you were cuckoo. It might ruin you and Kevin Kay both, and I couldn't see how you were figuring it. I didn't ask you, because the others were here, and by that time I had about concluded you were no longer capable of figuring."

Hicks stepped two paces away from the fire at his back, which took him closer to Griffin. "But when I heard from Sergeant Stebbins tonight how Nicoll had died, I realized that you had figured plenty. If Nicoll was going to die in a day or a week—exactly when didn't matter—your offer to pay him and guarantee Maddox risked nothing and would cost you nothing, even if it had been drafted by lawyers and signed. So it looked to me as if you knew Tuesday evening that Nicoll was going to die. I said before it was a ten-to-one shot, but now, looking at you, it's a thousand to one. Your two big mistakes were making that offer when I was present to hear it, and just dropping the capsule in the bottle. With the bottle right here in your dining room, you must have had ample opportunity to shake out some of the capsules, put yours in, and return the others. Then Nicoll would have died days later, probably after he had returned to the Coast, and that would have been different. Now it's this way. You understand what I meant, Paul, when I said that Kevin Kay was murdered by his own hand."

Griffin nodded. "Yes," he said clearly. "I understand."

"And you see how it is. There's not a glimmer of a chance. Are you going to try to fight it? Are you going to hang on until they get enough to lock you up?"

"No. I might if I thought I could get you to drop it and if these people hadn't heard it. No." Griffin left his chair and was upright, straight, tall, and lanky. He looked around at them. "It's all over, my friends. Amy, you little devil. Cynthia, you poor neurotic souse. Barry and Ernest, you lucky slobs, this will make the play, it will run forever. All right, Hicks, what?"

"You can tell me things. Or I can take you downtown in a taxi. Or I can phone and they'll come."

"Just a moment." He turned and grasped the arms of the chair he had occupied, a chair so big and heavy that it took a man to lift it and raise it above his head, which he did. With it aloft, he went across to the easel which held the life-size oil of Kevin Kay, and hurled the chair straight at its middle. The chair went right on through, making tatters of the canvas, and the easel toppled and crashed to the floor.

The Reluctant Client
Brett Halliday

June 1955

"This is Laura Jenson, Mr. Shayne. Mrs. Ralph Jenson." Her voice over the telephone was high-pitched and tremulous. She went on talking fast, as though she had spent some time nerving herself to make this call and planning exactly what she would say: "You won't recognize my name, but I need your help desperately. I don't know what to do. I'm so frightened and confused I . . . just don't know *what* to do." Her voice ended in a sort of wail.

"What kind of help do you need?"

"Your advice. I want to retain you to protect me from . . . being murdered."

"What about the police?" Shayne suggested. "They're better equipped than I. . . ."

"No!" There was real hysteria now. "I can't go to the police. It's Ralph, you see. I'm afraid *he's* going to kill me. Mr. Shayne, please let me talk to you. If you could come out tonight to the house . . . ?"

"I'm afraid I'm tied up tonight, Mrs. Jenson." The detective realized he spoke with a little more brusqueness than the occasion required but he detested hysterical wives who continued to live with men whom they suspected of planning to kill them.

"Oh God," it was a faint and despairing sigh. Almost a sob. "Couldn't you change your plans? I'll pay you anything. I'm so alone and afraid, and tomorrow may be too late."

"If you think there's really an immediate danger . . ." Shayne began grudgingly, and she broke in:

"There is. I know there is. We're on the Beach." She gave him a Miami Beach street address and went on breathlessly, "About eight o'clock? I'll be alone. My husband has a business appointment that will keep him late. If you only knew how wonderful it will be to see you . . ."

A grating, masculine voice broke in sardonically on the wire, "I'm sure he does know, my dear."

"Ralph!" It was a shriek of pure terror. "Are you on the extension? I thought you'd gone. I heard your car start up. . . ."

"So I caught you at it this time?" The grating voice was smug. "Calling your lover to make an assignation the moment you thought my back was turned. I left my car down the drive and slipped in the back way. Hello, you, whoever you are on the line. Speak up, damn it. I've got some things to say to a lousy skunk who slips into a man's house when he's away. If I knew who you were. . . ."

"Michael Shayne," said the detective grimly. "I'll be glad to discuss this any time you care to drop in."

"Please don't. No!" wailed Mrs. Jenson. "It isn't what you think, Ralph. I just called Mr. Shayne. . . ."

"I know. Asking him to drop in at eight when the coast was clear. Still listening, Shayne, if that's really your name? I advise you not to come. Tonight or any other night. Understand that?"

Shayne said calmly, "You can expect me at eight, Mrs. Jenson." He replaced the receiver of his office phone and sank back in his swivel chair with a grimace of distaste. Much as he disliked hysterical women, he had far greater dislike for jealous husbands who eavesdropped on their wives over extension telephones.

The grimace was still on his face and he was automatically tugging at his left ear-lobe when the door opened and Lucy Hamilton burst in excitedly.

His secretary was pretty and brown-haired and intelligent, and now she was frightened. "Michael Shayne!" she exclaimed. "I was listening in. You're not going there tonight."

"Of course I am," the red-head grinned at her. "I've got a client and I'm curious."

"But you heard what he said. He'll be there tonight and he sounds capable of anything."

"That," said Shayne morosely, "is exactly why I'm going. I was ready to discount the lady's fear until he stuck his oar in. Now I think she does need help."

He got up and sauntered to a steel filing cabinet behind the desk, yawning and glancing at his watch. "The sun's just sinking behind the yard-arm, angel. Let's have a drink and call it a day."

At seven-thirty that evening, Michael Shayne was alone in his Miami apartment leisurely sipping cognac from a wine-glass, with a tumbler of ice water beside him, when his telephone rang. He leaned his rangy body forward and stretched out a long arm to lift the instrument, said, "Shayne speaking," into the mouthpiece.

He recognized Laura Jenson's voice immediately. "Mr. Shayne. It's the first chance I've had to call you. Ralph just drove away. I'm calling from the upstairs extension and can see his car going down the drive. But I'm afraid he'll slip back later, and I don't know what he might do if he catches you here. I don't think you should come."

"Exactly why I should come, Mrs. Jenson. I'd like to meet your husband and tell him a few plain truths."

"You don't know him. It was awful this afternoon. Even when I told him who you were to convince him you weren't my lover."

"Did you tell him why you called me?" Shayne's voice was hard.

"Yes, I did. I can't live with fear any longer. I came right out and told him."

"Then I'm positive I had better come. See you in half an hour, Mrs. Jenson." Shayne hung up and finished his cognac. He took a sip of ice water and got up, opened a drawer of the desk in the center of the sitting room and took a short-barreled .38 automatic from it. He slipped it in the side pocket of his tweed jacket, rammed a gray felt hat down over his coarse red hair and went out.

Twenty minutes later he was across the Causeway and driving north on Ocean Drive watching for the street number Mrs. Jenson had given him. It was early fall and there was a pleasant coolness in the night breeze sweeping in from the ocean on his right. The season had not really started yet, many of the large hotels were still closed, and there was a relaxed feeling of torpid languor in the air. A half-moon rode high in a cloudless sky, the silvery light silhouetting palm fronds along the road as he drove.

The Jenson driveway was graveled and curving, leading gently upward to a two-story house of white stucco situated directly on the edge of the high bluff overlooking the white sandy beach and the ocean beyond. The drive forked as it approached the house, one fork leading on to a two-car garage at the side, the other curving in front beneath a vine-laden porte-cochère directly in front of the entrance.

Shayne stopped beneath the porte-cochère, cut his headlights and motor and got out. The night-silence was broken only by the muted sound of breakers on the beach beyond and below the house, and his heels sounded loud on the gravel as he circled the car to the flagstones in front of the double doors.

There was an overhead light and Shayne pressed the door button. The door opened inward almost instantly. Laura Jenson was a tall and striking brunette. She wore a long, blue velvet housecoat with a tight bodice and full skirt that flowed over full hips and long legs to her ankles. She wore heavy lipstick, but the dark shadows beneath large black eyes did not look like mascara.

She held the door open but blocked the entrance with her body, saying swiftly, "Mr. Shayne? I don't think you should come in. I really don't. You heard Ralph this afternoon. He's frightfully jealous. Always imagining things about me and working himself up into rages. I don't know what he might do if he came back and found you here."

"I think I should come in," Shayne told her. "You did call on me for help this afternoon."

He moved forward and she stepped back when his body was almost touching hers. With a little cry, she whirled from him, throwing both hands over her face and shuddering violently as she crossed a long, thickly-carpeted living room with open windows overlooking the ocean, and sank into a deep chair beside the fireplace.

Shayne closed the door and followed more slowly. It was a pleasant room in tans and grays, quietly luxurious, but without ostentation. Three floor lamps were lighted, and there were comfortable chairs and smoking stands, and a low-back settee across from the fireplace.

He dropped his hat in a chair near the door, moved to the settee and sat down gravely while Laura Jenson kept her hands pressed tightly to her face and struggled with convulsive sobs.

He lit a cigarette and said nothing until she straightened in her chair and took her hands away from her tear-wet face. Her large black eyes were luminous with moisture and her fingers writhed together in her lap as she tried to smile. It was a pitiable effort and it failed.

"I'm glad you did come," she said hoarsely. "I have to talk to someone. I'm at my wit's end about Ralph. I think he may kill me one day in a fit of—temper."

"Get away from him," said Shayne harshly. "You need to consult a lawyer, not a detective."

"But I love him," she said. "There's no reason for his jealousy. I thought if we could prove to him that I'm *not* unfaithful, that all his suspicions are groundless, that we could go on as we used to be. That's why I thought of a detective. One with your reputation." She leaned forward imploringly, her face twisted with anxiety to have him understand. "If you'd follow me . . . put a tail on me, isn't that the word for it?" She laughed nervously, "For a few weeks. Keep a meticulous record of everything I do and everyone I see. That should convince him, shouldn't it?"

"That's not a very good basis for a happy marriage, Mrs. Jenson." Shayne frowned and rubbed his jaw thoughtfully. "In the meantime, from what you said this afternoon I gather you'll be living in daily fear of death."

"I . . . I don't know," she said dully, leaning back and biting her upper lip. "Perhaps I exaggerated the danger to get you to come tonight. I just don't know."

The telephone on a stand beside her chair rang at that instant. She listlessly picked it up on the second ring and put it to her ear.

She jerked as though an electric current had shot through her, and her face showed abject terror as she listened. Her eyes sought Shayne and she gestured imploringly for him to come to her.

He crossed the room in two long strides and before he reached her side he heard a familiar grating voice emanating from the receiver at her ear.

She turned it slightly as he bent down so he could hear her husband's voice clearly, and spoke in a strangled tone:

"No, Ralph. I tell you he isn't here. I'm all alone."

"I don't believe a word of it. Why should I, the way you've lied to me before? Tell that damned shamus to get out of my house, Laura. Tell him to keep his nose out of my business, if that *is* the reason he's visiting you . . . which I doubt . . . you no-good slut."

Shayne's gray eyes were blazing. He put a big hand on the receiver and wrested it from Laura though she strove desperately to hold onto it. In a voice thick with fury, Shayne told her husband:

"Michael Shayne speaking. I suggest you come home and find out exactly why I'm here." He slammed the receiver down and Laura shrank away from him, moaning, "No. Oh, no. You mustn't. He'll kill us both. I swear he will. You don't know Ralph like I do. Please go quickly."

She arose and began to push him frantically toward the entrance, her face contorted with fear, voice rising in a shrill babble that was fast approaching hysteria.

Shayne's face was bleak, with deep lines etched in each cheek, his eyes hooded as he allowed her to push him toward the door.

He realized nothing would be gained by insisting on staying in the house. She was too near the breaking point to listen to reason or logic. He was convinced that something would snap in her mind if he stayed with her.

He caught up his hat near the door, said gruffly, "All right, Mrs. Jenson. For your sake, I'll go this time. But I'm going to make it a point to see your husband, and if necessary I'll file charges that will take care of him."

He was breathing deeply as he stepped outside and the door closed beside him. He moved slowly around his car, deciding that for Mrs. Jenson's peace of mind he would get in and drive away from the house down to the street entrance. There, unknown to her, he could park to block the driveway and have a talk with Ralph Jenson when he returned. Definitely, Shayne knew he was not driving away from and leaving Laura to face her husband alone on his return.

He was behind the wheel turning on the ignition when he heard the single shot from inside the house.

It took him seconds to jerk the right-hand door open and leap out with gun in hand. The front door was locked and stoutly resisted his first lunge against it. More seconds were wasted while he put two bullets into the lock. It gave under his shoulder after the second bullet and he burst into the living room.

Laura Jenson lay on the carpet in front of him with a bullet hole in the center of her forehead. One glance told Shayne she was quite dead.

There was no weapon in sight, no powder marks about the wound to indicate it was self-inflicted. Shayne wasted only a brief moment assuring himself of this, then ran down an unlighted hallway, past stairs on the right that led upward, through the kitchen where silvery moonlight streamed in the open back door.

Directly in front of the door wooden stairs led down to the white beach thirty feet below. There was no one in sight, now, and Shayne knew there had been time for the killer to run down the steps and along the beach to the right where a narrow street dead-ended against the ocean beside the Jenson estate. If he had parked his car there and sneaked up the rear way . . . even as Shayne thought this, he heard a motor start at the dead-end and saw headlights as it pulled away fast.

He trotted back to the living room to call police headquarters, then strode back to the rear, turning on lights as he went, investigating library, dining room and kitchen thoroughly.

Upstairs there was one large master bedroom on the ocean with twin beds and a telephone table between them. From the layout of the rear hall and the stairs leading off it, it was easy to see how Jenson had been able to slip in quietly that afternoon and get upstairs to the extension without being heard by Laura in the front living room.

Two smaller guest-rooms showed no signs of occupancy and were empty. Shayne went down and stopped at the foot of the stairs. Light gleamed on the bright brass of an ejected shell near the baseboard in the hall. From where he stood, he could look forward and see Laura lying in a direct line from that spot and the front door. The killer must have stood in the dark hall just about where he did, and fired the shot when Laura turned away from the door after forcing Shayne outside.

He swore silently as the scene vividly reconstructed itself in his mind. If he had insisted on staying with her despite her protests until her husband returned. . . .

He shrugged and walked slowly toward the living room as he heard a car coming up the drive. If he had a crystal ball he wouldn't be in the detective business.

He heard the car slide up with grinding brakes behind his, a door slam and running footsteps. He drew back along the front wall a few feet from the door and waited.

A tall man flung it open and burst in. He was bulky and middle-aged, with a broad face that was suffused with anger.

He plowed to a stop on the carpet, his eyes bulging and jaw drooping at sight of the dead woman directly in front of him. He cried out, "Laura," in a thick, disbelieving voice that retained the grating quality Shayne had heard over the phone twice that day, then whirled to face the detective who lounged against the wall.

"Shayne! You . . . my God, you've killed her." His jaw clamped tight and his eyes became murderous. Big fists balled up at his sides and he walked slowly toward the waiting redhead.

Shayne said, "Hold it, Jenson. I didn't shoot her. It was someone from the back door after I had gone out the front."

"I don't believe it." There was froth at the corner of Jenson's mouth. "I'm going to kill you with my two hands." He continued to shuffle closer.

Shayne lifted the automatic from his pocket and showed it to him. "The police will be here in a moment. We'll tell it to them."

"I'm not waiting for the police." Jenson leaped suddenly and without further warning. Shayne sidestepped and swung the flat of the automatic against the side of his head as he collided with the wall.

Jenson slid to the floor in a sitting position, shook his head stupidly and then braced both hands on the floor to get up. Shayne stepped back a few paces and said flatly, "Better just sit there, Jenson. Why are you sore about someone doing the job for you?"

Jenson pushed himself erect slowly as a siren sounded near the driveway. He said dully, "I would never have hurt Laura. I loved her."

"Hell of a way you had of showing it." Shayne moved to the door and flung it open to admit the Miami Beach Chief of Detectives with members of his Homicide Squad.

"Shayne, eh?" Peter Painter strutted in glancing past him at the dead woman. He was a small, immaculate man with gleaming black eyes and a pencil-thin black mustache. He said, "Take his gun, Sergeant. Why did you kill her, Shamus?"

"He was her lover," exclaimed Jenson violently. "He's been slipping in behind my back for months now. She was trying to break it off. He must have forced his way in tonight. . . ."

Shayne snorted loudly and gave his gun to the sergeant. He moved to the settee and sat down, disregarding Jenson who was talking excitedly. He told Painter, "When you're ready to listen to me, I'll give you the dope. In the meantime, I haven't touched anything except in this room. Better check fingerprints in the back and upstairs. I have a hunch the killer was hiding up there waiting for me to leave. You'll find an ejected shell in the hallway where he probably stood when he let her have it. Then I figure he ran out the back while I was shooting the front lock to get in. I heard a car start up and drive away on that dead-end street next door within three minutes after she was shot."

Painter nodded curtly and issued orders to his men. He had Shayne remain in the living room while he took Jenson into the library to get his statement. Shayne sat back quietly and smoked while men dusted the room for prints, an M. E. came and examined the corpse, pronounced her dead, probably from a .32 bullet that was lodged in her brain. The assumption was strengthened by discovery that the ejected shell in the hall was a .32.

Peter Painter returned in ten minutes without Jenson. His manner was aggressive and challenging as he planted himself in front of the redhead and sneered, "So you've started knocking off your dames when they get tired of you?"

Shayne grinned sourly. "Laura Jenson was a client. I met her the first time in my life at eight o'clock tonight. Have your stenographer take down my statement and keep your stinking wisecracks to yourself."

Painter's slight body quivered with anger. "I'll take your statement, and then I'm taking you in. First, give us your fingerprints for comparison."

Shayne stolidly gave them his prints and then began talking. He gave a comprehensive résumé of his two telephone conversations with Mrs. Jenson, and exactly what had occurred after his arrival at eight. "My gun's a thirty-eight, he ended wearily. "You'll find two bullets missing, two slugs in the front door and two ejected shells outside. You won't find my prints anywhere in the house except in this room where I spent a few minutes with Mrs. Jenson before her husband broke it up with his phone call. Get a set of fresh prints from the back door or the stairway banister or upstairs that don't match with Jenson's or the servants and then start looking for your killer."

Painter got to his feet and turned away without a word. In the rear, he conferred with his experts, and then returned triumphantly. He seated himself across from Shayne in the chair Laura had occupied earlier, and happily brushed a thumb-nail across the thin black line on his upper lip.

"This time is it, shamus. Why not admit you were having an affair with Mrs. Jenson and killed her in a jealous rage when she wanted to go back to her husband? We've got the whole story from him. He overheard her making this date for tonight, and she swore to him it was for the last time . . . to break it off.

"There's been no one else in this house tonight," he went on impatiently. "There's not a single indication that any intruder broke in and lurked here and escaped by the back stairs as you want us to believe. We have only your word for the car starting up and driving away on the next street. You were alone here where it happened, Shayne. You and the woman. Sure, the gun you handed over is a thirty-eight. You'd naturally think of bringing a decoy when you came to commit murder. Easy enough to toss the thirty-two into the ocean from the back door. And it'll be easy enough to dredge it up tomorrow, Shayne. You haven't one single thing to prove any of your story, and we have plenty to disprove it. Who else but an ex-lover had a motive to kill her?"

Shayne sighed and took a deep drag on his cigarette. "She was deathly afraid of her husband. I told you why she called me this afternoon."

"Sure. You told us. Her husband?" snorted Painter. "He called on the telephone from Fifth Street not more than two minutes before she was shot . . . according to your own testimony. You talked to him, damn it. Recognized his voice over the phone. You, by God, are his alibi." Peter Painter leaned back and chuckled happily. "I never thought I'd see the day. Talk about dumbness. *You were* the only person who could alibi him. If you'd kept your big mouth shut. . . ."

"Wait a minute!" Shayne sat upright, tugging at his ear-lobe while his trenched face became rigid in concentration. "Who dusted the upstairs room for prints?"

"Heckelman, I think. But what . . . ?"

"Get him in here," snapped Shayne.

Painter hesitated, then shrugged and called, "Heck!"

A neat young man entered from the rear and Shayne demanded, "Did you check the upstairs telephone?"

"Of course. We found prints from Mr. and Mrs. Jenson. No other traces."

"In exactly what order?" Shayne was tense as he shot the question. "Which had used the phone last?"

"Obviously, Mr. Jenson. We found partial prints of hers with his superimposed."

"That does it," said Shayne grimly. "Bring Jenson in here, Painter, and I'll explain exactly how he managed to murder his wife . . . using me to provide him with a perfect alibi."

"How crazy can you get? Even if he called from a phone next door, there wouldn't have been time for him to get here and do it. According to your own testimony."

"But he didn't use a phone next door. He used the extension upstairs where he was hiding after slipping in the back way after driving away at seven-thirty and parking at the dead-end next door. Go back to my statement," he went on angrily. "Mrs. Jenson said, 'I'm calling from the upstairs extension and can see his car going down the drive.' *How did his prints get over hers on that phone?* There's only one possible answer. He slipped back and used it later to establish his alibi."

"But you can't do that," protested Painter weakly. "It's impossible to call the same number from an extension."

"Any dick worth his salt knows that trick," Shayne told him. "Plenty of others know it too, and use it to call downstairs, though the telephone company doesn't volunteer the information to just anyone. Every telephone exchange in the country," he went on, "has a certain combination of numbers that works like this." He got up confidently and crossed to the phone beside Painter. He lifted it and dialed a series of numbers. Then he replaced the instrument and waited. In a moment the telephone began ringing shrilly. It continued to ring until Painter picked it up.

"Go upstairs and answer the chief," Shayne told Heckelman. "And then put the cuffs on Jenson."

Custody
Richard Deming

December 1955

When the bell sounded, I reached out and pushed down the alarm-clock button. The same bell kept ringing.

Sleepily I pulled on the bed lamp and reached for the clock again. Then I came three-fourths awake and picked up the bedside phone.

"Harry Maddon?" a voice inquired in my ear after I said hello.

When I said yes, the voice went on, "Lieutenant Grange of Homicide. I'm over at your former wife's place on Water Street. Know where that is?"

I came completely awake. "Of course, Lieutenant. What's up?"

"Could you get over here right away?"

"What's up?" I repeated.

"It'll keep till you get here, Mr. Maddon. Want me to send a car?"

"I have one," I said. Glancing at the clock, I saw it was two A.M. "Be there by two-twenty."

I took five minutes to throw a handful of water in my face, brush my teeth and dress. It was twenty blocks to my ex-wife Hazel's flat, but I pulled up behind the squad car parked in front of the building at exactly two-twenty.

Naturally, questions were racing through my mind all during the fifteen-minute drive. Lieutenant Grange had said Homicide, which presumably meant someone was dead. I wondered if Hazel, in a drunken rage, had finally killed her equally drunken second husband. Or vice versa.

There was a third possibility which I didn't like to think about. That Hazel, or George, or both of them had killed Tommy.

Even the thought of that possibility made my jaw muscles bunch with rage. I suppose most fathers love their sons, but my feeling for Tommy went beyond ordinary paternal love. He was all I had left from my wrecked marriage, and he was the only person in the world I really gave a damn about. His attachment to me was just as strong, I knew, and the most frustrating thing for both of us about the settlement was that I was to see him only on Sunday afternoons.

If anything had happened to Tommy, there was going to be at least one more murder tonight, I resolved.

But that fear left my mind a moment after Lieutenant Grange opened the door to me. Beyond him, sitting on the front-room sofa in pajamas and a robe, I saw Tommy.

Before I could even reply to the lieutenant's query of, "Mr. Maddon?" Tommy saw me too and flew across the room to throw his arms about my neck.

He started to sob onto my shoulder, and I patted his back and said, "Hold it, skipper. There's nothing to worry about now that your old man's here."

Leading him back to the sofa, I said, "Just sit down, Tommy, until I can find out what this is all about."

Obediently he reseated himself, but tears continued to trickle down his cheeks.

I turned back to the lieutenant, introduced myself and shook his hand. He was a tall, slim man of middle age with sparse, graying hair and a thin, intelligent face.

"You said Homicide, Lieutenant?" I asked. "What happened?"

"Show you in a minute," he said. "Main reason I called you over here is on account of the boy. Got room to put him up at your place?"

"Of course," I said. "For how long?"

He regarded me thoughtfully. "The kid says he'd like to live with you permanently. We had quite a talk, and he thinks his father's a pretty swell guy."

"I think he's a pretty swell guy too," I said. "There's nothing I'd like better than to have him permanently. I fought for custody when my wife and I were divorced. But it seems the courts automatically grant the mother custody if she wants it, even if she's a tramp. I've got Sunday visiting privileges."

"I don't think you'll have much trouble getting custody after tonight," Grange told me. "Come in the bedroom."

As we passed into the hall in the center of the flat, I saw through the open kitchen door that it wasn't Hazel who was the corpse. She was seated at the kitchen table in a dirty housecoat, swaying in her chair and feebly protesting being spoon-fed black coffee by an oversized cop in uniform. Her still attractive face was puffy from drink and her soft blonde hair hung in damp strings about her face.

When I paused in the hallway, the lieutenant said, "She's still blotto, but we'll have her sobered up enough to talk before long."

Then he opened the bedroom door.

The overhead light was on so that I got the full impact of the scene at once. George Kerry, Hazel's second husband, sprawled across the double bed in his pajamas. He lay on his back, so that I could see his gaunt face was unshaven, as usual, and his mouth sagged open to disclose his discolored and uneven teeth. The stain on his left breast was only a small round spot. I learned later that he hadn't bled much because the bullet in his heart had killed him instantly, and you stop bleeding after you're dead.

"Your former wife was sitting in that chair, passed out, when we arrived," Grange said, pointing to the flowered chintz easy chair diagonally across the room from the bed. "The gun was still in her hand, and the angle of the shot was such that it seems likely she was sitting there when she shot him. We haven't been able to get her coherent enough to get a statement from her yet, but we have the boy's account of what happened."

I frowned at him. "You mean you questioned a twelve-year-old kid about a thing like this?"

"There aren't any other witnesses," he said patiently. "We were gentle as possible with him, but we had to know the story. He'll probably have to testify in court too."

After a moment's reflection, I reluctantly accepted this. Though it went against my protective instinct, I realized that if Tommy was the only witness, naturally he'd have to testify.

"Just what happened?" I asked.

"The kid said it started early this evening. Both of them were drinking, which I gathered was a nightly routine, and they got in an argument over money. By nine o'clock they were screaming at each other. Once she slapped him and he knocked her down. That ended the argument up till bedtime, but both of them continued to tank up on opposite sides of the room and glare at each other. The kid says he went to bed in his own room at ten, but couldn't sleep. After a time he heard them stumbling around getting ready for bed, and guesses that was about eleven-thirty. Maybe fifteen minutes later the argument started again in the bedroom. Your former wife screamed something about killing Kerry, and then there was a shot. Everything was quiet after that, but the kid was too scared to go investigate for a good five or ten minutes. Eventually he screwed up nerve enough to go peep in their bedroom. The ceiling light was on like now, Kerry was where he is and the kid's mother was in the chair passed out. Some neighbors knocked about then to inquire about the shot, and Tommy let them in. The neighbors phoned us at twelve twenty-five."

"I see," I said. "Mind if I talk to Hazel?"

"We'll both talk to her, if she's in shape to make sense. Come on."

He preceded me into the kitchen and we stood watching the uniformed cop pour coffee into my ex-wife. He was no longer spoon-feeding her, but was holding the cup up to her lips, urging her to drink. As we watched, she managed to get a couple of swallows down, and spill a couple more. Then she pushed the cup away, rubbed the back of one hand across her mouth and groaned.

Setting the cup on the table, the cop said to the lieutenant, "I think she's beginning to come around, sir."

"Okay, we'll try her again," Grange said. Approaching Hazel, who had dropped her head backward against the back of the wooden chair and had closed her eyes, he said distinctly, "Mrs. Kerry!"

Hazel slowly opened her eyes and stared up at him.

"Can you understand me?" the lieutenant asked.

"Course I understand you," she said pettishly. "Who are you?"

"Lieutenant Grange. I'm a police officer. Do you know what happened here tonight, Mrs. Kerry?"

"Happened?" she asked vaguely. Then her gaze moved blearily to me. "That you, Harry? What are you doing here?"

I said to the lieutenant, "You're wasting your time. I've seen her in this state often enough to know you're not going to get any sense out of her for some hours yet. Until she sleeps it off."

Even as I spoke Hazel leaned her head back again and went to sleep sitting up.

"Guess you're right," Grange said disgustedly. To the cop he said, "Get a coat around her and run her down to Central District. Book her for investigation, suspicion of homicide. Better throw a toothbrush and some clothes in a suitcase for her. She'll probably be away from home a long time."

"Yes, sir," the cop said.

Back in the front room, I told Tommy to go get dressed and pack a suitcase, that he was going home with me. He had stopped crying, and now his face lit up with an expression of relief which almost approached happiness. Eagerly he ran to his bedroom.

"We think of kids as defenseless," the lieutenant commented. "But they can take a lot more than we give them credit for. They seem to have a capacity for forgetting unpleasant things the instant something new grips their attention. Few minutes ago he was in the depths of despair. Then you tell him he's going home with you, and it's like he's getting ready for a vacation."

"He never liked Kerry," I said. "It was shock more than grief that upset him. And he probably doesn't yet realize what this means to his mother. He's happy because he's always wanted to live with me. He practically lives for our Sunday afternoons together. If he'd had the choice, he'd have stayed with me from the minute Hazel and I separated."

The lieutenant said gloomily, "Probably the kid will be better off to be out of a setup like this, where he had to be a witness to drunken brawls. But it's a devil of a way to get a kid transferred to the parent he belongs with."

It was nearly four in the morning before I finally got Tommy settled in the spare bedroom of my apartment and he had dropped off to sleep. Then I reset my alarm clock for nine and went back to bed myself.

In the morning I let Tommy sleep. Mrs. Garret came in to do the semi-weekly cleaning at nine-thirty, just as I was finishing breakfast, and I told her Tommy was in the spare bedroom and not to awaken him. As I planned to be gone most of the day and didn't want the boy left alone, I arranged for Mrs. Garret to stay on until evening, give Tommy his lunch and generally supervise him.

Then I called the advertising agency where I work, told the chief what had happened and asked for a little time off. He said to take all the time I needed and that he'd spread my accounts around among the other boys until I was ready to come back to work.

Next I phoned Ed Harkness, who had handled my divorce suit against Hazel two years before. After I explained the situation and told him what I wanted, he said to meet him at Central District at eleven A.M.

I got there at ten of eleven. Ed showed up promptly on time. Ed Harkness was a short, round man of about my age, thirty-five, timid-appearing for a lawyer, but the appearance was deceptive. In front of a jury he could be as suavely self-confident as a con man.

After shaking my hand and expressing sympathy for this latest trouble, he told the desk man he was Hazel's attorney and asked to see her. Ten minutes later a matron brought her from the women's cell block and left the three of us alone in an interview room which had a barred window.

Hazel's appearance had improved considerably from the previous night. She wore a clean black knit dress which clung to her still voluptuous figure, her face was carefully made up and her blonde hair was brushed to fall loosely about her shoulders. But her hangover showed in the dark circles under her eyes and in the way her hands trembled uncontrollably.

She looked from Ed Harkness to me, and tears formed in her eyes. "They told me you'd gotten me a lawyer, Harry," she said. "After all I've done to you, you're still willing to help me. Why do you bother?"

What do you say to a question like that? That it was because I pitied her? That even now I still thought she was a basically fine woman whose only real fault was the drinking which had ruined both our lives and had done a fair job of ruining Tommy's?

I said, "No matter what you ever do, you're still Tommy's mother."

Wearily she sank into one of the three straight-backed chairs in the room and asked for a cigarette.

When I had lit it for her, she said, "They tell me I killed George and then passed out. Or maybe it was the other way around. I guess Tommy will be happier now. He always wanted to live with you instead of me, Harry."

Ed Harkness said, "What do you mean, 'They tell you you killed George,' Hazel? Don't you remember what happened?"

"I don't even remember getting ready for bed. I woke up in my cell this morning wearing a nightgown and a robe, but the last I remember, I was still fully dressed."

Ed looked from her to me thoughtfully. "You saw her last night, Harry. Would you say she was that drunk?"

I nodded. "As drunk as I ever saw her."

"Who else saw her in that state?"

"Lieutenant Grange, another cop, Tommy, whatever technical cops had been there before I arrived, I suppose. And I understand some neighbors were in the flat shortly after the shooting."

"Hmm. Maybe we can make the blackout dodge stick. If we can convince the jury she couldn't possibly have known what she was doing."

"You mean plead temporary insanity?" I asked. "Can you work that in a case of plain drunkenness?"

"It's a different law, but it's based on the same legal principle as temporary insanity. Under the law you aren't held to as great a degree of accountability when you commit an unpremeditated crime at a time when you aren't aware of what you're doing, as you would be if you were in full possession of your faculties."

He turned to Hazel. "You ever threaten your husband in front of anybody?"

Hazel made a rueful face. "Dozens of times. At the top of my voice. At one time or another everybody within a radius of blocks must have heard me yell that I'd kill him."

"That's not good," Ed said with a frown. Then more briskly, "All we can do is wait to see what the charge is going to be. Maybe the DA will only try for manslaughter. Or at the worst, second degree. If he decides not to attempt to establish premeditation, we may get away with a blackout plea."

Then he began to question Hazel about what she did remember of the evening. That wasn't much, except for the early part. She recalled slapping George and getting knocked down in return, and she remembered Tommy going to bed, because he came over and kissed her goodnight. But she couldn't recall getting ready for bed herself, or anything about the later argument in the bedroom which Tommy had said preceded the shot.

"I don't even know how I got hold of the gun," she said drearily. "I knew George had one, but I don't even know where he kept it."

"Has it been established as his gun?" Ed asked.

Hazel nodded. "I did that for them. They showed it to me awhile ago and I identified it. I'd seen George cleaning it a couple of times. It's a .38 revolver with a pearl handle. Shouldn't I have?"

"It doesn't matter," Ed said. "They'll double-check by tracing it from the manufacturer anyway. But from here on out I don't want you to say a word except when I'm present. Understand?"

Hazel said she did.

Ed told her he'd take up the question of bond immediately after arraignment if the indictment was for less than first-degree murder. He said the grand jury sat on Tuesdays and Thursdays and as it was now Wednesday, they'd probably consider her case tomorrow. Arraignment would probably follow immediately, or by Friday at the latest, so if she wasn't indicted for first-degree homicide he might be able to get her out on bond by the weekend.

He said there was no bond in first-degree cases.

The news didn't seem to cheer Hazel much.

That evening I tried to explain the situation to Tommy. I suspected that he hadn't as yet realized what might happen to his mother, but he was intelligent enough to know that people who kill end up in jail and, once he got over the shock of his experience, I was afraid he might start getting hysterical about what the law was going to do to her.

I sat him in the front room and examined him carefully before I began.

He looked up at me expectantly, but I could detect no sign of disturbance in him.

When I had decided he seemed sufficiently over the shock of his experience to talk about it calmly, I said, "Tommy, you're big enough now so we can talk man-to-man instead of just as father to son. You've been through an experience no kid your age should have to face, but it can't be undone. Have you thought yet about what changes are going to result from what happened last night?"

"Sure, Dad," he said. "Won't I live with you for good now?"

"Yes, of course. But I don't mean just that. You know what happened, don't you?"

"You mean about Mom shooting George? Sure. I was there when it happened."

I said, "Have you thought of what's going to become of your mother?"

He was silent for a moment. Then he said, "I guess they'll keep her in jail, won't they? Forever."

"Possibly," I admitted. "You may as well face that there's that chance right from the start. But I've engaged a lawyer for her, and maybe she'll go free if the lawyer can prove in court she didn't know what she was doing. We'll hope so anyway."

His eyes widened. "Then will I have to go back and live with her?"

In a tone of mild rebuke I said, "I don't think we ought even to consider that factor at this point. The important thing is your mother's welfare."

He looked so woebegone, I relented. "I imagine you'll be able to stay with me even if she's freed, skipper. I'll file a new suit for custody, and the fact that she killed her husband while under the influence of drink is bound to influence the court's decision as to which of us will make the best parent. But you do want your mother to get out of jail, don't you?"

He hesitated before saying dubiously, "Sure, Dad. If I can keep staying with you."

I frowned at him. "That's a funny way to express yourself. You mean you'd rather have your mother spend the rest of her life in jail than go back to living with her?"

Tommy looked up at me wide-eyed, his lower lip trembling. After a time he said, "You don't know how awful it was, Dad. The two of them always drinking and fighting. The other kids in the neighborhood all knew how they did, and they talked about it in front of me and made me so ashamed, half the time I felt like running away. Don't make me go back to her, Dad."

I felt a mixture of compassion at what he'd been through and shock at his seeming callousness to his mother's situation. "I'll keep you with me if I possibly can, Tommy," I told him. "But the important thing right now is your mother. I intend to do everything I can to save her."

Tommy looked down at his hands without saying anything.

"There's at least a chance this lawyer I hired can get her off," I said. "There's a law that if people don't know what they're doing, they can't be held responsible for it. Or at least not as responsible as when they do know what they're doing."

"Didn't Mom even know she'd shot George?" Tommy asked.

"She doesn't remember anything after you went to bed. Not even getting ready for bed herself. She doesn't even know how she got hold of the gun. She says she didn't even know where George kept it."

"In the top part of the kitchen cabinet," Tommy said. "Behind the stuff stored up there."

The remark didn't mean anything to me at the moment. It wasn't until after I had sent the boy off to bed a short time later, and was reviewing our talk in my mind in an effort to decide whether or not I'd been wise in making his mother's situation clear to him, that its full significance penetrated.

Then I summoned up a mental image of the kitchen cabinet he'd referred to from the few occasions I'd been in Kerry's flat. As I recalled it, the storage compartment at the top was just below the ceiling, where it couldn't be reached without standing on a chair. And Tommy'd said the gun was kept behind the things stored there.

I tried to visualize Hazel, so drunk she even swayed when sitting down, standing on a chair and groping past the clutter of items stored in such places for the gun. The picture refused to form.

Besides, Hazel claimed she hadn't even known where the gun was kept. There was no reason to believe she'd lied, inasmuch as she made no attempt to deny the shooting, and obviously thought she had killed George.

But Tommy had known.

Rising, I went into the spare bedroom, switched on the corner lamp and looked down at my son's face. He was sleeping peacefully, a smile of contentment on his lips.

There wasn't anything in the world that meant more to me than my son, I told myself. Nor anything in the world which meant more to him than I did. How much I meant, and the extent to which he was willing to go to be with me, I'd never before even begun to realize.

Switching off the lamp, I returned to the front room and collapsed into an easy chair.

"My God!" I said aloud, to no one. "What do I do now?"

Split It Three Ways
Walter Kaylin

March 1956

All Paulie wanted to do was take some money from this fellow.

"He's got a bar in Santa Monica close to the beach," he said. "There's a vacant lot across the street where he parks his car. All we've got to do is wait over there until he closes up. When he comes along, we take it from him. What do you say?"

We were having coffee in a drugstore on Figueroa Street, Paulie sitting across the table from Sal and me. He was wearing an Eisenhower jacket, a white shirt buttoned up to the neck and no tie. It was the first time we'd seen him since he'd gotten out of Leavenworth and he didn't look good, his face thin and blotchy, his eyes darting from one to the other of us until it gave me the jumps.

"Suits me," Sal said. "How about you, Willie boy?"

"Sure," I said. "Sure thing. Why not?"

"Now, you're talking," Paulie said, nodding very fast as though something had loosened up in there and he couldn't get it to stop. "Listen, we'll need somebody with a car. Larsen's a big guy and it'll take the three of us to handle him. How about Sylvia? That little Chev of hers really goes. Any kicks?"

"Not from me," Sal said. "She'll bring some class to the party."

If he meant it as a dig, Paulie was too wound up to notice it. You could see Sal was beginning to have himself a ball, though. After all, we were just kids when Paulie had been loose and wild and someone you were supposed to be very careful with. Now, here he was all sweated up about a routine-type thing. Of course, we hadn't seen him since he'd gone to Korea and then spent two years in Leavenworth for breaking up another GI and knocking him down a flight of stairs.

"All right, everything's all set, then," he said, getting up. "We'll meet at Floyd's at ten-thirty."

"Sharp?" Sal asked.

"Sure," Paulie said, not even knowing he was being ribbed. "Don't be late."

As soon as I got there, I could see it was going to be a bad night. They were all sitting in a booth and Sal had brought Gertrude. You could tell both he and Paulie were pretty sore. Gertrude was about seventeen and maybe there was nothing exactly wrong with her, but sometimes I thought there was nothing exactly right, either. She was square and chunky—something like Sal, himself—and all frozen in behind a white, fat face and eyes like green marbles thumbed into paste. She was wearing a mackinaw and black pants that tucked into her motorcycle boots.

Sylvia had her arm around Paulie's shoulders. She was a thin, dark girl and something of a drag. I mean she cried easy and got upset and even when we were kids we used to wonder why Paulie bothered hauling her around. Of course, she looked pretty good and dressed like a shark.

"Now, take it easy, honey," she said. "It won't do any good to get all excited."

Paulie was rolling an empty glass back and forth between his hands. His head was bent over it, but you could see a corner of his mouth twitching as though someone were tugging on it with a string.

"Here, I'll leave it to Willie," he said suddenly jerking his head up. "Did anyone say anything about bringing anyone else along, Willie? You were there."

"Well, what's the trouble anyway?" Sal said uneasily. You could see he felt maybe he'd pushed Paulie a little too far. "I forgot I had a date. Besides, all she'll do is sit in the car with Sylvia. What can happen?"

"It's not a way to do things," Paulie said looking down at the glass again. "You make arrangements, you're supposed to stick to them."

There was enough of a whine in it for Sal to move back in. He leaned forward and spoke as though he'd just learned Paulie's hearing wasn't too good.

"I said all she'll do is sit in the car with Sylvia," he said loudly.

"Well, be sure that she does," Paulie said and caught Gertrude's green-glass stare for a second, then turned away. "Let's get going," he said irritably. "For God's sake, how long are we going to sit around here?"

We drove past the lot across from Larsen's place and parked two blocks past it. Then we left the girls in the car and went back there. His car——a pre-war Olds—was about thirty feet into the lot from the sidewalk. We found a clump of rocks fifteen or so feet past it and sat down behind them. We had a fifth of rye and began passing it back and forth, every once in a while one of us standing up to look across the street and see how near he was to closing.

"The car's turned right for us," Paulie said. "He'll have to come around this side to get in. I can get over there in a second. You two stay behind me so I can get a good crack at him. When he goes down, be sure and grab his arms just in case. I'll get the wallet."

He had brought a length of lead pipe along. As we sat there drinking and waiting for Larsen, he got on his knees and tried a few swings, first one-handed, then two. You could see he couldn't make up his mind.

"You should have thought of that before," Sal said. "This is a hell of a time to be practicing."

He was getting edgy, too. I guess I was in the best shape of all of us. That's because somehow I wasn't in it as deep as either of them. What with the rye tugging them on, they were pretty close to going at each other when two couples came out of Larsen's place and a minute later the lights went out.

"All right," I said. "Now, let's cut out the racket. He'll be here in a second."

We moved around to the edge of the rocks, Paulie in front holding the pipe. I could see drops of sweat on his neck over the Eisenhower jacket. Sal was on my left, his mouth open and the smell of rye strong on his breath. Across the street, the door opened and a man came out and stood there a minute with his back to us, locking up. He looked big as a bear in his leather jacket, the moonlight gleaming on his bald head.

"Don't miss, for God's sake," Sal whispered. "That guy's a giant."

"Shut up," Paulie said without turning around. "Shut up, can't you? I know what I'm doing."

Larsen came toward us, picking his way around small rocks and singing "Stardust" in a high-pitched moony way, probably imitating something on his juke box. When he got close to the car, he took out his keys and came around it. As he put a key in the door lock, Paulie jumped for him, but too soon. Larsen saw it coming, jerked back and caught it on his shoulder.

"Hurry up," Paulie shouted throwing himself at him. He sounded frantic. "Hurry!"

We rushed at him and bowled him over, but holding him down was something else again. He was strong as a horse. I had him by one shoulder, but the way he was whipping that arm around, it was almost impossible to hang on. Sal was having the same trouble on the other side and Paulie wasn't getting anywhere trying to reach into his pockets.

"Can't you hold him?" he gasped, and all the time Larsen was pulling a leg up under himself and getting ready to try getting up. He wasn't hollering. He didn't look worried, or even sore. He'd probably been a wrestler or something. We were just like kids the way he was tossing us around. I knew if he ever got up we wouldn't have a chance with him. Then I felt someone move in next to me.

"Watch it," Gertrude said.

"What the hell—" I began, and then she stepped around me and kicked at his head. It caught him good and he went down on his back with blood leaking out of his ear. She'd caved in the side of his head, but even then he wasn't through. In a second, he was straining to lift himself again, his eyes rolling like he'd gone mad.

"I can't hold him," Sal shouted, and a second later Larsen had his arm free and was swinging it over at me. He'd thrown Sal and Paulie off him like they were mice and now instead of me having him, he had me.

"Grab him," I hollered, trying to squirm away and then, from next to me, Gertrude kicked at him again. He caught it full in the face and was probably through right there, but she gave him another to make sure.

Even then, he wasn't out, but he just lay there without moving while Paulie went through his pockets. His eyes were closed and he was shivering like a dog after a truck's hit it. His face was in awful shape. He just stayed like that until we had his money and were running to the car.

Paulie counted the money on the way out to the beach. He was sitting in front with Sylvia, the rest of us in the back, Gertrude in the middle. We intended staying out at the beach for half an hour or so, then coming back into LA by some other route.

"Seventy-two bucks," he said. "Well, I thought we'd do better than that."

He sounded tired and fed up, almost as though he wished the whole thing had never happened. I wasn't exactly singing myself, but Sal was feeling pretty good. He had his arm around Gertrude's shoulders, laughing and telling her she was the "greatest" all the way to the beach. If Gertrude heard him, she never showed it.

We parked a block away, then walked over to the beach and down to the water. Sometimes you see people picnicking out there, but this time it was too cold. The moon was still out, though, and we could see well enough to divide the money without lighting a match. The sand was too cold to sit on, so we stood up while Paulie began separating it into different-size bills.

"Seventy-two bucks split three ways," he said. "I figured it out in the car. Twenty-four bucks apiece."

"Why three ways?" Gertrude asked.

"Sal, Willie and me," Paulie said.

"Why not me?"

She was standing in front of him with her hands in her mackinaw pockets, her face looking like lumped dough in the moonlight.

"Look, nobody invited you in the first place," Paulie said and he pointed the hand with the money in it at her and you could see it shaking. "We would have taken him whether you were there or not and we wouldn't have had to almost kill the guy—"

She took one hand out of her pocket, a length of bicycle chain wrapped around her knuckles, and swung at him. It caught him on the forehead and for a second the link marks were clear as brands. Then the blood filled them in.

"Oh," Sylvia said and her hand jumped to her lips.

Paulie just stood there as though he couldn't believe what was happening. He began to shake his head and then she hit him again. This time he went down, but rolled over and got on all fours. He was starting to get up when Gertrude moved in on him again and lifted her knee into his face knocking him over on his back. When she stepped toward him again, I thought she was going to go on with it, but all she did was bend over and start picking up the money.

"What's a quarter of seventy-two?" she said when she had it all.

"Eighteen," Sal said.

She divided the money into four stacks, handed one to me, one to Sal and offered one to Sylvia who was on her knees dabbing at Paulie's face.

"Here," she said. "You want it?"

"No, that's all right," Sylvia said. "I don't want it."

"You sure?" Gertrude asked.

"I'm positive," Sylvia said firmly.

"Okay," Gertrude shrugged, putting the money in her pocket. "I'll keep both of them."

It was a quiet trip back to town. Even Sal didn't say anything. Once or twice he looked at Gertrude uneasily as though wondering what she'd pull next. Paulie rode with his head resting on the back of the seat, a handkerchief pressed to his face.

When we were close to downtown LA, Paulie said he wanted to *go* to Floyd's and get a drink. It was the first thing he'd said all the way. I said I could use one, too, and Sal said he'd go along. Sylvia said she'd pass it up and no one was about to ask Gertrude. We stopped in front of Floyd's and the three of us got out. Sylvia put her head out the window to kiss Paulie. She was smiling.

"I'm going to drop Gertrude off," she told him. "Don't you boys drink too much."

We went in and ordered a round.

"I never was able to hit a woman," Paulie said. "It's the one thing I never was able to do."

He looked terrible. It wasn't only that his face was cut up. He looked like an old man, all shrunken into himself and beat up, beat up from the inside out.

"Well, if one ever needed it, tonight—" Sal began.

"We could have used the dough," Paulie said moodily, paying no attention to him. "We were going down to Tijuana and celebrate me getting out."

We got our drinks and drank them, then put away a second round and ordered a third. They weren't doing us any good. I mean, Paulie was glooming in something all his own and Sal and I were wondering why we didn't forget it and go on home. Then Floyd's guy brought us the third round and, as he left the table, we saw Sylvia coming toward us.

She walked up to the table and dropped a roll of bills on it right under Paulie's nose. She was smiling at him, a strange, winner's smile I'd never seen on her before, her eyes shining like a big cat's.

"Thirty-six dollars," she said. "That should get us to Tijuana."

"Where did you get it?" Paulie asked. He looked puzzled and tired and a little tight.

"From Gertrude."

I felt everything inside my clothes begin to crawl. Sal's face looked wet and he didn't know he was holding a drink. Sylvia was leaning forward, bending in over Paulie till he had to back up to look at her straight.

"How?" he whispered.

"Don't you know?" she laughed. "My God, isn't it written all over her?"

Then Sal let his breath out in a long, low sigh and I bent over my glass.

"Jesus Christ," Paulie whined. "Jesus Christ, I can't keep up with anything any more."

He got up and went out of there without touching the money. As he went past the window we could see him buttoning up the Eisenhower jacket. I had a picture of him doing that a lot from then on, slouching in and out of places and buttoning up that old jacket.

"He'll be back," Sylvia said but she didn't look sure. Maybe she was thinking the same thing I was. I mean, all Paulie had wanted to do was take a little money from this fellow.

Seven Lousy Bucks
C. L. Sweeney

August 1956

The sound of the man being sick wakened him. He came out of his drink-drugged sleep slowly, painfully, gradually becoming aware of the dull throbbing ache at his temples, the stifling heat of the August night, the sick-sweet smell of the perspiration oozing from the pores of his flabby white body and soaking his underclothes and the sheet on which he lay, the gagging fumes of rotten whiskey coming up into his nose and throat.

He opened his eyes and looked into the darkness of the tiny bedroom. The night sounds of the city came through the open window on the dead night air and he lay there and heard them, not moving, staring into the blackness, his mind groping back into focus. Somewhere in the block a baby was crying, an automobile horn rasped impatiently at a busy intersection, a man's voice was raised in violent argument, a girl giggled excitedly as she was pressed back into the shadows of a doorway.

And above them all he heard the sound of the man being sick. Violently, retchingly, disgustingly sick.

He buried his head in the damp pillow, pulling the edges up around his ears, trying to shut out the sound, feeling his own stomach begin to writhe and groan in sympathy.

God, it was bad enough having Clare bring these bastards up to the apartment, letting them make love to her in the next room, his room, his bed, while he sweltered in this damned hot box. Now even that wasn't enough. Now they had to get sick, too.

He raised himself on his elbows, then with considerable effort forced his heavy body up and around until he sat on the edge of the bed. Sitting up, his head ached even worse and nausea came over him in sickening waves, flooding his senses, like the sound of the man in the bathroom. He fought his stomach down and fumbled frantically about in the darkness until he found the bottle. He held it to his ear and shook it and nearly laughed aloud with relief as he heard the reassuring gurgle. His hands trembling almost uncontrollably, he unscrewed the cap and pushed the bottle to his lips. Throwing his head back, he felt the stuff burn past his throat to his stomach, then the familiar warm, steadying glow. He shook his head in appreciation, wiping the back of his hand across his thick lips and the stubble of beard on his chin.

That was the ticket. He felt better. Not good, but better. He shook the bottle and there was a faint slopping. Good. Still some left. He'd need it worse later. He always needed the next one worse.

The man had stopped being sick now and he could hear Clare talking to him in that low, throaty, voice of hers. Hearing her, he felt a sudden surge of resentment. The least she could do was show a little common consideration. Bringing some guy up here and letting him get sick all over the place! This did it. This was the payoff. Who's she been bringing up here for months? College boys, office clerks, punks! Ten bucks here, fifteen there. The best had only left twenty-five, and he hadn't bothered to come back. Now she'd brought one that was sick! She wasn't trying. He'd told her before and he'd tell her again. Only this time so she'd remember it.

He listened. He could hear Clare moving about but the man was still quiet. He fumbled for a cigarette, found one and lit it. Ten lousy bucks! How could anyone live on that kind of money? When things had been going good, before they'd cracked down on the syndicate, he'd spent plenty of dough on her, all right. Clothes, jewelry, furs, car, swell apartment, the works. Even married her. He, Joe, Young Bookie Most Likely to Succeed, he'd married her. Best looking girl in the city, they said. Best looking call girl, they meant, but he'd married her anyway. Set her up in real style so she could be decent and respectable. All right, so now he was down on his luck. All right, so she did have to go back to work for a while. So what? She'd done it before, she could do it again. Typists and stenographers went back to work after they were married. One trade or another, what's the difference?

But ten bucks! Any high school girl with a build could do better than that.

He heard Clare walk up to the door, then knock softly.

"Joe," she said, "Joe, are you awake?"

Awake, he thought, she wants to know if I'm awake. How the hell could anyone sleep with that kind of racket going on. He reached over and flicked on the light. The sudden brightness burned against his eyes and he buried his face in his hands, letting the light trickle slowly through his fingers until he became accustomed to it.

"Joe," she said again, hearing the click of the light switch, knowing he was awake. "I brought a guy up here and he got sick. He's passed out on the bathroom floor." She waited, listening.

He did not move. His mouth tasted rotten and his head had begun to ache again. To hell with her. She'd picked the slob up. Let her take care of him.

"Joe," she said, pleading now, "I can't lift him. Help me get him up on the couch. Please, Joe?"

To hell with her.

"He brought a bottle with him, Joe. It's still half full."

He picked his bottle off the floor and held it to the light. Just one good slug left. Not half full. Not a lot of good slugs. Just one. A man couldn't travel very far on that. Like they say, you can't fly on one wing. He tilted the bottle to his lips and drained it. Then he stood up and walked to the door, his bare feet slapping against the floor. He turned the key in the lock. He always kept it locked. Didn't want some clown stumbling in the wrong room and finding him. He didn't give a damn about the guy but he had his pride, hadn't he?

He opened the door. Clare was standing there, still in her evening gown, the one he had always liked, the tight blue one. He stopped, framed in the doorway, and looked at her. By God, she was still a good looking dame. Sometimes he almost forgot, living like this. Still had her figure. He rubbed his hand across his sagging paunch. More than he could say. Still had those same long tapered legs, those same smooth soft curves of thigh and stomach, those same breasts, firm and full, that she'd had when he met her. What was the matter with these guys? Ten bucks. Ten lousy bucks. Didn't they know a woman when they saw one?

"He's in the bathroom," she said. "He got sick in the cab coming over. He drank a lot and it was pretty close in the cab."

The blonde hair was all hers, too. No bleach job. All hers, like the pink and white complexion. Still a good looking dame. He ran his tongue over his lips. The eyes a little dark and tired, maybe, a line or two here and there, but still a good looking dame. He felt a quick unaccustomed warmth.

"Come on, Joe," she said, urging, "help me get him up on the couch."

He suddenly reached out and pulled her to him, forcing her body against his, violently, brutally, crushing her lips beneath his own, running his hand across her bare shoulders, down the flesh-soft smoothness of her back, down. For a moment she went limp and then he felt her stiffen and push herself away. He reached for her again, breathing hard.

"Not now, Joe," she said, looking over her shoulder to the half open bathroom door. "Later. After we get him taken care of. Later, Joe." She backed away.

He looked at her. Damn. A man couldn't even make love to his own wife in his own apartment any more.

She was across the room. "Come on, Joe. Help me with him." She was smiling now, enticing, promising.

Okay, why make a big thing out of it. Get this joker out of the way. Then we'll see if she still remembers her Joe. We'll see.

He walked across the floor to the bathroom door. "Where's the bottle?" he wanted to know. "You said there was half a bottle."

"After we move him," she said. "I'll get it after we move him."

He wheeled, his frayed nerves snapping. "After we move him," he shouted, "after we move him. Everything is after we move him." He smashed his fist down on a small end table and a lamp teetered crazily and crashed to the floor. "I want a drink now!"

"Okay," she said, her practiced voice soothing, calm. "Okay, Joe, keep your voice down. I'll get it for you." She went into the kitchen.

He realized that he was trembling, and when she came back and held the fifth out to him he snatched it from her and put it to his lips, hearing the pleasant gurgle, feeling the warmth of it spread through his body, not putting it down until he felt the trembling pass. He took a deep breath of satisfaction, feeling new, whole, alive again.

She was standing there watching him. Just standing there, her eyes half-narrowed, something burning deep behind them. He tried to make it out. Was it hate? Loathing? Passion? Want? He gave it up. Why try to guess. He moistened his lips. He'd find out, no guessing, in a couple minutes now.

"All right," he said, suddenly impatient, "let's get this over with. Let's get this punk out of here."

She started toward him, to help.

"I'll take care of it," he told her, flexing his arms, swelling his chest. "I can handle him."

She stopped.

He pushed the bathroom door fully open and placed the bottle down on the floor inside. The man was lying on his back, on the floor, his head between the toilet and the tub, his feet toward the door. He was fully dressed. His clothes were rumpled and mussed but well-cut, his shoes newly shined. He looked like money. Not a lot, but enough. He wasn't too old, maybe thirty-five, not bad looking. There was a thick gold wedding band on his left hand and he was asleep and breathing deeply. Out. Out cold.

If there had been any mess, Clare had cleaned it up. Thank God for that. He wouldn't have been in any mood for what was coming if he'd had to take care of that, too.

He took the man by the feet and pulled him into the center of the bathroom floor. The leather of the shoes was warm and smooth in his hands. Good shoes, expensive shoes. Expensive. Money. Then he remembered. He looked over his shoulder at Clare, standing in the door. "How much did he pay you?"

She shook her head. "He didn't. We didn't do anything. He got sick first."

He snorted, looking down at the man, nudging him with a bare foot. "Hell," he said, "he owes you anyway. It wasn't your fault. You were willing." He knelt down and reached under the man and extracted his billfold. He stood up.

"No, Joe," she said, "he doesn't owe me anything. Put it back."

He ignored her, pulling the bills out, looking at them, counting them.

"Put it back, Joe," she said again, her voice hard now. "We don't have to roll anybody. We don't need money that bad."

He was tearing wildly at the billfold, ripping out the seams, throwing cards and papers about the room. Suddenly he slammed it to the floor and dropped to his knees beside the man, clawing, tearing at his pockets.

"Joe," she almost screamed, not understanding, "Joe, stop it!"

He looked up, still on his knees, his face grotesque with rage and frustration. "You know what he had? You know what this bastard was going to pay you?" He held the bills up and let them drop from his hand and fall on the man, one by one, as though they were pieces of filth. "Seven! Seven lousy goddam bucks!" He lashed out and hit the man full in the face with his open palm, hard.

"Joe," she screamed, frightened. "Cut it out."

"Cut it out," he shouted back, mimicking her voice. "Cut it out. You bring a cheap bastard up here to sleep with you for seven bucks and you tell me to cut it out." He slapped the man again, backhand this time, and a trickle of blood began to run down from the man's torn lip.

The man mumbled but did not move.

She flared at him, her voice not screaming now but again hard, cutting. "You put that money back, Joe," she said evenly. "You put that money back and leave him alone or I'm going to call the cops."

The words had a sobering effect but he laughed at her, derisively. "You're going to call the cops? You, with a customer out cold on the floor? Don't try to kid me." His eyes traveled over her until they came to her breasts and lingered there. He watched them rise and fall, sharply outlined, straining against the flimsy blue stuff of the dress. He reached over and picked up the bottle and took another long drink, not taking his eyes from her. "Anyway, Baby, you and I still have a little business to take care of."

Unsteadily, he got to his feet.

She was backing across the room, away from him. "No, Joe, no. Please. Not tonight."

He began to walk toward her, swaying, the bottle in one hand, the crushed bills which he had again picked up in the other. He held the money out to her. "Come on, Baby, I'm a customer. I've got money. Seven bucks. That's all we think you're worth—he," he jerked his head back over his shoulder, "and me, your husband."

Her face was taut, chalk-white, her nostrils distended. "You're not my husband. You're not anything." She spat the words at him, angry, crying, hating words. "You're not anything but a no-good drunken pimp."

The words staggered him, stunned him, words which he knew but had not wanted to hear, had not dared to admit, even to himself. He stood in the center of the floor, his chest pumping; the room beginning to spin wildly about him. Then a blinding wave of rage engulfed him and swept him up and he started for her, a deep animal cry in his throat, compelled to destroy this woman who had dared to name him for what he was.

She was almost at the hall door and she had half turned when the bottle caught her on the temple, bouncing off and shattering against the frame of the door. She crumpled to the floor, making no sound, no protest.

Instantly he was on his knees beside her, holding her in the crook of his arm, dabbing ineffectively at the ugly broken, bleeding bruise. "Clare, Clare, my God, I didn't mean to, Clare." Tears had already begun to form at the corners of his eyes and a sudden sob racked him.

She did not move. Her head hung back and her rouge and lipstick were garish on the pallor of her face. Her moan tilted the room, turning it, and everything was unreal, impossible, nightmarish as the red heat of anger consumed him.

Still holding her, he slowly lifted his eyes, blinking them, striving for focus, lifted them until they came to and rested on the legs and shoes of the man he had left in the bathroom. The shoes. The expensive shoes. Go ahead, lay there, you bastard. Sleep sound. You've got no worries. Your wife is safe in bed at home. So what if she is tired of you? You can buy someone else's wife for the night. Reasonable, too. This one won't get tired of you. This one isn't like your wife. This one's got to support a drunken husband who hasn't had a job in five years. This one needs the money. But seven bucks, you bastard. Where's your sense of values? You could at least pay as much for another man's wife as you do for your shoes.

He looked down at Clare. Her features were calm, reposed. He could not remember when she had looked so beautiful.

His eyes went back to the legs, down the legs to the shoes. And so that was all he had thought of her. Seven bucks' worth. Not even ten. Seven. Clare, not worth as much as the shoes he was wearing. His hand dropped to the floor and fastened around the neck of the broken bottle and slowly raised the six inches of ragged broken glass.

Gently he lowered Clare to the floor, smoothing her evening gown, the one he had always liked, the tight blue one, making her comfortable. She moaned but his eyes did not waver from the man.

He got to his feet then and began to walk toward the bathroom, slowly, steadily, the bottle neck in his hand, the sharp ragged edges outthrust. Seven. Seven lousy bucks. Seven bucks worth of woman. Seven bucks worth of wife. Sleep, you bastard, sleep and dream. Dream of the bargain you got this time. You'll never find another one like it again. Not ever, you won't.

The Secret
Stuart Friedman

September 1956

Raymond was wearing his Sunday suit because it was Sunday and sitting in the easy chair in his own room eating chocolate cake and drinking milk before bedtime and thinking how everything had turned out good, after all, which was how things always did turn out when you came right down to it.

It used to be he had bad habits like the wine-drinking habit and the cigarette-smoking habit and sinful-thinking habit, and he did not work hard and mind what he was told and everything would just seem to get him nervous. It used to sometimes look like he was not going to make good. But he had made good.

He worked hard and minded what he was told and got a lot of fresh air and all the food he could eat and all the milk he could drink and his own private room with curtains on the window and two pictures and a table and a bureau and two chairs and a looking glass and a heap of a bed and a free radio and Mr. Kettrick gave him fifty dollars every month so he could buy clothes and see movies and basketball games and buy all the brand new comic books he wanted. Things did not get him nervous here on the farm, and Mrs. Kettrick, who was Mr. Kettrick's wife, told him he was one of the family, and Agatha Kettrick who was Mr. Kettrick's and Mrs. Kettrick's young daughter had had a surprise party for his birthday when he was forty years old, and he had got a lot of presents—a necktie and three Sunday handkerchiefs and a scarf. What Raymond wished more than anything in the world was that his name was Kettrick, too.

Raymond took a couple of swallows of milk and filled up his glass from the pitcher and drank some more. There was one thing about him, he thought, and that was that he sure did like milk, and most of all he liked milk just before bedtime so he could sleep good and solid and be able to do his full day's work and keep on making good so Mr. Kettrick would be proud of him. He took another big bite of the chocolate cake and started to chew it, slow and easy, tasting all of the different flavors of the dough and the walnuts cracked up in it and the thick fudge icing.

When he was chewing he was happy and did his best thinking, and it was like Mr. Kettrick's cows who were chewing all the time and did not get nervous, and it was like Mrs. Kettrick's chickens who moved their heads all the time when they walked. Raymond guessed if your head moved from walking or chewing it kept the blood turned up toward your head so you could do your best thinking. Maybe if he could start to chew tobacco.... He frowned and shook his head. The tobacco-chewing habit was not a clean habit and Mrs. Kettrick would not allow him to have it. But maybe he could do like Agatha Kettrick did sometimes and chew chewing gum. The first thing tomorrow morning after the morning milking he would try to be sure not to forget to ask Mr. Kettrick if it would be all right to take up the chewing-gum habit.

He heard the quick clicketty-click of Agatha coming up the stairs in her first pair of high-heeled shoes. Raymond hurried up and licked his gooey fingers clean and picked up the fork that she had put on the plate for him to eat his cake with. He could tell by her step that she was not having a slow, sad mood, so she either felt frisky or else she had her spunk up. Raymond waited as she came along the hall and got a little nervous because she might be mad and start hitting him. Agatha never had got her spunk up at him, but he thought about it a lot of times how she might take a notion to beat him up and get him down and pull his ears. She was little and skinny and only a girl of thirteen years of age and not big and strong like him, but if she took the notion to do that to him she would just go ahead and do it, and it made Raymond nervous to think about that.

She rapped shave-and-a-haircut on his door and at the same time opened it and stepped in part way, "Hi, Raymond. Are you enjoying your cake?" she said in her teasy little voice.

"Yes, ma'am," he answered prompt and smiled back when she smiled. She had on a fat, whooshy, shiny dark green skirt and butter colored sweater and a jingle jangle of bracelets and sparkly swinging earrings and her cinnamon colored hair was passed through a napkin ring on the top back of her head and dropped in back like a horse tail and her face was round and clean and she had alive eyes that could be tender like a new calf's and she smelled good.

Suddenly, Raymond did not know if he ought to stand up, because even if she was just in school she had started to grow little titties on her chest and that made her a lady instead of a little girl. He got a little nervous and wriggled and started to get up, but she cried:

"What are you doing, Raymond? You don't have to get up. Don't let me bother you. I just looked in to see if you wanted any more cake or milk. H'm?"

"Oh, no. No ma'am. This will be plenty when I finish this. It is sure good cake."

"Better than Mama makes?" she said, teasy.

Agatha herself had made the cake, but if he would say it was best, and Mrs. Kettrick heard what he said . . . He wet his lips and frowned and did not know what to say. His eye got caught by her high-heeled shoe. She sure did have pretty legs, like girls in a bathing suit in the pictures. Then he thought that was sinful thinking and looked up higher at her skirt where her stomach was, and he stared at that place while she said in a laughy way:

"You don't have to answer that. I was just teasing."

"Yes, ma'am." He tried to think what it was he didn't have to answer, but when he was not chewing he did not do his best thinking. She was skinny under the fat skirt, but her stomach was swole out big as a melon. It was funny.

"You just quit that ma'am, Raymond. I'm Agatha and you know it very well."

He looked up and her face was so pretty to look at that a warm feeling went through his chest and he tried to think of something that he could do for her, and then it came to him.

"Agatha, I used to go to school and what I was the star pupil in was arithmetic. I could do multiplication tables, every one of them perfect clean through the sixes, and if you need any help studying arithmetic, you just come to me."

"Oh, Raymond, you're just a doll. Thank you very much. What I'm having trouble with is two times two."

"Two times two is four."

"Wonderful. Whew!" She fanned her face. "Now I'm relieved. If you hadn't helped me I just don't know what I'd do. I've got to go."

When she was gone, Raymond sat and ate up the rest of his cake and cleaned up all the crumbs from the plate and from his Sunday suit and ate them, and drank off the last drop of his milk. It was fifteen minutes till nine and time to wind the clock and set it. He had already been to the outside privy and had washed in the inside bathroom, and all he had to do was take off his clothes and hang them up neat and lay out his work clothes and turn out the light, and get in bed and go to sleep.

He lay in bed in the dark, but something had got him nervous and he did not sleep. He heard Agatha go downstairs, then come upstairs and go in her room, then down to the bathroom, then the toilet flushing, then the washing bowl water running. She did not come out for a long time. He thought she was washing her teeth and hands and face and putting on different kinds of salves and creams for ladies, like he had seen in the medicine chest. One time he had known a girl that had little titties and had wanted them to be big and so she put some kind of cream on them and rubbed them and they would look shiny and polished and he thought maybe Agatha was putting cream on herself that way. He turned over and tried to sleep, but he was still nervous and he did not know why. He heard Agatha come out of the bathroom and go in her room across the hall. He listened close when she shut the door and heard the clicky sound of her putting on the chain lock. Mr. Kettrick had got a chain lock for her door so if a thief came in the house to steal Agatha's watch and gold school pin and bracelets he could not do it. That was why Mr. Kettrick put the chain lock on Agatha's door.

Raymond got to worrying if he did not get to sleep quick, he would not have his full eight hours of sleep by the time it was time to get up and work. But he could not sleep. There was a tiny thump thump sound of Agatha walking around in her room, maybe in her bare feet, which she put red toenail polish on. And then he heard the snick of her light switch and her footsteps going to bed. He thought about her getting into bed, and then he remembered what had made him nervous. It was how fat her lower stomach was, like she had a melon under her skirt and he felt scared and wished it was not dark. If Mr. Kettrick would only let him sleep with the light on he could sleep.

But he couldn't sleep. All of a sudden the sinful-thinking habit came back on him. He did not know why, but there it was back on him. He had gone to church today and had done right all day, but there it was back on him. He got so nervous he just did not know what to do because Mr. Kettrick told him he could not get the bed dirty, but was to go down to the barn when the habit came on him. But it was too cold to get up and dress and go down to the barn. Then he thought maybe he could do it without anybody knowing, but right that minute he heard Mr. Kettrick coming up the stairs. Raymond waited, very nervous. He heard Mr. Kettrick try Agatha's door, and Agatha called out in a sleepy little voice who was it and Mr. Kettrick saying in the special soft voice he used on Agatha that it was just Daddy and good night and sleep tight and don't let the bedbugs bite. Then Mr. Kettrick opened Raymond's door and Raymond shut his eyes and made a snory sound and the light went on a minute, then went off. Raymond stopped being nervous and having bad thoughts that Mr. Kettrick wouldn't like and he went to sleep.

Raymond heard the tick that sounded just before the alarm went off and he turned off the alarm and got up quick before he would fall back to sleep. Mr. Kettrick did not like a hired man lying around like a perfumed woman past five o'clock. He dressed and pretty soon he heard Mr. Kettrick go down to shake the furnace. Raymond went down and outside and walked down to the cowbarn, and went up into the silo and threw down feed, all by himself, and pretty soon the gasoline engine that ran the milking machines was chuffing away and Mr. Kettrick yelled up that was enough silage. Raymond climbed down and started carrying silage to the cows in the stanchions. Then he helped give them their bran and soybean meal and salt and brought in the clean cans the creamery truck had left. Raymond hand-milked the raunchy little Jersey who would not hold still for the machine, and helped with the stripping after the machines were done. Mr. Kettrick said Raymond had a better way with cows than any hired man he ever had had and never gave a one of them a sore teat from wrong squeezing.

Going up to the house for breakfast, Raymond walked just like Mr. Kettrick with a long stride and a strong proud look on his face. They washed in the kitchen that smelled good of cereal and eggs and frying ham and potatoes. While Mrs. Kettrick was setting the bowls and platters on the big table, Mr. Kettrick went in the sitting room and switched on the radio for the farm reports, then came standing in the doorway looking at Agatha's empty chair. Raymond hoped she would not be sick again and not be able to eat breakfast like she had been every day the last week, because a gloomy feeling came over everything and Mr. Kettrick would not be in a jokey mood.

Mrs. Kettrick looked at Raymond and said: "Don't just stand, dear. There's nothing for you to do. Sit down at your place."

Mr. Kettrick went and shut off the radio when he heard Agatha open her door. She swung sluffing in houseslippers along the hall upstairs, and Raymond got nervous because Mr. Kettrick and Mrs. Kettrick both stopped moving and were listening. Agatha went in the bathroom. Then the sound came, like it had been every morning the past week. A gagging sound from Agatha's throat. She kept doing it, like throwing up and it made Raymond very nervous and he saw Mr. Kettrick and Mrs. Kettrick look at each other a long time like they were talking a silent, secret language and Mr. Kettrick's long, wide leather-looking face turned sort of gray, and he formed his lips like to say something, but nothing came out. He stomped over to his chair and sat down hard and opened the Bible quick and Mrs. Kettrick scooted onto her chair and bowed her head and Raymond bowed his. Mr. Kettrick read from the Bible, but it was not like his voice, and it scared Raymond. Then the Bible slapped shut and Mr. Kettrick said some more and Amen.

He looked at Raymond and said: "Aren't you hungry, Raymond? Ella, Raymond is not hungry, so we will just give his breakfast to the pigs." Mr. Kettrick said the same thing lots of times for a joke, only this time it did not really sound funny and Raymond could not laugh very hard. Raymond wished Agatha would be well and come down so everybody would feel good again, and talk and make jokes instead of just eating and eating without saying anything.

Then finally she did come down, with her little shoulders all slumpy and her mouth down at the corners. She had on her school clothes, a blouse and sweater coat and skirt and saddle shoes and she said:

"Mama, I can't hardly fasten my skirt. Will you let it out?"

Raymond looked at her lower stomach, and in her school skirt it stuck out more than ever.

"There's not time before the school bus."

Raymond jumped like he was shot because Mr. Kettrick smashed his fist down on the table bouncing all the dishes.

"She's not going to school today. She's sick."

"Oh," Agatha wailed. "I've *got* to go to school. I've just *got* to."

"Eat. You're sick. You'll stay home."

"But, Daddy . . ."

"Eat."

"I'm not hungry. I just want some black coffee."

"Hurry up, Raymond, and get down and turn the cows out and start cleaning the barn . . ."

"Can't I have no more milk, Mr. Kettrick, and some of that leftover pie?"

"Drink up. Carry the pie with you. Ella, wrap it up for him to carry. Get your coat on, Raymond."

Raymond got up and went for his sheepskin coat and put it on. "Can't I go first back to the . . ." He did not want to say privy in front of a lady, and he didn't know what to do because that's where he always did go first, and if he had to go down to the barn first when he always did it the other way it would make him nervous.

"Yes. Yes. You can go back there first. Now go on."

There was a "shoo" in Mr. Kettrick's voice and Raymond hurried out. When he came back, he came into the kitchen because he had forgot his pie. And he wished he had never stopped back inside. They did not see him because they were in the sitting room.

"You read the letter from Jim's wife last week, Agatha," Mrs. Kettrick said. "And you have the exact same symptoms she has. And *she* is going to have a baby."

"I don't care what that dumb thing has."

"That's shameful jealous talk, Agatha. Never mind. The point is, your stomach is swollen, and you're having the morning sickness . . . just like her. As if I didn't know the symptoms myself after five children. You didn't have your last period, either, did you?"

"I did. I DID!" Agatha yelled.

"Agatha. Look in my eyes and say that."

There was a long silence and Raymond got nervous waiting and he wanted to go back outside, but if he would move he was scared they would hear him.

"I tell you I didn't do anything bad. I didn't. I've been kissed. But I'm cool, just clinch and break clean, no B Pix, no heave-ho. I gave my sacred promise to Jim the very night before he got married. I promised Jim right in this room that I would not let a thing happen that shouldn't. I'd rather be *dead* than break my sacred promise to my own *brother*"

Raymond nodded and thought how Agatha never would break her sacred promise to Jim. Jim had got married just before Raymond came to work for Mr. Kettrick. Agatha got in sad moods because Jim had gone off and left her and she said that she would marry Jim herself if she was not his sister. Agatha liked Jim.

Mrs. Kettrick said: "You missed your period."

Agatha started in to cry like her little heart had broke and Raymond snuffed his nose and the corners of his eyes burned and he felt a sad feeling in his chest for Agatha.

"Yes," Agatha said. "I didn't have it. I've been so scared I could die . . . oh-oh-ooooooo" she cried. "I wasn't going to school. I was going to run away . . ."

"Agatha," Mr. Kettrick said. "Who did it?"

"Nobody, Daddy. I swear . . ." she stopped to cry some more. "I SWEAR. How could it happen? It couldn't . . ."

"Your Daddy would never turn his back on you in trouble, honey," Mr. Kettrick said. "Don't be scared to say the truth."

Agatha let out a choky, crying sound and came running in the kitchen, her face all wet and red and her eyes shiny wide and she did not even see Raymond as she picked up the Bible and went back in the sitting room.

"I swear on the Bible, Daddy. I swear my solemn sacred oath on the Bible. I didn't do anything. I didn't do a thing to have a baby and I don't know why I'm going to have one. I'll kill myself."

"Tush," Mrs. Kettrick said and laughed. "Come along. Let's go upstairs and wash your face. Then we'll go over to the doctor's . . . and you're not to think silly things like that . . . why, you talk like your folks would turn you out."

Raymond heard them going upstairs, and he couldn't make himself make a sound because Mr. Kettrick was sitting right in the sitting room not making a sound and would hear. Then Mrs. Kettrick came back down in the sitting room.

"George, I believe her."

"No. She's scared and lying, and trying to protect the boy."

"I know my children, George. And I know that my Agatha is not lying."

"Why, God damn it, Ella, talk sense. She's pregnant."

"Then it happened when she was asleep."

"Ahhh!" Mr. Kettrick made a snorting sound. "And not wake up? A young girl like that. A virgin girl. Talk sense. Nature put a mighty tough wall up to block the passage in innocent girls. She couldn't of slept through a breaking of her maidenhead."

"She didn't have a maidenhead, George."

"What are you saying?"

"She didn't. When she was ten it was broken. Remember when she fell off the tractor and was laid up in bed?"

"Is that a fact, Ella?"

"I said it. And I say it wouldn't be impossible for her to be attacked while she was sleeping."

"I put on that chainlock. And there's never the night I don't check it to see she hasn't forgot it . . ."

"Do you remember that first week after Jim got married? It was hot every night."

"Oh, my God!"

"Remember the night you heard her having a bad dream . . . ?"

"Good God, yes I do remember. She's opened her door to get some air through. I went in. She was whimpering and half-asleep. I sat down and patted her and she said she'd had a bad dream."

"That's what we thought it was. A dream."

"It never came to me that—"

"And the timing is exactly right. It's while Jim was on his honeymoon."

"Get her to the doctor. I'm going down to the barn."

Raymond stepped back quick and opened the door to the porch and just then Mr. Kettrick was in the doorway staring at him.

"I just come in this second," Raymond said, "to get my pie on the way to the barn."

"You were a long time back there." Mr. Kettrick stood and stared at him, not moving, just staring. Then Mr. Kettrick looked down at a shiny little puddle in the middle of the floor. Raymond knew there must have been a little snow on his boots that had melted off while he stood there. Mr. Kettrick walked into the kitchen and stood right over the puddle and looked at it and then at Raymond. Raymond saw Mr. Kettrick's jaw muscles clench and suddenly Raymond could not breathe. Mr. Kettrick looked up at his face and he smiled.

"Well, I guess you didn't take any longer back there than you had to. Go on and take your pie, and go to the barn."

It was already daylight, but things felt dark when Raymond walked down the lane to the barn. He held the slab of pie, careful, but he just could not take a bite of it, because back of him, maybe a stone's throw, he could hear the crunch crunch of Mr. Kettrick's boots on the snow. Crunch . . . crunch . . . crunch . . . coming steady and strong back of him. Raymond wanted to look around but his neck seemed locked. He did not want to look at Mr. Kettrick. Mr. Kettrick knew Raymond had been standing in the kitchen and had not told the truth about just coming in the house. But instead of scolding him for telling a story Mr. Kettrick had smiled and it made him scared.

The minute he got inside the barn, he began to eat the pie as fast as he could do it. When Mr. Kettrick came in Raymond had the pie all in his mouth, so both of his cheeks were bulged out. Mr. Kettrick snapped on the light and looked at Raymond and pinned Raymond's eyes to his. Raymond stood trying to chew, but wasn't able to, while Mr. Kettrick was looking at him. Raymond could see a lot of thinking going on. That made him nervous and he tried to get his eyes away from Mr. Kettrick's, but he couldn't. His hands started to shake and he thought if he had some wine, just this one time again, that was what he would like to have, but Mr. Kettrick did not allow the wine-drinking habit. Raymond wanted to say something and ask Mr. Kettrick if anything was wrong and why wasn't he moving or saying something. Suddenly, Raymond's voice was out of his mouth:

"I never done it. I never. Mr. Kettrick, I never. She is like my own little sister and I help her with arithmetic, all the multiplication tables clean through six, one times one is one, one times two is two, one times three is three . . ."

"What are you nervous about?"

"Because I didn't. I would take the Bible, too, and swear my sacred honor, too, and what I would like to take up is the chewing-gum habit. Can I, Mr. Kettrick?"

"Sure. Now, let's get to work. I know you are a good boy, Raymond, and would never hurt Agatha or tell a story to me. Let's get to work. I know you will always tell me the truth."

"Yes sir, Mr. Kettrick."

"And you're not a low, sneaking filthy animal who has to be wiped off the face of the earth. Let's get to work."

Raymond got to work.

He worked all day, good. At dinner there was just leftovers because Mrs. Kettrick and Agatha had gone in the car to the doctor. At supper he did not see Agatha, and Mrs. Kettrick was not hungry. But he ate good and did not look at Mr. Kettrick. After supper he went to the privy and then went to his room. The light was on in Agatha's room, but he did not hear her. At eight-thirty he did not go down to get a sweet and his milk. But after a while Mr. Kettrick opened his door and looked at him.

"How come you don't want something before bedtime, Raymond?"

"Mr. Kettrick, I just don't know why."

"Don't you?"

"No, sir."

"It's because there's a poison lie in you, Raymond, isn't there?"

"I was in the kitchen before and listened and heard."

"Fine. That's a little part of the truth. What's the rest, Raymond?" Mr. Kettrick came in and shut the door back of him and stood against it, not smiling. "Have you done any sinful thinking?"

"No." Raymond looked away. He looked back. "Some."

"Ever about Agatha?" His voice got hoarse and his eyes were mean, and Raymond was scared to say.

"No."

Mr. Kettrick went out and downstairs and Raymond sat feeling nervous, and then Mr. Kettrick was coming back up. He came in the room with a wedge of cake and milk. He put it down by Raymond and then sat down on the other chair and watched.

"Eat," Mr. Kettrick said, real soft. And he smiled, but it was not a right smile. There was a loud rumbling in Raymond's stomach. He picked up the cake, but his throat was all dry and he knew he would not be able to swallow and he thought maybe some milk would wet his throat and he drank some. It came back up all over his overalls. He looked quick and scared at Mr. Kettrick and mopped his overalls clean with his bandana. Mr. Kettrick stood up, smiling, and went to the door.

"Well, goodnight, Raymond," he said. "Sleep tight."

Only Raymond could not sleep tight. He could not sleep any at all. He heard Mr. Kettrick in the hall walking up and down, slow and soft. Then Mr. Kettrick went down the stairs and out of the house. Raymond got to sleep, and then suddenly he was awake. It was the sound that made him wake up.

The bull bellowing. He could hear him clear from the barn, because the bull was mad. And what always got the bull mad was when he was put in the short pen.

Mr. Kettrick had put the bull in the short pen to make him mad. And Mr. Kettrick would put Raymond in there with the bull.

Raymond knew what he had to do and that was to ask Agatha to help him. He got up fast and put on his overcoat so he would be covered proper. He opened his door careful, and listened and he did not hear anything, just from the barn the bull bellowing. He would knock soft on Agatha's door and wake her up and tell her to tell Mr. Kettrick who really did it to her, or else Mr. Kettrick would think it was him.

The hall was dark and shivering cold and Raymond squinched his eyes, looking up toward the front bedroom, thinking for a minute that somebody was standing up there like part of the black shadows. He listened and there was no moving or breathing and he guessed it was nobody up there. He knocked on Agatha's door. It sounded terrible loud. He did not hear Agatha wake up. He looked up toward the front bedroom, then knocked again.

"Who is it?" Agatha called. Raymond did not say anything, but waited and she came thumping in her bare feet that she put toenail polish on. He shivered and thought he saw something move up in the black shadow by the front bedroom. "Who is it?" Agatha said, close to the door. She opened it on the chainlock.

"Daddy," Raymond whispered.

"No it is not," Agatha whispered. "Raymond, you get right back in your room."

"Agatha, please leave me talk to you. Please. You got to say who really done it to you, Agatha. Your daddy will think it was me that did it bad to you, Agatha. He'll put me in with the bull."

"I can't tell him."

"You got to." Raymond heard his voice come out aloud almost sobbing. He got down on his knees at the part-open door and tried to reach his hand in to touch Agatha, but she shut it hard on his wrist. "Ouch! Oh! I never meant anything bad, Agatha. Can't you see me on my knees begging. Please, Agatha, or he'll kill me."

"No he won't. Now go away."

"Please!"

"I can't tell him. It happened when I was asleep. I know who, but I can't tell."

Suddenly, the hall light was snapped on and there was Mr. Kettrick standing with his shotgun looking at Raymond on his knees in front of Agatha's door.

Mr. Kettrick's face looked like Jehovah standing high with wrath and he said, "Raymond, get dressed. There is something down there bothering the bull. We will have to go and see about it."

"No." Raymond put his hands together like praying at church. "No. Please don't put me in there with him."

Mr. Kettrick walked close to him and put the end of the double-barrel 12 gauge shotgun by his head and said:

"Get dressed. And, Agatha, shut your door."

But she never. She opened it and ran out in her nightie crying. "Daddy, don't hurt him. It wasn't him. Don't. Don't."

"Then, who was it?"

"I can't in front of him."

"In your room, Raymond."

Raymond got into his room fast as he could and stood in there breathing hard and scared. He heard that bull a-bellowing, and then closer the bellowing of Mr. Kettrick.

He heard a slap and Agatha started bawling. "It was, it was, it WAS." Agatha said. "The night before he got married Jim came in and I was asleep, and partly awake. *It was* my brother. It was—"

There was another slap, and a big commotion and Mrs. Kettrick coming down the hall, and a lot of talking and yelling, then they all went in Agatha's room and slammed the door.

It grew quiet, only murmuring. Raymond sighed and sat down on the edge of the bed. Now they knew he had not done the bad thing.

There were footsteps in the hall. Raymond's door opened. Mr. Kettrick came into the room. He had the shotgun. "I told you to dress," he said.

Raymond had to dress. And march downstairs, and outside of the house. Mr. Kettrick marched back of him down the lane, pushing him sometimes. And the bull let out a bellow and Raymond could hear the slam of the bull's head hitting the pen.

They were almost at the barn when Raymond heard the car from back up toward the house, and then its headlights were shining across their backs and laying their shadows out long in front of them, and the horn was honking hard.

"George!" It was Mrs. Kettrick yelling. The car stopped and she got out and came running in her bathrobe. "George, you can't do it."

"Get back to the house, Ella. March, Raymond. March. Go back, woman, or I'll knock you down."

Raymond could not help it. He broke away and he started to run and it was the wrong thing to do. He knew it was the wrong thing to do when he did it, but he could not help it and then he was falling on his face and there was the fire from Hell burning him and he was dying and it hurt so bad to die that he started to cry.

They came up to him, growing fainter very quickly; the gun in Mr. Kettrick's hands seemed to be pointing at his head again and Raymond sobbed, "Don't shoot me no more," and the gun moved off without shooting.

Mrs. Kettrick said, "My God, the poor devil . . ."

Raymond tried to tell them, but no words came out. He tried to tell them to please carry him back up to the house where he belonged and not let him die out here in the cold all alone but right in his bed in his own private room like one of the family where he had made good and helped Agatha with the multiplication table clean through the sixes, one times one is one, one times two is two and everything had turned out good after all which was how everything always did turn out when you came right down to it.

Death Wears a Gray Sweater
Gil Brewer writing as Roy Carroll

November 1956

Walsh returned from work later than usual that evening, just at dusk. He drove through the suburbs of Compton, hoping he had forgotten nothing on the list of stuff Edith had asked him to pick up on the way home, and halted the two year old light blue Ford sedan at the intersection just across from his home. He felt tired. The planned celebration for his daughter Mary Lou's eleventh birthday, which would commence at eight with eager, young, howling, ice cream and cake festivities, would tire him still more. He looked forward to it with resignation.

Traffic streamed by. He turned his headlights on, sat there, idling the engine. His driveway was directly across the street. A bad place to turn in, especially with early evening traffic the way it was. He watched the cars roar by the intersection, looking for an opening.

"Dad!"

Mary Lou ran down the drive. She had on the blue, frilled party dress Edith had made. Though Walsh could see nothing of her expression, he knew what it would be like. Shining. Eager with anticipation. Did you remember the chocolate ice cream? The favors? You didn't forget the paper caps?

He flagged an arm at her out the window, and some of the tiredness went away.

"Hurry up, Dad!" she called, standing at the curb. "Mom wants to fix the table. They'll all be here. Hurry up."

"Right with you, honey."

Traffic gaped. Walsh knocked the shift into low and started across the street; then applied brakes sharply.

Something blue and dark and fast, with early headlights, came from nowhere, roaring. Mary Lou stepped into the street, waving at her father. She posed momentarily and lifted the edges of her full skirt, showing him how pretty it was, and he screamed at her, helpless in the wild roar from the blue car that did not swerve, did not brake at all—just hit her.

There was no noise, other than the roar of the engine. Mary Lou did not scream. There was no thump of bone and flesh against steel.

He sickened, his breath gone. He saw her sprawl into the air. He watched her strike against the curb, roll loosely up across his own driveway. The car that hit her was already a half block away, misty purple taillights glaring, still moving dreamlike in the midst of its invincible roar.

Walsh drove heedlessly across the street, parked, leaped from the car and rushed to his daughter. Traffic had lapsed completely; the street was numb and still. There was no sound of slammed doors from the house. Edith hadn't heard.

Mary Lou was dead.

For one awful moment he knelt there, holding the crumpled and suddenly changed body. It hurt him strangely that in that moment he could not think of her as lifeless; he could only think of how her new dress was ruined, and of how this would trouble her. Then he did know.

He started to pick her up; then laid her down. He straightened and stared at his home and something came up inside him—something strong and hellish—something he had never before known. He wanted to kill, maim, destroy. It was a feeling, not wild, crazed—rather an established singleness of purpose, fused like concrete. He turned and ran for his car, climbed behind the wheel and drove off, gas-pedal thrust against the floor.

The misty purple taillights were still in sight. At that same instant, they vanished.

Woods Boulevard, he thought. All through him there was this horrible patience as he urged the sedan toward the far corner.

He came around into Woods Boulevard neatly and fast. The misty taillights were far on up the road, but *they were there*. That was all he asked.

They wouldn't expect him to follow—anyone to follow. They would imagine it had all happened much too fast. They hadn't hesitated; if anything, they had increased speed the second they struck Mary Lou.

The road was deserted and dark. Woods Boulevard reached like a long slim finger out into the country, away from Compton. It was a hump-backed macadam road, sparsely spotted on either side with small frame houses, and wooded acreage that was gradually vanishing as the town expanded.

They? He realized he had seen more than one shadowed form in the speeding car that had wiped out his daughter's life.

His foot on the accelerator was flat against the floor. He felt insane; he couldn't think. He was unable to dwell on Mary Lou being dead. He knew it and that was all.

The other thing was different. He had to get them. Face to face. This was all he really knew.

He gained on them, but there was in no real satisfaction in this. He *knew* he would catch them.

The car up there with the misty purple taillights was not even a car to Walsh—and that somebody drove it meant nothing. The car was significant only in that it existed as something he must stop and wipe out.

He went past the closed, stock car race track, off beyond the parking area, to the right, the tall wooden fence pale in the moonlight.

The taillights vanished.

He sped on, took the turn and picked them up again. He was off Woods Boulevard now, on the hard-packed dirt stretch that led to the sand pits. The other car was only a quarter mile away.

Death Wears a Gray Sweater

They knew he was after them now. He could tell from the way they swerved occasionally with slight loss of control, and knew whoever was driving the other car was giving it everything it had.

The other car crossed a main highway, cut into the narrower dirt stretch that led among pine, oak and willow through the sand pits. Walsh followed, and a moment later his headlights leaped as the sedan rocked in ruts.

They had led him in here purposely. He knew that, too.

There was no sign of the misty purple taillights.

The narrow road curled past low sand hills. He muttered aloud, cursing them now, gunning the engine. He almost smashed into the looming, dark rear end of the other car. He threw his engine into neutral, flung open the door and leaped out.

"Get him!" somebody said. It was a young voice. There was nervousness in it.

He whirled into someone who clubbed him across the face, with something hard like steel. He grabbed for the person, saw a bull-shouldered figure in a gray turtleneck sweater, a white, grim face with a sprinkling of pale freckles in the headlights' glare.

Somebody yelled, "You hit her! You take care of him!"

"Don't worry," the one in the yellow sweater said.

"You killed her!" Walsh shouted.

"Get him!"

Arms and a heavy shoulder caught Walsh across the backs of his legs and he went down. He heard a girl call, "Hurry. I want to get home."

"Mash his head," the young male voice said.

Blood was warm on his face, in his eyes.

"Get him good, now. It's gotta be good."

Somebody grunted and he tried to dodge, rolling on the ground, but the hard steel caught him in the neck, just above the shoulder.

"You killed her," Walsh said. "I saw you. You'll never—I'll get you—"

Again he was struck. He came to his hands and knees, dazed now, unable to think, trying to concentrate.

"God's sake, hit him. Hit him!"

"Hurry up, will you?" the girl called.

He felt the brutal blows, realized them, but that was all. He was really unconscious before he flattened on the sandy ground. Through the welter of futility and blood and darkness, he sensed that they kept hitting him with whatever it was. On the head, on the back, on the head . . .

"Who's payin' for the drinks back at Molly's?"

"Shut up."

He heard their voices and then for some time he sensed nothing at all.

"Well, he's not hurt as bad as he looks. How he did this to himself—and why—I'll never know. Get him awake. I want to talk to him."

Walsh lay on his back and looked up at the night between shifting branches of trees. He saw the pale sky, the low stars, the thin filtering of a cloud—and the cold image of a bull-shouldered young man wearing a gray turtle neck sweater. He hurt plenty, but there was a kind of laughter inside him, too, as he remembered something else.

"He's come to," a man said.

A bright light glared in Walsh's eyes. He blinked, trying to focus on a still minutely spinning world.

"All right. Get him on his feet."

"They killed her," Walsh said.

"Yeah. O. K. Let's go."

"Maybe we oughta take him back to headquarters. He looks sick," a man said.

"Stand him up. I want a look at him."

Hands grasped his shoulders, swung him to his feet. He staggered, nearly fell, thinking only of that young freckled face and the gray sweater now. The misty purple taillights still spun through his mind. Nobody prevented him from falling, and he went to his knees.

"He'll get up," one of them said.

Walsh became conscious of shining boots, of brass, and the glare of a car's headlights. They were police. He wondered absently how they had found him?

"Blood and hair smeared on his front left fender," a man called. "Fender's smashed pretty bad, too."

"I want to vomit," another said. "Bring him along. We'll talk to him down at headquarters."

"You know what *I'd* like to do?"

"Yeah. But we can't."

Walsh got to his feet again, staring at them, wondering what they meant. He reeled, and when he spoke, his voice was blurred, for he couldn't articulate right yet.

"Save it," one of them said with disgust. "You weak-livered, hit-and-run bastards are all the same."

Walsh said, "What do you mean?"

A young man in a brown suit, carrying a felt hat in one hand, with dark hair and pained eyes, stepped up to Walsh. "Look," he said. "Whoever you are. Wait till we get back downtown, then you can tell us all about it and why you didn't stop. Right?"

Walsh grabbed the man's coat lapels, then let go, but stood looking at him. The words began to flow monotonously from his lips as he told them who he was, and what had happened. "Kids," he said. "Young kids, you hear me? I saw them kill her."

The man in the brown suit came to life a little. "Can you prove who you are?"

Walsh nervously got out his wallet, handed the man his identification. He was trembling, watching the other. But he wasn't seeing him. He was seeing something else—a gray sweater.

"Let's head downtown right now," the man said. "This might change things and we'll have to move."

At headquarters, Walsh explained everything and convinced them of his innocence. They cleaned his cuts, bandaged his head, and the brown-suited man took Walsh into an empty room. Walsh sat in a chair at a long table and looked at the man, the careful eyes, expressionless face.

"Like to run over things again with me?" the man asked. "My name's Adkins. I know what you must be going through, Mr. Walsh."

"You know I'm her father now?"

"Yes. You see, a girl called in, said the man who'd hit the girl out on Seventy-first was in the sand-pits. Said she'd seen it, wouldn't say who she was, and hung up. It's understandable now. Kids. Figured they could maybe swing the guilt over to you. Figured you'd seen them, maybe, and tried to catch them. Just Joe Citizen. They—well—" Adkins moved to a chair across the table and leaned on the arm. "We'd have seen how thin it really was, the way they—well—fixed your car so it would look like the—uh—"

"That's all right," Walsh said. "I'm all right. Say anything you like."

"Yes." Adkins stared at Walsh and frowned; then resumed talking in his mild voice. "Dented your fender, and so on. They didn't explain your being beat up. They figured anything to get us on your tail would be enough. It almost was, you see?" He paused. "Only they didn't know you were the kid's father."

Walsh said nothing. He glanced at the door; then toward Adkins again. He wanted to get out of here, fast.

Adkins cleared his throat, offered Walsh a cigarette. Walsh refused. Adkins lit one, and smoked, watching Walsh.

"What are you thinking about?" Adkins asked.

"When I can go. I want to see my wife."

Adkins smoked. "Look, Mr. Walsh. You say you didn't get a good look at any of them?"

"No. It all happened too quickly. I didn't see anything of them, really—they jumped me."

"They say anything?"

"Just yelling around," Walsh said. "There *was* a girl's voice."

"Trying for a lead," Adkins said, scowling at the floor. "Think back. The moon was up. It was dark, but probably with your car's headlights—Try and remember. Anything—anything at all."

"It was dark. I didn't see anything."

"Your headlights were still on when we got there, Mr. Walsh," Adkins said patiently.

"Oh? Well, I still didn't see anything." He walked around the table, looked at Adkins. "I'd better get on home. Edith—my wife—will want me."

Adkins smoked. Watched. Did not move.

"Look, Walsh. This is a pretty terrible thing, I grant you. I'm sorry about it. I want to do what I can. I wish you'd help me."

"How can I help you?" Walsh said. "I've told you everything I know."

"I'm worried about you," Adkins said, looking at his cigarette.

Walsh tightened his jaw muscles.

"You're not mad enough," Adkins said. "Why, Walsh? Why? Wouldn't you like to get your hands on those kids? Tear them apart?"

It burst past his lips. "Yes!" He cut it off sharply.

"That's what I mean," Adkins said. "See? It's all inside you—along with something else."

"I'm sorry," Walsh said. "I don't know what I'm doing. I—I'd better get on home."

Adkins sighed, ground out the cigarette in an ash tray on the table. "O. K.," he said. "Let's go."

They walked out through the building, down a sloping ramp, and into the parking area.

"You can take your car," Adkins said. "Here it is. We won't have to impound it now." He opened the door on the driver's side and looked at Walsh. "Couple of the boys—they washed it up for you."

Walsh turned quickly away, climbed behind the wheel, started the engine. Adkins slammed the door and Walsh looked out at him.

"Thanks," he said.

"Yeah," Adkins said. "You better get home to your wife. She's not doing so well, Walsh."

He knew they would follow him and they did. He was no more than two blocks from the Police Building when he picked up the cruiser in the rear view mirror, hanging well back, but yet staying close enough not to lose him.

All right. He had that worked out, too. And it wasn't right, maybe, because Adkins had been a good guy. But it didn't matter about how good he'd been. There was something Walsh had to do, and nothing could stop him.

It didn't matter who else had been in the car that had struck Mary Lou. The only person who mattered was the driver. And he knew who the driver was—at least he knew his face, and that gray sweater. He could change the sweater, but not the face. Somehow, Walsh didn't believe he'd bother to change the sweater.

Molly's. Where was *Molly's?*

But that would have to wait, too. First the gun. Not that he would use the gun, really. He had a better idea than that.

He took the shortest route toward his home. Now and then, passing through the streets he had driven over early this evening, thinking about Mary Lou's birthday, he wanted to cry. Something inside wouldn't let him cry.

The police car hung well back, and he made no effort to lose it. He drove home, but parked out front instead of in the driveway. He had to take the chance of Edith hearing him. There was a car in the drive, and one out front. Friends. Lights were lit all through the house.

He wanted badly to be with Edith, but it was impossible. He couldn't wait to do this thing that rode inside his mind. He had to do it now.

Walking toward the house, across the lawn, he watched, without turning, as the police cruiser slowed before his home, then sped up and drifted away along the street. They wouldn't bother him now. Adkins had suspected plenty. He'd known Walsh was withholding something.

Walsh ran around the side of the house and looked in the front windows, through the bushes. He saw Edith, and Jim Fleming and Jim's wife, sitting on the couch. Edith's eyes were red and she was trying to smile. Bert Lowell came through from the dining room carrying a tray of drinks.

Edith would be all right till he came back. She wouldn't ever have to know what he was going to do. Nobody would ever have to know. But he would never be able to live with himself if he didn't do it.

He softly opened the back door, moved quickly across the porch and through the kitchen to the pantry. He could hear them talking quietly in the living room. He found the gun, a .45 Colt automatic, checked the clip to make sure it was loaded, and hurried softly back out to the car.

As he got behind the wheel, somebody opened the front door of the house. He heard Bert Lowell exclaim, "Hey, somebody's out there! It looks like Irv!"

He drove away fast.

Molly's Tavern was on the outskirts of Compton, not too distant from Woods Boulevard. Walsh had looked it up in the telephone directory, and as he parked out front he was so excited his heart hammered.

He sat there for a moment, looking the place over. It was a roadhouse, the juke music from inside booming out across the night. Several cars were parked along the dusty stretch of road-shoulder beside the tavern.

He saw nothing of the blue car with the misty purple taillights. But it might be here. Maybe he didn't recognize it.

Through the dirty windows, he saw a bar, and young men and women dancing. It was dimly lighted inside, the red glow from ceiling-high bulbs casting gleams that somehow went with the loud booming music, and the angry-seeming voices inside.

Walsh unfastened his tie, took it off, opened his shirt. He had to keep on his jacket, because the big automatic would be too noticeable in a pants pocket. He ran his fingers through his hair, looking at himself in the rear-view mirror. He looked nasty, all right, what with the bandages and the splotches of iodine.

He went inside. He moved in a kind of haze, through which he searched for the gray sweater. Nobody paid him any attention. It was deafening in the tavern. He stepped to the bar, elbowed himself between a couple of kids not over highschool age, and ordered a bottle of beer. He paid for it and sipped slowly. Then he stopped.

Suppose this wasn't the right place? Suppose those words he'd overheard at the sand-pit when he was being knocked around by those kids had really meant somebody's house—or some other Molly's place. Maybe not even in Compton.

He drank some more of the beer, carefully checking every person in the room. Flashing-eyed young girls, with tight sweaters and swirling skirts, young men and boys in dungarees and loud-colored shirts, tanned faces with swimming eyes and too-long hair, faces that were excited with whiskey and devil-may-care.

There was no sign of gray sweater.

He waited. He had to wait. There was nothing else he could do.

He began to think about Mary Lou. He tried to control his thinking, switch it away, but he couldn't. He kept hearing her voice, the way she had called to him when he'd come home earlier in the evening. The scene of the car striking her as she attempted to show him her new dress.

He smashed the glass hard down on the bar. It didn't break, but the bartender came over and looked at him, a heavy-cheeked man with frank eyes, and a clean white shirt.

"Something the matter, mister?"

"No," Walsh said. "Nothing."

He felt frustrated. He had to find those kids.

"What happened to you?" the bartender said. "Not that it's any of my business, but you sure look a mess."

Walsh remembered how he looked, how he should act in a place like this. "I hung one on last night, got in a brawl. Wife's mad."

"I should guess," the bartender said.

"I was supposed to meet a young kid here tonight," Walsh said. "He wanted to buy a car I have for sale. But I don't know his name."

The bartender swabbed the linoleum-covered bar. "I know most the kids hang around my place, here. What's he look like?"

Walsh hunched on the bar, feeling the way his heart kept socking away. "Big guy," he said. "Dark hair—freckles. Big in the shoulders, like a bull. He had on a gray turtle-neck sweater earlier tonight."

The bartender frowned. "You mean Ernie Williams. Yeah. He was in just a while ago. Tying one on, too. He took some kids home. I think he had a date with his girl. He probably won't be back." The bartender leaned across the bar, wadding the bar rag. "That Williams kid's got a sweet little girl, you know? Right now he's probably out in the woods with her, too." He straightened up, looked around the room; then he went away, as if to a just remembered duty.

Walsh stared at his beer, sick inside now—more so than before. He went to the phone booth and checked the book for Ernest Williams' name, but it wasn't listed. He thought of asking the bartender where the boy lived, but he knew that wasn't the thing to do, either.

He waited. The kids began to thin out, boys and girls paring off, and heading for the door. He drank three beers, trying to keep his mind off Edith, how she was feeling, all alone, wondering where he was. It didn't help. Only he had to find Williams.

He started outside for some air. The place smelled of sweat and stale beer, rank perfume, and head disinfectant.

He was nearly to the door when he heard the bartender call out, "Hey, mister, there's the guy you were looking for!"

It was Williams. Big, bull-shouldered, still wearing the gray turtleneck sweater, shoving through whirling dancers near the door. A sexy-eyed blonde of about sixteen, wearing skin-tight pale dungarees and a white sweater, clung to Williams' arm.

Walsh started toward them, his hand on the gun in his jacket pocket.

The girl saw Walsh, let go of Williams' arm, said something and pointed in his direction.

Walsh was up to them now. "Outside," he said to Williams.

"You going to take that from him?" the girl said to Williams.

"Fly away," Williams said to the girl, shoving her toward the bar, "What's with you?" he said to Walsh.

"Outside," Walsh said. He got up close to Williams and rammed the muzzle of the .45 into the young man's side. Williams wasn't drunk, but he was close to it. He stank of whiskey and sweat. His face was sheened with sweat, his eyes shot with blood, the dark hair falling over his forehead. His lips curled downwards.

"Take off," Williams said. "You're drunk."

"Maybe you don't know what this is?" Walsh said, showing Williams the gun as he withdrew it partly from his pocket. "I promise you, I'll kill you right here if you don't get outside."

The girl stood off, looking at them. Williams glanced toward her and winked, then looked at Walsh again, and there was fear in his eyes that he did not want the girl to see.

"All right," he said. "We'll go outside, you want to."

They moved through the door and outside into the dusty parking area. Walsh felt a fine trembling inside his chest, but his hands were steady.

Williams turned and faced him outside, and he was plainly frightened now.

"Over there," Walsh said. "To that car. You saw that car earlier tonight, Williams."

"What the hell you talking about? I don't know you."

"You want to die right here?"

Williams' face was paler still, but tinged with red from the lights inside the tavern.

"Your girl won't do anything to help you," Walsh said. "Don't you realize that? She's probably on her way home right now. She should be."

"What—what you want?"

"Get in the car, there. Get behind the wheel."

They stood beside Walsh's car. Williams didn't move. The parking area just off the road was very quiet and there was nobody in sight, so Walsh took out the gun and showed it to Williams, muzzle first.

"Get behind the wheel, son. I'm going to kill you. But not right here." Walsh waited a moment and Williams still did not move. "But just the same," Walsh said, "it's up to you. You want to die right here, where your friends can come out and stare at the corpse?"

"You're crazy," Williams said. His voice was low, almost a whisper. "You've flipped."

"In the car," Walsh said.

Williams turned dreamily and slid behind the wheel of the car. Walsh moved rapidly around the front of the car, keeping the gun on Williams all the time, and got in beside him. He closed the door.

"Start the car and drive where I tell you."

"I don't want to go no place," Williams said.

"You'd better make it snappy," Walsh said. "My patience is running out."

Something in the sound of his voice reached the other, and he started the car and backed off the parking lot. Walsh directed him to the corner and told him to turn left, and then he began talking to him, slowly, each word weighted with emotion, but somehow monotonous, flat.

"You killed my daughter," Walsh said. "You didn't know that, did you? I'm not here because of what you did to me out there in the sand pits. That was nothing. I'm here because you killed my daughter—"

"Daughter?" There was the sound of shock, of understanding in Williams' voice. "Ah, what the hell you talking about?"

"Don't pretend you don't know," Walsh said. "You do know, and we both know it."

Williams was hunched over the wheel. He was big, full-grown, yet Walsh knew he wasn't even eighteen. He was just a kid, and the look of a kid was in his eyes, but that look was mixed and jumbled with a lot of things that added up to heavy experience. Watching him, Walsh saw the trapped and insecure expression on the boy's face. He knew those big hands were sweating on the wheel, and he knew that under that thick, greased mat of black hair the boy's mind was hard at work for a way out.

"There's no way out for you," Walsh said. "Except the one way. You know what that is. Take your next left and start out Woods Boulevard."

"Listen," Williams said. "What you want to go out there for, for cripes' sake?"

"Do as I say," Walsh told him. "And drive damned careful, because if you make a break of any kind I'll kill you right where you are."

Williams straightened his shoulders, turned and looked at Walsh. Walsh's face was dead white and strained.

"I think you're scared," Williams said. "I don't know what you're talking about, mister. But you're too scared to use that gun."

Walsh held the gun up and squeezed the trigger.

The shocking sound of the explosion in the small confines of the car nearly blew his ear drums. He had aimed directly across the front of Williams' face, out the far window.

The car swerved.

Walsh jammed the gun into the boy's side and shouted at him. "Drive careful, Williams. Next time you'll get the slug; it won't go out the window."

"I can't hear," Williams said. He whined a little now. He turned and stared at Walsh, shrinking toward the far door of the car. The car swerved again. Walsh's ears were ringing and there was a strong, pungent odor of cordite in the car.

"Turn in at the stock-car race track," Walsh said loudly. "Drive right through the gate in the fence."

Williams slowed the car, began to talk rapidly. "Look, mister—you got this all wrong. I'm sure you got it all wrong."

"You killed her," Walsh said. "You ran her down. You didn't stop. You killed her. I'm going to kill you, Williams."

"No," Williams said. "No, I tell you." He slowed the car still more. "It wasn't me."

"It was you. Turn in here."

Walsh found that he keenly enjoyed the young man's terror. With this realization, he shook himself reproachfully and remembered Edith and Mary Lou, and that Mary Lou was gone forever.

"Drive right inside there," Walsh said, as they came across the parking grounds outside the fence-enclosed race track. Dust funneled behind them, spreading damply out across the night-chilled darkness. They approached the gate. It was ajar. Walsh looked at Williams and Williams was hunched over the wheel, not mad, not trying anything—on the verge of tears.

Walsh did not feel sorry for Williams. He wanted to kill him now, more than ever before. And he knew Adkins, the cop, had known this, too. It was what had worried Adkins.

They came through the gate.

"Stop the car and get out," Walsh said.

Williams stopped the car, turned off the ignition, but didn't move from under the wheel.

"I said, get out," Walsh told him, jabbing the gun into his side. "Out."

Williams opened the door and stepped out. Walsh slid across the seat and climbed down behind him.

"Walk with me over to the gate," Walsh said.

They walked to the gate, and Walsh fastened it with the long wooden bar. He glanced at the broken padlock on the gate, and mused on how kids like Williams had probably broken it. Maybe Williams himself. He'd read in the papers how kids would come out here late at night and hold drag races. A lot of things had happened out here. Now there was going to be something new happen, and inside Walsh was a high and very wonderful keening of emotion.

He had the feeling of death-dealing. Of omnipotence. He looked at Williams' face, pale in the stark moonlight that spread like silver around the enclosure of the fence.

"We're all alone in here. Nobody but us," Walsh said. "Isn't that fine?"

Williams just looked at him. He did not speak, did not even try. He stepped backward slightly, staring at Walsh, his eyes wide, his mouth slack, dark hair hanging dank and sweaty across his pale forehead.

"I didn't mean it," Williams said.

"But you did it," Walsh said. He felt composed now, steady, sure of everything. He advanced on Williams. "Look around you, Williams. Look how it is in here. See the bleachers, the way the moonlight strikes them. Did you use to come here often?"

"You're crazy," Williams whispered. "You're crazy."

"No. Not at all. Or, maybe I am. What difference is that to you? I could say the same thing about you. Is it crazy because I'm going to kill you? Is that why you think I'm crazy?"

Williams did not speak. He turned wildly and looked around the vast circumference of moonlit track, fence, the center of grass, the shadowed and silvery bleachers, the signs: COCOA-COLA—PEPSI!—CARLING RED CAP—GEORGE'S GARAGE. Posters were plastered to the fence all around the track. Williams turned and started to run.

"Wait a minute," Walsh said.

Williams didn't stop, running toward the shadows of the fence to the areaway by the bleachers. Walsh lifted the heavy gun and fired twice into the ground near Williams' feet. Williams stopped running, turned and stood waiting.

"Just stand right there," Walsh said. He walked past the car and up to Williams. "I want to be sure you know why you're going to die," he said. "Tell me, do you understand?"

Williams broke now. He moved toward Walsh clumsily, his arms hanging. "Don't," he said. "Don't kill me. I never meant to hit that little girl. I never saw her. She stepped down off the curb that way. I never saw her. It was nearly dark, mister. You can't see good when it's like that. A car's lights were in my eyes."

Death Wears a Gray Sweater

"There were no cars, just then," Walsh said. "You killed her and you ran, and that's all that matters. You're one crazy kid that'll never kill anybody else."

"Stop it!" Williams yelled. "Stop talking like that! All you can say is kill—kill!"

"Walk through the inside fence, there," Walsh said, pointing to the low, white-washed fence that outlined the inside of the track. "Walk over onto the grass."

"What for?"

"Do it."

Williams sighed, and moaned quietly, then did as Walsh directed. Walsh ran softly back to the car, climbed under the wheel, started the engine and put the gun on the seat beside him. He shoved the car into gear and roared out across the track. He was satisfied. Williams knew why he would die, and that was all that mattered.

Williams knew everything now. He knew what Walsh was trying to do. He knew *how* he was going to die. For a brief instant, in the flash of the glaring headlights along the edge of the track, he stood rooted, staring.

Then he ran.

Inside the car, Walsh was laughing. He didn't know it, didn't hear the way it burst wildly past his lips, became one with the roar of the engine. All he knew was the urge to *kill—kill—kill . . .*

He didn't even really see the night out there; he just saw Mary Lou. And the need within him boiled stronger because Williams was trapped. It was Godlike and complete. The high board fence surrounded the track. The tall gates to the pit at the far end were closed, barred from the other side. There was a ten foot barrier in front of the stands and bleachers—and Williams was alone and pursued, like a beetle in a dishpan.

Walsh leaned out the window now.

"Run!" he shouted, slowing the car. "See if you can get away, Williams! I'm going to run you down!"

Williams lurched, stumbled, and fell almost in front of the car. But Walsh swerved aside, gunned in a vicious circle, and returned at high speed. *Scare him, too.* He felt and heard the splattering as mud and sand ripped beneath his wheels. The feeling of elation and strength grew. The sound of the engine was nepenthe to everything of sorrow inside him. But there was no real sorrow. All he could think of was killing Williams—that kid—that killer.

He bore down on him at full speed. Williams came to his feet, limping painfully now, and ran diagonally across the grassed inner circle of the track, screaming. The headlights glared on the barrier, angled up across the stands, painting the bleachers with silver.

Williams slowed. The car slowed. Williams began running faster, out onto the width of dirt track itself now. The car was directly at his heels.

Walsh saw Williams stagger slightly. He didn't want the boy off his feet when he struck him. He wanted him full of life, bursting with it, running full tilt. He slowed the car, stopped it, said nothing, waited.

Williams hesitated, reeling in the moonlight. He moved slowly along the track looking this way and that, walking jerkily. Still Walsh waited. He waited, and inside he was smiling.

Williams abruptly broke into a frenzied run toward the ten foot barrier in front of the stands. Walsh waited, watching the light bouncing off the sweater, watching the fine speed that Williams now had. Williams was out of the glare of the headlights now. Walsh knew that in the boy's heart was a promise of escape now. He was going to try and climb the barrier, the only chance he had.

And yet Walsh waited, waited until he was sure that Williams would feel certain of escape. Until that moment when Williams would be saying to himself, *"He didn't mean it after all, that crazy nut. He just wanted to scare me. I'll make the bleachers, then head for home"*

Now Walsh gunned the engine to life. He tramped the gas pedal to the floor and swerved straight at Williams. Williams was almost to the high board barrier in front of the stands.

Walsh drove directly at him, cutting down the track, the speedometer reading thirty—then thirty-five . . . forty-five . . . fifty. At fifty-five miles an hour, he bore directly down upon Williams.

He saw the young man leap, hang by his hands to the top of the barrier, frantically trying to climb. He saw the hands slip, tear loose. Williams fell, crouched, then turned with his back against the moonshot barrier in front of the stands.

And Walsh saw Williams' scream, but he didn't hear it. The glare of the headlights became brighter and brighter as he neared Williams. In another moment he would be a crushed mass of flesh and bone, mingled with wood-slivers and steel.

All Walsh saw was Mary Lou's lifeless, flying body, then Williams' screaming face as the car struck, smashing through the barrier. Walsh rode the brakes and the car rocked to a standstill as long torn strips of wood spun through the night. Walsh shoved himself off the steering wheel, put the car in reverse and backed free onto the track again.

Walsh sensed a fine trembling inside him as he got out of the car and walked around front. In the shattered glare of one remaining headlight, he saw that the boy's body, jammed and caught against the bumper and grille-work, had been dragged when the car had been backed out onto the track. Dark blood clotted the earth.

Over by the entrance gate there was the sound of another car, but Walsh did not look up. He stared at Williams' body with sick eyes. A police cruiser swung into the track and raced around to where Walsh stood.

"Get up," Walsh said softly. "You're free, you hear? It's all right. Go home—" He broke off, knelt beside the body.

The police cruiser stopped nearby. A young girl in tight dungarees ran toward Walsh as two uniformed cops and a plain-clothes man stepped from the car. The man in plain-clothes was Adkins. The girl's voice was edged with shrill panic. "*Ernie,* it's all right! I saw the gun when he made you go with him. I had to tell them. Ernie! I told them everything. We were looking for you when we heard the shots . . ." And then she stopped talking, could only stare.

"Get up," Walsh said softly, pleading.

One of the uniformed men leaned over Williams, straightened and shook his head. Adkins stopped near Walsh, his face expressionless.

"Get up," Walsh said to the mangled body. And he could see Mary Lou as she must have looked to Williams just before he killed her, and he knew no man could do that purposely. "A car's headlights blinded me." There *had* been another car. His own car, crossing the intersection. And he kept staring down at Williams, knowing he couldn't have done this, either. "I *couldn't* do it, don't you see?"

"You did, though," somebody said.

Walsh came to his feet, turned slowly and moved away.

Adkins motioned to the uniformed cops, then walked after Walsh, scowling.

Joy Ride
C. B. Gilford

April 1957

They felt a need for shining chrome and the feeling of mastery it gives to unleash roaring horse power on an inviting concrete stretch. The need was as deep as the yearning for a woman. It ate at their insides like a primitive hunger. And so they walked the dark streets looking for a way to satisfy this desire of theirs.

"Harv, maybe your old man's home by now and he'd let us have his car," Leech said. Leech wasn't his real name, but he was called that because of the way he stuck to his buddy.

"He ain't home, and he wouldn't let us have it anyway."

They walked on. Whenever they found a car parked in a shadowy place they tried its doors. But they weren't lucky. Car owners in that neighborhood had grown cautious. And they weren't professionals, so they had no skill with locks.

"Let's get a beer and forget it," Leech said after awhile.

"Who'd serve us beer around here?" Harv wanted to know. "But if we had a car we could go out to Andy's. He don't go for draft cards."

In front of Anarchios' Shoe Parlor they found a dusty 1939 Plymouth. Its windows were rolled down. They stood on the sidewalk and looked at it. Leech waited for Harv.

"I heard '39 Plymouths are easy to get started," Leech said.

"Junk," Harv answered disdainfully. "And the guys that drive 'em leave about a spoonful of gas in the tank. We can do better'n this."

They wandered. They drifted into an area where the street lights were dirty and the neon signs fewer, but their luck didn't improve.

"We should have taken that Plymouth," Leech said sadly.

"Shut up," Harv answered, his frustration bursting out as anger. Leech fell silent.

When they came to the Sperry Avenue junk yard, they were suddenly back in familiar territory. They had sold hub caps here. The place had a high wire fence all around it, but there was nothing inside for them anyway. Leech ran his finger along the fence as they walked, playing one of the oldest games known to boys. But the gesture produced little noise, and so Leech picked up a piece of iron pipe that lay outside the fence. Dragged along the fence, the pipe made an adequate noise, like a slow and tired machine gun.

"What the hell are you doing?" Harv exploded, finally waking to the noise. "Why the hell all the racket?"

Leech stopped the noise, but he didn't get rid of the pipe. He stared at it instead.

"Where'd you get that?" Harv asked.

"Back there."

They both got the idea at the same time.

They retraced their steps till they came to the place. There were half a dozen short lengths of pipe strewn over the ground. Harv picked up one, hefted it for weight and balance.

"We can get a car," he said finally, his voice soft, even trembling a bit.

"It's been done," Leech agreed, with the same trembling.

But they hesitated. They stood there, each with two feet of lethal metal in his right hand. A minute ago they'd been boys, wandering in search of luck. Now they were armed men.

"What do you say?" Harv asked after awhile.

Leech was nervous. He even giggled. "It's okay with me," he said. "How do we do it, Harv?"

"Don't you read the papers?"

"Sure."

"If it's two guys working together, each guy gets in on opposite sides of the car when it's stopped for a stop sign or a red light. When it's the only car around, of course."

"What if the doors are locked?"

"Then you run like hell and try some place else." Leech giggled again. He couldn't control himself. "What if they ain't locked?"

"You get in and convince the guy he ought to give us the car." Harv made small, but significant motions with the pipe.

"I don't want to hurt nobody," Leech said.

"Me neither. We just want a car."

They started walking. A clock in a store window said eleven-thirty. They headed back toward a slightly busier section, where there would be more stop signs, more traffic lights, and more cars.

They went unnoticed. They were big boys, and they passed for men. They wore identical dark blue jackets over white tee shirts. Leech wore faded levis, but Harv's trousers were a natty gray. There was little about them to attract special attention. They carried the iron pipes vertically next to their legs, always on the side away from the street.

There were no other pedestrians. Even the cars were thinning out. And the cops, if any existed, were somewhere else. The boys picked the first corner they came to that had a traffic light. Harv crossed the street. They both had a shadow to wait in.

The wait wasn't too long. The first two cars came as a pair. They stopped, but were allowed to speed on, when the light changed, unhindered. The third car had the light in its favor and didn't slow down. The two boys waved encouragement to each other. The fourth car came a moment later, and it was the only moving car on the street. It was an ivory and green hardtop, and it looked like it might have been bought yesterday.

There are people who say traffic lights ought to be turned off at a certain time at night, because late at night they no longer serve a useful purpose. Perhaps those people are right. But perhaps too they're not completely right. A red light might serve a purpose, though maybe not a useful one.

There was a man driving this hardtop, all alone. He didn't look like a very big man. And he was obviously a law-abiding citizen, because he stopped at the intersection even though there wasn't another car in sight. He stopped and he sat there dreamily, like a pigeon on a fence post. Harv whistled.

It was the signal, not pre-arranged, merely an inspiration. Harv came sprinting from across the street. Leech darted out of his shadowy spot. They arrived on opposite sides of the car at the same time. And neither door was locked.

The man was a fool. The doors shouldn't have been unlocked. And he shouldn't have shouted "Hey!" and started flailing around with his arms. He should have known that two strangers leaping into his car like that must have come on serious business. They could have had a gun or two. He could have been shot. But he shouted and flailed anyway.

The two boys both hit him. They had to, to shut him up. They weren't free-swinging, skull-crushing blows. The quarters were too cramped for that. Harv used a wrist motion, tapping the man over the ear. Leech's pipe scraped along the roof of the car and hit the man mostly on the shoulder. Leech pulled back to swing again.

On Harv's side there was a little blood on the man's head. Harv could see it because the opened door of the car kept the overhead light burning. The sight of the blood made him hurry, scared him a little. He pushed the man toward the middle of the seat and took the driver's place himself. Leech barely had time to throw himself inside before the car began to move. They ran through the red light, and they didn't get the doors closed till they were halfway down the next block. The car shot forward.

"Man, this baby has pick-up," Harv exulted, his hands clenched tensely on the steering wheel.

"Yeah!" Leech said.

The little man sandwiched in between them made no comment. Even if he were dazed or unconscious or had fainted, he couldn't have fallen over. He was wedged too tightly between the two blue jackets.

They paid little attention to him. Harv's pipe was forgotten on the floor. Leech still had his, but he wasn't using it to threaten the man. He was too fascinated by the speed of buildings and street lights whizzing by.

But it was Leech who came to his senses first. "Slow down," he said, "or we'll have the cops on us."

Harv's foot let up a little on the gas pedal. The whine of tires over cement grew softer. The outside world went by in a slower parade, its glare softened by the tinted glass all around them. The leather seats, the dials and gadgets, the green to match the exterior, everything new and gleaming—it even smelled new—were all sheer luxury. They squirmed sensually on the seats to express their pleasure. Leech flicked on the radio, and the music that came on was as soft and soothing as the leather of the seats. Paradise . . .

"Where'll we go?" Harv was asking. "Man, this thing is just screaming to go places."

"What about the Ferry Road?" Leech said.

And now a third voice talked. The little man who owned the car hadn't said anything. Maybe he had been dazed, in a state of shock. But maybe now the conversation woke him up. Maybe he had visions of his green hardtop hurtling along the Ferry Road at the incredible speed it was capable of, a speed he himself would never push it to. A drag race maybe . . .

"Let me out," he said. "Please let me out."

The sound of his voice surprised them. Suddenly Harv laughed. "Hey, Leech, I forgot about the guy"

Leech laughed too. It was funny.

"Please let me out," the little man said again.

"Let's get rid of him," Leech said.

Harv slowed and pulled toward the curb. They were in a residential area now, and there were plenty of shadowy places to dump an unwelcome guest. Harv chose one of them, turned off the lights as he slid smoothly into it. Leech opened the door on his side.

"Wait a minute," Harv said.

"What's the matter?"

"I just thought of something."

"Like what?"

"We put this guy out, and the first thing he does is call the cops and tell 'em his car's been stolen. Gives 'em a description and the license number, so every cop in town is looking for this car."

"That ain't good, is it?" Leech said.

"There's enough gas in this baby to ride all night. We don't want to waste it, do we?"

The little man chimed in again, and his voice was shaking. "I won't report it," he said. "I won't report it till morning."

"Like hell . . ." Harv sneered.

"But I promise."

"Shut up." Leech still had the pipe in his right hand. He showed it to the little man, and the little man didn't say anything more.

"Harv," Leech said. "Let's put him in the back seat. We can do that."

"Sure."

Leech got out. The little man, sensing what was expected of him without being told, climbed around the seat into the back.

Leech showed him the pipe again. "You give us any trouble," he said simply, "and you get this."

The little man, who by this time was probably feeling the pain of the earlier blows, wasn't in a fighting mood. Leech got back in, and the green hardtop rolled.

Nobody said anything now. The two boys up front surrendered to the luxury of the machine, and the man in the rear had his own thoughts. But it was a different kind of silence somehow. It could almost be heard above the soft croon of the radio. They had just about reached the Ferry Road, where there would be no speed restrictions, when Leech spoke up.

"I just thought of something," he said.

"You think?" Harv said. "What've you got to think with?"

Leech ignored the mild insult. "You know," he said, "the cops could be looking for this car anyway."

"How do you mean?"

"This guy could have a wife who's expecting him home by a certain time. When he don't show up, she could call the cops and tell 'em about it. She could tell 'em what kind of a car he was driving too."

Harv pondered. He hadn't thought of that possibility.

"Hey, mister," Leech said to the little man, "you got a wife or somebody at home waiting for you?"

There was just the slightest hesitation before the reply came. It was a noticeable hesitation, as if the little man were trying to think of the wisest thing to answer. "Yes," he said finally.

"He's lying," Harv said.

"Is she the kind to worry about you?" Leech asked the little man.

"I don't know . . ." There was a strange ring of truth in the statement which the boys could have missed. "I don't know . . ."

"He's lying," Harv said again. "Hell with him!" But the joy ride was spoiled.

"I got an idea," Leech said a few minutes later. "We could park on some dark street and let the air out of the tires and put this guy out for awhile with a little knock on the head and you and I could hitch home and we could get rid of this whole thing . ."

But they were on the Ferry Road, a four-lane divided strip, miles of smooth, uninterrupted concrete gleaming white in the headlights. It seemed that Harv's foot didn't even have to press harder on the gas pedal. The hardtop seemed to know that this was the reason for all its horsepower having been put under the hood. It became a thing with a life all its own, and it was as seductive as a striptease, each higher number on the speedometer another veil flung off, another mystery revealed.

"Take it easy, Harv," Leech said, as if afraid of his own ecstasy.

"I just want to see what it will do," Harv told him. "I just want to see . . ."

They passed everything on the road.

"Nice, huh?" Harv said.

"Yeah, but slow down, will you?"

"Why should I?"

"We can't have cops chasing us now, Harv. This is a stolen car, and there's the guy in the back seat."

Sure . . . the guy in the back seat. Always the guy in the back seat. The millstone getting heavier with every mile. They'd made a mistake somewhere. But how could they have gotten the car without taking its driver too?

Harv slowed down. The hardtop seemed reluctant. It wasn't easy to keep it under sixty. It was such a waste of a good car. And it wasn't much fun.

"Harv," Leech said.

"What? You thought of something else?"

"No . . . I just don't like this any more."

"Well, that's great. That's real great."

"What do they call this, Harv?"

"What do they call what?"

"The cops. If they catch us, I mean. What do they call it? Besides stealing a car. The guy in back, I mean."

"How do I know?"

"What'll they do to us if they catch us?"

"They ain't going to."

Leech grinned, a sickly grin. "Sure, sure . . . but just in case. I know lots of guys who've taken cars, Harv. They just get talked to most of the time. Those judges are real soft. So we took a car . . . that's all right. But what about the guy? We took him too. And we hit him a couple of times . . ."

"They call it assault, I guess."

"That ain't too bad, is it?"

Harv shook his head. But he wasn't sure. It made him relax just a little more on the gas pedal, and the hardtop dropped to fifty.

And a minute or so later it was Harv who said, "Do you think they'd call it kidnapping?"

Leech didn't answer. He stared straight ahead. The hardtop's powerful engine seemed to make no

noise at all at a mere fifty, and the only sound was the rush of wind going past.

"What do you think, Leech?" Harv asked again. His voice was the merest whisper, scarcely audible above the wind.

"I don't know. Maybe so. How do I know? That'd be something for the Feds, wouldn't it?"

The side road leaped into view almost without warning, but Harv took it anyway. He swung the steering wheel hard to the right, and the hardtop, low-slung road-hugger though it was, protested with a screech of tires. Harv had the wheel to hold onto, but Leech was thrown against him so violently that he almost lost the iron pipe. The back tires skidded, raising clouds of gravel dust. For a few seconds then they were plowing through soft dirt, till the car finally righted itself and dug gravel once again. Harv accelerated till they were out of sight of the lights on the main highway. Then he braked hard, and the car came to a jolting halt that almost unseated the passengers a second time.

Harv doused the headlights, and they were left sitting in the middle of a dark silence.

"Suppose they do call this kidnapping?" he said.

"That's what it is, kidnapping!" the little man in the back squeaked suddenly. Maybe it was wise and maybe it wasn't, his butting in like that. He just sounded scared.

"Shut up!" Harv yelled.

They sat for a minute and listened to one another's breathing.

"What do we do now, Harv?" Leech was fully surrendering leadership.

"I'm trying to think."

"We could do like I said. Put the guy out for awhile, and hitch back to town."

Harv thought for a moment. "Yeah, but what happens after that?" he wondered aloud.

"We forget about the whole thing."

"Sure, we forget. But does this guy forget, and do the cops forget?"

"They don't know who we are though."

"But this guy can describe us, can't he?" "I guess so . . . but they got to find us first." Harv considered again. All of a sudden he was feeling a healthy respect for cops. "That can happen," he said.

"But how?"

"How do I know? I seen it happen though. I seen 'em pick up guys six months after they do something. They got ways, Leech. I don't know how they do it, but they do it."

"I know what you mean," Leech said.

They sat for awhile again. In the back seat, the little man was perfectly still. If his knees were shaking, or if he was puking in his fear, he was doing it silently.

"There's a way," Harv said after a long time.

"What?"

"It ain't a good way, but it's the only way."

Harv spoke jerkily. "Everything depends on this guy telling the cops what we look like, okay? The rest don't matter. We can wipe off the places we touched in the car, so there won't be no fingerprints. And we can tell anybody who asks that we were watching a movie or just walking around, and nobody can say we weren't. Nothing can happen to us if this guy can't identify us to the cops. You know what I mean?"

Maybe Leech knew. Or maybe he didn't want to know. Because he didn't ask. He just waited.

And Harv had to say it. "We got to take care of this guy."

For maybe half a minute all three of them contemplated it. The naked truth, finally. The facts of life that any criminal, big or little, has to look at. You can get away with anything if they don't know you did it. Evidence is the thing that tells them you did it. And the best evidence is a witness. No witness . . . no evidence . . . no cops . . . no jail . . . nothing . . . you're clean.

But it was a big step, a step you can't back up from. They hadn't taken it yet. They hadn't even decided to take it.

All the little man in the rear seat knew, however, was that they were talking about killing him. He was in a spot where a lot of people have made a mistake.

"I won't tell the police what you look like," he started babbling. "I won't even tell 'em you took the car or hit me or anything . . ."

And because he promised them that he wouldn't, they knew beyond any doubt that he would.

It was Leech who made the first move. He wrenched the door open, slid out, and then reached in again for the little man. The little man screamed when the groping hand first touched him in the dark. He fought the hand. Leech had to drop the iron pipe. With both hands then he dragged at the little man, and the little man held onto the seat and wouldn't let go. It was an even fight for a moment, until Harv lunged over into the rear seat and pounded at the little man so that he had to let go. They dragged him, kicking and sobbing, out of the car.

They didn't know exactly how to kill a man. For a few seconds they just swung wildly at him in the darkness. Sometimes they hit each other. And finally it dawned on them that they couldn't kill him with their fists alone.

"Hit him with the pipe, Leech!" Harv yelled desperately.

"I haven't got it. It's in the car."

"Get it. I'll hold him. Get it, Leech!" Harv said.

Leech stumbled toward the hardtop. Somewhere on the car's floor, he'd dropped his iron pipe. He searched for it in absolute blackness. It seemed an eternity before the pipe came to his hand, cold metal, hard, hard enough to split a skull . . .

But he wasn't going to do this thing alone. Harv had to join in. Harv wasn't going to say later that Leach had done it all by himself. So he went looking for the other pipe, Harv's pipe. It was on the floor in front of the driver's seat. He took it with him, too.

When he staggered back with the weapons, Harv was yelling again. "Hit him with the pipe, Leech Go on and hit him."

"You got to hit him, too," he yelled back.

"Hit him with the pipe, Leech."

"I brought both of 'em. Here, take yours. You got to hit him first."

"Hell with it, Leech . . . hit him . . ."

"Take the pipe . . . take it . . ."

And suddenly the little man wasn't there any more. He had wrenched out of Harv's grip, and had melted into the deep black of the night. They heard him go crashing into the roadside brush and took out after him at once. But the racket they made drowned out or confused the sounds that they might have followed.

They made their way back to the car, deciding they would leave it just where it was. They hoped that the guy would come back and drive home in the car, that maybe because they'd left the car, he wouldn't call the police and would just forget the whole thing. And they told one another, by way of further comfort, that they were glad he had gotten away, because if he hadn't they might have killed him and hell that would have been murder . . .

When they reached the car, they got rid of the iron pipes, throwing them off into the darkness as far as they could. Harv throwing his in one direction; Leech in another.

And then they were walking along the Ferry Road in the direction of town. Their clothes were torn and there were cuts even on their faces where they'd run into sharp branches in the darkness. Every now and then Leech made a noise in his throat that sounded like he was crying.

"Will you cut that out?" Harv complained wearily. He'd been thinking of cops, the mysterious ways they had of picking up people. That no matter what, no matter where they went—how far—it was too late to get out of it now.

College Kill
Jack Q. Lynn

May 1957

There were three of them in the office. Three cops. And they kept walking around, hammering at me. From the right, from the left, from over me, yeah, even from down under.

Finally they shut up and one of them stood in front of me, smoking a cigarette. His name was Malone, and he was a pretty decent-acting cop, older but not tough-talking like the other two.

After a long time he said, "How the hell did you get in this mess, Lane?"

I considered it. Yeah, how the hell did I?

Matt Lane, the guy who could run over the biggest tackle the opposition had, *anytime,* the guy who made booting field goals look as easy as tossing pennies in a sack, the guy who could out-run a horse. That was me. Big Man on Campus at Crawford College.

And five days before graduation in June, the old man came around with a contract.

"Want to try coaching here, Matt?"

"Here?"

"Sure, here. Where else? We have a good bunch of kids coming up and you know our system inside out. We want you, Matt."

So I signed a contract and became an assistant coach at Crawford College. Then in July I married Anne Morrow, a black-haired, blue-eyed kid with a lot of body. She had her senior year at Crawford coming up, but we weren't waiting around until she graduated. The next thing, she got pregnant. We weren't sure in September, but by the end of October all of the doubt was gone.

We decided not to tell anybody about the baby, not then, not even Anne's folks who lived down-state. Anne was going home for a visit the second week in November and I planned to whip down there the day before Thanksgiving. We'd spend the holiday with her folks, and we'd tell them about the baby then. It would be one of those holiday surprises.

I put Anne on a train on Monday. The first two days she was gone I was okay. I kept busy with my physical education classes, slipped downtown to Joe's at night and had a few beers, then sacked in early enough to feel good the next day. Wednesday I was restless; it was too damn quiet around our apartment, and Wednesday night I drank as much beer as I could hold. Thursday started out the same, the beer and the grousing around, so I decided to go over to the college library to do a little research on some work I was planning for a master's degree.

An hour later I was at a table in the large library reading room when the girl got up from another table, put a book on the shelf near her, and reached for her coat which was draped over the back of a chair next to where she had been sitting. Her impact on me was jolting. I couldn't get my eyes off of her. She was tall; her skin was a honey-colored tan, and her hair, black as black can be, tumbled from beneath a green beret to very wide shoulders. Her high, full breasts strained against the thin fabric of her dress, and the dress was pleasantly shadowed where it caressed her thighs.

I stared hungrily, feeling excitement begin to knot my stomach muscles.

And then suddenly I found her staring right back at me without moving. It made me feel uncomfortable. I lowered my eyes and shifted in the chair.

She moved then. Shrugging into her coat, she walked toward the front door of the library. For a moment I sat mesmerized, then I started after her, leaving the book I had been reading open on the table. Outside the front door of the library, I put on my heavy jacket and stood on the top step watching her. She was crossing the street in front of me. I went down to the sidewalk. She opened the door of a blue convertible parked at the curb on the opposite side of the street and slid under the steering wheel. I caught a flash of nyloned legs before the door closed. And then, without looking my way, she was gone in a surge of power.

I was suddenly a different guy. I wasn't teaching physical education to a bunch of kids at a small midwest college. I didn't have a wife named Anne. And I didn't have a nice, warm, little apartment two blocks off the campus.

And all because that girl was burned in my mind. I couldn't stop thinking about her.

After my final class Friday afternoon, I went straight from the gymnasium to the library. But the girl wasn't there. Nervous and sweating, I hung around for over an hour, waiting.

The girl didn't show. My disappointment was so bitter I walked downtown to Joe's to drown it. An icy wind seeped right through my coat and crept into my bones, and the first snow of the season was coming down. It was a lousy day. Gray, cold, snowing, and no girl. I had to get the girl out of my system, but I didn't know how. I had another beer. Drinking didn't help. I walked out of Joe's at ten minutes after nine.

I saw the convertible as I hit the street. It was parked at the curb right in front of me. There was a shadow slumped behind the steering wheel and I saw a red cigarette glow in the dark. Then the shadow moved and the car door in front of me opened.

"Get in, Matt," the soft voice of the girl said.

I got in without saying anything. It was a neat car, new, with safety belts and all the trimmings. The girl dropped her cigarette out of the wing window, kicked over the motor of the convertible and pulled away from the curb into the line of traffic. At the first stop light she said, "I've been waiting over an hour."

"How did you know I was at Joe's?"

She laughed softly. "I know plenty about you, Matt Lane—now. I've made inquiries."

I twisted on the seat, opened my coat, and purposely put one knee against her thigh.

She didn't even give me a glance. "My name is Edie Jackson," she said. "My home is in New Orleans. I came up here to school because I wanted to be out on my own."

The windshield wipers whisking the snow from the window made the only sound in the car.

I got out a cigarette and fired my lighter.

"Light two," she said.

She didn't ask me to light two cigarettes. She didn't say please. She just said, "Light two."

I lit two and gave one to her. She glanced at me then and smiled.

"Do you always get what you want?" I asked.

"Almost always. My father is a very wealthy man. And he dotes on me."

"Other than your father?"

"Almost always."

"Like now?"

I saw her frown. "What do you mean?" she said.

"You saw me looking at you in the library yesterday afternoon and for some reason you decided I was for you."

She laughed softly.

"You've got it twisted, haven't you, Matt?" she asked. "Turn it around. *You* want me."

I didn't say anything then. I couldn't.

"Do I shock you, Matt? If I do, you'll have to get used to it. I'm like that. I say what I think, and I do what I want to do."

"I'm not sure I like you," I said slowly.

"But you *want* me. And that's what counts."

She turned the car off of the main thoroughfare onto a sidestreet. We eased along another block, and then she turned into a driveway. I had a look at the house as the headlights swept over it. It was a small place with an attached single car garage. She drove the convertible into the garage and switched off the lights. A light in the back seat popped on when she opened her door.

I reached out suddenly and grabbed her wrist. She had one long leg out of the car. Twisting in the seat, she looked at me and I saw her tiny mocking smile.

"You're taking a lot for granted, aren't you, Miss Jackson?"

"Am I?"

We sat there a long time without moving, measuring each other with our eyes. And then she said, "I live here Matt—alone. Your wife is out of town. Now, do you want to come in for a drink?"

"How old are you?"

"Eighteen."

"You're jailbait. I'm twenty-four."

Her face clouded and she gently twisted her arm out of my grasp. "That's something else you should know about me, Matt. I'm a woman. I'm eighteen in years, but I'm twice that age otherwise. I've had men, plenty of men. Not boys still wet behind the ears, Matt. I hate fumbling, sniveling boys. When I want somebody, he is a *man!*"

She got out of the car then and stood beside the open door, looking in at me. "Coming?"

We went into the house through a kitchen. She pulled the drapes across the windows in the front room before turning on a pair of lamps. I looked around. The room was expensively furnished. There was a fireplace in one wall; three logs were burning slowly. To my left was an open room that had been furnished as a study and behind me was the kitchen. To my right was a closed door.

"The bedroom," Edie said, following the line of my eyes. She smiled then and slipped out of her fur coat. Whisking the green beret off of her head, she said, "Your coat."

I shrugged out of it and she put it with hers in a small closet near the front door.

I looked her up and down then, making no attempt to hide the fact that I was taking a surface inventory. She was wearing slacks; they were dark green and showed off her figure.

My hands felt damp. I wiped them on my thighs.

She smiled and waved her arm toward a low sofa in front of the fireplace. "Make yourself at home, Matt. What'll you have to drink?"

"Anything."

She went into the kitchen. A moment later I heard the slam of a refrigerator door and then the crack of an ice cube tray being opened. I walked to the kitchen entry and stood there looking at her.

"Bourbon?" she said over her shoulder.

"With something sweet."

She mixed the drinks and we went to the sofa in front of the fireplace. I sat down.

"Do you like music?" she asked.

I shrugged my shoulders.

"I like the classics," she said.

There was a record player beside the sofa with a record on it. She clicked a switch on the player and music, low and soft, filled the room. Then she sat down beside me and put her leg against mine all the way up.

I looked at her.

"Why do you want me?" she asked over the rim of her glass, her eyes probing mine.

"Why does a man want any woman?"

"I don't know. That's what I want you to tell me."

I thought about it. Why did I want her? What crazy thing was it that had me sitting with her in the front room of her place? Me, a guy with a helluva sweet wife and a decent future. Why the hell was I here? Why was I jeopardizing everything I had and everything I might have? There didn't seem to be a logical answer.

"You can't tell me?" she said softly.

I stared at my feet. "No."

I felt her hand crawl over my thigh then. "Don't let it bother you, Matt," she said. "I've never had a satisfactory answer either."

I gulped my drink and put the glass on the floor.

"Matt?"

Twisting, I looked up at her. She was smiling cozily.

"I want to dance for you," she said.

"Dance?"

"You'll like it," she said softly.

Too puzzled to move, I sat there on the sofa watching her. She began to sway with the music coming from the record player. Her mouth was fixed in a half-smile, lips open, straight white teeth gleaming. Her eyes became slits. She whirled around the room, head high, breasts straining. I watched her, fascinated. And then she was back in front of me, her body swaying suggestively. I saw her hand go to the buttons on the front of her blouse. The buttons came open and in one swirling motion she stripped out of the blouse and flung it away from her. She wasn't wearing a bra. The naked half of her body was a honey-colored sheen in the lamplight, breasts tip-tilted. She turned her back to me. One hand opened the slacks above her hip and the slacks inched down. Suddenly she whirled around and the slacks dropped to the floor. She stepped out of them and danced forward and into my arms.

I wrapped one hand in her hair and jerked back her head. Her hands ripped open my shirt as I mashed my lips against hers.

Finally, I picked her up and carried her across the room. She kicked open the closed door.

It was dark in the room and hot. My body was wet with sweat. Edie stirred beside me.

"Cigarette?" she said, and her voice cracked.

I felt her groping toward the table beside the bed. She sat up and a moment later a match flared. She had two cigarettes in her mouth. I watched her light them and then she flicked out the match and stretched out beside me, putting an ashtray on her flat stomach.

We smoked in silence.

After a long while she said, "Tell me all about you, Matt."

I told her. And later, when I had finished, she sucked in a deep breath and said, "Will you stay with me all week end? We won't even have to *go* out of the house."

I put one arm around her shoulders and squeezed her. "You'll have to blast me out to get rid of me, baby."

She laughed softly then and sat up straight, spilling the ashtray. She reached for a lamp and turned it on, and then brushed the ashes out of the bed and looked down at me. She was smiling.

"I've got a secret," she said slyly.

"Yeah?"

She turned away from me and leaned over the side of the bed. I heard metal clicking against metal and I started to shove up on one elbow.

"No," she said without looking at me. "Just stay where you are."

I heard a sharp click then, and a whirring noise. After that her soft laughter. Then her voice: *Talk dirty to me, Matt. I love it.*

A shiver went up my back as I heard my own voice. The things I said almost made me sick.

Her voice came on again. Beautiful, Matt. More. Tell me more.

My voice was hardly more than a harsh, rasping whisper, but it was clear and audible.

Edie dropped one arm over the side of the bed and I heard a click. It became ominously silent in the room. I wasn't sure of what I was going to do. And then I was on her fast, my balled fist pounding viciously into her belly. A hard object smashed against my head, stopping me.

I flopped back on the bed as I clutched my head. Edie leaned over me; there was a glass ashtray in her hand. Her face was not a good thing to see.

"Don't ever do that again!" she shouted.

"You dirty, rotten—" The words flowed out of my mouth. Some of them I'd never used before in my life.

"You know all of the dirty names, don't you?"

I stared up at her. "Why, Edie? Why a tape recording?"

"It's a hobby," she said, grinning nastily. "A profitable hobby."

Quite a few things drifted into place then. And all of a sudden I thought I understood why she had been waiting for me outside of Joe's. Or did I?

"There's no rich father in New Orleans, is there, Edie?"

"My old man was a seaman. I never saw him in my life."

"And I guess you never lived in New Orleans. But—but why'd you pick me. A college boy. I haven't got a hundred bucks to my name."

I got to her with that. She frowned down at me and shook her head. Then, "I don't know. I don't really know why you. I guess maybe it was the way you looked at me in the library."

"Sweet Jesus!"

"I know you don't have money. Not my kind of money. But—"

She let it hang there, searching for words.

"I won't give you a dime, Edie."

"I don't want a dime—from you."

I pushed her away and sat up. "Okay, it's been fun. You've had your kicks. Now give me that tape."

She sat up on the edge of the bed and reached toward the floor. I turned my back to her and started to scoot out of the bed.

"Matt?"

I twisted around. She was up on one knee on the bed, leaning toward me. Her arm was raised high above her head. There was a spike-heeled shoe in her hand. I wasn't fast enough. The heel crashed down on my head. Blackness hit me fast. I didn't even have the sensation of sinking into the bed.

I wasn't sure how long I was out. When I came around I was only sure of the sharp pains, like shooting needles, stabbing my mind. I opened my eyes, blinked, and closed them.

"Headache, Matt?"

Her voice came from above me. I opened my eyes again. She was sitting on the edge of the bed beside me, smoking a cigarette. She had put on a white gown. It was diaphanous and under it every flowing curve of her tanned body was visible and beautiful.

"I'm sorry I had to do that," she said. "But I had to hide the tape."

"You bitch!"

She smiled. Calmly, she butted her cigarette in an ashtray on her lap and put the ashtray on the floor. Turning slightly, she leaned over me. The front of her gown parted and the ring dropped on my chest. I looked down at it. It was a plain gold ring, no stones, just a gold band. And it was looped in a heavy gold chain around her neck.

It was my wedding ring.

I reached for it and started to jerk the chain from her neck, but her hand covered mine, stopping me.

"I want it, Matt. At least for this week end." Her eyes bored into mine.

"For God's sake, why?"

"I don't know," she said with a tiny smile curving her mouth. "I don't really know."

My hand with the ring in it flinched and her grip tightened. "I said I want it, Matt. Now please be a good boy. Don't be difficult. Don't force me to mail our little tape to Morgansville."

"Morgansville?" I said in surprise.

"That's where your wife is, isn't it? Mrs. Matt Lane, care of T. M. Morrow, Morgansville, Illinois."

I loosened my grip on the ring gradually. Then, "Has it ever occurred to you, baby, that I might be quite capable of killing you?"

"Yes. Yes, it has. But if you stop and think about it, Matt, killing me will only make things worse for you. You'd be wanted for murder then. As it is, you're not wanted for anything—by the police. Right now all you have to do is be a real nice boy for one week end. Real nice to me. And then you get your ring back and a tape recording and a nice neat return to a dull life."

I heard it, but I couldn't believe it. People like Edie just didn't exist.

I said, "You're crazy, Edie."

She shook her head slowly, her face tight. "No, not crazy. Maybe sick, but not crazy."

"Sick?"

"Some doctors say nymphomania is a sickness. Maybe it is, maybe it isn't. I don't know. All I know is, I've had it as long as I can remember. Even when I was a little girl . . ."

There was a long silence and I didn't break it.

Finally, she said, "The only difference between me and most of the other girls like me, I'm cashing in on it."

"Okay," I said wearily. "I might have sixty-eight bucks in the bank. I'm not sure. But whatever is there, you can have. Just give me my ring and that tape and—"

She was shaking her head. "No. I told you, Matt, I don't want a dime from you."

"Well, my God, what do you want?"

"Just you, for the next two days and nights."

I could hardly believe what my ears had heard.

"You're a big man, Matt." Her hands rubbed my chest. "Muscular. Strong. I need you."

I stared up at her. And then suddenly it was all very funny. I began to laugh and I said, "I've been a lot of things in my twenty-four years, baby. But a stud for a week-end? Never."

She didn't say anything. She just put her head on my chest and stroked me slowly with one hand, as the full length of her was pressed tight against me. That changed my mind faster than anything she could have said.

We didn't leave the house until Sunday night. We didn't eat much, we didn't drink much, and we didn't sleep much. It was a crazy, unbelievable week end for me.

I tried to find the tape, of course, but without luck.

Early Sunday evening, Edie wanted to go for a drive. It was to be my last night with her. Monday morning she was to turn me loose with the tape and my ring.

The night was clear and cold. It was early. There was no moon, but the stars were out and the night was light. Edie drove the convertible north past the Crawford campus and out of town. There wasn't much traffic on the highway.

We eased along comfortable at forty miles an hour. Our conversation was idle and inconsequential. About ten miles north of town, we arrived at the river bridge. Edie slowed the convertible. We crossed the bridge, and then she turned off the highway onto a rutted lane. We topped a rise and dropped onto a deserted stretch of sand along the river. She stopped the car and switched off the lights. The only sounds were night sounds and the soft slapping of the slow-moving river.

Edie reached for me.

I looked at her in surprise. "Here?"

Thirty minutes later we were driving back into town.

"It's almost ended, Matt," she said softly.

"If I said that grieves me, I'd be a liar."

She looked at me. "Really, Matt? Don't you feel anything towards me?"

"If I told you how I really felt, baby—" It was then that I saw the figure of the man in our headlights. He was facing us in a half-crouched position, his arms thrown above his head as if to ward off the onslaught of the powerful body of steel almost on him.

"Edie, Edie, look out!"

I felt the violent swerve of the convertible as she jerked the wheel. The loud thump that I heard brought horror rushing up inside me. And then terror gripped me, for instead of stopping, Edie had tromped on the accelerator. I looked back through the rear window and was just able to distinguish a dark form sprawled in a circle of lamplight on the street.

"Stop, Edie! Good God, stop! You hit a man!"

"Shut up!"

She turned into a sidestreet at the first corner, raced two blocks, and then turned again. I sat in stunned silence all the way to her house. I guess I really didn't want to go back to the man she'd hit, not any more than she did. Inside the garage, she got out of the car quickly and pulled down the garage door.

I slid across the front seat slowly and got out.

Edie was in front of the convertible, examining it. "Smashed the fender a little on your side," she said, coming to me.

We walked into the house together. When we reached the kitchen, she moved up close to me and hooked her hands behind my shoulders. "I couldn't stop, Matt. I couldn't stop because of you."

"Because of me?" I said.

"What would it look like in the newspapers tomorrow? Your name and mine. Your wife—"

"But we might have been able to help that man, Edie."

"Sure. And then again, maybe he just got up and walked on home."

"Not him. I saw him. He was flat on the street and—"

She fastened her mouth on mine, stopping my words. I jerked my head away from her and shoved her away from me.

She straightened. The surprised look of realization appeared in her eyes.

"Matt, you're frightened!"

"You're damn right I am!"

"Don't be," she said, coming close to me again. "Please don't be. When a man's frightened he's no good—for anything."

I grasped her shoulders and threw her away from me. She hit a wall hard and slid down to the floor. Staring down at her, I was suddenly sick to my stomach. I thought I was going to vomit. I drew back my foot.

"No, Matt! Don't!"

The toe of my shoe sinking deep into her stomach was the best feeling I'd had in three days.

I went into the front room then and sat down on the low sofa in front of the fireplace. My thoughts were scrambled and I tried to get them in order.

A long time later I heard Edie crossing the front room behind me. She was sobbing softly. I didn't look around at her, and she didn't say anything. She went into the bedroom and closed the door.

That night I cat-napped on the sofa.

I was up early. The paper boy came up the front walk about six-thirty. I had to force myself to wait until he was out of sight. Then I got the paper off of the small front porch.

The story was right there on page one, a full column.

"Well?"

I looked up. Edie was standing in the bedroom doorway, staring at me. She was barefooted and in a robe that she held tight to her throat.

"He's dead," I said. "He died in the hospital about an hour after we hit him. He had three kids."

In a sudden flare of anger, I threw the newspaper at her. She came into the room and picked it up off the floor. I watched her read the story. Her face didn't reveal how she felt. When she had finished, she dropped the paper in a chair and went back into the bedroom.

I knew then what I had to do.

I stirred up the fire in the fireplace and put on another log. The story said there had been no witnesses, but the police had found some particles of paint on the dead man's clothing. They expected to be able to match the paint with that on the car that was involved.

Expected to match it!

I knew they *would* match it—eventually. And when they did, I'd be just as guilty as Edie.

There was only one thing for me to do. Only one out. I had to get rid of Edie and the convertible.

When she came back into the front room a long time later, she was wearing a red turtleneck sweater, tight-fitting white slacks, and moccasins. And in her hand was a tape recording. She walked right up to where I was sitting on the sofa and held the tape out to me.

"Good-by, Matt."

I took the tape without saying anything and threw it in the fireplace and watched it burn. Facing her then, I said, "My ring."

She stood in front of me. "Get it," she said, arching her back.

I don't know what she expected. Maybe she figured I couldn't touch her without wanting her. If that was it, she knew different right away. I slid my hand under the red sweater, at her waistline, and up until my fingers found the ring. Then I jerked. The chain cut into her neck all right, because she flinched. I pulled the chain out of the ring and threw it toward the fireplace. Then I put the ring on my finger where it belonged and sat down on the sofa.

"I thought you wanted to leave," she said.

"Tonight."

"Tonight?"

I didn't answer her.

I thought the day would never end. I killed most of it with a bottle in my hand. I didn't get drunk; I couldn't afford to do that. I just got a sharp edge and held it. Edie made a couple of stabs at quizzing me, but finally gave up. She prowled the house, restlessly. But I didn't let her bother me. I had just one worry. Would the cops somehow trace the murder car to Edie's place before dark? If they did . . .

I wouldn't let myself think about that.

At eight o'clock, straight up, I smashed an empty bourbon bottle on Edie's head. She had been sitting in a wing-chair with her back to me, reading a magazine. When I walked up behind her and hit her, she slid out of the chair and sank to the carpet without a sound. I dropped what remained of the bottle.

If the blow had killed her, it would have saved me further trouble. But it hadn't. I found her heartbeat, when I put my hand to her body.

I moved quickly. I got Edie into her fur coat and then shrugged into my own coat. I turned off all of the lights. Edie wasn't heavy. I carried her out to the garage and put her in the front seat of her convertible.

This was the risky part. If the cops were scouting around for a dark blue convertible, I was going to be in trouble.

I backed out of the garage and turned north. I stayed off of the main thoroughfare as long as I could and watched my speed and all of the neighborhood stop signs. My route took me behind the Crawford campus, but just two blocks beyond the college I had to swing out to the highway. I headed north again and drove at a moderate speed. I slowed at the river bridge, crossed the bridge, and turned off of the highway onto the same rutted lane Edie and I had been down Sunday night. On the sandy stretch of ground at the edge of the river I swung the convertible in a wide U turn, switched off the headlights, and drove back onto the rutted lane and stopped.

Dragging Edie out of the car, I stretched her out on the lane in front of the right wheel of the convertible, I had to be sure she died. And I had to be sure she died the right way. Then, before I could think about it too much, I jumped in the car and drove it over her body. I didn't hear a sound from her. I drove the car back and forth over her three times and then I got out again and stuck my hand inside her coat over her heart. Her chest felt like it had slipped a little to one side. There was no heartbeat.

Lifting her, I carried her around to the driver's side of the car and, finally, managed to shove her under the steering wheel. I hooked the safety belt around her middle, to make sure she didn't slip out of the car before I wanted her to, rolled down the window beside her, and kept the door open. Pushing against her, I was able to squeeze part way under the steering wheel. Then I drove to within a few yards of the highway, where I braked. I got out and walked up to the highway.

There were no headlights in either direction. I ran back to the convertible and squeezed in beside Edie again, drove the car onto the highway, and backed down the road several hundred yards. Switching on the headlights, I gunned the motor. The car rolled smooth. I hit thirty, forty, fifty miles an hour—and I was on the bridge. I swung the front door wide, whipped the steering wheel to the right and bailed out. The last thing I remembered was the crash as the convertible ripped through the bridge railing and plunged into the river.

I wasn't sure how long I was out. When I came around, all I knew was that I was flat on my face on the concrete. I rolled over and sat up. My hands burned smartly. My knees were cut open and there was a gash on my head just below my hairline. Blood dribbled down into my left eye, blinding me.

I finally got to my feet and staggered over to the hole in the bridge railing. It was too dark to see anything down below, but the bubbling sound coming up to me was loud. I turned then and that's when I saw the figure of the man walking across the bridge toward me.

"Hey, mister," the figure said, "were you in—" That was all I heard. I ran as fast as I could off of the bridge, went down through a ditch and over a fence into a field.

One hundred yards into the field I stopped running and turned toward town. It was slow going, but it was the only way. I couldn't risk being seen, and I had to get to my apartment before daylight.

I walked at a steady pace, vaulting the fences as I came to them. The highway was to my left and I kept it in sight. I hadn't covered too much ground when I saw the winking red light winging along the highway. I stopped and watched it until it was out of sight. If that was the highway patrol or an ambulance heading for the bridge, it meant somebody had already found the convertible.

The first red-gray streaks of dawn edged the horizon, when I hit the city limits. I followed the alleys to my apartment. I cleaned up. Much as I felt like it,

I couldn't chance going to bed. It was imperative I be on schedule all day. So I sat in a deep chair in the front room and chain-smoked cigarettes until the paper boy arrived.

It was all there, right on page one.

A girl, identified as Edie Jackson, 18, of New Orleans, had apparently driven her car off of the river bridge ten miles north of town. The county sheriff tentatively had identified her convertible as the car that had struck and killed a Crawford man on Sunday evening. The paint on the car matched the particles found on the victim's clothing.

I read the rest of the story fast.

Miss Jackson, a freshman student at Crawford College, was found strapped in a safety belt when sheriff's officers pulled the car from the river. She was dead.

The sheriff speculated that the girl may have become depressed after fleeing from the Sunday night accident scene and committed suicide.

However, an air of mystery surrounded the discovery of the car in the river.

Harold Stribling, an itinerant, was asleep under the river bridge when the car plunged off about eight forty-five last night. Stribling said he ran up to the highway to secure aid as soon as he realized what had happened.

On the highway, he claims to have seen a man who ran from the scene when he called to him. Stribling then went to a nearby farm house and called the sheriff's office.

Stribling told authorities he would not be able to positively identify the man, but . . .

I couldn't read any more.

I had a full schedule of classes that day. They were pure hell. I managed to get through the morning sessions; then shortly after one o'clock that afternoon a man walked into the gymnasium. I watched him with some apprehension as he talked to a student, and then the student pointed to me. The man came toward me.

"You're Matt Lane?" he said.

"Yes," I said huskily.

He showed me a badge. "You'll have to come downtown with me, Mr. Lane."

I'd never been inside a police station before . . .

Now the soft-talking cop named Malone was standing in front of me, smoking a cigarette.

"Let's start all over again, Lane," he said. "Did you know this Jackson girl?"

I got a grip on myself. "If you mean the girl," I said, "who drove her car off of the river bridge last night, no, I didn't know her."

"How come you know she drove her car off the bridge?"

"I read about it in the paper this morning."

"She was a freshman student at the college."

"I teach physical education and coach. There are no girls in my classes."

"You're positive then that you didn't know the Jackson girl?"

"Positive."

He sucked in a deep breath and looked at one of the other cops. "Play it, Simpson."

The cop pushed away from a wall and walked toward a record player. I leveled my eyes on him. What the hell was going on? The cop snapped a switch and the next voice I heard was Edie's!

Then my own!

I couldn't move. I tried to swallow. It was a frame!

I was being framed by someone who was dead!

The cop snapped the switch, cutting off the recorder.

"Now, Mr. Lane . . ." Malone said. He let it hang there.

I knew, of course, what Edie had done to me. The tape I had burned at her place the previous day—I hadn't played it to be sure that it was my own!

"We found several other tapes, Lane, but this particular one—"

"Okay," I said, interrupting Malone, "so I lied about knowing her. I just didn't want to get involved. I got a wife. You know how those things are. That's all—"

He cut me off. "There's a couple of things mighty peculiar about the Jackson girl's death. Medical examination turned up a large bump on her head. Too, her chest was crushed and the lungs punctured. She could have received these injuries in the crash, but—well, we found the girl strapped into the car by a safety belt. And we don't figure it's too likely she hit the steering wheel hard enough to crush her chest seeing as the belt wasn't broken."

He paused and looked at me steadily.

I wanted to run. But where?

"The truth of it is, Lane, we found tire marks on the girl's clothing, glass in her hair, and this in the front room of her house."

He opened a desk drawer and held up the top quarter of a broken bourbon bottle. He held it gingerly by the jagged edge.

"There are fingerprints on this, Lane. Are they yours?"

Hang on, boy, I told myself. Hang on tight. They still haven't got you cold.

But I knew they'd get me eventually. They always did. And before I knew it, I was talking, telling them everything.

They put it on tape. And later they had it on paper and the paper in front of me. They wanted me to sign my name.

I did.

He's Never Stopped Running
Aaron Marc Stein

June 1957

With men Rick almost never had trouble. If a man looks tough enough and he always goes his own way, never messing with anybody unless it's some guy who's gone out of his way to get in his road, it'll be like that. He did all right with women, too, and if he ever had any trouble there, it wasn't anything that couldn't be fixed by handing the dame a slap in the mouth. Mostly he took up with them in bars and sometimes it was in a dance hall, but always he knew all the answers. Grace, however, had him off base from the very first minute.

He was working this construction job and this one time he was sent into the job office to bring out some blueprints. She was in there and she got the stuff for him and she was wearing a thin pink dress and perfume and Rick in his work clothes and not knowing where the sweat on him stopped and the dirt began. He was standing away from her and trying to figure what he should do with his hands and that was a funny feeling for Rick, being self-conscious.

That time he told himself she wasn't for him and he worked at forgetting her, but it does look as though maybe she had other ideas about it. After that you never knew when she was going to be walking around the job except that it always seemed to happen it was Rick would have to pull over so she could get past or it was Rick had to give her a hand because she would be going across somewhere where the walking wouldn't be too good.

It was a night he was going to the movies it really started. He was fresh out of the barber shop and you know how that is. With a barber shave and the stuff they put on his hair, he was smelling pretty sweet himself. He was on line to buy himself a ticket and he happened to look back and he saw her. The way she was coming along, he thought she was going to go right on by and he wanted to say hello and he didn't know how without yelling it, so he skipped it. But then she hesitated and she looked at the posters and next thing she'd hooked on to the end of the line.

Maybe it was only his barber shop smell and not wanting to waste it, but there he was up to the window and buying two tickets. He walked back along the line and showed her the tickets, and it made him feel good that she knew him right off never having seen him before when he wasn't in his work clothes and when he had his hands and face washed. She said he shouldn't have done it and how she oughtn't let him, but he took her arm and she came off the line.

It was the kind of picture he would have walked out on half way through, but she liked it and he didn't mind staying even though she did sit all the time with her hands folded in her lap and her elbows pulled in and not touching him anywhere. Along about the time he stopped seeing the picture he laid his arm on the back of her chair and the rest of the time they were in the theater he worked at that, edging it closer all the time. His hand was within a half inch of her shoulder when they came to the place where they had seen it around. They were out on the street again without his even having touched her. That's how much she had him off base.

He did suggest a drink before he took her home and she thought that meant an ice cream soda. Because he didn't know any way to tell her it didn't, she had an ice cream soda. He did with a cup of coffee. He didn't know whether he liked the way it was going or not. To be with a girl that long and not put his hands on her even once, that was a new kick for him and he didn't understand it. He seemed to be doing all right and yet he wasn't.

Walking home, he took her arm and she let him keep it. That helped him decide. He was going to kiss her goodnight. He had to make his move sometime and what was there to wait for? It wasn't any good letting her think she was out with some high school kid who hadn't yet made his first jump out of the bees and flowers. He squeezed her arm a little and she tightened up just enough so that it brought the back of his hand close against her breast where he felt it soft and warm on his knuckles.

By the time she stopped walking and said this was it, he had been feeling perfectly natural with her. He was halfway toward reaching for her with his free hand to swing her around where she would be in his arms and under his mouth, when it hit him that they weren't in front of any house. It was this furniture store, a big one. He did swing her around, but then held her and looked down at her.

"I don't get to walk you all the way home, baby?" he said. "Why's that? Husband?"

Looking up at him, she laughed. "Silly," she said. "The light's still on in the back room. That means pop's still there and there's nobody home."

He laughed with her. "Big girl like you afraid to go home to a dark house?" he said. "No call to be afraid. You aren't alone. You've got me with you."

She wasn't afraid. It was only that she didn't have a key and with her father not home there would be no way she could get in. Rick was way off base again. He'd never imagined a girl who didn't own a latchkey and when she rattled the knob of the store door and her old man came out of the back room to open up for her, that threw Rick some more. Her father wasn't an old guy. Even under the green eyeshade he was wearing he didn't look old. For a man who wore one of those green eyeshades, he wasn't badly set up and he looked to Rick to be ten or at most fifteen years older than himself. Rick was trying to remember if he had ever thought about a dame having a father before and he couldn't remember. If dames had fathers they would either be dead or so old that nobody even thought about them any more.

She introduced him to her old man and they waited while he packed up to go home. While they waited, Rick was adding things up. The name on the store windows, the easy way Grace moved around the place—it wasn't just that her old man worked in this store. He owned it. Rick was back to not knowing what to do with his hands. He had never in his life known anybody who owned anything, not to talk to.

They went out the back way and the three of them walked over to the house together. It was no sort of walk, just through the back yard, and they said good night in the yard. That night Rick didn't make it even as far as the little back porch. He went away, writing the whole thing off. It was out of his league and he knew it.

After that, of course, when she walked around the job and it was Rick had to give her a hand across some spot where the walking wasn't good, she didn't just thank him and go on. She'd stop and talk, but Rick wasn't making any moves. All she had to do was come near him and every alarm bell he had in his head would start sounding off. This wasn't jail bait exactly, but it came too close.

Then after about a week when she asked him to come around to supper, she caught him flatfooted. He dreamed up a date for that night but then she wanted to know which night he could make it and he didn't know any answers to that one. He went around to supper. It was a nice house and all the furniture looked brand new and Rick asked himself why not with a whole big store of the stuff. After supper her old man went across to the store to work on his accounts and Rick helped her clean up the dishes. He might have kissed her that evening but, before he even got around to working toward it, she kissed him.

After that they were going steady, but it was a week or more before Rick could get over being surprised at how much she would let him love her up. He just couldn't figure where he should put her because there would be the nights when he came to the house and her old man would be across the yard working on his accounts and those nights they would be alone and everything would be warm and natural and easy. Come a night Rick took her out, though, and everything changed. Her old man never gave her the latchkey and it was always stopping by the store to see if he was still there and then it would be saying goodnight out in the yard with her old man waiting to go in and Rick not even touching her.

For a while Rick thought it was funny but that couldn't last long. It was getting him too itchy for him to laugh at it. He never knew whether he meant it to happen the way it did. It was just one of those things that had to happen like the sun coming up in the morning; and one of those evenings when her old man left them alone, it did happen. At the very last moment she made a try at fighting him off, but then it was much too late and there was never any sign Rick could read that told him she hadn't wanted it to be too late. And then right afterward she didn't reproach him or cry or anything like that. She just began talking about when they would get married as though he had asked her and she had said yes and it had all been settled between them.

It wasn't the first time a dame had pulled that one on Rick either. You laughed at them and you slapped them on the rump and they knew what the score was. If she didn't know and it was a babe who took to nagging him about it, that was one of the things a slap in the mouth could fix. This, however, was different.

It couldn't be as with others that she had made the mistake of tabbing him for a fall guy. It couldn't be that she was looking for the easy meal ticket. That job she had over on the construction, that was only for laughs. She didn't have to work, not with her old man and that store of his. These people had dough.

"Sure, baby," he said. "Sure. Sure thing."

She wanted him out of there before her old man came back across the yard and Rick wanted time to think. He kissed her hard and he left. He thought he wanted to get drunk and on the way home he stopped into a bar he liked. Somehow the whiskey didn't taste as good as he'd expected and he switched to beer. It was an off night and except for some couples in the booths out back who obviously didn't want to be bothered the place was empty.

Rick was telling himself he ought to leave town, not think about it, not wait for anything, just hop the next bus out, whichever way it was going. Although that wasn't his name for it, he knew his reflexes had been suspended too long, but now they were acting again and he couldn't be smarter than he would be if he just let them carry him along.

Maybe it was because they had been too long suspended or maybe it was because this one really was different, but something was happening to Rick that had never happened to him before. Always it had been the automatic act, the thing his muscles wanted to do and because they wanted it, he wanted it. Now he was feeling divided. His muscles wanted to hop that bus. He didn't know what he wanted.

He fell into talk with the bartender. They talked about the town and about business, about how the storekeepers were doing. It was a good town with good business. A man, he had him a little store in that town, there was a man who had it made. The bartender told him about some guys, guys they didn't know anything, not even how to wipe their noses for themselves, but these guys, they had an old man, he owned a grocery store, or maybe it was farm implements. So they go into the store with the old man and they still don't know anything but it never made any difference. The bartender offered to show Rick a dozen of these schmos, all of them driving Buicks.

"Maybe it was a time once in this country," the bartender said, "a fellow could get something started. Maybe it was once but it ain't any more. Nothing gets started anywhere now. It only gets passed on and you've got to be one of them it gets passed on to. Without that, brother, you're nowhere. Your wages go up, so everything you buy, it goes up more. You work your tail off and do you ever get ahead? Nah. You're lucky if you can even stay in the same place."

Rick didn't have more than a couple of beers, but by the time he was out of that bar, all his reflexes were dead. He had started thinking. He didn't even know who his old man was and, whoever he had been, Rick was certain of this much.

He hadn't ever had anything. Rick wasn't one of them it got passed on to. Rick was nowhere, working his tail off, and nowhere.

So here it was. This had come. Rick hadn't done anything to make it come. He hadn't planned it any more than he had planned that other thing, that one fight that started like any other fight and went along like any other fight with Rick trying to knock the other guy loose from everything he had mostly for no reason except that the other guy was trying to knock Rick loose from everything he had. Rick had never known why that one fight had to be different. He hadn't planned to cripple the guy. If he let himself think about it, he could even feel bad about that, but not too bad because it could just as easily have been the other guy who had done it to Rick. That was the luck of it and you didn't think much about luck.

Anyhow that one fight had been different and he had crippled the creep. Then the cops had had him in the station and that had been completely different. Those cops, they'd had everything under control. They didn't cripple Rick. They didn't even mark him so much that there was any of it left to show by the time they got him into court, but they had handled him all right. The way they had handled him, it made all the rest of it seem easy, even the two years in the pen.

Rick wasn't any good at thinking and he knew it. He didn't even know why all that stuff should be coming back to him now. It was years ago and half across the country and over and done with. Of course, he had never forgotten, not to forget so much that every time he just happened to see a cop the hair didn't move at the back of his neck, not so much that a cop just standing in the street and hitching up his pants didn't make him want to vomit a little because he could still see the way they had stood ringing him around and one after another in pairs they had taken their turn at him and he had known which pair would be coming at him next because they did it every time, hitched their pants up a little before they stepped out toward him.

Did he skip town or did he stay? That was what he was thinking about and none of this had anything to do with it. Leaving or staying, it was nothing to get up any sweat about. Rick couldn't even begin to count up how many towns it had been, towns he had worked in one time or another and this could be just another town. This wasn't anything special. It wasn't anywhere near as special as that town where he'd had the bad fight, or maybe it was.

This time Rick didn't want to move on. So he wasn't one of them it got passed on to. Grace was, and it was a house that was plenty big enough for three and who would keep it nice for her old man and cook for him and all if Grace went away with Rick? Her old man wouldn't want her going away and there wasn't anybody else. Anything got passed on, it would get passed on to her.

"I can be like a son to him," Rick said, thinking aloud, "except he's going to have to let me have a latchkey."

Hearing himself, he started laughing and he didn't think any more except for remembering the way she had been and thinking that it had been nice and he had never had it nicer.

The next morning he saw her at work and when his time came to knock off for lunch, she went to eat with him and it was as if that were the only way to do it. They made the eating quick and they were just going to walk along together in the sun the rest of the time before they had to go back, but Rick thought of something and they walked down to where there were stores and he wanted to buy her a ring.

She said, of course, he would, but he wasn't going to buy it in that store. Her old man would send him to a place where he would get a big discount. You didn't just go in off the street and buy something. That wasn't the way it was done. A jeweler wanted furniture and he came around to the store and got a discount. Any time they wanted something from him, the jeweler did the same. They got a discount.

"Nobody buys retail," Grace told him.

Rick grinned at her. He told himself that he was going to have to remember that. He wasn't nobody any more. It would be the same at the Buick dealer's. There would be a dealer who bought furniture and he would knock something off. This was a new world and Rick liked it.

"You've told him?" he asked.

"Yes. Over breakfast."

"How happy is he?"

"He'll get used to it."

"If he's worrying about losing you . . . ?"

"He'll get used to it."

"I wouldn't be taking you away from him. If he wants we should live in the house . . ."

"I told him. I'll stop working. Cooking for three's a lot easier than for just two."

"Then what's the trouble?"

"No trouble."

But there was. When Rick went around that evening, he knew it right away. The old man didn't break out a bottle so they could have a drink on it. He didn't clap Rick on the back. He didn't call him son. He didn't even call him Rick. He said nothing.

Rick forced it. "Gracie told you about us," he said.

"She told me. Let's not rush anything. You haven't known each other very long. You ought to know each other better."

Rick wanted to tell him how well they knew each other. He talked about the ring instead.

"Sure," the old man said, but that was all he said.

It went on that way for more than a week except that they weren't alone much any more. The old man had stopped going across the yard to work on his accounts. He would sit with them or, if he had to go over to the store, he would find some reason why they had to go with him, like moving a display around with Rick to help him heave the stuff.

Rick felt off base again, but every time he caught Grace's eye, she gave him a look that brought him back in. He took to putting his hands on her even if her old man was watching and, when he felt like kissing her, he kissed her. Her old man never said anything. He was pretending it wasn't happening.

Rick kept reminding him about the ring, but he always said "sure" just the way he'd said it the first time and nothing ever happened. He had Rick steaming and one day Rick just went out and bought the ring—retail. He gave it to her when he was walking her home after work, and she kissed him right out in the street even though he was still in his dirty work clothes and he hadn't shaved yet and his chin was even rougher than that because he had some bits of dried mortar stuck in his beard.

Always when he walked her home that way after work, he would go as far as the store and she would go in to get the key from her old man. He wouldn't go in with her. He would go on home and clean himself up and come back later. This time she wanted him to come in with her because she would be showing her old man the ring. The old man hardly looked at the ring. He handed her the key and told them to go over to the house. He was going to lock up and he'd be right over.

He was quicker than that. He caught up with them in the back yard.

"Give it back to him," he said.

"Now, look . . ." Rick began.

"Give it back to him," her old man repeated, "and ask him about Joliet."

Rick went blind. This was why they weren't to rush anything. He'd needed time, time to hire himself some snooper to get everything dug up and laid around. Grace had the key. She went up the steps and opened the door. She held it open for him. Blindly Rick followed her and went in. She still stood holding the door.

"Come inside, pop," she said. "We'll do this without the neighbors."

"Give it back to him," her old man said, as he came in and she shut the door behind him.

"We're getting married," she answered. "I told you we're getting married."

"Not to no con, you don't. Give it back to him. I'm going to throw him out, but give it back to him first."

"You throw him out, pop, and I go with him. You won't ever see me again. You won't ever hear from me again. It'll be like you never had a daughter. I'll be . . ."

She never got to say what else it would be because her old man slapped her across the mouth hard. A couple of drops of blood showed on her lip.

Rick caught him by the shoulder and swung him around. He started a kick toward Rick, but Rick was back with his reflexes again and this was something where he knew how to handle himself. He brought his heel down fast and hard on the old man's instep and the kick never got anywhere. The old man threw a punch and Rick took it on the side of his head and came back with an openhanded slap that sent the old man reeling.

The old man caught himself and grabbed hold of a chair. He came for Rick with the chair. Rick brought his hands up to protect his eyes and getting a grip on two legs of the chair he wrenched it out of the old man's grasp and flung it across the kitchen. It crashed against a cupboard and Rick heard the dishes in the cupboard go. He went off guard for a moment looking over his shoulder toward the cupboard and in that moment the old man tried again. This time he made a kick good.

"I wasn't looking at him," Rick thought, "but I'll bet he hitched his pants up first."

He swung on the old man and now it wasn't the flat of his hand. His fists landed and they landed again. The old man went down and stayed there.

Rick turned to Grace. "I didn't want to hit him," he said. "Honest. I didn't want to."

She took hold of his arm and squeezed. "I know you didn't," she said. "It's all right. I know."

Rick started for the door. "You coming with me?" he asked.

She hesitated for a moment. "Later," she said. "I can't just leave him. I'll get him fixed up and I'll come over to your place later. Go home and wait for me."

"You're going to have to make up your mind. Him or me."

Quickly she went to him and kissed him. "I don't have to make up my mind," she said. "It's you."

"He's got it right, that about Joliet."

"I don't want to know. Go home and wait for me."

Rick went home and, waiting for her, he began wondering how she would know where to find him. She had never been around to his room and he had never told her where he lived. He began thinking that it had just been a trick to get him out of the house. He couldn't see why it shouldn't be. How could she ever know how a man could have gotten to be a con and still not be all that different from everyone else, or wasn't he all that different? His muscles were pushing him again. The next bus out of town, he belonged on that.

He had begun throwing things in a bag when she came and he forgot to ask her how she had known where to find him. Rick went on with his packing. She had told him she had chosen and now she was proving it. She would go away with him.

"Yes, darling," she said. "Yes, if we have to, but I know him. He'll come around. Once he sees it means losing me, he'll come around."

Rick said he didn't care what her old man did. He kept saying that, but steadily with less conviction because there was this new thing and it had gone into his blood. There was the house and the store and them it got passed on to. He was, after all, her old man. She should know him.

Rick stayed. They saw each other on the job every day, and every evening she came out and met him. She even went to taverns with him and she drank beer and all the time she kept saying her old man would come around. Then there was the day when she was saying, I told you so. Rick was to come to the house that night. It wasn't just that she was asking him. Her old man had told her to ask him to come. Her old man wanted him.

He went. When he came to the house it was locked and there was nobody there. He hadn't expected to find Grace. She'd told him she'd be home later. It was her night to have her hair done, but her old man wanted to talk to him alone so they could get it all patched up man-to-man before she came home.

Rick guessed he would be over in the store and he walked across. He knocked at the back door and it swung away from his knock. Startled, he bent to look at the lock. It had been smashed. It was then that he smelled the smoke. He pushed into the office. It was dark. He found the switch and the lights came on. The office was empty and he saw the blood on the desk. He was looking at the blood, trying to understand it, when the lights went. The fire had gone through to the wiring.

Rick slammed through into the front of the store. There was a sharp reek of gasoline all around him and half way down the long space the flames roared upward. They leaped toward a row of sofas and even before the flames touched them, the sofas exploded fire. In the firelight Rick saw the old man. He was lying on the floor behind the sofas and what had happened to the top of his head explained the blood on the desk.

Rick grabbed up a chair to hold in front of him and shield his face from the heat while he went forward to pull the old man out of there. The chair upholstery was wet and the fumes of the gasoline bit at his throat. He threw the chair away from him and went into it empty handed. The old man's clothes were smoldering when he reached him. Rick picked him up and ran with him blindly for the back door. He staggered into the office and, as he went through the door, he heard another explosion of fire and the heat seared his back.

Carrying the old man outside, he set him down on the grass. That was the first he thought to see whether the old man was alive. He felt for the heart and the thump of it came up under his hand. The old man stirred. His eyes fluttered open and he looked at Rick.

"You let her do it for you," he gasped. "You let her do the dirty. You could never have anything as long as I lived and nothing after I was dead either, so you had to have it this way—each other and my life insurance and the store insurance, everything. I was sorry for the both of you because you were going to have each other. Now I'm sorry for you. You didn't have the stomach to leave me in there to burn alive. My daughter—she had the stomach for it. And now you've got her."

The old man's eyes closed again and Rick brought his hand up to wipe his mouth with it. Rick wiped gasoline all over his lips. The old man's eyes opened again. They were filmed over now and, when he spoke, Rick could only barely make out the words. They were that mixed up with the noises of dying.

"God help you," the old man said.

Rick didn't wait for her to come home. His muscles took over. He started running and he's never stopped running since.

Stolen Star
William Campbell Gault

November 1957

I got into the mess late and not by choice. The local papers were giving it more ink than the Japanese surrender and I can imagine it was front page news from coast to coast.

Laura Spain had been kidnapped. Laura wasn't the youngest star in the business but she still had her figure and enough looks to pull all the men over thirty into any theatre showing one of her pictures.

The thing had a bad odor right from the first ransom note. The local police are skeptical about publicity shenanigans; a jewel robbery out here is almost certain to be no more than that. But kidnapping?

It didn't seem logical that a sane citizen would go to that extreme for free ink, but then a sane citizen wouldn't fill a swimming pool with champagne for a party, either. And Laura had done that a few years back.

So the F.B.I. wasn't called in, but on the other hand, the local gendarmes didn't treat it as a gag, either. And woe to Laura, the D.A. was quoted as saying, if she had dreamed it up. She would be prosecuted to the limit.

The thing that made it seem fishy was the modest ransom the kidnappers were asking—twenty-five thousand—and the fact that Laura had been snatched right at her house and had evidently taken a rather complete wardrobe along for the trip. There were three dogs in that house, Dobermans, and two servants, one of them an ex-pug.

Well, it made good bar talk and there were as many opinions as there were people to voice them and nobody was shy about voicing them. It became a farce, almost, and kidnapping is nothing that should ever seem humorous. There are too many crack-pots who get ideas from the kind of spread this thing was getting.

Forty-eight hours after the first news break on the story, Hal Slotkin came to see me. Hal is a divorce and criminal lawyer, about as rich a barrister as this town knows and we had never done business before. And he didn't *send* for me; he *came*. He must have been worried.

"Mr. Puma," he said, "I have known of you for some time, by reputation."

"And I you, sir," I said. "Won't you sit down?"

He took a good look around my inexpensive office before sitting down, as though he'd been searching all the places that might hold a tape recorder.

He sat down and sighed. "Your ethics, I've been told, are unassailable and your courage immense." He was a short, fat man, and his language seemed a little pompous. But I was impressed, nevertheless. In a jungle, he had become king of his tribe.

"My ethics have been stretched from time to time," I told him, "and my courage ebbs with the years." Gawd, now he had me doing it.

He rubbed his fat neck with a pudgy hand and stared wearily at the bamboo shades behind me. Match-stick bamboo, Sears-Roebuck, five bucks a panel. He said, "It's been a hectic two days, hasn't it?"

"Not for me, sir," I said, "but as Miss Spain's attorney, I imagine you've had a busy time of it."

He nodded. "If I had it to do over, I'd have gone in for corporation law." He sighed. "Or probate work. I might have made a few dollars less, but I wouldn't be pampering my ulcers."

I didn't comment. I can never find the proper comment for the wailings of the wealthy. I tried to put some sympathy into my smile.

2.

He said suddenly, "How would you like to earn a thousand dollars for two hours work?"

"It would depend upon the work, Mr. Slotkin," I answered.

"Can you guess?" he asked.

"Delivering the ransom money? I thought you'd lost contact with Miss Spain's abductors."

"We had. Until half an hour ago."

"Have you informed the police?"

He shook his head. "I was expressly warned not to."

I said, "Mr. Slotkin, acting as an intermediary in a kidnapping case would not only lose me my license, it could put me in jail."

"Not if you're employed by Hal Slotkin," he said, "not in this town. I could include the Chief in our confidence, if you want me to."

"That puts a different light on it," I said, "but not the whole light. How do I know I don't get bumped? If Miss Spain is dead, the boys who killed her aren't going to hesitate about wiping out one poor private investigator. I might be able to finger them later, they'll realize."

"All right," he said, "I'll make it two thousand dollars." He shrugged. "It's not my money."

I chuckled. "You figure I wouldn't commit suicide for one thousand, but I might for two?"

"Somebody has to deliver the money," he said matter of factly. "If you don't want the job, I'll go elsewhere. If I'm forced to, by your refusal, I'm sure you'll keep this a secret until Miss Spain is safely home again."

"Of course," I said. "Give me a moment to think."

He nodded, and leaned his head back in the chair and closed his eyes. His face was pale and his neck flabby. He didn't look at all like the courtroom tiger of his legend.

I thought about the brake job I needed and the new tires, about the five hundred I owed the bank and the new suit I should have.

"Well?" Slotkin asked.

"Okay," I said. "What's the deal?"

"It's in the desert," he said, "near Canyon Springs. Flat country and they can see if they're being crossed, I suppose. By the way, don't get cute with this, will you? Just deliver the money and pick up Miss Spain."

"Of course," I said. "Why would I get cute with it?"

"I don't know. Maybe to grab a headline. That seems to be a disease in this town." He handed me a slip of paper. "Here's the address." He paused. "Don't deliver the money until you see Miss Spain, *alive.*"

"And if she's not in sight, I still get paid."

"You get paid right now," he said, and took out a checkbook.

He must have been sure they were going to deliver the girl or he never would have paid in advance. Which smelled a little, but it also led me to think I wasn't likely to run into any violence. And yet, I couldn't believe if the whole thing was a hoax that a man of Hal Slotkin's eminence would be a party to it. He had a reputation as a tricky operator but all his tricks were well within the law.

Any reservations still in my mind were quieted by the slip of paper he handed me next. *Pay to Joseph Puma, two thousand and no/hundredths.*

He told me I was to pick up the ransom money at his office in an hour. It would be a fairly bulky package as they were all small, old bills.

The bank was still open; I went over immediately and deposited the check. And then I phoned Tommy Verch. Slotkin hadn't stipulated I was to go alone, and Tommy could use the business. His office is in Venice and he doesn't get the carriage trade I do.

I said, "How much would you charge me to ride along on a little job tonight?"

"What kind of job?"

"I hate to say over the phone, but it includes delivering some money."

A pause, and then, "A headline story, Joe?"

"That's right."

Another pause, and he said, "You know my rate."

"Yes, but I'm getting two thousand dollars for the job."

"I'll up my rate then. Two hundred all right?"

"That's more than fair."

"You want me armed, Joe?"

"Absolutely," I said.

"I'm on the way over," he said.

When he got there, I said, "Maybe you'd better eat, first. I'm going over to pick up the money. When I get back, I'll park in the small lot behind the building here. You climb into the back while I go over to eat. That way, if I'm being watched, nobody will see you get into the back of my car. Once out in the desert, you can sit up again. Clear?"

He nodded. "You looking forward to trouble, Joe?"

I shrugged.

He said, "I'll go and eat." He went out, a stocky man of medium height with a flat and broken nose looking out of place in his thin face.

3.

Slotkin wasn't at his office when I got there; I was handed a package by one of his young associates. I'd brought a small grip and I carried the money with me when I went to eat.

The afternoon *Mirror-News* informed me that there were no new developments in the Laura Spain kidnapping. The earlier police skepticism, according to this piece, had disappeared and anxiety about Miss Spain's safety was growing. If nothing new developed by tomorrow morning, the F.B.I. would be called in.

One of Laura's former husbands was quoted as saying he still thought it was a gag. But that could be just the bitter words of a poor loser.

When I got back to the car, I could see that the blanket had been pulled down from the back seat. I got in, started the engine, and asked, "All safe, Tommy?"

"Roll her," he said. "It's the first job I've had in a month."

I rolled her, heading for the Hollywood Freeway which would take me to Highway 99, which would take me to the desert and Canyon Springs. The place I was supposed to make rendezvous was on this end of town. The road leading to it would be visible for miles, and I was supposed to arrive before dusk, *just* before dusk.

Delivery would be made as close to dark as possible, so they could use its cover to get away. But light was necessary for them to be able to watch all the roads. It would require good timing, and I hoped my tires would hold up. A flat would throw the time-table off.

Once off the freeway, I watched to see if any cars persisted in following, slowing and speeding in turn. When I was sure we were unwatched, I told Tommy, "You can sit up now, boy, for a while."

He grunted and came up off the floor, relaxing in the back seat. He said, "Where's the pick-up?"

"Right outside of Canyon Springs."

"Good pick for a desert spot," he commented. "They can go four directions from there. How do you figure it, Joe, a gag?"

I shrugged.

He leaned back. "Well, as long as I'm getting only ten per cent of the money, I hope I only get ten per cent of the lead they throw."

"It was your price, Tommy," I reminded him.

"I know, I know—and very welcome. So starving to death is no easier than being shot. Onward, moneybags."

I looked into the rear-view mirror to see if his comment had meaning, but he looked content and peaceful, his eyes closed. Well, if things went right, I could slip him an extra fifty.

I was doing a steady sixty-five, but traffic went blasting past me. The safest driving in the world should be in the desert, with its unlimited vision, but it had a horrible safety record.

I hit Beaumont at about the proper time and turned south a few miles beyond, down a less traveled road. Nobody followed. To the west and north, the mountains were beginning to show shadows, beginning to take the glare out of the sun.

In the back seat, Tommy stirred, took his .38 from its shoulder holster and spun the cylinder. He replaced it and said, "Maybe I'd better get out of sight again; this road is kind of deserted."

I nodded agreement.

He said, "If you want, you can give me a signal when you see the girl. I guess I could show after that, couldn't I?"

"Why antagonize them?" I asked. "If I need you to come up gunning, I'll holler."

A silence, and then he said, "You nervous, Joe?"

I nodded.

"Me, too," he said, and went down below the blanket on the floor.

We were coming to a crossroad now, a two lane asphalt strip that led east to Canyon Springs. A State Patrol car was parked here and I was glad Slotkin had paid me in advance. Because it could easily be a stake-out or a road block. And if it was, the kidnappers would certainly be alerted.

The car was off the road, over on the sand, and both troopers were sitting in the front seat. I slowed, waiting for a signal from them, but none came. I turned east on the crossroad, keeping a careful eye on them in the mirror.

Their car didn't move. I said to Tommy, "Just passed a parked State Patrol car. It might be a coincidence."

"I get my dough either way, remember," he said.

I didn't answer him. Ahead, the first buildings of Canyon Springs were coming into view. Far behind, the police car was still immobile. The purple dusk of the desert was shrouding the harshness of the landscape and one early star was visible in the east. We went over a culvert spanning a dry arroyo and ahead I could see a solitary cactus with a sign pointing toward some buildings to the right. *Air-conditioned cabins,* the sign read.

4.

There was a man standing next to the sign and he wore the red jockey cap I was to look for. I slowed, stopped and opened the door on the right side.

"I've brought the money," I called.

He was a thin man, fairly tall, with a long, narrow face and grayish stubble in the black of his week-old beard. He came over and climbed into the seat beside me.

"Up past the cabins," he said.

"There's a State Patrol car back at the turn-off," I told him. "What gives? I don't want to get into trouble."

"It's okay," he said. "Past those cabins, to the end of this road."

The cabins looked deserted as we went by, old-fashioned adobe buildings that probably couldn't compete today. Up the road, now, I could see a solitary, larger cabin, with two cars parked around in back of it. I couldn't read the license plates from here and by the time I got to the cabin, the cars would be out of sight behind it. Well, I wasn't being paid to learn anything.

I said, "I see Miss Spain before you see a nickel. I see her alive."

"Hell, yes." He chuckled. "But what if I told you to go to hell. What could you do?"

"I couldn't tell you right now. I'd have to decide about that when the situation came up."

"You armed, shamus?"

"Always," I told him. "Even on a publicity romp like this, I figured a gun wouldn't hurt."

"I'll take the gun," he said.

"No, you won't. The money's right there, all in small and dirty bills, like you wanted it. When Miss Spain comes with me, that goes with you, and everybody wins."

"The broad isn't here," he said. "Do you think we're crazy? When you hand over the money, we send out the signal and she'll be released. How crazy do you think we are, sitting here in the middle of nowhere with a broad that hot?"

"All right, then, I'll wait until I get word from her attorney that she's safe. Then you get your money. Okay?"

"Hand over your gun," he said, "and stop yacking, or I'll put a hole in you. Get to it, man."

"Okay, Tommy," I said clearly. "Now would be the time."

The man next to me whirled around—just in time for Tommy to press the barrel of his .38 in the middle of the man's forehead. Tommy said lightly, "Don't even blink, skinny. Don't even breathe heavy. I'm nervous."

The man stared and some obscene muttering came from his thin throat. I had my gun out, now, and I relieved him of the one in his hand. It was an army .45.

I asked, "Is Miss Spain here, or isn't she?"

"No," he said hoarsely. "Look, maybe I talked too rough. She's going to be all right, believe me. And there are plenty of guns in that house; so don't think you can get away with anything."

"I came to deliver the money," I said. "I came in good faith. Now listen carefully—I'm going to let you go up to the house. One of your men can come with me to Canyon Springs, one unarmed man. I'll phone Slotkin from there. The second he hears Miss Spain is released, I'll hand this man this satchel containing twenty-five grand. I'll even give him your gun back. My job was to deliver the money, not you hoodlums, and I'll go through with it. Is that clear?"

His eyes went from me to Tommy and back. "There's Tommy guns in that house; there's sawed-offs."

"And there's you," I pointed out, "sitting here courting a hole in your head. It's a hell of a situation, isn't it? Just because there's no honor among thieves."

Silence all around for a few moments.

Then I said, "I'm going to turn around so we're headed the way we came. I'm going to let you go—unarmed—up to the house and deliver my message. If you're not back in three minutes, with your hands well away from your body and empty, I'm going to go into town and get a lot of law out here." I nodded toward the door on his side. "Get out and go to the house, *now.*"

He got out and went trotting toward the house as I turned around and pulled a couple hundred feet down the road from the place. Tommy stayed in the back, watching everything through the rear window.

Without turning around, he said, "Gutty, aren't you? Do you believe him about the fire-power they're holding?"

"No. The rube sees too many movies. Old ones, on TV. Tommy guns, cripes!"

"Maybe, maybe," Tommy said doubtfully. "I still don't like it, Joe."

"It's rougher than I figured," I admitted. "I think I'll give you an extra fifty, Tommy."

"That's white of you," he said. "I wish that bastard would come out again."

"Maybe they'll send somebody else."

"Hell, no. We've already seen *him;* the fewer we can identify later, the better for them."

Tommy was right; in another minute, the same thin and grizzled gent came down the road toward the car, his hands well out from his body. I could see no sign of life from the cabin behind him.

He got in as I opened the door. He said, "I'll go with you. If you try to cross us, those guys will kill you, sure as you're alive this second. They've got your license number and they can find out who you are."

"I'll save them the trouble," I said. "My name's Joe Puma and my office is in Beverly Hills. If everything is okay, the money in that satchel is yours. You can take it out and check it right now."

"Don't worry," he said. "It's there. Or Slotkin will get what I promised you."

"It's my satchel," I said. "When I get the word, you'll get the money, but not the satchel."

He shook his head. "A cheap private eye, worrying about his crummy suitcase. What are you getting for the job, Sherlock, twenty bucks?"

"Fifteen and the gas," I said, "and twenty cents for every shell I have to use."

Tommy said, "Keep a civil tongue in your head, skinny. I don't like lippy hoodlums."

"Go easy on him, Tommy," I said. "The old gent's scared. He's lost his moxie and he's scared."

5.

Next to me, the thin man smiled and I thought there was some anticipation in it.

I was back on the two lane asphalt road that led into Canyon Springs and to our right was a modern motel and restaurant with a mammoth parking lot.

I said, "You stay in the car with skinny, Tommy. I'll take the money inside until I get in touch with Slotkin."

"Right," he said. "Park out of view of the highway, though."

I pulled around behind the ell the motel office made and took the ignition keys. It was almost dark now, and all the motel lights were on. I didn't want to bring skinny into that bright office; just seeing him would make any desk clerk in the country phone for the police.

I had the unlisted number Slotkin had given me and I phoned him collect. He must have been sitting on the phone; he answered immediately.

"Puma," I said. "What's the word?"

"Give them the money," he said. "She phoned me two minutes ago from a drugstore in Hollywood."

I told him okay and hung up. I went out to the car wondering how the police would like this; she had been free and in a public place *before* her abductors had taken delivery of the ransom.

I had an urge to keep the money and turn Skinny over to the local law, but I'd been paid to do a job, not act like a citizen. I wasn't proud of myself as I opened the door of the car.

"Well?" Skinny said.

"The money's yours, boy. Should I leave you here with it, or do you want me to take you back to the house?"

He smiled in the reflected light from the motel office. "Leave me here; you've been followed all the way."

I gave him the money, keeping the grip. He tucked the package under his arm and said, "Drive careful, shamus. There's a lot of desert ahead of you." He climbed out of the car and headed across the parking lot toward the road.

We watched him approach a three-year-old Mercury on the other side of the street. Tommy said, "Ornery bastard, isn't he? I don't think he likes me."

"We'll never see him again, probably," I said. "Want to climb up in front now?"

He shook his head. "I think I'll try to get some shut-eye. I'll curl up on the back seat."

The Merc was still parked at the curb when we headed out of town. It was dark now, and traffic would be light until we got back on 99. The state patrol car was no longer at the corner.

Easy money, *I thought*. But if the police swallowed this as a legitimate snatch, I'd have to believe that Slotkin owned the Department. It smelled every way but right. So, what was all that to me? I was paid.

It continued to bother me.

A half mile past the cut-off, I saw the lights beginning to move up from behind. For no reason at all, I said to Tommy, "What do you think Skinny meant about all that desert ahead of us?"

"Just words," Tommy said drowsily. "He had to sound tough."

"A car turned off back there from the Canyon Springs road," I told him, "and he's catching up. Be careful."

He sat up. "Why? Look, we paid, didn't we?"

"Sure. But both of us could put the finger on Skinny. I don't think he meant it that way. You were along, which he didn't expect. And he's one of those professional tough guys, remember."

Behind, the car's headlights grew closer. Another car was coming from the opposite direction, and I told Tommy, "See if you can get a look at that car behind in the headlights of this one coming. See if it's the Merc."

A few seconds after the car went past, Tommy said, "It's the Merc, all right, Joe. I'm going to lower this back window."

"Don't," I said. "If they shoot at us, it's better to have the windows closed. And don't you do a thing, Tommy, unless they shoot at us."

"I won't shoot unless they do," he said. "But I'm going to lower this window."

"As they start to go by," I said, "I'll hit the brakes. Be ready for that."

The lights grew and now they darted back at me from the rear-vision mirror. I waited until they began to swing out to pass before taking my foot off the accelerator.

I misjudged the speed of the car behind; it was next to us before I could touch the brake. I heard the blast of the sawed-off, and then another shot, but heard no answering shot from the rear seat before the third shot hit my shoulder.

The shock of it made me twist the wheel and the Plymouth went screaming to the right. I almost caught it in time. I would have caught it in time if the arroyo hadn't been there, and the thick concrete wall of the culvert.

The right front wheel caught that wall and we went careening end for end across the road and into the ditch on the other side. The last thing I remember was flying through the air, free of the car, my shoes lost from the impact. *The sand could be soft,* I thought; *the softness of the sand could keep me alive.*

6.

I didn't regain consciousness for two days. When I did, I was in a Los Angeles hospital and one of Hal Slotkin's associates was sitting in a chair next to the bed.

He smiled at me. "Feeling better?"

"I don't know. I don't know how I felt before. Where am I?"

He told me.

I said, "How about Tommy?"

"Tommy? Do you mean Mr. Verch?"

"That's right."

"He's—dead. He died before the car turned over."

I closed my eyes.

The young lawyer said, "Don't worry about a thing, now. All your bills here will be taken care of, and your car's almost all rebuilt by now. That'll be taken care of, too."

"Why?" I asked.

He smiled at me. "Why not?"

"I've a lot of regard from Mr. Slotkin," I said, "but I never for a second confused him with Santa Claus."

The young man smiled knowingly. "Maybe it's not his money. That needn't concern you. Your concern is to get well. Don't worry, now."

It concerned me. Tommy Verch was dead and that had to concern me. But I didn't argue with the young man. I never argue with anyone *before* they pick up the tab.

I'd been brought here from the hospital in Riverside, and I could guess I'd been brought here so it would be convenient for one of the Slotkin young men to remain at my bedside. I relaxed and tried to regain my strength and forget Tommy Verch. The nurse brought me all the papers; that was another expense somebody was shouldering, a private nurse. I had good coverage in all the papers.

And then, as frosting for this expensive cake, I was honored with a visit from Laura Spain. Complete with five photographers, seven reporters, two publicity men and a Slotkin representative. If she was coming to my bedroom as reward, you'd think the least she could have done would be to come alone.

She was certainly a beauty, and her advertised charm was not over-rated. If she had come alone, I think I might have forgotten Tommy Verch.

The morning after her visit, I walked out of the hospital with a Slotkin man, and my car, looking better than ever, was ready for me on the hospital parking lot.

There, the Slotkin man said, "If we can be of any further service, don't hesitate to call on us, will you?"

"I won't," I promised. "Maybe you could give me the West Side Station, huh, for my very own?"

He frowned. "I don't understand, Mr. Puma."

"Yes, you do," I said. "We all understand each other. Take care of yourself, young fellow." I patted his shoulder and got into my car.

He was still standing there, watching me, when I turned into the traffic heading west.

At my office, I checked the week's accumulation of mail and wrote checks for a couple of bills I'd owed for some time. I was writing a letter to my aunt when the phone rang.

It was Hal Slotkin. He said, "I've heard that you're not happy. Would you mind telling me why?"

"This phoney kidnapping rankles in my small soul, I guess, Mr. Slotkin."

"What makes you think it was phoney?"

I gave him all the reasons. The too early release of Miss Spain, Skinny not counting the ransom money and not being worried about the State Police and his not even looking in the back of my car before climbing into it.

"So, maybe he was an amateur."

"Maybe. An *armed* amateur, and a real tough, cool one. I don't think he was an amateur thug, though this may have been his first snatch."

Silence, and then, "Well, *I* only represented a client. I'm not involved personally. You believe that, don't you?"

"I think I do, Mr. Slotkin."

"So what difference does it make? You got paid and you're not the police."

"In a way, I'm a policeman. I'm licensed by the state. But that isn't important. Mr. Slotkin, the important thing is that a man is dead."

"And that's important to you?"

"Yes. Isn't it to you?"

"It used to be," he said. "I suppose it should be." He sighed. "Well, I guess we have nothing else to say to each other, Mr. Puma."

"I guess not," I said. "Thanks for the business, anyway."

I hung up and sat there, angry for no reason I could isolate, burning. I was no knight; I didn't even have a horse. Why should I burn?

I phoned Slotkin again, intending to ask for Miss Spain's unlisted phone number. His office girl said Mr. Slotkin was not in and Miss Spain's phone number was never given out to anybody.

Well, I knew where she lived; I went down and climbed into the rebuilt Plymouth.

7.

The house was low and probably the architect had tried to give the impression of a sprawling, western ranch house. What emerged from the drawing board was a low, red, shake-roofed home for a Hollywood star who entertains informally.

The maid asked, "Did you have an appointment, Mr. Puma?"

"No, I didn't. I'm just returning Miss Spain's recent visit to me. She didn't have an appointment that day, either."

The maid frowned. "Are you the—the—"

I nodded.

"One moment, please," she said.

In a few minutes, she came back to say, "This way, please."

It was a sunny day; Laura Spain was pool-side in a Bikini. Her body belonged to a younger woman, her face was slick with oil.

"Mr. Puma," she said, smiling. "How pleasant."

I stood at the pool's edge and looked down. "Is this where you had the champagne?"

"That's right. Though the story was exaggerated. We only filled it to a depth of three feet."

She was sprawled on a pad; I sat down next to her and said, "I've been thinking about this kidnapping, Miss Spain. The whole business smells of fraudulence."

Her young-old face stiffened. "Really? And why?"

I gave her the same reasons I'd given Slotkin.

She reached out and took a package of cigarettes from a low stand nearby. I lighted one for her. She looked at the water, and said, "I've no idea what the standard operating procedure for kidnappers is. You might be right about their lack of experience. But even if it was a monstrous publicity stunt, why are you concerned?"

I said wearily, "It's a sad civilization that makes me keep explaining that *a man is dead.*"

"Millions are," she said reasonably. "Thousands of men die every day, I imagine."

"Not violently in my car, working for me," I answered. "Don't you feel *any* responsibility for his death?"

She nodded. "Some. What can I do about it?"

"You could tell me who the men were you hired. I'm sure you didn't expect them to extend their services to murder."

Her face was stone. "I didn't hire any men. It was not a publicity stunt, Mr. Puma. And even if it were, would you actually expect me to implicate myself publicly?"

I took a deep breath. "No. But I had to take the chance." I stood up. "Well, I'll know the man if I ever see him again. And when I do, I'll know how to work the rest of it out of him."

She shook her head. "You sound absurd. You sound like Dick Tracy. This is 1957, Mr. Puma."

"Of course," I said. "I wasn't thinking of violence. I was thinking of a deal with him."

Her eyes were blank. "You were thinking of violence. That's your kind of operation, I would bet."

I said, "If you're still in touch with them, warn them to stay out of my way."

"I don't know them," she said lightly, "but from what I've seen of them, I can imagine you don't frighten them much. Good day, Mr. Puma. Don't hurry back."

I went out, fully aware that I had learned nothing, but I *had* left a message. And if she were involved and did forward the message, I wouldn't have to look for her abductors. They would find me.

Which was emotional thinking, adolescent thinking, but I wanted to meet Skinny again so bad I could taste it. And Miss Spain had set a wave of violence into motion with her fraudulent stunt; she couldn't escape the responsibility of that. Which absolved me from any concern for what justice might do to her career.

I had a pair of names and two addresses still to check. The first one I went to was a four unit apartment building on Olympic in Santa Monica. This was the address of Laura Spain's second husband. He was an assembler at Douglas Aircraft now, and the manager of the apartment told me he wouldn't be home until 4:30.

Her first husband was undoubtedly also working, but the place he worked wasn't far from here. He was a car salesman for a Venice Ford agency.

He was a big man, almost as big as I am. He wore an Italian silk suit and a hand-painted tie and an air of complete disillusionment. His face was florid, the face of a heavy drinker, but still handsome in a completely virile way. He was on the used-car lot when I drove up.

He said, "I'm due for a coffee break in five minutes. Hang around and we'll go across the street."

Five minutes later, in a crummy greasy spoon on the busiest street in Venice, Jack Dugan, Laura Spain's first husband, gave me the story of that early romance.

She was nineteen when he met her, a refugee from Oklahoma, a thin, tough, very attractive girl whose innocence was at least five years behind her even then.

I said, "I never got that picture from the fan magazines; I had the feeling she came out here clean as new snow and won a beauty contest."

He smiled. "Sure. Not that I'm rapping Laura, understand. She still sends me a buck now and then for auld lang syne and she's bailed me out of some monumental drunks. There's nothing cheap about the girl. It's just that she has this damned driving urge to stay way up there on top."

"We built a civilization on it," I said. "Knowing her, would she have the guts to pull a phoney kidnapping for ink?"

"For publicity," he said, "Laura would arrange to have Eisenhower kidnapped." He shook his head musingly. "And you know, she might get away with it, at that?"

"What was her family like? Did you ever meet them?"

He had. And he told me about them and I wondered why a man who still got a "buck now and then" should go into such detail to hand a private operative a case against his benefactor.

And because I wondered, I asked him. "Why give me all this? How can you benefit from giving me all this?"

"Benefit?" he said. "Look, I'm a drunk and a pitch man and a lot of things that aren't exactly admirable. But I'm still a human being, right?"

"Right," I agreed. "So—?"

"So a man is dead, isn't he? Isn't it important that a man is dead?"

"It always has been to me," I assured him, "but I was beginning to think I was old-fashioned." I smiled at him. "I'll pay for the coffee. And when I need a new car, I'll head this way."

"Do that," he said. "I might even rob you less than the others. Who knows?"

I left him, and went back to the office. I didn't think there was any need to look up Laura's second husband. She'd been young when she had married her first; he had her true story, the story she'd told him before she realized that in Hollywood, backgrounds are invented, not lived. He could be quite possibly the only man in the town who had her true story. Until now.

8.

I sat in the quiet office and nothing happened. I went out for lunch and came back and the place was still quiet. I had a hunch now who the skinny man was, and maybe if I sent the hunch out on the grapevine, it would stir up some action. But if I sent it out on the grapevine in this town, the damage would be done but Tommy Verch's killer might still be free.

That blast from the sawed-off had been meant for both of us. He hadn't shot out of pique; he was a pro. He had hoped to kill us both because either of us could identify him.

And if he was a pro, would he come here, into this best-policed town in America, Beverly Hills? There were a number of areas in the county where the police protection is not exceptional; this town would be dangerous hunting grounds. Of course, he didn't lack guts. He had a number of lacks, undoubtedly, but I was sure guts wasn't one.

Why should I sit there burning; solvent, fat and alive? What was Tommy Verch to me? A colleague, a brave and humorous man who lived as honestly as he could in a trade where that wasn't always good business. A man who had been forced to risk his life for two hundred dollars and lose. Tommy Verch was important.

I hadn't put my car on the lot; I'd left it parked right in front of this building so anyone who was interested could see I was in the office. I could have gone home and waited, but I had carpeting on the floor at home and that's harder to clean than the asphalt tile of the office.

The door opened and the hand in my lap stirred. It was Doctor Graves, the young dentist from the office next door. He said, "How about some golf tomorrow afternoon?"

"Maybe. I'll let you know tonight."

"What's the matter?" he asked. "You look nervous."

"I'm still not right. Had a concussion, you know. And a badly strained back."

"Maybe we'd better forget the golf, huh? The back—"

"I'll let you know tonight," I repeated. "How's everything otherwise?"

He yawned. "All right. I'm solvent. I sure get sick of looking into people's dirty mouths, though."

"I get sick of looking into their dirty souls," I said.

He chuckled. "Oi, a philosopher. Two hundred and twenty pounds of thought. You look like you're waiting for Armageddon." He winked. "Call me at home, Joe. Good luck, kid."

I waved my left hand. My right was still in my lap.

My mom had always insisted I had prescience, but my mom had a lot of peasant superstitions. I knew I was more certain than I had a reasonable right to that I'd see Skinny again. I thought I knew who he might be, and if I didn't see him, I would go to the police for help in looking up a picture of the man.

But analyzing what Jack Dugan had told me, it seemed logical that Skinny could be the man I thought he was.

In the windows behind me, the sun was now low and soon the mountains to the west would cut it from view. On the street below, the going-home traffic was noisy.

I heard footsteps in the hall going past; soon the offices on this second floor would all be vacant, all but this one. I lighted a cigarette and turned on the light. I stood by the window a few seconds, looking down at the traffic, and then came back to sit behind the desk again.

How much did Slotkin know? He was no dummy. Of course, in his business, it wasn't always wise to know too much. His job was leading people through the intricacies of the law, not writing biographies of them. He did his job well and was satisfied to stay within the limits of it.

If Tommy Verch hadn't died, I would have been happy to stay within the limits of my job, which had been to deliver some money.

It was dark now and the light overhead wasn't very bright. From the direction of Wilshire, I heard a siren and a clang of a fire truck.

From the hall outside, I thought I heard a pair of footsteps coming up the stairs. They grew louder, and they were very deliberate footsteps and now they were coming down the hall. I sat where I was.

The door opened slowly and quietly. If I hadn't been facing it, I wouldn't have heard it.

Skinny stood there. Shaved and wearing a cheap dark suit and no longer sporting the red jockey cap. His hair was black, not sprinkled with gray as his beard had been. He had one hand in his jacket pocket.

He came in and closed the door quietly behind him. "You made it, eh?" he said. "Tough guy. The way that heap went end for end, I figured you for a goner."

"I'm tough," I said. "Peasant stock. Where's your brother, waiting in the lot behind here, with the engine running?"

His face showed a momentary bewilderment. "Brother—? How'd you guess—" The face went blank again. "You don't know nothing."

"I know there was an Okie named Lorna Spangler who had a couple of no-good brothers," I said evenly. "A couple of punks who thought Dillinger and Nelson and that breed were the greatest Americans of their generation. The girl grew up to become Laura Spain. What happened to the boys? We could find out, I suppose. We could check."

He said nothing, studying me carefully.

"And when Lorna, or Laura, wanted somebody she could trust to pull a cheap publicity stunt, what better pair than these no-good brothers? Man, you've aged a hell of a lot more than she did, haven't you? You didn't take care of yourself like she did, bumming around, knocking off the kind of cheap jobs you're big enough for."

"You're trying to make me hate you, eh?" He looked at me with his head cocked to one side. "Why, shamus? What's your beef? You got paid."

"I'm sick of explaining it," I answered. "Why are you here now?"

"Unfinished business," he said. "You're not much, but you're still a finger."

"I was hoping you'd come," I said. "This thing was getting too personal. It was building into an obsession."

He smiled. "And here I am." In his pocket, his hand moved and came out holding the big .45.

In my lap, my hand moved and my .38 came up swiftly and I just kept pulling the trigger, even though the first shot caught him in the neck.

It's an asphalt tile floor.

His brother was waiting, the engine running, when the local gendarmes put the arm on him. They'd been watching the office, but not looking for a '57 Olds.

When they heard the shots, soon after Skinny had come up, they realized the man in the Olds could be their man.

If Skinny hadn't shaved, he would have been picked up downstairs because then they would have seen the gray in his beard. His hair was so black, it didn't seem logical to the men below that his beard could have any gray in it. His hair was touched up, we learned later.

I was glad Skinny had shaved. Because though he was guilty of murder and would have been eligible for the gas chamber, there was a possibility he might have avoided that.

There are an awful lot of smart criminal lawyers in this town.

Just look in the phone book.

Hooked
Robert Turner

February 1958

The fishing camp was down a rutted dirt road, about five hundred yards off the highway. Marchand had never been there before. It wasn't quite the way he had visualized it; not rundown and dirty, at all. It was really quite a place, well kept and prosperous looking, and Marchand could see how, living here, having a business like that, a man who wasn't too ambitious, didn't want too much out of life, the outdoor type who liked boats and water and people who went in for fishing, could be quite happy with it.

First there was a small, store-like building, with a sign over it that said you could buy all kinds of bait and rent tackle there and that they served food, beer and soft drinks. Behind that, closer to the water, was the house. It was a fairly new, modern looking house, in the $15,000 class. At the lake's edge there was a small pier and a half dozen trim, freshly painted small boats suitable for rowing or attaching an outboard.

Marchand parked the shiny new Cad Eldorado convertible near the store and settled back comfortably in the seat to wait. He'd gotten out here a little early, about fifteen minutes before Gladys had told him to be there.

In a few minutes a girl came out of the store, walked toward the car. She was barefoot and she wore jeans and a blue work shirt, the tails of it out and tied in a knot in front, baring her midriff and accentuating the most beautiful development Marchand had ever seen on a woman. He could hardly believe his eyes as he watched her walk toward the car. The jeans fitted her long, finely carved legs as though she'd been born in them.

For a moment, Marchand was almost afraid to look at her face. She had to be a hag in the face department, he told himself; there had to be *some* catch to a girl with a body like that being stuck way out here in the sticks.

But there wasn't. Under a smartly coiffed cap of sun-glistening, mahogany red, softly waved hair, was the most strikingly beautiful face Marchand had ever seen. The eyes were widely set and unbelievably dark and liquid looking, under their long, thick, spiked lashes. The brows were delicately winged. Under a small, saucily tilted nose, her mouth was full and moistly pouting, made for kissing.

Just before she reached the car, she smiled and her teeth were tiny and so even and white the smile almost blinded Marchand. He had had his share of lovely women in his twenty-seven years, showgirls and models some of them, but he'd never had one hit him like this at first sight. He thought it had something to do with the clean, wholesome, unspoiled look about her. Whatever it was, she had him flipping. He felt himself flushing and getting nervous and full in the throat like some silly school boy.

"Hi," she said. "Mrs. Marchand is still out on the lake but I imagine they'll be in pretty soon. You can wait out here or come on inside, if you like and have some coffee or a beer or something." Her voice was low and throaty, yet completely feminine.

Somehow, Marchand got words out without stammering, without his voice breaking with emotion; he never knew how.

"So you're a mind reader, as well as being beautiful," he said.

She laughed. "Not exactly. I recognized the car." She was close to it now and she trailed her fingers, lightly, lovingly along the glittering chrome trim. "How could I miss?"

"You like this buggy, huh?"

She shook her head, wonderingly. "It's almost too much to believe that people own things like this." Then she looked up at him. "I didn't know Mrs. Marchand had a son."

"She doesn't." He grinned crookedly at her. "I happen to be her husband."

"Oh!" She looked quickly away, flustered. "I—I'm sorry."

"Forget it. It happens all the time. It's what I get for marrying a woman almost twice my age."

"Mrs. Marchand's very nice," she said. "She's sweet."

"Yeah?"

"Well, I think she is. She's very nice to us."

"You old man Foster's daughter or do you just work here?"

"I'm his daughter. I'm Nila. I'm just home during the summer. I go to State."

"Oh."

"Oh, college is all right."

"Sure, except with a girl like you, it's a waste of time."

"What do you mean a girl like me?" her eyes flashed. "Just because my father runs a fishing camp here in Florida doesn't mean I intend to spend *my* life here, either, just because *he* goes for it."

"I didn't mean that," he said. "What I meant was, a girl with your looks doesn't need a fancy education to make out. You should be in New York or Chicago or L.A., right now, knocking down fifty an hour as a model, maybe working in TV, even the movies."

"Uh-huh," she said. "Listen, Mr. Marchand, girls with good features and a nice shape are a dime a dozen in those places. I know what the score is. Maybe if I had a lot of money to pay for a big time photographer for glamor shots, for a press agent, for the works in a high priced beauty salon once a week, for the kind of clothes it takes, for a top voice and drama coach. Without those things it'd be a rat race just like anything else."

"You shouldn't have any trouble getting somebody to finance you."

"That's a nice, polite word for it," she said. She saw him staring at the bulging front of her blouse. Her voice froze a little. "You mean somebody like you, Mr. Marchand?"

He looked up at her eyes again. They stared right back at him, steadily, almost defiantly. "Ray," he said.

"What?"

"My first name. Ray. Never mind the Mr. Marchand bit. I feel old enough, being married to a woman like Gladys, without that."

"Well, Ray, then," she said. "I'm sorry, Ray, but sometimes I get a little tired of guys coming in here and giving me the dumb little country girl treatment."

"Include me out of that group. I wasn't speaking for myself. Hell, Nila, I haven't got a cent of my own. My wife's the one with the rocks."

She started to say something but then, from the lake, there came faintly the sound of an outboard motor. They both looked out toward the lake and saw a boat, about a quarter mile out, heading in.

"Here comes your wife, now. I'll see you. I'd better get back inside. My father likes to have hot coffee waiting for him when he gets back."

He watched her walk away from the car. The view was even better from the back. Because the swing of her full-rounded, tight-jeaned hips was natural and not over-done, it was twice as provocative. Watching her, Marchand felt his pulse begin to pound and his head felt hot and swollen with the blood beating through it.

"Nila!" he called out.

She stopped and half turned around, the partway twist of her body accentuating its ripely curved beauty.

"I'll be out here again," he told her. "I think I could get to like this fishing routine. I'd need a guide to take me out in a boat, though; I'm a real square landlubber. You ever available?"

"Sometimes," she said and went on into the store.

2.

Through the windshield of the car he watched his wife, Gladys, and old man Foster, who owned the camp, tie-up the boat. Then Gladys, carrying a string of several bass, all of them over three pounds, and a couple of plump crappies, walked up from the dock. Behind her, carrying the outboard motor, was Pops Foster.

They made a good pair, those two, Marchand decided; his wife, a little plumpish but generally well preserved for a woman in her fifties and Foster, about the same age but not looking it with his big, lean, rawboned body; except for the iron gray hair at the temples and a ruggedly lined face. He watched Gladys look back at Foster and jabber something so that both of them laughed.

"What the hell have they got to be so damned happy about?" he asked. "Two thirds of their dull lives already shot and they gambol about, yakking and yokking it up like school kids. Just because they've been out in a dinky boat for a few hours, throwing out a silly plug and reeling it in; out and in and if they're lucky, a couple of stupid, slimy, smelly fish get suckered into snapping at the thing? Is that it? I don't get it. . . . Now, maybe a fishing party, out on the Gulf, in a fifty foot cabin cruiser, with lots of good booze and a couple of dollies along. . . ."

Gladys came up to the car and said, "Hi, Sweetie," and took the fish around to put in the trunk compartment. Then she came back and got into the car next to him.

"Been waiting long?" she said.

"Hours," he lied.

"I'm sorry. I didn't realize we were late, but Floyd—Mr. Foster—he got to telling me about going for muskies up in Michigan and the time just went by."

She leaned toward him, one hand on his shoulder, her lips puckered. "You were sweet to get the car fixed and run out here for me. Give Momma a kiss."

He was looking past her bent-forward head toward the Fishing Camp store and he saw Nila standing there talking to her father, only Nila was looking toward the car, at him and Gladys and she could see inside, he knew.

"Oh, come on," he told Gladys. "Act your age, will you?"

She looked up and saw the direction of his gaze and turned and looked the same way. "Oh, I see," she said. "You've met Nila. Cute-looking child, isn't she?"

"Yes," he said. "She's a walking, breathing doll. She's got me nuts, just looking at her."

Gladys laughed, heartily. "You!" she said. "I should have known you'd really go for that. I meant to tell you about her and watch you come out here, sniffing around, just for kicks."

"What do you mean?"

"Look, Buster, Nila Foster isn't one of those Tampa B-girls or peelers you're so fond of. You not only wouldn't get to first base; you wouldn't even get a turn at bat, with her. That's strictly hands off, honey, if I've ever seen it and it's going to stay that way until some court clerk hands her the piece of paper that gives her the right to some guy's name."

"Is that so? You know what I think, Gladys?" he said . . . She was getting under his skin so that he had to control his voice. "I think you're just trying to discourage me because you're afraid I might really go for something like that. Then you'd lose me."

Gladys stretched her plumpish, dungareed legs out under the dash and lit a cigarette. She blew smoke. "Ray," she said, "I thought we understood each other better than that. I couldn't lose you for a million babes like Nila; not for more than an hour at a time. You know why, don't you?"

"No, I don't. I know that *you* think you know why. How do you know I'm not sick and tired of being a rich old woman's husband? How do you know I don't want out?"

"Now, Ray, dear," she said, as though reproving a child. "You know not many things make me sore, but you're starting to get close. How would you like your allowance cut off for a week again?"

He told her what she could do with her allowance and smashed down on the gas pedal. The big Cad leaped forward like a live thing. In no time the speedometer was registering over ninety.

Sitting a little rigidly, now, Gladys said: "Wouldn't it be nice and convenient for you if we had an accident at this speed? That is, if I were the only one killed."

Gradually he slowed the car and neither of them said anything for a while. Then Gladys said: "Okay, honey, you win. I feel too good to fight, any more. Maybe you're right and you'll bowl Nila right over with your beautiful looks and flashy line. Okay?"

He didn't say anything.

"Only I still doubt it," she went on, "because if the old man even catches you sniffing around her, he'll kill you He's already thrown a drunk fisherman who asked Nila for a date, into the lake. Anyhow, she's the serious type, honey, not interested in just a fast hassle. It would take too much of your time."

He still didn't answer.

"But give a whirl, doll, if it'll make you happy," she said. "You know me, not a jealous bone in my big old body and, anyhow, we had it understood that you could have your little outside parties, so long as you're discreet and don't get too serious about anyone. Okay?"

There was no answer. Marchand didn't speak again all the way home. When they got to the house, he left the car in the drive and got out, without waiting for Gladys and went on inside by himself. He went straight to the room that had been turned over to him as a studio. He set up a clean canvas. For a number of hours he painted furiously, without stopping. When he finished, exhausted, he stepped back and examined what he had done. It was a rough but effective full length portrait of Nila Foster, as he had last seen her, half turned around to look back at him.

He saw immediately that he'd captured some alive quality that he'd never been able to put on canvas before. At the same time that it awed him a little, it brought out all the fury and frustration in him.

"Christ, what's the matter with me?" he said. "Blowing my stack over some dumb kid in a hick fishing camp!"

He slapped a brush into the oils and started splashing paint haphazardly over the portrait until it was obliterated. Then he went over and flung himself face down on the studio couch, breathing as though he'd just run a long, long way.

He lay there, thinking about Nila and the things Gladys had told him about her and the way it was with him and Gladys.

When he'd married her three years before, Gladys had been considered a hopeless alcoholic. He figured he had it made. In a few years she'd either drink herself to death or fall, have some kind of an accident and he'd be set for life. Even if it took ten years, he figured he could stand it. Then a crazy thing happened, as it sometimes does with alcoholics. She just quit drinking. Nothing spectacular happened to make her do it; she just suddenly seemed to wake up to what she was doing to herself and decided it was ridiculous. She had a little trouble sticking with it the first year but after that it didn't seem to bother her at all. It only bothered Marchand.

Then, a year ago, they'd come to Florida for a vacation and Gladys had fallen in love with the place and they'd settled here permanently and she'd gone off on this outdoor life, fresh water fishing kick. It didn't bother her that Marchand didn't share her enthusiasm. He had his painting, she said.

That was another thing. Marchand had thought that with financial security, not having to worry about working for a living, being able to devote full time to it that he'd develop the real talent he was certain he had. But that hadn't happened. If anything, his work deteriorated, became even less imaginative.

He lay there thinking about that and how different it would be, with a woman like Nila Foster. When he awoke, it was morning. . . .

3.

At three o'clock that next afternoon, he could no longer stand it. Gladys was going into town to shop and Marchand got out his Corvette and headed out for Foster's Fishing Camp. Before he could get out of the car, Nila saw him and came out of the store. He watched her walk toward him. Today, she was wearing a dress, a summer cotton frock that was even more maddening than the outfit she'd worn the day before, though it only hinted at, instead of displaying, the lushness of her figure.

"I told you I'd be back," he said.

She acted flustered, almost scared. "What is it?" she said. "Why are you here?"

He raised his brows in surprise. "Why, to see you of course. Why else?"

She glanced behind her, out over the lake. "Listen, my father knows you're a married man and your wife's one of his best customers. You'd better get out of here."

"Where is he?"

"Out on the lake, around the bend, netting minnows. But he's liable to come back any minute."

He grinned. "What are you so upset about? I just tell him I want to go fishing and I want you as a guide and I've come to make an appointment."

"Are you crazy?" she said. "He wouldn't let me go out on that lake with a strange man."

"Oh, come on, honey. You're over twenty-one, aren't you? How eighteenth century can you get?"

"You don't know my father."

"From what you're telling me I don't even want to."

She glanced apprehensively over her shoulder again. She stamped her foot petulantly. "Will you *please* go away. Please. Right now, before you get me into trouble." She sounded close to crying.

He reached out of the car and caught her wrist. She tried to yank it away once and then let it stay in his grasp. Her flesh felt very smooth and warm and through his fingertips he could feel her pulse racing.

"There's got to be some time I can see you. When he isn't here, maybe? He can't be here all the time."

She shook her head, frantically and tried to pull free from his grip again. Then, her voice desperate, she said: "If I tell you, will you go, now?"

"Sure."

"Well, Mondays. Mondays there isn't much business anyway, after the weekend and we close down. He has a man come in to clean the boats and the dock, work on the motors and he usually goes into town to buy new equipment. Come back Monday."

He let her wrist slip from his hand, then and without another word, without looking at him again, she turned and ran back to the store, disappeared inside.

Trembling, his heart pumping as though after some great exertion, Marchand somehow managed to start up the car and swing around and drive back to the highway. All the way home he sang into the wind rushing past the windshield of the sports car, at the top of his lungs. He hadn't done anything like that since he was a kid of sixteen.

That night for the first time in months he was really, genuinely pleasant with Gladys. He took her out to dinner and then to a movie in town. He didn't see much of the movie, though. He kept thinking about Nila, what it was going to be like with her; he kept going over every wonderful, delightful detail of what it was going to be like, again and again. . . .

4.

The coming Monday, it wasn't anything like he had dreamed it would be. It was the worst day he'd ever spent in his life, for a while.

She was there, all right, and her father wasn't. The only other person at the Camp was a Negro, working on the boats and Nila told Marchand not to worry about him; that he couldn't get her in trouble with her father because the Negro was deaf and dumb.

She was wearing white sharkskin shorts, the kind, buckled at the sides so tightly that the edge of the material bites into the flesh and so snug all around that a man wonders how the girl ever got into them and why they don't split with her slightest movement. And for the first time Marchand really saw her legs. They were tanned not too darkly, so that they looked burnt but were the color of a Malayan woman's. The thighs and calves were in perfect proportion. No muscles or tendons showed and yet there was not the slightest flabbiness either; just taut-skinned fullness, roundness. Her waist was so tiny it cut in sharply from the arch of her hips.

The first moment he looked at her that day, Marchand just stood there shaking his head, an awed expression on his face. She gave a short, slightly self-conscious laugh but he knew that his obvious admiration pleased her.

For a few moments they talked the meaningless, fencing, preliminary small-talk of strangers and then Nila said: "We can go out in a boat, if you'd like. I've figured out a way so that we won't be caught even if my father should come back a little early."

"Swell," Marchand said. "What's the bit?"

She told him that at the far end of the lake there was a small strip of beach to land a boat and a path leading from it to a side road. She had already towed a boat up there and left it. Now, if they drove up to that path in Marchand's car, when he was ready to leave, she'd drop him off at the strip of beach again and come back alone in the boat. She said that she often went out on the lake alone, when her father was away and he wouldn't think anything about it.

On the dirt road, near the almost unnoticeable-from-a-distance path that led to the lake, they got out of his Corvette and started through a dense stand of jackpine and punk trees and live oak, dripping with moss. Fallen needles were a soft carpet under their feet and the Florida summer heat was softened to an almost-coolness. Walking behind Nila, Marchand felt as though the two of them, here, were all alone in the world and always had been and would be and the excitement of that was almost unbearable to him.

Several times he stopped her and moved close but it didn't do him any good. She didn't make a big routine out of it. She just looked at him, softly and whispered: "No, Ray! Please, no. Please?" And so he let her alone. If anybody had ever told him anything like that could happen, he would have gone into convulsions of laughter.

They went out onto the lake in the boat and just drifted. They were in a large cove cut off from sight from the main part of the lake and the houses and fishing camps around it. There was nothing but the thick, high breeze-waved reeds around the shore and here and there a tangle of dead tree branches reaching gnarled and twisted, out of the water and herons and cranes standing in the shallows, patiently, waiting for minnows. The sun was hot on them but the over-the-water breeze kept them from perspiring. And they sat, she at one end of the boat, he at the other and talked.

He told her about the way it was and had been with himself and Gladys. She told him how it had been very rough for her and her father and it had been only in recent years that they'd had any kind of comforts. Pops Foster had started his camp with a couple of broken down old boats and a crude shanty, with only one room.

"That's why I'm sticking through college," she said. "I don't know how, but I'm going to get a lot of money, somehow, for my father and me. Maybe I'll marry somebody with money; maybe I'll figure some way to make it. I might even try it the way you said, Ray, going to New York or California. I've been thinking about it since you mentioned it."

They talked a lot and then came the time when there seemed nothing else to talk about and suddenly he got up and moved to her end of the boat and sat beside her. "Nila." he said, very quietly, "Why won't you let me kiss you? You know how bad I want to, don't you? You know how it is with me, don't you, how it's been since the first second I saw you? Girls always do."

She turned her head away. She didn't answer.

"It's the same with you, too, isn't it?" he said. "Guys know, too. . . . And you *want* me to kiss you, so why won't you let me? I've never asked before, Nila, but I knew I had to with you. You'll let me, won't you?"

"No. Ray." she said.

"Why not? There isn't any reason, really, not any good enough reason."

"Yes, there is. Once I kiss you, Ray, I'll be finished; you could do anything you wanted to me or with me. I can't have that. You're married, Ray. I've always done everything all at once and big and for keeps. When I love a man, it's going to be that way, too. And it can't be that way with us, Ray, don't you see?"

"No," he said. "All I see is that we've got to have each other or we'll both go crazy."

It became something he couldn't control then; the hot beautiful nearness of her was too much for him.

She fought him and the strength of her surprised him. It also made him that much more desperate and determined to have her. When both of them fell to the floor of the boat, she stopped struggling quite so hard. Then, a moment later, so suddenly it surprised him, her furious writhing and twisting was no longer against what he was trying to do but with it, helping him.

5.

His head was in her lap and she was finger-combing his thick, tousled black hair. He said: "I don't know, Nila. I just don't know. Don't think I haven't thought about it, before I met you, even. I've wanted out for a long time, now but there just isn't any way. Sure, I could probably get some kind of a divorce but I wouldn't get any real loot out of it. I'd be lucky if I even got her to pay the costs. She's a stubborn old gal and if she got really riled-up, which she would, she'd fight me all the way."

Nila didn't say anything.

After a while Marchand said: "I don't expect you to understand. Anybody who hasn't really *had* a lot of money, couldn't possibly. You don't know how wonderful it is, honey. Christ, I could never go back to being poor again. Not ever."

She sighed. "I don't blame you. I guess I do understand and I wouldn't want you to, even. If we did it that way, you'd be miserable in a few weeks and then I would, too. Remember I told you I want money, too."

"Aw, hell," he said. "We'll think of something. We'll work something out." He reached up to pull her head down to kiss him.

She pulled away. "Will we, Ray? I don't think so. I think it's pretty hopeless. I'm not sorry for what happened this afternoon. I'm glad. But it's not going to happen again. I'm not going to see you any more, Ray. This was crazy and it was wonderful while it was happening, but it's over now. I mean that."

He protested, argued, but it did no good. She remained adamant and finally she had to leave and he walked back through the pine-scented, cool, silent woods alone to his car.

The next week was hell for Marchand. He fought it every way he could; he got drunk; he went over to Tampa and blew his whole week's $400 allowance from Gladys on a whole roomful of B-girls; he fought with Gladys constantly, but none of it did any good. He thought of Nila all the time, when he ate, when he drank, even when he slept. And as Monday came closer, he knew that no matter what, he had to see her again.

Monday afternoon, he drove out to the camp and he almost went insane when he found that Nila wasn't there. He finally learned, through the gesticulations of the deaf and dumb Negro, working on the boats, that Nila had taken one of them and gone out on the lake. Then, after much futile motioning and trying to convey his idea, unsuccessfully, he finally got through to the Negro that he'd pay him to fix a motor on one of the boats and let him go out. The Negro said no, until he saw the twenty dollar bill Marchand held out.

Marchand found her, lying on the small strip of sandy beach, in the cove, where they'd rendezvoused the week before. She must have heard the sound of the motor coming toward shore, but she never looked up. Even when Marchand beached the boat and walked over to her and kneeled beside her, she didn't look up. She lay with her eyes closed. She was wearing a strapless black bathing suit, zipped down one side.

Marchand said: "Why weren't you there, Nila? Why did you do that to me? I almost went crazy when you weren't there."

She didn't answer for a moment and he watched the deep rise and fall of the slopes of her breasts, overflowing the top of the swimsuit, showing an edge of whiteness against the tan. Then she said:

"I was afraid to be there. I guess I knew you'd come and I knew I wouldn't be able to refuse you, yet I *couldn't* see you again."

"You *are* seeing me, though. Right now."

"Yes," she said. "Even with my eyes closed. The way I've been seeing you all week."

He lowered his face against her throat and fastened on a small pulse beating there. His hand fumbled for and found the zipper of the suit. "Nila, Nila, Nila," he whispered . . .

The idea came to him, afterward, when Nila wanted them to go swimming off the little beach and he had to admit to her that he'd never learned to swim. She stared at him, amazed, as though she'd never heard of such a thing. He was a little embarrassed about it. Almost defensively, he said:

"Hell, lots of people can't, Nila."

"I suppose," she said. "I guess I've just never met any of them before."

"You've met one other," he said. "My wife. Gladys can't swim a stroke, either."

"She can't?" Nila said. Then a strange, dreamy look came into her eyes and suddenly she turned her face away. "Oh," she said. "That was terrible, awful! I—don't know what's come over me."

"What?" he said. "What are you talking about?"

"What I was thinking." She still couldn't look at him.

"What was it?"

"About your wife. It—was a terrible thing to think of, Ray, but I—well, I just couldn't seem to help it. Forget about it, please, will you? I don't even want to talk about it."

"Maybe we should talk about it." He took hold of her shoulders, his fingers digging in. "What were you thinking about Gladys, Nila? Something about the fact that she can't swim? You were thinking about her going out on the lake, all the time, weren't you? You were thinking how convenient it would be if something would happen; if a storm would come up and the boat would turn over and sink or something, weren't you?"

"No, Ray!" she said. "No, no, I wasn't."

"Yes, you were." He was talking almost breathlessly now and his mind seemed to be going wild. He was suddenly full of a weird excitement.

"All right." She turned back to face him and her lower lip protruded a little, defiantly. "It was wrong, of course, but maybe I was. Maybe I was even wishing it *would* happen, but it won't, of course."

"You mean because your father is always out there in the boat with her. Is that what you mean?"

"Of course. He's a very powerful swimmer."

"Yeah," Marchand said. He turned away from her and began pacing up and down the beach. Then he came back and stood in front of her. "But your father doesn't *have* to be out there in the boat with her from now on. Why couldn't I suddenly decide to take up, fishing? Why couldn't I start going out there in the boat with her?"

She pulled back away from him, her eyes very large and frightened looking, her mouth O'd. "Ray!" she gasped. "What are we talking about? Are we out of our minds or something? We've got to stop talking like this."

"Do we? She could fall out of the boat, couldn't she? If I happened to rock it at the wrong time or something? The lake is pretty deep, isn't it, in places?"

She nodded. "Out in the middle, it's very deep. But this is silly, Ray. It's just crazy talk. Even if it wasn't, it would be stupid. It would be so obvious. They'd get you for it, Ray. After all, the circumstances *would* be suspicious, you so much younger than Gladys and she's so wealthy. It would look awfully bad, Ray."

"Why, for Christ's sake?" he said. "It would be an accident."

"They'd wonder why you couldn't save her. You could reach out an oar to her. Then there are those two seat cushions, you know, the ones the law says have to be there, one to a person. They're life preservers, you know, filled with cork or kapok or something. All you'd have to do would be to throw her one of those."

"Yeah," he said. "You're right, I'm afraid."

She moved into his arms and she was trembling all over, now. "Ray, Ray, we've got to stop this. We can't do anything like that and you know it. You *know* it!"

"Wait a minute," he said. "The life preservers, those cushions. You've given me the answer."

She looked up at him, her eyes still frightened.

"Don't you see, honey," he said. "It's a natural. I don't push her, at all. The boat tips over. I tip it. But before I do, I get hold of her cushion, as well as my own, on some pretext. When we're both in the water, I'll shove the boat away so she can't hold onto it. I'll have both cushions. . . . Later, I'll tell them that one of the cushions just floated out of reach when the boat tipped over. I'll tell them I tried to get to her but she went down before I could reach her. With me not being able to swim, either, it's a natural. That day, before we go out, I'll make some kidding remark to your father about neither one of us being able to swim."

She pressed her whole body against him, now, her fingernails digging into his shoulder blades. "Oh, no, Ray, no!" she whispered. "Please, no, Ray. Stop it! Stop it!"

"Stop it?" He felt filled with a vicious, terrible exhilaration, the way he imagined it would feel to be soaring on some narcotic. "You can't stop something like this, Nila. It was *meant* to be—the whole thing. Don't you see?"

"No," she said again but there was less spirit in the protest, this time.

"Nila, you know how much she's worth?"

She shook her head.

"Over three quarters of a million dollars. Do you have any *idea* what it's like to have that kind of money?"

"But—would you get it, Ray, if—"

"Of course. She has no living relatives, not even distant ones. And she's never made a will. Her lawyer's got after her about it a number of times but she just treats it as a joke. She says she's nowhere near ready to die. You don't know her. She won't even admit to herself that she's beginning to get old. Not seriously."

"You'd never get away with it, Ray."

"You're crazy; it can't miss. Now I'm on the right track, all the little pieces are beginning to fall into place. You'll be on shore, watching that day. You'll see the whole thing. She stood up, we'll tell them and leaned over too far to pull in a fish and, when she lost her balance, started to fall, she grabbed the edge of the boat and capsized it."

"It'll still look funny, Ray. I mean, you're suddenly going out with her like that, when you've never cared anything about fishing."

"I've thought of that, too, Nila. That's easy. It won't happen the first time I go out with her. Sure, I'll suddenly decide to take up fishing, to be more companionable to my wife, but what's wrong with that? Especially if the accident doesn't happen until we've already been out on the lake together three or four times. We'll make it the fourth trip, definitely."

"But suppose, even though you do go out with her, fishing, she still insists on taking my father along as a guide?"

"All right. If she wants him to go along the first time or two, okay. I let him. But then I just tell her I don't want him along any more; I just want the two of us to be alone for a change."

She rubbed her mouth softly against his shoulder. "I don't know, Ray. It's such a horrible thing to do, to even think about."

"Look," he told her. "Dreaming about getting rich, getting that kind of money by working hard for it, through a lucky break or something, is kid stuff. It's pipe-dream stuff. It never happens. You've got to have the guts and cold nerve to pull something big, to go *after* the money, to let nothing stop you. You think we'll ever get it any other way—either of us?"

She stepped back away from him and closed her eyes and put the back of her hand against her forehead.

"All right, Ray. All right. But don't let's talk about it any more. I feel a little sick and my head's starting to hurt. We can't rush right into it, anyhow. Let's think it over for a week."

"All right, honey," he said. He smiled, faintly. He was pretty sure he'd sold her. Any thinking she did about it from now on, would be the right way.

7.

That night he started right in, priming Gladys, so that she wouldn't be suspicious, later. He bought a paperback book about fresh water angling, at a drug store. He asked Gladys a lot of questions about the sport.

She looked at him curiously, said: "What's the pitch, lover. This is out of character for you."

"Maybe I'm just getting smart," he said. "I've been thinking a lot about it. I figure there must be something to this fishing gimmick, so many millions of people seem to get a charge out of it. I don't want to miss anything, but how'll I know, if I don't look into it a little."

She shook her head, wonderingly. "For the first time since I met you, you really surprise me; you've caught me off guard. Well, you won't last long at it, that's one sure thing. You just aren't the type, Handsome—even though there isn't supposed to *be any* type."

"Well, I figure a little sunshine and fresh air and mild exercise might be good for me, too. I feel pretty edgy and kind of rundown, these days. No interest in anything, even my painting, you know. Maybe it would be like a kind of therapy."

"Maybe," she said. "You'll try it once, probably, and that'll be it."

Two days later, Marchand went fishing with his wife. Gladys bought a spinning outfit and some plugs for him from Nila, in the little store. Nila scarcely looked at him, all the time and he knew for sure, then, that she was going along with him.

Pops Foster went out with them, that first time. Marchand was surprised to find that he was a likeable old guy, who knew how to handle a boat and seemed to have an uncanny instinct about where they'd find fish. He had a laconic, dry sense of humor, too, Marchand learned and seemed to be surprisingly intelligent in a shrewd, native sort of way. Following Foster's advice, carefully, Marchand landed his first fish, a three and a half pound bass, on his fourth cast. In a little less than three hours they had taken their limit and in spite of himself, Marchand was excited and happy about the expedition. He didn't have to fake it.

On the way back, Foster watched Marchand examining the catch and said: "Reckon the bug's bitten your mister pretty hard, Miz Marchand. You probably won't be able to keep him away from the lake, from now on."

Gladys chuckled. "If I hadn't seen it, I wouldn't have believed it. But the real test'll be when we spend a few hours out here some day, one of those bad days, and don't even get a strike. That separates the men from the ribbon clerks in this sport."

Marchand just grinned at them.

That night, in bed, he thought about all that had happened. But by then he'd forgotten the excitement of the sport, itself. Another, greater excitement seized him. The first big step had been taken. And both Gladys and old man Foster had been sold on his enthusiasm. There would be no cause for suspicion on that score. He wished he could see Nila alone for five minutes, just to tell her how well it was going. But he knew that wouldn't be wise. It would be best to stay completely away from her from now until it was all over and probably even for some time after that. It might even be best if they waited until the end of the summer and she started back to College, before he saw her again. It would probably look bad for him to go back to the lake where his wife had drowned. Just thinking about waiting that long before he could hold Nila's hot young writhing body close to his own again almost made him sick; made him feel empty and depressed. But he would have to be patient.

Two days later, Gladys was ready to go fishing again. She didn't seem surprised that Marchand volunteered to go with her.

She just shrugged and said: "After today, you'll probably have had it. We probably won't have much luck. There's quite a wind and the lake will be plenty choppy. But we'll see."

They got out to Foster's camp about three o'clock in the afternoon. There was no sun; the sky was completely overcast and a stiff wind was blowing off the lake. On the way out, Marchand had suggested that this time they go out alone. He said that he wanted to see what he could do by himself, without a guide supervising his every move. Gladys didn't seem too surprised and offered no protest.

Both old man Foster and his daughter, Nila, were on the dock, when Marchand and his wife shoved off, with Gladys sitting in the stem, operating the outboard. Just before they did so, Gladys shouted over the roar of the motor: "Floyd, keep your fingers crossed that we don't run into a snag and bust a hole in this scow. Neither one of us can swim, you know."

Floyd Foster showed his big strong teeth in a grin and shouted back: "You won't be in any danger. A lot of the lake is shallow. Anyhow, you've got those cushion life preservers."

Then the motor roared louder and they eased away from the dock. Gladys increased throttle as they cleared the narrow canal leading into the dock and got out onto the lake proper. Out on the water the wind was stiffer than ever and as the 15 horse motor revved up to full speed, the lake's choppy whitecaps slapped viciously against the raised prow, as though determined to pound the little craft to pieces.

When Marchand saw that instead of following the shore line toward one of the coves where they'd fished the last time, Gladys was heading straight out toward the deep center of the lake, his heart began to wallop crazily against his ribs.

Cupping his hand about his mouth to be heard over the shriek of the wind and the roar of the motor, he shouted: "Where are we going?"

"Out in the middle," Gladys shouted back. "When it's windy and choppy like this, the fish often stay out in deep water. We'll give it a try out there for half an hour, anyhow, using deep-running plugs. Okay?"

He shook his head. The excitement in him was beginning to get unbearable. Everything was setting it up for *today*. If he had the nerve to take advantage of it, he wouldn't have to wait for two more trips. *It could be today*. He remembered Gladys' remark to Foster about them not being able to swim. She was steering. Foster would remember that, tell the police that, so they'd know it was Gladys' idea to go out into the deep middle of the water. It was made to order for him, today. All he had to do now was find the final courage to go through with it.

In another few minutes, they were in dead center of the lake and Gladys cut the motor. When they drifted to a stop, heading into the wind, Gladys threw out the stem anchor.

"Hurry up and get that bow anchor in, too, honey-bunch," she told Marchand. "So we won't keep swinging around."

He watched her, standing up there in the stern, leaning way over, easing the heavy anchor down into the water. Something inside of him, shouted: *"Now! Now! You've got a perfect opportunity and the longer you wait the more likely you are to lose your nerve. A thing like this, you do fast, at the first big chance and the less thinking about it the better."*

Then he glanced back toward the shore and his heart felt as though it had dropped into his stomach. Two figures were still standing on the dock, watching them out here. Nila *and* her father. They would *both* see what he did if he did it now. He couldn't do it, now.

"Goddamn that old goat," he thought. "Why can't he stop gawping and go back about his business?"

Angrily, he reached down and picked up the chained cinder-block that was used as the bow anchor, squaring a little, to put the strain of the weight on his legs instead of his back. He didn't ease the anchor into the water the way Gladys had. In his temper, he heaved it in with a great splash that sloughed water over him and into the boat. At the same time, the effort to heave the heavy block and the sudden release of its weight, made him lurch, almost lose his balance. He had just recovered it and was about to turn around when he felt something digging into the small of his back. He twisted his head, yelling in protest.

Unbelievingly, he saw Gladys holding an oar, the blade of which she'd set against the middle of his spine and now her face was twisted partly in an evil grin and partly from the strain of her effort as she shoved against the oar with all her might.

Marchand felt himself being thrust ludicrously off balance, his arms, flailing. He felt the sound of his own screaming being whipped away from his mouth by the strong wind as he went headlong over the side of the boat.

Just before he hit the water, he twisted and saw Gladys still standing in the boat, clutching one of the cushion life preservers against her chest and hurling the other one out of the boat on the opposite side from him.

He hit the water and had a momentary surprised awareness that it wasn't cold; it was actually luke warm, near the surface. He went under and a quantity of the brackish tasting water rushed into his mouth before he could close it, choking him, making his eyes feel as though they would pop. He thrashed violently and finally surfaced. When his head broke into the air, he coughed out water and tried to gulp in air. He was looking squarely at the boat, swung around so that it was almost ten yards away from him, now and saw Gladys, holding the cushion preserver against her chest with one hand and clutching the gunwale of the small boat with the other, while she stood, furiously rocking the boat, trying to capsize it. Marchand was starting to go down again, when he saw the boat go over, saw Gladys pitch into the water, still clutching the life preserver, a good twenty feet away from him.

As Marchand started to sink again, he flailed frantically, trying to force himself toward her. But the effort only made him seem to sink faster.

The last thing Marchand thought was what a prize fish he had been. Just like a stupid, greedy, unsuspecting bass, he'd gone for the lure they'd thrown in front of him—Nila. And now that it was too late, Marchand could see how a woman like Gladys could get tired of him and fall for a man like Floyd Foster, her own age, her own type.

The fact that he knew now, for sure, that Nila had been in on it from the first moment, had suckered him so beautifully from beginning to end, was a blow so sickening that he almost welcomed the big swelling, swelling blackness that was filling his head to bursting.

One Hour Late
William O'Farrell

April 1959

It was late spring. The Southern California season had ended only the week before but the afternoon was hot. The prowl car from the sheriff's sub-station drove slowly down the beach road. It passed Point of Rocks, and a few miles farther south pulled off the road at the foot of Martinez Canyon. It parked there, facing the highway and partly hidden by a concrete bridge, in a position to observe traffic approaching from three directions. Cars came south from the sub-station and Point of Rocks, north from Palisades City, and from straight ahead down the winding canyon road. The location was a good one, from the point of view of the two deputies in the car. The shopping center on the far side of the road was a traffic focal point.

The parking spot had further advantages for one of the deputies, the man who sat erectly on the right. He was dark and good-looking, and his black eyes stared expectantly at the small cafe next to the supermarket. His name was Tommy Riggs. The big round face of the other deputy, the one who sat behind the wheel, was placidly expressionless. His name was Earl Bingham, and he didn't have the driving curiosity that Tommy had. Some people, and Tommy was among them, believed that when Earl was physically awake he was still half-asleep.

They sat there for twenty minutes, from two-thirty until ten minutes to three, and all that time Tommy watched the cafe. Customers came and went, but whoever or whatever he was waiting for did not appear. He gave an irritated glance at the Swiss cigarette lighter Earl was playing with, and turned his attention to the row of beach houses on his right.

There were fifteen or twenty of these, built close together in a straggling line along the road. The nearest was about twenty yards away. Tommy knew the weather-beaten, wooden house. It had recently been bought by a man named Warren, who had divided it into two apartments, one above the other. Warren lived in the lower level and rented the upper half to an artist and his wife. From where he sat, Tommy could see the upper bedroom window. The same look of irritation he had given the cigarette lighter crossed his face. He disliked and disapproved of artists. Tommy disapproved of any man, for that matter, who apparently had to work less hard than he did. He shifted his position, looked past the house down at the beach. He muttered an exclamation and leaned forward, watching the couple on the sand.

There's no law forbidding a man and girl to make love in public, within reasonable limits. But when the man is married and at least thirty-five, and the girl a year or two below the age of consent—well, a thing like that, it makes a guy's blood boil. Tommy said so, in anger and disgust.

"What do you mean?"

"You saw those two down there!"

Earl nodded. "He kissed her. What you mean, it makes your blood boil?"

Tommy, intent on what was happening delayed his answer. The man trotted across the sand and disappeared around a corner of the Warren house. The girl waited for a moment, then sauntered after him. She, too, disappeared, and Tommy turned back to stare at the cafe.

"I mean it makes you sick."

"Why?"

"You saw what happened. She's just a kid. You know what's happening right now?"

Earl thought about it. He nodded doubtfully. "I guess so," he said.

But he guessed wrong. What had actually happened and what was happening at the present moment, was not at all as Tommy had imagined. It was ten minutes before three. The motivation of the scene the deputies had just witnessed was only slightly tinged by sex, and it had no sexual outcome. Its beginnings lay in nothing more serious than a restlessness that had come over Dave Russell thirty-five minutes before . . .

At two-fifteen Dave had taken a half-hour break. The decision to knock off was not reached easily. He had to talk himself into it. He wasn't satisfied with the way his work was going. The magazine cover he was doing had a posed quality, lacking life.

He left his drawing board and went out on a narrow exterior stairway that climbed to the porch behind the kitchen. The porch was on a level with the beach road and, beyond it, he could see fast, thick traffic. This part of the beach was getting to be as cluttered as a business street in town.

He got his swimming trunks from the clothesline and turned back to the stairs. These descended to his own door, and then continued down to a sandy enclosure that served as both patio and front porch to the lower half of the duplex. The lower half was where Lu Warren—now that his wife, Amy, had gone home on a visit—lived alone. Dave went down the steps, his right shoulder brushing the side of the house, his left hand on the banister. If he had raised his hand he could have touched the wall of a similar but empty house next door. He returned to the living room to peel off his paint-smeared sweatshirt and khaki trousers.

After his swim, he would hang the trunks on the line exactly as they had been before. They would be dry when his wife came home at six; Helen need not know that he had taken time off from his work. The only think lost would be a little more of his self-respect—which, it seemed to him, was already wearing pretty thin. Helen had made more money in the past year than he had.

This slump was not entirely Dave's own fault. The market for his stuff had been unsettled by the easy popularity of TV. These things happen, and invariably adjust themselves in time. In time Dave also would adjust to changing conditions, but meanwhile his ebbing confidence was beginning to affect his work. He would gladly have taken a job, any job, except for the fact that his painting was the only thing that might pull them out of their present hole.

In a way, it was too bad that this was so. A job, if it accomplished nothing more, would at least have returned them to an equal, companionable level. Formerly they had swum together. Now Helen worked while he swam alone, and concealed the evidence of his loafing. It was an unpleasant, furtive situation all around.

Dressed for the beach, he wound a towel around his neck and frowned at the hand still holding it by one end. It was a strong hand with long, thin fingers. His fingers were as skillful as they had ever been. They had mastered their techniques so thoroughly that they could work without conscious direction from his mind. And there was certainly nothing the matter with his mind. His tanned body was well-muscled, he was thirty-four years old and married to an attractive woman with whom he was in love. He had been a successful commercial artist for thirteen years. This was a period during which he should have been turning out the best work of his life, and he was doing nothing of the kind. He shrugged, and went to take a swim.

Barefoot, Dave ran down the rest of the wooden steps to the sandy enclosure at the bottom. He started across it to the beach, and stopped. A girl was blocking the way, sprawled out in a deck chair. She looked as though she were about sixteen. Her short blonde hair was so light that it was almost silver. She wore a tight, black strapless swimming suit, and stared up at him with sullen but curiously beautiful gray eyes.

The french windows at the far end of the patio were open, but this was Friday and Dave knew that his landlord was not at home. Lu worked at an aircraft plant inland and about ten miles away. The girl was probably a young friend of his wife.

Dave nodded, waiting for her to move her legs. They were stretched across the only gap in the low concrete wall. She did not move.

"Hi," she said.

Dave smiled. "Didn't know anyone was here."

She shrugged. "I'm here. All of me—two hands, two feet, ten fingers and ten toes." She wriggled them. "Got nothing else to do so I just finished counting 'em. You going someplace?"

"For a swim."

"I can't swim. Not much swimmin' where I come from," she said.

Her voice and diction were straight out of the Ozarks—nasal, high and slurred. Lucius and Amy Warren had both come from Western Arkansas. The connection established itself in his mind as he waited for her to let him pass.

She continued to study him, lying motionless in the deck chair. He said, "Pardon, please," stepped across her outstretched legs and went out on the sand.

The tide was on the ebb. The waves had left behind them a small embankment about two feet high. He dropped his towel on the embankment and sat beside it, his feet on the wet sand. He did not know the girl had followed him until she appeared from behind and sat down at his side.

"Like the beach?" she asked. "I can't get used to the fishy way it smells."

She carried a bulging beach bag from which she was taking a pack of cigarettes. "Hey," she said. "It's okay. I'm a sort of cousin of Lu Warren's. Thelma. You're that artist, ain't you? Got a match?"

He shook his head.

"Never mind. I got one here." She found a box of matches and lit her cigarette.

There was no shade, and the hot sun had only declined slightly. Already there was a fight film of perspiration on Dave's skin, but Thelma seemed unaffected by the heat. She sat on her heels, slender legs folded lithely underneath her, leaning back for balance on her right hand and arm. Her left forefinger drew concentric circles on the sand, but her gray eyes did not follow the motions of her finger. They rested fixedly on him. He noticed that the sullenness had left them. It had been replaced by an expression he found difficult to define. Her eyes were interested. They contained a hint of calculation, but this was overbalanced by a wistful quality. More than anything else, they were alive and aware of their aliveness. Her slightly parted lips disclosed good teeth. She had a short, straight nose with nostrils that pulsed in rhythm with her breathing. Her body was fully developed. There was a vaccination scar high on her right leg.

Dave got up quickly. "Think I'll take a dip," he said.

The wave broke as he plunged into it. The cool salt water buoyed him up to greenish fight. He was facing seaward when his head broke surface, and he dived again to swim beneath a second wave. The ocean was relatively calm next time he came up. The backward toss of his head was unnecessary and done from force of habit; it had been years since he had worn his hair long enough to have it wash across his eyes. He swam straight out, and presently swerved to look back at the beach.

Thelma sat where he had left her. She was rummaging in her bag again, and had the settled appearance of a person who had found a place that suits her and intends to stay. His self-allotted thirty minute break was nearly up, and he swam back slowly. She rose and carried his towel to him as he waded through the surf.

"You swim good," she said.

"Thanks." He saw that she was holding a pencil and a large pad of paper, evidently taken from her bag. "Writing letters?"

She shook her head. "Who'd I write to, and who'd bother to read my letter if I did? Got nothing and nobody. An hour late and a dollar short, that's me." She held out the pad with simulated coyness. "Draw my picture . . . Dave?"

He did not want to. That little pause before she spoke his name, and the soft way in which she'd drawn it out into two syllables, making it sound like "Day-yuv," warned him off. But he had learned that it often consumes less time to grant a small favor than to frame a plausible excuse.

"Okay." He accepted the pad and pencil, and wound the towel around his neck. "Sit down."

"Here? What's the matter with your studio?"

"I don't have a studio."

She sat down, disappointed. "Thought your wife was out."

"She is. Look straight at me. Now turn your head a little to the left." Dave sketched with rapid competence. The girl was stiff, too conscious of the fact that he was studying her as a subject rather than as a female. In an effort to relax her, "When did you come to California?" he asked.

"Six months ago." She was thinking about herself now, and her face was animated. "But I just run into Lu last week. Lucky thing I did. I was working at the five-and-ten in Palisades City. I'd just got fired when he come ambling in."

"Why'd you get fired?"

"Well, they didn't exactly get a chance to fire me. I beat 'em to it. You know something? You're sort of cute," she said.

She was leaning forward, looking straight into his eyes. Dave, susceptible to her expression as a man, accepted it whole-heartedly as an artist. Something happened to his fingers. They took on independent life. He finished the rough sketch, put his initials at the bottom and handed her the pad.

"Portrait of a promising young girl," he said.

She examined the sketch and got up very slowly. But her breathing was rapid and color tinged her cheeks. "Hey," she said in a low, wondering tone, "it's me, all right. It's the way I really am." Before he could guess what she intended, she ran forward, threw her arms around him and kissed him wetly on the lips. "Gee, thanks!"

Dave disentangled himself. "Glad you like it." He went away from her, trotting across the sand. He crossed the little patio, ran up the stairs. Without pausing to shower or dress, he went directly to his drawing board. He had recaptured something down there on the beach; it was a feeling he had mislaid what seemed a long, long time before. He wanted to get it down in line and color before it slipped away. If it did slip away. Maybe this time he would be able to hang on to it.

After he had gone, Thelma stood for a quarter of a minute, looking at the flight of stairs he had just climbed. Then she followed him as far as the patio, and went through the french windows into the lower section of the house.

But, of course, the two deputies in the prowl car got a totally different impression. And that impression gave rise to an idea in the deviously working mind of Riggs . . .

Anything that Tommy said or did was perfectly okay with Earl. He knew that he was—well, say inexperienced; and he admired his partner. Tommy had taught him practically everything he knew about his job. There were lots of little extras to be made; the trick was to make them without getting caught. Little by little, just by keeping his ears open, Earl was catching on. When Tommy told him to stop clicking his lighter, he stopped doing it. "Going to get this fixed tonight," he said, and put it in his pocket. When Tommy said the blonde girl was jail-bait, and that a guy who'd take advantage of her like that ought to be jugged, Earl nodded in slow agreement.

"She's beautiful." He pronounced it *beauty-full*, reaching forward to turn on the ignition.

"The guy's one of these artists. Probably got a dozen models running after him. You and me, we get what's left." Tommy spat through the open window. "Where you going?"

Earl had started the motor. "Been an hour since we went down to the pier. Figure we got time for one more round. Okay, Tommy?"

"You're driving. Suit yourself."

The prowl car eased into the southbound traffic. Tommy studied the Warren house as they drove past. There was parking room for three cars beside a gate that opened on a flight of wooden steps. Near the gate was a small porch on a level with the road. A kitchen window opened on the porch, but it was screened. Tommy tried, but it was impossible to see inside.

They turned around at the pier, completing the southern leg of their tour, and were back at the foot of the canyon by three-thirty. There was still time for a trip to Point of Rocks before knocking off for the day. Tommy grunted affirmatively when Earl glanced at him. Ten minutes later Earl swung the car in a U-turn and parked off the road.

Tommy opened the car door and got out. The high tide had left ankle-deep pools of water on the beach fifty feet below. Children played in the pools, watched by their sun-bathing parents. A zigzag path, starting at his feet, led down to where the children were. Beyond them was the gray mass of Point of Rocks, a pile of jagged boulders stretching out into the sea. A few fishermen had climbed out to the end. They sat stolidly on uncomfortable bare rock, exposed to sun and wind. Tommy was exasperated by a patience he could not understand. The poor morons would sit there all day long, and make a big production of it if they caught so much as a single fish—a fish that could, when you counted in the cost of their tackle, time and transportation, be got a lot cheaper in the market. It just went to prove what he had always known: that people, taken as a whole, were pretty stupid. A smart operator could always make out without breaking his back or even trying very hard.

The idea which had been churning in his mind this past half-hour took recognizable form and floated to the surface. There was a chance that cradle-snatching artist might be parted from a few coarse bills. But it would have to be worked smoothly, if it was worked at all, and the layout would have to be well cased first. Tommy grinned. Maybe he could talk the girl into co-operating. An investigation under such circumstances might turn out to be fun. Like Earl had said, the little blonde was beauty-full.

He turned to the right, looked north along the wide curve of the bay at the little settlement where the sub-station was located. The cluster of buildings was similar to the one at the foot of Martinez Canyon. There was a post office next to the sub-station, a grocery store, a restaurant and cocktail lounge, a service station. About a dozen houses were on the hill above the settlement. Tommy, since he had split up with his wife, lived in a rented room in one of these. The road north of Point of Rocks was relatively new. It had been chipped out of the palisades only six years before, and was shorter by ten miles than the old road winding inland over the mountains. There was no beach. The new road ran high above sea-pounded rocks.

Earl called diffidently, "How's about it, Tommy? Getting late."

Tommy got back in the car. They reached Martinez Canyon at quarter to four, fifteen minutes before the end of their shift. Earl parked on the beach side of the highway, as he always did, and Tommy resumed his alert surveillance of the cafe. Above the door of the cafe a sign, bright green on a white background, read, *MILDRED'S PLACE. GOOD EATS*. On the plate-glass window in frosted letters had been written, *TRUCKERS WELCOME*. Two trucks and an ice cream wagon had stopped in front of it. The ice cream man was doing a good business selling to people from the beach.

A woman came to the door of the cafe. Wiping her hands on her apron, she blinked at the declining sun. She was about thirty-five, a year or two younger than Tommy, and she was well-built and had good, regular features. Once she had been pretty, but her freshness was all gone. Her neat brown hair was gathered at the nape of her neck and tied with a ribbon, but the dull colored ribbon was strictly for utility. She looked harrassed, and continuous worry had burned deep lines in her face.

Earl cleared his throat. "There's Mildred."

"Blow the horn."

The horn blared out. The woman shielded her eyes against the sun and turned toward the sound. Tommy waved. She looked directly at him and, without acknowledging his salutation, went back inside. The afternoon was still warm, but she closed the door.

Tommy chuckled. "She'll be sorry."

"You hadn't ought to treat her that way, Tommy. She's sort of nice."

"You married to her, or am I?"

"You are. I just—"

"You just shut up. I'll treat her any way I like."

Mildred walked through the opening in the counter, past the two truck drivers who were having early dinners, and went into the kitchen. Hazel, her white-haired helper, was busy at the stove. Hazel glanced at her as she walked silently to the window and sat down in a chair. From the window she could see the supermarket, Manny's beer joint and a good stretch of the highway, but nothing she saw stirred her interest. A person walking a tight-rope doesn't pay much attention to the scenery. She's got all she can do to keep her balance and stay alive.

"What's the matter, honey?" Hazel asked. "Feeling punk?"

"I'll be all right."

"You'll get over it. You always feel punk every time you get a letter from the kid."

Ralph's letters arrived regularly once a week. One was like a carbon copy of another. He never complained. Complaints would have been edited by the reform school censor. On the other hand, he never really told her anything. "I'm well and hope you are the same . . . Nothing much to say except I wish I was home . . . They treat me pretty good . . . Your loving son." He never mentioned Tom Riggs. Not even when Mildred had written that she and Tom had separated and that she was considering a divorce. Ralph utterly rejected his stepfather. That's possible when hundreds of miles separate you from the person you reject. It's not so easy when every day you have to see, and sometimes talk to, the man you hate more than anything on earth.

Familiar sounds came in from the front. The cash register rang, the truckers slammed the door as they went out, a couple came in and ordered hamburgers and cans of beer. Mildred started to get up but Hazel said, "I got it, hon," and she sat down again. Hazel was nice. On days like this she did more than her fair share of the work.

There was a lull when no customers entered the cafe. Hazel came into the kitchen, stood beside her. She looked out the window, too. She said, "There's Lu Warren's cousin-or-whatever-she-is. Like to know what Amy thinks about her staying in the house. Going to the market." Hazel gasped audibly. "Well, I'll be—!"

The blonde girl, dressed in sandals, white shorts and a pink halter, had not been headed for the market. Passing the beer joint, she had suddenly turned in.

Hazel was indignant. "Got a mind to tell Lu Warren, just to see him burn!"

"It's not a saloon," Mildred said quietly. "Manny doesn't sell hard liquor. You drink beer yourself."

"There's a world of difference between sixteen and sixty, dearie. And she ain't a day older than sixteen."

Three-quarters of an hour went by. More customers arrived and left. Hazel took care of them. Mildred remained in her chair. Once she made an effort to rise, but sank back again. She felt incapable of movement, drained. But her mind was active, surveying her problem from every conceivable angle, and from every angle meeting the same high, barricaded wall. She did not see Thelma come out of Manny's place, but she probably would not have noticed if she had.

The front door was opened briskly and Tom Rigg's voice boomed through the cafe. "Mildred here?"

Hazel didn't answer. Mildred heard approaching footsteps. Then a moist hand was rested heavily on her shoulder.

"Hi."

She sat rigidly. "Take your hand off me, Tom. I don't want you to touch me, and I don't want you in my kitchen."

"Baby, why don't you give in?" He burlesqued a noisy sigh. "You know you're crazy for me. Why don't you break down and tell me so?"

But when she swung around to face him, he jerked his hand away. He went over to the ice box and got a can of beer. She studied him as he punctured it and drank.

He still held a physical fascination for her, and she despised herself for feeling it. He was shallow, cheap and cruel, but he was also strikingly handsome. One of his ancestors had been an Indian; it showed in his slightly Oriental features, his dark coloring and black hair. He had changed from his uniform at the sub-station. In slacks and a loud sports shirt, he looked like what he had been before he'd joined the force: a salesman on a used car lot. A good but disappointed salesman. Tommy had been able to move jalopies as fast as anybody in the trade, but every time he tried his hand on new cars—especially expensive ones—he failed to make it. People who bought Lincolns, Cadillac and Jags seemed to prefer a subtler form of pressure. They shied away from overbearing charm.

Mildred saw his amused eyes watching her above the tilted beer can. She stared back at him. "What're you doing here? You got anything to say, you can tell it to my lawyer."

"Hell with lawyers. You're my wife. Man's got a right to come in his own place."

"I'm not your wife. This restaurant belongs to me."

"We're still married. This is a community property state." He finished his can and tossed it in the wire receptacle beside the sink. "This is the day you're supposed to hear from Ralph. Get a letter?"

"Yes."

"They treating him all right?"

"He says so."

"You got me to thank for it. I got friends up there."

"You want me to thank you for something, Tom? Get out and don't come back."

He shrugged. "Of course, if you don't want him treated right I might be able to arrange that, too."

Mildred got up slowly. "You'd like to do that, wouldn't you? You've always hated Ralph."

"Now, hold on—!" A flush crept from the collar of Tommy's shirt to spread across his face. "I did everything I could to help that punk. He was guilty—"

"Of what? He didn't even know that car was stolen." She walked toward him with purposeful, unnerving deliberation. "Guilty of trying to protect himself after you'd run the car off the road and killed his friend?" Her right hand dipped into her apron pocket. "Ralph never owned a switchblade in his life."

Tommy had backed up against the sink. He watched her pocket. "You gone crazy, woman?"

Hazel's head came through the open service panel. "Mildred, you okay?"

"I'm okay. Everything's okay." Mildred's hand was no longer hidden in her apron. Hazel glared at Tommy, withdrew her head.

"Like mother, like son. Screwy." Tommy edged away from the sink, went over to the window. "Switchblades! Getting so it ain't safe for a man to open his mouth."

"You're safe," Mildred told him. "You'll stay safe just as long as your friends are good to Ralph."

He grinned, his confidence restored. "You want that, why don't you try being nice to me? You ought to see my new room, Milly. Got a color TV, twenty-one inch. Private entrance, too. Feel like a short drive up the coast?"

"I don't feel like a drive of any kind with you."

"You will, one of these days. Can't hold out forever, baby. Let's have another beer."

Mildred got a can from the ice box punched it and held it out to him. But Tommy was no longer interested. Suddenly he had become intent on something on the far side of the window. Mildred looked past his shoulder. She saw the blonde girl, Lu Warren's cousin, standing in front of Manny's. Thelma was a little drunk. She was talking to Dave Russell, smirking and swishing herself around in a way she probably thought was cute.

Mr. Russell seemed to be listening politely, but he only took it for about twenty seconds. Then he went into the supermarket. Thelma wrinkled her nose as she turned toward the beach road. She was evidently going home.

Mildred was still holding out the can. "Take your beer, Tom. I got to go to work."

Tommy didn't take the can. He turned from the window, crossed quickly to the ice box, slipped out a six-pack and hurried from the kitchen. He acted like a man with something on his mind. Mildred didn't ask him what it was. She was too glad to see him go.

But a moment later, when she saw his yellow convertible turn into the beach road, she nodded as though she'd known that he was up to something of the kind. And didn't care.

"Hazel, you want a can of beer?" she called.

A girl's got to have her kicks. Beer's okay but it wears off fast, and a girl is left feeling even lower than she was before. With nothing to do but sit on the beach and nothing to look at but the crazy ocean, and nothing to look forward to but Lu coming home and preaching at her like he was a shouting Holy Roller trying to get her to repent.

Give a girl a chance. First let me do something to be repentful for, Thelma told herself as she walked home. She giggled. I'll be as repentful later on as right now I'm full of beer.

It wasn't easy walking alongside the road. There were all kinds of little hills and hollows. Her feet kept climbing up on one and slipping down into the other and once she sort of lost her balance just before she reached the gate. She was leaning against the gate when she saw the yellow convertible. It must have sneaked up on her; it was standing only a couple of feet away. A man was grinning at her from behind the wheel.

"Hi, honey. Want a lift?" he said.

He was good-looking. Not the way Dave Russell was. You had to study Dave close before you realized he was as good-looking a fellow as you could ever hope to meet. This fellow's crazy looks reached out and sort of slapped you in the eye.

"Don't need a lift," she told him. "I'm already home."

His teeth, set against the darkness of his face, were white as skimmed milk. The wider he grinned, the whiter his teeth got. "Home's a place to come back to. How're you going to come back if you don't go places first?"

"Now if that ain't just what I was thinking! Mister, it's the awful, lousy truth. You take me places?"

"I'll take you, honey, and bring you back again. Climb in."

Thelma climbed in. There was a cold six-pack on the seat. She lifted it to her lap. The car swung in a U-turn, drove past the supermarket, turned right into the canyon road.

"There's an opener in the glove compartment," the good-looking fellow said. "My name's Tommy. What's your pretty name?"

On this particular late afternoon, Dave Russell for a change did not resent the fact that, in a sense, he was doing his wife's work while his wife did his. The painting promsed to turn out even better than he'd hoped. He was like a man who, having risked his last quarter on a slot-machine, unexpectedly lines up the three jackpot symbols. Running into Thelma a second time had not especially disturbed him. He was sorry about what was happening to her, as he would have been sorry to see rust forming on a piece of gleaming, well designed equipment. But, after all, he did not own the equipment. It was not his business if she let herself grow up to be a tramp.

He wheeled his groceries to the cashier's desk. They were whisked from the bag and put into a paper sack. He peered through the glass door before carrying the sack outside. Thelma was not in sight. He was on the sidewalk before he remembered that he hadn't bought dessert.

The ice cream man was getting ready to move on. Dave caught him as he closed the side-panel of his truck.

"Pint of chocolate, please." In surprise, he added, "Well, hello! When did you take on this job?"

It was Ken Hurley, a young man who had formerly worked in the service station. He and his wife lived about six houses south of the Warrens' place.

"Do it every year, soon as the warm weather starts. Pump gas during the winter months."

Dave paid him for the ice cream. "Like it?"

"Why not? Keeps me outside and not too far from home."

He slammed the side-panel, got into the driver's seat. He raised his hand in casual salute, let in the clutch. As the truck rolled away it automatically began to play a tinkling little tune. Dave smiled, listening. It was good advertising, that particular nostalgic number. It brought back memories of childhood. He hummed it, crossing toward the house. *Oh Where, Oh Where Has My Little Dog Gone?* It made him think of long, hot summer days—and cold ice cream.

He went through the gate and down the steps, entered the living room and carried the groceries to the kitchen. The house was built in a manner conforming to the steep hillside; in order to get to the kitchen, he had to climb another flight of narrow stairs. He set the groceries on the sink, put the ice cream in the refrigerator and glanced through the screened window at his trunks hanging on the line. They were quite dry now. On impulse he returned to the living room and placed his almost finished picture where Helen would be sure to see it as she came in. She would like it. He told himself the pleasant things she would say about it, and went back to the kitchen where he made preliminary preparations for dinner. He was an indifferent cook, but Helen more than made up for his lack of skill. She always put the finishing touches no their meals.

A few minutes later he heard their Rambler come to a stop beyond the window. He saw the car door open, and returned to the living room. Helen seemed unusually slow coming down the stairs. He opened the front door, stepped out and called.

"Need any help?"

Helen smiled, but it was a tired smile. Her left hand rested on the banister. "I'm a little beat. Hard day at the shop and the traffic's tough."

Dave felt quick concern. He climbed to take her hand. It was an extremely feminine hand but he sensed resistance in it, as he had sensed resistance in many of Helen's reactions during the past few months. He let go immediately, a little hurt.

But that, he knew, was behaving immaturely. When a man's wife comes home tired he doesn't, or shouldn't, sulk. He held the door open, turned back with a smile.

"Little surprise for you," he said.

Helen entered the living room. She hesitated when she saw the picture. Dave shut the door.

"Well—like it?"

"It's good," she said, with no particular enthusiasm. "Quite good. Mind if I rest a few minutes? Then I'll fix dinner. I have to work tomorrow."

"Tomorrow's Saturday!"

"Maybe it'll only be for a few hours in the morning. I'm lucky Victor doesn't have me working Sundays, too."

She walked to the little stairway that mounted to their bedroom. Dave lifted his hand uncertainly as though to stop her. But he let her go.

Helen resisted an impulse to slam the bedroom door. She eased it shut, crossed to the dressing table and grimly inspected her reflection in the mirror. It had happened, as she had known it would happen the first time Dave caught sight of that little blonde girl from downstairs. Helen had only seen her once herself, the night before when they'd passed each other on the outside staircase. But even that small encounter had been enough to put her on her guard. There are females who regard all marriages other than their own as personal challenges; their own they usually regard as unavoidable inconveniences. Thelma—that was the name Lu Warren had used when he had called her from below—was one of these. Okay, Helen could accept that. What she could not accept was the fact that Dave—who was *her* husband!—had proved himself to be in no way different from any other husband, any other man. Susceptible? He could not possibly have met that predatory child before this very morning—and already he had painted her portrait, had the damn thing nearly finished!

Helen went to the closet, got out a pair of white silk lounging pajamas and dropped them on the bed. She started taking off her clothes. She was a smart woman, in several senses of the word. She dressed smartly; as buyer for a woman's shop, that was an essential part of her business. She was beautiful, but she was also clever. It was her cleverness that she would have to call on now. Thelma might have her teen-age freshness and resiliency, but she—Helen reminded herself—had experience, self-control and brains.

Furthermore, it was entirely possible that she was allowing herself to become agitated over a trifle. Dave might have seen in the girl an interesting subject for a picture, nothing more. Very likely, during the course of the evening, he would mention having spoken to her—politely, casually—and having noted her pictorial possibilities. That would be Helen's cue to compliment him, slip him the happy needle, tell him what a really fine job he had done.

Helen sat on the foot of the bed, reached for the pajamas, started to pull them on. With one foot lifted to plunge into the trousers she abruptly paused.

If only the damned picture didn't absolutely reek of sex!

His wife was the only woman Dave had ever known who felt about good, natural things—the sun, the sea, music and the correct proportions of vermouth and gin—as he did, and did not think it incumbent on her to chatter about them. But now, when it came to a critical appraisal of his painting, she was carrying taciturnity too far. "Quite good," she had said. If there was one word he hated, it was that affected adverb, *Quite*. He sat on the couch and lit a cigarette.

Before he had time to finish it, there were footsteps on the stairs and she was back again. She had changed to white silk pajamas. They set off her brown hair and dark sun tan, and she stood before him in an attitude of amused contrition. Dave frowned, knowing that she was not contrite, but unable even as he frowned to keep from thinking how her long legs and perfect figure could do anything she liked with any kind of clothes.

"Your picture's wonderful, Dave. It's the best thing you've ever done."

Dave got up and kissed her warmly. "Sit down, working woman. I'll fix dinner."

"Oh, no you won't! I'm hungry. Whip up a couple of martinis, if you like."

Getting his mixing implements together, he had an impulse to tell her about Thelma. But he repressed it. He would find a more suitable occasion later on—make a joke of how he had met, and talked to, and drawn a quick sketch of Lu Warren's little cousin on the beach.

But of course he didn't do it. That would have called for an explanation of how he had happened to be on the beach in the first place, an explanation that would in effect have been a semi-apology. He didn't feel that an apology was indicated, and he saw no reason for ruffling the tranquility of what had turned out to be a pleasant evening. Helen became oddly quiet about ten o'clock, and they went to bed at eleven. It was illogical but Dave, as he undressed, had all the symptoms of a queasy conscience.

It must have been the same symptoms, whatever caused them, that kept him awake. He lay still, waiting first for the little muscular spasm that always signified Helen's "jumping off to sleep," and then he lay still for another three-quarters of an hour, afraid that any movement might awaken her. He grew increasingly tense. He wanted a cigarette, he wanted a drink of water, and these two wants combined to make any immediate prospect of sleep unlikely. At last, with infinite care he slipped out of bed and tiptoed to the living room. He stopped there long enough to light a cigarette, then climbed to the kitchen, not having bothered to turn on the lights.

There was no light in the kitchen, either, but none was necessary. He went unerringly to the sink, felt for and found a glass, turned on the tap. He stood there for a moment, sipping water and discovering that he wasn't thirsty after all and had started back to the living room when he heard a car stop by the gate.

He would have paid no attention if, simultaneously, he had not heard Thelma's petulant, slurred voice.

"Home?" It came blurred through the window screen, and it was obvious that she was drunk. "Whatcha bring me here for, hon?"

"You change your mind too much." The man's voice was heavy with resentment. "Say you'll go to a motel, then say you won't. Now you can go to bed by yourself."

"See you tomorrow?"

"I'll think about it. Go on, now—scram!"

There was a pause, followed by the sound of a scuffle. A car door slammed. Dave heard the motor accelerate, then fade away. All this happened before the girl began to scream.

"*You* scram! Hear me, you old goat? Scram! Scram . . ." Her anger dwindled as quickly as it had risen. She chuckled, talking softly to herself. "Should of asked Dexter when you had the chance, old goat. He could of told you. Knows all, sees all—sees it in the stars." The gate creaked and Dave moved closer to the window. He looked out.

He could just make out her figure, a shadow darker and more opaque than the shadows that surrounded it. She wavered past the window and beyond his line of vision, but he heard a soft thud as she sat down abruptly on the steps. She started humming to herself.

It was no recognizable tune she hummed, and it was interrupted after only a few seconds by a man who came running up the stairs.

"Drunk!" It was Lu Warren, whispering furiously. "You get down to bed!"

Thelma laughed. "Whose bed? How you, Cousin Lu?"

"Shut up!" There was a sharp crack; he must have slapped her face. "You're no kin of mine, you little wench!"

Her protest ended in an unintelligible gurgle. It sounded as though Lu had clamped his hand across her mouth. Dave heard her heels thump as he half-dragged, half-carried her down the steps.

She broke loose once and screamed, "Le' me go, you ol' devil! I'll tell Amy—"

He silenced her again. Her heels bumped rapidly for a moment, then there was nothing to be heard except diminished traffic on the road and surf breaking on the beach. Dave let out pent-up breath, grateful that Lu had been able to handle her without awakening Helen. He returned to the living room and was halfway across it, tiptoeing toward the bedroom, when the lights switched on.

Helen stood by the light switch. Her hair was dishevelled but she was wide awake.

"What time is it?"

"About twelve. Sorry you woke up," he said. "Lu Warren had a little trouble with his cousin."

"His what?"

"Girl who seems to be visiting him. Supposed to be a relative but, from what I overheard, could be she isn't. She came home swacked."

"I heard that much," Helen said. "In fact, I heard too much. Why on earth are you up wandering around the house at this hour?"

"I got up to go to the kitchen—"

"This is hardly a time of night to start a long discussion about nothing. Are you coming to bed?"

Dave said huffily, "I don't want to disturb you. I'll stay here on the couch."

"Well, really—!" Helen would have said more, but she caught sight of his expression. She shrugged, switched off the light and climbed the bedroom stairs. Dave stretched out on the couch. It was lumpy and the pillow had been designed for purely decorative purposes. He blamed Helen for what he knew would be a long, uncomfortable night.

In the morning, as usual he awakened first. He dropped his feet to the floor and sat up stiffly. There was a crick in his neck, and he was tempted to let Helen fix her own breakfast for a change. But his better nature joined with his own need for a cup of coffee, and he went to the kitchen to fill the percolator and put it on the stove.

Waiting for the first beige spurtings to turn brown, he reviewed the little tiff. The danger of such a misunderstanding, and even of a serious argument, seemed to be always with them lately. It lay just below the surface, as a shark might swim around and under a small boat. He would have to watch himself. He didn't know why it should be but, under the present unnatural conditions, responsibility for domestic peace seemed to be all his.

He opened a can of orange juice, poured coffee and arranged a breakfast tray. He braced his shoulders and carried the tray into the bedroom. Helen was still sleeping. But her face looked fresh and rested, and her sleep could not have been very sound. As he placed the tray on the bedside table, her hand reached out and touched his lightly. That was all. No more was necessary. He sat on the bed, handed her the orange juice and watched her fondly as she sipped.

It was a bright morning with a blue sky and no smog, and Dave was interrupted only once. There was a knock on the door about ten-thirty. He opened it, and experienced something like psychic panic when he recognized his visitor. It was Thelma. The girl showed no signs of a hangover. Her bright hair was covered by a red babushka. She wore her strapless swimming suit and had assumed a model's pose—hand on hip, weight on her right leg, left knee forward and slightly bent. Her provocative gray eyes were amazingly innocent.

"Hi, Dave. Going for a swim?" she asked.

He shook his head. "Sorry, I'm working."

"You hear me when I come in last night?" She grinned. "Up on cloud seven, wasn't I?"

"You were feeling no pain."

"Maybe no, but that crazy Lu sure was. Still is. Well," she said, "I'll be on the beach, happen you change your mind."

"I won't."

She giggled. "That wife of yours sure got you hog-tied, ain't she?"

"Now, you look here—!"

"Never mind. I dig it, Davy. You know where to find me later on."

She undulated down the steps. Dave closed the door with unnecessary violence and wondered, as he did so, whether the violence was directed entirely at Thelma or partly at himself. He was honest enough to admit that he did feel a little flattered by the interest of a young and pretty girl, but he was also realistic. He wanted nothing more to do with her. It was lucky that his painting only needed a few finishing touches, or, in his confused state, he might have botched the job. As it was, he completed it within two hours, and then did something he refrained from doing as a rule. He mixed a cocktail before lunch.

It was a self-congratulatory gesture of celebration, and he carried the martini to the living room. He was holding it when there came a second rapping on the door. This time it was Lu Warren.

Warren was a thin man who dressed habitually in khaki shirts and trousers. He was a care-ridden fifty with an accent that was the male equivalent of Thelma's. He had a nervous, fretful manner, and Dave had noticed the same manner in Amy Warren. He had wondered what common calamity had formed the worry-lines in their lean faces, and since last night he had suspected that it was each other. That might partly explain Thelma's presence in the house while Amy was away.

"Hello, Lu," Dave said. "What's on your mind?"

"Want to ask you something, Mr. Russell. You're friendly with my . . . cousin?" There was a significant pause before he spoke the final word.

"Friendly?"

"Well, you drew this picture, didn't you?" The sketch Dave had made the day before was thrust into his hand. "Just one thing I want to know," Lu said. "Was it you that took her out last night?"

The creaking of the gate at the head of the stairs attracted Dave's attention. He looked up. Helen was standing there. She had come home unexpectedly and, by her expression, she had heard what Lu had said.

Lu had also seen her. He nodded curtly. "Hi, Miz Russell." He scowled at Dave. "Talk to you about it later." He turned away.

"You'll talk about it now. The answer's no. I heard her come home last night, and I heard you. I heard everything you both said. Like me to repeat the conversation?"

Lu took a backward step, alarmed. "Needn't take that attitude, Mr. Russell. I was just asking."

"You've been answered." Dave ignored him, holding his left hand out to Helen. "Glad you came home early, darling."

Helen said nothing. The cocktail glass in Dave's right hand assumed the proportions of a gallon jug as she came slowly down the steps.

The prowl car cruised north on the stretch between the breakwater and Martinez Canyon. Tommy Riggs was driving. Earl Bingham sat beside him, a placid mass. Earl did not notice the beautiful blonde girl, but Tommy did. She was standing at the gate beside which he had picked her up the previous night. He almost drove past before deciding to give the kid another break.

"Hi, Thelma. How you feel?" he called.

She shrugged a bare, indifferent shoulder. Earl, leaning forward to get a better look, saw that she had a red dingus on her head and that she was wearing a tight black swimming suit.

"Ain't that the girl was on the beach yesterday?" he asked.

Tommy said off-handedly, "Correct."

"You know her?"

"Spoke to her, didn't I? Name's Thelma."

Earl thought about it for a minute. As Tommy turned in to park beside the bridge, he said, "You didn't know her yesterday."

"Yesterday's twenty-four hours ago."

The car was stopped, as usual, facing the highway. Earl waited until Tommy had set the brakes. "You must of met her last night, then."

"That's right, Earl. That brain of yours is working overtime today."

"Yeah," Earl agreed soberly. "Yeah, it is. How'd you make out with her?" he asked.

An expansive grin lit Tommy's handsome face. "Now you've embarrassed me. As a gentleman, I can't answer that. But I'll tell you this much—she's no different from any other dame, you know how to handle 'em. I know how." He opened the car door. "You got any more questions, prepare to ask 'em. I'm going over to see Mildred."

The furrows in Earl's narrow forehead grew deeper. "I got one more question, Tommy. Yesterday you was talking about the guy that kissed her on the beach. You said seeing an older man making a play for a kid like that—you said it made you sick."

"Did I say that?"

Earl nodded. "Then you go and make a play for her yourself. How come?"

"Well, I'll tell you," Tommy said. "With me, the circumstances are entirely different."

"What circumstances?"

"It's simple. That artist and I are two entirely different people. He's him, I'm me. What's right for me is wrong for him and maybe vice versa, maybe not. It all depends." He jumped out of the car. "You think that over for a while."

Earl watched him swagger across the road. He thought it over. If it had come from anyone but Tommy, he would have said it didn't make good sense. And Tommy or not, he was getting tired of having his questions answered in a sort of fancy double-talk. Just because a fellow thinks slow doesn't mean he doesn't think good, when he thinks.

There was a breeze from the east. Smog settled over the beach like a dirty cotton blanket. The brilliant, energetic day turned glum. Swimmers bundled up their gear, drove home. Dave and Helen went about their individual tasks, treating each other with self-conscious courtesy. Dave got together the materials necessary for wrapping his picture for the mail. Helen compiled a grocery list and crossed the beach road to the supermarket. Walking, she had a tendency to come down hard on her heels.

It was only too clear now that, during the daylight hours while she'd been working, Dave had spent his time lounging on the beach. Playing around with a vicious little juvenile delinquent, drawing pictures of her, arousing Lu Warren's protective jealousy. He could rationalize his behavior all he pleased; the fact remained that he had deliberately concealed the truth about the girl. He hadn't even mentioned that he'd met her. And, since he had concealed their acquaintanceship, it was perfectly obvious that what existed between them was a good deal more than that. It was much more likely—

Helen got that far in her angry reasoning, and no further. She suddenly realized to what end her suspicions must inevitably lead her, if they turned out to be true. A lonely, bitter end. A vacuum, because life without Dave would be no more than that.

She had already paid for her groceries. They boy was putting them in a heavy paper bag. She caught up the bag and almost ran out of the store. A truck slammed on its brakes, just missing her as she crossed the road. She ran through the gate and down the steps. The front door was standing open. She went in.

She came to an unbelieving halt. Dave was leaning out of the window, talking to someone below him on the beach. She knew who it was even before she heard the hateful, whining voice.

"Lu's gone to Palisades City. And your wife ain't here, so why not, Davy? I'm lonesome. Come on down."

Helen was not conscious of having made a sound, but she must have done so. Dave whirled around. She studied his guilty face for a long moment, then turned and crossed the living room to the bedroom stairs. Silently, with natural dignity. The door at the head of the stairs always stood open. She locked it as Dave started up the steps.

He banged on the door. She lay face down on the bed, hands over her ears. She could still faintly hear his muffled voice, sense from its changing tone that he was growing angry. But she was too hurt even to attempt a reply.

The noise stopped after a while but she still lay motionless. An hour passed before she got up, washed her face. She went down to the living room prepared to suffer through an explanation and, perhaps an abject apology, but it was too late by that time.

Dave had gone.

There were only a few customers in the cafe and Hazel was taking care of them. Mildred sat beside the kitchen window, fingering a letter. The letter had arrived only that morning, but already she knew it by heart. Unlike Ralph's other letters, this one said something. It said too much.

"Dear Mom,

I'm sending this out by a guy they're turning loose, a friend of mine, so the screws won't get a chance to read it. When I wrote you before that everything was fine and they were treating me okay, I was lying, Mom. Maybe I would deserve to be treated this way if I was guilty, but I'm not guilty. Tom Riggs framed me. He was jealous because he knew you loved me, and he picked up Hank's switchblade after he run us off the road and Hank got killed, and he planted the switchblade on me and swore I pulled it on him. I never did, and I would have told the judge what happened but I thought you was sold on Riggs, so I thought what the hell.

Mom, I'm breaking out of here. This friend of mine they're turning loose is going to get a car and come back and pick me up. There's a place in the wire I can get through, and what I want you to do is pack a suitcase and have it ready when I phone. I'll phone you Monday night. Please don't worry. Everything's all set.

                                           Your loving son . . ."

Mildred put the creased letter in the pocket of her apron. She tried to decide what she should do, and was incapable of reaching a decision. She didn't want Ralph to try to escape. Even if he were successful, the act of escaping would place him in defiance of the law. And no boy, no man, can defy the law without warping something in his character. Something deep inside Ralph that had been straight would be forever twisted out of shape.

On the other hand, she could not bring herself to notify the school's authorities. That would have been treachery. Her lips moved, forming silent words.

Mildred was praying, not knowing that she prayed.

Palisades City is a boardwalk beach town. Until a half-hour after midnight its boardwalk, which is really a broad cement sidewalk lined on both sides with tawdry shops, is a rowdy, garishly illuminated pedestrian thoroughfare. At half-past twelve the colored neons are turned off as though someone had pulled a master switch. After that, only the street lamps are left. They shed a cold synthetic moonlight over shuttered stores and empty benches, all waiting for the returning crowd to bring them back to life.

Dave came out of the Palisades Theatre at ten minutes before twelve. He had sat through the feature picture twice, and had no idea of how he could further pass the time until Helen might reasonably be presumed to have gone to bed. He did not want to go home until that happened.

The center of the boardwalk was occupied by a long line of benches. He went to one of them and sat down. The Rambler had been left in a parking lot two blocks away; in another hour he would reclaim it and drive home. All he had to do was sit still for another sixty minutes. But sitting still was more difficult than he had thought.

His mind was in rebellion, and his eyes were as restless as his mind. Fleetingly they noted individual faces in the crowd, a shooting gallery directly ahead and, no its right, an open counter piled high with salt water taffy. On his left a sign above a crimson door read, *The Beach Bar—Cocktails*, and beyond that another sign called attention to the offices of *Dexter*. Somewhere Dave had seen or heard that name before. He got up and crossed to the twenty-foot store front.

There were no windows, only an open double door across which a black star-spangled curtain had been drawn. A tripod beside the door held a large black placard. In the center of the placard was a photograph of a bearded man who wore a turban. This was presumably Dexter, and grouped around his photograph were a number of glossy prints of moving picture celebrities. All of these were autographed, and curiously all the autographs were in the same scrawled handwriting. Five-pointed tinsel stars were scattered among the glossy prints and, at the bottom of the placard, silver letters read, *The Man Who Guides The Stars*.

The phrase stirred Dave's memory. He recalled the circumstances in which he had heard the name before. Thelma had mumbled it when she had come home drunk the previous night.

Everything revolved around that damned girl. She was omni-present, he thought bitterly, and he was aghast that only that afternoon he had been a little flattered because she had displayed an interest in him. One of her favorite words came back to him: Crazy. It would aptly have described his addled state of mind. He went back to the bench, looked at his watch. Only twenty minutes had passed. The time was ten minutes before twelve.

The world had shrunk for Thelma. She lay on the beach and vaguely wondered why she had ever let herself get steamed up about the things she didn't have. Everything she wanted was right here within reaching distance. Her back itched. She rubbed it against a small convenient boulder that had become embedded between her shoulder blades. A couple of feet away, beside a shallow pool left by the tide, there was a bottle. The moon was so bright that she could see how full the bottle was. The moon was peeking at her over the top of Point of Rocks. It was close. Her right forefinger stirred the shallow pool. If she felt like it, she could have lifted her finger and poked the old moon in the eye.

A man lay on the sand beside her. His arms were around her so tight it hurt her ribs. She tried to remember what his name was. He'd told it to her a day, an hour, a week before, but she'd forgotten it. Ask her right now what he looked like, and she couldnt' even tell you that. It didn't make much difference. He was a man.

She wriggled out of his arms and rolled away, for no better reason than to see what he would do. She giggled when he did what she'd expected. He reached out and grabbed, just missing her, and the shadows mixed with moonlight painted funny pictures on his face. His hair was mussed up, so that it looked as though he had two horns sprouting from his forehead. Like a billy goat, or like a bull. She took a drink from the bottle, screwed the top back on again. It was so comical she laughed out loud. She took the red babushka off her head and dangled it in front of her, the way she'd seen a bull fighter in the movies do. She remembered an old song she had learned when she was just a kid. She sang it to him, giggling, waving her babushka in the moonlight.

> "'Toreador-a, don't spit on the floor-a,
> Use the cuspidor-a, that's what it's for-a . . .'"

She was only doing it for kicks, but it turned out that he wasn't fooling. All of a sudden he made a big jump and landed right on top of her, and started getting fresh. Real fresh. That wouldn't have been too bad if only he'd been nice about it, but he wasn't a bit nice. He was rough, and Thelma wasn't the kind of girl that was going to stand for being treated rough. She told him so and tried to shove him off, but he didn't pay the least bit of attention. He was pressing all the wind out of her and it was getting hard to breathe, so she lifted up her forefinger and poked him in the eye. The left eye. And before he could do anything about it, she poked him in the other.

It was funny how he acted then. He didn't make a sound. He got up on his knees and, for a minute, she thought she'd taught him a good lesson and that he would treat her nicer after that. He couldn't have been seeing good, but he still kept hold of her with one strong hand. The other hand fumbled around beside him on the beach. He picked up something, and Thelma saw it was the boulder she had used to scratch her back. She tried to roll away, but he had her pinned down tight. He lifted the boulder and slammed it hard against her head.

That was another funny thing; it didn't really hurt much. It dazed her, though, and scared hell out of her. And maybe it knocked her out—but only for a second. She knew what was happening when she felt his hand start yanking at her hair. But it was as though it was happening to somebody else, not her. There'd been a mistake somewhere. She'd never hurt anybody. She was just Thelma, out for kicks, an hour late and a dollar short, and she tried to explain this, but he rolled her over and pushed her face down in the pool. She yelled then, yelled loud, but the only sound that got out was a sort of roaring bubble. Water choked the rest.

Dave did not notice the sudden semi-darkness when, within minutes of each other, all the neons were clicked off. He looked up after a while and found himself alone on a deserted boardwalk. It was time to start for home.

He got up wearily and returned to the parking lot. On the beach road going north, he had to slow down because of a gang of men in hard shipworkers' helmets who were staring apprehensively at the overhanging palisades. Since the spring rains there had been trouble with landslides, and Dave recognized the men as a work crew bent on preventing traffic tieups before they happened. As he was waiting for the signal to resume normal speed, he heard a shout and felt a sharp jolt against the car. He stopped, knowing what had happened: a boulder had rolled down the palisades and hit his right front wheel. There was no damage.

That did not prevent the foreman from taking down his name and license number. When he was permitted to go ahead, it was with the understanding that he might be called upon to testify to the foreman's competence and to the accidental nature of what had happened. That was all right. He did not expect ever to be called. There was no other incident on his way home. He reached there at twenty minutes after one.

The window of the bedroom was dark, and now glow came up the exterior stairway from the Warrens' place. Dave had to feel his way past the porch and down to his front door. He unlocked the door and let himself into pitch-blackness, made his way uncertainly to the couch. He took off his jacket, shoes and trousers, and lay down in his shirt and shorts.

He lay down but did not immediately go to sleep. Seconds later he heard the soft shutting of the bedroom door. Helen had been awake; she had waited in the darkness until he came home. Dave smiled grimly in the direction of the unseen ceiling. He closed his eyes.

They opened again at twenty minutes before two. He verified the time by looking at the radium dial of his watch. It was less easy to be certain of what had awakened him but, listening, he heard footsteps passing the front door. There was no other sound except that of the sea.

The footsteps went heavily, slowly down the stairs. Dave thought of them as heavy because the steps creaked under their weight. A picture formed in his mind of a grotesquely fat man tiptoeing down to the beach.

He fell asleep and dreamed of the fat man standing knee-deep in surf, washing away layer after layer of adipose tissue. When the man returned to the house, he was no longer fat. His footsteps, as they climbed the stairs, were stealthy but brisk and light.

Dave was suddenly wide awake. The sounds were real; they were not part of his dream. Footsteps were again passing the door, this time going up. It was ten minutes before two. He got up, exasperated, went to the kitchen and looked out of the window.

It was too dark on the beach road to see much. Another car had pulled in behind the Rambler. Someone had opened the door, was climbing behind the wheel. It was a man; Dave could tell that much, no more. The car was only a black hulk. He could not even be certain of its make.

He turned away—and was stopped by an odd tinkling sound. At almost two in the morning an ice cream truck should be in its garage, but Dave distinctly heard familiar notes. They formed the refrain, *Oh Where, Oh Where Has My Little Dog Gone?* he had heard the afternoon before.

He went back to the window but by that time the truck had passed beyond his range of hearing. The car that had been parked behind his own was just starting to drive off. Dave did not wait to see it disappear. He returned to the couch, fell instantly asleep and did not wake up again until six-thirty in the morning.

He was still tired. Normally he would have slept for another couple of hours. Some unaccustomed deviation from routine must have pulled him back to consciousness. There was an appreciable lapse of time before he became aware of what the deviation was. Helen's most prized luxury was having her breakfast coffee in bed. But this morning the familiar odor was already perceptible in the living room.

It was a bad sign. It probably indicated an unwillingness on her part to accept any favors from him, even so slight a favor as making morning coffee. Dave pulled on his shoes and trousers. If the cold war was going to continue, he might as well get dressed. He approached the kitchen warily.

Coffee was bubbling in the percolator and Helen was busy at the kitchen table. A wicker hamper was on the table and she was making sandwiches. She looked up as he came in.

"Picnic today," she announced. Her voice was gentle and subdued. "We need a change of scene. I'd like to go up in the hills to our old place. Maybe when we come back we'll be more like we used to be." She smiled uncertainly. "Okay?"

"Okay."

"Sometimes you provoke me beyond the limits of my patience. But I love you," she said, after they had kissed.

The canyon wound inland for thirteen miles, climbing between rocky hills that were high enough to be small mountains. The last few miles were up a steep grade until, just below the crest, they reached what Helen had referred to as their "old place." They had come here often during the first years of their marriage, a shady spot fifty yards off the road, from which the surrounding country unfolded far beneath them like a lumpy green and yellow bedspread. There were no rusty cans or other evidences of previous picnickers; apparently few people wandered this far from the road. They ate their lunch in privacy and an atmosphere of renewed serenity, and Dave gave her a detailed account of how he'd spent the previous evening. He told her about the footsteps and the ice cream wagon, too.

"And don't say I was dreaming. I actually heard them. I was as wide awake as I am now."

"Wider, by the way you're yawning."

He nodded. "That reminds me. It's time for my siesta now."

There was a beach mat in the car. He spread it on the grass and lay down on it. He slept with his head on Helen's lap.

The sun sets early in the mountains. At six, when they went back to the car, it was already getting dark. They ran into sunlight again, however, as topping the crest they came for a moment in sight of the sea. They drove inland five more miles, then doubled back southwest, and they had dinner at a restaurant overlooking the ocean. It was a good dinner. Afterwards, they started for home by what they thought was the shortest route, along the beach.

But the road was blocked; the expected landslide had taken place. They were forced to detour inland and return through Martinez Canyon. Lights were burning in both sections of the house when they finally reached home. A sheriff's car and a police cruiser were parked beside the gate.

Helen touched Dave's hand. Her voice was puzzled. "Why the police? You suppose Lu's in trouble?"

"Lord knows." He indicated two deputies standing at the gate. "They'll tell us."

Dave stopped behind the sheriff's car. Before he could slide from under the wheel a deputy was at his side.

"Russell?" He was a flashily handsome man, his features aquiline as an Indian's.

Dave nodded.

"This your wife?"

"This is Mrs. Russell."

The deputy opened the car door. "Bingham," he called, "take this woman down to the lieutenant." His hand closed forcefully around Dave's wrist.

A second, massive deputy showed up on the right side of the car. He said, "This way, ma'am." Helen silently climbed out.

Dave controlled his anger. He waited until she had been escorted through the gate. "Am I under arrest? If so, for what?" he asked.

"Ask the lieutenant. He's waiting to talk to you."

"Unless I am under arrest, take your hands off me," Dave said.

The first deputy grinned. He twisted Dave's wrist and gave it a vicious jerk. As Dave came out of the car, his left arm was doubled painfully behind his back.

"Goddamn kid-killer." The deputy ran him forward and around the car; he was pushed through the gate. "Get down there," the man said, and shoved him down the steps.

There was a dazed period wherein things happened, he was pushed and pulled, and voices spoke to each other, but it was like watching the screen of a drive-in movie from far away. He saw moving figures but could not distinguish one from another. He heard blurred sound but could not make out words.

Then abruptly there was silence and the scene swam into focus. He stood in the middle of the living room. Deputies stood beside him, one on either side. In front of him was a lean man with graying temples. At first glance he appeared to be intelligent, but Dave was in no mood to take people at face value. He reserved judgment, concentrating on the fact that the man, although obviously a policeman, wore well-cut civilian clothes. That might, or might not, be an indication that he was less brutal and moronic than the others. Helen leaned against the wall. Her eyes were anguished, her face was pale and drawn.

"It's the truth, Lieutenant!" she was saying. "My husband was at home last night!"

"Not all night, Mrs. Russell," the lean man said gently. "We have a witness who saw him about one o'clock." He turned to Dave. "I'm Lieutenant Morgan, temporarily attached to the sheriff's sub-station. I'll need your statement."

"I'd give it to you, if someone would tell me what the statement is supposed to be about."

The lieutenant frowned. "Don't you read the papers? Thelma Grant was found this morning—murdered."

The name meant nothing. "This is ridiculous," Dave said. "I don't know anyone—" Then a message Helen had been trying to flash to him suddenly grew clear. He took a quick step forward. "You mean Lu Warren's cousin?"

Lieutenant Morgan nodded. The breath went out of Dave. He felt as though he had been kicked in the solar plexus. "So help me," he said slowly, "I hardly knew her. This is the first time I ever heard her full name." He took another step. The handsome deputy stopped him by grabbing at his arm. "You say she's murdered?"

"That's what we're trying to establish," the policeman said. "Mind coming along?"

Dave frowned at the hand clasped around his arm. "Do I have any choice?"

"We just want a few people to see you, and to ask some questions. I'd appreciate it if you came willingly. It would make things easier."

"By all means, let's make things easier," Dave said.

Morgan nodded to the deputies. "Mr. Russell will ride with you. I'll follow. Want to talk to Mrs. Russell for a minute."

The deputy jerked Dave's arm. "Let's go." Dave said nothing. He allowed himself to be led out.

He was hit the instant the front door shut behind them, hit hard back of the ear. He fell forward, landing on the steps.

"Take it easy, can't you?" The voice of the deputy named Bingham seemed to come from a great distance. "You don't know he's guilty. Nobody knows that."

"As far as I'm concerned, he's guilty," Tommy said.

Helen waited for Dave to call but the hours passed and the telephone was silent. A clock ticked, waves tumbled on the beach, the tide ran out, and still there was no message. At two o'clock she lifted the telephone but, after holding it for half a minute, slowly replaced it in its cradle. She went back to the couch, picked up the evening paper. She shuddered as again she saw the glaring headline, GIRL'S BODY FOUND ON BEACH. The paper came out while she and Dave were in the mountains.

She sat on the couch and for the sixth time read the story. It was a sensational story. The body, dressed only in panties and brassiere, had been discovered about breakfast time that morning. It was lying, hidden from the house where the girl had been visiting, at the foot of a small embankment near the sea. Thelma's other clothes were neatly piled some distance away. A preliminary medical examination had disclosed the presence of water in her lungs, and police had first supposed her death to be suicide or accidental drowning.

Helen raised her hand to the venetian blind. If she had lifted the blind she could have seen the embankment at the foot of which Thelma's body had been found. She did not lift it. She went back to the story.

Two hours after the discovery of the body, a red babushka identified as Thelma's had been picked up miles to the north at Point of Rocks; and a more thorough examination, conducted about the same time, had shown a swollen bruise on the girl's head. The babushka was torn, and other signs of a struggle had been found in the area. Thelma, it now appeared, had been knocked unconscious shortly after midnight and her head held under water in one of the pools left by the tide at Point of Rocks.

Lucius Warren, brought in for questioning, had admitted that the girl was not a relative. He had met her in Palisades City where she had been employed as a salesgirl. He was being held tentatively on a charge of contributing to the delinquency of a minor. Police, acting on information furnished them by

Warren, were looking for David Russell, an artist who occupied the upper part of the Warren house and who was said to have been on familiar terms with Thelma Grant.

Familiar! The hateful word stirred Helen into action. She dropped the paper, went to the phone and told the operator to ring the substation.

She gave her name to the man who answered, and told him she was calling about her husband. "He hasn't come home. I don't know what to do."

"Hold the line, please." There was a pause while the man asked muffled questions. Then he spoke into the phone again. "They took him to the city, Mrs. Russell. They haven't booked him yet, if that's what you mean."

"Of course they haven't booked him!" Helen sounded more indignant than she felt; actually she was relieved. "He didn't take his car. I just wanted to know what time I can pick him up."

"Couldn't tell you, ma'am," the man said.

Helen hung up and walked to the ship's clock hung decoratively on the wall beside the bedroom stairs. She checked the time; then she straightened magazines on a table at the far end of the room. She moved like a somnabulist, and, when she suddenly climbed to the kitchen, her action was compulsive, governed by no motive known consciously to herself.

In the kitchen she opened the refrigerator. It contained, among other items, a plate of cold sliced meat left over from the picnic. She was not hungry but she crammed two slices of tongue and one of turkey in her mouth, and was only stopped from eating more by the creaking of the gate out by the porch. Someone was coming down the steps.

She almost fell in her hurry to get to the door. She pushed it open and ran out.

"Dave!"

The man on the steps continued downward. She knew instantly that it was not Dave, but he had come within six feet before she recognized Lu Warren.

"Mr. Warren, have you seen my husband?"

"I seen him." Warren's voice was bitter. "Told the cops about him, too." He passed her and kept on going down the steps. "Hope they put him in the gas chamber. It's what he deserves."

Helen's hand groped blindly for the banister. She watched the landlord until he had reached the sandy patio and passed from sight. Then she returned to the living room and lay down on the couch, forearm covering her eyes. Her eyes ached with the pressure of accumulated tears, but she did not cry. There would be time for crying later. Lots of time.

It was dawn when Dave finally came home. Helen heard him on the stairs, but this time she did not go running to the door. She sat up and waited. He saw her as soon as he came in.

He smiled faintly. "Tough night? I know how you feel."

She said. "Sit down. Tell me what happened."

"Isn't there any coffee?"

"I'll make some. You sit down and rest."

When she returned with the coffee, he was asleep sitting in his chair. Her instinctive pity put up only a token struggle before anxiety completely routed it. She set the coffee down and shook his shoulder.

"Wake up, dear."

He woke as a hunted animal wakes—standing, poised to run. "What's the matter?"

"That's what I want to know," she said.

He sat down again, sipped coffee, lit a cigarette. She noted the dark circles under his eyes, and gave him all the time he needed. When he seemed more relaxed, she said, "Tell me about it. Start from the beginning."

He gave her a lopsided grin. "They questioned me. Know what a police questioning consists of? The same old questions asked over and over again for hours and hours. It seemed to disappoint them that I kept on giving the same answers. Finally they let me go—drove me home, as a matter of fact. That's all for tonight. My present status is a polite form of house arrest. I'm supposed to be here when they want me."

"Why?"

"Look, darling—they have to have a suspect. The public expects it of them. It's a rule. Lu Warren's out. At the time she was murdered he was looking all over the place for her, and people saw him. Ken Hurley, among other people. They may still get him on that contributing charge, but not for murder. He's clear on that."

"You're not?"

He shook his head. "Lu spent a lot of time upon the road last night. I wasn't home at the time the murder was committed, and he knows it. Then there's the foreman of a gang of road workers. He talked to me at one."

"But how about the ice cream wagon? How about those footsteps you hear?"

"I told all that to Morgan. Told him about Dexter, too." Dave shrugged. "He said he'd look into it . . ."

His voice trailed off. She had to prompt him. "Well?"

"I don't think he believed me. He didn't seem impressed." Dave got up. "I'm going to have to go to bed."

"When does Morgan want to see you again? What about?"

"Ask him. He'll be here at eleven. Please, Helen," he begged. "I've got things to do. Before I do them I have to get some sleep."

She let him go. By that time it was half-past five, and she'd had no sleep herself. She lay down on the couch but could not keep her eyes closed. At eight she got up. She could no longer be inactive, waiting submissively for terrible things to happen. What Dave had described as a polite form of house arrest did not apply to her.

Dave seemed to be sleeping. She hurried from the house and down the road to the cottage occupied by the young man who drove the ice cream truck. She'd known Ken Hurley, as Dave had, when he'd worked at the service station. Her heart beat rapidly as she knocked on the cottage door.

No one came to open it. She called, "Mr. Hurley—!" but there was no evidence of life beyond the door. She didn't give up. It had been a good try, and she could come back later.

Helen went back to the house. She called the shop and left word for Mr. Victor that she would not be able to work that day. Hanging up, she heard Dave coming from the kitchen. She turned toward the steps.

She started to explain, "Just calling—" and broke off in surprise. "You're going out?"

He nodded. "All dressed up to have my fortune told. Morgan didn't believe me about Dexter. I'll have to see the guy myself."

"You're not supposed to leave the house. Morgan will be here at eleven."

"So will I. Fresh coffee will be ready in a minute. If Morgan expected me to stay in one place," Dave said, "he should have kept me in his jail."

There are some people a guy just naturally hates on sight. They affect you like an overdose of raw corn liquor. Tangle with one of them, and you wake up next morning with all the symptoms of a hangover. Tommy Riggs woke up Monday morning with a dry mouth and a headache. If it hadn't been for Dave Russell, he would have got to bed earlier and slept better. He would have wakened feeling fine, ready to go to work.

But work, today, wouldn't have been a good idea anyway. Some of the people at the sub-station—Corporal Gonzalez in particular—were gunning for him. Tommy had to keep a jump ahead of them. Right now he had to get himself in a position where he could just sort of casually mention what he had been doing Friday and Saturday nights. Block any thought of a connection between Thelma and himself before it could get started. There was no telling what might happen if word that they had known each other got around.

It would be easy enough. Mildred and Earl could be counted on to give him alibis. Mildred was nuts about him, and Earl would do anything that Tommy said. Nobody had actually seen him with Thelma, so he didn't have to worry about that. Tommy dressed, and drove his yellow convertible down the beach to Mildred's place.

He turned the motor off, staring moodily across the road at the window of Russell's bedroom. What a racket! Russell was probably still asleep while he, Tommy, had been forced to haul his backside out of bed at dawn to make a third-rate living. Around noon, Russell would get up, slap a little paint on canvas and sell the canvas for a couple of thousand bucks. It wasn't fair.

But the hell with thinking about Russell. What he had to concentrate on right now was being nice to Mildred. And what she'd always liked best was a little sweet talk about the future. She needed something to build on, hope for. He got out of the convertible, opened the door of the cafe.

"Hey, Mildred!" he called.

It was Hazel's day off. Mildred sat in the kitchen by herself. She turned as he came in, and Tommy saw that something must have happened. There were new lines in her face, and she looked old. He gave her a winning smile.

"Honey, I got a proposition to make. You interested?"

She shook her head. "No proposition of yours would interest me."

Tommy's voice dropped in pitch, became utterly sincere. "You just listen for a minute. I do a lot of horsing around, but actually I'm a very serious type," he said. "A family man, you know? I don't like the way things are with you and me. I live all by myself up in this room, and all I do is sleep and look at television and go to work. And I don't like the kind of work I'm doing now. It's got no future in it, understand?"

Mildred said quietly, "You're a little late worrying about your future. That was all decided long ago."

"You may be right. I always felt I was intended to do something big." He smiled ingratiatingly. "Well, what I got to say boils down to this. How's about you and me getting together again? I could come down here and run this restaurant. Maybe I could handle a few cars—clean ones, strictly high-class—on the side. When Ralph gets out, and if he's learned his lesson, I might be able to throw a job his way. All we need is a little capital; we'd have it made. So how's it strike you, Milly—pretty good?"

There was a silence. Then Mildred got slowly to her feet. "Get out. Get out, you son of a bitch," she said.

Tommy was so shocked that he started to obey. He had turned toward the front door before he thoroughly realized that she had meant what she had called him, and he got mad.

"Hey!" He turned back quickly.

"Nobody, least of all a goddamned woman, can call me that!"

Her hand was in the pocket of her apron. "Tom, I haven't even begun to tell you what I think of you. You don't want to hear it, you'd better get out fast." She took a slow, determined step in his direction. "You framed Ralph."

"That's a lie!"

"It's the truth. I know that now. I know a lot about you, and every bit of it is bad. How about that little blonde girl that got murdered—Thelma Grant?"

Tommy shivered. It was as though someone had poured a bucket of ice cold water down his spine. "Well, what about her? I didn't even know the girl," he said.

"Is that what you'll tell the district attorney? I don't think he'll believe you. I saw you with her Friday. Suppose I tell him so?"

"This is a sample of what you'll get," he said, and clipped her on the jaw.

She crumpled to the floor. Tommy looked at her a moment, then suddenly he got frightened. He hadn't meant to hit her. He didn't like to hit women, as a rule. He'd have a hell of a job now, talking her into doing what he wanted. It might be better to wait a while before he tried. He went out to his car.

But he was nervous. His mind was working frantically, much faster than it usually did. He'd thought he was safe but, if Mildred had seen him with Thelma, it followed that other people might have seen him, too.

Abruptly, he remembered Dexter. He hesitated a moment. The fortune teller didn't know his name. There was a possibility that Dexter wouldn't remember him at all. Just the same, he had to make sure. There was no use trying to do anything with Mildred until he had made sure. He started his convertible, turned south into the beach road.

Just before he reached the Warren house, a Rambler nudged into the traffic ahead of him. Dave Russell was driving it. Tommy scowled, wondering where Russell was headed for. Then, as the blocks passed and the Rambler anticipated every turn that would take both it and the convertible to Palisades City, that icy feeling began playing up and down Tommy's spine again. Even before the Rambler turned into the parking lot near Dexter's place, Tommy knew it was a good thing he hadn't gone to work. He had to get to the fortune teller before Russell did.

The telephone booth was in front of a drug store on the east side of the boardwalk. From it, Tommy could see the entrance to Dexter's place. That damned attendant in the parking lot had held him up. Russell had beat him by a whole half-block.

Tommy was dialing the telephone as he watched. He heard it ring, heard the gruff voice of Corporal Gonzalez at the sub-station up the coast.

"This is Riggs," he said. "Corporal, I don't feel so good. Doctor says I shouldn't work today."

"I feel for you, Riggs, but I can't quite reach you. Bingham got less sleep than you did, but he's on the job."

"Swear to God, that's exactly what I told the doctor. Said it'd look funny as hell, my partner working and me not. You want to talk to the doctor, Corporal? He's right here."

"No, I don't want to talk to any doctor. But there is a matter I'd like to discuss with you. A personal matter. At your convenience, of course."

The connection was broken but Tommy still held the receiver to his ear. As long as he looked like he was talking, nobody would pay any attention to him in the booth. He was sweating, although the day's heat had not yet begun. That damned Gonzalez had the knife in him, all right!

He was still at the telephone when Russell came out of Dexter's. Russell headed back toward the parking lot. Tommy darted from the booth as soon as he was out of sight.

He ran across the boardwalk, did an about-face, and walked right back into the booth again. He'd nearly run into a guy he knew, Dick Swope, a plainclothes man attached to the city force. A disturbing possibility occurred to him. Swope might be standing on a plant outside of Dexter's place.

But why? How could first Russell, and then Swope, have known that he'd brought Thelma here to have her fortune told? It was all very confusing, but Tommy dismissed the idea of personal danger after a moment's thought. For one thing, Swope was paying no attention to Dexter. His interest was centered on a cute little redhead he'd just run into on the boardwalk. Tommy watched the detective sit down beside her on a bench. Swope's back was turned. Once more Tommy left the booth.

And once more he was forced to return to it. A couple of yokels—they looked like honeymooners—stood giggling in front of the black placard until the old fortune teller, complete with beard and turban, came out and roped them in.

Swope was still on the bench when those two came out again. But he was making good time with the redhead; Tommy knew from experience that a man in Swope's position couldn't think of two things at once. He didn't bother to take precautions. He hurried over to Dexter's, brushed the yokels aside, went in the door.

Dexter met him in the tiny, curtained reception room. He bowed, touching his forehead, lips and heart. "Good morning," he said, his accent as thick as it was fake. "You are deeply disturbed, sair. I 'ave known that you were coming. I 'ave seen it in the stars."

He was a slight old man. Tommy rushed him through a second door into the rear, private room. He shut the door, turned the key and popped a chair beneath the knob.

"I'll get to you in a minute," he said, as the old man mouthed silent, frightened words. He crossed to the window, opened it, looked out. A stationary ladder descended from the window to the beach. Dexter had provided himself with an emergency exit. He'd been smart, but not smart enough.

Tommy shut the window. He returned to the trembling fortune teller. "Remember me?" he asked.

"You ... you ... No! I never seen you in my life!" Dexter's accent was forgotten. He was so agitated he could hardly speak.

"That's the right answer, but you took too long to say it. Now we got to make sure, next time somebody asks you, you come up with the right answer and come up fast."

Tommy took a blackjack from his pocket and went scientifically to work.

It was only a little after ten when Dave got home, but a police car had parked beside the gate and a uniformed policeman waited at the wheel. Dave wasn't worried. If Morgan wanted to get tough, he had material now with which to soften him. He got out of the Rambler, went down the steps and entered the living room. Lieutenant Morgan was with Helen.

As far as he could tell, Helen was perfectly at ease. She was sitting on the couch, drinking coffee and talking to the lieutenant. Morgan rose as Dave came in. The policeman's face remained expressionless but, as Dave approached, he saw that Helen's calm had been assumed. The sight of him had brought relief into her eyes.

"Lieutenant Morgan's been waiting to talk to you," she said.

Morgan nodded. "Mr. Russell, I understand you went to call on Dexter. I thought I asked you to stay at home."

"What did you expect?" Dave shrugged. "Somebody had to talk to him."

"Dexter's place has been staked out since six this morning. He was the next man on my list. Now—" Morgan sighed, went over to the phone. "Mind if I make a call?"

He dialed a number. "Lieutenant Morgan. Have Swope bring Dexter in immediately." He read the number from the telephone. "Call me back."

He hung up, and thoughtfully recrossed the room. "Well, Mr. Russell, what did you find out?"

"Two things," Dave said. "Thelma was there Friday evening with a man."

"Description?"

"No luck. That rear room of his is heavily curtained and he keeps the lighting dim. The man stood over in the corner. Dexter couldn't see his face."

"Curious. Even a shadow in a corner has dimensions," Morgan said. "If it talks, it has a certain kind of voice. You said you found out two things, Mr. Russell. That's only one."

Dave said quietly, "The man with Thelma was a policeman. He wasn't wearing his uniform, but Thelma had been drinking. She let it slip."

There was an intense but only momentary silence. Dave looked at Helen, and she looked back at him. Morgan had been smoking. He crossed to an ash tray, snubbed out his cigarette.

"May I have more coffee, Mrs. Russell, please?" he asked.

Grudgingly, Dave admitted to a sneaking admiration for the lieutenant. Morgan had poise. He gave no indication that he had just lost his Number One suspect and, as a substitute, been handed one of his own men. He stirred his coffee, sipped it black.

"We'll wait a minute. Maybe Dexter will be able to tell us a little more," he said.

The telephone rang as he was putting down his empty cup. "That's probably for me." He crossed the room to answer it.

"Yes? . . . Speaking." Dave, watching, saw quick anger form in the policeman's eyes. He saw the effort with which Morgan fought it down. "Well, you know what to do. Tell Swope—" he said, and checked himself. "Never mind. I'll talk to Swope myself."

He hung up and turned to Dave. "Dexter's not talking to anybody. He's on his way to the hospital with a fractured skull."

"An accident?" Dave got his answer from the expression on Lieutenant Morgan's face. "Hey, wait a minute—you're not accusing me! Somebody must have done it after I left. Somebody—"

"That's right, Mr. Russell. Somebody. I'll have to go now. Will you stay put this time, or must I lock you up?"

Dave had been pushed around too long. "On what charge? You can't lock me up without a reason. Do you have one?"

Morgan ticked off several. "Material witness, suspicion of murder, assault with a deadly weapon. How about—?"

"Never mind. You win," Dave told him. "I'll stay put."

There were people on the beach but Tommy saw them only as mobile obstacles between which he must make his way. He went north, plodding through soft sand toward questionable refuge. Fear prodded him so sharply that once he lost his head and broke into a run.

But he got hold of himself almost immediately, and slowed to an inconspicuous walk. What the hell was the matter with him, anyway? He was a cop; he knew that a cop's attention is always attracted by a running man. Particularly when the man doesn't seem to be running anywhere. The cop instinctively looks to see who's chasing him.

There wasn't anybody chasing him, that he knew of. He had a good head start. He'd got out of the window and down the ladder a split-second after the first knock on the door. He had gone so fast that he'd been halfway down when he'd heard the shouted, "Open up—police!" He had not heard Dexter's answering shout.

Why hadn't he heard it? He hadn't hit the old man often or very hard. He'd pulled his punches, or meant to pull them, because he didn't really give a damn about Dexter one way or the other. All he'd wanted was to throw a scare into the guy. Scare him enough so he wouldn't blab the little that he knew.

But when you came right down to it, what did Dexter know that was worth blabbing? He might be able to say that Tommy was tall and dark, and had been wearing a sports shirt, but they could walk along the beach and drag in a thousand guys that looked like that. Fingerprints? Prints must be so thick in Dexter's greasy shack, the chances were a hundred to one against them finding a single positive.

So he was safe, or reasonably so, and all he had to do was get out of the neighborhood, act natural and fix up those two alibis. Just the same, he wished Dexter had sung out when that knock came on the door. The old guy had either been too scared to answer, or—

Tommy refused to consider the alternative. His head was still splitting and Palisades City was a half-mile behind him now. He wanted a drink. But all they sold at the makeshift stands along the beach was beer. The bars were on the far side of the boardwalk, and he didn't want to go up on the boardwalk yet. He stopped at a stand and bought a can of beer.

It tasted like carbonated quinine water, but he got it down. He came to the crowded pier at last, and had a double shot of bourbon at a bar. The whiskey warmed him, cleared his thinking. He knew exactly what he had to do.

There was a liquor store across from the end of the pier. He bought a pint of bourbon, put it in his pocket, went to the corner and caught a southbound bus. The bus line paralleled the boardwalk. He got off a block east of Dexter's place, walked to the parking lot and got his car. Then he drove inland, approaching Martinez Canyon by a roundabout route. He parked behind Mildred's cafe, drank from his bottle and got out of the car. He opened the kitchen door of the cafe, but did not enter.

"Mildred—" He kept his voice low as he called.

She was in the kitchen, as he'd figured she would be; it wasn't time for the lunch crowd yet. She looked at him with sullen resentment from the far side of the stove.

"Come back to hit me again, Tom? Didn't you do it hard enough last time?"

"Honest to God, Mildred, I wouldn't hurt you for the world. Wouldn't have touched you if you hadn't gone haywire on me. What you said—about me and Ralph, remember—it just wasn't true."

"Why did you come back?"

"There's a little something you can do for me. No trouble, honey, or I wouldn't ask you. Just give Earl a message."

"Earl?"

"Earl Bingham. He's probably parked across the road. Will you do that for me?"

"Why don't you do it for yourself?"

"There's a reason, a good reason. Just get Earl off by himself and tell him I want to see him. I'll be in Manny's joint next door."

"Suppose he isn't there?"

"Tell him when he comes. I'll wait. And Mildred, anybody asks you, I been in and out all morning. I want to talk to you, too, as soon as I've seen Earl. See you later," he said, forcing a hard quality into his voice. "Let me give you some advice—don't cross me up."

Mildred said quietly, "The way you're acting, something tells me you're crossed up already. Can't say it breaks my heart."

"I could break your heart, if that was what I wanted. I hope you won't make me," Tommy said.

He left her, slipping around the corner of the cafe and into Manny's. He bought a can of beer and carried it to an empty booth. There was a window on his left. A thick curtain was drawn across it. He parted the curtain and looked out.

It took a moment for his eyes to adjust to bright sunlight after the gloomy interior of the bar. When they did, he saw Earl in the prowl car across the road. Earl was alone. Mildred stood beside the road waiting for a break in the traffic that would enable her to cross. The break came, but the prowl car moved away before it did. It merged with southbound traffic, headed toward the breakwater and the pier.

Never mind. Earl would come back, although that landslide might slow him down a little, and if Mildred knew what was good for her she would be waiting for him when he did. Tommy dropped the curtain, and immediately parted it again.

The scene was unchanged, but now he was able to identify a couple of people he had only glanced at casually before. The ice cream wagon was parked in front of Mildred's place. A man was standing beside it talking earnestly to the driver. Dave Russell!

Tommy slapped the curtain back in place. He took the bottle from his hip pocket, helped himself to a slug and chased it down with beer. He put the bottle back, and for a time did absolutely nothing. He didn't even think.

He knew that something was wrong at least a quarter of a minute before he was able to put his finger on exactly what it was. The knowledge felt, at first, like an emptiness in his stomach. Then, with realization sudden and complete, he stiffened as though he had been given a severe electric shock. The breath went out of him. He clapped his hand to his right hip pocket. Nothing was in it but the pint of whiskey. The left pocket contained only a handkerchief.

His blackjack was gone.

"But I heard you!" Dave insisted. "Early Sunday morning. You drove past my house."

Ken Hurley answered impatiently. "You couldn't have heard me. I'm always in bed by ten-thirty. That's my rule."

"Then someone was driving your truck. I recognized that little tune it plays."

Hurley shook his head. "Every evening all trucks get turned in to the company garage. The garage is locked. There's a watchman in the place all night."

"But—?"

"Say, tell me something, will you? What's everybody picking on me for, anyway? Lieutenant Morgan gave me the same line. I told him just what I've told you." After a moment, he added coldly, "Sometimes, or so they tell me, people hear things that just aren't there. Particularly when they're under a strain."

"Oh, for God's sake!" Dave said, and turned away. Abruptly, he turned back. "Hey, wait a minute. You told Morgan a lot more than that. You alibied Lu Warren, said you saw him on the road. How could you have seen him if you were in bed?"

Hurley's shrug expressed disgusted resignation. "Okay, okay—Morgan knows, so I might as well broadcast it to the world. Saturday night the wife and I had a small difference of opinion. She threw a book at me and ran out of the house. I met Warren when I went out to see which way she was heading. When she came home around two, I saw him again. Asked him what he was doing. He said he was looking for his cousin. Satisfied?"

"If the police are, I suppose I'll have to be. I'm also satisfied," Dave said, "that I heard an ice cream truck, but you've convinced me that it wasn't yours." He went home, not nearly as convinced as he had said he was.

Helen came down from the kitchen. "Find out anything?"

"I drew a blank." He told her Hurley's revised story.

She said thoughtfully, "That's not necessarily a blank. He's a big part of Warren's alibi. If he and Lu turned out to be friends, or if—"

"Please, darling," he begged, "we can't go around suspecting everybody. Let it rest."

She sighed. "I really botched things, didn't I?"

"Botched things—you?"

"This whole thing started because of my darned jealousy. If I hadn't nagged you so, you would have stayed home Saturday. You would never have been dragged into this. It's all my fault."

Dave was astonished. "Careful, girl—humility's rich food."

"I can swallow it. It's taken something like this horrible murder to make me see the truth. Darling, you know those long strings of colored electric lights they hang on Christmas trees? I'm like they are."

"You're prettier."

"No, I'm trying to be serious," she said. "The tree's all lit up, everything is lovely. Then one tiny light flickers—and the connection's broken. The whole string goes out. That's me. We're getting along fine. Then some small thing happens, and it may not even be your fault. But suddenly there's no more light and you're the world's worst heel. How can two people who love each other, as we do, act like that?"

"I don't know," he said, "but I do know one thing. We're not going to do it any more." He put his hand out, and she took it solemnly. "Agreed?"

"It's a deal," she said.

They had a light lunch. Afterwards, Helen refused to let him help her with the dishes. The telephone rang as she started carrying them to the kitchen. She put the dishes down to answer it.

"Yes? Oh, hello, Mr. Victor. No, I was standing right here by the phone." She was silent for what seemed to Dave a long time. Occasionally she frowned. "I understand," she said at last. "You'd better wire them. Hammerschlag & Vincent; my address book's on the desk." Her frown was deeper this time, really troubled. "Oh, Lord! Will you hold the line a minute, please?"

She cupped her right hand over the instrument. "I've goofed," she whispered. "Darling, would you mind terribly if I ran into the shop just for an hour or two?"

"Go right ahead." He waved permission with a lightness that he did not feel.

Helen spoke into the phone again. She told Victor to hold everything, that he could expect her at the shop within an hour. But as she talked, her eyes were fixed questioningly on Dave. He turned away, looked out the window. He was no longer listening but he knew when she hung up. He knew what she was going to say before she spoke.

"Dave, the way you looked just now—are you *sure* that you don't mind?"

He turned back after a moment, smiling. "Mind? Of course, I mind. You're not the only one whose wiring is a little faulty. But run along, darling. My lights may have flickered for a second, but now they're screwed in tight."

"Okay." She was responding slowly to his smile. "I'll leave as soon as I've done the dishes."

"You'll leave now. I'll do the dishes, and have a good time doing them," he said.

Tommy heard someone speak his name. He opened his eyes. Mildred was standing beside the table. He shook his head in an effort to clear it, and felt for his bottle. It was empty. Someone had stolen his liquor while he slept.

"You take my liquor?" he asked Mildred.

"No. And after you've heard what I've got to tell you, you better lay off the bottle. I talked to Earl Bingham."

Earl. The necessity of seeing him, and all the pressing reasons that made it a necessity, swept over Tommy in a nauseating wave. "Where is he?"

"He can't come here. Not until much later, after work. He says they found your blackjack. There's an all-points out to pick you up."

"Oh, my God!" Tommy struggled to rise, but couldn't make it. He fell back heavily against the booth. "Why would they do a thing like that to me? I'm a cop, just like they are. They're my friends!"

"You don't have friends, Tom, unless maybe Earl is one. Outside of him, all you've got is a lot of people that you've used."

Mildred left him. She went back to the cafe, and did not permit herself to think of him again. That wasn't hard; she was utterly preoccupied by something more important. This was Monday. In a few more hours, with the coming of darkness, her son planned to escape. If it took all night, she would wait beside the telephone to hear from Ralph.

At half-past six Dave crossed the road to the super-market and bought a can of roast beef hash for dinner. He bought canned stuff because it would be easier to prepare, and he chose the smaller size because Helen had just telephoned that she and Victor were still trying to straighten things out at the shop.

Something about an order from Hammerschlag & Vincent that had been shipped to the wrong address. She would have dinner in town and come home afterwards as soon as she could get away.

Dave had accepted it serenely. Only a few hours before, he realized, the message would have left him wallowing in resentment. Now he could take it, not only without wincing, but without feeling that his masculine pride demanded at least a token wince. He left the market with a small bag of groceries, shouldering the glass doors open wide.

"'Evening, Mr. Russell," a man said.

The man was getting out of a parked car. Dave recognized him as one of the deputies he had ridden with last night. The fairly decent deputy, as opposed to the one who had clouted him behind the ear. A huge man in uniform, he seemed even bigger in civilian trousers and white shirt.

"Hello, Bingham. Thanks for holding your partner back last night."

The deputy looked sheepish. "Tommy wouldn't of really hurt you. He's a nice fellow, just sort of . . . excitable."

"He's that, all right. You know why I haven't filed a complaint against him? I hope to be clear of this mess soon," Dave said. "Then I'm going to find him off duty and out of uniform. I'm going to take him apart. You tell him that."

"I'll tell him, Mr. Russell, but he ain't going to like it," Bingham said.

Trying to pound something into Earl's thick muttonhead was like slapping water with a stick. He just sat there on the other side of the table, meaning well, but nothing you said to him left much impression. Tommy sighed, went over it again.

"Look, Earl, maybe you better write this down and study it. Friday night I was with Mildred. I haven't talked to her yet, but I know she'll back me up. Saturday night—well, where was I then?"

A frown formed slowly on Earl's narrow forehead. "I know what you want me to say. You want me to say you was with me."

"That's it! I knew you'd get it, given time. We bought a six-pack of beer and drank it on the beach. That's where I lost my blackjack. Then we drove up to Santa Barbara just for the ride. At three A.M. you drove me back to my place and spent the night. Got it?"

Earl nodded, and Tommy gave him a relieved smile. He killed the rest of a can of beer. "Wish I had a decent drink."

Earl pulled two full pints of bourbon from his pockets. He pushed them across the table. "Mildred told me you was drinking. Figured you'd be needing a pickup about now."

"If you wasn't so ugly, Earl, I'd kiss you." Tommy stowed away one pint, opened the other and tilted it against his lips. "Well, now we got everything settled, haven't we?" He drew the back of his hand across his mouth.

Earl shook his head. "It won't work. Morgan's already asked me about both nights. Told him I went to a picture show Friday, and then went home. Did the same thing Saturday; it was a real good show. Asked me if I'd seen you. I told him no."

Tommy didn't move. Only his sick eyes betrayed the way he felt. All his plans, and all the hopes founded on those plans, had suddenly been smashed. Mildred might have alibied him for one night, but not for both. Hazel would have known that she was lying. She wouldn't have let Mildred get away with it. She hated Tommy for some reason he had never been able to understand.

Earl was still talking, but his voice was only a semi-intelligible rumble in Tommy's ears. "I'd do anything to help you, if I could. If I'd known what you wanted me to tell Morgan, I'd of told him exactly what you said. I'm sure sorry."

"You're sorry."

Earl nodded. "You're my friend. Everybody knows that. Why, Morgan put a tail on me hoping I'd lead him to you. It's okay," he raised a reassuring hand. "I shook him. But I'm taking a chance just being seen with you. That's all right, too. Us cops got to stick together. I want to help you all I can."

"How?"

"You better hole in somewheres. This'll all blow over." Earl paused, and after a moment added, "It'll blow over, that is, if you didn't really kill that girl."

"Hey!" Tommy sat up straight. "What is this? You know damn well I didn't kill her!"

Earl soothed him down. "Sure, Tommy, sure. I know you didn't, and I got a pretty good idea who did."

"So have I. Russell."

"Well, maybe—maybe not. Maybe it's another fellow doesn't live so far from here. People don't know, but he's been having trouble with his wife. Had his eye on Thelma. Anyway," Earl said, "you better keep away from Russell. Next time he sees you, he says he's going to take you apart."

Tommy leaned forward, his elbows heavy on the table. "Did he actually say that?"

"Sure did. Not ten minutes ago, out here in front. Hold on, Tommy." Earl rose, gently restrained his friend. "You can't tangle with him now. Where's your car?"

"Back of Mildred's. Why?"

"You better stretch out in it and get a little sleep. Then find yourself a place to hide."

"Just like that, huh? Where?"

Earl said thoughtfully, "You got a private entrance to your room. They already went there to look for you. If you was to leave your car somewhere, your own place might be the safest place there is."

There was a short silence. "I'll think about it," Tommy said.

"You do that." Earl asked one more question just before he left. "Say, Tommy—tell me the truth. Where was you Saturday night?"

Tommy stared at him furiously. "It's sapping Dexter they want me for. That's all. I had nothing to do with that blonde girl. I didn't even know her, understand? You remember that, and keep your nose out of places where it don't belong."

"Sure, Tommy—anything you say." The big deputy left the table, walked out of the beer joint. Tommy was alone. He thought about the girl he'd had a date with Saturday night. There was a fat chance of getting Maria Gonzalez to give him an alibi. If Corporal Gonzalez knew the truth, he'd beat hell out of his wife. And if he didn't do the same to Tommy, he'd certainly have Tommy's job. It was a terrible thing to be suspected of something that you haven't done, and not be able to prove you haven't done it because what you *had* done was, from certain prejudiced points of view, almost as bad.

Tommy pushed Maria from his mind and concentrated on the guy who'd really killed poor Thelma. He was going to have to have a showdown with Dave Russell, beat the truth out of him if it was necessary. But Earl had been right about one thing. Before he tackled Russell, before he did anything, he was going to have to get a little sleep.

At ten minutes past seven the pay telephone in the front part of the cafe rang shrilly. There was only one customer at the counter. Mildred went over to the phone. Her movements were unhurried. She had been waiting hours for this moment, and she had schooled herself not to betray excitement. Her hand was steady as she lifted the receiver and held it to her ear.

"Hello," she said, expecting to hear Ralph's voice.

A woman answered. "This is Western Union. I have a telegram for Mrs. Mildred Riggs."

"This is Mrs. Riggs. Read it to me," Mildred said.

There was a pause. Then the woman said slowly and with terrible distinctness, "Message follows. 'Regret to inform you Ralph accidentally killed while attempting escape. Please wire as to disposition of body.'" A shorter pause. "The telegram is signed—"

"Never mind," Mildred said. "I know who signed it."

"Would you like us to mail you a copy?"

"I don't care. It makes no difference."

She hung up. The customer was drinking coffee. "Leave your money on the counter," she told him. "Shut the door when you go out." She went into the kitchen and sat down beside the window, her accustomed place.

She was sitting there when Tom Riggs came out of the beer joint. She saw him stand unsteadily for a moment, staring at the house across the road. Then he lurched around to the rear of the cafe. Presently she heard him climb into his car. He slammed the door but did not drive away.

An indeterminable period of time went by. It could have been three minutes or three hours. Mildred didn't know. She was waiting for something—something significant—to happen. She did not know what it would be, but she knew that it would happen, and that she would recognize it and be guided by it when it did.

Then Tom Riggs snored, and apparently was awakened by his snoring. The car door creaked as he opened it and got out.

Dave went up to the bedroom, and changed to pajamas and a dressing gown. It was a gesture supposed to show that he wasn't a bit worried. But he was worried. It was ten o'clock and Helen had not yet come home.

The doorbell rang. He was running down the stairs before he realized that it could not be Helen who had rung it; she would have used her key. That only increased his anxiety. She might have been in an accident. This might be someone bringing him the news. His hand was damp, turning the knob.

The door was violently pushed open. The deputy named Riggs stood there. He was no longer handsome. His face was lined and puffy, his half-closed eyes were red. He looked as though he had been drunk, and shortly might be drunk again, but right now he was sober. Fairly sober. He took two lumbering steps into the room.

"Smart boy, Russell! Murder Thelma, then make 'em think I did it!" He swung a powerful but misdirected fist.

Dave hit him twice. The first blow caught him in the belly and won a spray of vomited bourbon. The second, as Riggs doubled up, came from below to connect with the point of the deputy's chin. He went down but, falling, he wrapped his arms around Dave's legs.

They were strong arms. Dave tried to smash his knee into Rigg's face, but the dragging weight threw him off balance. He fell, but managed to free himself. Once more he slammed his fist against the sagging chin. He sat on top of Riggs and banged his head against the floor. Suddenly all resistance stopped. The man's head lolled to one side. He had passed out cold.

Dave slapped him, first on one cheek then the other. There was no response. He got up, went to the kitchen for a glass of water. Returning, he poured it on the upturned face. Riggs gasped. His eyes came into bleary focus. He stared at Dave.

Dave nudged him with his foot. "So now they think you did it, do they? Well, that figures. A cop was at Dexter's Friday night with Thelma. You're a cop. Suppose you tell me all about it, friend."

Comprehension came back slowly to the staring eyes. "Gimme a drink."

Dave grinned. "What would you like? Water, whiskey, gin?"

"Whiskey."

"There's a whole fifth in the liquor cabinet. But you'll have to earn it. Want to talk?"

"Got nothing to lose. Gimme a drink," Riggs said. "I'll talk."

Dave crossed to the cabinet. He filled a shot glass, and brought back both the glass and bottle. Riggs gulped the whiskey. He got groggily to his feet, held out the empty glass. Dave refilled it. Riggs threw the second glass of whiskey in Dave's face.

Alcohol seared his eyes. Through a burning haze, he saw the deputy stagger toward the door. Half-blind, he plunged after him. He almost caught him on the outside stairs, but Riggs kicked backward. His heel hit Dave in the chest. Dave saved himself by grabbing at the banister, but the delay had given Riggs too big a start. He had already crossed the road when Dave got up to the gate. Riggs was running in the general direction of Mildred's cafe, and Dave started after him. He stopped when he heard his name called softly.

"Mr. Russell?"

It was man's voice. Dave thought he recognized it. It came from the shadows on the far side of the gate.

"Let him go, Mr. Russell. They'll pick him up now. Poor fellow hasn't got a chance."

"Bingham?"

"Yes, sir. Hope Tommy didn't hurt you. I tried to get here sooner. Had trouble with my car."

Dave's eyes had adjusted to the night, and they no longer burned. He could see Bingham quite distinctly now. The deputy stood beside an old sedan. It was a black Buick with a damaged right rear fender. There was something about its presence here, and about Bingham's presence, that didn't fit in logically with the time and place.

"Why didn't you warn me Riggs was coming? You didn't have to drive; you could have phoned."

"Didn't have anything for sure to tell you; I didn't know what Tommy was going to do. He was in bad enough trouble. Didn't want to make it worse."

"He's in trouble, all right," Dave said. "And so are you. You're a deputy sheriff. Riggs is wanted for murder. Why didn't you grab him? You practically had him in your hands."

The huge deputy was silent. He produced a pack of cigarettes, methodically opened it. He offered a cigarette to Dave.

Dave shook his head impatiently. "Well?"

"Just couldn't do it, Mr. Russell," Bingham told him. "Deep down inside me, I still can't believe that Tommy killed that girl. Sure, I *know* he did it, but knowing ain't believing. Anyway, I can't arrest him. He's my friend."

There was another silence, longer than the one that had preceded it. Then Dave said, "He's no friend of mine. I'll have to telephone Lieutenant Morgan, Bingham. I'm going to do it now."

Bingham shrugged. "I see what you mean. It all depends on how you look at it. I won't try to stop you. Guess it's the only thing you can do."

Dave turned away, feeling no sense of vindication or of triumph. Feeling, on the contrary, unsatisfied. Something was lacking, but what it was he didn't know. He would do what he had to do. From then on it would be up to the police. He started toward the little gate.

Then he stopped, becoming suddenly and absolutely rigid. From close at hand—from very close at hand—there came a tinkling little tune. Dave had an instant of total recall. It was two o'clock in the morning and he was standing in the kitchen, in the dark. Outside, beyond the kitchen window, a man had just climbed into a car. Its motor started and Dave distinctly heard familiar notes. They formed the refrain he had always associated with the ice cream wagon. *Oh Where, Oh Where Has My Little Dog Gone?*

Dave turned back slowly. He looked at the deputy, at the cigarette lighter in Bingham's hand. That's where the tune was coming from, the lighter. It was one of those Swiss gadgets that played when its top was open. In the excitement of discovery, Dave stared at it too long.

He looked up to see that Bingham was watching him, and he saw that Bingham knew he'd been found out. Neither man spoke. After a moment, Dave turned away again.

This time he hurried. When he heard footsteps close behind him, he broke into a run. He ran down the steps and slammed the front door as he went in. He crossed to the telephone. He had just picked it up when the door shuddered under the impact of Bingham's heavy shoulder. He dialed rapidly.

The door burst open. There was a gun in Bingham's hand as he came in. The gun was pointed at Dave's stomach.

"Put the phone down, Mr. Russell," Bingham said.

Dave dropped it in its cradle. When Bingham told him to turn around, that's what he did. Something heavy crashed down on his head. He heard a groan, and vaguely recognized the sound of his own voice. Then the room tilted up on end and slid away.

Helen turned into the beach road from the canyon at twenty-eight past ten. There was a light still burning in Mildred's cafe as she passed. That was unusual, but Helen was so angry that she didn't even notice. She was furious with Victor for keeping her so late. Goodness only knew what Dave would say when she got home.

A car was parked just beyond the little gate, and she slowed down to stop behind it. Her headlights illuminated the crumpled fender of a black Buick sedan. The Buick moved out as her car crept up on it; it made a fast U-turn and headed north. The Rambler slid into the place where it had been. Helen climbed out and started down the steps, coming to an abrupt stop as she neared the door.

The door stood open, and something was the matter with it. Light streamed through the doorway from the living room. She went down the rest of the way and saw that the door was hanging awry on its hinges. She walked past it, looked up the stairs toward the kitchen. No sound came from the kitchen; it was dark.

"Dave—?" She ran up the stairs.

The bed was unrumpled. His shirt and slacks were lying in a chair. She looked in the closet. His pajamas and dressing gown were gone. Where, dressed only in a dressing gown and pajamas, could Dave have gone at this hour of the night? And who had broken in the door?

She remembered the black Buick with the crumpled fender. Panic clogged her throat.

She ran down to the telephone. She told the operator to connect her with the sheriff's sub-station, that it was an emergency.

A red-hot spike had been driven through Dave's skull. He was burning up but his forehead, curiously, was cold. And wet. There was a rumbling nearby crash of heavy surf. He opened his eyes and, by the gritty feel of it, knew that he was lying face downward on damp sand. His hands were locked behind his back. He moved them, but only for a couple of inches. They stopped then, the metal was tight around his wrists.

He rolled over on his back, willing the pain to go away. It didn't go, but presently it became supportable. A man stood near him, thick legs spread apart. It was Earl Bingham.

The deputy must have heard him move, but he paid no attention. He was staring northward, up the coast. Dave knew where he was now, on the beach near Point of Rocks, beside one of the pools left by the receding tide. One of the pools in which Bingham had drowned Thelma. By turning his head and craning back his neck, he was able to see what the deputy was staring at. There were red flares on the road ahead.

"What is it, Bingham?" he asked. "Your first glimpse of hell?"

The deputy looked down at him. "Trouble of some kind. Don't know what. Sorry you woke up, Russell. Hoped I could get this over with before you did."

"Must you get it over with?"

Bingham's voice, when he answered, was puzzled and surprised. "Well, sure. What else can I do?"

"I don't know what you hope to gain. They're sure to catch you. I don't know why you killed Thelma. Tell me, Bingham—why?"

"I am not as slow-thinking as everybody says I am. Fellow gets tired of always being pushed aside, seeing other fellows get the gravy, the good-looking girls. There was something special about Thelma. She was beauty-full. Tommy didn't see that; all he saw was another dame, and he treated her like one. He didn't have no trouble. So I tried, but she just laughed at me. Made me pretty mad. Guess I sort of lost my head."

"What makes you think she didn't laugh at Tommy, too?"

"Because he told me. He told me she was easy. Tommy wouldn't lie to me. He's my friend."

Dave looked past the deputy at the zebra-shadows on the beach. He had thought he'd seen one move, but now it was quite still. He kept on talking, and tried to keep Bingham talking. Kill time. Hope that something, anything, would happen. It was the only thing left.

"Riggs is your friend, but you went out of your way to make him look bad. You wanted him to be suspected. Why?"

Bingham chuckled. The muscular spasm accompanying the chuckle was like a small earthquake. "Sure played that one smart. Yes, sir—Tommy might've pulled that trick hisself."

"How smart can you get? Would you have let him go to the gas chamber in your place?"

The earthquake chuckle gradually subsided. "Why not?" Bingham said. "I don't want to die, and it's what Tommy would of done to me. He's told me so a hundred times. He always said a guy's got to look out for hisself."

He reached down then to put his hands beneath Dave's arms, to drag him over to the pool. For an instant he was in a vulnerable position. Dave drove his right foot up with all his strength.

Bingham's breath whooshed out of him. His hands went to his crotch; he doubled over. Dave tried to get his legs out of the way. Too late. The deputy landed on them as he fell.

His huge arms encircled them and held on tight. Presently, when his breathing had grown normal, he got back on his feet. This time when he approached, it was cautiously, from Dave's head. The shallow pool was less than a yard away. One heave pulled Dave up beside it. A big hand grabbed his head and pushed it down. Dave tried to shout, and gagged on brackish water. He breathed, and water rushed into his lungs. He had not known there could be red flares beneath the surface of the water. But they were there, lots of them, when they should have been up on the road. He watched them, growing strangely incurious as time passed.

One by one the red flares all went out.

The mindless night was alive, groping and sentient. It seeped through the kitchen window, dimming the single electric bulb suspended from the ceiling. Mildred knew that when the light was gone, when the darkness was complete, she would go, too. Not bravely, not with a gallant gesture. The night would simply take her over. She would cease to be.

Someone opened the front door of the cafe. "Anybody here?" a man's voice called. She got up slowly, went to the service panel remembering that she had not locked the door.

"Sorry. Closed for the night." She looked through the service panel at the man who had come in.

He was dressed in working clothes: high laced boots and a yellow metal helmet. The helmet was shaped like those worn in the First World War. He turned in the direction of her voice.

"Have to use your phone." He had already started toward it, feeling in his pocket for a coin.

Mildred pulled her head back from the panel, heard him dial, heard the bell ring as he dropped his dime. "Put Mike Collins on. Emergency," he said.

Five seconds passed while his fingers impatiently tapped the coin box. Then he spoke urgently. "This is Art. Mike, you know that fault a half-mile north of Point of Rocks? It gave way twenty minutes ago." A pause. "The biggest yet. Knocked out the whole road—nothing left but a sheer drop to the rocks. Better get the gang here on the double."

He listened, nodded briskly. "Yeah, set up a road block—route traffic through Martinez Canyon. Will do. I already got flares going. Hurry up."

He hung up, started for the door. Mildred came into the front part of the cafe.

"What happened?"

"Landslide," the man said. He hurried out.

Mildred returned to the kitchen. She took a switchblade from the pocket of her apron, and dropped it on a table. The knife was part of her defiant, bitter past; she wouldn't need it any more. She took her apron off and hung it on a nail. She picked up a bright scarf from the table and tied the scarf around her head. There was something almost coquettish about the manner in which she adjusted it and tied the knot. She smiled at her reflection in a mirror. She might have been a young girl going to a dance.

She didn't bother to shut the kitchen door as she went out. She walked around the parked car, opened the door, got in behind the wheel. Tommy was huddled in the corner of the front seat, head drooping on his chest. He didn't awaken until she had started the car, backed up and turned into the beach road.

He stirred then. His head came up, but it was at least a minute before he spoke. "Well, what do you know! Old Mildred," he said thickly. "You taking me for a ride?"

"That's right."

"Cops looking for me, Milly. Where we going?"

"We're going home," she said.

A man shouted at them as the car sped north. He wore a yellow helmet, and Mildred swerved to avoid hitting him. A few yards south of Point of Rocks three cars were clustered together off the road. Two of them bore the official insignia of California, but Mildred didn't notice that. She was staring eagerly through the windshield at red brilliance on the curving road ahead. The brilliance came from flares. Black moving dots were silhouetted against them. The moving dots grew larger, became distinguishable as men. One of the men threw up his arms in an arresting gesture. He shouted; there was a whole chorus of warning shouts. Mildred ignored them. Her eyes were fixed on a wide gap in the road ahead.

Beyond the gap was nothingness. The flares were on both side of the brink. Their redness had a stimulating effect on Tommy. He started bragging about his twenty-one inch color television as the car shot into space.

It was a hot day. The window by Dave's bed was open.

A young man stood by the window studying a chart. He wore a stethoscope around his neck. When he saw Dave looking at him questioningly, he smiled.

"Awake, Mr. Russell?"

"What hospital is this?"

"St. Mark's. It's eight o'clock in the morning. Your temperature is normal, and if you don't let yourself get excited you'll probably be discharged this afternoon."

"How did I get here?"

"The usual way, an ambulance. Don't talk too much, Mr. Russell; I'll tell you anything you want to know. You can thank your wife for being here. She telephoned Lieutenant Morgan, described Bingham's car. They'd been looking for it already. Morgan showed up at Point of Rocks in time to pull your head out of the water; the ambulance crew got the water out of your lungs. Bingham's in jail. He's a celebrity. His picture's in all the papers, and he's making the most of it. That's all, I think," the doctor said. "Or is there something more?"

Through the window came familiar notes, a tinkling little tune. It passed. Dave listened until it had faded in the distance. It was a hot day, but it wasn't ice cream that he wanted.

"Where's my wife?"

Down and Out
Joe Gores

June 1959

In San Francisco, when you've stopped shaving every day and your hand shakes reaching for that first quick one, they'll say you're headed south of Market. It's like going north of the bridge on Clark Street in Chicago or down Washington Avenue to Second in Minneapolis; liquor stores outnumber everything but pawnshops and at night only the bars are bright. Cops work in pairs here, and winos sleep on street corners until the wagon takes them to the drunk tank at Kearny and Washington. Any night, south of Market, you can find them: the snowbirds, the drunks, the whores, the bullies . . . and the men who are scared so deep down in their guts that they're almost beyond fear.

The men like me.

I was sitting in a slophouse on Third over a tired piece of pie and a cup of muddy jo when I saw two guys arguing outside. The grey-haired one wore a white shirt, sport jacket, and rumpled trousers. His tired whiskey eyes peered from a lined face that had been stepped on for more years than Williams has been with Boston. The short dapper Mexican sported a blue suit, white shirt and red tie, cowboy boots, and two days' whiskers. One hand waved a nearly empty Tokay bottle; the other tried to fit his new white Stetson onto the old bird's head.

Just as I came out he spread his arms wide and ran into a parking meter. Then he tried to drag the old guy down Third.

"G'wan. You got me in trouble once already. I ain't goin' down there with you."

After the Mexican had wandered off, he saw me and hollered, "Hey, sport!"

Coming over, he added: "I had just enough for a good bottle of Tokay, and then I went and give it to that Mexican. Found out afterwards that boy has plenty of glue—folding glue. Struck me as prob'ly a swell feller when he's sober." His faded blue eyes stared worriedly after the Mexican. "Hate to see that boy go south of Market with that glue. He don't know this town, an' what the hell is he gonna find down there except trouble?"

I couldn't answer that one. Figuring it for a touch, and being a soft-hearted slob, I separated myself from a couple aces.

"Here, Pops. Have yourself a ball."

"I didn't ask for this." His face got wistful as he palmed the two bucks. "Name's Kiely, sport—live at the Wessley on 22nd and Third. Ever out that way . . ."

He stopped there as if afraid of pushing it too much, treated me to a gentle smile, and slouched off. Just another grifter among the Third Street juice-heads and happy girls and silent drifting Negroes. In the bars I found the usual sad guys sucking away on draft beer with their pockets full of dust and their heads full of ghosts. I took in a triple feature, any seat in the house for 35¢.

Around midnight I started hiking out Folsom toward the Mission District where I lived. In a dark deserted stretch between the puddles of streetlight, a lean black 1956 Lincoln slid up to the curb, its exhaust murmuring poh-poh-poh in the cold night air. A heavy blue-chinned face with a fat cigar screwed in the middle of it was poked out the window.

"Give ya a lift, boyfriend?"

Before I could say no, the door was open and the short fat guy who belonged to the face was on the curb beside me. A switchblade gouged my belt buckle.

"In, boyfriend."

His blue chin joggled the spitty cigar up and down like a frayed brown finger waggling. Under his blue topcoat were stuffed twenty-five extra pounds of soft Italian cooking, but with the knife he was plenty tough for me just then.

His partner took the Lincoln down Eighth with the lights to Bryant, then cut left towards the waterfront. He had the build of a fast light-heavy, wavy blond hair, and cold blue eyes that seemed to focus on something a foot behind me.

"Call me Emmy," suggested the stubby Italian, working the cigarette lighter nonchalantly. This was old stuff to him.

"Listen," I said, "You have the wrong guy. You made a mistake."

Leaning forward, Emmy spoke around me.

"He says we make a mistake, Earl."

Earl didn't say anything. Settling back against the cushions, Emmy announced with finality: "We ain't made no mistake, boyfriend . . . Right, Earl?"

Earl went right on not saying anything. He swung the Lincoln into the dead end on First Street across from the squat grey mass of the Seaman's Union, and parked facing out towards Harrison with dimmed lights.

"What's the handle, kid?" he asked.

"Rick. I told you, you got the wrong guy."

"Make it easy on yourself, kid. Tell us about Kiely."

"I never even heard of him." I was sweating by then.

On the corner was a dive with a red neon sign above the door. Two guys came out, glanced incuriously at the Lincoln, and angled across Harrison. I didn't move. Beside me Emmy made wet noises on the end of his cigar like a baby with a new bottle.

"We knew he was in town." Earl's voice sounded detached, as if he was trying to remember the last man he'd gunned down. "Tonight we spotted him talking with you on Third, but we lost him."

"Then we make you again comin' outta the flics," put in Emmy.

"Hell," I said, remembering. "Was that Kiely? He's just a juice-head, bummed me for a buck."

"Did he say where he lived?"

After a second I said in a steady voice, "No—nothing. Not even thanks."

Earl began to drum on the steering wheel with his fingers. Then, abruptly, "Okay, kid, I guess you're straight. Emmy, let him out."

As I slid out, Emmy shoved his face close to mine. With his saggy jowls and droopy outer eye-lids, he resembled a well-fed bloodhound.

"Right down Harrison without trying to look-see the license plates, boyfriend."

"Can the musical comedy act and get to hell in here," snapped Earl.

I told him thanks and he laughed and I walked down Harrison feeling like a tin duck in a shooting gallery with his pulley broken, even though I knew it was silly. No one shot at me. After half a block I stopped to light a cigarette: the Lincoln was out of sight. Cupping the match my hands shook, but not nearly as much as Keily's would have shaken.

The Wessley was an upstairs flophouse two and a half blocks from the Third Street precinct station where the bus had dropped me. When I paused under the single lightbulb over the hotel's street entrance, a big car slid in to the curb in the next block and cut its lights. Nobody got out. I had the street to myself.

There was a worn matting on the creaky stairs and the stuffy office was empty. Ajax Kiely, by the register, had room twenty-seven. The Wessley smelled old and worn out, like a tired miner after a day in the pits. A strip of faded maroon carpeting wandered down the narrow hall and around two right-angle turns to dead-end at twenty-seven. Nobody did anything when I knocked.

I went downstairs, outside, and into the saloon next door. It was an old-fashioned place with high ceilings; plain heavy glass bowls filled with hard-boiled eggs were set out on the mahogany bar. On my side of the plank were two Italian laborers, on the other a balding heavy-set barkeep who looked like he could have stopped Dempsey in his day. In that neighborhood he probably had a blackjack on his hip and a loaded .32 under the beer cooler.

In the mirror I was broad and tired and white around the mouth, friendly as a truck driver out of work. It was nearly two A.M.

"What's yours, Jack?"

"I want to talk with a guy named Kiely."

"Kiely?" He made it sound like the name of an unknown animal.

"Right . . . Ajax." I pointed at the ceiling and waggled my thumb like Matt Dillon with his six-gun. "Number twenty-seven, upstairs."

"Uh huh." His dirty towel moved the dust around on top of the bar. "You better go ask at the kitchen."

Through a connecting doorway was a darkened delicatessen with another doorway in the rear from which shone dingy yellow light. I could smell garlic and steak frying. The tiny cluttered kitchen barely held a black iron cook stove and a fat Italian woman with a fine assortment of chins. Her hair was pulled back in a wispy bun and her stabbing blue eyes hadn't missed a buck since we went off the gold standard.

"I ain't doing anything but sandwiches tonight."

"Fellow name of Kiely lives upstairs in twenty-seven. Has he been around?"

"You from a finance company?"

I wrinkled up my nose without answering, as if someone had hung a herring under it.

She flopped over the sizzling steak, cut it enough to peek in, took down a heavy platter and reached for a loaf of French bread with an economy of motion that would have shamed an efficiency expert.

As she cut the bread she said: "Harry had some trouble out front last week. He don't like to answer questions much." She shoved the platter with the sandwich on it into my hands. "Tell the guy on the end he owes me a buck. Kiely's out back."

Beyond a washed-out green curtain at the end of the tavern was a big barren room with long tables pushed back against the walls to open the unvarnished floor for Saturday night dancing. There were wooden booths along the left wall and in the second one was Kiely, sopping up gravy from a cleaned plate with a slice of French bread.

When I slid in across from him he looked up and grinned.

"Didn't expect you tonight, sport." He gestured at the plate. "Man hadn't ought to never neglect his diet. Learned that when I was batting .300 with the Chi Sox."

I said: "Listen, there's something—"

"When the war come along I got out of baseball, sport—enlisted in the Air Force and captained a flying squad in Australia." He hacked his piece of apple pie in two and stuffed half of it in his face. Red-brown flakes of crust spilled down his shirt front. "Ain't ever liked a Limey since then. Bought a jug of juice off one on the bus, I did, for ten bucks American. When I opened it I found it was tea. Since then—"

I repeated patiently, "Two guys. They want you. I thought you might be faintly interested, but I wouldn't want to interrupt you."

His fork hit the plate and spanged off on the floor. In the bar the juke box started blaring.

"Two guys, huh? Earl an' Emmy, ain't it? By God, they did it again." Suddenly his words were bullets. "What's your angle, sport? How'd they slice it for you?"

"To hell with you, Mr. Kiely."

I started to slide out of the booth but he grabbed my arm.

"Sorry, sport. It started in Philly and it's gone through New York and Chicago and Miami and New Orleans and L.A. Spend three years on the bum with death lookin' over your shoulder, an' it does somethin' to you."

"Okay, Pops. Forget it. I get these impulses."

He nodded.

"I seen this Earl kill a man in Philly. There was a lotta money an' I got it, never mind how. When I shake him it'll be women an' likker an' fancy hotels an' flunkies shinin' old Kiely's shoes . . ." His voice stopped, lowered. "You ever seen eighty grand, sport?"

He clawed open the top buttons of his shirt and I saw a small leather pouch slung around his neck on a cord and hung under one arm. He took out a flat metal key with the number 181 stamped in it and laid it reverently on the table between us.

"There she is, sport. Safe deposit box. But only old Kiely knows the bank an' the city an' what name she's under."

There wasn't much for me to say. Looking at the key lying in one of the rings his water glass had made, I thought about what a man might do with eighty grand. But I remembered Earl's eyes and competent killer's hands, and was glad I wasn't Kiely.

When I looked up he was watching me.

"I know, sport: you're thinkin' that Kiely's eighty grand ain't done him a hell of a lot of good. You're right. It ain't." His blue eyes sharpened with hate, like a hustler's when the guy she's been working for drinks turns out to be a John from the vice squad. "But once you start runnin' it ain't easy to stop. An' it ain't just the money, neither; Earl needs me dead cause I can finger him for that old Philly kill."

"Look, Pops," I said suddenly, "Give me until tomorrow morning and I can raise maybe a double sawbuck to get you out of town."

He regarded me for a long time without speaking; then one forefinger slid the key across the table to me.

"I got a feelin', sport. Gimme this tomorrow mornin' at the bus depot. Now c'mon up to the room an' tell me about Earl."

"I don't want that key, Pops."

"This way, sport, if he . . . finds me tonight I can't tell him where it is, 'cause I won't know. I tell ya, I got a feelin'."

So I stuck the key in my pocket and followed him up the back stairs. His room was typical of a Third Street flophouse: faintly sour with dead cigar smoke and narrow as a reformer's mind, with newspapers cluttering the unmade bed just inside the door. In front of the window was a worn-out easy chair that had been there when Rockne was coach at Notre Dame. The thin brown shade was drawn and the closet door stood open just enough to let a mouse out. The nap of the brown patterned rug was thin as a depression dime. It was a room to have nightmares in.

"They'd give a lot to know that what they want is right here," said Kiely, switching on the light. I turned back to slide the night chain into its metal groove and he added, in a sudden high breathless voice, "When I was playin' ball with a fellow in Philly name of Moran . . ."

He stopped abruptly, with a sigh. As I started to turn from the door there was the splitting painless sensation of being struck on the head: then there was nothing at all.

Obscenely gay printed flowers were strewn across the sides of the cheap tin waste basket and the brown carpet tickling my nose smelled mouldy. A very large wasp was monotonously sinking its stinger into the base of my skull. When I rolled over I was not ashamed to groan. Kiely regarded me thoughtfully from the broken-down easy chair.

"What the hell?" I said to him. "What the hell?"

Somehow I answered the bell for the tenth. My shoe skittered something across the rug to rattle against the wainscoting. It resembled the knife that Emmy had held against my belly earlier that evening. I remembered the cigar smoke odor and looked at Kiely. His shirt wore a new red necktie. As I watched, the end of the necktie lengthened and dripped twice in his lap. I'd fingered Kiely after all.

Outside a lightly-touched siren growled throatily. I recalled that the precinct station was only two and a half blocks away. An anonymous phone call, probably. Hide the knife. I drifted over, picked it up, and slid it into my pocket. There was blood on my jacket sleeve. *What the hell?* I thought then, *I can't hide Kiely.*

"Pardon me," I said aloud.

Feet pounded up the echoing stairs by the front desk. I went around Kiely to lean against the window. It burst outward with a lovely shattering sound, taking the shade with it. Shockingly fresh air, heavy with mist, stung my sluggish brain.

A heavy fist made the thin door quake and a voice like Tarzan's bellowed: "Police! Open up in there!"

From the window sill I cannon-balled into darkness. My heels crunched in a pail and flipped it over, landing me tail-first in a shower of stinking garbage. I dodged through a junk-littered yard to the back fence, and, though my legs were wobbly, made the top on the first try. When I paused to curse the slivers in my hands, a flashlight beam from Kiely's window probed the yard frantically and voices shouted, so I went on over.

The ground was low and wet, the night foggy. At the bottom of a shallow muddy embankment I found railroad tracks. They led me to the 25th Street intersection; here I turned uphill, away from Third, and climbed towards the Potrero Terrace Housing Projects. The cement government prefabs waited emptily for the wreckers to come, grey and cold and ghostly in the swirling mist. I found a pay phone and called a Yellow.

Sweating out my cab in the shadow of a big warehouse at the foot of Connecticut, I rolled my jacket into a tight bundle with the blood inside and the knife still in the pocket. When a prowl car rocketed past on Army Street, siren and spot blazing, I didn't try to flag it down.

My shoes echoed hollowly on the cement ramp of the all-night auto park in the basement of the Bellingham Hotel on Sixth and Mission. A husky Negro about my own age was dozing on a cot in the bright cramped office by the foot of the ramp. He resembled Harry Belafonte and had the name of the garage stitched in neat red script across the chest of his blue mechanic's coveralls.

His sharp eyes opened, focused, lit up.

"Man," he said, "Little cool to be running around outside without a jacket." He sat up, rubbing his eyes, then reached for the desk drawer where the bottle was stored. I shook my head.

"Where you flopping now, Nat?"

"Dump over on Geary and Octavia. Why?"

"I need a pad for a few days."

He took a key from his pocket, dropped it on my open palm.

"Third house from the corner, yellow with lots of gingerbread. Front room on the ground floor. Don't let the landlady see you, man. She's death on Whites bein' in there. Bad trouble?"

"Bad enough. A guy got dead." When his eyes widened I added: "I didn't do it, Nat."

"Man," he said softly, "I didn't ask. You just naturally can't stay out of trouble." He stood up to reach an army field jacket down off a hook screwed into the unpainted wall. "Be sunup when I leave here, won't need this."

I laid my jacket on the chair. "Can you get rid of this thing, Nat? There's blood on it, and a knife in the pocket."

"This the knife that—"

"Ya."

"I'll call you a cab, man; you look like hell."

It was four o'clock.

A little Negro girl skipped down the sidewalk, wearing a bright red cloth coat, her hair sticking almost straight out in two tight black braids. She was happy. Behind her came three Negro boys and one Chinese boy, all dressed in gaudy windbreakers and brown corduroy trousers. Two of them carried school books. Golden sunlight slanted across the sidewalk; no town is lovelier than San Francisco when the sun shines. Nat came up the street from the bus stop, whistling. Under his arm were school books, too; law school on the G. I. Bill.

Over steaming coffee fresh off his hot plate I told the whole story, ending with the key in my hand. He shook his head.

"Old soft-hearted Rick," he said.

"And eighty-grand."

"When you went to warn him you didn't know about any eighty grand. How the devil you figure those cats found the old man's pad?"

"Earl didn't believe that I didn't know Kiely's place," I said bitterly, "So they just followed me out there. It must have been the Lincoln I noticed pulling in down the street just after I got there."

"So they read the register, jimmy Kiely's lock, and wait in the closet. When Kiely says that what they want is in the room—bingo!"

"Not they," I corrected. "Just Emmy, and I bet Earl waited outside in case Kiely got away. He never would have knocked off the old man without making sure of the money first. When I woke up the room had hardly been disturbed."

Nat poured out more coffee and leaned back on the bed. Suddenly he sat bolt upright, making the springs whine protestingly.

"Hey, man, just before Kiely got it . . . what's he say?"

"Something about Philly and a ballplayer named Moran. Nothing there that . . ."

I stopped and looked at the key in my hand.

"That's it," shouted Nat excitedly, "He was plenty sharp. The loot is in safe deposit box 181 at some bank in Philly under the name Moran."

"There're a lot of banks in Philly."

"We can beat that. The big thing now is that this cat Earl is going to realize that Kiely probably gave you something that he wants. Better stick right here, Rick. I'll poke around tonight before work, see what I can find out."

Later, as he was at the door, I called softly, "Nat—thanks."

His grin was huge. "Old army buddies—and eighty grand." Then he laughed and went out the door.

I never saw him again.

Time passed slowly. The papers gave Kiely's killing the usual skid-row treatment—a couple inches on page two. The Giants were looking good and Silky Sullivan had dropped dead in the Derby. They were drafting 10,000 men this month.

The floor wore a green carpet and someone had laid rose pink paint over the wallpaper. I found a jug in the closet. How many banks were there in Philly with safe deposit boxes? A team of patient men could cover them in time.

By eight-thirty the bottle was dry. I walked through the fog to the Chinese store in the 1100 block of Geary, averting my face when autos passed. In the hall at Rick's place a colored teen-ager was pleading with a colored woman in her thirties in front of her open door. The hall smelled like the halls in every cheap rooming house in the world. They stopped talking to stare at me with flat observant eyes from across the racial gulf that only love or friendship can really span.

I had a few belts and switched on radio station KOBY: Jerry Lee Lewis and Fats Domino, everybody rockin' and rollin' and havin' a ball. Sometime before midnight I fell asleep in the chair.

When a newscaster awoke me at six A.M. I wished that he hadn't:

> Nathaniel Webster Doobey, 28, colored, address unknown, was found by a cruising patrol car early this morning in a doorway off Jessie Street behind the Seventh Street Post Office. There were eleven knife wounds in his chest and abdomen, and four knuckles of his right hand were broken, indicating he had defended himself until overcome by loss of blood. Doobey died in the police ambulance without regaining consciousness. Robbery has been advanced as the motive behind the brutal slaying . . .

I took a hooker from the bottle for my hangover, then doused my head in cold water at the washstand in the corner. The single weak bulb over the sink gave me back a yellow and terrified face from the wavy mirror. It hadn't been a robbery; I was next. Maybe he'd spilled where I was hiding. Run.

Nat's dresser gave me enough money to get to Philadelphia. His sport jacket was just a little tight across the shoulders and I fitted into his grey flannel slacks. A cruising cab picked me up in front of the Cardinal Hotel on Geary and Van Ness.

The one-way fare to Philly left me nine bucks. I tried to concentrate on a magazine at the Greyhound bus station on Seventh while I waited for the bus, but it didn't work. Dead faces kept blurring the pictures. I'd fingered Kiely. Earl had probably worked on Nat personally; he was the type who couldn't quit cutting once he was started. Nat had planned a law practice in the Fillmore District, with an office on O'Farrell Street. They shouldn't have left him bleeding his life away in a dirty gutter. My hands had shredded the magazine. I tossed the woman some change and walked out into the waiting room.

They were all people going places, intent on business or a vacation, people laughing or sad or not giving a damn. But going places. Then I admitted it: I wasn't going anywhere. Not yet I wasn't. San Francisco was my town, and somewhere in that town were Earl and Emmy, searching, asking questions. They would be silently noted—and remembered.

The evening rush hour crowds were thinning when I stopped to light a cigarette for the legless man who peddles pencils on Market Street. He has more of my dimes than the phone company. My feet hurt. The legless man rested on his neat square castored board, never turning his heavy handsome head but cataloguing every person who passed. As I bent over him with the lighter he said:

"The fat one came out of Western Union two hours ago, Rick. He had a Yellow Cab waiting."

At the cab stand by the bus depot it took me half an hour to find the guy I wanted. He was a tall stooped number with brown hair and a Los Angeles vocabulary. Five bucks made him use it.

"Ya, this guy you're talking about, like he bar-hopped down around Third and Folsom quite a while. Kept me waiting, Clyde, like he didn't stop for a drink. Looking for someone, y'know what I mean, Clyde?"

"Then where'd he go?"

"Ya, like I finally dumped him at the Rockwell on Jones and Eddy. Cheap, Clyde . . . no tip. I don't dig that jazz. You a private peeper or something, Dads?"

When I went away he reburied his nose in his movie magazine as if it was a schooner of beer. The fat man running the newspaper stand in the middle of the block stopped me to say that Stan wanted to talk to me. I figured it might be important.

Stan is a steady honest Bohunk from the Old Country who's sold papers in Market and Kearny since I was old enough to remember. He and his fat Polish wife have had me over to dinner a couple times. He was wearing a blue sweater, huddled up in the corner of his square green booth as if he was cold.

"This Nat, he always stop here buy paper on way home from work. Then maybe two hours sleep, go college." His faded eyes blinked, once, rapidly. "I hear this fellows you look for do this thing to Nat."

"That's right, Stan."

He nodded.

"Tall one, hard eyes, he walk by here maybe two three hours ago. Down Third he go."

"Looking for me."

"Other one—fat one. . ." He blew out his cheeks like a squirrel's and patted his belly above his gold watch chain. "Rockwell Hotel bar, Eddy Street, there he drinks. The Lincoln in the parking lot is, between Larkin and Leavenworth on Eddy. No attendant."

He wouldn't take my four bucks.

"You good boy, Rick. I think you do one thing a man have to do sometimes. I tell Mama you ask after her."

"You tell her that, Stan."

When I went on the shrouded streets threw the sound of my impatient footsteps back at me. Men of chilled smoke hurried by in search of warm rooms and good drinks and maybe soft women to make them human again. On Alcatraz Island the foghorn bellowed desolately about being out in the Bay on such a night. Swirled pearl hazed the streetlights. Somewhere in that murk was Earl, moving as a hungry cat moves, his fist full of bills and his flat blue eyes full of death.

After checking out the Lincoln I called Emmy at the Rockwell bar. His voice was mushy, as if it was being strained through one of his wet chewed cigars.

"Ya?"

In a high rapid staccato I said: "You one of the guys looking for a joker named Rick?"

"Ah . . ." His ponderous brain moved around inside his thick skull like a fullback at a ballet lesson. "Ya, I—ah . . . wanta talk to him."

"You talked to a shine last night on Jessie Street. That kind of finger is going to cost you."

He breathed cautiously into the phone, finally said:

"You got something on him we pay good."

"Okay. Meet me at the '76' station on Franklin and Pine in twenty minutes. Bring a car and be ready to travel. I'll talk when I see some green."

"I oughtta wait until—"

"This Rick is checking out tonight. He's got his mitts on something big. Be there." I hung up.

The narrow parking lot was sandwiched between two red brick office buildings that must have seen the '06 'quake. It was dark and only held a dozen cars. When Emmy waddled up he was panting and sweat glinted on his forehead. I waited until he was bent over the door lock, then came out from between the Lincoln and the wall.

I judo chopped his shoulder with a force that numbed my hand. He sprawled sideways against the Lincoln, his hand dipping under the blue topcoat and coming out to flick a deadly steel finger at me. The blade slid white-cold across my hand, missing the tendons. Then my fingers locked around his wrist. I broke his left thumb when it tried to gouge my eye.

For thirty seconds we hung there, motionless as flies mating, while the veins swelled on our necks and the sweat began to burn my eyes. Then Emmy grunted and gave back a step. I bent him across the hood and turned his hand in toward his own stomach. He sobbed. His foot growled on the gravel. We slid over sideways against the fender. Our arms writhed like snakes: then his wrist twisted with my grip and my hand thudded against his belly.

Emmy stopped panting and let his hands drop to his sides. He stared down, dumbly. The handle of his new switchblade was a grotesque horn growing from the center of his lower abdomen.

"Oh Jesus!" There was a terrible urgent despair in his voice. The words were not a curse. "Oh Jesus Christ!"

His right hand groped for support, making opaque smears on the black polished hood of the Lincoln. The backs of his fingers were matted with dark hair. Harsh noises came from his throat and he sat down on the gravel suddenly, like a fat man at a picnic. I backed out from between the cars, unable to look away.

From the entrance of the lot came a coarse male voice, whiskey-burred: "This is the one."

I sprang back between the cars and huddled over Emmy, clamping my hand over his mouth to shut off the slow agonized sounds.

"This—fog!" came a woman's loose voice. "Which—car is it? Down at the end by the Lincoln?"

My fingertips gently touched the switchblade's cold handle.

"That ain't it." Their long shadows danced on the gravel. They picked the car on the other side of the Olds against which I was leaning. I released a long breath and let go of the knife. The woman was giggling drunkenly; there was sudden movement and slopping kissing noises. Finally their light blinked on, the motor grumbled, and the car pulled out with its wipers snickering at the haze.

A warm tickle made me look down and see blood; my hand jerked back from Emmy's face as if it had been burned.

He stared at me in the faint light.

"Hey . . . hey . . . boyfriend . . ."

Then his lips blew some small pink sad bubbles and he died. His glassy eyes regarded me like a pair of thoughtful cocktail onions. I took a deep breath and began.

When I stood up the knife was in one hand, blade glistening, and his hotel key was in the other. I walked over four cars and threw up against the door of someone's new Ford.

Here at the Rockwell I came straight through the lobby without glancing at the desk, bouncing the room key in my hand. No one seemed to notice me. I took the stairs up here to the third floor and found this room.

That was an hour ago. Maybe the cops have found Emmy by now and loaded him on the meat wagon. Or maybe Earl found him first, got into the Lincoln, and drove quietly away. But I don't think so.

I think Earl will be up. If he's found Emmy he'll be moving warily now, looking back over his shoulder into the fog. Because he'll know then that I'm not a frightened wino like Kiely or an inoffensive guy like Nat. He'll know that only one of us can live.

The knife is held low along my side, the way I learned on the streets out in the Mission District as a kid. When the door swings open I will be hidden for the instant it will take to slide the blade into Earl's kidneys . . . if he hasn't found Emmy.

There is the clang of the elevator doors: the boy is saying, "Good night, sir." Silence.

Is it Earl, padding down the hall on noiseless feet like the tiger I used to watch at Fleishaker Zoo on Sunday afternoons? Does he know? In my mouth is the taste of fear, as if I have been chewing on a brass cartridge case. I am so frightened I am beyond fear: I am almost calm.

The key is in the lock! It is Earl! In a dozen seconds I'll know if he's found Emmy and is prepared for me.

In a dozen seconds . . .
If I'm alive.

Wrong Pigeon
Raymond Chandler

February 1960

He was a slightly fat man with a dishonest smile that pulled the corners of his mouth out half an inch leaving the thick lips tight and his eyes bleak. For a fattish man he had a slow walk. Most fat men are brisk and light on their feet. He wore a gray herringbone suit and a hand-painted tie with part of a diving girl visible on it. His shirt was clean, which comforted me, and his brown loafers, as wrong as the tie for his suit, shone from a recent polishing.

He sidled past me as I held the door between the waiting room and my thinking parlor. Once inside, he took a quick look around. I'd have placed him as a mobster, second grade, if I had been asked. For once I was right. If he carried a gun, it was inside his pants. His coat was too tight to hide the bulge of an underarm holster.

He sat down carefully and I sat opposite and we looked at each other. His face had a sort of foxy eagerness. He was sweating a little. The expression on my face was meant to be interested but not clubby. I reached for a pipe and the leather humidor in which I kept my Pearce's tobacco. I pushed cigarettes at him.

"I don't smoke." He had a rusty voice. I didn't like it any more than I liked his clothes, or his face. While I filled the pipe he reached inside his coat, prowled in a pocket, came out with a bill, glanced at it and dropped it across the desk in front of me. It was a nice bill and clean and new. One thousand dollars.

"Ever save a guy's life?"

"Once in a while, maybe."

"Save mine."

"What goes?"

"I heard you levelled with the customers, Marlowe."

"That's why I stay poor."

"I still got two friends. You make it three and you'll be out of the red. You got five grand coming if you pry me loose."

"From what?"

"You're talkative as hell this morning. Don't you pipe who I am?"

"Nope."

"Never been east, huh?"

"Sure—but I wasn't in your set."

"What set would that be?"

I was getting tired of it. "Stop being so goddam cagey or pick up your grand and be missing."

"I'm Ikky Rosenstein. I'll be missing but good unless you can figure some out. Guess."

"I've already guessed. You tell me and tell me quick. I don't have all day to watch you feeding me with an eye-dropper."

"I ran out on the Outfit. The high boys don't go for that. To them it means you got info you figure you can peddle, or you got independent ideas, or you lost your moxie. Me, I lost my moxie. I had it up to here." He touched his Adam's apple with the forefinger of a stretched hand. "I done bad things. I scared and hurt guys. I never killed nobody. That's nothing to the Outfit. I'm out of line. So they pick up the pencil and they draw a line. I got the word. The operators are on the way. I made a bad mistake. I tried to hole up in Vegas. I figured they'd never expect me to lie up in their own joint. They outfigured me. What I did's been done before, but I didn't know it. When I took the plane to L.A. there must have been somebody on it. They know where I live."

"Move."

"No good now. I'm covered." I knew he was right.

"Why haven't they taken care of you already?"

"They don't do it that way. Always specialists. Don't you know how it works?"

"More or less. A guy with a nice hardware store in Buffalo. A guy with a small dairy in K.C. Always a good front. They report back to New York or somewhere. When they mount the plane west or wherever they're going, they have guns in their briefcases. They're quiet and well-dressed, and they don't sit together. They could be a couple of lawyers or income tax sharpies—anything at all that's well-mannered and inconspicuous. All sorts of people carry briefcases. Including women."

"Correct as hell. And when they land they'll be steered to me, but not from the airfield. They got ways. If I go to the cops, somebody will know about me. They could have a couple Mafia boys right on the City Council for all I know. It's been done. The cops will give me twenty-four hours to leave town. No use. Mexico? Worse than here. Canada? Better but still no good. Connections there too."

"Australia?"

"Can't get a passport. I been here twenty-five years—illegal. They can't deport me unless they can prove a crime on me. The Outfit would see they didn't. Suppose I got tossed into the freezer. I'm out on a writ in twenty-four hours. And my nice friends got a car waiting to take me home—only not home."

I had my pipe lit and going well. I frowned down at the grand note. I could use it very nicely. My checking account could kiss the sidewalk without stooping.

"Let's stop horsing," I said. "Suppose—just suppose—I could figure an out for you. What's your next move?"

"I know a place—if I could get there without bein' tailed. I'd leave my car here and take a rent car. I'd turn it in just short of the county line and buy a secondhand job. Halfway to where I'm going I trade it on a new last's model, a leftover. This is just the right time of year. Good discount, new models out soon.

Not to save money—less show off. Where I'd go is a good-sized place but still pretty clean."

"Uh-huh," I said. "Wichita, last I heard. But it may have changed."

He scowled at me. "Get smart, Marlowe, but not too damn smart."

"I'll get as smart as I want to. Don't try to make rules for me. If I take this on, there aren't any rules. I take it for this grand and the rest if I bring it off. Don't cross me. I might leak information. If I get knocked off, put just one red rose on my grave. I don't like cut flowers. I like to see them growing. But I could take one, because you're such a sweet character. When's the plane in?"

"Sometime today. It's nine hours from New York. Probably come in about 5:30 p.m."

"Might come by San Diego and switch or by San Francisco and switch. A lot of planes from Dago and Frisco. I need a helper."

"Goddam you, Marlowe—"

"Hold it. I know a girl. Daughter of a chief of police who got broken for honesty. She wouldn't leak under torture."

"You got no right to risk her," Ikky said angrily.

I was so astonished my jaw hung halfway to my waist. I closed it slowly and swallowed.

"Good God, the man's got a heart."

"Women ain't built for the rough stuff," he said, grudgingly.

I picked up the thousand-dollar note and snapped it. "Sorry. No receipt," I said. "I can't have my name in your pocket. And there won't be any rough stuff if I'm lucky. They'd have me outclassed. There's only one way to work it. Now give me your address and all the dope you can think of, names, descriptions of any operators you have ever seen in the flesh."

He did. He was a pretty good observer. Trouble was the Outfit would know what he had seen. The operators would be strangers to him.

He got up silently and put his hand out. I had to shake it, but what he had said about women made it easier. His hand was moist. Mine would have been in his spot. He nodded and went out silently.

It was a quiet street in Bay City, if there are any quiet streets in this beatnik generation when you can't get through a meal without some male or female stomach singer belching out a kind of love that is as old-fashioned as a bustle or some Hammond organ jazzing it up in the customer's soup.

The little one-story house was as neat as a fresh pinafore. The front lawn was cut lovingly and very green. The smooth composition driveway was free of grease spots from standing cars, and the hedge that bordered it looked as though the barber came every day.

The white door had a knocker with a tiger's head, a go-to-hell window and a dingus that let someone inside talk to someone outside without even opening the little window.

I'd have given a mortgage on my left leg to live in a house like that. I didn't think I ever would.

The bell chimed inside and after a while she opened the door in a pale blue sports shirt and white shorts that were short enough to be friendly. She had gray-blue eyes, dark red hair and fine bones in her face. There was usually a trace of bitterness in the gray-blue eyes. She couldn't forget that her father's life had been destroyed by the crooked power of a gambling ship mobster, that her mother had died too. She was able to suppress the bitterness when she wrote nonsense about young love for the shiny magazines, but this wasn't her life. She didn't really have a life. She had an existence without much pain and enough oil money to make it safe. But in a tight spot she was as cool and resourceful as a good cop. Her name was Anne Riordan.

She stood to one side and I passed her pretty close. But I have rules too. She shut the door and parked herself on a davenport and went through the cigarette routine, and here was one doll who had the strength to light her own cigarette.

I stood looking around. There were a few changes, not many.

"I need your help," I said.

"That's the only time I ever see you."

"I've got a client who is an ex-hood; used to be a trouble-shooter for the Outfit, the Syndicate, the big mob, or whatever name you want to use for it. You know damn well it exists and is as rich as Rockefeller. You can't beat it because not enough people want to, especially the million-a-year lawyers that work for it, and the bar associations that seem more anxious to protect other lawyers than their own country."

"My God, are you running for office somewhere? I never knew you to sound so pure."

She moved her legs around, not provocatively—she wasn't the type—but it made it difficult for me to think straight just the same.

"Stop moving your legs around," I said. "Or else put a pair of slacks on."

"Damn you, Marlowe. Can't you think of anything else?"

"I'll try. I like to think that I know at least one pretty and charming female who doesn't have round heels." I swallowed and went on. "The man's name is Ikky Rosenstein. He's not beautiful and he's not anything that I like—except one. He got mad when I said I needed a girl helper. He said women were not made for the rough stuff. That's why I took the job. To a real mobster, a woman means no more than a sack of flour. They use women in the usual way, but if it's advisable to get rid of them, they do it without a second thought."

"So far you've told me a whole lot of nothing. Perhaps you need a cup of coffee or a drink."

"You're sweet but I don't in the morning—except sometimes and this isn't one of them. Coffee later. Ikky has been penciled."

"Now what's that?"

"You have a list. You draw a line through a name with a pencil. The guy is as good as dead. The Outfit has reasons. They don't do it just for kicks any more. They don't get any kick. It's just bookkeeping to them."

"What on earth can I do? I might even have said, what can *you* do?"

"I can try. What you can do is help me spot their plane and see where they go—the operators assigned to the job."

"How can you do anything?"

"I said I could try. If they took a night plane they are already here. If they took a morning plane they can't be here before five or so. Plenty of time to get set. You know what they look like."

"Oh sure. I meet killers every day. I have them in for whiskey sours and caviar on hot toast." She grinned. While she was grinning I took four long steps across the tan figured rug and lifted her and put a kiss on her mouth. She didn't fight me but she didn't go all trembly either. I went back and sat down.

"They'll look like anybody who's in a quiet well-run business or profession. They'll have quiet clothes and they'll be polite—when they want to be. They'll have briefcases with guns in them that have changed hands so often they can't possibly be traced. When and if they do the job, they'll drop the guns. They'll probably use revolvers, but they could use automatics. They won't use silencers because silencers can jam a gun and the weight makes it hard to shoot accurately. They won't sit together on the plane, but once off of it they may pretend to know each other and simply not have noticed during the flight. They may shake hands with appropriate smiles and walk away and get in the same taxi. I think they'll go to a hotel first. But very soon they will move into something from which they can watch Ikky's movements and get used to his schedule. They won't be in a hurry unless Ikky makes a move. That would tip them off that Ikky has been tipped off. He has a couple of friends left—he says."

"Will they shoot him from this room or apartment across the street—assuming there is one?"

"No. They'll shoot him from three feet away. They'll walk up behind him and say, 'Hello, Ikky.' He'll either freeze or turn. They'll fill him with lead, drop the guns, and hop into the car they have waiting. Then they'll follow the crash car off the scene."

"Who'll drive the crash car?"

"Some well-fixed and blameless citizen who hasn't been rapped. He'll drive his own car. He'll clear the way, even if he has to accidentally on purpose crash somebody, even a police car. He'll be so goddam sorry he'll cry all the way down his monogrammed shirt. And the killers will be long gone."

"Good heavens," Anne said. "How can you stand your life? If you did bring it off, they'll send operators to you."

"I don't think so. They don't kill a legit. The blame will go to the operators. Remember, these top mobsters are businessmen. They want lots and lots of money. They only get really tough when they figure they have to get rid of somebody, and they don't crave that. There's always a chance of a slip-up. Not much of a chance. No gang killing has ever been solved here or anywhere else except two or three times. Lepke Buchalter fried. Remember Anastasia? He was awful big and awful tough. Too big, too tough. Pencil."

She shuddered a little. "I think I need a drink myself."

I grinned at her. "You're right in the atmosphere, darling. I'll weaken."

She brought a couple of Scotch highballs. When we were drinking them I said: "If you spot them or think you spot them, follow to where they go—if you can do it safely. Not otherwise. If it's a hotel—and ten to one it will be—check in and keep calling me until you get me."

She knew my office number and I was still on Yucca Avenue. She knew that too.

"You're the damnedest guy," she said. "Women do anything you want them to. How come I'm still a virgin at twenty-eight?"

"We need a few like you. Why don't you get married?"

"To what? Some cynical chaser who has nothing left but technique? I don't know any really nice men—except you. I'm no pushover for white teeth and a gaudy smile."

I went over and pulled her to her feet. I kissed her long and hard. "I'm honest," I almost whispered. "That's something. But I'm too shop-soiled for a girl like you. I've thought of you, I've wanted you, but that sweet clear look in your eyes tells me to lay off."

"Take me," she said softly. "I have dreams too."

"I couldn't. It's not the first time it's happened to me. I've had too many women to deserve one like you. We have to save a man's life. I'm going."

She stood up and watched me leave with a grave face.

The women you get and the women you don't get—they live in different worlds. I don't sneer at either world. I live in both myself.

At Los Angeles International Airport you can't get close to the planes unless you're leaving on one. You see them land, if you happen to be in the right place, but you have to wait at a barrier to get a look at the passengers. The airport buildings don't make it any easier. They are strung out from here to breakfast time, and you can get calluses walking from TWA to American.

I copied an arrival schedule off the boards and prowled around like a dog that has forgotten where he put his bone. Planes came in, planes took off, porters carried luggage, passengers sweated and scurried, children whined, the loudspeaker overrode all the other noises.

I passed Anne a number of times. She took no notice of me.

At 5:45 they must have come. Anne disappeared. I gave it half an hour, just in case she had some other reason for fading. No. She was gone for good. I went out to my car and drove some long crowded miles to Hollywood and my office. I had a drink and sat. At 6:45 the phone rang.

"I think so," she said. "Beverly-Western Hotel. Room 410. I couldn't get any names. You know the clerks don't leave registration cards lying around these days. I didn't like to ask any questions. But I rode up in the elevator with them and spotted their room. I walked right on past them when the bellman put a key in their door, and walked down to the mezzanine and then downstairs with a bunch of women from the tea room. I didn't bother to take a room."

"What were they like?"

"They came up the ramp together but I didn't hear them speak. Both had briefcases, both wore quiet suits, nothing flashy. White shirts, starched, one blue tie, one black striped with gray. Black shoes. A couple of businessmen from the East Coast. They could be publishers, lawyers, doctors, account executives—no, cut the last; they weren't gaudy enough. You wouldn't look at them twice."

"Look at them twice. Faces."

"Both medium brown hair, one a bit darker than the other. Smooth faces, rather expressionless. One had gray eyes; the one with the lighter hair had blue eyes. Their eyes were interesting. Very quick to move, very observant, watching everything near them. That might have been wrong. They should have been a bit preoccupied with what they came out for or interested in California. They seemed more occupied with faces. It's a good thing I spotted them and not you. You don't look like a cop, but you don't look like a man who is not a cop. You have marks on you."

"Phooey. I'm a damn good-looking heart wrecker."

"Their features were strictly assembly line. Neither looked Italian. Each picked up a flight suitcase. One suitcase was gray with two red and white stripes up and down, about six or seven inches from the ends, the other a blue and white tartan. I didn't know there was such a tartan."

"There is, but I forget the name of it."

"I thought you knew everything."

"Just almost everything. Run along home now."

"Do I get a dinner and maybe a kiss?"

"Later, and if you're not careful you'll get more than you want."

"A rapist, eh? I'll carry a gun. You'll take over and follow them?"

"If they're the right men, they'll follow me. I already took an apartment across the street from Ikky. That block on Poynter and the two on each side of it have about six lowlife apartment houses to the block. I'll bet the incidence of chippies is very high."

"It's high everywhere these days."

"So long, Anne. See you."

"When you need help."

She hung up. I hung up. She puzzled me. Too wise to be so nice. I guess all nice women are wise too. I called Ikky. He was out. I had a drink from the office bottle, smoked for half an hour and called again. This time I got him.

I told him the score up to then, and said I hoped Anne had picked the right men. I told him about the apartment I had taken.

"Do I get expenses?" I asked.

"Five grand ought to cover the lot."

"If I earn it and get it. I heard you had a quarter of a million," I said at a wild venture.

"Could be, pal; but how do I get at it? The high boys know where it is. It'll have to cool a long time."

I said that was all right. I had cooled a long time myself. Of course I didn't expect to get the four thousand, even if I brought the job off. Men like Ikky Rosenstein would steal their mother's gold teeth. There seemed to be a little good in him somewhere—but little was the operative word.

I spent the next half-hour trying to think of a plan. I couldn't think of one that looked promising. It was almost eight o'clock and I needed food. I didn't think the boys would move that night. Next morning they would drive past Ikky's place and scout the neighborhood.

I was ready to leave the office when the buzzer sounded from the door of my waiting room. I opened the communicating door. A small tight-looking man was standing in the middle of the floor rocking on his heels with his hands behind his back. He smiled at me, but he wasn't good at it. He walked towards me.

"You Marlowe?"

"Who else? What can I do for you?"

He was close now. He brought his right hand around fast with a gun in it. He stuck the gun in my stomach.

"You can lay off Ikky Rosenstein," he said in a voice that matched his face, "or you can get your belly full of lead."

He was an amateur. If he had stayed four feet away, he might have had something. I reached up and took the cigarette out of my mouth and held it carelessly.

"What makes you think I know any Ikky Rosenstein?"

He laughed a high-pitched laugh and pushed his gun into my stomach.

"Wouldn't you like to know?" The cheap sneer, the empty triumph of power when you hold a fat gun in a small hand.

"It would be fair to tell me."

As his mouth opened for another crack, I dropped the cigarette and swept a hand. I can be fast when I have to. There are boys that are faster, but they don't stick guns in your stomach. I got my thumb behind the trigger and my hand over his. I kneed him in the groin. He bent over with a whimper. I twisted his arm to the right and I had his gun. I hooked a heel behind his heel and he was on the floor. He lay there blinking with surprise and pain, his knees drawn up against his stomach. He rolled from side to side groaning. I reached down and grabbed his left hand and yanked him to his feet. I had six inches and forty pounds on him. They ought to have sent a bigger, better trained messenger.

"Let's go into my thinking parlor," I said. "We could have a chat and you could have a drink to pick you up. Next time don't get near enough to a prospect for him to get your gun hand. I'll just see if you have any more iron on you."

He hadn't. I pushed him through the door and into a chair. His breath wasn't quite so rasping. He grabbed out a handkerchief and mopped at his face.

"Next time," he said between his teeth. "Next time."

"Don't be an optimist. You don't look the part."

I poured him a drink of Scotch in a paper cup, set it down in front of him. I broke his .38 and dumped the cartridges into the desk drawer. I clicked the chamber back and laid the gun down.

"You can have it when you leave—if you leave."

"That's a dirty way to fight," he said, still gasping.

"Sure. Shooting a man is so much cleaner. Now, how did you get here?"

"Screw yourself."

"Don't be a crumb. I have friends. Not many, but some. I can get you for armed assault, and you know what would happen then. You'd be out on a writ or on bail and that's the last anyone would hear of you. The biggies don't go for failures. Now who sent you and how did you know where to come?"

"Ikky was covered," he said sullenly. "He's dumb. I trailed him here without no trouble at all. Why would he go see a private eye? People want to know."

"More."

"Go to hell."

"Come to think of it, I don't have to get you for armed assault. I can smash it out of you right here and now."

I got up from the chair and he put a flat hand out.

"If I get knocked about, a couple of real tough monkeys will drop around. If I don't report back, same thing. You ain't holding no real high cards. They just look high," he said.

"You haven't anything to tell. If this Ikky guy came to see me, you don't know why, nor whether I took him on. If he's a mobster, he's not my type of client."

"He come to get you to try to save his hide."

"Who from?"

"That'd be talking."

"Go right ahead. Your mouth seems to work fine. And tell the boys any time I front for a hood, that will be the day."

You have to lie a little once in a while in my business. I was lying a little. "What's Ikky done to get himself disliked? Or would that be talking?"

"You think you're a lot of man," he sneered, rubbing the place where I had kneed him. "In my league you wouldn't make pinch runner."

I laughed in his face. Then I grabbed his right wrist and twisted it behind his back. He began to squawk. I reached into his breast pocket with my left hand and hauled out a wallet. I let him go. He reached for his gun on the desk and I bisected his upper arm with a hard cut. He fell into the customer's chair and grunted.

"You can have your gun," I told him. "When I give it to you. Now be good or I'll have to bounce you just to amuse myself."

In the wallet I found a driver's license made out to Charles Hickon. It did me no good at all. Punks of his type always have slangy pseudonyms. They probably called him Tiny, or Slim, or Marbles, or even just "you". I tossed the wallet back to him. It fell to the floor. He couldn't even catch it.

"Hell," I said, "there must be an economy campaign on, if they sent you to do more than pick up cigarette butts."

"Screw yourself."

"All right, mug. Beat it back to the laundry. Here's your gun."

He took it, made a business of shoving it into his waistband, stood up, gave me as dirty a look as he had in stock, and strolled to the door, nonchalant as a hustler with a new mink stole. He turned at the door and gave me the beady eye.

"Stay clean, tinhorn. Tin bends easy."

With this blinding piece of repartee he opened the door and drifted out.

After a little while I locked my other door, cut the buzzer, made the office dark, and left. I saw no one who looked like a lifetaker. I drove to my house, packed a suitcase, drove to a service station where they were almost fond of me, stored my car and picked up a Hertz Chevrolet. I drove this to Poynter Street, dumped my suitcase in the sleazy apartment I had rented early in the afternoon, and went to dinner at Victor's. It was nine o'clock, too late to drive to Bay City and take Anne to dinner. She'd have cooked her own long ago.

I ordered a double Gibson with fresh limes and drank it, and I was as hungry as a schoolboy.

On the way back to Poynter Street I did a good deal of weaving in and out and circling blocks and stopping, with a gun on the seat beside me. As far as I could tell, no one was trying to tail me.

I stopped on Sunset at a service station and made two calls from the box. I caught Bernie Ohls just as he was leaving to go home.

"This is Marlowe, Bernie. We haven't had a fight in years. I'm getting lonely."

"Well, get married. I'm chief investigator for the Sheriff's Office now. I rank acting-captain until I pass the exam. I don't hardly speak to private eyes."

"Speak to this one. I could need help. I'm on a ticklish job where I could get killed."

"And you expect me to interfere with the course of nature?"

"Come off it, Bernie. I haven't been a bad guy. I'm trying to save an ex-mobster from a couple of executioners."

"The more they mow each other down, the better I like it."

"Yeah. If I call you, come running or send a couple of good boys. You'll have had time to teach them."

We exchanged a couple of mild insults and hung up. I dialed Ikky Rosenstein. His rather unpleasant voice said: "Okay, talk."

"Marlowe. Be ready to move out about midnight. We've spotted your boy friends and they are holed up at the Beverly-Western. They won't move to your street tonight. Remember, they don't know you've been tipped."

"Sounds chancy."

"Good God, it wasn't meant to be a Sunday School picnic. You've been careless, Ikky. You were followed to my office. That cuts the time we have."

He was silent for a moment. I heard him breathing. "Who by?" he asked.

"Some little tweezer who stuck a gun in my belly and gave me the trouble of taking it away from him. I can only figure why they sent a punk on the theory that they don't want me to know too much, in case I don't know it already."

"You're in for trouble, friend."

"When not? I'll come over to your place about midnight. Be ready. Where's your car?"

"Out front."

"Get it on a side street and make a business of locking it up. Where's the back door of your flop?"

"In back. Where would it be? On the alley."

"Leave your suitcase there. We walk out together and go to your car. We drive the alley and pick up the suitcase or cases."

"Suppose some guy steals them?"

"Yeah. Suppose you get dead. Which do you like better?"

"Okay," he grunted. "I'm waiting. But we're taking big chances."

"So do race drivers. Does that stop them? There's no way to get out but fast. Douse your lights about ten and rumple the bed well. It would be good if you could leave some baggage behind. Wouldn't look so planned."

He grunted another okay and I hung up. The telephone box was well-lighted outside. They usually are, at service stations. I took a good long gander around while I pawed over the collection of give-away maps inside the station. I saw nothing to worry me. I took a map of San Diego just for the hell of it and got into my rent car.

On Poynter I parked around the corner and went up to my second-floor sleazy apartment and sat in the dark watching from my window. I saw nothing to worry about. A couple of medium-class chippies came out of Ikky's apartment house and were picked up in a late model car. A man about Ikky's height and build went into the apartment house. Various people came and went. The street was fairly quiet. Since they put in the Hollywood Freeway nobody much uses the off-the-boulevard streets unless they live in the neighborhood.

It was a nice fall night—or as nice as they get in Los Angeles' spoiled climate—clearish but not even crisp. I don't know what's happened to the weather in our overcrowded city, but it's not the weather I knew when I came to it.

It seemed like a long time to midnight. I couldn't spot anybody watching anything, and no couple of quiet-suited men paged any of the six apartment houses available. I was pretty sure they'd try mine first when they came, and if Anne had picked the right men, and if anybody had come at all, and if the tweezer's message back to his bosses had done me any good or otherwise. In spite of the hundred ways Anne could be wrong, I had a hunch she was right. The killers had no reason to be cagey if they didn't know Ikky had been warned. No reason but one. He had come to my office and been tailed there. But the Outfit, with all its arrogance of power, might laugh at the idea he had been tipped off or come to me for help. I was so small they would hardly be able to see me.

At midnight I left the apartment, walked two blocks watching for a tail, crossed the street and went into Ikky's dive. There was no locked door, and no elevator. I climbed steps to the third floor and looked for his apartment. I knocked lightly. He opened the door with a gun in his hand. He probably looked scared.

There were two suitcases by the door and another against the far wall. I went over and lifted it. It was heavy enough. I opened it. It was unlocked.

"You don't have to worry," he said. "It's got everything a guy could need for three-four nights, and nothing except some clothes that I couldn't glom off in any ready-to-wear place."

I picked up one of the other suitcases. "Let's stash this by the back door."

"We can leave by the alley too."

"We leave by the front door. Just in case we're covered—though I don't think so—we're just two guys going out together. Just one thing. Keep both hands in your coat pockets and the gun in your right. If anybody calls out your name behind you, turn fast and shoot. Nobody but a lifetaker will do it. I'll do the same."

"I'm scared," he said in his rusty voice.

"Me too, if it helps any. But we have to do it. If you're braced, they'll have guns in their hands. Don't bother asking them questions. They wouldn't answer in words. If it's just my small friend, we'll cool him and dump him inside the door. Got it?"

He nodded, licking his lips. We carried the suitcases down and put them outside the back door. I looked along the alley. Nobody, and only a short distance to the side street. We went back in and along the hall to the front. We walked out on Poynter Street with all the casualness of a wife buying her husband a birthday tie.

Nobody made a move. The street was empty. We walked around the corner to Ikky's rent car. He unlocked it. I went back with him for the suitcases. Not a stir. We put the suitcases in the car and started up and drove to the next street.

A traffic light not working, a boulevard stop or two, the entrance to the Freeway. There was plenty of traffic on it even at midnight. California is loaded with people going places and making speed to get there. If you don't drive eighty miles an hour, everybody passes you. If you do, you have to watch the rear-view mirror for highway patrol cars. It's the rat race of rat races.

Ikky did a quiet seventy. We reached the junction to Route 66 and he took it. So far nothing. I stayed with him to Pomona.

"This is far enough for me," I said. "I'll grab a bus back if there is one, or park myself in a motor court. Drive to a service station and we'll ask for the bus stop. It should be close to the Freeway. Take us towards the business section."

He did that and stopped midway of a block. He reached out his pocketbook, and held out four thousand-dollar bills to me.

"I don't really feel I've earned all that. It was too easy."

He laughed with a kind of wry amusement on his pudgy face. "Don't be a sap. I have it made. You didn't know what you was walking into. What's more, your troubles are just beginning. The Outfit has eyes and ears everywhere. Perhaps I'm safe if I'm damn careful. Perhaps I ain't as safe as I think I am. Either way, you did what I asked. Take the dough. I got plenty."

I took it and put it away. He drove to an all-night service station and we were told where to find the bus stop. "There's a cross-country Greyhound at 2:25 a.m.," the attendant said, looking at a schedule. "They'll take you, if they got room."

Ikky drove to the bus stop. We shook hands and he went gunning down the road towards the Freeway. I looked at my watch and found a liquor store still open and bought a pint of Scotch. Then I found a bar and ordered a double with water.

My troubles were just beginning, Ikky had said. He was so right.

I got off at the Hollywood bus station, grabbed a taxi and drove to my office. I asked the driver to wait a few moments. At that time of night he was glad to. The colored night man let me into the building.

"You work late, Mr. Marlowe. But you always did, didn't you?"

"It's that sort of a business," I said. "Thanks, Jasper."

Up in my office I pawed the floor for mail and found nothing but a longish narrowish box, Special Delivery, with a Glendale postmark.

I opened it. It contained nothing at all but a new freshly-sharpened yellow pencil, the mobster's mark of death.

I didn't take it too hard. When they mean it, they don't send it to you. I took it as a sharp warning to lay off. There might be a beating arranged. From their point of view, that would be good discipline. "When we pencil a guy, any guy that tries to help him is in for a smashing." That could be the message.

I thought of going to my house on Yucca Avenue. Too lonely. I thought of going to Anne's place in Bay City. Worse. If they got wise to her, real hoods would think nothing of raping her and then beating her up.

It was the Poynter Street flop for me. Easily the safest place now. I went down to the waiting taxi and had him drive me to within three blocks of the so-called apartment house. I went upstairs, undressed and slept raw. Nothing bothered me but a broken spring. That bothered my back. I lay until 3:30 pondering the situation with my massive brain. I went to sleep with a gun under the pillow, which is a bad place to keep a gun when you have one pillow as thick and soft as a typewriter pad. It bothered me so I transferred it to my right hand. Practice had taught me to keep it there even in sleep.

I woke up with the sun shining. I felt like a piece of spoiled meat. I struggled into the bathroom and doused myself with cold water and wiped off with a towel you couldn't have seen if you held it sideways. This was a really gorgeous apartment. All it needed was a set of Chippendale furniture to graduate it into the slum class.

There was nothing to eat and if I went out, Miss-Nothing Marlowe might miss something. I had a pint of whiskey. I looked at it and smelled it, but I couldn't take it for breakfast, on an empty stomach, even if I could reach my stomach, which was floating around near the ceiling. I looked into the closets in case a previous tenant might have left a crust of bread in a hasty departure. Nope. I wouldn't have liked it anyhow, not even with whiskey on it. So I sat at the window. An hour of that and I was ready to bite a piece off a bellhop.

I dressed and went around the corner to the rent car and drove to an eatery. The waitress was sore too. She swept a cloth over the counter in front of me and let me have the last customer's crumbs in my lap.

"Look, sweetness," I said, "don't be so generous. Save the crumbs for a rainy day. All I want is two eggs three minutes—no more—a slice of your famous concrete toast, a tall glass of tomato juice with a dash of Lea and Perrins, a big happy smile, and don't give anybody else any coffee. I might need it all."

"I got a cold," she said. "Don't push me around. I might crack you one on the kisser."

"I had a rough night too."

She gave me a half-smile and went through the swing door sideways. It showed more of her curves, which were ample, even excessive. But I got the eggs the way I liked them. The toast had been painted with melted butter past its bloom.

"No Lea and Perrins," she said, putting down the tomato juice. "How about a little Tabasco? We're fresh out of arsenic too."

I used two drops of Tabasco, swallowed the eggs, drank two cups of coffee and was about to leave the toast for a tip, but I went soft and left a quarter instead. That really brightened her. It was a joint where you left a dime or nothing. Mostly nothing.

Back on Poynter nothing had changed. I got to my window again and sat. At about 8:30 the man I had seen go into the apartment house across the way—the one with the same sort of height and build as Ikky—came out with a small briefcase and turned east. Two men got out of a dark blue sedan. They were of the same height and very quietly dressed and had soft hats pulled low over their foreheads. Each jerked out a revolver.

"Hey, Ikky!" one of them called out.

The man turned. "So long, Ikky," the other man said. Gunfire racketed between the houses. The man crumpled and lay motionless. The two men rushed for their car and were off, going west. Halfway down the block I saw a Caddy pull out and start ahead of them.

In no time at all they were completely gone.

It was a nice swift clean job. The only thing wrong with it was that they hadn't given it enough time for preparation.

They had shot the wrong man.

I got out of there fast, almost as fast as the two killers. There was a smallish crowd grouped around the dead man. I didn't have to look at him to know he was dead—the boys were pros. Where he lay on the sidewalk on the other side of the street I couldn't see him; people were in the way. But I knew just how he would look and I already heard sirens in the distance. It could have been just the routine shrieking from Sunset, but it wasn't. So somebody had telephoned. It was too early for the cops to be going to lunch.

I strolled around the corner with my suitcase and jammed into the rent car and went away from there. The neighborhood was not my piece of shortcake any more. I could imagine the questions.

"Just what took you over there, Marlowe? You got a flop of your own, ain't you?"

"I was hired by an ex-mobster in trouble with the Outfit. They'd sent killers after him."

"Don't tell us he was trying to go straight."

"I don't know. But I liked his money."

"Didn't do much to earn it, did you?"

"I got him away last night. I don't know where he is now. I don't want to know."

"You got him away?"

"That's what I said."

"Yeah—only he's in the morgue with multiple bullet wounds. Try something better. Or somebody's in the morgue."

And on and on. Policeman's dialogue. It comes out of an old shoe box. What they say doesn't mean anything, what they ask doesn't mean anything. They just keep boring in until you are so exhausted you flip on some detail. Then they smile happily and rub their hands, and say: "Kind of careless there, weren't you? Let's start all over again."

The less I had of that, the better. I parked in my usual parking slot and went up to the office. It was full of nothing but stale air. Every time I went into the dump it felt more and more tired. Why the hell hadn't I got myself a government job ten years ago? Make it fifteen years. I had brains enough to get a mail-order law degree. The country's full of lawyers that couldn't write a complaint without the book.

So I sat in my office chair and disadmired myself. After a while I remembered the pencil. I made certain arrangements with a forty-five gun, more gun than I ever carry—too much weight. I dialed the Sheriff's Office and asked for Bernie Ohls. I got him. His voice was sour.

"Marlowe. I'm in trouble—real trouble."

"Why tell me?" he growled. "You must be used to it by now."

"This kind of trouble you don't get used to. I'd like to come over and tell you."

"You in the same office?"

"The same."

"Have to go over that way. I'll drop in."

He hung up. I opened two windows. The gentle breeze wafted a smell of coffee and stale fat to me from Joe's Eats next door. I hated it. I hated myself. I hated everything.

Ohls didn't bother with my elegant waiting room. He rapped on my own door and I let him in. He scowled his way to the customer's chair.

"Okay. Give."

"Ever hear of a character named Ikky Rosenstein?"

"Why would I? Record?"

"An ex-mobster who got disliked by the mob. They put a pencil through his name and sent the usual two tough boys on a plane. He got tipped and hired me to help him get away."

"Nice clean work."

"Cut it out, Bernie." I lit a cigarette and blew smoke in his face. In retaliation he began to chew a cigarette. He never lit one.

"Look," I went on. "Suppose the man wants to go straight and suppose he doesn't. He's entitled to his life as long as he hasn't killed anyone. He told me he hadn't."

"And you believed the hood, huh? When do you start teaching Sunday School?"

"I neither believed him nor disbelieved him. I took him on. There was no reason not to. A girl I know and I watched the planes yesterday. She spotted the boys and tailed them to a hotel. She was sure of what they were. They looked it right down to their black shoes. They got off the plane separately and then pretended to know each other and not to have noticed on the plane. This girl—"

"Would she have a name?"

"Only for you."

"I'll buy, if she hasn't cracked any laws."

"Her name is Anne Riordan. She lives in Bay City. Her father was once Chief of Police there. And don't say that makes him a crook, because he wasn't."

"Uh-huh. Let's have the rest. Make a little time too."

"I took an apartment opposite Ikky. The killers were still at the hotel. At midnight I got Ikky out and drove with him as far as Pomona. He went on in his rent car and I came back by Greyhound. I moved into the apartment on Poynter Street, right across from his dump."

"Why—if he was already gone?"

I opened the middle desk drawer and took out the nice sharp pencil. I wrote my name on a piece of paper and ran the pencil through it.

"Because someone sent me this. I didn't think they'd kill me, but I thought they planned to give me enough of a beating to warn me off any more pranks."

"They knew you were in on it?"

"Ikky was tailed here by a little squirt who later came around and stuck a gun in my stomach. I knocked him around a bit, but I had to let him go. I thought Poynter Street was safer after that. I live lonely."

"I get around," Bernie Ohls said. "I hear reports. So they gunned the wrong guy."

"Same height, same build, same general appearance. I saw them gun him. I couldn't tell if it was the two guys from the Beverly-Western. I'd never seen them. It was just two guys in dark suits with hats pulled down. They jumped into a blue Pontiac sedan, about two years old, and lammed off, with a big Caddy running crash for them."

Bernie stood up and stared at me for a long moment. "I don't think they'll bother with you now," he said. "They've hit the wrong guy. The mob will be very quiet for a while. You know something? This town is getting to be almost as lousy as New York, Brooklyn and Chicago. We could end up real corrupt."

"We've made a hell of a good start."

"You haven't told me anything that makes me take action, Phil. I'll talk to the city homicide boys. I don't guess you're in any trouble. But you saw the shooting. They'll want that."

"I couldn't identify anybody, Bernie. I didn't know the man who was shot. How did *you* know it was the wrong man?"

"You told me, stupid."

"I thought perhaps the city boys had a make on him."

"They wouldn't tell me, if they had. Besides, they ain't hardly had time to go out for breakfast. He's just a stiff in the morgue to them until the ID comes up with something. But they'll want to talk to you, Phil. They just love their tape recorders."

He went out and the door whooshed shut behind him. I sat there wondering whether I had been a dope to talk to him. Or to take Ikky's troubles on. Five thousand green men said no. But they can be wrong too.

Somebody banged on my door. It was a uniform holding a telegram. I receipted for it and tore it loose.

It said: "On my way to Flagstaff, Mirador Motor Court. Think I've been spotted. Come fast."

I tore the wire into small pieces and burned them in my big ash tray.

I called Anne Riordan.

"Funny thing happened," I told her, and told her about the funny thing.

"I don't like the pencil," she said. "And I don't like the wrong man being killed, probably some poor bookkeeper in a cheap business or he wouldn't be living in that neighborhood. You should never have touched it, Phil."

"Ikky had a life. Where he's going he might make himself decent. He can change his name. He must be loaded or he wouldn't have paid me so much."

"I said I didn't like the pencil. You'd better come down here for a while. You can have your mail re-addressed—if you get any mail. You don't have to work right away anyhow. And L.A. is oozing with private eyes."

"You don't get the point. I'm not through with the job. The city dicks have to know where I am, and if they do, all the crime beat reporters will know too. The cops might even decide to make me a suspect. Nobody who saw the shooting is going to put out a description that means anything. The American people know better than to be witnesses to gang killings."

"All right, loud brain. But my offer stands."

The buzzer sounded in the outside room. I told Anne I had to hang up. I opened the communicating door and a well-dressed—I might say elegantly dressed—middle-aged man stood six feet inside the outer door. He had a pleasantly dishonest smile on his face. He wore a white Stetson and one of those narrow ties that go through an ornamental buckle. His cream-colored flannel suit was beautifully tailored.

He lit a cigarette with a gold lighter and looked at me over the first puff of smoke.

"Mr. Marlowe?"

I nodded.

"I'm Foster Grimes from Las Vegas. I run the Rancho Esperanza on South Fifth. I hear you got a little involved with a man named Ikky Rosenstein."

"Won't you come in?"

He strolled past me into my office. His appearance told me nothing. A prosperous man who liked or felt it good business to look a bit western. You see them by the dozen in the Palm Springs winter season. His accent told me he was an eastener, but not New England. New York or Baltimore, likely. Long Island, the Berkshires—no, too far from the city.

I showed him the customer's chair with a flick of the wrist and sat down in my antique swivel-squeaker. I waited.

"Where is Ikky now, if you know?"

"I don't know, Mr. Grimes."

"How come you messed with him?"

"Money."

"A damned good reason." he smiled. "How far did it go?"

"I helped him leave town. I'm telling you this, although I don't know who the hell you are, because I've already told an old friend-enemy of mine, a top man in the Sheriff's Office."

"What's a friend-enemy?"

"Law men don't go around kissing me, but I've known him for years, and we are as much friends as a private star can be with a law man."

"I told you who I was. We have a unique set-up in Vegas. We own the place except for one lousy newspaper editor who keeps climbing our backs and the backs of our friends. We let him live because letting him live makes us look better than knocking him off. Killings are not good business any more."

"Like Ikky Rosenstein."

"That's not a killing. It's an execution. Ikky got out of line."

"So your gun boys had to rub the wrong guy. They could have hung around a little to make sure."

"They would have, if you'd kept your nose where it belonged. They hurried. We don't appreciate that. We want cool efficiency."

"Who's this great big fat 'we' you keep talking about?"

"Don't go juvenile on me, Marlowe."

"Okay. Let's say I know."

"Here's what we want." He reached into his pocket and drew out a loose bill. He put it on the desk on his side. "Find Ikky and tell him to get back in line and everything is oke. With an innocent bystander gunned, we don't want any trouble or any extra publicity. It's that simple. You get this now," he nodded at the bill. It was a grand. Probably the smallest bill they had. "And another when you find Ikky and give him the message. If he holds out—curtains."

"Suppose I say take your goddam grand and blow your nose with it?"

"That would be unwise." He flipped out a Colt Woodsman with a short silencer on it. A Colt Woodsman will take one without jamming. He was fast too, fast and smooth. The genial expression on his face didn't change.

"I never left Vegas," he said calmly. "I can prove it. You're dead in your office chair and nobody knows anything. Just another private eye that tried the wrong pitch. Put your hands on the desk and think a little. Incidentally, I'm a crack shot even with this damned silencer."

"Just to sink a little lower in the social scale, Mr. Grimes, I ain't putting no hands on no desk. But tell me about this."

I flipped the nicely sharpened pencil across to him. He grabbed for it after a swift change of the gun to his left hand—very swift. He held the pencil up so that he could look at it without taking his eyes off me.

I said: "It came to me by Special Delivery mail. No message, no return address. Just the pencil. Think I've never heard about the pencil, Mr. Grimes?"

He frowned and tossed the pencil down. Before he could shift his long lithe gun back to his right hand I dropped mine under the desk and grabbed the butt of the .45 and put my finger hard on the trigger.

"Look under the desk, Mr. Grimes. You'll see a .45 in an open-end holster. It's fixed there and it's pointing at your belly. Even if you could shoot me through the heart the .45 would still *go* off from a convulsive movement of my hand. And your belly would be hanging by a shred and you would be knocked out of that chair. A .45 slug can throw you back six feet. Even the movies learned that at last."

"Looks like a Mexican stand-off," he said quietly. He holstered his gun. He grinned. "Nice smooth work, Marlowe. We could use you. But it's a long long time for you and no time at all to us. Find Ikky and don't be a drip. He'll listen to reason. He doesn't really want to be on the run for the rest of his life. We'd trace him eventually."

"Tell me something, Mr. Grimes. Why pick on me? Apart from Ikky, what did I ever do to make you dislike me?"

Not moving, he thought a moment, or pretended to. "The Larsen case. You helped send one of our boys to the gas chamber. That we don't forget. We had you in mind as a fall guy for Ikky. You'll always be a fall guy, unless you play it our way. Something will hit you when you least expect it."

"A man in my business is always a fall guy, Mr. Grimes. Pick up your grand and drift out quietly. I might decide to do it your way, but I have to think. As for the Larsen case, the cops did all the work. I just happened to know where he was. I don't guess you miss him terribly."

"We don't like interference." He stood up. He put the grand note casually back in his pocket. While he was doing it I let go of the .45 and jerked out my Smith and Wesson five-inch .38.

He looked at it contemptuously. "I'll be in Vegas, Marlowe. In fact I never left Vegas. You can catch me at the Esperanza. No, we don't give a damn about Larsen personally. Just another gun handler. They come in gross lots. We *do* give a damn that some punk private eye fingered him."

He nodded and went out by my office door.

I did some pondering. I knew Ikky wouldn't go back to the Outfit. He wouldn't trust them enough if he got the chance. But there was another reason now. I called Anne Riordan again.

"I'm going to look for Ikky. I have to. If I don't call you in three days, get hold of Bernie Ohls. I'm going to Flagstaff, Arizona. Ikky says he will be there."

"You're a fool," she wailed. "It's some sort of trap."

"A Mr. Grimes of Vegas visited me with a silenced gun. I beat him to the punch, but I won't always be that lucky. If I find Ikky and report to Grimes, the mob will let me alone."

"You'd condemn a man to death?" Her voice was sharp and incredulous.

"No. He won't be there when I report. He'll have to hop a plane to Montreal, buy forged papers—Montreal is almost as crooked as we are—and plane to Europe. He may be fairly safe there. But the Outfit has long arms and Ikky will have a damned dull life staying alive. He hasn't any choice. For him it's either hide or get the pencil."

"So clever of you, darling. What about your own pencil?"

"If they meant it, they wouldn't have sent it. Just a bit of scare technique."

"And you don't scare, you wonderful handsome brute."

"I scare. But it doesn't paralyze me. So long. Don't take any lovers until I get back."

"Damn you, Marlowe!"

She hung up on me. I hung up on myself.

Saying the wrong thing is one of my specialties.

I beat it out of town before the homicide boys could hear about me. It would take them quite a while to get a lead. And Bernie Ohls wouldn't give a city dick a used paper bag. The Sheriff's men and the City Police co-operate about as much as two tomcats on a fence.

I made Phoenix by evening and parked myself in a motor court on the outskirts. Phoenix was damned hot. The motor court had a dining room so I had dinner. I collected some quarters and dimes from the cashier and shut myself in a phone booth and started to call the Mirador in Flagstaff. How silly could I get? Ikky might be registered under any name from Cohen to Cordileone, from Watson to Woichehovski. I called anyway and got nothing but as much of a smile as you can get on the phone. So I asked for a room the following night. Not a chance unless someone checked out, but they would put me down for a cancellation or something. Flagstaff is too near the Grand Canyon. Ikky must have arranged in advance. That was something to ponder too.

I bought a paperback and read it. I set my alarm watch for 6:30. The paperback scared me so badly that I put two guns under my pillow. It was about a guy who bucked the hoodlum boss of Milwaukee and got beaten up every fifteen minutes. I figured that his head and face would be nothing but a piece of bone with a strip of skin hanging from it. But in the next chapter he was as gay as a meadow lark. Then I asked myself why I was reading this drivel when I could have been memorizing The Brothers Karamazov. Not knowing any good answers, I turned the light out and went to sleep. At 6:30 I shaved and showered and had breakfast and took off for Flagstaff. I got there by lunchtime, and there was Ikky in the restaurant eating mountain trout. I sat down across from him. He looked surprised to see me.

I ordered mountain trout and ate it from the outside in, which is the proper way. Boning spoils it a little.

"What gives?" he asked me with his mouth full. A delicate eater.

"You read the papers?"

"Just the sporting section."

"Let's go to your room and talk about it. There's more than that."

We paid for our lunches and went along to a nice double. The motor courts are getting so good that they make a lot of hotels look cheap. We sat down and lit cigarettes.

"The two hoods got up too early and went over to Poynter Street. They parked outside your apartment house. They hadn't been briefed carefully enough. They shot a guy who looked a little like you."

"That's a hot one," he grinned. "But the cops will find out, and the Outfit will find out. So the tag for me stays on."

"You must think I'm dumb," I said. "I am."

"I thought you did a first-class job, Marlowe. What's dumb about that?"

"What job did I do?"

"You got me out of there pretty slick."

"Anything about it you couldn't have done yourself?"

"With luck—no. But it's nice to have a helper."

"You mean sucker."

His face tightened. And his rusty voice growled. "I don't catch. And give me back some of that five grand, will you? I'm shorter than I thought."

"I'll give it back to you when you find a hummingbird in a salt shaker."

"Don't be like that," he almost sighed, and flicked a gun into his hand. I didn't have to flick. I was holding one in my side pocket.

"I oughtn't to have boobed off," I said. "Put the heater away. It doesn't pay any more than a Vegas slot machine."

"Wrong. Them machines pay the jackpot every so often. Otherwise—no customers."

"Every so seldom, you mean. Listen, and listen good."

He grinned. His dentist was tired waiting for him.

"The set-up intrigued me," I went on, debonair as Milo Vance in a Van Dyne story and a lot brighter in the head. "First off, could it be done? Second, if it could be done, where would I be? But gradually I saw the little touches that flaw the picture. Why would you come to me at all? The Outfit isn't that naive. Why would they send a little punk like this Charles Hickon or whatever name he uses on Thursdays? Why would an old hand like you let anybody trail you to a dangerous connection?"

"You slay me, Marlowe. You're so bright I could find you in the dark. You're so dumb you couldn't see a red, white and blue giraffe. I bet you were back there in your un-brain emporium playing with that five grand like a cat with a bag of catnip. I bet you were kissing the notes."

"Not after you handled them. Then why the pencil that was sent to me? Big dangerous threat. It reinforced the rest. But like I told your choir boy from Vegas, they don't send them when they mean them. By the way, he had a gun too. A Woodsman .22 with a silencer. I had to make him put it away. He was nice about that. He started waving grands at me to find out where you were and tell him. A well-dressed, nice-looking front man for a pack of dirty rats. The Women's Christian Temperance Association and some bootlicking politicians gave them the money to be big, and they learned how to use it and make it grow. Now they're pretty well unstoppable. But they're still a pack of dirty rats. And they're always where they can't make a mistake. That's inhuman. Any man has a right to a few mistakes. Not the rats. They have to be perfect all the time. Or else they get stuck with *you.*"

"I don't know what the hell you're talking about. I just know it's too long."

"Well, allow me to put it in English. Some poor jerk from the East Side gets involved with the lower echelons of a mob. You know what an echelon is, Ikky?"

"I been in the Army," he sneered.

"He grows up in the mob, but he's not all rotten. He's not rotten enough. So he tries to break loose. He comes out here and gets himself a cheap job of some sort and changes his name or names and lives quietly in a cheap apartment house. But the mob by now has agents in many places. Somebody spots him and recognizes him. It might be a pusher, a front man for a bookie joint, a night girl, even a cop that's on the take. So the mob, or call them the Outfit, say through their cigar smoke: 'Ikky can't do this to us. It's a small operation because he's small. But it annoys us. Bad for discipline. Call a couple of boys and have them pencil him.' But what boys do they call? A couple they're tired of. Been around too long. Might make a mistake or get chilly toes. Perhaps they like killing. That's bad too. That makes recklessness. The best boys are the ones that don't care either way. So although they don't know it, the boys they call are on their way out. But it would be kind of cute to frame a guy they already don't like, for fingering a hood named Larsen. One of these puny little jokes the Outfit takes big. 'Look guys, we even got time to play footies with a private eye. Jesus, we can do anything. We could even suck our thumbs.' So they send a ringer."

"The Torri brothers ain't ringers. They're real hard boys. They proved it—even if they did make a mistake."

"Mistake nothing. They got Ikky Rosenstein. You're just a singing commercial in this deal. And as of now you're under arrest for murder. You're worse off than that. The Outfit will habeas corpus you out of the clink and blow you down. You've served your purpose and you failed to finger me into a patsy."

His finger tightened on the trigger. I shot the gun out of his hand. My gun in my coat pocket was small, but at that distance accurate. And it was one of my days to be accurate myself.

He made a faint moaning sound and sucked at his hand. I went over and kicked him hard in the chest. Being nice to killers is not part of my repertoire. He went over backwards and sideways and stumbled four or five steps. I picked up his gun and held it on him while I tapped all the places—not just pockets or holsters—where a man could stash a second gun. He was clean—that way anyhow.

"What are you trying to do to me?" he said whiningly. "I paid you. You're clear. I paid you damn well."

"We both have problems there. Yours is to stay alive." I took a pair of cuffs out of my pocket and wrestled his hands behind him and snapped them on. His hand was bleeding. I tied his show handkerchief around it. I went to the telephone.

Flagstaff was big enough to have a police force. The D.A. might even have his office there. This was Arizona, a poor state, relatively. The cops might even be honest.

I had to stick around for a few days, but I didn't mind that as long as I could have trout caught eight or nine thousand feet up. I called Anne and Bernie Ohls. I called my answering service. The Arizona D.A. was a young keen-eyed man and the Chief of Police was one of the biggest men I ever saw.

I got back to L.A. in time and took Anne to Romanoff's for dinner and champagne.

"What I can't see," she said over a third glass of bubbly, "is why they dragged you into it, why they set up the fake Ikky Rosenstein. Why didn't they just let the two lifetakers do their job?"

"I couldn't really say. Unless the big boys feel so safe they're developing a sense of humor. And unless this Larsen guy that went to the gas chamber was bigger than he seemed to be. Only three or four important mobsters have made the electric chair or the rope or the gas chamber. None that I know of in the life-imprisonment states like Michigan. If Larsen was bigger than anyone thought, they might have had my name on a waiting list."

"But why wait?" she asked me. "They'd go after you quickly."

"They can afford to wait. Who's going to bother them—Kefauver? He did his best, but do you notice any change in the set-up—except when they make one themselves?"

"Costello?"

"Income tax rap—like Capone. Capone may have had several hundred men killed, and killed a few of them himself, personally. But it took the Internal Revenue boys to get him. The Outfit won't make that mistake often."

"What I like about you, apart from your enormous personal charm is that when you don't know an answer you make one up."

"The money worries me," I said. "Five grand of their dirty money. What do I do with it?"

"Don't be a jerk all your life. You earned the money and you risked your life for it. You can buy Series E Bonds. They'll make the money clean. And to me that would be part of the joke."

"*You* tell *me* one good reason why they pulled the switch."

"You have more of a reputation than you realize. And how would it be if the false Ikky pulled the switch? He sounds like one of these overclever types that can't do anything simple."

"The Outfit will get him for making his own plans—if you're right."

"If the D.A. doesn't. And I couldn't care less about what happens to him. More champagne, please."

They extradited "Ikky" and he broke under pressure and named the two gunmen—after I had already named them, the Torri brothers. But nobody could find them. They never went home. And you can't prove conspiracy on one man. The law couldn't even get him for accessory after the fact. They couldn't prove he knew the real Ikky had been gunned.

They could have got him for some trifle, but they had a better idea. They left him to his friends. They turned him loose.

Where is he now? My hunch says nowhere.

Anne Riordan was glad it was all over and I was safe. Safe—that isn't a word you use in my trade.

Hangover
Charles Runyon

December 1960

I couldn't feel the hammers in my head when I woke up. But I knew they were poised to thud into the base of my skull the moment I lifted my head from the pillow. My nose felt stuffed and swollen, as though someone were pinching the bridge tightly between thumb and forefinger.

I heard a noise in the kitchen. Something made of tin tipped over, rolled for what seemed like an hour, then hit the floor with a sound like the cymbals in a Wagner overture. My head began to throb. I tried to deal with the noise passively, without moving: "Marian! Are you in the kitchen?"

The only answer was a metallic echo, the kind you get from an empty house. I forced an eye open and saw that the opposite bed was empty. The spread lay neatly folded at the foot. The sheet was turned back as crisp and smooth as glass, ready to receive her body. But Marian hadn't slept there; she'd been gone for nearly two weeks.

I closed my eyes, and fragments of despair dropped like lead weights into my mind. I'd been thinking she came back last night. She smiled down at me the way she always did before coming to bed; with her eyes, hardly moving her lips. She was wearing the pale blue nightdress I'd given her two months ago on our tenth anniversary . . .

Hell, I must have dreamed it. I wanted her home, and that's the kind of impossible wish that keeps distilleries in business.

I felt a warm weight pressing against my back. I turned quickly, but it wasn't Marian. This girl's hair was the same dark auburn color; but Marian had never let her hair get into such a tangled mess, *with* matted rat's nests above the ears.

I drew away from her. She frowned in her sleep and moved toward me. I slid out of bed, pulled on my robe and looked down at her. She was somewhere between twenty and twenty-five. If she was pretty, I couldn't see it; not with her face lumpy and sagging in sleep. Her upper lip arched outward to reveal two slightly protruding teeth. A line of saliva trailed from her mouth to the pillow, where it mixed with lipstick and formed a stain the color of diluted blood.

I hated to deal with her now; even the intimacy of conversation made my stomach queasy. But I wanted her out of my house, so I shook her shoulder.

"Baby . . ." Without opening her eyes, she rolled her tongue around her mouth. "Let's sleep a little longer, baby."

I could feel my patience slipping away. I hated that sticky, stupid, shopworn endearment; in thirty-five years I'd come to tolerate everything but being called "Baby." I shook her until her eyes popped open. "What's your name?"

"God, did you wake me up for *that?*" She jerked the sheet over her head. "Marian . . . you been calling me Marian."

I jerked the sheet off her head. "Dammit! That's my wife's name."

"I know, Baby, I know." She kicked off the sheet and stretched, her legs forming a straight line from toe to torso. "I'm Sandra. You can call me Sandy."

She gave me a heavy-lidded smile she probably meant to be sweet and seductive. To me it was like having syrup smeared on my face. Her nakedness aroused me somewhat less than a tree with the bark stripped off, though she had the fleshy, over-blown kind of figure that's supposed to be the American dream. She wasn't my dream and that's why her presence threw me. I couldn't remember where I'd picked her up or why. My last sharp memory was coming home from the office Wednesday and feeling the emptiness of this house hit me like a fist in the stomach. I knew I couldn't spend another night talking to the furniture, so I'd gone out and started throwing down vodka martinis.

"Okay, Sandy," I said. "Where'd I meet you?"

She raised her eyebrows. "Hey, you really had a blackout. I'm a hostess at the Dolly Bar."

I frowned and shook my head. I couldn't place it.

"That's a strip joint on Fourth street. Don't you remember *that?*"

"Would I ask if I did?"

"Aw . . . Baby's got a hangover, hasn't he?" She slid off the bed and started toward the door. "I'll get you something for that."

"Never mind. Just tell me when and why you came to my house."

She stopped in the door and turned. A hip stuck out and she cupped her palm over it. "Okay. You came into the Dolly Wednesday night. You bought me a few drinks, then a . . . former friend of mine tried to move in and you hit him. You hit him several times before they threw you out, and I liked the way you handled yourself. I took you with me to my hotel and next morning we came out here."

"What time was that?"

"About eleven."

"*Eleven?* Oh, Jesus." I saw myself staggering into my new tri-level house with a B-girl on my arm. That sort of thing wasn't done in Elysia. It was really PTA and cub scout country—even though its name conveyed a vision of satyrs and fat-hipped Greek women dressed in bunches of grapes. Elysia meant home and family to the men who worked in the city, and I'd broken one of the club by-laws. "Did anyone see you?"

"Well, I guess." Sandy shrugged. "You didn't tell me to sneak in." She paused. "Look, if there's any more questions, I'll be in the john."

She walked away and slammed the bathroom door. A second later I heard a glass shatter in the kitchen.

I padded barefoot down the half-flight of stairs, walking with a bent-knee shuffle to stabilize my aching head. In the kitchen, I found that Marian's gray cat had overturned a flour canister and was anointing the room with white paw prints.

I cornered her and imprisoned her under my arm. I rubbed her behind the ears and surveyed the kitchen.

It was a mess. Odors of stale food and liquor rose from a sink piled high with dirty dishes and glasses. The stove held a stew pan filled with black pebbles which once were beans. I wondered what Marian would have said; she was the kind of woman who jumped up from the table and started washing dishes before they even cooled.

I saw two plates on the table. One held a puddle of gray grease with a slab of bacon in the center, garnished by a long, auburn hair. My stomach did a half-gainer; eating with Sandy was even less appetizing than sleeping with her.

The cat mewed. "All right, kid," I said. "You first, then the other one."

I shuffled through the long living room and found the front door open. The carpet around it was damp; the door had stood open all night and it had rained. I set the cat on the lawn and nudged her away with my toe.

Around the front steps lay proof that life in Elysia had flowed on without me. Several milk bottles warmed in the sun; I tried to count them but they kept moving. Two newspapers formed a wet, gluey mass on the sidewalk. A third lay near the door, crisp and dry and smelling of ink as I picked it up. I read the date beneath the flag: *Tuesday, July 19.*

Five days, I thought. *A drop of sweat traced a cold path down my spine.* Oh, Jesus. Five days gone like bootleg liquor down the drain.

I dropped the paper and stood there trying to remember. Nothing came but sweat, cool and clammy under my robe. The sun was a white-hot rivet tacked on a sheet of blue steel. It couldn't have been much past eight in the morning; I still had time to get to the office. But I remembered the winter sales program I was supposed to have presented to the board last Friday, and I knew that one more day would add little to the devastation.

I raised my eyes and saw my car crosswise in the drive. The back wheels rested on my neighbor's lawn. Now the whole damn town would know. Two women walked past, pushing empty grocery carts. They stared at me, then walked on with the studied concentration of students coming late to class. I was suddenly aware of my bare legs sticking out beneath my robe.

I went inside and slammed the door on the painful sunlight. I needed a drink. My nerves were rubbing together, rasping like the hind legs of a cricket.

The bar was a half-flight down in a basement room with sand-colored tile on the floor. The walls were lined with desert murals, and I reached the bar feeling like I'd just trekked across the Quattara depression on my hands and knees.

But the bar held no bourbon; no scotch. I searched beneath it for the exotic liquers Marian had stocked against the day I reached the level of a party-giving executive. I wondered if she was sitting in her hotel room now, regretting that she'd ripped apart all those detailed blueprints for the future.

All the bottles were empty; we'd even drained the tall, slim containers of fiery Metaxa. Apparently we'd finished up on creme de cacao: I found two glasses containing a brown, concave residue, dry on the edge and damp in the center, like a pond in a drought.

I prowled the room and found a beer mug containing an inch of bourbon and a shredded cigaret butt. I fished out the butt, gulped down the bourbon, and shuddered like a volcano about to erupt. I swallowed three times before the bourbon gave up and decided to stay down.

After a minute I felt well enough to climb the stairs and call a cab. I felt even better when I'd done that; it would be a relief to get Sandy out of my house.

When I hung up, I found myself looking at the words I'd scrawled on the pad a week before: *Regent Hotel, CA-72700*. The number had cost me an eighty-dollar detective fee, but I'd never used it. I kept reminding myself that it was Marian who got caught cheating; not me. She had to come to me.

I got up and walked upstairs, away from the telephone. Outside the bedroom, I found my suit. It was crumpled, damp and muddy. I lifted it with a bare toe and saw that it had bleached the hardwood beneath it, as skin is bleached by a bandage. I couldn't imagine what fuzz-brained impulse had driven me out into the rain. Maybe Sandy would know . . .

I found her in the bathroom, standing under the shower with her back to me. Behind the portiere of needle-spray she looked like Marian—though a Marian drawn with thick pencil strokes that made my chest ache for the original. I felt a curious urge to shove the girl's head under water and hold it there.

Instead, I tried to make my voice pleasant but brisk. "About finished?"

She halted in the act of lathering her belly. She turned, suds squeezing out between her fingers. "I like it slow, Baby." She smiled with one side of her mouth. "Wanta wash my back?"

I stretched out my hand and jerked the shower curtain together. Once I'd washed Marion's back; but that honeymoon ritual had been shelved several years ago. "Hurry up," I said. "I called a cab."

"A nice big Cadillac and you use a cab?"

I could feel my tiny supply of patience seeping away. *"You'll* use it, Sandy—the minute it gets here."

"Wearing nothing but soap bubbles?" She ripped off a laugh that tweaked my nerves like a fingernail drawn across a blackboard. "Anyway, I can't leave you, Baby."

"Dammit! My name is Greg. Greg Maxwell."

"I know, Baby . . ."

"Don't call me that!"

"You liked it yesterday."

I walked to the washbasin and started throwing cold water on my face. Talking to Sandy was a pointless ordeal; she'd leave when the cab arrived. I wondered how much money she'd want . . .

I wiped off the mirror and looked at my dripping image with detached, alcoholic disdain. I looked like someone who sang hymns in a skid row mission; a red-haired joker whose big frame hung loose inside an expensive bathrobe, as though tacked together by a hurried carpenter. The pallid face was patched here and there with red-black stubble, interspersed with tiny razor nicks.

I looked down at my hands. The knobby knuckles were scraped raw; the nails were cracked and chipped and tipped with black, dirt-filled crescents. I remembered my wet, muddy suit in the hall, and tried to recall what happened yesterday.

But yesterday was gone. So was the day before, and the day before that. Five days were lost, buried deep among three billion brain cells. A strange, violent character had taken over my body; an idiot who enjoyed being called baby, and went for women who measured an axe-handle or more across the hips. Now he sat back in my mind and smirked from a perch atop a filing cabinet full of memories. *"Get out of here, Maxwell,"* he was saying. *"Those five days were mine, old buddy."*

"What?"

I jumped at the sound of Sandy's voice. "I didn't say anything."

"You said something about getting out of here."

"Oh, Jesus." My mind was splitting apart; I couldn't remember saying anything. I put both hands to my forehead and squeezed. "Sandy . . . What was I doing in the rain?"

"Don't you even remember *that?*"

I clamped my teeth together. "Sandy, all I know is that my suit's in a wet, muddy heap in the hall."

"Oh. Well . . ." She was silent a minute, then the shower curtain screeched. She came to stand behind me, enclosing me in her aura of scented bath soap. "You did that Friday night when the guy came to see why you hadn't come to work."

"What guy?"

"Gosh, I don't know his name . . ."

"Dammit! What did he look like?"

"Bug-eyed little fella. Kept eating candy."

"Candy . . ." My mouth went dry, and my skin felt hot and prickly. My boss was Harvey Reed, sales manager. His protruding eyes gave him a look of never quite believing what he saw. He chewed mints chain fashion to blunt a craving for cigarets. "Go on," I told her.

"Well he didn't stay long. He acted kind of teed off . . . didn't even taste the drink I fixed for him."

I whirled to face her. "Why the hell didn't you stay out of sight?"

She froze in the act of wiping her left ear. "Gee . . . I was trying to *help*. You said he was your boss and I wanted to treat him nice . . ."

"Oh, for God's sake!" I turned back and gripped the washbasin. Harvey was a nut on family integrity: *"A man who can't run his home has no business dealing with customers."* I remembered him saying that, looking like a surprised chipmunk with the mint tucked in his cheek. "Okay, Sandy. So he saw you. Now how'd the rain get into the picture?"

"I . . . Are you sure you wanta hear?"

I spoke softly, watching my lips move in the mirror. "Sandy, for the last time, I wouldn't be asking if I didn't."

"Okay. Okay. Jesus, I wish you'd get drunk again. You're a lot more fun when you're drunk." She sighed. "Well . . . so when the guy left, you followed him outside telling him he couldn't fire you because you already quit. You had a lot better job with United Oil, you told him. When he drove off you was standing on the lawn yelling at him—"

"Yelling?"

"Yeah, you were giving him hell, only I couldn't hear you so clear in the house. Then it started raining and you got down on your hands and knees and dug your fingers into the lawn. I went out and asked what you lost. You said we were about to fall off the world and you wanted me to help you hold on . . ." She started to laugh, then cut it short, "I'm sorry, but you did act . . . kind of funny."

I shook my head, trying to clear it. Dark fragments of memory swirled like storm clouds; I remembered feeling that the earth was tipping away from the sun, pitching me into darkness. I'd been afraid of losing contact and flying off into cold, deep space without Marian there to anchor me . . .

"Was it a good job?" asked Sandy. "I mean . . . I guess it was, but you mentioned the deal with the other company . . ."

"I made it up, Sandy. Now let's drop it." The concern in her voice sickened me. I didn't want sympathy; that's why I couldn't go back to the office. I'd mail my resignation; let them believe the story about United Oil. I might even be able to get on there, with a good recommendation—

Oh, sure. Harvey would grab at a chance to recommend me: *"Good man, Maxwell; aside from his drinking problem. Can't blame the boy, of course, considering his domestic situation."* Damn, damn, damn. Nobody would touch me with a ten foot pole.

An electric shaver whirred, sawing at my nerves. I had a vision of Marian shaving her gently tapered legs. She didn't like me to watch her; shaving was a masculine act that made her feel coarse and indelicate.

I turned to see Sandy with her leg propped on the edge of the bathtub, running a tiny electric shaver along her thick calf. For a moment I watched it chew away the faint stubble, then it dawned on me that it was Marian's shaver. I jerked the cord from the wall plug and the whirring died.

Sandy looked up with her mouth open. "What the hell . . . ?"

"Where'd you get that shaver?"

"Why . . . you gave it to me last night."

Last night. I'd been almost sure that Marian had taken it with her; apparently I was mistaken.

I held out my hand. "Let's have it."

She gave it to me, watching my face. I wrapped the cord around the shaver and put it in the medicine cabinet; I'd have to clean it later, when my stomach settled. The air in the bathroom was mushy with the scent of bath soap.

"Did you bring any luggage?" I asked her.

"A suitcase, like you told me."

"Good. I'll help you pack."

She blinked in surprise. "Baby, *wait* a minute . . ."

"Clean up in here first. Then get dressed." I walked to the door. "And stop calling me baby."

I walked into the hall and took a deep breath. It didn't help much; I was sick with the knowledge that I'd thrown away ten years of work Friday night.

I found Sandy's cheap pasteboard suitcase in the bedroom and prowled through the house, carrying it open under my arm. Sandy had treated the place like a burlesk runway. I found shoes in the living room, a negligee in my den, and underwear in the basement bar. They were black, sleazy garments that clung to my fingers.

I was nearly finished with the house when I heard a dog barking out back. It wasn't ours; Marian didn't like dogs. I went out and found our neighbor's Dalmatian spraddled on the naked black earth at the edge of the unfinished patio. He was growling at a Beagle I'd never seen before.

I yelled, and they ran off. Then I wondered why the hell I bothered. The patio was Marian's idea; another page torn from her futures book. She'd had it started during my last two-month trip around our sales divisions. The night I came home, I'd found her with the contractor who had the job. He wasn't building a patio then . . .

I went back inside and slammed the door. The next owner could finish the patio. Let him worry about the house and its twenty-five year mortgage. I couldn't handle the payments without a job.

I'd have to move into a cheaper home in a different neighborhood. I had to start fresh in another job; maybe I'd even go back to pushing doorbells. *Damn.* I missed Marian. I needed her calm, realistic approach to problems; without her I was like a centipede with each leg trying to run in a different direction.

First I had to get rid of Sandy. I walked upstairs and found her wet footprints leading to the bedroom. She hadn't cleaned up the bathroom. In the bedroom, I found Marian's closet open, the clothes disarranged. I felt anger rise inside me.

I found Sandy in the kitchen drinking coffee. She wore the blue nightdress I'd given Marian on our last anniversary. I felt a stab of disappointment that Marian had left it behind, then the disappointment changed to anger. "Stand up," I told Sandy.

She rose slowly, her face blank.

"Now take off the robe."

Her face twisted in confusion. "But you *told* me to wear it yesterday."

I covered the distance between us in two quick steps. I gripped her arm and said: "Slip it off gently. I don't want it damaged." Gradually I tightened my grip until she began to move. "That's it. Now the other arm . . . easy."

When it was off she dropped back in her chair, rubbing her arm. "Your hands are strong, you know that? You oughta see the other marks you gave me." Her lower lip trembled. "I didn't mind them, though. You know why? Because you made me feel like a wife and I went for that. All of a sudden you change . . ." Her eyes grew shiny and her face became pouchy and ugly.

I watched a tear roll down her cheek and felt my skin crawl. I didn't want her tears. "Isn't your cab here yet?"

"Sure." Her mouth twisted. "It's under the table."

"If it doesn't come you can walk. Now get dressed. I want you out of here when my wife comes back."

"Your *wife?* But you—" She closed her eyes for a minute, then opened them. "You sent her away because you caught her cheating on you."

"I didn't actually *catch* her . . ."

"She didn't deny it, you said." I didn't want to argue, but the urge to justify myself pulled me in like quicksand. "Sandy, I'd been away for two months. During that time I wasn't exactly a . . . perfect husband myself. Anyway, I don't care what she did. She's coming back."

"What about your promise?"

"Promise?"

She stood up, and her weak mouth seemed suddenly firm. "You said we'd go to Mexico. You'd sell the house, draw your money out of the bank, sell your stocks . . ."

"Oh, hell. Don't you realize I have no job? The house is mortgaged, I still owe money on the car, I've borrowed against my stocks. Sandy, you're trying to con the wrong man. I'm damn near broke."

Her chin came up at that. "I'm not trying to con you!"

"Then why don't you leave?"

"Because . . . you said you hated your wife because she was a cold, efficient machine. You liked me because I was warm and passionate and . . . and sloppy."

Suddenly I was tired of the conversation. "Listen, whatever happened during those five days, it's ended. I'm a different man. I've turned inside out. What I hated before, I like now. What I liked before, I now hate. You understand?"

"You hate me?"

"It isn't your fault, Sandy. It's just the way it works out."

"Thanks a lot." She walked to the door, then turned to face me. "You should've stayed drunk, Baby."

She walked out and up the stairs, grabbing her suitcase on the way. I watched her disappear into the bedroom, feeling as though I'd just detached a terrier from my leg.

While I waited for her to come down again, the cab arrived. I went out and told him to wait, then went back inside. I paced the long living room, impatient now that I'd decided to get Marian back. She'd be grateful, I thought, though she wouldn't show it. She'd be anxious to please, and I'd accept that. I'd have her make chocolate brownies and bring me coffee in bed. I'd loaf for a day or so, warm and musty under the covers with the soft feel of flannel. We'd make small talk and lazy daytime love. Though she thought there was something perverted about love in the daytime, she wouldn't deny me. Later I'd tell her about the job and we'd decide what to do . . .

Sandy came down then, clad in a black sequined gown that must have been her working dress. It covered her just a little better than nothing, but I didn't care. I felt almost grateful to her, the way you feel toward a bore when he goes out the door after a long, trying evening. I pressed a twenty into her hand and said, "That's for the cab, Sandy."

She looked down at it sullenly, then stuffed it into her purse and walked out, the gown tight across her haunches. I hurried to the phone and dialed the Regent Hotel. "Give me Mrs. Maxwell's room," I told the operator.

"Just a moment, sir."

I drummed my fingers on the telephone stand while I waited. In my mind I saw Marian sitting in her room. Her small white hands reposed in her lap, palms up. Her nose had a faint blush of red on the end, just where it began to turn up. She'd been crying, or was about to cry. After a moment she rose, picked up her purse, and walked to the door. She paused before the mirror; a small woman fashioned without waste of bone and flesh. Her dark auburn hair was pulled back from her temples, the comb-marks straight as plow-furrows on bottomland. On top the hair lay in careful, frozen curls, like a stylized Chinese drawing of the sea. She lifted her hand to touch an imperfection visible only to herself. Suddenly the phone rang . . .

The operator's voice pierced my ear. "Sorry, sir. Mrs. Maxwell checked out yesterday."

My stomach flipped over and a drop of sweat rolled slowly down my back. "Did she . . . leave an address?"

"No sir. Sorry."

I replaced the receiver, tasting a bitterness in my throat. I couldn't think; my mind was like an electrical appliance which had been struck by lightning. It seemed to give off smoke and a faint buzzing sound, but no power.

I heard a noise behind me. I turned to see Sandy standing there.

"I knew she wouldn't be there," she said. "She came here last night."

I could only look at her.

"You . . . sent her away again," said Sandy.

My mouth went dry. I thought of Marian coming home, hoping to be forgiven, finding me in that insane, drunken state and the house ravaged by a four-day orgy. "What . . . what did I say to her?"

"Gee, I don't know. You shoved me into the bathroom when she came. A long time later you came in and said she wouldn't get in our way again."

My face felt tight, as though someone had grabbed the skin at the back of my head and pulled, slitting my eyes and pulling my lips tight across my teeth so that my words came out blurred and fuzzy:

"Was that when I gave you the shaver and the nightdress?"

"Yes." Slowly her eyes grew round. "Baby, you look like you need a drink."

"Oh, Jesus. Jesus Christ." I squeezed my eyes shut and pressed my forehead against the cool, firm wood of the telephone stand. The memory came back all at once, like light returning to a city when the current is restored. It was bright, vivid and unbearable . . .

The argument had lasted a long time, and we'd moved from room to room. Now we faced each other on the patio, and my voice was hoarse and my breath was ragged. Marian was stiff, sober, and firm as a tree; she'd seen the house, she'd sensed the other woman's presence, and now she was leaving. "This time, Greg, I'll never come back." I screamed curses at her. She regarded me with a cool, quizzical expression that drove my fury higher until there was only hate swirling in my mind. I knocked her down and pried a stone from the patio, lifted it above my head, and smashed it down with all my strength. Afterward, as I pried up more stones, I laughed at the way my hands were shaking.

Sandy's voice came to me from a distant, peaceful land, speaking with a sweetness that curdled my soul. "Let's get drunk, Baby. Don't worry about her. I'll stick with you. Always."

I heard dogs on the patio, fighting again. This time I knew what they were fighting over.

How Much to Kill?
Michael Zuroy

February 1961

"So this is it," said Sam Tuttle, the public-relations man, casting diagnostic eyes over the development. From the road off which Cummins' car was parked they had walked about a half-mile into the property. "This is the dream stuff you want me to tout. A piece of Florida at a low, low price. Anybody can afford to be a landowner now. Take that first step towards independence and retirement. What's wrong with the deal, Sheldon? What's your gimmick?"

The unassailable dignity of Sheldon Cummins' square-cut face did not change, but he attempted no pretense with Tuttle; Tuttle had worked for him before. He merely replied, "That concern you, Sam?"

"It does. I'd like to know what kind of trouble I might get into."

"It's not too bad. Not bad at all. Nice-looking property, wouldn't you say? I've got roughly two thousand acres in here, mostly level, crossed by babbling brooks, dotted with charming little ponds, off a good U.S. highway, a short ride to beaches, resort areas, shopping towns and industry. Ideal location and a clear title; every buyer gets an ironclad deed. Minimum plot is one-eighth acre. Streets, as you see, are marked out."

Tuttle bent his head to let some of the rain water spill from his hat brim. For several days the weather had been unsettled, vacillating between fine drizzles and heavy downpours. The rain was falling harder now. Still fairly dry in their raincoats, the two men stepped beneath the shelter of a tree. Tuttle glanced at the occasional rough signs projecting from the brush and tall grass. The closest sign read, "Beachcomber Drive."

"Picturesque," observed Tuttle. "Who wouldn't want to live on that street? You going to actually build the streets, Sheldon?"

"Hell, no. I've had them surveyed and marked. That's it."

"Maybe someday the town that collects the taxes will build them, eh? Maybe someday next century, after a fat assessment. But meanwhile the streets are neatly drawn on your plot maps. Let the buyer beware. Well, that doesn't throw me, Sheldon, but I think there's more to your gimmick than that."

"Why so?"

"I look at it like this," said Tuttle. "Here's two thousand acres of good-looking land in one of Florida's more desirable locations. Empty. No buildings, no improvements on it. There are a lot of legitimate real estate developers in Florida—if you'll pardon the distinction. Some of them sell mail-order. But none of them have touched this parcel, and they haven't just overlooked it. You picked it up for next to nothing, if I guess right. Something's extra special wrong about this land. What is it?"

Cummins looked at Tuttle, his thick eyebrows crawling a little closer to each other, like caterpillars. It wasn't Tuttle's curiosity he disliked as much as his attitude. He never had liked Tuttle, he remembered. For an instant he toyed with the idea of booting Tuttle off his property, but his keenly developed acumen as to his own self-interests stopped him. He needed the younger man right now. He needed favorable publicity. He didn't know another public-relations man as competent and as unscrupulous as Tuttle, and anyone who would take on this job would have to be unscrupulous.

There was a lot of money involved here. This was the biggest operation he had ever promoted—by far. It was so big that it frightened him. No one would guess that under his distinguished front beat a frightened heart, but it was true. He was far out of his league—and alone. He didn't think there was anything as lonely as manipulating a million dollar operation by yourself. Or as worrying.

How he worried! He'd worried every step of the way, over even the smallest decision, over every cent he'd put out. It would be a miracle if he came out of this without an ulcer.

But if things worked out he'd be a millionaire, actually a millionaire. The stake was worth the grief. If things went wrong, he was through. Everything he had and could raise was in this venture.

He said, "Sam, it's been raining a while now. Look there, at that wash coming along that little gully. Look beyond it, there's another one, and another one. Look there, at that brook. Notice how wide and rapid it's become? This is a flood basin, Sam."

Tuttle nodded comprehendingly. "Thought it was something like that."

"Ninety-five percent of the year this area's all right. The rest of the time it's flooded. You can't put a house on this property. The rains hit the hills, miles of them, and they all drain into this basin. Looks like Niagara Falls when the run-off is heavy. Flash floods hit every now and then."

Tuttle swivelled to face Cummins. "Hadn't we better get out of here then? I've read about these flash floods. Read where only a little while back a fellow in a car was swept off a road and drowned."

"Relax," said Cummins. "I know this property. There's a little ridge crossing it from the road, no more than fifty feet wide at best. It's the only ground that never gets flooded. You could hardly tell, but we're standing on it now. We're safe enough. There's even an old shack the surveyors have been using not far along the ridge."

"All right." Tuttle's sharp face went thoughtful. "So what are you asking for one of your damp-dry eighth-acre plots?"

"One hundred dollars."

Tuttle nodded. "Doesn't sound like much. Let's see, two-thousand acres at eight-hundred an acre . . ." He whistled softly. "Better than a million and a half dollars!"

"Don't forget the streets, Sam."

"O.K. Subtract the streets. Subtract your land investment and all your expenses. Subtract say two-hundred thousand give or take fifty all told. You're still way over a million."

Cummins said, "And capital gains taxes?"

"You ought to still clear over a million."

Cummins again repressed his irritation with Tuttle. He lit a cigar. "You through figuring my deal, Sam?"

"Yes, I'm through. And in answer to your implied question, yes I'm interested. I don't foresee trouble. It's not too much of a swindle."

"No swindle, Sam," said Cummins slowly. "The customer gets the land. Maybe it's a little shock when he finds out he can't build on it, but he still owns the land. He's only put a hundred dollars in it. He can pitch a tent in nice weather and go hunting or fishing. He can talk about his Florida property. Maybe some day a flood-control job will happen around here, and then the property will really be valuable."

Tuttle snorted. "Flood control! I wouldn't want to hold my breath until. But it's not too bad a swindle, Sheldon. What do you want me to do?"

The rain turned abruptly into a heavy cascade that gushed through the foliage that had been sheltering them. "We'll be drenched!" yelled Tuttle. "Let's get back to the car."

"Too far in this rain. The shack's a lot closer. Come on."

The two men pounded along the ridge, the hissing torrent driving through their rain-coats in seconds. The shack showed up, and Cummins fiddled with the lock and they burst in.

The shack had once been used as a dwelling and contained several rooms in one of which the surveyors had stored some equipment. The floors sagged and were covered with dust, dried mud and woods debris, and the walls leaned, but the roof still managed to shed water, and the men took off their wet coats and hung them on a couple of the nails that bristled from the walls. They were silent a while, listening to the fury of the downpour, strumming on the roof shingles as it swept across, slapping at the crusted window panes and leaving flowing streams of water that obscured the outside.

"We're liable to see some flooding before this is over," said Cummins. "But, to go on with our business, all I want from you, Sam, is a good press, and I mean nationwide. Most of this land is going to be sold mail-order. Sure, some buyers will come in person, but the odds are they'll see the property at its best, and for a hundred dollar investment they won't be doing much investigating. Mainly, it's the advertising campaign that'll be doing the selling, so it's got to be top-flight, and believe me, it is. It's wrapped up now, all set to go, waiting for the word from me. We ran a couple of test ads, and the percentage was pretty.

"But advertising needs support to gain public confidence. You know how it is, Mr. Doakes reads our ad and sits there dreaming how phenomenal the offer is, if he could believe it. Then he starts forgetting it, and turns some pages, and surprise, right before his eyes is a dignified little news article on our beautiful development. That does it. Doakes has learned to trust us. He digs for his money. That's where you come in, Sam. I want those dignified little articles."

"Can do," said Tuttle. "How much?"

"Five thousand now, two payments of ten thousand each as the work progresses."

"Not enough." Tuttle's reaction was automatic. "That's only twenty-five thousand. I'll take fifty."

Cummins glared. "Don't try to hold me up, Tuttle. The job's not worth that much. It's no sweat for you and I know it. I'm offering you more than enough."

"A job with a smell costs more. Let's hear another offer."

Cummins' resentment began to boil. Tuttle was a nasty little profiteer and a wise-guy to boot. If there were any handy alternative he'd tell him off. He needed Tuttle all right, but he didn't appreciate being black-jacked, and maybe someday he could return the favor. Meanwhile, he forced himself to dissemble.

The bickering went on, seeming as endless almost as the hard driving rain, but at last they agreed on a figure of thirty-seven thousand. When it was settled, they grew impatient to get back to Cummins' car, but the rain refused to let up, so they waited, until finally there came an abrupt cessation of its violence. Through the windows they saw the sky lighten a very little, and the sound outside changed to a delicate unsteady patter. They were donning their raincoats when the new sound began.

"My God!" said Tuttle. "What's that?"

It was a far-off roar that rushed rapidly and irresistibly, swelling as it came until it had grown to a frightening thunder that seemed to submerge and surround them, holding interminably, finally to lessen to a huge rustling.

Cummins watched Tuttle's paling face maliciously. He didn't feel too comfortable himself, but it was good to watch the man fighting against panic. "Flash flood," he explained at last.

"Well then, let's get the hell out of here! What are we waiting for?"

"According to my information this ridge has never been under water. This shack's been standing here a good fifty years, so we should be all right. Let's take a look."

The men went out, took a few steps and halted. The narrow strip of dry land which was the ridge still meandered before them, but everything else on either side was under water. It was as though they were standing within a restless lake across the surface of which white, foaming streams still rushed down from the heights.

"My God," repeated Tuttle. "And this is what you're selling! What makes it come so fast?"

"Same principle as a rolling snowball. Water flows together as it descends from a thousand different sources." Cummins headed back along the ridge, but unhurriedly, aware that Tuttle was still afraid, savoring and prolonging Tuttle's fear. Tuttle could not give up his dignity and run; he had to stick with this pace.

Therefore it was quite some time before the two men reached a view of what had happened out on the water.

Cummins saw it first, his suddenly rigid back bringing Tuttle to his side. Cummins' immediate reaction was that of a surprised bystander, but then the implications grew clear and a sick feeling pushed into his middle. Why? he thought. Why right now?

"Looks like kids!" Tuttle was shouting in his ear. "Two boys."

The figures stood a couple of hundred feet across the turbulent water on what had been a knoll, except that it was now about a foot under. The water raced and splashed over the boys' knees as they hung on to some brush. They began waving and calling frantically at sight of the men.

"How soon'll the water go down?" yelled Tuttle.

Cummins looked at him grimly, and pointed at the white streams still roaming over the lake, breaking into spray where they divided around the trees that rose from the flood. "Still going up."

"The kids will drown. We've got to get help."

Cummins grabbed Tuttle's arm. The blind fool, he thought. Doesn't he understand? "No time. It's up to us. The surveyors keep some line in the shack. Let's get it." He turned and ran heavily, aware that after a pause Tuttle followed.

When the line was secured and fastened to a tree at a point opposite the marooned boys, Cummins rapidly stripped. Tuttle eyed him with a peculiar expression. "You really going in, Sheldon?"

"What the hell does it look like?"

"I take my hat off to you. I didn't think you had it in you. I wouldn't step into that torrent for anything."

Cummins looped the line around his waist and ungracefully splashed into the flood. He gasped at the cold shock and struck into the turbulence. His muscles felt the strain at once and water surged into his nostrils. He was only a fair swimmer and he was too heavy but he forced his arms alternately ahead with savage persistence until it seemed that he had been swimming a very long time. Then he looked up and was stunned to discover that he had lost ground. The travelling water had moved him below the boys, although he was some distance from the ridge.

Cursing his stupidity in not allowing for the flow, he turned back, gained the ridge and flopped upon the ground, gasping, waiting until his breathing had slowed, paying no attention to Tuttle's talk.

When he was ready he plunged in again a good distance above his first position. He noted that the boys were now submerged almost to their waists. He had to get them out on this try.

He swam powerfully, but tried to avoid haste, to conserve his strength. Soon his eyes lost all sight but that of the plunging water which struck at his face. There was no sound in his ears but the rushing and roaring of water.

While his body fought for its life, steadily losing power against the tireless water, his mind grew curiously calm and detached, as though this diminished world in which he struggled could make no demands upon it. Was he being a fool, he wondered? His mind deliberately weighed this, while he admired the clarity of his thinking. He had come to the fork in the road, his mind told him. He had rejected the easy path that led to—nothing. It was now all out, and nothing suffered to block him, even the risk of his own life. He was not being a fool.

Now it seemed impossible that he could lift each arm one more time. He was out past the edge of endurance, almost past the edge of consciousness, but the thought held fast: those kids must not drown.

He made it, of course, that single-minded purpose driving him to his object. After he dropped his feet onto the knoll, he fastened the line to the sturdiest and highest limbs he could find among the brush, praying that it would hold. He sized up the kids quickly and sent the larger and huskier of the two back along the line by himself.

He waited until he was sure the kid was making it, then started the other one off, staying right with him. Twice the force of the water began to tear the boy off the rope, but Cummins grabbed him and held him, bulling him along until he regained his grip.

"Why, you're a hero, a blasted hero," Tuttle told him when the boys were safe on the ridge, sitting huddled together, resting. "That was a fine thing to do, Sheldon."

Cummins regarded him contemptuously, and swivelled his head to make sure the boys were out of hearing range. "Save your praise, Sam," he said. "I did it for only one reason—a million dollars."

"Clear that up, will you."

"You slipping, Sam? You can't be that dense. Suppose the two little punks drowned on my property. That's news, isn't it? Headline news a lot of places. The national papers would carry something on it. Florida Flash Flood Drowns Two Youngsters in Real Estate Development. I might as well fold up and steal away after that. Nobody would pay a dime for this property. You don't think I want to spend my declining years selling insurance, do you?"

Tuttle bowed satirically. "Forgive me for misjudging you. Ever the promoter, eh Sheldon? As a public relations man the aspect you mention should have occurred to me, but I was too concerned about the boys' danger. Foolish of me. I must be, as you say, slipping."

"Now, this way," went on Cummins, "it doesn't matter too much if the boys chatter about what happened. A close shave is hardly news. Oh, it might make a local paper or two, but that's about all. The kids are alive, that's the main thing. Corpses we don't need around here."

"I admire your logic," said Tuttle. He glanced at Cummins meditatively. "You'd do anything for money, wouldn't you, Sheldon?"

"For enough money. Like anybody else. Don't you go superior on me, Sam, we're all the same, all of us humans. The only difference is the price. Everybody has their price, five hundred, five thousand or five million. For me a million does it. I'd do anything for a million. You didn't jump in after those boys because there was only thirty-five thousand in it for you. Not enough."

"Plus the fact that I can't swim."

The rain began to patter down more strongly again, and Cummins looked worriedly over at the boys. Couldn't have them contracting pneumonia either; had to get them under shelter. They'd return to the shack.

When they were all inside the old building, Cummins regarded the youngsters keenly. They seemed to be about fifteen or sixteen years old, neither too well built although one was slightly taller. The taller one had a broad jaw, open blue eyes and freckles. The other was spindly-looking with sharp features and a narrow head and a weak button of a chin. His eyes seemed perpetually half-closed and flat.

"We want to thank you again for pulling us out of there, Mister," said the spindly one. He said it reluctantly, as though grudging the necessity.

"That's all right, that's all right," returned Cummins genially. "As long as you kids are safe. Where you from?"

"New York." The boy pulled up a leg of his worn jeans and scratched casually.

"New York. That's a long way off. What are you doing all the way down here?"

"Seeing the country."

"Where are your folks?"

The boy jerked a thumb at his companion. "Joe there, he doesn't have any. Mine are still in New York, I guess."

"You guess? What did you do, run away?"

The boy shrugged. "Nothing to run away from. The old man's a booze hound. My old lady, well let's forget her. They ain't missing me."

"What's your name?"

The boy's grin was almost a snarl. "Elias. Elias Smith. That's Joe Jones over there."

"Oh, come on!"

The boy nodded his head vigorously, grinning. "Sure, that's us. Smith and Jones. Jones and Smith." He laughed.

"Now don't get smart," said Cummins heavily. "What were you doing on this property?"

"Sight-seeing."

"I'm losing my patience," said Cummins.

"Well, for Chris-sake, what do you want, a big fancy story? We turned in off the road to sleep last night, that's all. Say, what are you, a cop or somethin', Mister?"

"No, I'm not a cop, I'd just like to know."

"Hey, he's just nosy," said the other boy.

The spindly one cackled. "Sure, nosy. So this is what happened, nosy. We couldn't stay dry account of the rain, so in the morning we walked in a ways looking for a better spot. We found one and settled down and all of a sudden there was this wall of water, looked about ten foot high coming down on us. Joe and me, we got to that little hill. The other guy didn't make it."

The silence stretched while Cummins absorbed the words. "What other guy?" he asked slowly, at last.

"The other guy, the other guy. Herb, the other buddy. The water caught him."

"There were three of you? You're telling me that there were three of you?"

The boy appealed to Tuttle. "Hey, has this lad got all his marbles? Ain't I just finished tellin' him there was another guy?"

Suddenly Cummins struck the boy a back-handed blow across the cheek that sent him sprawling. "Enough of your sass. Talk straight, now. What happened to the third boy?"

The boy who called himself Smith lay on the floor as he had fallen, his eyes growing flatter and more heavy-lidded. He did not appear otherwise angered or surprised at the blow; he appeared used to blows. He said softly, "I guess Herb got drowned. That straight enough for you? Anything else you want to know?"

This was too much, Cummins thought. After all he'd been through, to end up with a drowning on his hands was too much. "Let's take a look around," he said to Tuttle dully. "You boys wait. We'll be back."

The men walked the ridge carefully, not speaking, watching the water and the ragged water line along the ridge. After a while they came upon it, as Cummins had known they would. It was a soaked blob of denims, and when Cummins turned it over with his foot, there was the young drowned face.

"Pity," said Tuttle.

"Yes, a pity," said Cummins bitterly, not meaning it the same way.

After a silence, Tuttle said, "I guess this blows your million all right."

Cummins was thinking hard. "I don't think I'm through yet, Sam." His mouth worked. "Suppose nobody finds out about this drowning?"

The two men stared at each other, each working out this line of thought in their own way.

"We bury the body in the muck," Cummins went on. "It'll never turn up. The kid was a nobody, like the other two. The chances are there'll never be any inquiry made after the little bum. There isn't anybody gives a damn about kids like these or knows where they are. So another drifter disappears."

"You want me to keep quiet?"

"That's right."

"For a price?"

"That's right. You got a price, Sam."

Tuttle nodded. "Certainly I have. You know me that well, Sheldon. How much?"

"Seventy thousand."

Tuttle whistled. "Just for keeping my mouth shut. Well, well. It's tempting, but risky. What about the other two boys?"

"I admit that's a weak point. I was thinking we could give them some money and a couple of tickets out of the state."

Tuttle shook his head slowly. "No good. They can talk wherever they are. Sooner or later those boys are going to run foul of the police. How do you know what they'll say then? No, Sheldon, the story's too apt to come out."

Cummins looked at him broodingly.

"Count me out," Tuttle said regretfully. "It's a nice piece of change, but I don't want to be accused of hiding a body. Besides, if the story came out it would really queer your little deal, wouldn't it?"

"I agree with you, Sam," Cummins said in a strained voice. "It won't do. But there's another way to make sure the boys won't talk."

Tuttle grinned. "Oh, sure, we can . . ." But then he saw Cummins' eyes, and the grin died.

"Yes," said Cummins, "there's another way."

"Now don't be fantastic, Sheldon."

"Fantastic! I tell you, Sam, this means a million dollars to me. One million dollars! For that price I'll do it."

"Forget it, will you. You don't think for one moment I'd go along?"

"You've got a price for this too, Sam."

"Not for this."

"Less than an hour's work, Sam. Two lousy little bums. They're no use to themselves or anybody else anyway. We'd be doing society a favor. We could plant the three of them so deep in the muck they might as well have vanished into thin air. Nobody's going to bother wondering about them. Hell, they'd be dead right now if I hadn't rescued them. So I made a mistake. I'll just correct that mistake."

"I wish you'd stop talking this way."

"What's the price, Sam? Two hundred thousand?"

"I admit I've pulled some shady stunts in my time," said Tuttle, "but I stop short at murder, at any price. Now cut it out, Sheldon. You're not a murderer and you know it."

"You're absolutely right," replied Cummins. "I have no desire to murder anybody. It makes me sick to think about it. But I'm telling you again, Sam, for this much money I'll kill. How about three hundred thousand?"

"Look, Sheldon, why don't you simmer down? Forget it, and I'll see what I can do about squashing the story."

Cummins shook his head. "There's nothing you can do or you would have mentioned it before. A kid drowned in a flood in a big real estate development? That story won't squash once it gets out. I'm convinced this is the only way. Don't try holding me up, Sam, I'm warning you. I'll go four hundred thousand and that's my limit. Are you going to accept it?"

"No."

"All right, Sam," said Cummins softly. "I gave you your chance." He raised his powerful hands and placed them on Tuttle's throat. Tuttle tried to jerk back, but the hands tightened. "You're crazy, Sheldon," Tuttle yelled and swung his fist against Cummins' head, but the blow seemed to make no impression.

Cummins began to squeeze, ignoring the man's struggles, and slowly Tuttle sank to his knees and his back arched, so that Cummins had to bend over him while he squeezed. Cummins went to his own knees to ease the uncomfortable position. After a while he took his hands away and rose to his feet and Tuttle's body collapsed on the ground.

It was the only solution, Cummins thought. It might be taking a chance, but he had chosen to go all out and he would have to accept the risk. He estimated that the odds were with him. Tuttle was a lone wolf, and since this job was on the shady side it was unlikely that he had discussed it with anyone. He had no car here; he had arrived by plane. It would simply be a case of a man disappearing, a man whose connection with himself would remain private. If ever questioned he would give the proper answers. It would occur to no one to search this property, and in any case, Tuttle's body would never be found.

Next, the boys. Unfortunately, he had no weapon with him, but if necessary he would take care of them with his bare hands also. However, he seemed to remember something about the surveyors' supplies. He knitted his brow, trying to visualize. Yes, he remembered. There was an axe.

He decided on his course of action. When he entered the shack he would walk casually to the storeroom and get the axe. They would be unsuspecting, so that he could kill at least one of them without a struggle. After that, the axe would make short work of the other, even if he tried to fight.

Cummins reached the shack, opened the door and stepped in.

The kids were sitting on the floor, backs against the wall. "Hey!" said the skinny one. "Look who's here." He rose, grinning sarcastically and sidled over to Cummins. "Where's the other fellow?"

"He won't be back," Cummins said shortly. "Had some business."

The last thing Cummins saw was the knife the kid pulled . . .

When the body was still the boy began going through the pockets. "I don't know if you shudda knocked him off," the taller boy said doubtfully.

"Why not? Looks well-heeled, don't he?"

"Yeah, but after all he saved our hides."

"Because he was a dope. If he wasn't a dope he wouldn't have got it now. That's what I keep tellin' you, don't be a dope. He rubbed me the wrong way anyhow." The boy came up with a fat wallet and cackled. He counted the money and looked up, his flat eyes taking on a glitter. "Two hundred and thirty-eight dollars," he said, awe creeping into his voice. "It was worth knocking him off. Jeez, for that much money I'd knock off anybody."

Deadly Triangle
Les Collins

April 1961

Death walked with the three through the scattered but thick patches of scrub oak and manzanita; the sun would soon set in the hills that surrounded San Jose Valley, ending a particularly hot summer day.

The feast-or-famine vegetation was typical of the California coast ranges. The clothes of the two men and one woman were typical hunting outfits. The dominant thoughts were atypical: one would die.

They seemed two of a kind, Frank Morriss and Jim Thomason. Two—but only one Pat. She'd married Frank.

At the mouth of a small valley. Frank halted. Nervously, he gulped from a canteen. "We'll find some up there." He lifted his chin in gesture at the head of the dry stream.

Pat and Jim followed his line of sight, up the steep hill. Dense brush thirstily sought what little moisture remained close to the ground surface.

"What do you think?" Frank asked.

"Your party, Frank. You always were better at hunting than I," Jim Thomason said, with a quick, sidewise glance at Pat.

Frank, wiping perspiration from his forehead with his sleeve, grinned. "Yeah, but that was when I was in condition—"

"When we both were in condition." Jim patted a very slight bulge at his waistline. "Fifteen years is a long time ago, measured against hunting men."

"But today you're hunting deer, remember?" Pat asked impatiently. "And they won't bring up any 88's or SS reserves." She softened then. "The hearth grows cold, men, and despite your talk, the wheelchair isn't waiting. Believe me, 34 is not ancient."

"I'm 35 today!" Frank objected. "Have you forgotten so soon?" Pat hadn't, of course; the new Winchester Special in his hands was a reminder.

"She was complimenting you, dope!" Jim said. "Anyway, this practical female wants us to shoot the deer instead of waiting for them to die of old age. What is your Estimate of the Situation, Sergeant Morriss?"

The tall man smiled appreciation at the old standard joke. It had begun on a snowy night in France when Jim, a new replacement scared green on his first patrol, had asked the tough, experienced sergeant the question. Jim didn't know the sergeant's experience was all of two months and that Morriss was equally scared. His reply—"The Situation calls for us to run like hell!"—drew the men together afterwards, when they could laugh about it.

"If we go around the hill on either side, swing down and take 'em from behind, they'll move in this direction," Frank said, "Pat, hold the spot. We'll flush 'em, and they'll come right at you. Just shoot the males, though—What's wrong? Why the strange look?"

"I can shoot only one more male," she said levelly, "The game warden—"

"All right, all right! Shoot only one more, then." Frank turned to Jim, who was mopping his brow. "The troops are falling apart! What's bothering you?"

"Nothing. Too much sun, maybe."

"When didn't you have this reaction, Jim? Always scared before and after—but I'd have no one else beside me during a fight. Forget the flip-flops in your stomach, and take the west side. I'll go east."

"Like Hannibal at Cannae!" Jim was suddenly enthusiastic. "Double envelopment; you always were a good tactician—"

"And you always did read too much," Pat interjected dryly. "We haven't an awful lot of time left."

Frank nodded. "True, we haven't much time left at all. Let's move out."

Patricia Morriss sat on a fallen tree trunk, ideally placed at the mouth of the valley. From here, she could shoot anything that came down. Anything?

I guess I should have kissed him, she thought, I should have. At least, I could have said goodby. Yes, I could have kissed off 11 years of marriage. Frank, why did you force me to this? Thou shalt not kill, thou shalt not commit adultery . . . am I a monster? I begged you, but you wouldn't give me the divorce. Why was it always a fight between us, even to this?

She watched her husband's retreating back until he was gone, striding boldly around the hill. Jim had already disappeared. Jim, smarter than Frank, much more easily manipulated—Jim would do it.

Funny, but she'd never noticed before how they'd leaned on Jim. Always knowing, but never recognizing how he'd helped, they just assumed he'd be standing by. There were hundreds of incidents—did Frank and Jim remember?

The dance that evening so long ago: both men entered together. For a few moments, as she watched from across the floor, they stood shoulder-to-shoulder, eyeing the setup. Jim spotted Pat before Frank, approached, hesitantly asked for a dance.

She accepted—and immediately sensed weakness in Jim. When Frank cut in, she knew she was right. Frank was the strong personality in the team. They danced twice more; he wouldn't give her up, even when Jim returned. She was so beautiful in those days.

The three wound up at the punch bowl, arguing, then drinking. The sorority punch was properly spiked, Frank and Jim grew thick-tongued.

Finally, there came the inevitable question and Frank's answer: "The situation calls for us to run like hell. You start out." She spent the rest of the evening with Frank. As most returned veterans, he was more mature than the campus boys; the type she wanted, he would be a good husband.

Pat called the moves; for two years, she was with both men. It seemed as though the duo had become a trio. Jim was dangled enough to arouse Frank's competitive instinct. And then, one evening just before graduation, Pat sensed a crisis.

When they arrived in San Francisco, less than an hour from campus, Pat noticed fitfulness in her escorts. Frank was impatient; Jim, tense. She suggested Ernie's for dinner, and both growled; didn't she know by now that the budget was restricted?

Jim intervened, cut off a potential argument, deftly pushed them to one of the North Beach spaghetti joints—the kind infamous for poor, if plentiful, food. Their somber mood continued during the meal until, with startling suddenness, Frank abruptly proposed to Pat.

This, then, was what had caused their edginess: Frank had transmitted his excitement to Jim, who must have known instinctively what was coming. Jim had reacted, and Pat picked up the mood from both of them.

It was her decision: Frank or Jim? No decision, really. Poor second-best Jim! She'd known he loved her, and she said so. But it was to be Frank. Jim had colored, smiled sadly, and said, "I guess, sergeant, this is one situation where *I* run but you can't."

There followed the usual maudlin scenes. Pat wondered briefly why men acted in such fashion; they were silly. Jim had the role of Good Sport and Good Friend; he played it beautifully the rest of the evening, actually for the following 11 years.

It was only a few months ago that she asked Frank for a divorce. The marriage had gone bad. For one thing, he was ungrateful. He'd been set up in business with some of her father's money, yet lately he'd stubbornly refused to do what she wanted. Frank argued with her constantly. When Pat bought the house as a surprise for him, he was displeased that he hadn't been consulted.

And why should Frank want children so much? He suggested them several times, even though she replied that children would ruin their fun, and could come later. Another thing: why didn't Frank arrange to be home the once or twice she'd have dinner guests? Obviously, he had no use for her friends and was humiliatingly blunt about it.

He'd even begun to work late, much too late, at the office.

Frank, Pat discovered, had become completely intractable. It was shocking that he wouldn't give her the divorce; instead he suggested they try to work out their differences. She knew it was hopeless.

The next day, she lunched with Jim. He could always be counted on; it was surprising that even with his weak personality, he had become successful in advertising.

She was sure Jim still loved her; he was sympathetic about her marital problems—sympathetic and properly upset, but with a calculating look. They began to see each other with increasing frequency. Fairly soon, they were entangled—the usual entanglement of a disappointed suitor—and she suggested what had to be done. It was almost as though she were hypnotized, and she hated herself while planning this hunting trip.

Hunting trip? Pat was suddenly back in the present. Surely both men were on the hilltop by now, and she had to look as though she were waiting for deer. "Happy birthday . . ."

Jim Thomason left first, trudging toward the red sun. He glanced once, quickly, over his shoulder, but the others were already out of sight.

I hope she kissed him, he thought, she should have. Born, married, died—11 years. A rotten world, a rotten life . . . and I have to take it. I'm a monster, or is human life really that important? Frank, why didn't you give her the divorce? You always were better at tactics than I; unfortunately, I was always a better shot.

Jim paused to check the 30.06. The bolt action was smooth; Remingtons were made with integrity. He loaded the magazine, but kept the chamber empty. Then, cautiously silent, he continued through the brush. It was like France, except then Frank was on his side.

France, Frank, the football team—the night we met Pat. I remember how we arrived, stood shoulder-to-shoulder in a post-adolescent bravado that covered basic shyness. My first sight of Pat: she *was* beautiful from across the room.

How did I beat Frank to her? He was much faster than I at the quick size-up. My feelings as I approached Pat: this was The Girl, I thought over and over.

Finally, after walking through molasses for a million years, I was asking her to dance. You accepted, Pat, but what happened? The moment you were in my arms, the wonderful, youthful, haze disappeared. Was it a foreboding, a preview of today? Later, at the punch bowl, when Frank said, "The situation calls for us to run like hell, or we won't start out," I think I realized even then—

The dry underbrush crackled up ahead, alerting Jim. He was gripping his rifle too tightly, sweating too much. Deer, for sure; Frank was right. Quietly, he worked the bolt back and forth, putting a cartridge in the chamber. Perspiration stung his eyes, and he wiped it away. Annoyed, he knew he had to relax, move slowly.

Move slowly? I did, for two years. Until that night in the city. We were all tense; there was some silly quarrel about where we'd eat, ending as usual at North Beach—sure, Italian food, romantic setting, night-life of the nongods. And everyone snapping at everyone else.

We'd almost finished when Frank suddenly dropped his fork. This would be uncomfortable; I knew what he was going to do even before he proposed, and it was obvious Pat accepted. But—I remember now!—my feelings were a strange mixture of relief and sorrow.

I must have spoken aloud because Pat started talking; told me I loved her. Did I? Yes, with reservations.

Somewhere, appropriately, I said, "Sergeant, this is a situation where I run but you can't." It was supposed to be funny, but Pat didn't like the sound of it. Guess Frank didn't either.

During the evening, I managed to express my loyalty to both of them. Or perhaps not—Pat was talking quite a bit.

She was always a good talker, but she failed when it came to the divorce. These 11 years were good years, fun years—why this sort of an ending? From that day a few months ago, when Pat called and invited me to lunch, the pattern seemed obvious and inevitable.

She told me the whole story; in her words, Frank's infidelity, gaucherie, stubbornness, and the rest. I felt sorry for both of them—and for one second, I saw Pat as I had that night we first met.

Funny, but with one break in your armor, you leave yourself wide open. I don't like to think about what happened next, Frank; it was betrayal. Unplanned, but still betrayal: of you, of Pat, of me.

So I am responsible for what today brings—

Today? *Now.*

Jim was excellently positioned. "Happy birthday!"

He brought the rifle up, aimed, and slowly squeezed the trigger.

Frank Morriss watched Jim walk toward the sunset, then swing out of sight around the hill. Silently, he turned to Pat, a mocking look in his eye.

"I'd better take off myself."

She nodded, deep in thought.

Frank began the long walk to and up the east shoulder of the hill. I wish she'd kissed me, he thought, or maybe I should have kissed her. I gave her the chance; I gave Jim one, too—and now . . . He shrugged. Thou shalt not kill, true, but what *is* the solution? I can't lose her to another man. God! despite everything, I still love her.

Frank stopped suddenly, instinctively, at the buzzing noise. A small, Coast Range rattlesnake was coiled on guard, less than six feet away. Shaking its tail, its head and neck upright and poised for a strike, the rattler glowered malevolently at him.

Though the snake wasn't really a threat, Frank felt the usual chill at the back of his neck. He eased to a stoop, his fingers fumbling for, and finding, a heavy rock.

By then, the snake had buzzed angrily a few more times and uncoiled. It glided regally eastward, an imperious look proclaiming its victory. Frank, gripping the rock, could have thrown it accurately enough to break the rattler's neck. Instead, the man let go, hardly hearing the dull thud of rock against soil.

Snake, why should I kill you? You're as frightened as I, so today we are brothers. You don't kill a brother—or someone as close as a brother. Stay alive, snake. I am older; I came to life 13 years ago, so I'll be the one to die soon.

Came to life! Jim and I hit that dance with only one thought: available, makeable, age-of-consent females. We couldn't know the dance would not be over for so many years.

I'm sure I saw Pat first—and stood, stunned. By the time I'd recovered, Jim was already talking to her. How could the son of a bitch do something like that?

Hold it! Am I talking about Jim? The guy who picked off the mortar squad when the rest of us were hugging holes in the ground, too frightened to move. Jim's a friend; besides, I could always talk him into doing what I wanted. Pat danced with me the rest of the evening.

OK, we *should* have run like hell, and maybe today wouldn't be here. I couldn't leave her, Jim. She was like a picture that I'd made up and never thought could exist. Bells going off in my head, alarm bells, telling me to get away. Instead, I stayed, with my guts churning. I wanted to strangle you when you spoke to her; I floated when she gave me her full attention. Pat was man-hunting; I vowed she'd stop as of then.

She nearly did, too. My only competition for the next two years was Jim. Always there, always forming the trio. Damn you! Couldn't you see?

No, not even the night I proposed. That restaurant you dragged us to—tawdry, run-down, covering dirty wallpaper with a blanket of "atmosphere." You knew, and you wanted to stop me.

Without realizing it, Frank worked the lever of the carbine. Then, hooking a strong thumb over the hammer, he pressed the trigger and gently, slowly released the hammer. The Special now had a cartridge in the chamber, and could be fired quickly. There'd been little noise: a *click-snick* of the assembly, barely audible, gave Frank godlike power. He moved on.

You lost, Jim; I won. And so we were married and I lived unhappily ever after. Pat is headstrong; domineering without ability to dominate; add her father's money. It took me a long time to realize I was a kept patsy—pushed around at her whim, too puppy-dog grateful to know it.

As soon as I caught on, the marriage went sour. She didn't want kids; actually, I was acting in that capacity, and she couldn't stand it when I showed independence. Suddenly, she wanted out.

Conveniently enough, Jim, in all that time you never married. Why?

Divorce? The hell I'd give her one! Maybe it was time for her to grow up. I suggested it in that battle we had.

Well, you don't argue with children, you tell them. The divorce was out. I'd matured. Finally had control of the business; next, I'd control my family . . . including the kids she'd bear me.

Pat said it was a fine curtain speech, but unfortunately I was too weak. Was I? The next few months would tell.

Then came the shock of the day when I accidentally discovered she'd been seeing Jim! My best friend! And my wife . . .

"I loved you both. But: It's my: birthday."

Frank aimed carefully.

Two almost-simultaneous shots echoed in the canyon, disturbed a circling hawk, frightened a doe, made no impression on the omnipresent manzanita, and very quickly dulled to nothing in the late-afternoon winds of the Coast Ranges.

A voice from a thousand miles away: "Run like hell?"

An answer, tremulous as though aged: "No, not from this one. We'll tell them it was a hunting accident."

Unconscious habit, born in days of fear that were never expected to return, with greater intensity drew them shoulder to shoulder. Pat, sprawled back over the fallen tree, lay unmoving where two tiny motes had pushed her. The bullet holes, like two bleeding close-spaced eyes, were an inch and one-half apart.

The Big Haul
Robert Page Jones

August 1961

It had begun to rain when he picked up Highway 77 outside of Friersville. Now, nearly a hundred and fifty miles west, water rattled down on the tomblike cab of the big tractor like showers of hail.

The driver—his name was Johnny Womack—chewed at a sandwich. He had nearly white hair, cropped close to his head like fine toothbrush bristles, but his face was young. The jaw was lean and hard, faintly corded with muscle. He had dark gray eyes. They squinted against the glare of an onrushing car. Cursing softly under his breath, he cut his speed back to forty, left it at that after the car had passed. He was satisfied to be making even forty through the drifting sheets of water.

The big rig moved well. It was nearly seven years old, one of the old stick-shift jobs, with ten forward gears—but it was dependable. And it was nearly his.

If he didn't miss any more payments.

He thought about the empty van in back. His lips made a bitter expression. He had hauled a full load of cotton to Denver, hoping to get some kind of load for the trip back to El Centro, without success. It had been a bad deal from the start. The cotton run hadn't paid well and he had been forced to come back empty.

And there was Emma. This would be the first time in ten years that he wouldn't be returning to her. Emma. His lips made the bitter expression again. Not that he blamed her. Ten years is a long time to hang around while your husband is on the road—especially with bills coming in faster than money. Even when two people are in love, it's no good without money. And he knew now, had known ever since she ran out on him, that she hadn't been in love with him—not really in love.

He took another bite of sandwich and put the uneaten portion on the seat beside him. He felt let down and depressed. His face half bitter, half angry, he shook his head. The thought slipped in and out of his mind that he had felt let down and depressed for most of his life.

He rolled on, still knocking off forty, headlights stuck out before him like the probing antenna of a giant bug. The rig was running low on gas. He would reach Stanton around midnight and he could tank up there. Maybe. The oil company had let his credit card expire—he owed them nearly three hundred bucks—and he had only a few dollars left in his pocket.

Shifting hands on the wheel, he groped under the dash for the big .45 suspended there from metal clips. He had bought the gun for protection on long overnight hauls. Emma had wanted him to have it. He hefted it in his hand. The metal gleamed in the glow from the dash-lights. He remembered the first time he had held a gun. A long time ago. He had been a little boy. He had picked it off the floor by the body of his father.

Shrugging, as if to resolve some problem that bothered him, he hefted the gun and then put it back in the clips.

He would hock it, if he had to, or sell it. That would be better than using it; He had spent part of his youth in a reform school. It had taught him something. If he ever used a gun, it would be for something big. Something really big. Like a million dollars.

He laughed out loud. A million bucks was more money than there was in the world.

2.

There were three of them. One was a soldier. He wore his tailored summer gabardines with the deliberate casualness of one who could never quite accustom himself to army discipline. The gabardines were obviously of expensive quality. They were the kind that the officers wear. But the shirt bore no insignia rank—only the collar brass of an enlisted man.

He was younger than the others. His narrow, colorless face was heavily pockmarked, as if the skin had been gnawed by a rodent. He said softly, "Quit sweating, Wibber."

"Who's sweating?" The man called Wibber mopped at his face. He was very fat. He lay sprawled on his back on the cheap hotel room bed, perspiration-stained Western hat perched on his mountainous stomach, looking straight at the ceiling. "I just don't want us to screw up, that's all. I know this town. I know how they'll react to a heist like this. It'll be the biggest thing ever hit this place . . . and I don't aim to get caught in the middle."

"You don't know nothing. None of you know nothing. If you did, you wouldn't be scrabbling for peanuts in a penny-ante berg like this." The soldier—his name was Sammy Travis—reached for his cigarettes. His fingers were slim and white, almost like the fingers of a woman, only the tips were stained dark yellow with nicotine. He got to his feet and said tersely, "What time is it?"

The third man—his name was Bernie White—looked at his watch. He had the dirt-clogged nails and blunted fingers of a man who works with engines. He said, "Twenty-seven after."

"Three minutes," Travis said.

Wibber moaned softly and swung his feet to the floor. The bedspread was sweat-sopped where his body had lain. He said, "How can you guys stand it?"

Travis said, "Eh?"

"How can you stand it?"

"Stand what?"

"The heat?"

White said, "You should take off some of that blubber. It ain't hot."

Travis didn't answer. He went to the window and pulled back the drapes. Sunlight came in. What might have been a smile pulled at his lips as he said, "Right on schedule."

Wibber and White joined him at the window. For exactly four minutes they watched something that was going on in the street four floors below. Then, without speaking, Travis closed the drapes and walked to the dresser. He took out a half pint of whiskey and divided it equally into three glasses. When he had distributed the glasses, he sat down in a chair and lit a cigarette.

Travis' glass was empty and he was on his third cigarette when the phone rang. Before lifting the receiver he looked at White. "Time?"

White said, his voice edgy, "Eleven after."

"Exactly thirty-seven minutes." Travis let the phone ring three times, lifted the receiver, then replaced it without talking into it. The ringing stopped. He said purposefully, "All right. Let's try to get it straight in our minds."

"We've checked the timing on every run for the past three months, and it's consistent. That's important. Perfect timing is the difference between the right way or wrong way of doing a thing." Travis grinned acidly. "That's one of the things they taught me in the Army."

"I ain't convinced." Wibber grunted on the bed. "Knocking off an armored car ain't like maneuvers. Christ, every successful armored car heist in history has been an inside job, and we ain't on the inside."

"And that ain't an armored car." Travis lit a cigarette from the stub in his hand. The gesture was quick, nervous. "It's a 1938 klunker that's about to rust off its axels. Hell, if it wasn't for the Army payroll, it'd be carrying nothing but cash receipts from the Saturday night Bijou."

Wibber grunted, fanned his face with his hat.

Travis said, "Now then. Here are some of the things we know. The semi-monthly payroll for the base, discounting civilian employees who're paid by check, is about seven hundred and fifty thousand dollars. Cash. Beautiful green cash. Almost all of it in small bills."

"How do you know?" Wibber stopped fanning.

White said, "Wibber, weren't you ever in the Army?"

"What if I wasn't?" Wibber fanned. "What's so goddamned hot about the Army?"

"If you were," Travis interrupted, "you'd know something. Three quarters of a million, divided into a couple of thousand pay envelopes, ain't much. Twenties, mostly, except for some fifties they use for the officers."

Travis laughed softly at his own humor. "The money is transferred to the base by the local armored transport service. Big deal. Three quarters of a million clams floating around in a klunker that would fall apart if you leaned on it. The trip from the bank to the base takes thirty-seven minutes. Add four minutes at each end for transferring the dough and it gives us exactly forty-five minutes from vault to vault. Forty-five minutes to knock this hick town on its ear."

Wibber said, "You've worked on the car, Bernie. What do you think?"

"It's old. But it's tough." White looked at Travis. "We won't be able to crack it open. If we're going to stand any chance at all, we'll have to think our way in."

"Just like that, huh?" Wibber mopped his face again, eyes still pinned on the ceiling. "There are two security guards to handle the transfer at the bank—three, counting the regular bank guard—and the whole U.S. Army is on hand to unload. What do you figure they're gonna be doing while we clean house?"

"So we don't hit 'em during the transfer," Travis said quietly. "We wait until they're out on the road. Then—"

"One thing that's still bothering me," White broke in. He stabbed his finger at a red line on the roadmap spread between Wibber's feet. "Route 77 is the only road in or out of Valerie. A hundred and eighty miles to the California border, nearly the same distance to the nearest town east, and nothing but sand in between. Assuming we figure a way to make the heist . . . how do we get the dough out of the state?"

Travis pulled back the curtain and looked down into the street again, at the busy sidewalk in front of the First Trust and Savings Bank of Valerie, where less than an hour before he had watched canvas sacks containing seven hundred and fifty thousand dollars loaded into an armored car.

He stood at the window for several minutes. When he turned to look at the others his face was expressionless. He half closed his eyes as he said, "Working out the details is my problem. You two just make sure you're ready to go . . . two weeks from today."

3.

Bernie White slammed closed the hood of the big tractor, motioned for Womack to cut the engine, and walked around by the pumps.

"Sounds like maybe you got a bent rod," he said.

Womack cursed softly. "You sure?"

"Nope." White shifted a wad of something in his mouth. "I'll have to get inside and take a look."

"How long will that take?"

White shrugged. He mopped his face and neck. "Can't tell. I'm the regular mechanic, but the boss is off today, sick; so I've got to handle the pumps, too. Depends on how many people come in for gas. Hour, maybe."

"Okay."

"You in a hurry?"

"Yeah." Womack was in no particular hurry, but he didn't want to be stuck in this burg any longer than was absolutely necessary, not with heat shimmering up out of the pavement like steam in a Turkish bath. He climbed down out of the tractor and said, "Where can I drink a beer and cool off?"

"Frank's Place is about as cool as any." White pointed a puffy, freckled forearm. "It's about two blocks down the main drag. Can't miss it. You want I should come and get you as soon as I take a look?"

"Yeah. If I'm not back by then, you come and get me."

White watched the big truck driver walk down Mainstreet toward Frank's Place and thought how good a beer would taste. Then he went in by the grease rack for his tools. An armored car—PHILLIPS ARMORED TRANSPORT SERVICE said the sign on the side panels—was up on the rack.

White moistened his lips and looked for a long moment at the truck. They brought it in every week to be serviced and, although White had only worked at the garage for four months, he knew it like the back of his hand.

It was an old model, squat and ugly, like some thick-skinned prehistoric animal, but one which, if you could ever slit open its belly, would spew forth three quarters of a million clams.

In spite of the heat, White was whistling a happy tune when he walked back outside to work on the rig.

4.

Frank's Place may have been as cool as any, Womack thought—but that wasn't very cool.

It was a combination bar and cafe like a dozen Womack had stopped at along Route 77 in Arizona. The shades had been drawn in a vain attempt to keep out the heat. The only fight was from imitation candles, made even more feeble by cheap cardboard shades, on the bar and in the booths along one side. Womack sat in a booth. The seats were covered with imitation leather, decorated with livestock brands, like the old West.

A thin-faced guy in a white apron sat on one of the bar stools reading a newspaper. He was slightly built, about forty-five, with protruding shoulder blades.

The only other person in the place was a girl. Womack couldn't help thinking that she didn't belong there. That is, she looked like she should have been at the bar in some swanky New York hotel, instead of in this hick-town greasy-spoon.

She was sitting at the far end of the bar, wearing an obviously expensive cocktail dress, absently twirling a frosted glass. The glass was fully nine inches tall. It contained a smoky, pink-colored liquid. Her dress was green, with thin, rhinestone-covered halter straps that looked as if they might snap under the strain. She wore expensive shoes, separated from the dress by what looked like yards of sexily-curved legs.

The skinny guy with the apron came over and stood disinterestedly while Womack glanced at the menu.

"Soup. And a beer."

"What kind of beer?"

"Any kind. Hamm's."

"Chicken or split pea?"

"Chicken. And some crackers."

He took a pad from his pocket and wrote on it. "Chicken. You want the Southern fried steak or ravioli?"

"Just the soup."

Tight Face looked at him disgustedly. "You want dessert?"

"No."

Womack grabbed a handful of sugar cubes and stuffed them into his pocket. The way his money was holding out, the sugar might be his only other meal between Valerie and El Centro. If he ever made El Centro. He wondered how serious the trouble with his rig was . . .

He lit a cigarette and looked at the girl. She had swung around on the stool and was gazing at him openly, elbow on the bar, cheek resting in the palm of her hand. Like the dress, and the fancy beehive hairdo, she looked expensive. Too expensive. He'd never been able to afford dames like that. With a faint smile he realized that he hadn't even been able to afford Emma—and she had come pretty cheap. Emma. He wondered how long the little bitch had been playing around while he was on the road . . .

The girl got off the stool and crossed the room to the juke box. It was still light out, but she obviously had been drinking for most of the afternoon. She handled her body provocatively, like a stripper on a stage, accentuating the rising, full breasts and narrow waist and rounded hips. She selected an Ella Fitzgerald record and went back to the bar. While she listened, she continued to look at Womack. It made him uncomfortable. Before the record was over she took her glass and slid into the seat opposite him.

She fumbled in her purse for a cigarette, put one in her mouth, and looked expectantly at him. He lit it.

"That stool wasn't very comfortable," she said softly. "Do you mind?"

"No." He answered guardedly. He had forgotten how stupid this sort of thing could be.

"Car trouble?"

"Not exactly."

"Truck trouble, then."

"How'd you guess?"

"Why else would anyone stop in Valerie?"

Womack glanced around, thankful for the diversion. "So this is Valerie."

"Uh-huh. Practically all of it . . . unless you like Western movies." She closed her eyes, opened them, let them roam flirtatiously over his face. The look triggered a powerful response from somewhere deep down inside of him . . .

Christ, *he thought*. She oozes sex like a toothpaste tube. Those eyes, that hair, those breasts . . .

"On your way to L.A.?" she asked.

"El Centro."

"In a hurry to get across the desert, I'll bet."

"Uh-huh." His soup and beer arrived. He broke open the crackers and sat slurping the soup, thankful for something to do. He was beginning to feel kind of foolish.

"That's too bad," she said pointedly. She reached over and tugged absently at the curled white hairs on the back of his hand. "If you were going to be around for awhile I could show you the town. What there is of it."

Womack looked at her. He felt the response again . . .

She smiled, gave him a searching look with slanted, green-tinted eyes. She reminded him somehow of Emma, except that she had nearly-black hair, while Emma was a blonde. But the figure was the same, full and ripe-breasted, yet softly female.

He said, "Maybe next time."

"You mean next time your truck breaks down." She laughed over her drink. Somehow she managed to make even holding a glass look sexy. She was obviously a fun-loving girl with fun-loving ideas stuck in a no-fun town.

Womack looked at his soup. He had to force himself to eat. Under different circumstances a beautiful bundle like this would have had him dusting off a pitch. But, even though this one seemed willing, there was nothing in it for him. Not with the way things were—with a few dollars in cash and a hand full of sugar cubes between him and El Centro.

Womack drank the top off his beer.

She lifted her own glass and said, "What'll we drink to?"

"Anything you say."

"Okay." She beamed. "I'll drink to you and you drink to me. Okay?"

"Sure." He took another swallow of his beer.

She put down her glass.

"You act like you've got a wife in El Centro."

"You could call it that—" Emma was no wife, no wife at all. Not anymore. He didn't even know whether she was in El Centro or not.

"Is she pretty?"

"I guess she's okay." He began chasing a chunk of chicken. It was lousy soup.

"Prettier than me?"

Her voice was so low that Womack didn't understand the words. But there was something in her tone that made him lift his gaze from the soup. He looked at her.

She was leaning forward, elbows on the table, offering him an unimpeded look down the front of her dress. It was worth the look. He had known that it would be.

"Well," she said lazily. The alcohol had made her voice husky. "Is she?"

5.

Womack found himself thinking bleakly of Emma. How stupid could a guy be? There were other dames—like the one sitting opposite him. There had *been* other dames. But not this time. Not with his truck on the blink and only a few bucks in his pocket. He said, "Listen. You're a beautiful girl. You don't have to prove that to me."

"I was beginning to wonder—"

"Under different circumstances you'd have me falling all over my feet, but under different circumstances you wouldn't even know I was alive, all of which goes to prove something."

"What"

"That Valerie probably is even duller than it looks." He drank some of his beer. He felt suddenly relieved—and disappointed. "What you need, kid, is a change of scenery. Buy a ticket on a bus. Go somewhere—anywhere—it doesn't make any difference. Go where the bright lights are. Win a beauty contest and get in the movies—"

"I've been in the movies," she said acidly. She got to her feet, stood smoothing the dress over her hips, picked up her drink. She smiled, but the warmth was no longer there. "Well, have a nice trip . . . to El Centro."

She turned, wobbling slightly, and headed back toward the bar.

"Wait—" Womack half rose to his own feet, settled back down with his beer, suddenly contented to let things ride.

He signaled for the waiter, making a mental calculation of how much he owed, and dug a couple of bills from his pocket. He was still waiting for his change when the man from the garage came in.

Bernie White acknowledged Womack with a nod, strode straight to the bar, and ordered a beer. Perspiration gleamed on his face. He downed the beer with one tilt of the glass, Adam's apple working, then sat down opposite Womack in the booth. There was beer foam on his lip. He said, "How long did you drive with the rod bent?"

"How the hell do I know?"

"Well, don't make no difference now."

"It's bad, eh?"

"Pretty bad." He swiped at the foam with his hand. "She been pulling hard on the grades?"

"No. No worse than usual."

"Well, I can fix 'er. But it's going to take a couple of days to get 'er running good."

"How much?"

White took out a scrap of grease-smeared paper with some writing on it. "Got it figured right here. Parts and labor should run you around a hundred and seventy-five bucks. Of course, that's just an estimate, but I always figure kind of heavy."

Womack sat there, thinking absurdly to himself, it might as well be a hundred and seventy-five thousand. Because, either way, I ain't got a chance in hell of getting my hands on the dough.

"Okay?" Womack had no choice. "Fix her up."

"Don't worry." White *got* to his feet. "I'll have her running sweet as sugar."

Womack picked up his change and made another mental calculation. With the cash remaining in his pocket, and if he also picked up the dime he'd left as a tip, he would be worth exactly twenty-three dollars.

He left the dime where it was. It wouldn't do him any good. Neither would the twenty dollars remaining in his pocket. During the next couple of days, if he was to get his truck back to El Centro, he would have to figure a way to get his hands on some real dough. In the meantime, he could sleep in the rig.

Womack was about to follow White outside, when he noticed the girl again. She really had a sensational body. He thought about the way her breasts had looked inside the halter of her gown, startlingly white and pink-tipped, and a faint warning bell sounded down inside his stomach somewhere.

He didn't heed the warning.

6.

They had a few drinks together at the bar, beer and whatever it was she was drinking, while the bartender fed an occasional nickel into the jukebox. They were his only customers and he apparently wanted to keep them around.

At exactly seven o'clock he turned on the television screen high up over the bar. The fights were on. Womack found that he could barely hear the sound over the blare of the jukebox. He didn't care. You don't have to hear the fights. But it seemed strange to see the two men pawing at each other to the drains of the *Missouri Waltz.*

Womack gradually became engrossed. During one of the frequent commercials he turned his head slightly to look at the girl sitting next to him. Since joining her at the bar, they had said very little, just small talk. Her name was Lila. That much she had told him. Lila, a slender, dark-haired stranger with slanting green eyes and a sensuous mouth.

She stared up into his face. There was something strange about her, something different. Every word he had said, no matter how trivial, she had listened to attentively. It was as if it was important to her to have someone to talk to. And, yet, she had seemed contented to just sit while he watched the fights.

Womack took a swallow of beer and said, "You like the fights?"

Before she could answer, their attention was diverted by a soldier entering from the street. He was short and stocky, with damp sweat-spots under his arms and beneath his belt. He looked directly at Womack and the girl, as if he were using them to adjust his eyes to the reddish glow within the bar, then sat down on one of the stools. When he had paid for his beer he fished a dime from the change on the wet-stained bar and walked back to an inside phone booth in the rear.

Womack looked at the girl once more. Her face was very white, her eyes wide and frightened, and he wondered if she was going to be sick. He said, "Are you okay?"

"Yes." She sipped her drink. "It's the heat. It makes me a little woozy at times."

"Would you like to go somewhere else?"

She started to speak and hesitated—

"Some place where we can get a little air. It'll do you good."

"I thought you wanted to watch the fights."

"They're a couple of pugs."

"There's a place out on the highway . . . the *Blue Note*. They only have a band on Saturdays . . . but there's a dance floor and a jukebox. We could drive out there."

"No wheels." Womack grinned. "Isn't there someplace close?"

Lila nodded. "No. But we can take my car."

"Okay. Drink up."

They finished their drinks, had a final round for the road, then got to their feet. Womack felt a pleasant constriction building in his throat. He was dimly aware that he was getting drunk. He decided that he didn't give a damn.

He settled the bill and followed her outside and down the street to her car. It was a new Thunderbird convertible, white, with the top down. Somehow the car didn't surprise him. It went with the expensive dress and the forty dollar shoes and the sophisticated-sounding sigh she exhaled as she pressed close beside him.

Womack heard the warning bell again. It sounded in his stomach, causing the muscles there to tighten. It was all wrong somehow. A girl with this much class . . .

He said, "Some rig."

"It's all mine."

"Lucky girl."

She laughed. "Would you like to drive it?"

Womack opened the door for her and helped her in, then walked around and slid under the wheel. When he pulled away from the curb he could feel the tremendous, silent power under the hood. It never failed to give him a thrill.

Lila edged closer to him. Her shoulder touched his. The wind pulled at her skirt and rippled the halter of her gown, exposing flashes of milky flesh, startlingly white against the dark tones of her arms and shoulders. Her hair brushed his face. It had a smell of wild flowers in it.

There was not much traffic on the road, only an occasional car, and the road was straight. Womack put his foot down hard on the accelerator. The car lept forward.

Lila laughed softly. There was excitement in her voice as she said, "Not too fast, Johnny"

He let the needle hover at eighty. The hell with it. He felt good.

He glanced into the rear-view mirror once, noticed a set of headlights and wondered vaguely why the car behind them was following so close, then dismissed it from his mind.

He continued out Route 77 to a point where it intersected with a secondary county road. Near the intersection were a couple of acres of gravel-covered land with a shoddy motel and a combined gas station and cafe. A sputtering neon light alternately blinked *The Blue Note* . . . . GAS . . . *The Blue Note* . . . GAS . . .

Womack swung the Thunderbird onto the parking lot, gravel spraying the underside of the fenders, and stopped beneath the drooping branches of a tree that grew between the motel and the cafe. As he got out he noticed that the car he had seen in the rear-view mirror was stopping also.

It wasn't until the car's doors swung open that Womack saw the sheriffs star painted on one of them. The two men who got out and started toward him were strangers. One was big and burly, with a thick neck and shoulders, the other nearly as tall but lighter and small-boned. They were obviously county deputies. Despite the boots, and the big campaign hats, they lacked the sharpness of state troopers.

The smaller of the two said, "Hold it, Mister."

There was no doubt about it now. They had been following him. Womack wondered why. He had had the Thunderbird over eighty on the straightaways, but there had been a minimum of traffic, and there was no posted limit. What bothered him now was the fact that he had been drinking.

Stuffing a cigarette in his mouth, to disguise the alcohol on his breath, Womack walked forward to meet them. Lila watched him from the car. Even in the dim light, Womack could see that her face had gone white again.

The deputies halted directly in front of him. The big one shoved his hat away from his forehead, wiped at his face with a balled handkerchief, and smiled through rotten teeth.

Then, before Womack could return the smile, they began beating him with their fists.

7.

A half-forgotten recollection of his childhood flashed quickly across Womack's mind. He had stood this way many times before, on the streets of New York's West Side tenement section, while fists lashed out at his face. Nothing had changed. Someone was trying to hurt him and he knew only one thing: fight back, fight until he no longer had the strength to lift his arms. He staggered backward. A fist crashed into his face, bringing blood into his mouth, and another fist landed sickeningly against his temple. Gravel crunched beneath his feet. There was a muttered curse. He spit some of the blood at a face that bobbed suddenly before him—he didn't know which—and slammed his own right into the pit of a muscular stomach. He struck out again, blindly, his vision blurred by a sudden burst of pain. He felt a second burst of pain, exactly as before, and went to his hands and knees. He couldn't see the ground. He was aware of nothing but the pain.

A heavy boot landed against Womack's ribs. His arms and legs crumpled beneath him. The boot landed again and he rolled over on his back. Pain waved through his eyes. He saw the dark outlines of the two men standing over him.

One of the men was holding something white against his face.

"Come on," the other one said. "Let's get the bastard into the car."

They each took an arm, hauled Womack to his feet, and put him into the back of the car. He was on the floor and he pulled himself to his hands and knees again. He felt very sick. He was aware of the car being put into motion. Then something solid struck the back of his head and he was no longer aware of anything.

Womack heard the voice before opening his eyes.

It said, "What in Christ's name is the matter with you guys? Can't you make a simple pinch without getting your dumb faces kicked in?"

Womack opened his eyes—gingerly. The voice belonged to a very fat guy seated behind a battered wooden desk. He had a round, florid face, and his hair had receded to a few strands over each ear. A badge with the word *Sheriff* was pinned to the front of his sweat-sopped khakis.

Womack moved his head. The two deputies stood against the far wall. They were looking at the sheriff. The small one held a bloodstained handkerchief to his nose. Blood was splattered down the front of his shirt.

The burly one said, "Christ, Wibber—"

"Don't Christ me."

"How did we know the bastard was going to start swinging at us?"

"That's just it. You didn't."

"We did the best we could."

"Then I'd hate to see your worst." Wibber shifted his gaze from Womack to the two men. "Now get into some uniforms that don't look like you been killing chickens in them."

Wibber waited until the door had closed. Then he looked at Womack and said, "You a tough guy, Womack?"

Womack, tongue-tied by the pain in his head, only sat there.

Wibber went on. "Maybe you think this is some kind of hick town, that we don't know how to handle tough guys, is that it?"

The base of Womack's skull was a dull consistency of pain. He sat upright in his chair and said, "It might interest you to know, Sheriff, that your trained apes out there came at me first."

The sheriff's western hat sat before him on the desk. He shoved it to one side, leaned forward, and put his weight on his elbows. "Now, why would they do that?"

"I'm hoping the judge will ask that question."

Wibber smiled mockingly.

"It ain't funny. Your guys jumped me out there and I'm going to find out why."

"That's your story."

"You're goddamned right that's my story." Womack could feel the anger flooding in over the pain. "It's the story I'll tell in court . . . when I sue you for putting these bumps on my head."

Wibber held onto an impulse to raise his voice. He said, "You're not going to sue anybody, Womack. Not in this county. Because you're getting out of it."

"Now listen—"

"You listen, Mister." Wibber looked at him disgustedly. "We got laws to protect the citizens of this town. They're strict laws and we make 'em stick. We don't hold with drunks behind the wheel of a car . . . and we don't like transients molesting our women."

So that was it, Womack reached for his cigarettes. He should have known. He *had* known. But he had been too stupid to heed his own warning. A dame like that—with a too-high price tag—had to belong to somebody big. Maybe, Womack thought, she belongs to this fat bastard with the badge.

"So I'm a sex maniac, eh?" Womack said thickly.

Wibber was silent for a moment, gazing at Womack through small, hard eyes. Then he said, "I don't know, Womack. Is that what you are?"

Womack blurted out, "Come off it, Sheriff! Quit talking nonsense. Hell, if anything, the broad picked me up. We had a few beers. What's the law against that?"

Wibber belched, his face tight with pain, and rubbed his stomach. "It's like I said, Womack, that's your story."

There was no use talking. Womack could see that now. The cards were stacked. They had always been stacked against him. He said resignedly, "So I made a mistake."

"Eh?"

"I said I made a mistake."

"You bet your sweet life you made a mistake."

"Okay. Okay." Womack studied the backs of his hands. They were covered with thin scratches. He said, "It ain't exactly going to break my heart to leave this town. I wouldn't be here now if my rig hadn't broken down. As soon as it's fixed, in a couple of days, I'll be moving along."

Wibber's stomach seemed to be bothering him. He belched again to make himself feel better. He said, "If you're smart, Mister, you'll be moving on right now. Tonight."

"I can't do that, Sheriff. And you can't make me. If you want to lock me up . . . that's something else. But you had better make darn sure you can make it stick."

"Say, listen, don't you worry about that. I can make it stick. You damn right. We know how to take care of punks in this county."

"Is this your county, Sheriff?"

"Just what does that mean?" Wibber's voice was a rough whisper.

Womack paused to light his cigarette. "I was just wondering who owns you, Sheriff."

Wibber's face turned purple. He was obviously thrown off stride. He blurted, "One more crack like that and I'll lock you up right now. I mean it."

"So go ahead, Sheriff. You're dying to do that anyway. Lock me up . . . and see what it gets you."

"That's all you've got to say?"

"I've got a question."

"What is it?"

"When can I go?"

Womack's wallet was on the desk. Wibber picked it up and thumbed through it. "Johnny Womack, eh?"

"That's right."

"When can your rig roll?"

"Day after tomorrow."

Wibber tossed the wallet to Womack. "You make sure you're out of town by then."

8.

It was like waking up after being drunk the night before—only *really* drunk—when you don't remember what happened and you're conscious only of the killing pain in your head.

Womack listened to the knocking on the window of the tractor and debated about opening his eyes. He didn't want to open them. But the fist pounding against glass only aggravated the ache in his head so he climbed down from the sleeper finally and opened the door.

The sun wasn't up yet. Womack was glad for that. This way he could gradually accustom his eyes to the light.

Bernie White, dressed in clean coveralls and a black skull cap with the words *ABC Garage,* stood with his hand on the door. He said, "Didn't know you were going to sleep in the rig. There's an extra cot in the back of the garage. You could have used that."

"Thanks." Womack looked at the dark sky. The stars were still out. "What time is it?"

"Five-thirty." White already had a wad stuck under his lip. "Thought I'd get an early start. Maybe have 'er running for you by tomorrow morning."

"That would be just fine."

White grinned at him. "Rough night, eh?"

"Yeah. Pretty rough." Womack touched his face.

"The washroom is unlocked if you want to clean up."

"Thanks."

There was no warm water in the washroom but Womack shaved anyway, using the coarse latherless soap, careful to avoid the bruises on his face. When he had finished he toweled off and examined his face in the mirror. There was a nasty bruise under one eye and his fingers discovered a deep cut at the base of his skull but, aside from those two things, no serious damage. Only the pain.

He ordered a plate of eggs in a little diner directly across the highway from the garage. From his stool at the counter he could see Bernie White's legs sticking out from under the tractor.

He used to like to watch the sun come up on the desert. It always gave him a thrill. There was something clean and fresh and invigorating about the air in the morning, before the sun made it stale. But this morning he felt nothing, absolutely nothing.

The eggs were tasteless and the coffee like scalding water. He looked at the date on a soiled calendar over the grill and with a bitter grimace remembering that it was his birthday. *Happy birthday, sucker.* Johnny Womack, the guy everybody said was going to set the world on fire, broke, wife gone, stuck in a two-bit burg with a broken-down rig and no dough to cover the tab.

Womack gave a short, hard laugh.

He put down his cup and looked across the highway. White had crawled out from under the tractor. The mechanic was talking to someone over by the pumps. Womack knew right away who it was. He cursed softly under his breath.

White was talking to the sheriff. Wibber looked very big and imposing and official in the western hat. It was only a few minutes past six and already the sheriff was mopping at his neck with a diaper-sized handkerchief. It was going to be hot. The sheriff stopped talking once and gazed over at the diner. Womack couldn't see his face beneath the wide hatbrim but he got the impression that Wibber was looking directly through the window at him.

Womack wondered if trouble was boiling up again.

He found that he didn't much care. He had the feeling that there would be nothing but trouble for him now wherever he went. Thanks to Emma, he hadn't a dime to show for the ten years he'd saved so that he could have his own rig, because she'd skipped out with everything—every last cent. It was an even chance now that he would have to get rid of the rig or be chewed up with finance charges.

Womack had a sudden vision of the gun concealed beneath the dash in the big tractor. For a moment, the vision gave him confidence, and he knew that everything was going to be all right. But the confidence was replaced by a sudden sense of fear. He took a sip of coffee, its bitterness like black bile in his throat, and reached for the sugar.

He was thinking like a fool. He was being ridiculous. He wasn't about to risk another stretch in reform school—in prison, this time—for some penny-ante heist.

He had a second cup of coffee and watched the sun come up and felt the sweat forming damp spots under his shirt.

9.

When Sammy Travis unlocked the door at four-thirty that same afternoon, Lila was in the bathroom, adding tapwater to a couple of highballs.

"I heard you coming up the stairs," she said. "I figured you might want one of these."

He didn't wait but went in the bathroom.

Lila had her hair tied back in a loose pony tail and she was wearing a robe. She handed him a glass and he took a long swallow before saying acidly, "You been wearing that robe all day?"

"It's hot. I was getting ready to take a shower."

He put a hand on her arm and pulled her around to face him. She didn't move. He said, "I told you not to go out last night."

She looked nervous and on edge. He could tell that she had already been drinking. She said, "We going to fight?"

"It's up to you."

"I don't want to fight, Sam." Her eyes softened.

He released her arm.

She walked past him into the bedroom. "What's the sense of staying home all the time? You're never here."

"I'm in the Army, remember?" He followed her. "I ain't no general, either. I come to town whenever I can."

"Whenever you're not chasing around after some girl."

"That sounds great, coming from you."

"What's happened to us, Sam?"

"You can answer that as well as I can."

"Thanks."

"What's the matter with you, anyway? You weren't this way in New York."

"This isn't New York, Sam." The room had twin beds. She sat down on one of them. "What am I supposed to do, just sit around this crummy room while you play soldier?"

"I told you. It won't be for long."

"It had better not be."

"What's that supposed to mean?"

"You're the smart guy. You figure it out."

Travis removed his tie and sat down on the bed, not looking at her, and said, "Who was the guy?"

"How do I know? He seemed like an okay guy. He wanted to have a few drinks and dance. What's wrong with that?"

"You tell me."

"Don't make it sound dirty." She looked at him. "I don't sleep with every guy who comes along."

"Only the ones who ask."

"You've got a rotten mouth."

"It's a rotten world."

"Only because you think it's rotten, Sam." A look of sorrow came over her face. "Why can't you be like other people? Why do you have to own everyone so completely? Like Sheriff Wibber. He had that man almost killed last night . . . because he's afraid of you . . . of what will happen to him if he doesn't do exactly as you say."

"Wibber's a hick."

"You say that because you own him. But you can't own everyone, Sam. Not everyone. I hoped that being drafted into the Army would teach you that."

"The Army's no different than anything else, baby. Only bigger." He sipped his drink and stretched out on the bed. "And before I get through . . . it's going to be three quarters of a million bucks poorer."

The thought seemed to please her. She spread her robe on the bed so that the air would get to her bare legs. She sipped her drink.

"Sam?"

"Eh?"

"I didn't fix anything to eat."

"I don't want anything."

"I thought maybe you could take me out."

"Sure, baby. Sure."

"Sam, honey—"

"Eh?"

"Sweetie."

"What?"

"I love you."

Travis lit a cigarette, following her every movement, as she got out of the robe. She wore nothing but a bra and panties underneath. They were very brief and very white against the mahogany brown of her skin. Travis said, "You've got one hell of a body, baby."

"It's not bad," she admitted. She unfastened the bra, teasing him, walking toward the bathroom like a stripper on a stage.

Lila finished undressing in the bathroom with the door closed and while he listened to the shower running Travis sipped his drink and smoked. It was only a matter of days now. Nine, to be exact, and there was still one gaping hole in his plan. But he was confident that he would find a way to plug it. He had to. This was the big one . . . the million dollar heist that would make him a legend.

Travis laughed out loud. In exactly ten days he and Lila would be in Mexico with all the time and all the money in the world, and nothing to do but live it up.

"That's the coolest I've been all day," Lila said as she came out of the bathroom. She was naked. Water still glistened on her body. Her breasts looked very big and cold and dominating. There was a strong scent of gardenias in the room.

Travis put down his glass and stared at her, fascinated. She opened her mouth. He got to his feet and pulled her to him.

"Sam, don't, you'll get all wet."

"Who cares?"

"Sam—" She melted against him, whispering fiercely, her eyes tightly closed.

There was a knock on the door.

"Christ—" Travis released Lila, removed an Army .45 automatic from the drawer of the bedside table, and went to the door. Without opening it, he said, "Who is it?"

"It's me. Open up."

"Who?"

"Wibber." The voice was clattery. "For Christ's sake, open the door."

Travis stuffed the .45 into his hip pocket, released the night latch, and stepped back as Wibber came into the room. He said, "What's the idea coming here?"

For a moment Wibber stood there rooted, his puffy eyes slitted, riveted on Lila.

She hadn't expected Travis to open the door. It had happened so quickly that she was still frozen by the bed, completely naked, water dripping from her body onto the napless carpet.

"My God, Sam. My God," she moaned slowly. Her eyes pleaded. "Don't you even care?"

Travis said acidly, "Shut up and get your robe on. Nobody asked you to stand there."

Savagely, Lila pulled the cheap chenille spread from the bed, used it to cover her nakedness. Walking into the bathroom, she slammed the door.

Wibber eyed the water on Travis' khakis. He licked his lips. He said, "I sure picked a bad time."

"I told you never to come here without calling first."

"I figured you'd want to hear what I got to say."

"Whadda you mean?"

"It's about the guy we picked up last night. The one that was . . . bothering . . . your wife."

"I didn't tell you to beat the guy."

"You said you wanted him out of town."

"Yeah. But I didn't tell you to beat him. We don't want any trouble right now."

"Don't worry."

"What about him."

Wibber reached for his handkerchief and grinned. "Only that the bastard is the answer to our problem."

Later, after they had discussed Wibber's idea, Travis forced his mouth into something probably meant to be a smile and said, "It might just work."

"Hell. I know it'll work."

Wibber was pleased. It made him proud that Travis liked his plan. Not that it actually was his plan—White had given him the main idea and he had simply added the details—but at least now maybe Travis wouldn't think he was the only guy in the world with any brains.

Travis said, "One thing bothers me."

"What's that?"

"How do we know he'll go along?"

"He'll go along." Wibber grinned out of the corner of his mouth. "I've done some checking. The guy's got a record. And he's obviously down on his luck."

"That ain't no guarantee he'll come in on a heist like this."

"We got the best guarantee in the world."

"What's that?" Travis looked at him.

"A chance at three quarters of a million bucks."

10.

On Thursday morning, the day the rig was supposed to be ready to roll again, Womack went to a loan company on Mainstreet.

A perspiring, slightly bald man with distrustful eyes stood behind a waist-high counter that ran the full length of the room. Beyond the counter was a row of four wooden desks, three of which were also occupied by perspiring, slightly bald men. At the fourth desk a girl in a white blouse and pleated white skirt sat working an office calculator. In one corner was an open, chest-high partitioned office with a cardboard *Manager* sign affixed with tape to the opaque, pebbled glass.

Womack stopped in front of the man behind the counter and said, "I'd like to borrow some money."

"Do you have an account, Mr. . . . ?"

"Womack."

"Have you borrowed from us before?"

"No."

"What amount would you like to borrow?"

"Three hundred dollars."

"I'm sorry." The man smiled thinly. "We limit first borrowers to one hundred dollars. If you would like to fill out this application . . ."

Womack looked at the form. "How soon can I have the money?"

"Are you a resident of Valerie, Mr. Womack?"

"No."

"Of Arizona?"

"California."

"Oh." The man looked at him distrustfully. "It normally takes three to four days to process out-of-state applications."

Womack looked at the form again. It reminded him of the complicated, meaningless forms he was required to fill out upon entering the reform school.

"Never mind," he said. "I'll be leaving town today or tomorrow."

"I'm sorry." The man's eyes narrowed further. "If you would care to speak to our manager, Mr. Marmor . . ."

"No thanks."

Womack gave the man a hard look and headed for the door. He walked down Mainstreet to the *ABC Garage*. White was standing by the big tractor, wiping his hands on a grease rag, a wad of tobacco stretching one cheek out of shape. He smiled and kicked one of the big tires with the toe of his shoe. "All ready to roll. Plenty of guts, too. I had 'er out on the road this morning."

"How's the compression?"

"Went up two or three points at least."

"That's good."

They went into the cluttered office. White presented Womack with the bill. The estimate had been fairly close. The job came to a little over one hundred and eighty.

Womack said, "Can I mail you a check? I'm a little short on cash."

"I ain't supposed to do that, Mr. Womack." White took a Coke from the dispenser and popped the cap off. "The boss is out sick, or you could talk to him, but I reckon he wouldn't mind if I took your check . . . now."

"I doubt if it would be much good."

"Sounds like the trucking business ain't much good right now." White put his feet on the desk and eyed Womack critically.

"Business is bad all over."

"Buddy, you're right. You're so goddamned right it hurts." White swallowed half of the Coke. "It's them union bosses. A bunch of racketeers. Crooks, just lousy crooks. Stuffing their own pockets while the rest of us work our tails off."

"You're telling me."

"Did you ever think what it would be like to have all the cash you wanted? Think of the liquor you could drink . . . and the thick steaks . . . and the women. For Chrissakes think of the women."

Womack looked at him, his face blank.

White continued, his voice hoarse, a funny gleam in his eyes. "Suppose, just for the hell of it, you knew of a way to get your hands on some real dough. Cash. Lots of it. Say three quarters of a million dollars. Maybe a million. Think what you could do with that kind of dough . . ."

They talked for the better part of an hour.

In the end it was easier than even Wibber had imagined.

11.

There were four of them now.

They met late at night in the rear of the *ABC Garage,* behind carefully locked doors, with only the light from one naked bulb to illuminate the map spread on a greasy workbench. Big, perspiring Wibber. Bernie White, his face drawn, his hands swollen from hours of frantic last-minute preparation on the rig. Sammy Travis, nervous and irritable, smoking incessantly—but whose nerves suddenly jelled when he held a gun in the face of danger. Womack, hands thrust into the pocket of his jacket, thinking oddly of his father's suicide and of Emma, his wife, and of the twelve bitter years in a reform school. And there was Lila—actually, Lila made it five—standing apart from the others but very much a part of the group.

"This whole deal," Sammy was saying, "depends on everybody—I mean *everybody*—doing exactly what they're supposed to do at exactly the right time."

He looked at Womack.

"If anybody screws up—if anybody loses his head and panics—he's going to have to answer to me. I mean it. So you all had better understand that from the start."

Travis' eyes left Womack and made a quick tour of the others. There didn't seem to be any argument. He looked at White and said, "Bernie, you're the key to the whole exercise. You carry off your end and we should be able to walk through without a scratch."

"Don't worry about my end." White's voice carried complete conviction. "It's all taken care of. They brought the truck in yesterday . . . just like always . . . to have it serviced. I've been working on it for three months now. It'll be like cracking an egg."

"I guess I came in late," Womack said. "You want to tell me how you plan to crack it?"

There was silence and then Travis said, "You tell him, Bernie."

"Sure." White's voice was intense, a curious blend of pride and suspicion, as he said, "You know the problem. Two armed security guards accompany the Army payroll in the truck. Besides the driver, there's a guy sealed in the back, armed with a sawed-off shotgun and a .38 Special."

"It's the guy in the back that's the kicker," Wibber interrupted.

"That's right," White went on. "No matter what happens to the driver . . . we've got to take care of the guy in back before we can get our hands on the dough."

Womack said, "That's one of the things that have been bothering me. How do you figure on getting him out?"

Wibber's thick lips opened in a grin. "That's the beauty of the whole operation. We don't!"

"Huh?"

"That's my idea," Travis said. "Instead of wasting a lot of valuable time trying to bust open that truck . . . we seal the guard *inside*. . . . where he can't do us any harm. Not bad, eh?"

"Not bad," Womack said. "Only what's he going to be doing with that shotgun while we're loading the truck into the van?"

"Bernie."

"That's my department again." White opened a drawer in the workbench, removed a heavy object wrapped in an oil-soaked rag, and held it under the light. "I machined it right here in the shop after hours. This one and four others like it. They screw into the gun ports in the back of the truck. There's enough steel in each of them to stop a bazooka shell. And once they're in they can't be loosened from the inside."

Womack whistled softly.

He said, "You mean the gun ports are threaded?"

"They are now." White looked at him and grinned.

"That ain't all," Travis said. "There's an ignition cut-off switch and an emergency brake in the back of the truck. That's so the guy riding shotgun can stop the truck and kill the engine if anything happens to the driver."

"They don't mess around."

"Neither do we." Travis lit a cigarette. "Bernie here has taken care of that too."

"What if they check out the truck each morning. The way they check an airplane before taking off."

"They won't find a thing," White said. "I've rigged both the ignition cut-off and the brake so they'll work just fine . . . until I loosen a bolt and a couple of wires beneath the truck."

Womack said, "Sounds like you've got it pretty well covered."

"We told you we did."

"One more thing."

"What's that?"

"How about the driver?"

"I've been waiting for you to ask. It's the sweetest part of the plan." White's humor soared. He looked at Travis. "Tell him, Sam."

Travis half smiled. He said, "It's like Bernie says. The driver is the easy part, a pushover, perched in there behind the armor plate and bullet-proof glass like a sitting duck. He won't even know what hit him."

There was a silence and then Wibber giggled faintly. He said, "I get a bang out of just thinking about it."

"What's amusing the sheriff," Travis said, "is the fact that the cab of that truck is like a fortress. Armor plating like a tank and safety glass that'll take six .38 slugs point blank at the same spot and not even wrinkle."

"I'm afraid I don't get the joke."

"Don't you?" Wibber laughed out loud. "Man, there ain't no safety glass in that truck."

Womack looked at White.

White grinned and said, "Wibber's partially right. Safety glass don't look no different than regular plate. I replaced the pane of glass on the driver's side with regular plate the last time I serviced 'er. Took me about eleven minutes. Then I cleaned all the windows as usual . . . so the phony wouldn't look no different from the rest."

"You know the rest of it," Wibber said. "All you got to do is get in that rig of yours and drive on to glory."

Womack looked at Wibber. "I ain't exactly sure what your part is, Sheriff. You going to be around during the actual heist, or is your job just making suggestions?"

"You ain't one to talk, Womack," Travis said quickly. "If it wasn't for Wibber here, you wouldn't be in on the operation. It was his idea."

"I was just wondering."

"Well don't." The two men locked eyes. "Any questions of that kind will come from me. Wibber has an important part in the operation. If he didn't, he wouldn't be here, so forget the smart remarks. You just make sure you're ready to roll when the time comes."

Womack braced himself against the workbench, his arms spread beside him, fingers pressing hard into the greasy wood. The fingers quivered in spite of his pressure to keep them still.

After tomorrow, *he thought,* there'll be no more kidding yourself. After tomorrow you'll be a thief—maybe even a murderer—and it won't be like in the war. Kill a guy in the war and they pin a medal. But tomorrow will be different.

Womack looked at the others, at Lila who stood slightly apart, smoking silently. His mind went to Emma, back over a life that had led him to this, and he raised his hands.

Womack's eyes swept over the others, a half smile on his face, as he said, "I'm ready to roll right now."

12.

Julio Silvera looked at his five-year-old daughter. She sat with him at breakfast, studying him with warm brown eyes, round face resting in the palm of her hand.

They had a way—especially at breakfast—of communicating by means of a mystical, silent language known only to father and daughter. This morning something in Julio's eyes was saying, "Don't put so much jam on your toast."

And in his daughter's eyes: "I love you, Daddy."

For some reason—perhaps it was faint uneasiness that drained the appetite from his stomach—the silent line of communications seemed to be breaking down so that Julio, wrinkling his paper impatiently, said aloud, "Finish your milk, Debbie."

Carole, his wife, came in from the kitchen. She looked immaculate even in the worn-out robe, hair pulled straight back and secured with a rubber band, then falling to her shoulders in a long pony-tail. She was very fair. He liked the lightness of her hair and complexion. It always gave him a strange sense of satisfaction when others, startled by the contrast of his own dark skin, turned to stare.

Carole poured the coffee and sat down opposite her husband. Moving the jam jar out of the reach of her daughter, she said pleasantly, "Drink your milk, Debbie."

"Carole—"

She looked at him and he could tell—had known all morning—that she sensed something on his mind. He had been a fool to wait this long to tell her. Now he didn't quite know how.

She waited and when he didn't speak she said, "Have you talked to Mr. Phillips? I mean . . . about your vacation."

I might as well get it over, *he thought.*

"There won't be any vacation. Today is my last day."

"Julio!"

He shrugged. "I told you when I took the job it might only be temporary. Mr. Phillips wants to retire. He's tired. And starting next month the Army is going to handle the payroll transfer. I think that's what finally made him decide. The Army's his biggest account. Without the Army, he'd just be losing money anyway."

"And us?" She looked up, her eyes wet. "What about us?"

"We'll make out okay." He tugged at his daughter's pony-tail and, bending over, kissed her lightly on the nose. He repeated the process—it was part of the morning ritual—with his wife. "I stopped off to see Mr. Burton last night. He's short-handed at the lumber yard again. He wants me to work through the summer and maybe stay on permanently if business picks up."

"Did he say how much he'll pay?"

"No. We've just been talking, kind of. I'll *go* by and see him again tonight."

"Well. I'll miss seeing you in your uniform. You're really very handsome, you know." She adjusted the collar of his shirt—*Phillips Armored Transport Service* said the triangular patch on the short sleeve—and stood back to survey the effect. "But I don't mind telling you that I'm a little relieved now that it's all over. I never liked the idea of your being responsible for all of that money. It's just too risky."

"No more risky than a lot of jobs." He grinned. "If it was, the pay would be better."

Carole walked as far as the back screen porch with her husband, kissed him lightly, and watched as he backed their second-hand Volkswagen out of the garage.

Although it was the beginning of another hot day in July, inexplicably, she shivered.

13.

Lila and Sammy Travis checked out of the hotel before breakfast on that same Tuesday morning. They left in the white Thunderbird and Lila was driving. She was dressed in shorts and a sleeveless blouse. Sammy wore a sportshirt, open at the neck, and a pair of lightweight golf slacks. His jacket was tossed over the seat between them. The inside pocket contained his three-day-old discharge papers. He reached over and patted the pocket. Then, placing his head back on the seat, he smiled as the warmth of the early morning sun touched him. Lila found a parking place on Main street and the two of them went into a cafe and ordered a leisurely breakfast. Their watches had been carefully checked. They had time to kill.

Bernie White ate breakfast in the little diner across the highway from the *ABC Garage*. He was neatly dressed and he had a battered suitcase. Yesterday had been his last day at the garage but Mr. Hitt, who was back on the job now, had allowed him to sleep overnight on the old Army cot. He had four eggs, over easy, a side order of country sausage, fried potatoes, toast and coffee. He reflected that it had been this way when he was in the war. He had always been hungry just before going into action. A picture came into his mind. It was of a man in his company who had been killed during the Battle of the Bulge. The bullet had smashed the man's face so that he could not breathe. He had choked to death. The thought did not affect White's appetite. He put the image from his mind and continued eating.

Womack went without breakfast that morning. Waking up a little before eight a.m. he walked along Mainstreet until he found a barber shop that was open. He had a shave, trying to relax, but his mind spun crazily. He closed his eyes beneath a steaming towel and listened while the barber filled him in on the news. It was bad, as always. Somehow, the thought that the world was in a mess seemed to cheer him. When he came outside the sun was up full and for some reason he felt better. He walked south for a block and a half, past the cafe where Lila and Sammy sat over a leisurely breakfast, then west for two blocks to where the big rig was parked. As he climbed behind the wheel he looked at his wristwatch. Exactly nine-fifty. Right on schedule. He kicked the engine over and crawled out into traffic. Five minutes later he hit the highway. The sun broiled white and hot on the concrete. He could feel the sweat forming damp spots under his arms and beneath the belt around his waist. For a moment he had the feeling that the whole thing was ridiculous, that no one in his right mind could possibly take a thing like this seriously, that he should laugh at the whole deal and keep right on rolling until he hit El Centro. But for Johnny Womack the feeling passed.

Sheriff Adam Wibber woke up that morning in a tangle of sodden sheets, sweltering and suffering, gas pains like gnawing worms in his stomach. He heard someone groaning and realized that it was himself. Still groaning, he got to his feet, and walked into the kitchen. He stood in the middle of the floor, his two-hundred-and-forty pound body stripped to the waist, his bare feet splayed out over the faded linoleum. For one brief, unpleasant instant, he thought of his wife, Sarah. They had been divorced for over twelve years and in all of that time he thought of her only when confronted with the prospect of getting his own breakfast. He took a pan from the stack of pans in the sink and started water boiling for his cereal.

An hour later Wibber left the house and got into the tan-and-white car with the star on the side. He drove very carefully leaving Valerie and headed west on Route 77 until it intersected a secondary county road. He checked his watch. It was ten thirty-two. At ten forty he got out of the car. Lighting a phosphorous flare, he dropped it onto the highway, in the westbound lane. Then he dug out his handkerchief and mopped the sweatband of his western hat.

He belched, thinking that after today he would never again have to fix his own breakfast.

14.

In the sweltering, glass- and steel-enclosed cab of the armored car, Old Man Phillips—his first name was Cornell—removed his battered uniform cap and placed it on the seat. He wiped his lined face, thinking that this was the last time he would have to bake through the day in an oven on wheels. He would receive no gold watch when he retired, had no family to spend his extra leisure time with—but he had had enough of working.

Turning his head slightly, Phillips glanced through the small window separating the body of the truck from the cab. Julio Silvera sat on the small seat that, hinged down from the wall. A sawed-off shotgun rested across his knees. Phillips sighed. He felt a faint pang of guilt, closing up shop this way, leaving the kid high and dry. Not that there was anything he could do. It was fate that the Army had decided to transfer the payrolls themselves from now on. And there was nothing anybody could do about fate . . .

When Phillips returned his eyes to the road he saw the flare and flashing red light.

"What's up, Mr. Phillips?" Julio's voice, filtered through the bulletproof steel mesh of the voice vent, had a recorded sound.

"Don't know." Phillips brought the heavy truck to a stop, engine idling, and glanced alertly over the surrounding terrain. "Looks like the Sheriff. Got a flare in the road. Must be a wreck up the highway somewhere."

"See anything?"

"Not a thing."

Wibber crossed in front of the truck, dabbing at his neck with his handkerchief, and slowly approached the gun vent in the door of the cab. Phillips watched him. He had never cared much for the sheriff. He looked at Wibber's uniform, soaked through with perspiration, and imaged that he could almost smell his body odor through the gun port. His voice sounded surprisingly loud through the vent as he said, "What's the trouble, Sheriff? Wreck?"

"Uh-huh. Bad smash-up about two miles up the road. Some bastard rammed a produce truck pulling out of the Wilbert place. Cabbages all over the place." He laughed. His eyes were little round holes of heat in the perspiring face. "Guy following the first car barreled right into the wreckage. Got the road pretty well blocked."

"Anybody killed?"

"All but one. They're trying to cut him loose with acetylene. Take another hour probably. Passenger cars can get around by driving on the shoulder, but the sand is soft, so we're routing the trucks and heavy vehicles over the old Murray Road."

"That's kind of a long way around, ain't it?"

Wibber shrugged. "Better'n waiting here all day. Not that I give a damn. You can do what you want."

Without further words, Phillips released the clutch, backed the truck a few yards and turned onto the connecting road.

Wibber watched until the truck disappeared around a turn in the road. Then, working quickly, he scuffed out the flare and tossed the dead end into the brush. He had been lucky. Only a few cars had come along and he had waved them through without explanation. And there had been no other trucks.

He whistled happily as he drove back toward town.

15.

At exactly ten-fifteen Bernie White settled his bill at the diner and, pausing long enough to purchase cigarettes from a vending machine, went outside and stood by his suitcase near the edge of the highway. It was a beautiful day.

Three minutes later Lila and Sammy Travis picked up White in the Thunderbird convertible. The radio was playing. White tossed his suitcase in the rear seat, jumped in beside it. Then the three of them drove to where Womack had parked the tractor-van on the old Murray Road.

Lila stopped just long enough for Travis and White to get out. A few minutes later she was back on the highway heading for El Centro.

Womack was having trouble with the truck. At least, to anyone who happened along on the road, it would appear that way. The heavy, left-hand hood was raised and Womack, a greasy towel spread over the fender, was working on the engine with a big wrench.

Without speaking to Womack, Travis and White went around to the rear of the van and, opening the big double doors, jumped up into the interior. Then they closed the doors behind them.

They found two flashlights in a rack just inside the van. Moving quickly, but with practiced precision, the two men made a last minute inventory.

At the far end of the van, near the cab, an army cot had been set up and bracketed to the floor. Two blankets lay folded on it. Underneath was a box of medical supplies. White flashed his light quickly inside. On top was a package containing a half dozen morphine, sureties. At one end of the cot were two large jars of drinking water and several cardboard cartons of food.

"No beer?" White's guttural laugh sounded very loud in the closed van.

"In a couple of hours you'll be able to buy all of the beer in the world. A swimming pool full of beer, with dames in it, swimming back and forth naked."

"Man! I'd dive right in. I'd—"

Travis dug out a key, unfastened the lid of a government issue footlocker, opened it. They shined both of the lights inside. It was the stuff Travis had swiped from the Army: two carefully-oiled submachine guns, two .45 automatics, an assortment of ammunition clips.

Travis removed one of the submachine guns and cradled it in his arms. Closing the footlocker, he crossed over to where an acetylene tank and two cutting torches were secured by rope and metal hooks to the side of the van. Smiling thinly, he patted the side of the tank, then he motioned for White and the two men jumped back down to the road.

Womack was still pretending to work on the engine. He was surprisingly calm. In fact, he wasn't at all nervous, and that fact alone seemed to disturb him. He should have felt *something*. The knowledge that there was danger in what he was about to do, that he might actually die during the next few minutes, should have terrified him. But he felt good. Felt fine.

Travis came over and grinned at him. "Jittery?"

Womack shook his head.

"Good." Travis looked at White. "How about you?"

"Not me." White smiled at him wryly. "It'll be just like at the Bulge. Only them Kraut tanks had thicker skins."

"Remember, anybody panics . . ." Travis caressed the stock of the submachine gun to make clear his meaning. Then, motioning for White, he walked through a shallow gully and squatted down behind two rusted oil drums that had been placed in a dense thicket.

White, carrying a long metal device and dragging a heavy burlap sack, knelt beside Travis. It was a good hiding place. They had selected it only after several trips along the road.

Travis looked at his watch.

White wiped his glistening face with a corner of the burlap sack. It left a red welt on his cheek. He said, "You reckon Wibber will handle his end okay?"

For a long time, Travis didn't answer.

He looked at his watch again. He dug out a handkerchief and mopped at his face.

Then, when he saw the armor-plated truck appear several hundred yards down the road, he smiled thinly and said, "Don't worry about Wibber. Just make sure you get under that truck when I open up with the chopper."

16.

It was exactly ten fifty-one when Old Man Phillips brought the armored car to a stop several yards behind the apparently stalled rig.

He swore under his breath. If he had lived a few minutes longer he might have reflected on the coincidence of another delay so soon after the first. But his first thought was of the heat It became almost unbearably hot whenever he stopped completely.

The van blocked almost two-thirds of the road. There was a possibility that he could drive around. He put the truck into gear. He was about to inch forward when he saw a blur of movement out of the corner of his eye. He looked. A man was standing beside the road. Phillips swore when he saw what the man was holding. He thought, *the fool. He must be crazy* . . .

Travis squeezed the trigger on the submachine gun. The Army had spent hours teaching him that. But his aim was bad. The first bullets hammered against metal. He raised the barrel slightly. The sound the bullets made was deafeningly loud. They smashed the phony safety glass. They tore apart Phillips' head, killing him instantly, before his brain could register the excruciating pain.

While Travis still squeezed the trigger, White was on his feet, running headlong toward the rear of the armored car. His eyes were wide with terror. The sack was painfully heavy and it slammed against his knees. He stumbled ahead. The air was saturated with the smell of burned powder.

Stumbling, panting, White closed the distance between himself and the truck. He felt his heart beating faster. At one of the windows in the side of the truck a dark face appeared for a split second. He felt the impact of a bullet tearing through the fleshy part of his forearm. He made an incredible leap forward, sack held before him like a shield, kicking wildly with both legs until he was safely under the truck.

White lay there, pain stabbing savagely through his arm, listening. There was a sudden stillness. He raised his head and gazed along the ground. He saw Womack, framed between two long rows of tires, lying in a similar position under the big tractor.

"White!" Womack's voice sounded choked with dust. "You hit?"

White did not answer right away. A strange lethargy prevented him from moving. He thought he heard scratching noises from inside the truck. He raised his head to listen. Blood was trickling down his arm. He felt weak and sick.

"White!" Travis was pinned behind the thin protection of the oil drums.

"Okay! Okay!" White answered impatiently. Slowly, he twisted his body, so that he was lying with his head toward the rear of the armored car. He took care of the emergency brake and the ignition cut-off. Then, gritting his teeth, he began to inch forward.

"White!" Travis' voice was clattery. "We ain't got all day!"

"You want to come out here and take care of it yourself?" White turned his head and spit. Just like that bastard! He cursed himself for a fool for having been talked into this part of the operation.

When he was almost directly beneath the rear bumper he took two half-inch steel bolts from his pocket and inserted them into freshly-bored holes in the truck frame. Then, with the door bolted closed, he went about the business of plugging the gun ports.

The metal bar was very ingenious. It was Travis' idea. The two-inch metal plugs fit into a ratchet device at one end, allowing White to screw them into the gun ports while lying on his back on the ground, with only his head and arms sticking out from under the truck. Even partially exposed this way, he was perfectly safe, because the man in the truck could not fire directly down at the ground.

There was one gun port in the back, two on each side, five in all. The pain in White's arm made the going slow. He had to stop several times. Once, while he lay there catching his breath, he heard the thud of bootheels on the metal directly above his head. Suddenly the terrible thought struck him that the man might be able to open a trap door in the floor and shoot him while he lay helplessly on his back. He ignored the pain and began to work faster.

When he finally crawled out from under the truck, Womack and Travis were waiting. The big double doors of the van were open. Travis looked at White's shoulder and said, "Bad?"

"I don't know. It hurts like hell." Womack ripped the sleeve of White's shirt and examined the wound. He said, "It's not too serious. The bullet didn't stay in. But you should do something to stop the bleeding."

"Not now. Let's get moving first."

Without further words, Womack and Travis pulled out two heavily-constructed, steel-and-wood tire ramps from the back of the van. They were heavy and it took several minutes to get them into position. They had to be bolted to the frame of the van.

When the ramps were in position, White climbed into the front seat of the armored car; He had to move the body of the dead driver before he could get the truck into gear. He began to inch forward. Womack, standing inside the van, directed him with hand signals. In a matter of seconds, the car was inside.

White could not leave the front seat of the armored car without looking through the connecting window at the guard. It gave him a sudden chill. The guard, a surprisingly young-looking Mexican kid, was seated calmly on a seat that folded down from the wall. He was holding a sawed-off shotgun.

White looked into the man's eyes. The expression he saw there made him clinch his teeth. It was as if the man were already dead.

While White stared, fascinated, the man raised the shotgun and fired it directly at White's head. The sound it made was like a grenade going off. Shot rattled against the shatter-proof glass like birdseed.

Despite the pain in his arm, White threw back his head and laughed.

When he climbed down from the front seat of the armored car, the big van doors were closed, and the rig was moving.

17.

From start to finish—from the instant Old Man Phillips brought the armored car to a halt to the instant Womack swung the rig onto Route 77 and began barreling west—the operation took nearly nineteen minutes. That was exactly nine minutes longer than Travis had estimated. And, in their race to get the money out of the area, nine minutes could spell the difference between success and failure.

By eleven-twenty a.m. the telephone lines between the bank, Army post and sheriff's office had begun to overload. It was as if a bomb had landed on Mainstreet. There were frantic charges and countercharges, admonitions and threats, declarations and denials.

Then the general himself got on the phone.

"Is this the sheriff?"

"Yes, *sir*"

"You're in authority? I mean . . . this sort of thing falls under your jurisdiction?"

"Well, sir, it does until somebody tells me it don't."

"What does that mean?"

"The FBI will take over eventually. In the meantime . . . I reckon I'm in charge."

"What's your plan of action?"

"Plan?"

"What are you doing about the armored car?"

"We're looking for it, General."

"Now, see here, Sheriff." There was a tone of annoyance in the general's voice. "A truck that size can't simply disappear. Not in the middle of the desert. The idea is preposterous."

"That's the way we look at it, General." Wibber grinned into the telephone. "We've set up roadblocks on every road leading out of the county. They try to drive the money out . . . we'll nab 'em."

"You are of the opinion that the vehicle is still in the county?"

"That's right. It has to be. Even if they took the money out of the truck, they'd need a car, or another truck to carry it. You can't stuff that kind of cash in a lunch pail or a paper sack."

"Obviously."

"My guess is that they've hidden the armored car out in the desert someplace . . . it's a big desert . . . waiting for things to cool down so they can smuggle the money out a little at a time."

"How about an airplane? Maybe they flew the money out—"

"Not a chance. We've checked with the airport and I've got a man out there now. Nothing's taken off for the past hour and a half."

"The bus station, then. Or the train—" The general was getting frantic.

"We've covered all that. Everything is under control. The only thing to do now is wait." The sheriff belched, not bothering to take his mouth away from the telephone, and rubbed a hand over his stomach. "It's like I said, General. They'll lie low for a while . . . then try to skip the dough out a little at a time. Trickle it out. I know both of those security guards personally, General, and I know just how they'll react. They won't be able to sit tight for long. They'll get restless and make their move in a day or two. And when they do . . . you'll get your pay, General."

"I'm not worried about my pay." The words sounded as if they came through clinched teeth. "The Army has been robbed of a great deal of money. I want it returned. Now . . . what makes you think the security guards were responsible?"

"You mean, how do I know it was an inside job?"

"That's right."

"Well, now. General." Wibber couldn't suppress a chuckle. "It had to be an inside job . . . unless somebody figured out a way to steal a three ton armored car right off a crowded highway. And that ain't possible."

18.

Route 77 is a good truck road, straight and flat, with only an occasional hill. Womack kept the rig rolling at sixty-five—five miles faster than called for in the plan—in order to make up time. A lot still depended on timing. Still, he fought down the urge to drive even faster. He couldn't risk being stopped by a cop. Not now. Not with the load he was carrying.

He flicked a half-smoked cigarette through the window, reached in his pocket for some gum, while he fitted together in his mind the remaining segments of the plan. He raised no questions, made no guesses, made no attempt to evaluate their chances. He simply ran his finger down a mental checklist, his mind curiously numb.

Lila would be waiting with the Thunderbird in El Centro. According to the plan, she would meet them at a junction on the other side of town, then follow them along Highway 80 into the mountains. There was a road near Laguna that led to an abandoned logging camp. It was wide enough and straight enough to handle the big logging rigs. That's where they planned to get rid of the armored car and divide the money.

Afterwards, they would go their separate ways—Lila and Sammy Travis to Los Angeles in the Thunderbird, Womack and White back to El Centro in the rig. And Wibber? Womack wondered about Wibber. Supposedly, when things cooled off, he would join Travis in LA to get his share . . .

That was Wibber's problem.

Womack wasn't sure that he heard the siren. Glancing into the rear-view mirror, he spotted the patrol car about a quarter of a mile back, red light flashing. He came as near to panicking then as he ever had. Every nerve told him to push the gas pedal to the floor. His hands tightened on the wheel He knew that if he ran now it would be the end.

Gritting his teeth, he braked the rig gradually, pulled as far to the right as he could. The car was right behind him. It's siren wailed. He pushed a button under the dash that activated a red warning light in the van.

Womack could see the faces of the troopers as the car rushed past. They were looking straight ahead. One of them had a rifle wedged stock-down between his legs. They were obviously hurrying to set up a roadblock somewhere ahead . . .

Womack reached for the button under the dash, flicked it twice, then resumed his normal speed. He concentrated on his driving. He didn't want things to go wrong because of him. The plan was too good. Too perfect. There wasn't a flaw in it. He looked at his watch again. Things were going off like clockwork.

Sweating, his face lined with concentration, Julio Silvera leaned close to the inside of the armored car, his ear a filter, sifting the faraway roar of the engine for a sound that might tell him something.

It was pitch dark in the hot cubicle, like the inside of an empty boiler, but he had managed to study the faces of the two men as they taped newspaper over the windows. He wouldn't have to worry about recognizing them again. Their features were filed away in his brain. The problem now was staying alive . . .

With a frustrated sign, Julio groped his way back to the folding seat, and gave himself over to trying to work out a plan. His uniform was saturated with sweat. He couldn't think clearly. The heat was beginning to fog his brain.

The interior of the van was lighted by two naked bulbs suspended from the ceiling at each end. They gave off only enough light for the two men to work by.

Bernie White crouched near the box of medical supplies. His face was twisted in pain. There was a bandage on his arm. Rolling up his sleeve, he jammed the hollow needle of a morphine surette into his arm at a point just above the bandage, then squeezed the morphine into his blood. In a few minutes the pain was completely gone and he was able to continue with what he had been doing.

He spent the next few minutes attaching a fifteen-foot length of garden hose to the exhaust of the armored car. He was thankful for the morphine in his system. It made this part of the job a little easier. Still, his fingers quivered in spite of his efforts to keep them still. He tried thinking about the money. Three quarters of a million dollars. He grinned. He was actually taking part in one of the biggest heists in criminal history. Hell . . . the Bulge was nothing compared to this.

And a lot of guys had to get killed at the Bulge, he rationalized. Besides, this part of the plan was Travis' idea. He had to hand it to Travis. Travis was ruthless—without feeling, even—but he left nothing to chance.

At last White got the hose attached and passed the other end up to Travis who was stretched in a prone position on top of the armored car. There was only a foot and a half of space between the roof of the armored car and the top of the van—but Travis had been able to climb on top with amazing agility.

With aluminum foil and masking tape, Travis had sealed off the three air vents on top of the car. Poking a hole in one of the pieces of foil, he inserted the end of the hose, then he climbed back down.

"Okay, partner," Travis said. "Turn 'er over."

White looked very pale. He said, "You do it. My arm is killing me."

"Sure, Sure." Travis grinned acidly. "Remember. Just like the Bulge."

Travis climbed into the front seat of the armored car, put his foot on the clutch pedal, shifted the transmission into neutral. Then he started the engine . . .

Julio felt rather than heard the engine start. He was trying desperately to think but the heat was making his head grow dizzy. Sweat trickled down his face. He opened his eyes wide but there was absolutely no light in the truck. A sudden fear rose in him. He had the feeling that it would always remain this dark for him. Frantically, he got to his feet and began groping around the truck.

Travis let the engine run for fifteen minutes, checking the hose connections frequently, careful to insure that none of the deadly carbon monoxide leaked into the van. The sound of the engine was low and steady. Once Travis thought he heard a faint moaning and cat-like scratchings from the inside of the armored car. He pressed his ear against the warm metal. But there was no other sound.

At the end of the fifteen minutes, Travis climbed back into the cab of the armored car. Peeling the masking tape away from the connecting window, he flashed his light into the back. It illuminated what appeared to be a dozen canvas money sacks. Sprawled awkwardly on his face, as if he had been shot crawling under barbed wire, was the young Mexican kid. He didn't even twitch.

Smiling thinly, Travis cut the engine, got out of the cab.

"Is he dead?" White asked.

"You try it in there for fifteen minutes."

"The crazy bastard."

"Eh?"

"Any guy takes a job hauling that kind of dough . . . he's bound to get it sooner or later."

"Sure."

For the next ten minutes the two men used the acetylene torches on the heavy armor plating of the rear door. When they had sliced through the locking mechanism, Travis stepped to one side, removed the .45 automatic from the belt of his trousers. Pulling the action back, he eased a bullet into firing position.

White looked at him, thinking the bastard wouldn't take a chance on a three-cent lottery.

Nevertheless, White opened the door slowly, as if he were entering a nursery and was afraid of disturbing a sleeping child. The current of foul air hit him in the face. For a moment he hesitated. He flashed his light inside, ran the beam over the canvas money sacks, held it on the dark oblong of the guard sprawled like a ragdoll.

Then a strange thing happened.

White blinked his eyes in terror.

The guard raised his head slowly from the floor.

There was nothing White could do. He stepped back a pace. The sight of the guard's face, staring at him through grotesque eyes that were like flower blossoms, shocked him. He opened his mouth to express some half-formed thought but before he could speak the guard shot him in the chest. The second shot caught White in the jaw, abruptly closing his still-open mouth, but failing to stifle the scream that reverberated through the van.

Julio's visibility was hampered by the flat eyepieces of the gasmask. It was the thing that cost him his life. He had to turn his head slightly to bring the gun to bear on Travis. Before he could fire again, before he could take aim, Travis shot him. The bullet went through the center of the gasmask, between the anonymous eyepieces, into the brain.

Silvera managed to fire one more shot. But he was already dead, the tightening of his finger a reflex, sending the bullet thudding into a money sack.

Travis pumped another bullet in, just to make sure, then stood looking down at White.

"I kept trying to tell you," he said aloud. "Carelessness can mean the difference between living and dying. You should have listened. You should have paid attention to what I told you . . ." Then a startled expression came to Travis' eyes. He coughed spasmodically.

20.

Gradually, as she sat waiting in the Thunderbird at the junction of Route 77 and Highway 80, a lot of things came clear to Lila. Actually, her feelings had been crystalizing over the past few weeks. But it was during those precise moments, while she waited for the big van to appear over a low hill, that she realized with certain finality that everything was wrong. All of it. This impossible robbery, her life with Sammy, all of it wrong.

Before her, so deep that she could not see the bottom of it, was a black abyss. She could no longer ignore it. There was still time for her to turn her back, to walk away, but she knew now that she could no longer pretend that the blackness didn't exist.

She looked for the twentieth time at her watch. It was an expensive watch, a gift from Sammy. She found herself absently counting the jewels in the band and she felt a sudden coldness in her chest and in her mind. It was so hopelessly ridiculous, so terribly idiotic, that for a moment she thought about starting the car and heading back for New York. Or she might go visit her mother in Biloxi.

Somehow the thought left a foul taste in her mouth. She had never cared for her mother and father and they had cared little about her. There would be nothing but unhappiness if she went home.

What then? She no longer fooled herself. It would always be the same with Sammy. The money, if they were successful, would change nothing. They would go right on living the same meaningless life, doing the same meaningless things, regulating their existence by the turn of a card or a senseless whim. And why? For love?

It was odd how her life had been shaped by incidents rather than true feelings. She had slept with Sammy because she liked his looks, had lived with him because she had nowhere else to live, had married him because marriage offered a solution to her problems.

Now, this way, she knew there could be no solution . . .

She was about to start the engine of the car when she suddenly saw the rig—its lights came on, went out, came on again—rumble past with a faint tap on the horn. Without realizing it, Lila sighed deeply, her mind curiously numb. Almost without thinking she moved the Thunderbird into the line of traffic.

The rig was almost a half mile ahead.

As she pressed down on the gas pedal, she had the momentary sensation that she was driving headlong over the side of a bottomless abyss.

21.

It was nearly dark when Womack stopped the rig next to a ramshackle lumber shed in the logging camp. The dirt road continued on for about a hundred and fifty yards, sloping down sharply, ending at a big pond where they intended to get rid of the armored car.

According to Travis, the pond was about thirty feet deep. Womack got out of the tractor and walked down by the edge of the water. It was very muddy. A couple of ducks floated near a marsh on the far side.

Womack walked back up the slope. His shoes left dark pock marks in the wet dirt. They would have to be careful about that.

Before he got back to the rig, Lila drove into the clearing, parked the Thunderbird under the overhanging branches of a tall pine tree. The camp was surrounded by pines. They reminded him of the pines that grew around the CCC camps where he worked for a few years after leaving the reform school.

The big double doors of the van were still closed. Womack pounded on the metal with his fist. There was no sound from inside.

"Travis!"

Still no sound.

"White!"

Womack got the .45 from the tractor, pumped a shell into the chamber, and approached the doors. They had risen quite a few feet from the floor of the desert and there was a chill in the air.

Womack was aware of Lila standing beside him.

"What's happened?" she said.

"I don't know."

"Why don't they open the doors?"

"I don't know."

Standing there in the clearing, Womack was touched by fear, enveloped by it. But there was only one thing to do, and he did it.

As the doors opened, a stifling wave of carbon monoxide poured out. Coughing and chocking, they stared incredulously into the van. Then Lila screamed shrilly. The sound of it came down like a club on Womack's head. He slapped her and the scream broke off in the middle, punctuated by the sudden, stifling silence.

They were dead—all of them: White, sprawled face down just inside the van; the young security guard, staring unblinkingly through blood-spattered goggles; the armored car driver; and Travis—entangled in the canvas money sacks he had been removing from the truck, his thin face twisted and blue.

"Go back to the car," Womack said.

Without a word Lila turned and walked away over the blanket of pine needles.

Womack's mind was suddenly alert. He would have to work fast. Climbing up into the van, he removed the remainder of the money sacks from the armored car, put the two bodies inside with the guard. When he jumped back to the ground there was a sticky mess on his fingers.

It took a full five minutes to back the van down to the edge of the pond. The slope was very muddy. Muck rose up over the rear wheels, but he continued backing slowly, until the van was actually part way out in the water.

He had to wade through water up to his knees in order to get inside the van again. The work wasn't easy. But he managed. When the heavy planks were in position, they formed a ramp leading right down into the water. Starting the engine and shifting into reverse, he backed the armored car until the rear wheels were part way down the ramp. Then he pulled on the emergency brake and got out. He made sure the front wheels were straight. Then he opened the door, released the brake, and shut it quickly. The car rolled down into the water, descending very slowly at the last, but continuing down until it was finally out of sight.

Womack climbed back in the tractor and lit a cigarette. His fingers shook. He gritted his teeth. The worst of it was over. There would be deep tire tracks, on the slope, and he would have to be careful to smooth them away, but except for that he was finished.

He took a few drags on the cigarette and started the engine.

The rig wouldn't move!

Again and again he tried to gain some traction on the muddy slope, but the tractor only sank deeper into the muck, as if something below the surface of the mud were trying to devour the rig.

Womack shut off the engine. His clothes were soaked. He shivered. He could feel nothing at all. The crowns of the pine trees made a scratching noise in the wind. After a while Womack got out of the rig abruptly and walked over to the Thunderbird.

Lila looked as if she might faint. She was very pale. He opened the door and got in beside her. For a while there was no sound but the swish of the trees. Then Womack said, "The rig is stuck. I can't get it back up the slope."

She didn't answer. It was as if she hadn't heard. She hesitated a moment and said, "Are you sure they were all . . ."

"Dead?" he said acidly.

"Yes." He realized that it was the first time they had really spoken since that night in the cafe. "Both guards. And White. One of the guards shot him twice . . ."

"And Sammy?"

"Sammy, too." He didn't tell her how Sammy had died. He didn't want to talk about it. He said, "What now?"

"I don't know."

"We could head north. San Francisco, maybe."

"We?"

"Of course."

She looked at him, amazed.

"Listen." Womack's mouth was grim. "We're in this thing together. Until we get in the clear . . . if we ever do . . . we might as well stick together."

"Why?"

He hesitated a moment; "Because I'd feel safer if you were with me."

"You mean you don't trust me."

"I'd feel safer, that's all."

"And the money?"

"The money belongs to us now."

"I want half." There was a strange tone in her voice. She looked at him suspiciously.

"Are you crazy?"

"No." Her mouth was grim when she answered. "The money is the only thing that matters to me now. I figure I'm entitled to half. I want it. Suddenly I want it more than anything in the world."

Womack said hesitantly, "We can work that out later."

"And in the meantime?"

"It's like I told you." He reached over and removed the keys from the ignition of the car. "In the meantime we stick together."

Womack walked back to the rig. It was getting dark. He transferred the money from the sacks to several of the cardboard cartons that had contained food. It gave him a strange sensation to actually handle the money and he swallowed once from emotion.

Using his flashlight, he removed the registration papers and license plates from the rig and tossed them out into the center of the pond. With a hammer and chisel he mutilated what identifying marks he could find on the engine. He would never be able to prevent them from tracing the rig, he knew, but this way he might delay them for days—weeks maybe.

There were six cartons of money. Womack made six trips between the Thunderbird and the rig. By then it was completely dark. The silhouette of the pine trees emerged pitch black against a sky sprinkled with stars.

Womack removed two suitcases from the trunk of the car and put them on the back seat. It was very cold and he began to shiver. He put the money cartons in the trunk.

Lila was smoking quietly when Womack got into the car. He studied her face; in spite of the darkness he could make out her expression, and her calmness impressed him.

She said, "There are some clean khakis in the suitcase. You had better get out of those wet trousers."

"I'll stop at a filling station on the road." He started the engine. "Right now I want to get out of this place."

In the beam of the headlights, the rig looked like a giant ox stuck in a mudhole, waiting patiently to die.

Womack could not shake off the feeling of sadness as he spiraled down the mountain road to the highway.

22.

The first thing they did was get rid of the Thunderbird. It was in Lila's name—a gift from Sammy. They traded it for a three-year-old Ford and eleven hundred dollars cash. Actually, they needed the money. It would be a long while before they would want to touch any of the cash from the robbery.

The used car dealer helped Womack transfer the cartons of money. When he had loaded the last one in he wiped his fat, bespectacled face and said, "What are you carrying in there . . . bricks?"

"Yeah." Womack smiled at him. "Bricks."

The trunk wouldn't close all of the way. They had put the suitcases in also. Womack waited while the salesman got a ball of heavy twine, then fastened the trunk lid securely, trying not to work too fast—trying not to give the impression of someone in hasty flight.

They gassed up in town and had a quick meal. When they emerged from the cafe, Lila stopped abruptly, rummaged through her purse. When she had found what she wanted, she scrawled the words *Just Married* in cherry red lipstick on the door of the car. Then she repeated the message on the opposite side.

"There," she said, smiling thinly, and returned the lipstick to her purse. "Who would ever think we were a couple of criminals?"

Womack looked at her, tried to read some other meaning in her eyes, discovered nothing.

Two hours later they turned onto Highway 101, headed north toward San Francisco. It was getting late and there was a slight fog. Womack could hear the ocean breaking on the beach to his left. The sound was like a drumbeat. He could feel his lips compressed to a taut line. His shoulders ached. He thought, *relax. Get a grip on yourself. The worst is over. From now on in, things are going to be rosy as hell . . .*

Lila stirred beside him. She had tried closing her eyes but whenever she did she saw the huddled figures on the floor of the van. The image frightened her. She had never before seen a dead man. She felt a sudden chill. She had put a coat on over the playsuit and she pulled the collar around her throat.

Deliberately, she looked at the man next to her, wondering at the events that had brought them together. They hadn't spoken since leaving Riverside. She found that she wanted to talk. She said, "Do you know anyone in San Francisco?"

"No. It will be better if we don't."

"What will we do?"

"I don't know." He said nothing for several moments. Then: "Find someplace to live."

"You take it for granted that I will live with you?"

"Why not?"

She looked at him silently. Then she said calmly, "If you don't know why not, you're a bastard."

He remained silent, saying nothing.

She looked at him. It was almost as if Sammy were beside her. She wondered if all men were the same. Her mind concentrated on the men she had known—her father, the ugly years with him in the small, cluttered waterfront apartment. The few casual boy friends. Sammy.

There was a hollow, drawn feeling in her stomach. She searched for an explanation. When she could find none she began to cry softly.

Womack noticed her crying and said, "What's the matter?"

"Can't you see?" Her voice was distant. "I'm frightened."

"Don't worry."

"I can't help it."

"Go ahead and cry, then. It'll do you good."

"They're going to catch us."

"That's crazy."

"No it's not. We can't possibly carry this much money around without being caught. Boxes of it. It's so . . . unbelievable . . . somehow."

"We'll hide the money."

"It won't do any good," she said tonelessly.

"Dammit! Knock it off. We've got no choice now." His anger surfaced quickly and then subsided. He said quietly, "We're both tired. We should stop for the night."

They lapsed back into silence. The fog grew thicker. He could no longer make out the sand dunes to the left of the road. But he could still hear the ocean, and the wind had an odor of seaweed.

In Santa Barbara they looked for a place to stay. The first four motels were full. The fifth one had a room left and he registered as man and wife. It was a small room, but clean, with twin beds.

"It's the only one they had," he said when they were inside.

"Is it?"

Her sarcastic tone unsettled him.

He said, "I stopped because I thought you were tired. We can drive all night for all I care."

She gave a forced laugh.

Angrily, he turned and went into the bathroom. When he returned, a few minutes later, the room was empty. The door stood open. He cursed savagely and ran outside, his face white as plaster, his head filled with one thought.

She sat waiting for him, the engine running, headlights cutting yellowly through the fog. He got inside and was slammed against the seat as she jerked the car forward. In a moment they were back on the highway.

"You could have driven off without me," Womack said.

"I know."

"Why didn't you?"

"Because I wanted you with me."

Her voice sounded different. Her face, too, was different. He studied her face. It really was, he thought, remarkably beautiful. The passing headlights and the wind coming in through the open window played tricks in her hair. He wanted to touch it, to feel it against his face, and he discovered that, it wasn't just the money that made him glad she had waited.

He wondered if she had meant what she said. That she had wanted him with her . . .

Womack looked back at the road and saw the car. It came at them out of the fog. It wasn't until the headlights were almost on top of them that he realized that Lila wasn't in her own lane, that she was heading straight for the other car, so close that there was no time even to turn the wheel.

During the last few seconds, even as the darkness washed its black waves over and around him, the questions formed in his mind.

Was it an accident? Had she gotten confused in the fog?

Or was this the reason she had waited for him . . .

23.

Later, the police estimated that nearly a thousand dollars had been picked up by the thrill-seekers who stopped to look at the wreckage. But the rest of it was recovered by an alert state trooper who found the cardboard cartons in a shallow gully about thirty feet from the point of impact.

The trooper—his name was Carter—locked the money into the trunk of the patrol car and radioed into headquarters. He was instructed to make a thorough search of the area.

Another patrol car pulled off the highway behind Carter. He knew the two troopers who emerged. He told them about the money as they moved down into the gully.

The Ford sedan lay on its side. Most of the people crowded around it. The front end was completely pushed in. The trunk lid had sprung open.

"Anyone alive?" one of the troopers asked.

Carter said, "The woman in the Ford keeps moving. We'll have to wait for the wrecker so we can cut 'em loose."

The trooper shone his light on the lipstick-scrawled writing. He whistled through his teeth.

"Poor bastards." They heard a moan from inside the car. "But in a way it was a break for us."

"Huh?"

They walked over to where an old-model pick-up truck lay on its back. The body of a man was pinned underneath. The body of another man lay under a blanket nearby.

Carter shone his light on the man under the truck. He wasn't a man, really; just a kid, barely out of his teens. Carter said, "If it hadn't been for the accident, we might never have caught them."

"It don't seem possible, somehow."

"What doesn't?"

"That a couple of juvenile delinquents could pull off one of the biggest heists of the century . . . *and with a broken-down pick-up.*"

They walked back up to wait for the wrecker.

Eye-Witness
Charles Sloan

October 1962

A guy can spend a lifetime elbowing through throngs of people and still be lonely. Like a bum in a packed flophouse; or sharing a nigger-lipped butt with a dozen others in a nine-by-nine drunk tank; or sacking a park bench with another panhandler and getting a sweat-stinking foot in the face every time he rolls over. Surrounded by humanity, yet all alone—a Daniel Boone of the concrete canyons.

I was that way until one good thing happened to me, just one—when I met Myra. She was a model with a thrill-loving zest for life that sparked right out of her photos. She had been kept busy in front of the lens and behind it, with every guy in town after her. Only she married me, big footed, pug-ugly me. For eight weeks I felt like the sun had finally started shining. And then they took her away from me . . .

The squad room was throbbing with the city's aches and pains when I finished my last report of the day. I signed it—Detective Lieutenant David Fleers—and dropped it into a drawer. When I looked up, Captain Klegg was angled over my desk.

"Who're you taking with you on the Endze transfer tonight?" he demanded.

I snorted. "You know there's nobody available."

He started shaking his sparsely-haired round head. "You can't run that detail alone. Not when every gunbird in the streets may be waiting to transfer Endze to the morgue instead of the state pen."

I took out a cigarette and almost lit the filter tip. I was overworked and tired as Eddie Klegg and every other bull in the Third Precinct. Two months ago, on the day after my wedding, a twenty-year old mother and her baby had been run down during a robbery. Since we started the crackdown, I'd been pushing every man on the squad double-shift.

"I can't spare two men for a simple transfer," I said.

"Nothing's simple about getting killed. The syndicate can't chance Rudy Endze turning pigeon. Cartello could have you and Endze for the price of one executioner."

I shook my head. "Cartello's not that dumb."

Chris Cartello was the top slice off the local cheese, boss of Circle Bay's crime Organization. After a month of our cleanup, I'd received an "anonymous" phone call:

Pick up all the punks you want, Fleers, but stay out of my affairs. Or I'll yank the lid off something hot enough to blow you out of the department and clear out of town.

I ran as tough a squad as Captain Klegg would allow, and then some. I'd smacked around my share of punks, but I was clean. After the call, I cracked down all the harder.

I shook my head at Klegg again. "I don't think Cartello will try anything. If he does, I can take care of it."

Klegg sighed and rubbed a hand across his eyes. Muscle moved under his rolled sleeves. "When are you going to quit sweeping the gutters by yourself, Dave?"

I felt my jaw muscles bunch. We'd gone over all that too often for me to answer him, times when he'd told me to take it easy, leave a little for somebody else. I stood up, patted the holstered .38 clipped to my belt, and picked up my hat. "Is that all, Eddie?" I asked calmly. "I'd like to spend some time with my wife before I pick up Endze."

Klegg nodded. "Yeah, that's all." He gave me a tired smile. "Say hello to Myra for me."

They were waiting in my car.

Chris Cartello was on the passenger's side of the front seat. He was bland, handsome with a dark thinness, lips set beneath a delicate black mustache. He didn't resemble the public conception of a hood who lived off the profits of dope, prostitution, pornography, illegal booze—even hired killing. He was the good-looking executive surrounded by women at the country club dance. He flashed a mouthful of capped teeth at me. "Climb in, Lieutenant." He waved a magnanimous hand at the other side of my car.

The other two were in the back seat. One I didn't know, a scrawny cadaver with a massive forehead and the expensively-cut clothes of a gun-carrier. The other was Chris Cartello's brother, John, the syndicate's second-in-command. He was big, burly, with neither his brother's looks nor brains.

I climbed in behind the wheel. I reached across Chris Cartello and opened his door. "Get out. You're stinking up my car."

Cartello's mouth tightened. He yanked the door shut. "Don't push me, Fleers. You been a thumb up my nose for a long time now."

"I haven't even got a good start on you yet."

"You locked up eight of my runners in the past couple months. You're costing me a lot of cash, Fleers."

"Don't break my heart."

He stuck a rigid finger under my nose. "I'll break more than that, wise guy. I told you a month ago I could stop you." He pulled the finger back and ran its tip along his mustache. "But I'm willing to do it an easier way. Give him the envelope, Johnny."

"Sure." John Cartello took a long, white package from his inside coat pocket, leaned forward and slid it across my shoulder. It dropped into my lap. "Live it up, copper," he said.

I looked at him in the rear-view mirror. His eyes bored into the nape of my neck with a cold, inbred loathing for anything connected with the law. But when they switched to his brother, they became greedy pig eyes. It was no secret that John Cartello wanted to run the organization—a job he would have if it wasn't for his brother.

I picked up the package.

"You've been working too hard, Lieutenant," Chris Cartello said. "There's enough money there for a second honeymoon for you and that sexy little bride of yours. Hell, if I had a broad like that, I'd be home chasing her all the time." He winked and jabbed me in the ribs with a thumb. "Those blonde fluffs are really hot stuff, huh, Fleers?"

Anger was suddenly tight across my temples, like a hangman's noose that had slipped too high. I could feel it in my throat and knew I couldn't control my voice, even to tell him to take his hand off me. I held the bribe in my left hand. Slowly, so he could watch me, I spat on the envelope, twice, to get it just right. Then I swung around and slammed it into his face. It sounded like a flat hand slapping water.

In the mirror, I could see the startled faces of John Cartello and the cadaver. Their hands moved toward shoulder rigs. Right there in front of police headquarters, they would have gunned me, maybe gotten away with it. Only I was expecting it. I had my own gun pointed at Chris Cartello's stomach.

"Hold it!" I shouted. "I'll put lead in him, so help me."

John Cartello's eyes skipped to his brother in indecision. For a few seconds I wondered just how badly he coveted his brother's kingdom of crime. But the slight hesitation was enough. Their guns lowered.

Chris Cartello was dabbing at his face with a handkerchief. A little shiver ran through him. "You're playing games with the wrong guy, Fleers," he croaked hoarsely. "Now I'm gonna fix you."

My voice was steady now that action had rinsed away the peak of my anger, but it held an edge like a jagged switch blade when I said, "I don't take bribes, you lousy punk. And don't mention my wife again with your filthy mouth."

"I'm gonna fix you." Cartello spoke absently, as though to a ghost he could no longer see nor hear. "I was gonna have somebody else take care of it, but now I'll do it myself. I'm gonna get you where it'll hurt most."

I leaned forward and pressed the tip of my gun against his belt buckle. "I hope you try, Cartello. I hope you try in person. Then I can do a blast job on you with everything legal."

His mouth whitened at the corners, but I didn't pride myself that it was fear. He stuffed his handkerchief away. He whipped the package of money off his lap with a vicious backhand. Climbing out of the car, he smoothed down his mustache and walked away. John Cartello and the cadaver started to follow.

"Hold it." I scooped the package off the floor and tossed it onto the back seat. "Take this crap with you."

John Cartello shrugged. He picked up the envelope.

I put my gun away and turned to face him. "You should have let me kill him. It would have made you a big man in the gutters, instead of a flunky."

He attempted a smile that never reached his eyes. "Maybe some other time, Fleers," he said and stepped outside.

I drove home, the wheel sticking to my sweaty hands. The Cartello boys always affected me that way. I couldn't stand the kingpins, the hot-shots who think their feet don't stink. I despised everything about them, and I couldn't help myself.

Thirty-eight years ago, my old lady staggered into a slop joint on lower Third, for just one quick-one because of the March chill. As usual, she had more than one. Only this time her labor pains were just minutes apart. The bartender delivered me atop some beer cases in the storeroom. I was named after him.

They used to kid me about it, her and the old man. He was a two-bit pigeon who ended up wading the river with cement sneakers. Then the old lady hustled barflys until her alcohol count blew off the top of her skull. I grew up in squalor, among drunks and whores and addicts and out-and-out tramps, fighting for corners to hawk papers and waking up putrid from my own blood in alleys, with the few cents I'd earned gone. It had a lot to do with what I became, with what Eddie Klegg often accused me of being—a compulsive lawman, a lonely cop who can't let up on the addicts and whores and drunks, or the pushers and hoods and killers who stomp a guy even when he can't be ground any farther into the dirt than he is already. Only I never thought of it that way. It was a search for something clean, just one infinitesimal thing in the world to make it all worth while.

When I found Myra, it was like a drink of cool, fresh water that cleansed away the sour taste of my past, and of things like Cartello and his organization of filth.

As I pulled into my drive, I wondered how I was going to tell Myra about working tonight. This was the fourth time Since I'd known her that I'd handled transfers myself. I wasn't in too big a hurry when I started into the house.

She was lying across the bed when I came out of the shower. As always, she had the ceiling lights, the dresser lights and the three-way lamps on either side of the double bed all switched on full. Even under that merciless glare, her complexion was soft and smooth. I knotted the towel about my waist. I let my eyes roam along her legs to the mound where the red silk robe whitened against the thrust of hip; up over her breasts to the slim oval of her face—pretending surprise that she was watching. I winked, but she wasn't having any.

I stuck fists on my hips. "I'll use a pillow."

She frowned. "What?"

"To cover your face," I said, "if it freezes like that."

"Bull," she said sullenly, but a sheepish half-grin curled the corners of her mouth.

She rolled over, facing the window on the far side of the room. A grass-carpeted, shrub-decorated patio with a louvered fence shielded the window from all angles, letting us keep it open, the blinds up for the slightest draft, even while we dressed or slept. I watched the breeze finger Myra's blonde hair, felt again the shock that flickered through me when I was near her, that made me want to hold her, say,

Myra, Myra, I love you . . .

I reached out and touched her. She interlocked her fingers with mine, and pulled my arm across her body. "You promised we'd go out tonight," she said against my knuckles.

I sighed. "I know. I forgot about the Endze transfer."

"Every time you make a transfer, you're gone all night." She let go of my hand and rolled back, straining the thin robe. She propped her head on one arm. "We haven't been out together in six weeks."

"I know, Myra. I'm sorry."

"Don't be sorry, Dave. Just take me out. Let's have fun tonight, just us."

I gestured helplessly. "I can't. Not tonight."

She sighed, long, deeply. Her teeth nibbled her forefinger, like a small child lost in thought. I was thinking how nice it would be to kiss the wistfulness off her mouth when she swung erect on the bed, long thighs flashing, her full lips set in sudden resolution. "Dave, I want to model again."

It took me off guard. "You know how I feel about that. You said you'd stop working when we got married."

She fluttered her long hair impatiently. "I have to do something. Dave, I've been so darn lonely!"

"I don't want men oggling you."

"But I had my picture taken hundreds of times before we were married! You weren't jealous. You thought it was all right then."

I shook my head. "I never thought it was all right. And I've been jealous of you ever since we met." I turned and began digging underclothes out of the dresser. "Besides, you're my wife now. That makes all the difference."

I knew how she felt. She had expected romantic adventure, like the night of our third date, four months ago. Pitch dark, a lonely street, the sudden impaling of a mugger and victim by my headlights. He blackjacked me twice before I got him. Myra's eyes had shone, stunned with the melodrama of a cop's life. She ran tender fingers over my bruised face, but I could feel her heart pounding with excitement.

I could have told her then that a cop's wife has little but empty, waiting hours, but I didn't. I needed her to shut away the lonely hours I'd spent myself, just being alive. And when you find someone as wonderful as Myra, you don't care how you get her, nor what you have to do to keep her.

Since our wedding, I'd been working seven days a week, coming home late at night only for exhausted sleep. It was hard to realize I had something to do with my time besides pressuring the syndicate or the independent hoods, pounding at every case until I had the pieces shoveled behind bars. It was hard to remember that I was a husband now, too.

Myra's warm breast touched my arm. "Dave," she said softly, "couldn't someone else deliver that prisoner, just this once? It's important to me."

My heart hammered against my ribs and I half turned to pull her into my arms. Then I remembered Captain Klegg's words of caution in the squad bay that afternoon, and Cartello's threat as he sat in my car. I shook my head miserably. "If Cartello tries anything tonight, I should be the one to take care of it. I started the whole mess."

Her breath came hot, sharp against my back. She spun away, her negligee flying. "You don't have to spend every waking minute taking care of your job, do you?"

"Myra," I said helplessly, "don't . . ."

"I'm sick of sitting around this house alone all the time! I don't even know any of the neighbors, except to say hello."

"I know. I . . ."

She had her hands on her hips, her chest thrust out, and angry determination had squared the lines of her face. "Well, I'm going out tonight, with you or without you." Her lips twisted. "But you can bet I won't be alone for long."

She was being carried away now, flinging bitter words that I knew she didn't mean, angry words spawned during the long nights she had spent alone. But that knowledge didn't ease the sting of what she said.

"Don't," I said tightly, reluctantly angry myself, now. "Don't talk like that."

"I can pick up a dozen men anytime I want them."

"Stop it, Myra!"

"And from all the satisfaction I've been getting out of you lately, I'd *need* a dozen men . . ."

I was on her. I knotted my fist in her hair, jerked her face up close to mine. Brutal pressure forced her head back, tightened the smooth skin of her throat, pulling her eyes into elongated slits. She gave a sharp cry of pain and raked her nails along my hand.

"If you so much as look at anyone else, I'll kill you." My voice was a choked rasp. "I swear I'll kill you!"

"Dave! Let go!"

"I lived with animals like that, women who put out to anything in pants—even my own mother!—just for a free drink or a sick thrill." I wrenched her head farther back. She moaned deep in her throat. "Don't ever say anything like that again! Don't even joke about it!"

I shoved her away and turned to lean on the dresser, exhausted. And I was suddenly ashamed. I waited until my breathing was even. Without facing her, I said, "I'm sorry, Myra. I hadn't any right to do that. It's just I'm tired and on edge . . ."

Silence. My heart throbbed in panic.

. . . if I lost her . . . My God, if I lost her . . .

A sighing rustle of silk "Dave." Softly.

I turned.

The robe was froth at her feet. Her body was bold, glorious in the bright light. She offered her hand, led me to the bed, down, into the breeze from the window.

"I didn't mean it, Dave. I wanted to hurt you," she whispered contritely. "I was just afraid you didn't love me. You haven't told me for so long . . . love me . . . I love you . . ."

I stretched for the table lamps, but she pulled me back. Her lips were swollen, ripe in the bright pool of radiance. Her eyes held the same emerald gleam of excitement I'd seen on the night of the mugger.

"You know I like lights when you love me." She smiled wickedly, impishly. "Lots and lots of lights . . ."

I used my own car for the transfer. I cuffed Endze to the U bolt I have welded below the dash. It let me keep both eyes on the road. The trip normally took three hours, but this time I made a stop.

Rudy Endze was a convicted dope peddler. If he talked before Cartello got to him with a bribe or a bullet, I might have a wedge into the syndicate. I picked a deserted country road and cut the lights.

Endze was a half head over my six foot, solid. He broke the silence of the night only once, a groan hardly loud enough to drown out the chirp of the crickets. I was methodical, careful about bruises. The bracelets kept him from resisting.

Finally, defeated, I started the motor. I lit two cigarettes with the dash lighter, stuck one into Endze's mouth.

I watched him suck hungrily at the butt. "One thing about you, Endze," I said, "you can take it."

He looked at me with pain-ridden, heavy-lidded eyes. "We'll see how good you are, Fleers, when Cartello gets through with you."

Even in the dark, my face must have scared him. He wriggled against the far door. "You'll never get anything out of me, Fleers," he said quickly.

I uncurled my fists and jerked the cigarette out of his mouth. I threw both butts out of the window, and got the car off the berm onto the road.

For all my bravado with Eddie Klegg that afternoon, I breathed easier when I passed through the gates of the big cage. There had been no sign of Cartello or even a syndicate gun. Cartello might be going to try to take me, but evidently tonight was not the night. There was a touch of impatient anger, too, that nothing had happened. Someone else could have convoyed Endze. It had even been wasted time trying to get anything out of him. I could have been with Myra. And laying over at the prison until morning suddenly seemed like a stupid waste of time. By driving hard, I could be home by 1:00 A.M.

Only I got behind a lot of night-rolling trucks. Between that and the stop I'd made, I didn't make it until two o'clock.

I had to park at the curb because my driveway was filled with police cars.

I sat behind the wheel and took in the patrol cruisers, the house with every window aspew with light, the uniformed men glimpsed now and again behind them. I got weak. It hit me suddenly, like the smash of a nightstick across my brain.

I'm gonna fix you. Fleers. I'm gonna get you where it hurts the most.

The trouble was, I'd always been alone. I'd never had anyone to protect except myself. When I was threatened, it was a personal thing that I took care of when the time came.

Now there was Myra.

Her name was a breath in my throat. "If he's hurt her . . ."

I scudded from the car, sprinted across the lawn.

"Hold it, buddy!" A light swept my face. "Oh!" The voice was confused now. "Lieutenant Fleers . . ."

"What happened?"

"There's been a killing. I mean, your wife . . ."

I bolted past him to the door, flung it wide. The place was jammed with cops. Every eye turned toward me. The room became still as the sigh of a corpse. I sorted the faces, picked out Klegg's just as he started toward me.

"Where's Myra?" I demanded.

Klegg grunted. "She's okay. For now, at least."

My legs went limp. I dropped onto a hallway chair.

"What happened, Eddie?"

He said it quickly, bluntly. "Chris Cartello is dead. It looks as though Myra shot him."

I stared up at him. Finally, I worked a cigarette out of my pocket and into my mouth. Klegg had to hold the match. I almost gagged on the smoke. "Where's Myra?" I asked again.

"In the kitchen with a doctor. But I want you to see this first." He turned and walked across the living room. I followed him. It was like wandering through a twisted copy of my home by Salvador Dali, with surrealist policemen and equipment scattered bent and askew over the furniture. It couldn't be real. Not murder . . . not here . . .

There were clothes on the floor of the bedroom, a man's crumpled suit and the red negligee Myra had worn earlier tonight. A sheet-covered form sprawled half-on, half-off the double bed. The sheet didn't conceal the blood spattered on the spread, nor the pool that had gathered on the floor. Klegg walked over, grasped a corner of the sheet, glanced at me. I nodded.

It was Chris Cartello. He wasn't handsome anymore, not at all the lady's man. His nearly pupil-less eyes stared up at the intersection of wall and ceiling because of the odd angle that his head hung over the edge of the bed. The only thing he wore was a generous coating of his own blood. His chest, stomach and face were punctured with bullet holes.

Klegg dropped the sheet. I walked to the dresser and ground out my cigarette in an ashtray. I had seen dead bodies from one end of the city to the other, in alleys, bloated in bathtubs, in automobiles, even the pieces of one stuffed behind the altar of a church. But none had given me the sick revulsion of this one on my own bed. On Myra's bed. Our bed.

"Tell me, Eddie," I said thickly.

He nodded. "I'll tell it the way it happened to me, so you'll know I was only doing what was necessary," he said carefully.

"Just tell the goddamn story!"

"Yeah. We got a squeal at 12:35. A woman, unknown at the time."

"What do you mean, 'At the time'?"

"I'll get to that. The woman witnessed a murder. At this address—your's. I tried getting you at the prison, but you'd already gone and you weren't driving a radio car. We found Cartello just like this, nude, six .32 slugs in him. Myra was packing a suitcase. She was half-dressed and completely hysterical."

"What the hell did you expect?"

Klegg raised his eyebrows, shrugged.

I asked the next question with my throat tight, hating Klegg for making me ask. "Did the witness say who shot him?"

"I don't know. She didn't give her name until she turned up at the D.A.'s office. She's there now, and I haven't heard anything more."

"Then why does it look like Myra killed him?"

He made this one blunt, too. "We found the murder weapon on the floor. Myra's were the only prints on it."

I stared at him, waiting for him to burst out laughing, tell me this was a horrible, monumental joke rigged up with Myra because I'd left her tonight. But I knew it wasn't. Not with Chris Cartello's blood soaking my carpet.

I sucked in a long breath. "Let me see Myra."

"Go ahead."

I stopped at the door and turned back. "Who's the witness, Eddie?"

"Amanda Evans," Klegg said. "She says she was Chris Cartello's girl friend."

When I entered the kitchen, Myra gave a small whimper and jumped up from her chair at the table. I held her. It was a long time before she stopped crying. The doctor poured two cups of steaming coffee and set them on the table.

"You're the best medicine right now," he said. "Get her to drink this."

He left us alone.

I got her back to the table and had her drain both cups. I refilled them and kept one for myself. I scraped my chair around next to hers. "I've got to know, Myra."

She shook her head violently. "I can't! I've told it so many times!"

I cursed Klegg under my breath. I pulled her gently toward me. "Once more, Myra. Please."

She looked at me for a long time and then nodded. She squeezed her eyes shut and tears ran out beneath the lids. "Just so you believe me, that's all."

"Everyone believes you."

"No. Not the others."

"I'll believe you, Myra. I know you. I love you."

She hugged my hand to her breast, touched my lips with her fingertips. "That's the only hope I have," she said.

She told the story quickly, biting her lip to recall things she must have wanted to blot away forever . . . a bath . . . getting into her robe . . . a noise from the patio . . . when she turned, he was already through the window.

"He said he'd choke me if I screamed," she said, her eyes tightly-closed. "He . . . oh, Dave! . . . he tore off my robe . . . pushed me onto the bed. I was so frightened! I couldn't move. He took off his clothes and he . . . tried to . . . he climbed onto the bed . . ."

Myra's eyes flew open. "That's when he was shot. From the window. Terrible, loud explosions. I screamed. A gun came flying through the window. It hit me and I grabbed it and threw it on the floor . . . and . . . and that's all. He almost fell off the bed and blood was all over everything. Dave, hold me!"

I tried to soothe her. Once she had finished, I never wanted her to go through it again. But I had to know.

"Who was at the window, Myra?"

She shook her head. "I had all the lights on in the room. It was hard to see anything outside. I heard someone run across the patio. I went to the front room window, just as a man climbed into a car at the curb and drove away."

"Did you get a good look at him?"

"No." Her forehead wrinkled. She looked at me, as though unsure of something. I held her away from me.

"What else, Myra?"

"I . . . noticed another car parked in our drive. Another man ran from the direction of our patio—right after the first car drove away—and got into the second car and drove away."

"Did you recognize him?"

"He was just a shadow, but . . ." She frowned again.

"But what?"

"I think he was carrying a camera."

A camera. Was that Cartello's threat—obscene pictures of Myra to use against me? It was fantastic, but no more so than the way it had backfired on him. If I had given in, to protect Myra, Cartello would have finally been rid of me. If I hadn't knuckled under—if I had let him distribute the pictures for stags and smokers—letting me keep my badge would have been like giving me a legal license to kill Cartello. The D.A., the commissioner—they wouldn't have held onto me with lead-lined gloves.

I stayed with Myra after they booked her. She felt better when daylight flooded her cell. A sun shaft hazed the edges of her hair, forming a fuzzed frame of gold about her face. I kissed her swollen eyes.

"I love you, Myra."

She tightened her arms about my neck and kissed me with a desperate eagerness. "Help me, Dave. No matter what happens, what they say about me, just love me . . ."

"I'll always love you," I whispered.

Klegg tried to persuade me to turn over the case to someone not emotionally involved, but I shook him off. He finally gave me every man he could spare. We came up with nothing.

I put most of the pressure on the one man who had profited most by Chris Cartello's death—the new boss of the syndicate, John Cartello. We couldn't shake his alibi for the night of the murder. A dozen witnesses were ready to swear that John Cartello had never left his newly-inherited nightclub, The King's Room. The witnesses were all employees of the club.

The trial was brief, deadly, a walk-away for the prosecution. Bartenders, taxi drivers, waitresses—people easily bought by John Cartello—testified that Myra and Chris Cartello had been a cozy couple all over town for the past six weeks. They even had testimony from the clerk who made up the duty roster for our squad, testimony that showed I had been on double-duty for two months, making it easy enough for Myra to play around without my knowing it. But the most damaging evidence came from Chris Cartello's girl friend, Amanda Evans, the woman who had reported the shooting.

> *You are employed at The King's Room, Miss Evans?*
> *Yes. I'm a song-stylist.*
> *Christopher Cartello hired you?*
> *That's right. Four weeks ago.*
> *In only four weeks, you fell in love with him?*
> *Yes. With each other.*
> *Did he have that effect on other women? Was he handsome, charming enough to persuade a woman to have an affair with him—even a married woman?*

Objection!
Sustained.
Were you with Christopher Cartello on the night of the murder?
Yes.
Tell us about it.
Well, when I first started at the club, Chris had been seeing another woman. When Chris and I realized we were in love, he told her but she wouldn't listen to him. Finally, Chris decided to go to her home and have it out with her. I went with him, waited in the car. I heard shots inside the house. I ran to a window. I saw her standing beside a bed holding a gun. Chris was bleeding...
They were both unclothed?
Yes. She ... probably forced him to undress at gun point, to shame him. She was like that!
Objection!
She filled him rather than give him up!
Objection, your honor!
Sustained. The witness will confine herself to the questions.
The woman you saw holding the gun over Christopher Cartello's body—is she in this room?
The court will note she indicates the accused, Mrs. Myra Fleers.

Myra told her story, just as she had told it to me. Myra, built for the excitement she aroused in men, with a body that had made her a top model—a body that caused almost instant resentment among women, like seven of the jurists the prosecution had managed to empanel.

Myra was sentenced to die in the gas chamber.

The cell was bleak, uninviting as the bed of a coffin. Myra sat on the edge of the cot, her eyes withdrawn, hands clenched, her mouth restrained in mute, incredulous horror.

"I didn't kill him," she murmured thinly.

I took her hands. I almost recoiled from the slick, icy touch of her flesh. I wanted to pull her into my arms, warm her, but her body was unyielding. I kissed her. Her mouth was cold as the lips of the dead. Holding her, suddenly, unbearably, it was like embracing a corpse, her afterbreath tainted with the odor of the grave.

I sank to my knees, my face buried in her lap like the child I felt, and, God help me, my terror was not alone for her. I had been lonely before, but if they took her away from me now, I would be a dead man walking.

She bent above me, capping my head with soft breasts. She rocked, holding me, and she said, "I really didn't love him. They lied."

... over and over and again ...

The King's Room was aroar with party. I stood on the dais overlooking the sunken lounge until I found him in the crowd. He was taller than anyone around him, the punks and hoods, the behind-kissers that always gathered around scum like John Cartello, like pus encircling a sore. His head was thrown back in laughter.

Amanda Evans was no longer just a hired singer. She clutched Cartello's arms as though she had written the nine-points law. She was dressed in a black sheath, not at all the garb of a mourning lover. Her eyelids drooped over the alcoholic sheen in her eyes. I'd checked her, but found nothing I could have used in court—just enough to convince me she had lied. She was a small time road canary with unknown combos, and even those jobs she got more on the strength of her back than her voice; a bed hopper who bounced on any mattress stuffed with enough money; the sort who would commit perjury for the right price; a slut with no right to speak my wife's name.

I stood looking down at them, feeling my anger build. Anger that Myra was locked in a cell because of the word of a whore; anger that Myra was to die while vermin such as this still collected like dross on a cesspool; anger that I had let it be so.

I went down three carpeted steps and toward them. The crowd parted, became silent as some of them recognized me, whispered to others. Cartello turned, frowning.

"Hey, now!" His thick lips gashed open. "The prize fuzz of the Third Precinct! Greetings, Lieutenant."

"I want to talk, Cartello," I said. "Alone."

"Go to hell! Unless you got a warrant, you got no right here. I sure didn't invite you."

Amanda Evans tugged at his arm. "Hey, lover, don't holler on him. He's got enough troubles." She gave me the coy leer of a coquettish drunk.

Cartello guffawed. "Ain't it the truth?" He scooped a glass from a waiter's tray. He shoved it at me. I took it with reflex action. "Well, Johnny Cartello can let bygones be bygones. Welcome to the party, boy scout."

Amanda Evans lurched forward, her square bodice dipping as she clinked her glass against mine. "Here's to that pudgy little wife of yours." She looked up into my eyes and I wondered if she could see the hate welling in me, like smoke in a glass tube. "Long may she live!" She hiccupped.

"Yeah!" Cartello roared. "As long as they let her, anyway. Drink up, Fleers. This is a celebration. The law put the kibosh on my brother's killer today."

I threw the drink with the same reflexive action I had used to take it. Liquor splashed across Amanda Evans' cleavage. She screeched as the ice cubes slid between her breasts. I still gripped the glass. I swung it in a backhanded arc toward Cartello's face. It shattered against the side of his head and the shard in my hand sliced across his upper lip.

Motion, as Cartello's goons started toward me, the cadaver with the wide forehead in the lead. My shoulder took Cartello in his stomach while he still had his hand up to his slashed lip. He went over and down with me astride his chest. The muscle boys kept coming. I had my gun out but even that didn't stop them. They knew as well as I did that I couldn't take them all. Cartello rolled and bucked beneath me. From behind, someone took hold of my hair and throat.

I shoved the barrel of my .38 into Cartello's mouth. I could feel parts of his teeth snap away and the gun sight gouge his tongue.

I let pressure whiten my finger on the trigger.

Cartello became very still. He went cross-eyed trying to look at the gun and my face at the same time. Beads of moisture spotted his face.

The hands let go of my throat.

"That's right, boys," I said quietly. "Just take your goddamn hands off me."

Slowly, I pulled the gun from Cartello's mouth. The metal was slimy with spit and blood. I kept the muzzle about an inch from the tip of his nose. I said, "Tell them to line up across the room."

He tried to keep his eyes on the gun and motion with them at the same time. It didn't work. He spit blood and ivory chips and choked, "Do it!"

Everybody went away.

I tapped Cartello's nose with the gun. "Tell me about it, Cartello."

"A . . . about what?"

"About how you killed your brother."

"No! No, I didn't . . ."

He was lying beside pieces of the whiskey glass I had thrown. I took hold of his jaw and rocked his head sideways and down, grinding it against the floor. When I let his head swing back, his cheek was raw, with broken glass embedded.

"Tell me," I repeated.

He shook his head, his eyes and lips alive, dancing with pain. "I didn't. I tell . . ."

I gave him the gun, hard, against his bloody cheek, driving the glass deeper. His mouth came open in a silent shriek of anguish that couldn't get past the vomit in his throat. His sickness gushed out and mixed with blood and glass and teeth on the floor.

When I asked him again, he gave the right answer.

"Okay! I . . . killed him."

I tried to keep the surge of exhilaration and relief out of my voice. "Let's hear it."

Cartello tried to clear his throat. He spit some of the mess onto the floor and swallowed the rest. Then he told me.

Chris Cartello had been working for six weeks on a plan to fritz me—I knew what that was: the blackmail photos of Myra—and John Cartello suddenly had a foolproof way to take over the syndicate. He followed Chris, shot him through the window of my bedroom while wearing gloves. He hit Myra with the empty gun so she would pick it up, cover it with her fingerprints. He ran, got Amanda Evans to call headquarters and report the shooting. He paid for her false testimony to the District Attorney and later at the trial; testimony that put Myra on a non-stop trip to the gas chamber and set John Cartello up in business.

I sat on his chest and listened. When he finished, I hit him again with the gun. This time, the pain put him completely out. I phoned headquarters, keeping my gun on Cartello. Nobody tried to stop me. Nobody said a word.

But Captain Eddie Klegg had plenty to say. He stood braced in front of me as I sat on a barstool, his fists wedged into his sides, and roared, "What's next with you, Fleers? Judge, jury—you going to buy some cyanide and start your own gas chamber, too?"

I took a deep drag on my cigarette and snorted smoke. "I did more in a half hour than the whole force accomplished since the murder. I got the killer's confession."

"You think it will stand up in court?"

"He admitted the killing. Before witnesses."

"Witnesses! Gunsels, whores and hoods, you mean. Everyone here is on syndicate payroll."

"How about the hired help? And the freeloaders? There's bound to be one honest one among them."

Klegg's mouth came open, as though he had so many things to say he didn't know where to start. He spread his hands helplessly. "The only thing they'll testify to is that you beat John Cartello with a gun."

"You know his confession is true."

"No. I don't. And you don't either. Not now. What would you have done with a crazy man beating your face to a pulp?"

"I'd have told the truth," I said, but I couldn't bring my eyes up to Klegg's. I dropped my cigarette into a glass of whiskey.

"You'd have admitted anything to save yourself," Klegg said.

"Everything he said checks out," I insisted.

Klegg sighed. He walked around and sat on the stool beside me. He shoved the whiskey glass away with a grimace. "I should have kept you off the case, like I wanted to in the first place."

"That's easy for you to say. What the hell does Myra mean to you?" I was sorry even as the words came out, but I couldn't stop them.

Klegg's face grew taut and then as quickly relaxed into the features of a tired old man. "That's what I mean," he said sadly. "You don't even know what you're saying, let alone doing, or you'd never have pulled this clown act."

"I'm sorry. I shouldn't have said that, Eddie."

"Don't be sorry for me, Dave." Klegg swung around to face me. "Besides getting yourself busted, you may have used up Myra's last chance."

On the day Myra was transferred to the state pen, Cartello's lawyers forced my hearing. I got off with indefinite suspension and bust to harness bull. Klegg was right about one other thing, too. Unless I could get proof that Cartello's confession was true, it looked as though I had used up Myra's only chance.

I had to find the eyewitness, the man Myra had seen run from the patio carrying a camera. If Chris Cartello had been planning to use pictures of Myra against me, he would have had to use someone he could trust, yet someone capable of getting the kind of shots he would need. One man filled that bill—the photographer the syndicate used in their million dollar pornography business. I didn't know him, couldn't even be sure that he would be the eyewitness Myra had seen. But it was a fresh start. The only one I had.

I hit the ears and the stoolies: I wanted contact with the syndicate's smut man.

Two weeks without word—at home without even the activity of the squad room to occupy my mind. I lay in the dark, and sucked smoke deep and thought:

This is a cop. Your mother hustled and your father was a punk. So you pushed too hard at anything that reminded you of them, even the wheels and the kingpins. And now you're up to your chin in your own crap and somebody's making waves. If Myra dies, it will be you who pushed the pellet down the chute, and her time is growing shorter.

I rolled off the couch. I scooped my gun off the coffee table, shouldered into my coat, left the house. I had to find that eyewitness.

I grabbed two fistfuls of his shirt and jacket and rammed Jebbo Williams into the wall. No one paid any attention but the barkeep and when he got a look at my face, he walked to the opposite end of the bar and poured himself another stiff one. The little stoolie let his eyes float around in their own blood until they were aimed up at me.

"Why am I being hung up, Jebbo?" I asked. I twisted the shirt, squeezing the folds of skin on his neck, shutting off his wind. "Why has everybody clammed up about the smut man?"

He bobbed his head frantically. I eased up.

"We . . . we got orders! Not to give you anything. Me, I don't know the guy, anyway."

"Find out."

He shook his head so hard that spittle flew off the corners of his mouth. "I even mention it, I'm fish food. Anyhow, the syric's got it the smut man ain't around no more."

My hands grew cold. "Dead?"

"More like hidin' out. If you want him, the organization's got to put the blast on him, right? So he turtles."

It made sense. And if they were that eager to keep him away from me, it could mean I was on the right track. I let go of Jebbo Williams and stepped back. I left him heaped on the floor like dirt never swept up.

My beard was already three days old and my mouth was thick from the taste of whiskey and cigarette smoke washed down with black coffee, so my breath must have smelled just right. I wore rags that didn't fit. I headed into the back alleys and clip joints, the brothels and the fleabags, among the type of places where I was born and grew up—a wino with kicks for dirty pics. It was like sinking into a quagmire.

I studied the cards passed from hand to hand, obscene photos imprinted on decks of playing cards. I watched movies on screens of soiled sheets until I began to know their categories: "doubles", "three-ways", "frenchies", "mob scenes"; began to recognize the same thin plots even at the first framed segments: "the doctor and nurse", "the milkman", "the sex circus", "the baby sitter", "a day on the farm". I thumbed through "comic" books and illustrated "novels", even helped a dirty, whiskered old man assemble a picture puzzle of distorted lust. I watched and listened and I came up with a face repeated often in the pictures, a mulatto named Arlene Hutton.

I first saw her in a crowded room polluted with smoke and sweat and the fumes of cheap booze. I sat on an upended beer case, my hands gripping my thighs in revulsion that passed for the wet-palmed grips of lust the others had on their wine bottles.

A big shouldered gorilla sat beside me, his lips wet with anticipation as the picture leaped against the cracked plaster of the wall. It was a "black and white special", involving a white man and a sooty-skinned mulatto. The girl was young, no more than twenty-two, her features snub and pert. Her figure was full and dusky against the white backdrop of the bed, beside the man.

The ape prodded me with an elbow. "Boy, how'd ya like some'a that?"

The girl's popularity was evident by the number of productions she "starred" in. If anyone would know the syndicate's smut man, it would be Arlene Hutton.

It took me another three weeks to find her, while Myra's execution drew nearer and panic began to grip me.

We ended up half drunk in her apartment. I was shaved, scrubbed and suited. Arlene Hutton grew out of her low-cut white dress like a cocoa-toned Venus.

"You been a bash, man," she said throatily. She pushed away from the door and let her weight hang against me. "Let's take it together." She ground lips and body into mine. My flesh crawled. I stepped away. She opened her eyes, frowning.

"How do I know I can afford it?" I asked.

She put her hands behind her back. Seconds later, she stood clad in white panties and spike-heeled shoes, her dress trailing from her arm like a matador's cape in the dust. "Man," she gurgled, "can you afford not to?"

The only light spilled through the window from the neon-lighted city outside. It was enough for me to recognize the body with which I had become so familiar during the last few months. She posed, dusky skin accented by the white scanties, and gurgled again. "I better fix you a cold drink, big man." She hip-strutted away.

By the time she got back, I was on the couch with my deck of cards spread across the top of the coffee table. She handed me my drink and turned, breasts swaying, to stare down at her own image repeated over a half-hundred times in the obscene cards.

"I want to make sure I get my money's worth," I said. "Pick a card, any card."

She took a long pull at her drink. "So that's how you knew me. What do you think of them?"

I watched her face in the neon glow. "They're professional, all right," I said carefully. "Who's the shutterbug?"

She gave me her body in profile as she drained her glass. "A syndicate photographer. He uses me for all his best ideas. And he pays top dollar."

She set her glass down among the cards. She came down onto my lap. "But then I always throw myself into my work, big man. You'll see."

Her lips and hands, her whole body began touching me, caressing . . . age-old arts I had seen her use in movies, in the cards strewn on the table, ways of prostitutes the world over, things my mother must have done . . .

I flung her away, scoured at my lips with my hand to erase a taint that steel wool wouldn't remove. She sprawled on her back across the low coffee table, legs akimbo in mimic of the foul pictures scattered around and under her. Alcohol and anger mixed within me. I had the illusion of Arlene Hutton spiraling away, swelling back, laughing, flaunting her naked body, her hands seeking me with carnal urgency . . . while Myra waited to die . . .

I leaned over Arlene Hutton, one knee on the table between her legs.

"What . . . what is this?" she whimpered. "I thought you wanted to . . ."

"The only thing I want from you is the name of the man who created this filth." I swept the cards away. They flew, fluttered, demons from the mind of a madman.

Her eyes darted from my face to the butt of the gun that hung beneath my coat. "Are . . . you a vice dick?"

I took hold of her naked shoulders and pulled her face close to mine. I told her who I was. I told her what I wanted. If Myra died because I couldn't find that eyewitness, I swore that Arlene Hutton would die, too, the way any woman deserved to die who sold herself, gave herself like a dog in heat. She hung from my fists. I shook her, whipping her head back and forth, until fear was a liquid thing spilling out of her eyes. Her lips moved in spasms and I had to strain to hear when she whispered,

"Kopecchi . . . his name . . . Harold Kopecchi . . ."

I let her fall back onto the table and stood up. I was half-turned when the blow came. I twisted enough to see the scrawny cadaver with the massive forehead—the bodyguard who had accompanied Chris and John Cartello when they attempted to bribe me. And beyond, the apartment door I had never locked.

He swung the butt of a .45. It took me behind the ear with the seeming force of a paper bag inflated with air, but it drove me forward into darkness. I felt only the soft cushion of Arlene Hutton's body as my face fell against her.

I woke up looking into Captain Klegg's face. I saw Arlene Hutton's face, too, as they carried her out on a stretcher. Her pug nose had been splintered and one closed eye had a sagging, hollow look. She was unconscious, her breathing forced. If the desk clerk hadn't heard her one muffled scream, she would have been dead.

I told Klegg what had happened, but an APB got nothing. They locked me up for assault, and I think Klegg half believed it. I could see him remembering what I had done to John Cartello.

John Cartello . . . trying to frame me for murder, just as he had framed Myra . . .

Arlene Hutton lasted for a long time. Three days before Myra's scheduled execution—when my sanity hung thin—Arlene Hutton regained consciousness long enough to free me. She died choking for air between stitched and swollen lips.

It had been too much for the D.A., the commissioner, some of the council. I was free, but my services were no longer needed on the police force.

I had told Klegg about Harold Kopecchi. He had dug up a mug shot on the photographer from an old extortion rap. An APB had been posted when I was first booked—with no results.

When I walked out of the station, I was alone and without a badge. But I still had my gun and the mug shot of Kopecchi, with 54 hours to do what an entire police force had been unable to do in months—find an eyewitness to substantiate John Cartello's confession of murder. Two days and six hours to save Myra from the gas chamber.

Kopecchi's studio was set four steps below street level. The door was locked. Inside, framed portraits hung on walls and stood on shelving and counters, still and dusty. I could feel empty hysteria squeeze at my insides. I tried the door again, rattling the knob, throwing my shoulder against it and shouting, "Kopecchi!", again and again.

I pressed my forehead against the cool glass of the door and waited for my weakness and panic to drain away. I went up onto the sidewalk and walked away. If I hadn't started moving, I might have screamed. I'd checked the directory. The studio was the only address listed. But I had to find him. I had to find Harold Kopecchi.

I went through the shop that night. Bottles, trays, a few other things were scattered about the darkroom, as though Kopecchi had left in a hurry, taking only a few important items with him. Nothing else. Not one thing to assure me I had even a dead man's chance in the sun to save Myra.

O God! Myra! Myra . . . Myra . . .

My hands began to shake and I was sick in the bathroom before I left.

After a while, I moved in a daze, stopping only for the stinging impetus of alcohol, not daring to check the time, aware only that seconds were ticking away.

I showed Kopecchi's picture to taxi drivers, bus drivers, at railroads and airports, in restaurants and flophouses, in barrooms and stores, until I began to scream at the shaking heads with the uncaring faces, *my wife is going to die, goddamn it, can't you understand, they're going to kill her, I've got to find this man . . .*

9:00 P.M.

In five hours, Myra would die.

I stood at a bar. A terrible lethargy of failure and despair numbed my muscles until I could barely lift my glass. Myra was going to die and I was dying with her. My dying tasted of hate, hate that began a long time ago with my birth, a hell-flame fed by my mother and father, by Cartello and Amanda Evans, by Arlene Hutton, who died the way she had lived, her body outraged even in death. Only now the hell-flame flickered, because Myra was dying, the one good, sweet taste of life I had ever had.

I ordered another drink. I paid no attention when the barroom door opened; paid less attention to the man who entered and began staring at me while he nursed a beer. He walked up beside me and brushed my arm. I shook him off, snarled, "Get the hell away."

"Okay, buddy. It's just I thought I knew you."

I took in his gorilla's build and flat face, the ape who had sat beside me in some smoke-filled sty on the night I had first seen Arlene Hutton in a stag film. "I've never seen you before," I lied. I lifted my glass and threw the whiskey down my throat. "Just leave me alone."

He snapped his fingers. "Hey! Yeah, I saw you at some stags once. You remember me—Joey Phipps?" He hauled his glass along the bar until our shoulders touched. He dug under his leather jacket and came out with a handful of wallet sized pictures.

"You look sicker than a dog throwin' up into the wind." He nudged me. "Just throw a gander at these, buddy. They'll put the oyster juice back in ya." We were alone at the end of the bar. He fanned the pictures out before me.

My eyes moved automatically over the corruption. I raised my hand to push them away—and stopped, my eyes riveted to a picture of a woman facing away from the camera, the hands of an unseen man reaching for her. The woman was nude, with only her back showing as she knelt on a bed. But I knew her. God, I knew her! It was Myra, my Myra, in our bedroom where Chris Cartello had been shot to death. I snatched up the picture and dug my fingers into the gorilla's arm.

"Where did you get this?"

"Hey, man, leggo the limb!"

"Where did you get this picture, damn you!"

"Ouch! Man, if it works you up like that, it's yours! I don't like it, anyway." He jerked away and rubbed indignantly at his arm. "I got this set off a little guy, comes in here about once a week."

"When? What night?"

"Lemme see . . . yeah, tonight. He should be in tonight. Ten, eleven, usually."

I held my breath, dug into my pocket for the dog-eared mug shot of Harold Kopecchi. "Is this the man?"

"Yeah, that's him! Man, he's always got some hot ones."

"Do . . . you know where he lives?"

"Nope. Ran into him by accident, right here. Lucky, huh?" He gulped the last of his beer, wiped his mouth on his sleeve and nudged me again. "Look, pal, I can't stay tonight. If the little guy's got something special, get me some, too, okay? I'll make it good with ya." He scooped his pictures off the bar. He tapped the picture of Myra that I still held. "You keep that one, but don't forget, huh?" He winked. "Keep zippered up, buddy," he said and left.

9:45 P.M.

Myra was to die at 2:00 A.M.

He arrived at 11:10, a little man with searching eyes that took in everything in the room, like miniature cameras. He nodded to the bartender and walked to a back booth with high wooden wings. He carried a crinkled-leather brief case with a tiny lock snapped through the hasp. He laid it down and slid out of sight into the booth. The bartender went across the room with a bottle of beer and a glass on a tray. I followed him. He put down the load and I dropped a bill onto the tray.

"Take it out of there," I said, "and keep yourself and the change away from here."

When he'd gone, I sat down across from Kopecchi. He lit a cigarette with a kitchen match and watched while I tilted his bottle and let beer foam into his glass.

"Joey Phipps says you got the real stuff," I said.

"Ah!" His eyes crinkled at the name. "You want to buy some pictures, my friend?" He tapped the brief case with a dirty-nailed finger. "I have the best, sir."

I dropped the picture in front of him, the shot Joey Phipps had given me. "I want some more like this, Kopecchi. Of Myra Fleers and Chris Cartello."

His face went white and he had a lot of difficulty swallowing the mouthful of beer he had just taken. Carefully, he set down his glass. His eyes angled up from the picture until he was looking at me from under raised brows. It was hard to believe that so much white could show around an eye without its popping out of the socket. He tried to scramble out of the booth. I gripped the edges of the table and swung around beside him, knocking him back against the wall. I had my gun out for him to see. He put his hand against the muzzle.

"Don't," he said. "Please."

"I want information, Kopecchi." He was fascinated by the gun. It took a while for my words to penetrate. "Information? You're not from John Cartello?"

I pointed at the picture beside the beer bottle. "That woman is my wife. She's supposed to die tonight because of John Cartello."

"You're not going to kill me?" He squeaked it out, like a mouse that just avoided a snapping trap. He tugged out a handkerchief and wiped his face on one clean corner. "What do you want?"

"Did you see Chris Cartello die?"

He studied me warily, gave a feeble nod.

I wagged the gun. "Don't make me dig it out of you. I haven't got time. Who shot him?"

"I thought your wife . . ."

I punched his gut with the gun.

"John Cartello!" he blurted. "I saw John Cartello kill his brother." He wiped his face again. "I was taking pictures through the window. There was plenty of light. The woman had every light in the room on . . ."

I wasn't paying the least attention. I wanted to laugh. I wanted to cry. I wanted to kiss Kopecchi's feet. Hell, I wanted to kiss his behind!

I had an eyewitness! Myra was free!

I glanced at the barroom clock. 11:45. I could spare another hour and a quarter before I called Klegg to have the governor stop the execution. This time I wanted everything in a tissued and bowed package—not a fiasco like the night I'd beaten John Cartello. I needed more than the picture Joey Phipps had given me, a shot of a woman with her face turned away from the camera. I had to see the movies Kopecchi had taken of Myra and Chris Cartello.

Kopecchi told me the rest of it in the taxi.

The picture I had was a single frame from the movie. While Kopecchi had been taking the movie, a car arrived, parked at the front of my house. Kopecchi hid among the shrubs. John Cartello entered the patio, fired into the bedroom. He threw the gun inside, ran to his car and drove away, without seeing Kopecchi. The photographer needed only a glance to know Chris Cartello was dead. He escaped in the car Chris Cartello had left in the driveway. Somehow, John

Cartello found out about Kopecchi. Kopecchi fled, hid, coming out only to sell enough smut pictures to exist.

I leaned back against the seat. It all fit with Myra's story at the trial. I was the only one who had believed her. But then, I loved her. I would make it up to her, all the lost time. I would spend every spare moment trying to wipe away the horror she must have known, alone in her cell. I'd make it a second honeymoon, and this time I'd spend it with her instead of the city's gutter scum.

We pulled up in front of Kopecchi's hotel at 12:15.

The smell of soiled clothing blended with the faint odor of photographic chemicals and sweat and stale cigarette smoke—the smell of a giant's bad breath. The room was pitch black. I had the sensation of walking into an underground garbage pit. Kopecchi flipped on the lights. The room was as dirty as it smelled. Two blankets had been nailed across the window, making a photographer's darkroom of sorts. I picked out the cleanest of two cluttered chairs, cleared it, and dropped down onto the ripped and faded print covers. My last iota of energy was gone now that I had the proof to save Myra.

Harold Kopecchi chain-lit another cigarette, ground the first butt into the rug. He opened a bottle from the dresser, and splashed some of its contents into a paper cup.

"Gin?" he asked, motioning with the bottle.

"No. We haven't time."

He swallowed his drink and threw the crumpled paper cup onto the bed. Harold Kopecchi's body seemed to be about as clean as his soul. It was ironic that I'd found the man mainly responsible for the pornography that littered the city all the way from grade schools in the slums to the back room orgies of drunken socialites—and he was the one man in the world who could save Myra's life. A man who didn't deserve to be buried in the earth that Myra walked.

He set up a projector on a bed table and aimed it at a blank wall. He took a flat metal cannister from a locked drawer in the dresser, fished a small can out of a top drawer. He opened the film container and laid it on the dresser. He poised the small can over the film and struck a kitchen match on the thumb nail of his free hand.

I started up out of the chair.

"Sit down!" he commanded.

I dropped back, my palms cold with sweat.

He nodded at the can. "This is lighter fluid. I can easily destroy the film."

"What do you want, Kopecchi?"

"I want protection from the syndicate."

"You'll get it."

"And your promise that I will not be prosecuted for my—err—art work, for the organization. After all, if it were not for me, your wife would be only a painful memory by tomorrow morning."

"If you save my wife, Kopecchi, I'll do everything in my power to protect you from the organization and the law."

The match burned out between his fingers. He looked suddenly quite helpless and confused. "How . . . do I know you will keep your word?"

"You don't."

I leaned back. Klegg had asked me when I was going to let up. I could tell him now. Neither Kopecchi nor the law held any interest for me anymore. I had nearly cost Myra her life—my reward for trying to make the city streets safe. They even took away my badge when I fought back against the frame. Well, now they could all rot together—the D.A., the commissioner, all the self-righteous citizens, along with the whores and hookers and hoods—and I'd be able to walk past the garbage heap they made without even holding my nose against the stink. And as soon as Kopecchi told his story to the officials, he could hop on the pile himself. That's one thing the nightmare had done for me. I could quit trying to make the world pay for the sour mess my life had been right from the word go. I'd soon have Myra again, and nothing else mattered.

"Would you get the lights?"

I turned, startled. Harold Kopecchi had the film threaded through the projector. He held one grimy-knuckled finger on the machine's switch and was looking at me expectantly. I shut off the lights and stumbled back to my chair in the dark. The only thing visible was the glowing tip of Kopecchi's cigarette, like a tiny peephole into hell.

A click. A square of brilliance seemed to erupt out of the wall and leap along a funnel of cigarette smoke until it was sucked into the cyclopean eye of the projector. The machine whirred, the square of light dimmed and a figure moved upon the wall.

Myra.

She expanded, filling the scene, as though the camera were a lover moving soundlessly toward her, taking her in with hungry eyes. The scene steadied. Myra posed before her full-length mirror, her back to me, the front of her body in reflection, She was fastening her silk robe, pale skin glimmering like flecks of stars through the thin material. The cloth clung to the bath-dampened curve of her hips and breasts, clearly outlined in the bright lights of the bedroom. A small frown crossed her forehead. She turned, her negligee closed now. The scene leaped away, spread, and another figure walked into view.

Kopecchi's voice sounded above the rattle of the projector, abrupt, jangling after the mute pictures on the wall. "I used a zoom lens. I think I did a fine job, under the conditions. That mirror trick, for example. Of course, it was a good thing Mr. Cartello was right about there being enough light. Watch this next scene . . ."

His voice droned on, but I heard no more. I was watching the picture, watching Myra and Chris Cartello. She glided toward him, a soundless specter of beauty. Her arms lifted from her sides, spread, hands reaching toward him.

She touched him. Her fingers traced gentle paths along his arms until they joined and clasped behind his neck. She was smiling, lips formed in the taunting pout of a woman who knows a man's desire and is willing, eager to fulfill it. She mashed her open mouth against his, her eyes closed with the savagery of the contact. Her eyes opened again, her lips and body alive with the kiss, and in her eyes was the excitement, the same hungry intoxication I had first seen on the night I captured the mugger; the same frenzied ardor that had filled her eyes each time we had loved.

I gripped the arms of my chair, my fingers entities with life of their own, the nails tearing the chair cover. Blood ran wet on my chin from the lip I clenched between my teeth. I wanted to scream, *Enough!* I wanted to smash the projector, destroy the lies that it splattered upon the wall. I tried to close my eyes, wrench my vision from the lighted square, but I was held, stricken by the sudden knowledge of how alone I'd always been, and never really known.

I watched her disrobe, the silk falling away, held now only by her hands, slipping now to the floor. I watched her help him with his clothes, lead him to the bed, her body already in sensuous movement as she dropped eagerly down.

Not being forced down. *Willing.* Eyes not wide with fear. *Desire.* Body not shrinking. *Demanding.*

... the trial witnesses ... people I thought had lied ... who had seen them together on nights I had spent fighting the syndicate, the whole world ... nights Chris Cartello had spent setting this up to ruin me with the department ... and even in death, he was destroying me in a way he had never hoped for, could never have guessed ...

I watched Myra's mouth go slack with passion, watched and remembered the other movies I had seen, of prostitutes, whores like Arlene Hutton who used her hands in the practiced ways of whores, the way Myra was using her hands before me.

Myra ... my Myra ... the one good, clean thing in my life ... my innocent, loving bride of two months ...

The film chattered to an end. Darkness slapped at me like a living hand, leaving only a searing afterimage of the final scene printed on my eyes, the frozen phantoms of Myra and Chris Cartello, embraced.

From the dark, a demon's eyes, the fiery tip of Kopecchi's cigarette, the faint, oh, so faint devil's mask of his crimson-tinted face as he sucked at the cigarette between his lips.

Kopecchi.

Eyewitness.

The one person in all the world who could save my wife. Who could prevent Myra's writhing, gasping death under a smothering cloud of gas.

I aimed my gun at the glowing spark of fire in Kopecchi's mouth I started to sob as I pulled the trigger.

The Red Herring
Richard Deming

December 1962

The *Holt and Bancroft Manufacturing Company* was a long, one-story brick building with a truck ramp at one end. Matt Gannon walked up the ramp, past the open double doors of a shipping room to a door just beyond it which had a sign above it reading: OFFICE. A bell tinkled when he opened this door and went in.

A platinum blonde of about thirty was seated at a desk behind a low counter. She possessed both a stunning figure and a lovely face, but she was so made up she looked enameled. Pancake makeup, crimson lip rouge and blue eye mascara were laid on with a heaviness which would have been more appropriate for a nightclub stripper than a business-office receptionist.

Glancing up at the sound of the bell, the woman flashed Gannon a show-business smile. "Good morning," she said throatily.

"Morning. I'm Matt Gannon."

The blonde's smile widened. "How do you do? I'm Alice Emory."

"A pleasure," Gannon said gravely, and waited.

The blonde waited too, her gaze moving over his rangy frame with interest. It settled on the sun-bleached forelock which he could never keep from curling downward across his forehead in an unruly wave, no matter how often he combed it back. This seemed to intrigue her, for her eyes remained fixed on it.

"Matt Gannon, the private investigator," he prompted.

Her gaze dropped to his eyes. "You're a private detective?" she asked in a delighted tone.

He said patiently, "Mr. Holt's expecting me. He said just to give my name."

"Oh, you have an appointment with Mr. Holt? He didn't mention it."

"Well, I'm mentioning it," Gannon said, still patient. "Will you ring his office, please?"

"He's not in his office," Alice Emory said. "He's in Mr. Bancroft's."

Gannon tired of the game. Glancing around, he saw three doors at the far end of the room. The center one, glass-paned, he could see led to a hall. On either side of it were doors paned with frosted glass. One was lettered EDMUND HOLT, PRESIDENT, the other ARTHUR BANCROFT, VICE PRESIDENT.

Murmuring, "I'll find him, thanks," Gannon headed toward the door labeled ARTHUR BANCROFT.

The blonde's smile disappeared. "Wait!" she called. "I'll have to announce—"

The rest of it was cut off because Gannon had opened the door, walked in and shut it behind him.

Two men of about fifty were in the room. The man behind the desk had the trim figure and outdoor tan of an athlete. Iron gray hair worn in a crew-cut framed a face cut from granite. The other man, leaning against a file cabinet alongside the desk, was soft and plump, with a double chin and a little round bald spot at the rear of his head. A pair of gold-rimmed glasses rode far forward on a long nose too thin for his plump face.

The granite-faced man frowned at Gannon. The plump man merely looked surprised.

"I'm Matt Gannon," the investigator said. "Your receptionist didn't seem to want to announce me, so I came on in." He looked at the plump man. "You Edmund Holt?"

The man nodded. "That woman," he said testily. "As a receptionist she ranks about zero."

Gannon said, "She wasn't expecting me. According to her, you forgot to mention our appointment."

"I left a note on her desk," Holt said with a touch of heat. "As usual, she was off on a coffee break. It wouldn't occur to her to read anything left lying on her desk." He turned to the other man. "Art, how long—"

"She does her job," the granite-faced man interrupted. "Why don't you get off her back?"

Edmund Holt made an irritated gesture. Turning back to Gannon, he said, "We've been having a little disagreement about my engaging you, Mr. Gannon. Art—" He paused, then completely changed direction. "But I haven't even introduced you. This is my partner, Arthur Bancroft."

"How are you?" Gannon inquired, and was rewarded with a distant nod.

Edmund Holt said uncomfortably, "Art isn't very enthusiastic about my calling in a private detective. He doesn't think we're in any real danger."

Gannon said in a cold voice, "When you make up your mind, give me a ring," and turned to leave.

"Wait," Holt said hurriedly. "I want to engage you on my own, even if he doesn't agree."

Gannon slowly turned around again. "Then suppose we go into your own office."

Arthur Bancroft said on a faint note of begrudging apology, "I didn't mean to be rude, Gannon. It's just that I think my partner is blowing up a tempest in a teapot. Sit down and we'll explain the situation to you. I think you'll agree with me."

With a shrug Gannon moved to a chair before the desk, seated himself and lit a cigarette. "Go ahead. I'm listening."

Plump Edmund Holt said, "A little background information is necessary for you to understand the situation. Do you know anything about our company?"

"You manufacture electronic devices, don't you?"

The plump man nodded. "One of our biggest items in recent years had been a cheap, compact radiation detection device similar to the Geiger-Muller Counter, but based on a different principle. Originally we planned to manufacture it for amateur uranium prospectors, but we were able to produce it so cheaply that department stores all over the country stock it in their toy departments. It's sensitive enough to pick up the radiation from a luminous watch dial, yet it retails for only about three dollars. It isn't really a toy, but kids seem to go wild over it. It's made us a great deal of money."

"Uh-huh," Gannon said.

"The device was invented by a man named Gerald Greene. As a matter of fact it's called the Greene Radiation Counter. We bought the patent from him about five years ago. It was an entirely legal transaction, but he feels he was cheated."

"What did you pay for it?"

There was a period of silence before the man behind the desk said dryly, "Five hundred dollars."

Gannon hiked his eyebrows. "Outright? With no royalty clause?"

Edmund Holt said in an embarrassed voice, "It was a speculation. We had no way of knowing it would be so successful. We contemplated the sale of perhaps a few hundred units to uranium prospectors, and we risked several thousand dollars in just tooling up to manufacture it. Greene understood the speculative nature of our investment. If it hadn't accidentally clicked as a toy, he would think he made a good deal."

Arthur Bancroft said sardonically, "Stop trying to whitewash the deal, Ed. We took Greene. It was all legal, but nevertheless we took him." He turned stony eyes on Gannon. "In most legitimate business deals somebody gets the worst of it. I have no apology to make for being a smarter businessman than Greene. We got the patent as cheaply as we possibly could. Any other manufacturer would have done the same thing. It's called private enterprise."

Gannon leaned across the desk to punch out his cigarette. He said dryly, "And now you think Greene's out for revenge?"

"Think?" Holt said. "He means to kill us."

Straightening, Gannon looked at the plump man. "He's threatened you?"

"See what you think. Show him the letter, Art."

The granite-faced man reached into his top desk drawer and brought out an envelope. He handed it to Gannon.

The envelope hadn't come through the mail, for there was no stamp nor postmark on it. Typewritten on it was: *Edmund Holt and Arthur Bancroft*. Below that was typed: *Personal*.

Removing the single folded sheet inside the envelope, Gannon noted that it too was typed. It read:

Dear Vultures:

At last count my little invention had made your company a net profit of a hundred and twenty thousand dollars. How are you going to spend that in Hell? It interests me, because that's where you're going.

The note was unsigned.

Looking up, the private investigator asked. "What makes you so sure this is from Gerald Greene?"

Bancroft said, "He personally brought it in and left it with our receptionist. He didn't give his name, and she'd never seen him before, because she wasn't with us at the time we had dealings with Greene. But her description of the man tallies with Greene's. Besides, the Greene Radiation Counter has made us about a hundred and twenty thousand in the past five years, so obviously that's the invention referred to."

"When was this delivered?"

"Yesterday morning," Bancroft said. "We were both in our offices, but he didn't ask to see us. He just handed the envelope to Alice and asked her to make sure we got it."

Gannon thoughtfully pushed back his forelock, only to have it instantly fall forward again. "This isn't necessarily a threat. Maybe he means you're both going to Hell when you eventually die of natural causes."

Edmund Holt gave his head an emphatic shake. "It isn't the first threat. Two years ago he hired a lawyer to see what he could do about getting more money out of us. It never got to court, but the lawyer called us in for a conference. When we showed him the contract, he advised Greene that he didn't have a leg to stand on. Greene went into a rage. He screamed that he'd kill us both."

Gannon said dubiously, "Then he waited two years to carry out the threat? And decided to warn you of what's coming?"

"He told us he'd warn us," Holt said. "I remember his exact words. He yelled, 'It won't be today or tomorrow. Maybe I'll have to wait years. But I'll kill you vultures if it's the last thing I do. And I'll let you know when it's coming, so you can sweat a while.' This letter is his way of letting us know."

Gannon refolded the note and thrust it back into its envelope. He eyed the man behind the desk curiously. "Why are you so willing to dismiss this, Bancroft? What makes you so sure he isn't dangerous?"

"The man's sixty-seven years old and weighs about a hundred and twenty-five pounds," Bancroft said with contempt.

"That's big enough to squeeze a trigger."

Bancroft made a dismissing gesture. "I think he's senile. I can't take the threat of a doddering old man seriously."

The investigator shrugged. "Have you showed this to the police?"

Both men shook their heads. Holt said, "I thought a private detective would be more discreet. I do take the threat seriously. Will you look into the matter for me, even if Art isn't interested in engaging you?"

Gannon said a trifle gruffly, "Frankly I don't have much sympathy for either of you. It seems obvious that you cheated the old man outrageously. But even sharp dealers have the right of protection against cranks. I'll check up on the man."

Arthur Bancroft frowned at the private detective's blunt words, but Holt merely looked faintly embarrassed.

Gannon said, "Where do I find him?"

"We haven't the faintest idea," Holt said. "He moved from town right after his unsuccessful attempt to shake us down. We didn't know he was back until he brought the note in yesterday."

"What's his last known address?"

"We don't even have that on file. He had moved from the address in the contract at the time we met with his lawyer. Perhaps the lawyer would know. He's a man named Marcus Wade in the Bland Building."

Gannon took a small notebook and a pencil from his pocket. "Description?"

Holt said, "Art's already given you his age and weight. He's about five eleven, thin, slightly stooped and has a full head of white hair. He has blue eyes and wears thick-lensed horn-rimmed glasses."

After jotting the information down, Gannon unfolded his long form from his chair. Casually he stuffed the envelope containing the note into his inside breast pocket. Neither man made any objection.

"I'll give you a ring as soon as I locate him," he told Holt, and walked out.

CHAPTER II

In the outer office the blonde Alice Emory said with a pout, "I bet you got me in trouble."

"I tried," Gannon said. "But Mr. Bancroft seems to like you."

She gave him an unconcerned grin. "He's nice, isn't he? Not like Mr. Holt."

If Holt had his way, she'd be fired, Gannon thought. He wondered if the woman knew she was a source of disagreement between the partners.

Taking out the envelope and showing it to the girl, he said, "I understand this was delivered to you yesterday."

Peering at it, she nodded. "About ten A.M. by an old man."

"What did he say?"

"Nothing much. He just asked me to be sure both partners saw it. I took it in to Mr. Holt."

"How did the old man act? I mean was his manner pleasant, or angry, or what?"

A thoughtful expression grew on her face. "Sort of formal, I'd say. He was very polite."

"How was he dressed?"

She thought for another moment before saying, "Kind of shabbily. He wore an old seersucker suit and his shirt collar was frayed."

Gannon contemplated her for a moment, then remarked, "You're not a very curious woman, Alice."

Her plucked eyebrows went up. "Why do you say that?"

"Don't you wonder why I'm asking all these questions?"

Gannon got the impression that she flushed, though her pancake makeup was too heavy for the flush to show, so he couldn't be sure.

She said primly, "I was waiting for you to finish. If you're finished, I'll ask. What's this all about?"

"Just routine," Gannon said with a grin, and continued on out.

Marcus Wade was a thin, dark man with horn-rimmed glasses. He greeted Gannon with cordial reserve, asked him to have a seat, then placed the tips of his fingers together and stared at the investigator expectantly.

Gannon handed over his license. When the lawyer had examined it and had returned it without comment, Gannon said, "I'm trying to locate an ex-client of yours. A man named Gerald Greene."

When the lawyer looked blank, Gannon added, "An inventor who wanted to sue *Holt and Bancroft Manufacturing* a couple of years back."

"Oh, yes," Wade said, light dawning in his eyes. "We only had a couple of contacts. He didn't have any case at all. I don't believe he's in town any more, but I can give you a two-year-old address, if you think that would help."

Rising, he went to a file cabinet, searched and drew out a manila folder. He read off an address on Franklin Avenue. "I think it's a rooming house," he added.

Gannon scribbled the address in his notebook. Thanking the attorney, he left.

As Marcus Wade had suggested, the Franklin Avenue address was a rooming house. The landlady informed Gannon that Greene had moved eighteen months previously. He had left a forwarding address in Indianapolis.

By then it was lunch time, so Gannon stopped for a bite to eat, then checked into his office on Figueroa Street in downtown Los Angeles. It was only a cubbyhole of a place, but it was clean and well ventilated and the ancient furnishings were in relatively good condition. A cumbersome oak desk took up half the small room. Next to it, so that he could swing around without rising from his desk chair, was a standard typewriter on a stand. Against one wall were three gray file cabinets. The only other furnishings were a client chair in front of the desk and three more lined up against the wall.

Seating himself behind the desk, he called his answering service. There had been no calls. Then he called information. There was no local phone listed under the name Gerald Greene. His next call was station-to-station to the

Indianapolis address given him by Greene's former landlady. A pleasant female voice answered.

"My name is Mathew Gannon," he said. "I'm calling from Los Angeles. I'm trying to locate a Gerald Greene."

"My goodness!" the woman said. "He hasn't lived here for a year."

"Are you a relative?" Gannon asked.

"I'm the landlady. This is a rooming house."

"Do you have his present address?"

"Why, I suppose he's still at the State Hospital."

"The State Hospital?"

"The mental hospital. That's where he went from here. He was committed after the arrest, you know."

"No, I didn't," Gannon said. "What arrest?"

"When he was picked up for molesting all those women."

"I see," Gannon said. "Where is this hospital?"

"Right here in town. Hold on a minute and I'll look up the number for you."

There was a few moments of silence, then the woman reeled off a telephone number. Jotting it down, Gannon thanked her and hung up.

He placed a person-to-person call to the hospital superintendent and got through almost at once.

"Dr. Cordovan," a crisp voice said in his ear.

Gannon explained who he was and that he was trying to locate Gerald Greene.

"I remember the man," the superintendent said. "He was released as cured about two weeks ago. I'd have to know why you want him before we can release any information, however."

"I'm trying to keep him out of trouble," Gannon said. "He's here in Los Angeles and he's threatened a couple of people. I don't know his local address, so I'm checking back. I thought you might have it."

"He's been threatening people?" the doctor said in surprise. "We don't consider him dangerous."

"He has an old grudge against these particular people. Do you have an address?"

"I can look it up. As I recall, he went to live with a relative down your way. The reason I remember him is that he was moving out of state. Released mental patients have to get special permission to leave the state within a year of their release. And there has to be unusual circumstances before we'll permit it. In this case there was no place else for him to go and he had insufficient funds to take care of himself. Hold on while I pull his record."

After a few minutes' wait Dr. Cordovan returned to the phone. "The relative is a niece, the daughter of a deceased sister. Her name is Mrs. Mona Jarvis." He read off an address in the twenty-nine-hundred block of Ashbury Street in Los Angeles.

Gannon scribbled down the address. "Why was he committed, Doctor?"

"Well, the immediate reason was that he was picked up several times for following strange women and making indecent suggestions. But the diagnosis was premature senility. Greene was once a brilliant man, I understand, a sort of self-educated scientist. He once invented some kind of electronic device which he sold for pennies, but was extremely successful commercially. But in recent years he's started to *go* into what you laymen call second childhood. An unnatural preoccupation with sex is a common symptom of senility among men who are not really aged physically. When I say he was released as cured, what I really mean is that we don't consider him dangerous. His interest in sex is all in his head. It's extremely unlikely that he'd attack any woman. But he isn't really cured. You don't cure senility."

"I see," Gannon said. "Thanks a lot, Doctor."

"You're welcome," Cordovan said. "I hope you manage to locate him in time to keep him out of serious trouble."

Hanging up, Gannon left the office, locking the door behind him.

The house on Ashbury Street was a small, neat, one-story home with a white picket fence around it. A dark young woman with a sleeping baby in her arms sat on a porch swing.

Mounting the porch steps, Gannon asked, "You Mrs. Jarvis?"

"That's right," she said with a pleasant smile. Her gaze fixed on his sun-bleached forelock and he self-consciously pushed it back. It didn't stay.

"I'm looking for Gerald Greene," he said. "I understand he's your uncle and stays here."

The smile disappeared. "My husband and I are looking for him too, mister. You a cop?"

"Private." He held his license before her.

She examined it dubiously. "Mathew Gannon, eh? Pleased to meet you, Mr. Gannon. What's Uncle Jerry done? Woman trouble again?"

Gannon said mildly, "I just want to talk to him."

The woman blew a fly from the sleeping baby's forehead. "So would I. He was supposed to come back last night."

"Back from where?"

"He was invited to some fishing lodge over the weekend. An old friend, he said, but he just brushed me off when I asked who. Said I wouldn't know the man. As excited as he was, I half suspected it was really a woman. In Indianapolis a while back he was in trouble for bothering women, you know. I thought maybe he'd finally run into some woman who took him up instead of yelling cop. Then I decided that was silly. What woman would want a sixty-seven-year-old man, even with a roll of money?"

"He had some money?"

"About two hundred dollars. He said he'd collected an old debt. I don't know who it was that paid him."

Gannon thoughtfully pushed back his forelock again, only to have it flop back in place. "When did he leave for this fishing lodge?"

"About noon Saturday. Said he'd be back Monday night, but here it is Tuesday. He packed a weekend bag and took off in a taxi."

"Notice what kind?"

"A Yellow. Is he in some kind of trouble, Mr. Gannon?"

The investigator saw no point in worrying her. He said, "I've been retained to locate him by a company he once sold a patent to," which was the literal truth, insofar as it went.

"Oh." she said in a relieved tone. "Will there be some money involved?"

"I don't think it's likely," Gannon said dryly. "If he shows up, will you phone my office?" He handed her a card.

"Sure. Will you phone me if you catch up with him first?"

"Of course," he said. "Thanks for your time."

He walked back to the gate, pushed through it and climbed into his car. Mona Jarvis shifted the baby in her arms and waved to him as he drove away.

CHAPTER III

Ashbury Street was a considerable distance from Gannon's office. He stopped at the first tavern he saw and phoned his answering service.

The girl on the switchboard at the answering service said, "You had a call not more than thirty seconds ago, Mr. Gannon. A Mr. Edmund Holt wants you to call his office right away. He says it's extremely urgent."

"Thanks," Gannon said. Hanging up, he dropped more money in the phone slot and dialed the *Holt and Bancroft Manufacturing Company.*

Alice Emory answered and put him through to Holt immediately.

"Hello, Holt," Gannon said. "What's up?"

"Can you meet me at my home right away?" Holt said tensely.

"Why?"

"My wife just phoned that a package came in the mail for me. We don't get our mail delivered until one P.M. She's a curious woman, so she started to open it, even though it was addressed to me. She stopped halfway and phoned me. She thinks it's a bomb."

Gannon said sharply, "Did you get her out of the house?"

"Of course. I told her to leave it right where it was—she started to open it on the dining-room table—and get outside. She'll be waiting for us in front."

"What's the address?"

Gannon was glad he hadn't driven back to his office before checking with his answering service, because Holt lived on Fletcher Drive, just off San Fernando Road. The tavern from which he was phoning was on San Fernando Road about three fourths of the distance between his office and Holt's home.

"I'm not more than ten minutes from there," Gannon said. "I'll see if I can make it in five."

He made it in six minutes.

Edmund Holt's home was an expensive, two-story brick building with a spacious lawn around it. A plump, middle-aged woman in a house dress was standing on the sidewalk out front when Gannon pulled up.

Getting out of the car, he said, "Mrs. Holt?"

"Yes," she said nervously. "You must be Mr. Gannon. My husband said he was going to call you."

"He's on his way here too," Gannon said. "But we won't wait for him. Give me the layout of the house and tell me where the package is."

"It's on the dining-room table. Right inside the front door is a small lobby. Go left into the front room. There's an archway from there to the dining room."

"Okay," Gannon said. "I'll take a look. No one is inside, I hope."

She started to shake her head, suddenly looked horrified. "Stanley!"

"Who's Stanley?"

"My cat. My God, we've got to get Stanley out of there!"

She was starting toward the house when Gannon grabbed an elbow. "Take it easy, Mrs. Holt. I'll look for Stanley."

He strode up the walk, up the porch steps, took a deep breath, opened the screen door and went in. He let the screen door close gently behind him.

Cautiously he moved into the front room only far enough to lean forward and peer through the archway into the dining room. His blood curdled at the sight he saw there.

A small, narrow package about ten inches long, two wide and an inch high rested on the very edge of the table. The paper wrapping had been torn from one end of the package to expose two cylinders which looked remarkably like two half sticks of dynamite. A huge black tomcat sat on the table playfully slapping at the package with one paw.

As Gannon stood frozen, the package teetered over the table edge and fell.

Gannon did a back flip into the lobby, landing on his shoulders, making a complete somersault and as lightly as a cat coming to his feet again in the room across the lobby. Tensely he waited.

Nothing happened.

After a few moments he tiptoed across the lobby, leaned forward and peered through the archway again. The package lay on the floor. Crouched a few feet from it, ready to pounce, was the black cat.

"Skat!" Gannon hissed.

The cat came erect, his back arched and his tail shot straight upward. He hissed back.

Gannon took a step toward him. The cat broke for the kitchen and disappeared. Gannon retreated to the lobby again, glanced around and spotted a phone on a small end table. He dialed Madison 5-7911.

When a voice said, "Police department," Gannon said, "Homicide, please."

In Los Angeles the Homicide Division has twenty-one separate functions aside from the investigation of dead bodies. One of them is to investigate explosions. Technically their interest begins only after a bomb has gone off, but Gannon had a friend in Homicide and he was in no mood for splitting hairs. When someone answered the phone at Homicide, he asked for Lieutenant Harry Gloff.

A moment later the lieutenant's gruff voice said, "Gloff speaking."

"This is Matt Gannon, Harry. I've got a possible bomb for you. Better get the bomb squad over here fast."

"Where?" Gloff asked.

Gannon gave him the address. "Make it snappy, Harry. I have to keep it in sight because there's a cat who thinks it's a toy."

"A what?"

"Cat. He just gave me heart failure by pushing it off a table. I scared him into the kitchen, but he may be back."

"You get in the damnedest situations," Gloff growled. "Stand by. I'll have the bomb-disposal squad moving in thirty seconds. You can give me the details later."

Within three minutes there was a radio car at the scene, but it was closer to twenty before the bomb-disposal truck pulled up in front of the house. Meantime Gannon took periodic peeks at the package on the dining-room floor. Once the tomcat appeared in the kitchen doorway, but another hissed "Skat" drove it away again.

Two men were on the bomb-disposal detail. They came in empty-handed, listened silently to Gannon's explanation of the situation, then one moved cautiously into the front room while the other waited in the lobby.

The first man returned and said, "Looks like a spring job. Luckily she opened the end where the detonator wasn't. Two half sticks of dynamite, it looks like. Guess we better put on the suits."

Gannon said, "There's a cat in the kitchen who thinks it's a toy. I'll stay here to keep him away until you're ready."

Both men shrugged. "Be back in a couple of minutes," the one who had gone to look at the bomb said.

When they returned, they looked like men from outer space. Heavy asbestos suits encased them from head to toe and they wore steel helmets which completely covered their heads and necks. Shatterproof glass allowed them to see out. One man carried a pair of scissors, the other a screw driver and a pair of pliers.

"Okay, mister," one said in a muffled voice. "Better get outside."

"Glad to," Gannon said fervently. "Good luck."

Quite a crowd of neighbors had gathered out front by now. A couple of more police cars had arrived, and uniformed men were keeping the sidewalk out front clear by herding everyone to the opposite side of the street. Gannon spotted the plump figure of Edmund Holt standing next to his equally plump wife. Just in case the bomb experts made a mistake, an ambulance was standing by across the street.

As Gannon crossed the street, a burly figured moved from the crowd to meet him at the curb. "What's the story, Matt?" Lieutenant Harry Gloff asked.

"It came in the mail, Harry, addressed to Edmund Holt." He nodded toward the plump man. "That's Holt over there."

Gloff stared at the man for a moment, then turned back to Gannon. "Any idea who sent it?"

"Yes. An old fellow named Gerald Greene has a grudge against Holt and his partner. The *Holt and Bancroft Manufacturing Company*." Taking the threatening note from his pocket, he showed it to the lieutenant.

Gloff frowned when lie finished reading the note. "What's his grudge?"

Briefly Gannon explained the background situation. He had hardly finished when the two men of the bomb-disposal detail re-appeared from the house. Both were carrying their helmets instead of wearing them. One held a piece of wrapping paper, the other the twin cylinders which comprised the bomb.

Going over to their truck, they set the paper and cylinders in the front seat, then went around back and placed their helmets in the rear of the truck. They began to strip off their asbestos suits.

Gloff and Gannon crossed the street to the truck.

The lieutenant showed his I.D, and asked, "What's the story?"

Both men completed folding their asbestos suits and stored them in the rear of the truck before answering. Then one said, "A spring job, Lieutenant. It had a spring-activated firing pin attached to the detonator. The way it was supposed to work, tearing the paper on the detonator end would release the spring, driving the firing pin into the detonator. Only it was a dud."

"A dud?" Gloff repeated.

"The spring wasn't set. It wouldn't have gone off even if she'd opened the right end. Here, I'll show you."

Opening the front door of the truck, he picked up the firing mechanism from the seat, where it lay separate from the twin cylinders. The device was a ten-gauge shotgun cartridge with slim but strong-looking steel springs attached to each side. The ends of the springs were connected to a thin steel plate with a pointed firing pin welded to its under side. At the moment the plate rested flat on the base of the shell, but slightly off center, so that the pin projected down alongside the shell.

Placing a finger over the shell's detonator cap so that it couldn't accidentally be fired, the bomb expert forced the small steel plate upward. A small metal bar no bigger around than the lead of a pencil was hinged to the under side of the plate. When it dropped to a vertical position, its free end resting on the base of the shell, the plate containing the firing pin was suspended above the detonator cap.

"Now it's armed," the bomb-disposal man said. "There was a wire attached to that small metal bar, with its other end taped to the inside of the wrapping. Tearing the paper would jerk the wire, then *Bam!* Except it wasn't cocked. The pin was in this position." Carefully he returned it to the position it had been in when he first showed it.

Gloff said, "Let's see that wrapping paper."

Reaching into the front seat again, the man handed it to him. It was ordinary brown paper which had been sealed with brown tape. An address sticker had Edmund Holt's name and address typed on it, but no return address. There was forty cents worth of canceled stamps and the postmark was local. Stamped in ink above the address label was: FIRST CLASS MAIL.

Gannon said, "He sent it first class so it wouldn't be opened for inspection."

The bomb expert took the paper back from Gloff's hands. "We have to turn this other stuff in to the crime lab, so we may as well save you the trouble and turn this in too."

Gannon suddenly had a thought which brought a startled expression to his face.

"Harry," he said urgently. "Another one of those things may have been delivered to Arthur Bancroft's home. We'd better get on the phone fast."

CHAPTER IV

Now that the bomb danger was over, the police had allowed the crowd of spectators to cross the street. Mr. and Mrs. Holt were standing near the bomb-disposal truck talking with neighbors.

Striding over to them, Gannon said to Holt, "What's your partner's home phone number?"

The man looked surprised. "I don't know offhand. It's on a desk pad inside." Then a startled expression formed on his face. "You don't think—My God! Art went home sick this afternoon. If another of these things came in the mail—"

He broke off abruptly when Gannon took him by the elbow and started dogtrotting him toward the house. The burly form of Harry Gloff lumbered after them.

Inside Edmund Holt hurriedly leafed through a desk pad next to the phone. Locating the number he dialed it.

Standing next to him, Gannon could hear a female voice ask, "What number are you calling, please?"

Holt repeated the number he had dialed.

"Sorry, sir," the operator's voice said. "That number is temporarily out of order."

Slowly Holt dropped the phone back into its cradle. He stared at Gannon white-faced.

"I remember him mentioning once that his mail arrived about two in the afternoon," he said in a hushed voice.

Gannon glanced at his watch. It was just three. "What's his address?" he snapped.

"It's on Riverside Drive, only about a half block north of Fletcher. I'll have to look up the exact number."

"Never mind," Gannon said as Holt reached for the desk pad. "We'll find it."

Slamming open the screen door, he headed for the street at a long-legged run. Harry Gloff tore after him, puffing to keep up. As Gannon jerked open the door of his car, Gloff jerked open the other door and tumbled in.

It was only about a five-minute drive to Arthur Bancroft's home if you observed traffic laws and drove at normal speed. Gannon made it in two minutes flat.

It wasn't hard to pick out his home, because the street in front of it was crammed with so many vehicles, they had to park a quarter block away. When they saw the conglomeration, both men slowly got from the car, knowing there was no longer any need to hurry. Clustered in front of the house was a fire truck, an emergency rescue vehicle, an ambulance and two police radio cars,.

The home was about the size of Edmund Holt's, with a large wooden veranda. The veranda was littered with broken glass from a burst picture window, the front door had been blown from its hinges and lay on the porch, and there was a ragged, window-sized hole in the wall between the door and the picture window.

Police were holding back curious onlookers, but a cluster of people stood on the lawn within the circle. Gannon recognized Arthur Bancroft, a homicide cop named Sergeant Lennox and a police lab technician named Sam Mosby. The others in the group all wore firemen's helmets.

"Wonder how the devil he escaped the blast?" Gannon muttered to Gloff as they worked their way through the crowd.

"Who?" the lieutenant asked.

"Arthur Bancroft. He's standing there all in one piece."

A uniformed policeman, recognizing Gloff, opened an aisle through the bystanders to let him and Gannon through. They joined the group on the lawn.

Sergeant Lennox nodded to Gannon and said to Lieutenant Gloff, "A bombing, Harry. Shortly after two, but we didn't get the call until twenty minutes ago. The husband was in too much of a state of shock to think about the police, I guess. He was still trying to raise the operator on a phone whose box was blown from the wall when we got here. Said he was trying to call a doctor. Some neighbor finally called the fire department, though nothing was on fire. They called us after they got here."

Arthur Bancroft's face was no longer granite-hard. He merely looked sick. In a dull voice he said to Gannon, "I killed her. I should have opened it myself. It was meant for me."

Gloff looked inquiringly at Lennox. "What's he talking about?"

"His wife," Lennox said. "The bomb came in the mail, addressed to him. Only she opened it."

"I told her to," Bancroft said in the same dull voice. "She said, 'A package came for you, dear,' and I said, 'Well, open it and see what it is.' She never would have otherwise. She never opened my mail without permission."

Gloff asked, "How'd you escape the blast?"

"I was outside," Bancroft said shakily. "I came home from the office with a headache. On the way I stopped at a drug store for some aspirin, but I left the bottle in the car. The mailman came just as I walked in the back door. Emma brought in the mail and told me about the package. Just then I remembered the aspirin. I told her to open the package and went back outside to get the bottle. I was in the garage when the thing went off."

Lieutenant Gloff said, "Let's take a look," and headed for the veranda.

Gannon and Lennox followed the lieutenant inside. The front doorway led directly into the front room.

It was a gruesome sight. The body, lying in one corner, was so mutilated, the only indication of sex was a high-heeled pump on one foot. The other pump lay in an opposite corner. The room was a shambles of broken furniture and the walls were spattered with blood.

A few scraps of brown wrapping paper near a shattered end table indicated where the woman had opened the package. A phone was still balanced precariously on the remains of the table, but the phone box had been blown from the wall.

Lennox said, "Sam has already taken pictures. As soon as he collects all the bomb fragments he can find, I'll let them take away the body."

Making a grimace, Gloff turned and walked out again. The others followed.

Harry Gloff said to Sergeant Lennox, "We already know who sent the bomb. We just came from another house that got one, only it was a dud. Put out a pickup on Gerald Greene." He turned to Gannon. "What's that address, Matt?"

Gannon gave Lennox the Ashbury Street address. "He lives with a niece named Mrs. Mona Jarvis. But I don't think you'll find him there. He's been missing since Saturday."

Lennox jotted down the address and asked, "What's the guy look like?"

Gannon gave him the description.

There was nothing further either Gloff or Gannon could accomplish at the scene. After pausing for a moment to drop a word of sympathy to Arthur Bancroft, Gannon drove the lieutenant back to the Holt residence, where his car was parked.

After dropping off Harry Gloff, Gannon drove back downtown to the main office of the Yellow Cab Company on West Third. He asked to speak to whoever was in charge of dispatch records and was referred to a genial gray-haired man named Elmer Hewitt.

After explaining who he was and that he was working with the police on a murder case, Gannon said, "Around noon Saturday one of your cabs picked up a fare in the twenty-nine-hundred block of Ashbury Street." Taking out his notebook, he read off the exact number. "Will you look up the dispatch record on it?"

"Sure," Hewitt said.

Opening a file drawer, the man leafed through dispatch slips for a few moments, finally pulled one out. "One passenger to the Coast line Bus Depot."

Gannon was pleased. The Coastline was a small, independent bus company which ran lines only to communities within about a fifty-mile radius of Los Angeles. There was a much better chance of a ticket seller remembering an individual customer there than there would be at a large station such as Greyhound.

Thanking Elmer Hewitt, Gannon left and drove to the Coastline Bus Depot.

There was only one ticket cage in the tiny depot. A young, brown-haired woman with a cutely turned-up nose was on duty in it. When Gannon showed her his license, she looked him over with interest.

"My," she said. "I've never known a private detective before."

He grinned at her. "I've never known a Coastline ticket seller before."

She emitted a small laugh which just escaped being a giggle. "What can I do for you, Mr. Gannon?"

"Were you on duty at noon last Saturday?"

The girl nodded. "I come on just at noon."

"Do you recall selling a ticket to a man about sixty-seven years old? Five feet eleven, a hundred and twenty-five pounds, thin and slightly stooped. Full head of white hair, blue eyes and thick-lensed glasses."

An indignant expression grew on her face. "Do I! The old lecher asked for my telephone number!"

"That's the one," Gannon said with a wry smile. "Where'd he buy a ticket to?"

She thought for a moment. "Ventura. I'm sure of that because he took the one o'clock bus, and that's the only one that leaves at that time." She smiled a little ruefully, "It's always either old men or young smart alecs who want my telephone number. Never anybody interesting." She gave him an encouraging smile.

"That's life," Gannon said with amused sympathy. "Who's the driver on that run?"

She made a small face at him for ignoring the hint, then shrugged philosophically. "Harold Rourke. This week he's on a different schedule. He should be in a little before four thirty." She glanced at a wall clock, which said five after four. "He might be in the coffee shop right now. A big fellow with red hair."

"Thanks," Gannon said, and headed for the coffee shop.

Only one man in bus driver's uniform was in the shop. He sat at the counter alone with a cup of coffee before him, a big man with red hair and a square Irish face. Gannon slipped onto the stool next to him.

"You Harold Rourke?" he inquired.

The man swung sidewise to examine him. "Uh-huh."

"My name is Matt Gannon. I'm a private detective." He exhibited his license.

"Well, well," the bus driver said with interest. "A private eye. I thought they were only on television. What's on your mind?"

A waitress interrupted to ask what Gannon wanted. He ordered a cup of coffee.

When the girl moved away, Gannon said, "Last Saturday you had an old man on the one P.M. run to Ventura." He repeated the description he had given the ticket girl. "Remember him?"

"I'll say I do," Rourke said grimly. "I had to move the old fool. The woman he sat next to came forward and complained that he kept pressing his knee against hers. I made him come up front where I could watch him. Hope he isn't a friend of yours."

"I've never met him," Gannon said. "But I'm kind of looking forward to it. Did he mention anything about what he planned to do in Ventura?"

The waitress brought Gannon's coffee and the bus driver waited until she moved away again. Then he said, "The only conversation I had with him was when I made him move. But I think he must have been visiting a daughter. The babe who met him at the bus couldn't have been a girl friend. She was too much of a doll to bother with such an old guy unless he was her father."

"What did she look like?" Gannon asked with interest.

"A platinum blonde in her late twenties or early thirties. It was hard to tell her age with all the gook she had on her face. She was a real doll except for that. It made her look like a burlesque queen. As a matter of fact, I figured that's what she probably was. A stripper."

"Well, well," Gannon said softly. "You've really been a help. Can I buy you a second cup of coffee?"

"I have to check in at the office. I drive out in fifteen minutes. Thanks anyway."

"Thank *you,*" Gannon said. "You don't know how much of a help you've been."

CHAPTER V

It was sixty-five miles to Ventura, but it was freeway all the way. Gannon left the Coastline Bus Depot at a quarter after four and, by holding the speedometer needle at ninety all the time he was on the freeway, managed to make the Ventura City Hall at a quarter after five, fifteen minutes before it closed.

In the city clerk's office he asked a female worker if they maintained an alphabetical list of property owners.

"Our records are by plat number," she said. "But the tax roll is alphabetical. Try the tax assessor's office."

A middle-aged female clerk in the tax assessor's office was just getting ready to close up. Giving her his most charming smile, Gannon introduced himself and asked if there was any beach property listed in the name of Alice Emory. She graciously consented to look.

After checking the tax roll, the women shook her head. "Sorry, Mr. Gannon."

The answer was a disappointment. According to Mona Jarvis, her Uncle Gerald had been going to the "fishing lodge" of a friend over the weekend. Since he had subsequently been met at the Ventura bus depot by a woman answering Alice Emory's description, it was logical to assume she had taken him to some kind of beach cottage or cabin. He had been sure some sort of beach property would be listed in her name.

Then he had another idea. "How about either Edmund Holt or Arthur Bancroft?"

She checked again, regretfully shook her head a second time.

"Well, thanks anyway," Gannon said disappointedly, and was turning away when the woman said, "There's something listed under the *Holt and Bancroft Manufacturing Company.*"

Gannon swung back to the counter. "What is it?"

"There's no indication on the tax roll as to what the property consists of, but from the address and assessed valuation, I'd guess it was a beach cottage."

"That's what I want," he said with satisfaction. "It should have occurred to me that it might be company owned. It's an old tax dodge to charge vacation homes as a business expense. What's the address?"

The clerk wrote it on a piece of paper and handed it to him.

"Thanks," Gannon said with a smile. "Sorry I kept you overtime."

"Anytime at all," she said with sincerity. "I enjoyed being able to help."

The cottage was at the far edge of town at a point where the beach was a mixture of shale and gravel instead of sand. Because of the poor frontage it was relatively isolated, few people apparently having cared to locate cottages there. To the right the nearest cottage was a good hundred yards away. In the other direction a stand of palm trees and weed-grown undergrowth hid whatever was beyond.

The cottage was a small, one-story frame building built like a box. It was locked up tight and no one answered to his knock. Peering through a front window, Gannon saw a simply-furnished front room with open doors off it leading to a kitchen and a bedroom. An unmade double bed he could see through the open bedroom door suggested that the place had recently been in use.

Tire marks alongside the cottage were relatively recent, since it had rained the previous Friday. They had to have been made not earlier than Saturday.

Gannon was certain this was the "fishing lodge" to which Gerald Greene had been taken by his "friend." The next question was what had happened to him after he got there?

He circled the cabin, scanning the ground in all directions, but could detect nothing to indicate freshly-disturbed ground. His gaze touched the cement top of a cistern behind the building and he moved over to examine it.

The cistern was topped by an iron manhole cover. Prying it off, Gannon peered downward. Six feet below he caught the smooth reflection of water.

That would be silly, he thought. Even murderers aren't likely to pollute their water supply. And the water in it suggested that the cistern was in use. He let the cover bang back in place.

Circling the building again, he tried its various windows and was gratified to find a bedroom window unlocked. Pushing it up, he climbed inside.

A quick search of the place disclosed nothing of interest. There were no personal papers of any kind; not even a single letter. There was some fishing equipment in one of the closets, including a hefty tackle box. A bottle of reel oil in the latter had leaked all over the lures, and in examining its contents, Gannon got oil on his hands.

There was a small bathroom off the bedroom, and he entered it to wash up. It contained a small shower, he noted, and there was an electric water heater, but it wasn't turned on. He had to content himself with a cold-water wash.

Outside again he made another circuit of the cottage, then gave up. He drove back to Los Angeles.

Periodically, up till ten P.M., he called Alice Emory's phone number, but there was no answer. Eventually he tabled the matter until the next morning.

In the morning he was shaving when an idea occurred to him. Staring at the hot water flowing from the open water spigot, he thought of when he had washed his hands at the cottage bathroom. There had been no sound of an electric pump turning on, even though he had run water for some time. And with a cistern you can't run water through pipes without a pump to build pressure.

City water must have been piped into the area since the cistern was dug, he thought. Which meant the cistern wasn't used any more.

Quickly he finished shaving, dressed and phoned his answering service that he wouldn't be reachable all morning. Then he rolled a pair of swimming trunks in a towel and left the apartment. A block away he stopped at the filling station where he habitually traded and borrowed a heavy tow rope.

A little over an hour later he was again at the cottage owned by the *Holt and Bancroft Manufacturing Company*.

Glancing around to make sure no one was in sight, Gannon re-entered the cottage by the same route he had used the day before. In the bedroom he stripped and donned the swim trunks. Outside again he pried up the manhole cover over the cistern.

Lifting the tow rope from the car trunk, he looked around for something near the cistern to tie it to. When he failed to spot anything, he climbed in the car and backed it close to the cistern. He tied one end of the rope to the rear bumper, dropped the other end down the manhole. Grasping the rope, he lowered himself into the hole.

The water was nearly chin deep. Groping outward with one foot, he immediately located a bulky object which gave slightly to pressure. Submerging, he examined it with his hands. It felt like what he had expected to find: a human body.

The corpse was weighted down by an iron bar across its chest and another across the ankles. When he heaved the bars aside, the body slowly began to rise to the surface.

Getting his head above water, Gannon looped the rope around the corpse's chest, then pulled himself out of the hole. He hauled up the body, untied the rope and returned it to his car trunk. Barely glancing at the corpse, he re-entered the cottage by the bedroom window, took a cold shower, toweled himself down and dressed.

It was the idea of immersion in the same water where a corpse had lain for several days which brought about the shower, not fear of contamination. For there had been no odor of decay in the cistern. Although he didn't have a squeamish stomach, the very thought of the thing made him want to scrub himself thoroughly and instantly.

Outside again he tossed his trunks and towel into the back seat, then went over to examine the body. It was very little bloated, considering that it must have been in the cistern between forty-eight and seventy-two hours. The clear rain water in the cistern seemed to have preserved the body.

There was no doubt that the dead man was Gerald Greene, for the description tallied perfectly except that there were no glasses. Probably they were still at the bottom of the cistern, Gannon thought, but he had no desire to search for them.

Kneeling, he studied the corpse more closely. There was no sign of a wound or of strangulation. Greene had every appearance of having drowned. Gannon wondered if the eventual plan had been to throw the body into the Pacific and, if it was ever found, let the police assume it had either been suicide or an accidental drowning.

Rising, he stared down at the dead man moodily for a few moments more, then climbed in his car and drove away. A quarter mile from the cottage he stopped at a filling station and used the phone to call the Ventura police station.

A nasal voice said, "Police headquarters, Stone speaking."

Gannon said, "My name is Matt Gannon. I'm a private detective from Los Angeles. I just pulled a dead man from a cistern at a beach cottage." Tersely he described the location of the cottage.

"I'll send somebody right over," the desk man said. "Stand by there."

"I can give you everything I know over the phone," Gannon said. "Better take this down. Ready?"

"Go ahead."

"The victim's name is Gerald Greene, age sixty-seven, local address care of Mrs. Mona Jarvis in the twenty-nine hundred block of Ashbury Street, Los Angeles. Mrs. Jarvis is a niece. He's currently wanted for a murder he didn't commit in Los Angeles. I'm heading back there now to clear both murders up. I'll contact you again as soon as I have all the answers. Meantime if you have any questions about Greene, you can check with Lieutenant Harry Gloff at the Los Angeles homicide division."

"Wait a minute," Stone protested "You can't report a dead man, then just walk off."

"I'll be available any time you want me," Gannon said. He reeled off the address and phone number of his Figueroa Street office. "Right now I have more important things to do than stand around repeating what I just told you."

He hung up.

CHAPTER VI

Dropping more coins in the phone slot, Gannon made a long-distance call to Los Angeles police headquarters and asked for Homicide.

When he got Lieutenant Gloff on the phone, he said, "This is Matt Gannon, Harry. I'm phoning from Ventura. I just found Gerald Greene in a cistern at a beach cottage owned by the *Holt and Bancroft Manufacturing Company.*"

After a moment of surprised silence, Gloff said, "Dead?"

"No," Gannon growled. "He was hiding from the police under five feet of water."

"Very funny," the lieutenant growled back. "You didn't say there was water in the cistern. What was it? Suicide?"

"He looks drowned. But a cistern seems an odd place to drown yourself. Besides, he was weighted down and the lid was on the cistern. I don't think he could have managed it without help."

Gloff was silent again, apparently thinking. Presently he said, "You say this was on some property owned by *Holt and Bancroft?*"

"Uh-huh. A beach cottage."

In a slow voice the lieutenant said, "In a way I've been expecting something like this, Matt. Ever since I read the lab report on the second bomb this morning."

"Oh?"

"They managed to rebuild it in the lab. How, when it was practically granulated, I don't know. But they pull some amazing stuff. It was a little different than the one Holt got. It had detonating devices on *both* ends, so it would blow no matter which end of the package was opened."

"That's interesting," Gannon said.

"Yeah. I got to thinking about the bomb Holt received not being armed, and I wondered if maybe it was meant not to *go* off. Maybe it was a red herring."

"I've been thinking that since last night," Gannon told him. "Ever since I learned who Greene went to visit Saturday."

"Who? We talked to Mona Jarvis and she said he was weekending at the fishing lodge of some friend. Only she didn't know what friend."

"Alice Emory met him at the Ventura bus depot."

"Alice Emory?" Gloff repeated in a puzzled tone.

"*Holt and Bancroft's* receptionist. I forgot you haven't met her."

The lieutenant sounded even more puzzled. "You think she rigged this whole thing?"

"I think she helped, Harry. Suppose you meet me at *Holt and Bancroft* in about an hour and a half. I don't suppose Arthur Bancroft showed up at his office today because of his wife's death, but we ought to have both partners there. Can you pick Bancroft up?"

"Sure. But who'd this Emory woman help? Holt?"

"It has to be one of the partners, Harry. Which, I'm not sure. She didn't seem very friendly with Holt, but that may have been a cover-up to conceal their connection. We'll decide when we get her together with both partners."

"All right," Gloff said. "See you in an hour and a half."

As Gannon pulled away from the filling station, he heard a siren in the distance. As it drew nearer, he realized it was coming straight toward him.

Ventura police en route to the cottage, he decided. He turned off on a side street and detoured around the approaching police car.

When he arrived at the *Holt and Bancroft Manufacturing Company* right on schedule, he spotted Harry Gloff's car already parked in front. The lieutenant had just arrived too, for he was getting out one side of the car and Arthur Bancroft was getting out the other side. Crossing the street, Gannon joined the pair.

"Hello, Gannon," Bancroft said with a jerky nod. "The lieutenant hasn't explained what this is all about. Do you know?"

"No more than he does," Gannon said. "You'll hear about it inside."

In the outer office the blonde receptionist was seated behind the low counter. She looked surprised to see Arthur Bancroft and a trifle wary at sight of Gannon. Gloff she examined without recognition.

After introducing her to the lieutenant, Gannon asked, "Mr. Holt in?"

"Yes, sir. I'll ring him."

"Don't bother," Lieutenant Gloff said ponderously. "We'll just go on in. You come along too, miss."

"Me?" she inquired, raising her plucked brows.

"You," Gloff confirmed.

Looking a bit upset, she rose and came from behind the counter. Leading the way over to Edmund Holt's office, she knocked on the door.

"Yes?" Holt's voice inquired.

Opening the door, she said, "Mr. Gannon and a police lieutenant are here with Mr. Bancroft, sir."

"Come in, gentlemen," Holt said, rising from behind his desk.

They all filed into the room, Gannon last. He closed the door behind him. Holt glanced at Alice Emory in mild surprise that she was remaining.

"The lieutenant said he wanted me here too," the blonde said in a steady voice.

Shrugging, Holt resumed his seat and waved the others to chairs. Alice and Bancroft took seats, but Gannon and Gloff remained standing.

Gloff said, "I've called you all together to discuss a murder. Or, rather, a couple of murders. We've just discovered the body of Gerald Greene."

The blonde receptionist emitted a little gasp. Arthur Bancroft's stony face registered surprise. Edmund Holt looked startled.

Gloff said, "Matt, tell them where you found Greene's body."

Gannon looked the group over. In a quiet voice he said, "In a cistern behind a cottage up in Ventura. The cottage is listed on the tax roll as belonging to this company."

Both partners stared at Gannon. "Our company cottage?" Holt said in a high voice.

Bancroft asked, "How the devil did he get there?"

"He was lured there," Gannon said. "He thought he was going to spend an exciting weekend with a woman."

"What woman?" Holt demanded.

"Your receptionist, Alice Emory."

The partners turned their gazes on the blonde, who suddenly looked as though she were going to faint.

Gannon said, "It wasn't Monday morning that Gerald Greene showed up at this office. It couldn't have been, because he was dead by then. He came here days earlier. As a guess, I'd say about last Friday."

Edmund Holt asked puzzledly, "What are you talking about?"

"Greene didn't bring in that threatening note," Gannon explained. "He came in to make one more stab at getting some money for his invention. Alice let him in to see one of you partners. Which one, we'll get to in a minute."

"I certainly didn't see him," Holt said.

"Nor I," Bancroft chimed right behind him.

"One of you did," Gannon assured them. "And you were surprised to see the change in him since his last appearance a couple of years back. He had become a senile old man. He didn't do any threatening. He was just after a handout. I doubt that you would have given it to him, except that something happened."

"What?" Holt wanted to know.

"I suspect you saw him make some kind of pass at Alice, and this gave you an idea. You called Alice aside and instructed her to play up to the old man and invite him to spend a weekend at her 'fishing lodge.' Then, in order to put him in a holiday mood, you gave him a couple of hundred bucks. I'm not certain of the order of events, but something like that must have happened. I imagine that after his session with you he lingered in the outer office to ogle Alice, and that's when she made her pitch. He was a pushover, of course. It was all in his head, but he was willing to chase anything in skirts at any time of the day or night."

Alice said faintly, "It isn't true. I didn't—"

"You met him at the Ventura bus depot on Saturday afternoon," Gannon interrupted harshly. "We've established that by a witness. You took him to the beach cottage. There you either murdered him yourself, or helped."

"No," she said in a whisper. "I just delivered him and left. I didn't know—"

Abruptly she halted and stared at Gannon, appalled at her admission.

Gannon said, "The threatening note was probably typed right here in this office. The police will be able to establish that. Alice was instructed to say the old man delivered it personally. That set the scene. Over the weekend, while the shop was closed, the bombs must have been constructed here. There are tools enough in the place to build an arsenal. Monday evening they were dropped in the mail in order to assure delivery Tuesday."

Gannon paused and Gloff cleared his throat to get attention. "All right," he said. "Which one of you did it?"

"I certainly didn't," Arthur Bancroft said indignantly. "Why would I send a bomb to myself?"

"Why would I either?" his plump partner echoed.

The lieutenant gave the latter a wolfish smile. "As a red herring, Mr. Holt. Yours was a dud."

Holt's mouth dropped open. Bancroft scowled at him.

Gannon slowly shook his head. "You're assuming that the bomb mailed to Bancroft accidentally killed the wrong person, Harry. My guess is that it was meant for Mrs. Bancroft. Holt's bomb was a dud simply because Bancroft had no reason to kill his partner, but it would have looked suspicious for only one partner to receive a bomb."

Everyone looked at him.

"Bancroft arranged it beautifully to look like an accident," Gannon went on. "He came home with a headache, stopping en route for aspirin and timing his arrival home just as the mailman got there. Probably he parked up the street until he saw the mailman coming. He deliberately left the aspirin in the car, so he'd have an excuse to be out of the house when the bomb blew. He had to be home when it arrived in order to instruct his wife to open the package. Because, as he himself told us, she never touched his mail without permission."

Gannon looked at Alice Emory. "You may as well point your finger, Alice. You're hooked as an accessory no matter which is guilty. Am I right?"

The woman started to cry. Between muffled sobs she whispered, "I didn't know he was going to kill the old man. I thought I was just going to be his wife. He promised to marry me if I'd help him."

Edmund Holt stared at his partner in horror. Arthur Bancroft sat perfectly still, his stony face expressionless. But his eyes refused to look back at his partner.

After the cuffs were on, Harry Gloff said to Gannon, "How'd you figure it was Bancroft, Matt? I was guessing that Holt wanted to get rid of his partner."

"Simple," Gannon said with a grin. "Holt engaged me to investigate the threat. Bancroft wanted to ignore it. I didn't think a killer would be simple-minded enough to hire me to catch him."

Vegas...and Run
Don Lowry

June 1963

"Good morning, Mr. Jarvis, Mr. Morton and a Happy New Year to you—Mrs. Jarvis, Mrs. Morton. You both look so charming. How did you leave Hollywood?"

"It seems, from the crowd here in the lobby tonight, that all Hollywood's here, Drake," I replied to the Thunderbird's assistant manager, as I nodded casually to unknown faces in the gala New Year's Eve crowd, "and a good New Year to you—not, however, I hope, at our expense."

The swank Las Vegas strip hotel's greeter quipped and bantered suavely with us as he smoothly expedited our registering for two adjoining suites and gave us the important guest treatment—springing from a post-reservation credit rating investigation of the genuine E. M. Jarvis and R. C. Morton, two movieland executives whom we were impersonating. Our own *pre*-reservation investigation had checked out the two Hollywood executives just as thoroughly and we knew not only their triple A Dun and Bradstreet rating but also that the two men and their wives were aboard the Jarvis yacht on a South Pacific cruise that New Year's Eve.

From the V.I.P. reception I had a feeling we were "in" and that we had made no slip-up so far.

But unlike other holidaying couples, we switched roles the minute the bellhops left the suites.

"Grace and Jean—take your bags into the other suite and get dressed. Larry and I have work to do before we start out," I told the girls who were posing as our "wives". This wasn't a New Year's Eve party for us. Instead it was strictly business—a hundred thousand dollar's worth. The girls were Hollywood extras, hired with a story that we were gamblers who needed them for a front in a professional, but legitimate, gambling raid on the strip casinos. They had the appearance and the mink to play the roles and the role-playing was all we asked of them. Paid cash-on-the-line in advance, they agreed to come along for the act with an understanding that they could walk out the minute there was any "funny stuff". We were out to take the casino operators in a counterfeiting switch—not to seduce a couple of middle-aged actresses.

"OK, Larry, let's get with it—we have ten hours to take ten casinos for ten G's apiece."

"And so far it looks good, Billy—like the script says," smiled Larry.

I laughed when I looked up at him from my own dressing.

"What's funny, jokester?"

"You look like a prosperous businessman in that dinner jacket. The boys back in Leavenworth wouldn't recognize you."

"Drop the stir talk, Bill, those two broads have ears and they can get curious."

"You got a point," I admitted as I unlocked the attaché case with the queer traveler's checks. "Here they are for the first stop."

I locked the case back up again and carefully locked it back inside a Gladstone bag. It still held ninety thousand dollars in counterfeited traveler's checks and we didn't want a snooping maid or house dick admiring our offset work.

"It's been a long road, Larry," I said to my former cell mate, "and if we don't run into a rumble tonight it will be a plush one from now on."

"As I said like the script—and there'll be no rumble. Be careful what you say in front of those two broads. We need them for a front but we don't want them blowing the whistle on us. All set? We stop for champagne before we go into our act—like the rest of the crowd here tonight, we're on a holiday."

"I'll get the broads."

Jean and Grace, looked the part and the real Mr. Jarvis and Mr. Morton would have been proud of them in their roles of wives for the night. For a moment I contemplated what they had termed "funny stuff" if we had time and the thought of blowing this caper for a romp on the bedsheets shocked me back to reality. I knocked on the girls' door.

"Ready, Jean—Grace?"

"And waiting," quipped my "wife," Jean.

"Just a minute, Bill, I want to get the girls straight once more on their act."

Larry had felt from the beginning the one weak part of our entire plan was the wife act and he wanted to be sure.

"I'll run it down to you girls again so you'll know your script before the action starts."

I lit cigarettes for the girls as Larry made like a set director.

"First, as we explained in LA., we're professional gamblers and we can only get the action we want if the operators here remain in the dark on that point. We're posing as Hollywood businessmen and you're playing the role of our wives. No tricks; no gimmicks; and nothing illegal—so there's no chance of trouble for you. I'm E.M. 'Ernie' Jarvis and Bill's R.C. 'Bob' Morton. Grace, you're Mrs. Jarvis and Jean, you're Mrs. Morton. Play it that way for the rest of the evening. All you have to do is act like impatient wives of well-heeled businessmen who want to gamble while you want to party it up for the holiday and get on to see the sights at another hotel. But the only time you 'want to get on to another hotel' is when we give you the signal—with the handkerchief wiping the forehead. Keep to the script and there's a G note bonus for both of you. Any questions?"

"Nope. Just an observation."

"What's that, Grace?"

"You look good enough to be a husband, darling."

"Thanks baby," quipped Larry, "but this is strictly business tonight. We'll party some other time."

"I've got it straight," was Jean's uncommunicative reply.

"We'll join the partying crowd in the lounge. Like champagne, Jean?" I asked my "wife".

"Love it, Mr. Morton."

The girls were naturals for their parts, fitting into the game as if they'd been in on its planning back in the penitentiary cell at Leavenworth.

"Nice to have you with us, Mr. Morton. Good evening, Mr. Jarvis—Mrs. Morton, Mrs. Jarvis. Happy New Year," was the head waiter's welcome. How the genial and very professional Swiss came up with the names was beyond conception and as he led us to a reserved table I marveled at the smooth operation of the hotel on a crowded New Year's Eve. I hoped the security system of its cashier's department was less efficient in its operation.

While Larry and the "wives" made like typical holidaying guests, I sipped the imported champagne and let my mind wander back to the eight-man cell in the federal bigtop where tonight's caper had originated.

Both Larry and I had been well versed in the counterfeit racket. We'd served three bits for making queer and each time were scooped by Treasury agents who traced us through pushers who bought queer from us and did the canary act to cut their own time when they were knocked off. We'd never worked together before but a Los Angeles fence brought us together in Leavenworth. George Zakaras was one of the more careful L.A. fences and I'd been surprised to find him inside the walls in the federal bigtop.

"Billy Mortel! I heard you were back," was his greeting when I ran into him on the big yard after getting out of quarantine.

"Hi, George. How'd Uncle Whiskers get you east of the Rockies?"

"They said I shipped some hot furs across the state line, Billy."

"You appealing?"

"Yeah, I got 'em in Circuit Court now but I'll probably spring before I get a hearing. I'm only doing a nickel."

"Hope you make it, George," was the only reply I could think of to avoid the usual jailhouse attorney's prolonged dissertation on the possibilities of freedom via pseudo-legal technicalities. Next to the slamming of cell doors there's nothing more painful to the ears of a yardbird than the moans and wails of a jailhouse writ writer.

"I got a guy I want you to meet, Billy. You know Larry Jennings?"

"I think so, George or I've heard of him—pretty good with the queer, I'm told. Is it the same guy?"

"Yeah, that's Larry. And he's good people."

It was less than a month before Larry and I were in the same cell with George Zakaras. The eight-man cell in A Cellhouse held the best-behaved convicts in the building—we were too busy laying plans for the future to break any jailhouse laws. The other five, hand-picked over the years by George, were, like Larry, "good people". Bobo Martelli and Ben Sill were two west coast bank robbers who spent their time debating how to overcome past errors that FBI agents had been quick to discover. Jose Garcia and Chico Estevan were laughing off twenty-year sentences for transporting heroin. Ed Sims, a Frisco bartender who had mixed his drinks with girls, had fallen under the Mann Act, was finishing up his nickel, still trying to live down the quaint nickname, "Pimp". Even the deputy warden once observed, "How did that crew ever get together in the same cell?"

Long after lights-out, Larry and I had whispered plans for this swindle—for more than nine years. Before prison gates closed behind us we knew every move and the risks involved. Larry came up with the idea:

"I think I've got the answer, Billy."

"You and the warden."

"No. I'm serious. This one will work."

"OK, brain, spell it out," I whispered, leaning closer to Larry's bunk. It was midnight and talking in cells was a 'shot' if the screw made you on his rounds.

"We always fall when a pusher spills his guts. Let's do away with pushers. Make a bundle and push it ourselves in one big cleanup."

"You're dreaming, Larry. Go to sleep. You know how long you last trying to push queer. The first time a bill turns up, Uncle Whiskers turns on enough heat to give every pusher and counterfeiter in the country a sunburn at night without a star or moon in the sky."

"Listen to me, Bill. This is different. By the time there's any heat, we're long gone."

"I'm listening."

"I get out before you do. I'll get the shipment and paper together in the east and ship it to the Midwest. I'll buy it a piece here and a piece there and keep down any heat from suspicious suppliers who play ball with the Treasury people. When you get out we'll run off enough to lay at one shot and get out."

"You make it sound easy, Larry. Spell it out."

"Hundred dollar traveler's checks. Each one numbered consecutively, bound in the same folder like the real ones."

"Oh, hell, Larry, you're flipping your lid. That's the worst kind of heat. You show your face every time you cash one of them and anyway, how are you going to number them in sequence?"

"There won't be any heat and I've got the numbering problem solved. We don't cash them one at a time. We lay them by the book at the one place where books full are cashed at a time without the bat of an eyelash—at Las Vegas on a New Year's Eve. There won't be any heat until January 2nd and by that time we'll be gone. And we don't cash them. We buy hundred dollar chips. Want to hear more?"

I was wide awake by this time.

"Keep talking."

"We make our plates to cover a series of checks with a different number on each one. We each lay 5 G's in checks at one casino. From ten different spots on the strip or in town we walk away with a total of a hundred G's. We can use the same plates for each on the sequence of numbers in each book and they get so much traffic in those joints on New Year's Eve that they haven't time to be phoning around town checking with other casino cashiers."

From that night on, Larry and I spent nine years whispering through the nights, planning and plotting. We didn't hurry when we got out of Leavenworth and we waited a year before we contacted each other. We were known counterfeiters with long records and we knew the Treasury agents would put us to bed and get us up until such time as they felt satisfied we were out of the racket. I worked in a machine shop in L.A. and Larry worked for a printer in St. Louis, carefully making reports to federal parole officers each month to eat up our Conditional Release time. We talked to each other on long distance each weekend and carried on the plotting.

"You got some broads lined up out there, Billy?"

"All set and ready to go. And I've picked two Hollywood businessmen who never go to Vegas and who spend every holiday on their yachts. How're the plates coming, Larry?"

"They're finished, Billy. I'm going to run the stuff this weekend."

In the worst way I wanted to fly to St. Louis and look at the results but Larry wouldn't hear of it.

"Hell, no. You'll see them when we're ready. They'll be letter perfect. You look after the set-up in L.A. and Vegas. I'm trusting you for that. You leave this end to me. I'll be out there just before Christmas. OK, Bill?"

"OK, Larry. Here's a pay phone number where you can get me next Saturday at three in the afternoon."

I gave him another pay telephone number. We were taking no chances and used different booths in different areas of each city every time we talked.

I passed up dozens of broads before I picked Jean and Grace to make like our wives for the Vegas weekend. Some were too young; others didn't look the part of prosperous businessmen's wives or didn't have the clothes; and others wanted to know too much. I hung around Hollywood bistros until bartenders thought I was a regular. If the Treasury people were on my tail they must have figured I'd turned lush. Larry came into town Christmas Eve.

"Merry Christmas, Bill," was his nonchalant greeting at the Pasadena bus stop. He hadn't even wanted me to meet him there, claiming a one-in-a-hundred chance of recognition by the law could blow the whole thing wide open. He didn't even bring the checks with him but had mailed them on addressed to a post office box I'd rented. We picked them up and drove out to a Laguna motel where we planned to spend the holiday with a couple chicks I'd passed up for the Vegas wife act but found ideal for the real thing on a lost weekend.

"Close those drapes and let's have a look at the stuff, Larry. I can't wait."

With the pride of a craftsman—legal or illegal—Larry unwrapped the Christmas-wrapped package and handed me a book without a comment. He knew his counterfeiting product would speak for itself. After a long and careful examination, I let out a long, quiet whistle:

"They're perfect, kid!"

And they were, from the black binding of the folders to the sequence of numbers in each book. I couldn't find a flaw.

"Careful and don't mix them up, Bill. They're in sets—one set for each book but duplicated for each casino. Pack 'em back up. When we unwrap them again it will be at Vegas—ready for action."

We partied over the weekend and holiday at Laguna and concentrated on the broads and booze, setting aside the tension, planning and plotting of a decade which was to culminate in a week's time.

The week between Christmas and New Year's was a busy one—all work and no more partying. Trips to tailors for final fittings; shopping for the type of haberdashery and jewelry that would be worn by the Hollywood executives in whose names I had made reservations in Vegas; intercepting the confirmation of reservations which I knew would be mailed to the two bigshots; checking to make sure the two men and their wives were aboard their yachts and beyond reach of telephoned checking by careful Las Vegas hotelmen; and a couple dates with Grace and Jean to clue Larry up with them and keep them sold on the idea that we were a couple of professional gamblers interested in a gambling raid rather than a counterfeiting swindle on the Vegas strip. The week flew by.

"Come off Cloud 9, Bob, before the bubbly water takes your mind off the dice," laughed Larry through the sophisticated banter of the holiday crowds in the lounge. From then on, for the rest of the night, we were Bob Morton and Ed Jarvis.

"Watch for my signal, Jean, and make with the 'come on, honey, let's go some place else,' when you see it. You with me?"

"I'm with you, dear, and good luck."

Little did she know the kind of luck we needed. We sauntered casually towards the cashier's cage. In our first move, we were blessed with luck. Drake, the assistant manager, was talking with some guests in front of one of the cages.

"Enjoying yourselves, Mr. Jarvis—Mr. Morton?"

His recognition registered with the alert cashier and paved our way.

"It's impossible to do otherwise, Drake. Your staff is on its collective toes. Good organization."

He beamed with the compliment.

"Can I help you?"

"We'll depend on Lady Luck for that, Drake. You might introduce us to your cashier," I suggested as I produced my folders of traveler's checks.

"Certainly, certainly—Johnson, will you look after Mr. Jarvis and Mr. Morton?"

His request was a combined order and an expression of "the sky's the limit" approval.

"What'll you have, gentlemen?"

"Hundred dollar chips, please," as I began to sign check after check.

I didn't even tear them out of the folders but pushed them through the wicket to the cashier as quickly as I completed the signatures. Without taking his eyes off the checks, Johnson unhesitatingly tore them from the folders; riffled through the stack to tally it up and pushed me out fifty hundred dollar chips.

"Good luck, sir," he smiled in a business-like manner as he went through the same performance with "Mr. Jarvis."

Larry and I worked our way through the crowd towards a dice table and waited our turn to get into the action. Jean and Grace, at Larry's signal, came over and watched us win and lose a few chips—I actually made a few passes and picked up a couple thousand dollars while Larry blew a little. I wiped my forehead with my handkerchief.

"You boys can't have all the fun," laughed Jean, "come on, Bob, let's see some of the sights."

Grace chorused in and hung on Larry's arm like a loving and possessive wife, "Let's see some of the excitement, dear."

Larry and I reacted like typical husbands and went along with the "wives".

Back in the lounge our same table waited for us and the same waiter welcomed us back with the respect due guests whose credit cards demanded it. While he was repeating our order for champagne, we sent the girls to cash in the chips—at a different cashier's cage. They fitted in like veterans.

"This is a new mink for me," laughed Grace.

"I'll leave by the side door," quipped Jean.

Back in our suites, we made ready for another raid on another casino.

"Go powder your noses, girls, Bill and I have more preparations to make for more action at the tables," Larry instructed Jean and Grace. "We'll pick you up in a few minutes."

"Now the real test comes, Bill. We're walking into every joint on the strip cold turkey, with no friendly assistant manager to back our play. At these other places, we're only well dressed strangers. All we've got is our appearance, the broads and the traveler's checks. These other spots haven't checked out our credit and if they shy away from the traveler's checks we fall back on our credit cards to sell them on doing business."

"And no local references, Larry. We don't refer anybody to the Thunderbird. If Drake finds out we're laying this paper up and down the strip he'll start comparing notes—and those notes will be the numbers on queer checks. All set?"

"No. Wait 'til I get these bills in my money belt. If we get a rumble, there'll be no time to double back here and the five G's will be getaway dough."

"Before the night's over, there won't be room in that belt for the roll you'll have. I'm going to let Jean carry mine as it piles up. She has a purse big enough to pack a cash register in."

"Never trust a broad, Bill."

"I'm trusting my eyes, Larry, and I'm not letting her out of my sight. Might be a good idea to keep your eye on Grace too. As the night goes on they may get ideas. Make sure they don't get in any conversations with housemen or any strangers. And no phone calls."

The four of us strolled down the strip among gay New Year's Eve crowds, heading for the Sands, our next stop. A crowded lobby and packed casino helped our, act. We were just four more, among a milling mob of mink stoles and white shirt fronts and the hectic action at dice tables kept housemen, special deputies and cashiers from their usual observation.

We left the girls at the bar and elbowed our way to cashier's cages. The action was so heavy we had to wait in line. I took one line; Larry the next one, and we carried on a casual conversation to dispel suspicion of special duties and housemen standing around.

"Hundred dollar chips, please. Traveler's checks OK?"

"Yes sir." and the cashier pushed a ballpoint under the wicket. I used my own gold-plated pen and let him take it in, with the *R. C. Morton* signature along its barrel. Cuff links and Omega filled in the picture. He didn't ask for credentials and tore the checks from their folders with only a flashing glance at their numbering sequence. He didn't even look up from under his green eye shade to wish me luck as I thanked him and looked for Larry.

"Any trouble?" he asked with his eyes.

"Let's see how our New Year's luck is, Ed." was my reassuring reply.

We didn't even wait to get our hands on the dice at this spot. After a few side bets against the house, we exchanged looks which said the heavy, action-hungry crowds were cover enough to get out without prolonging the act. We walked to the bar to pick up Jean and Grace.

"Still lucky, boys?"

My reply to Jean was in the form of instructions to cash in the chips. They hadn't even seen us at the tables and I realized they had been out of our sight. Watching them was an impossibility. The girls cashed in the chips and we moved out with the crowds.

"Let's go back to the Thunderbird for a few minutes. Something I want to check on," suggested Larry.

Back in the suite we ditched the girls again and talked over the new problem. So far there was no need to hurry or panic.

"You see it like I do, Bill?"

"The broads—the crowds?"

"Yeah."

Larry was right. We couldn't keep track of them in the thick, elbow-together New Year's Eve crowds in the casinos. And we couldn't let them out of sight.

"Can't take them to cashier's cages with us. At two more stops they'll know we're pushing paper. If they have larceny in their hearts, they'll want in. If not, they'll scare and blow the whistle."

Larry summed the problem up in these words and left it hanging in the air for my solution.

"Alright, we'll watch them. We go to the cages one at a time and one of us will stay with the girls. It slows the action but it's safe that way. Buy the idea?"

"It's the only way, Bill. Get the girls and meet me at the entrance. I'll pick up a U-Drive. And bring the rest of those checks. We don't get back here again 'til we're done."

At the Dunes we ran into the first stumbling block of the night—a cashier who backed away from the checks when he found out the amount involved. I went through with the play.

"You'll have to see the manager, sir. I can't even handle traveler's checks for that amount unless your credit is established here."

As I turned from the cage, a houseman approached me.

"Can I help you, sir?"

I knew a signal of some kind had been exchanged. It could be a polite pinch or a courtesy. I had to gamble simply because it was impossible to bolt.

"Yes, you might direct me to the manager's office. I want to cash some traveler's checks."

He took me instead to an assistant manager's office, where he introduced me to either a credit manager or an assistant manager in charge of the casino.

"What can we do for you, Mr. Morton?"

"Sell me some chips so I can try my luck at your tables. Your cashier's policy doesn't include my traveler's checks," I replied as I brought out my folders and credit card container.

He examined the latter and was impressed.

"If you'll fill out this card, Mr. Morton, you won't have any problem the next time you visit us."

He handed me an application for credit at the Dunes which I happily filled out, wondering if the real Mr. Morton would appreciate the addition to his long list of credit cards if he ever received this one in his office mail.

"Go ahead and sign your checks, Mr. Morton and I'll take you back to the cashier. I'm sure you understand this sort of policy. Hope we haven't inconvenienced you."

"Not at all," I smiled as I looked up at him from my signing bee.

I thought I might as well pave the way for Larry and save him the momentary scare at the cage.

"If you have the time, Mr. Thorpe, I'd like you to meet the wife and another couple with me. Do you know Ed Jarvis, president of Acme Productions? He and his wife are with us."

"No, I don't, Mr. Morton. But it will be a pleasure to meet them and Mrs. Morton."

I almost broke out laughing when I saw the look of alarm in Larry's eyes as we approached him and the girls at the bar.

"Jean, this is Mr. Thorpe, the assistant manager here. Mr. Thorpe—Ed Jarvis—and Mrs. Jarvis."

"It's always a pleasure to meet new friends from Hollywood," said Thorpe as he shook hands with Larry.

"Join us," Larry invited the assistant manager who by now was completely sold on our authenticity.

"Thanks, I must get back to the office. This, as you can see, is a busy night. Nice to have met you and a Happy New Year to you."

Before he could turn away, I set the stage for Larry, "Better go with Mr. Thorpe, Ed." and, turning to Thorpe. "Ed will need your assistance as I did. Think you can help him?"

"It will be a pleasure. Traveler's checks, Mr. Jarvis?"

Larry moved right along with the pitch and joined Thorpe, "I suppose, if we're to try our luck at your tables, I should trade some of them for chips. Be back in a minute, Grace."

I noted the girls were too busy with their own drinks and taking in the sights of the bar to grasp our conversation and, with an arm around each of them I joined them at the bar.

"Night, Mr. Thorpe, and a Happy New Year to you! We'll wait here for you, Ed."

He exchanged greetings again with me and the girls as he walked away with Larry. So far, it really was a *Happy* New Year's Eve.

"Go ahead, Eddie. I'll stay here with the girls. Try your luck."

Larry walked towards one of the dice tables and I watched to see if a houseman or special deputy was tailing him. It was impossible, in the holiday crowd of the casino, to determine who was watching who so I gave him ten or fifteen minutes and sent Grace after him. They came back laughing. I looked at him with a questioning look.

"What gives?"

"I couldn't lose—made—five straight passes!"

I took my turn and dropped a G note's worth of chips. Back at the bar once more, we sent the girls to cashing the chips, keeping an eye on them this time. We eased out through the crowd and strolled to the parking lot as if we were actually on a holiday.

With only minor variations it was the same performance until we hit the Inn. Grace and Jean were showing the effects of floating up and down the strip on champagne and were on the verge of becoming a hazard rather than a help in the act. I drew Larry aside.

"We better get some food into those broads—they're looped and carrying forty-five G's of our dough in those purses. What do you think, Larry?"

"Wanna knock it off and miss this one?"

From the tone of Larry's voice, I realized he too was feeling the effects of liquid refreshments.

"No. We eat and get back to work. This is the last stop. OK?"

"Let's go."

On the way in to the dining room, where we had to wait in line, we met—of all people we didn't want to meet—Drake from the Thunderbird.

"Travelling around, folks?"

"Hello, Drake," I smiled. "Yes, the girls want to do it up right. See you are too." He had a carrot-topped chick on his arm that would have been an asset to any floor show on the strip.

"It's a New Year's morning custom here, Mr. Morton. We make the rounds of the competition. I see Thorpe over there from the Dunes. I'll bring him over. Do you know him?"

Larry took over fast. Obviously he wasn't feeling his booze as much as I had thought he was. He knew, as I did, if Drake and Thorpe got together with us there'd be trouble of the kind we couldn't stand.

"Yes, we met him. But say, Drake, if the others will excuse us for a minute, can I speak to you. Something important."

"Of course, Mr. Jarvis," replied the always polite and ready-to-serve assistant manager from the Thunderbird. "Excuse me for a minute, Bette," he smiled to the red head, "you're in good hands."

Larry had him by the arm, friendly-like, but I knew it wasn't a friendly move. I noted that Thorpe had gone into the restaurant through the reserved entrance and kept up a conversation with the three girls. I didn't know what Larry had in mind but hoped, whatever it was, it would be quiet. I saw him and Drake walk out the front door. At least he was making progress. We were just about to reach the head of the line into the restaurant when he came back.

"A change in plans, girls. We'll have to go back to the Thunderbird," Larry explained. "Drake asked me to give you a lift back, Bette. Said something urgent came up that he had to look after."

"The bum," was the only comment offered by the red head.

A few beads of sweat on Larry's temples and a chalkiness in his complexion told me that both he and Drake had run into "something urgent". I couldn't ask questions in front of the girls and hurried the pace to the U-Drive.

We left Bette at a table in the lounge at the Thunderbird with a promise to join her and Drake in a few minutes. Back in the suite, Larry became all action.

"Get your bags, girls. No time to change. We'll pick you up right away—we're pulling out." Larry closed the door between the suites.

"What happened?"

"Pack up while I get a bellhop. We have to get out of here—fast."

"I asked what happened, Larry," while I began throwing clothes into a bag. Larry whirled to the other suite door and called at Grace and Jean.

"Heh, girls, bring that dough in here."

Whatever had happened, Larry had his wits about him. I'd forgotten the money in the girls' purses. They dumped it on the bed and I could detect a sobered and frightened look on their faces as they saw the pile of hundred and five hundred dollar notes piled on the bed. They too were wondering what had happened back at the Inn.

"Here you are, kids, a G note bonus for each of you. We're as good as our word."

"But, wha . . ."

Before Grace could phrase her question, Larry cut her off.

"Get packed—the bellhop'll be here right away." and he shut the door behind them. I was sorting out the bills.

"Throw the dough in a bag, Bill."

"Clue me up, Larry. What happened back there with Drake?"

"What the hell do you think happened? I dumped him on the parking lot and pushed him under a car. Now will you make with the rush?"

I scooped the bills into a bag and finished packing, asking questions all the time.

"Do we still make it from McCarron Field?"

"No, Bill, we can't take a chance. If that car moves and they find Drake's body, the airport will be sewed tight. The plane doesn't leave for another hour and by that time there'll be more heat on the strip than on a hot stove lid."

"How do we get out? That red head will blow the whistle on us as soon as she hears something has happened to Drake."

"We drive."

"Larry, we'd never make the California line. It's a one road route to Barstow and they'll block it off. Come up with a better answer than that trip across the desert."

"Alright, Billy, I'll come up with one, but it's a helluva long shot and it means some fast moving for me and some fast acting for you."

Larry picked up a bottle of Ballentine's and took a long drink from the bottle. He had dropped his suave swindle act.

"Can you keep those three broads quiet for a half-hour or longer? Entertain them and stall until I can go over to the Inn and get that goddam body out of sight?"

He took another long swig as if he was fortifying himself for the body-moving job.

"Do I have an alternative? If you got the guts to go back to the Inn, I'll keep these three broads entertained if I have to provide them with a barrel of champagne. Can you do it?"

"If I'm not back in half-an-hour, you'll know I couldn't. Keep those broads in line," Larry hurled the words at me as he pulled the door open and left.

"Jean—Grace—more last minute changes. Larry's gone back for a private game and wants us to wait for him and Drake in the lounge."

Jean wasn't buying it.

"Look, Bill, I'm getting scared. You sure this is just a gambling trip?"

"Like I said, baby—and no funny stuff," was the best reassurance I could come up with off the cuff.

Grace wasn't the worrying type.

"Who cares, Jeannie. We got paid Let's get with the bubbly stuff. Makes a good breakfast."

"Come on girls, Bette will be waiting in the lounge."

But when we got to the lounge, the red head wasn't there and I began to get jittery. But when I thought of the jittery job Larry was carrying out, I calmed down. A new waiter was at our table and I asked him if the "young lady had left a message."

"I just came on duty, sir. I'll ask the head waiter. May I take your order first?"

"We want some champagne. For six. We're waiting for the rest of our party. But I would appreciate it if you'd ask the head waiter about the young lady who was here."

The head waiter himself came over in answer to some signal I couldn't detect from our waiter. He too was new with the shift.

"May I help you, sir?"

"Yes, a young lady was waiting for us here, and I wondered if she left a message."

"I'll check with the captain—he may have her message at his desk."

The never-go-to bed crowd had not thinned out and I turned back to Jean and Grace. They had sobered in the last half-hour and either fear or suspicion had given them a tense, strained appearance, unnatural in a holiday crowd. When the waiter poured the champagne, I proposed a toast for the night's good luck at the tables—and crossed my fingers hoping for good luck for just a few more hours.

Then, across the room, under a spot light, I saw a beautiful sight—the red head standing at a mike. She was getting ready to sing with a combo and waved gaily to us. Just as she waved, the head waiter arrived back with the news that there was no message. I gave him a sawbuck and explained who the missing "young girl" was and he joined in our laughter. Even Jean and Grace sensed a feeling of relief and joined in the laughter. Grace whispered in my ear,

"I hope Larry hurries back. I feel like having a real party now."

And Jean was getting warm and more than friendly, holding my hand beneath the table.

"Do we have to go back to L.A., dear?" she asked.

"'Fraid so, honey," I smiled at her, and hoped to hell we'd get the chance to get back there and away from a swindle that had turned into murder.

By the time Larry got back, we were part of the pre-dawn celebration. He wasn't hurrying which made me feel our luck was lasting.

"Luck hold out?" I asked.

"Everything's cool, Bill," was his only reply as he sat down. "Ready to go, girls?" asked Larry.

"Spoilsport," Jean and Grace chorused together, and Grace threw her arms around him.

"We wanna stay and live it up for a while, baby—les play a little—you boys had your lucky night—les have sumfun."

Larry grinned. "You people have been having a party."

I caught his look. "Let's go girls. Party's over." and I rose to help Jean from her chair. And right at that moment, the red head came back.

"Bring Mr. Drake back with you, Mr. Jarvis?"

"No, honey, I left him at the Inn. Have a goodbye drink with us. One for the road and the New Year."

Larry changed like a chameleon, and didn't want to leave the singer with any doubts that would bring any heat on us right away. We sat for another round and made like holidayers. Larry and I smiled and laughed—and sweated. I didn't know right then how much time we had and Larry couldn't tell me.

We checked out and paid our bill with good currency, explaining to the Thunderbird cashier that there was no point in cluttering up charge accounts with the night's tab when we had pockets filled with good Thunderbird cash. It was the first honest statement we made all night and the girl laughed and congratulated us on our winnings.

I had a few minutes alone with Larry in the suite before leaving and learned of his "clean-up" job while I'd been keeping the girls happy.

"You get rid of him?" I asked.

"I did," was Larry's terse reply, "put him to bed."

"Put him where? I thought he was d . . ."

"Under a blanket of sand. He was."

"Any heat? Any rumble? Can we afford to take a chance at the field?"

"No. No. Yes. In that order to all three questions. I told you everything's cool—or cold—depending how you want to look at it," shot Larry, as he picked up the crock of Ballantine's again.

I'd known Larry for over ten years and it suddenly dawned on me that I had a pretty cool operator for a partner.

Grace and Jean were asleep on their feet as we boarded the plane at McCarron Field for L.A. They didn't wake up 'til we reached L.A. and Larry and

I spent the trip whispering about the next move. Getting rid of Drake meant abandoning former plans and some fast and drastic changes.

"Anybody see you move him?"

"I don't think so. If they did, I made like he was a drunk. Kept talking to him all time as I was pulling him into the car. But what the hell's the difference. He'll turn up missing and that red head will talk. He'll be tied to us in twenty-four hours; sooner if somebody kicks up that sand at the edge of town; and within forty-eight hours at the latest when those queer checks start to bounce. There's only one thing to do when we dump these broads at their apartment—move and keep moving." Larry closed his eyes and let his head drop back against the plane seat head rest.

"We'll be landing in a few minutes, Mr. Morton. Shall I wake the ladies?" asked the stewardess.

"I'll do it honey. Thanks." and I turned to the seat behind us to wake Jean and Grace.

"Happy New Year, kids," I laughed.

"Pass the aspirin," was Jean's only reply.

"Wise guy," quipped Grace.

I glanced anxiously around as we passed through the airport terminal building and I noticed Larry pacing up and down as we waited at the baggage area for our bags.

"For a couple big winners, you two boys are not very lively," observed Jean while we walked to the cab stand.

"Just another night's work, honey," I yawned, and helped her into the cab. We wanted to make sure they got right back inside their apartment in North Hollywood and knew they'd sleep for a day and a night once we got them there.

"It was fun," were Jean's parting words.

"Call us and we'll do it again," were Grace's goodbye words.

"That, baby," I thought, "will never happen."

Larry and I changed cabs downtown and took another cab to my apartment. Inside we threw the bags in the center of the floor and slumped down in chesterfield chairs as the sun began to shine in.

"We did it, Larry."

"Yeah, wonder what the take was? Too bad we couldn't make that last hit at the Inn."

"Larry, Larry, if you hadn't moved fast back there, the take would have been a trip back to the bigtop or over to the Rock. You count it and I'll make some coffee. Then we pack and get out."

"I could sleep for a week, Bill. Throw me your keys."

I brought a pot of coffee from the kitchen and watched Larry sorting the bills.

"Take time out for some coffee?"

"Set it over there, Bill, this is stimulant enough for me."

Larry didn't even look up from his counting. I kicked off my shoes; ripped off the black tie and settled down to suck up the hot, black coffee and watch him. His face was a study in strained concentration and his hands moved like a bank cashier's, snapping each bill as he counted the loot. It took him half an hour and in that time he didn't utter a word or a sound. I didn't disturb him. He made two separate piles on the bed and let out a long, series of peppy whistles.

"Fifty-two G's apiece!"

"You sure, Larry?"

"Damn right, I'm sure."

"You realize that means we picked up fourteen G's at the crap tables? if we'd gone in those joints on a shoestring trying to beat those tables, we'd come out tapped. We throw some hundred dollar chips around for a front, not caring if we win or lose and what happens? We win. What do you think about that?"

"I'm thinking about something else, Bill. If I'd any idea we were over the hundred G mark, I'd have bypassed the Dunes and we'd never have run into Drake. And I'd never had to dump the guy. Pour me some of that java."

"It's done, Larry—the little world that might have been. No point in thinking about it—or him—now."

"I know. We got other things to think about. Heat from a pile of counterfeit checks is one thing, even without a rumble. But the heat that's going to be turned on for dumping that hotel man is something else. Good gawd almighty—think about it—the FBI for moving that queer across a state line and lamming after the caper; private law from that traveler's check corporation; the Las Vegas law; and all the law in the country that plays ball with them."

"You missed the real heat, Larry."

"Whatinhell did I miss that counts?" Larry asked with a derisive grin.

"The heat from the people behind the hotel association in Vegas. Those boys would hardly stand still for being slipped with the queer checks. They'll jump up and down when they learn one of their assistant managers got it in the process. And they'll tie us in with Drake's killing before tomorrow morning. The FBI will have it on teletype by tomorrow but the assorted mobs behind those casinos will have it on the grapevine before them. Get the picture, Larry?"

"I don't need a painting of it. Got any Benny? I don't see any sleep in the picture for another couple days."

We finished the New Year's morning breakfast—coffee, Benny and cigarettes—making new plans to lam. We had planned to head for Central America but knew now there'd be as much heat from the law there as anyplace else. We were both known to have lammed there before and the murder rap was on extradition treaties from Mexico to Costa Rica—and points south.

"We get off the continent in forty-eight hours, Bill, or we're done. Right?"

I agreed. We tossed possibilities back and forth for half-an-hour and decided to head north to Vancouver and from there to the Orient.

"Larry, we've got to get out of this apartment. I don't think there's any heat on yet. But it's no damn time for guessing games. This will be the FBI's first stop if they start looking for a counterfeiter on the west coast." I looked down on the street as I talked but couldn't see anything suspicious.

"OK, Bill, pack—and pack light—and let's get the hell outta here."

We changed our clothes and took the elevator to the basement where my car was parked. We drove to Chico Estevan's place on La Jolla and parked in the alley.

"Bill, Larry—come on in. Long time no see. Siddown. I fix a drink. I know you don't want any Horse."

We gave him an opportunity to express his Latin emotions at the sight of two former members of the Leavenworth cell in which he'd flattened out a double sawbuck and then I cut him short.

"No drink; no fix, Chico. Business this morning."

"What you want, Billy?" The heroin smuggler knew the score well enough and could be all business when necessary.

"I've got a car in the alley that I want driven and parked at San Ysidro to make like Larry and I've gone across to Tijuana. I want to be sure it gets there and gets parked—right away."

"Eees it hot, Billy?"

"No but it can damn soon be. No questions, Chico. There's a C note for getting it there by noon. You got anybody that's reliable?"

"Sure, and you know'm. Remember Jose?"

"Garcia? Is he around?"

"I get'm for you." he let go with a tornado of fast Spanish to his son who returned with Jose Garcia. We had to wait out another reunion speech from Jose.

"Billy and Larry got job for you, Jose. Drive heap to the border for a C note. You wanit?"

"For a C note I drive it to Guatemala and bring it back full of H. Where is it?"

I gave the keys to Jose and Larry handed him five twenties before I could pay him.

"Your car, my dough, Bill," was his only comment but I knew what was in Larry's mind. He didn't want me flashing any big bills. Chico and Jose were jailhouse friends—who would knife a friend for a tenth of what we were packing.

"You guys must be hot," quizzed Chico.

"No. Just that heap. See you around, kid."

We watched Jose pull out of the alley and left.

"Think he'll take it to the border, Bill?"

"Your guess is as good as mine. I think so. If he does, we get a break. If he doesn't, there's not a helluva lot we can do about it. The way I see it, we keep moving like the law's right behind us and don't take anything for granted, Larry. Still want to take a chance on the airport?"

"We want to get to Frisco before there's any heat. Georgie Zakaras is the only connection we know out here for papers and passports. We can't get off the continent without them. You think of a faster way to get to Frisco?"

Larry flagged down a cab and I left his question unanswered.

"Statler Hilton," I replied to the cabbie who didn't want to talk any more than we did. When he stopped for a light on Wilshire, he asked.

"Want to hear the eleven o'clock news?"

"Don't mind," I came back with, "it'll be the first news of the New Year." I could feel Larry stiffen.

"Crime, crime, nothing but crime. What a way to start off the New Year," observed the philosophical cabbie.

But the crimes we had committed last night and this morning were not on the news and we walked into the airline office in the Hilton like we had a license. Our luck was lasting, even if we were pushing it, and we got on a flight that put us down in San Francisco early in the afternoon.

"Don't sit next to me on the plane, Bill. And when it lands in Frisco, don't walk with me or make like we're together. Keep me in sight. I'll take a cab to the Music Box on Geary Street and you can pick me up there or at the hotel across the street if you lose me. I got a hunch this is just the calm before a helluva storm for us. OK?"

"OK, Larry." and I slept all the way north until the stewardess woke me to fasten my seat belt for landing. Even the Benny couldn't overcome the demand for sleep. I caught Larry's eye as we were waiting to leave the plane but he only nodded his head imperceptibly and I followed him into the airport building. Cautious glances ahead didn't turn up any sign of law and I managed to get the cab behind Larry's as it pulled away safely into the traffic.

"The Music Box on Geary Street," I told the driver and kept my eye on Larry's cab to see if he was tailed. After a couple miles, I relaxed. So far no heat and we were getting farther from where the heat would start.

"Any news?" I asked Larry when I found him scanning a paper in the hotel lobby.

"The usual," was his casual reply. "Let's go."

"Same cab?"

"No. You know Georgie's address. Pick me up there." Larry walked through the lobby and out the door with the paper folded under his arm. I stopped at the news stand for some cigarettes and noticed transistor radios in the showcase.

"Do those sets work on a plane or train?"

"Oh, yes, sir, they'll work anyplace. They're guaranteed."

I bought one, thinking, "I'll never be around to get my money back, baby, if it doesn't work."

I got out of the cab a block away from the address George had given me when he left Leavenworth.

"I own the house, Billy, and if I'm not there, my old lady can tell you where I'll be," were the instructions of George Zakaras when he left us at Leavenworth. He ran a sideline to his fence—letter-perfect, forged credentials and passports for the underworld.

I walked around the side of the brown frame house and knocked. The inside curtain moved and the door opened.

"All you guys use side doors today. Come on in, Billy."

George must have been up all night too and he was still celebrating.

"Happy New Year, kid. You look good," George bellowed with an arm around me.

"Larry here?"

"Yeah, he's upstairs, looking out the window for you. How come you sneak up the alley? Who you hiding from, Billy boy?"

I laughed and let him talk. I didn't know what Larry had told him and, as far as I was concerned, the less told the better. Larry was stretched out on a chesterfield with a drink in his hand.

"Make it OK, Bill?"

"No trouble. You?"

"Just got here ahead of you, Bill."

"You guys on the run? What's the score?" asked George as he walked over to me with a drink.

Larry took it from there. "Sit down, Georgie, we've got business with you—paper business."

"Everybody's got business with Georgie. Today we party. It's been a long time and we were in that drum a long time together. We live it up today and tomorrow we talk business. You like that, Larry?"

"No, I don't like that, Georgie." and Larry reached over to turn down the blaring television.

George turned serious, "Trouble? Heat?"

I got in the picture, "Bad trouble. Bad heat, Georgie—"

"You guys drive up here on the lam. You're nuts. This house is the hottest spot this side of Mission Street. And if the law's looking for you where do you think they go? Your Uncle Whiskers' sheet pegs your old cell partners. If they even think you're in this town, they'll be here," George raved.

"So let's get the hell out of here, George, we still got business with you. You know this town. Take us to a spot where we can talk and not worry about the law moving in," Larry was on his feet talking chin-to-chin with Zakaras.

George moved like the house was on fire. His last words to his wife as we went out the side door were,

"I'm in Sausalito if anybody wants to know." He kept going, ignoring her shouting and questions.

He led us up one alley and down another and finally down a set of basement steps at the rear entrance of what could only be a jive joint from the noise above us. Three or four mid-day drinkers were at a dingy bar and the few couples at tables didn't look up through the fog of smoke as George pushed through to a locked door. He pulled out a key ring and fumbled for one of a dozen or so keys. Inside was a roll-top desk and a few chairs. He sat down at the desk and whirled around in the swivel chair.

"Alright, my lamster friends, spell it out. What do you want?" George was cold sober now—all business, if a little breathless from the eight-block ducking-and-dodging through the Frisco tenderloin.

"Two passports, birth certificates, Social Security cards, driver's licenses, a couple credit cards and anything else you can come up with to stand up under nosey questioning by strange bulls," Larry ran it down to him.

"And you want it on the fly," sneered George. "How come the big rush. What you running from, boys?"

"You don't want to know that, Georgie. How long will it take you to come up with this paper?" I asked.

"How do I know? It means finding people and a lot of other things. Today's a holiday. You guys sure must be hot."

Larry was on his feet again. "Look, George, this is going to be a working day for you and whoever you need to come with what we need. Price doesn't mean a gawdam thing. Speed does. You with me?"

George's eyes narrowed, "Two grand from each of you and maybe I can come up with what you need by tonight."

"You got a deal—with an extra G note if you can make it before eight o'clock," Larry shot back at him.

"Boy oh boy, you bastards must be awful hot!" said George in a quiet voice. "Maybe too hot to handle?"

Larry counted out the bills and laid them on George's desk, "That'll take the heat off us as far as you're concerned, Georgie. Now get us some action—fast. You just got paid."

George looked at the banknotes; folded them and put them in his pocket. "You don't look so hot to me, boys."

And he gave us action, dialing number after number 'til he got all his connections together. He even brought in some broad with a camera for the passport shots. George played the host as well as the organizer, getting two steaks sent in—our first meal in almost twenty-four hours. Larry slept in a straight-back chair and I kept my ear to the transistor set. Six o'clock and nothing on the air. So far nobody had tripped over that blanket of sand left by Larry on the outskirts of Vegas but I knew, by now, a helluva a hunt was going on around that town for Drake. By now that broad would have told the hotel people that we were the last people he was seen with. The heat had to come soon.

"Where you going?" George got up to leave the office and Larry woke with a start as soon as the swivel chair creaked.

"Tell the bartender to bring it in," was Larry's curt comment. "Tell him to bring two—and some sandwiches."

George opened the door and called to the bartender, "Mike, bring in two crocks of Bourbon and send out for a dozen ham on ryes."

I kept my ear to the transistor and said nothing.

"Won't be long now, Larry," George broke the silence, "You sure must be sweating a bad one out."

"Like I said, George, you don't want to know," I broke in. I knew Larry wouldn't stand much pushing around and I wanted to see the phony credentials in our hands before curiosity got the best of George.

The bartender brought in the booze and sandwiches and laid an evening paper on the desk. I read the headline, word for word, with George, "COUNTERFEITERS LINKED TO HOTELMAN'S SLAYING".

George's face turned to a sickly shade of white and he just stuttered as I grabbed the paper from him. Larry saw my move and jumped across the room. We read the news report in silence with George peering over our shoulders. I could feel his arm shaking. Some of the subheads jumped out to tell the story: Tied to slaying through singer—May Be in Mexico—Traced to Los Angeles.

"At least, Jose got that car to the border," was Larry's only comment.

"There's all your answers, Georgie," I grinned at the shaking fence and tossed the paper on to his desk. He grabbed it and spelled out the words through his bifocals.

"Maybe you'll get us some action now, Georgie," laughed Larry, "you know the rap for harboring?"

Zakaras grabbed the phone and dialed with a palsied hand.

"Benito, how long you going to be on those passports? You got the rest of the stuff ready? Get it over here fast."

"Half an hour and your papers'll be here," was George's only comment. He rubbed his face with his hands and poured a glass full of Bourbon.

"Do I know the rap for harboring? he asks me," George blurted out, talking to himself. "Do you guys think your big heat—or mine—is from the law? Let me ask you a question, 'Do you know what those casino people are doing right now?' They're turning their own kind of heat on you. They'll track you down any place you go and nail you while the law's sorting out tips from stool pigeons. They'll gun you down so gawdamn fast you'll think you're a couple clay pigeons in a Mission Street shooting gallery. You got any idea who's behind those casinos? What a pair of dumb bastards. Here, take this dough, I wouldn't be caught dead with it—and that's the only way I'd be if I was caught with it. Harboring? Hell, I'd do twenty-five on the Rock to get away from the mobsters who are on your tails right now."

One thing about Larry. He didn't shake. "Thanks for the refund, Georgie. I was wondering what I was going to do with you after those papers showed. But I don't have to do anything now. The paper did it for me. You're so gaw-damned scared that you wouldn't admit having seen us if the reward was a cool million. Stay that way, Georgie, and don't ever get any ideas. And keep the rest of your paper hustlers in mind—even if you have to dump them into the Bay one by one. Get the picture?" Larry was pouring himself a drink while speaking his piece to George and he didn't even raise his voice.

George almost fell out of his chair when a quiet knock sounded on the door, in spite of the fact that he knew the coded knocking. It was the papers and whoever brought them didn't come in. George dumped them out of a brown manila envelope on to the desk. We looked them over and examined them closely. For a hurry-up job it was good counterfeiting and forging and both Larry and I were qualified to judge both arts.

"You'll never get to use them," quivered George.

"We'll try," returned Larry.

"Sure you won't take the dough for them?" I asked the shook-up fence and paper man.

"Billy, I wouldn't handle any of that dough under any circumstances. Just do me one favor—forget you ever knew me. For the record, you never saw me after I left Leavenworth." Georgie was really shook.

"Don't worry about us, George. We never saw you. How the hell do we get out of here?" was the only farewell offered by Larry.

"Wait a minute, boys. I can get you out through the boiler room and up another set of stairs. I hope to God nobody in the bar recognized you."

"Let's go, George. Nobody can see through that smoke." I wanted to get out and away from the scared jelly belly.

He led us through a dust-filled boiler room, along a slimy tunnel and up a set of stairs opening from another building across the alley.

He had a natural spot from which to operate his "business" but I wondered how he could stay in the racket with such a complete lack of guts when the going got rough.

"Just a minute 'til I look out," George cautioned before he moved aside to let us out the door. Then he pulled it back shut. "I wouldn't trade places with you guys for all the dough in Vegas. Now, don't forget—you never saw me. Get out and good luck—you poor suckers."

"See you in hell, Georgie," Larry quipped as we moved into the alley in a fine drizzle of rain. The alley air smelled good compared to the den we'd spent the afternoon in.

"Where to, Larry?" I asked as I pulled my coat collar up from the rain and Frisco night air.

"Out of this part of the town, quick—in separate cabs. You remember Ben Sill's address?"

I gave it to Larry and hoped my memory was correct. We were on our way to test the friendship of another former cell partner.

"Meet me there. We'll see if he scares as easily as Georgie. If I get a rumble, keep going. I'll do the same if I see a tail on you. OK?"

"We'll play it by ear, Larry and handle what we meet when we meet it. There's a cab. Flag it and I'll see you at Ben's place." He stepped out to stop the cab and I ducked back into a doorway.

It took me five or ten minutes to pick up another cab and the driver gave me a suspicious look, probably as much from the pickup area and from my rainsoaked appearance as from anything else. But I wasn't taking any chances.

"Let me out at Turk and Eddy," I replied to his, "Where to, Mac?"

I switched cabs twice before I headed for Ben's place across the Bay Bridge. And when we got there I told the driver to pull on by. I walked in the opposite direction until I saw the cab disappear and then turned and walked back to Ben's house. No one was around in the suburban neighborhood so I walked right across the grass and looked in. Ben and Larry were sitting talking. I tapped at the window and saw Ben get up to go to the door. I also saw Larry pull his .38 from his coat pocket. I walked over to the porch and was met with laughter from Ben Sill.

"You tap on windows in this neighborhood and you'll fall on a Peeping Tom rap, Billy. Come on in."

Ben had heard the news reports and knew the score.

"I sort of figured you boys were south of the border by now. That's what the law figures according to the news flashes. Said your car was found at San Ysidro across from Tijuana."

Larry ran the car plant story down to Ben.

"Where do you go from here?" was Ben query after Larry finished telling of Jose's performance.

"We want to get north to Vancouver and then try to make it to Hong Kong," I explained, as if it was a wish for a weekend trip to a resort.

"What can I do to help?" Ben asked without any show of fright.

"You know the kind of heat we bring with us, Ben?" Larry asked.

"Hell, I'm hot myself. I live here with the wife under a phoney name and the neighbors think I'm a fruit buyer. I've been on the lam since a year after I sprung. I hung up my C.R. time and got a rumble from a score in St. Louis. Don't worry about me. But you want to get out of this part of the world. I've got an idea. Want to listen?"

"Keep talking, Ben, you're doing OK," Larry said.

"Rest up here tonight and tomorrow I'll drive you to Seattle, packed in a load of fruit. I've got the truck, the papers, and I make the occasional run with a load of fresh fruit up north whenever I want to move out myself. I can stand a stop on the highway and I know the route."

We tossed the idea back and forth 'til midnight and the more we talked about it the more I liked Ben's plan to plant us in a truckload of tomatoes for the trip up to Seattle.

"We'll make it worth your while, Ben. You sure you know what you're getting into? What do you do if the law stops you and says, 'Unload.'?" asked Larry with more than an academic interest in the possibility.

"I tell them to unload it themselves if they want to and duck when they get to you people. It's your party from then on and they'll be so gawdamn busy with you, they won't notice me shooting them in their backs. I've got some extra artillery you can pack in there with you and if a road block gets that suspicious—which I don't think they will—there'll be only one answer—spread tomatoes and law all over the highway. I can't stand a pinch any more than you can but somehow or other I got a feeling I can make it without that kind of trouble. I know the guys at the highway stations and they know my truck. Besides I'll pick up a legitimate shipment of tomatoes from a wholesaler and I'll have a good bill of lading. Want to give it a try?"

"Sounds OK to me. What do you think, Bill?"

"Come tomorrow morning we'll be just a couple 'hot tomatoes'. I'm for it," was my reply.

"Alright then, we'll try it. Now let's get some sleep. I'll load up at the market at three in the morning and come back over here to load you in. You look like you could use some sleep. Come on, I'll show you the shower and your bedroom. You can relax here." And Ben yawned as he began turning off lamps in the living room.

"Think he's on the level, Bill?" Larry asked in a whisper when I came back from the shower. He was cleaning his .38 and his question was matter-of-fact rather than excited.

"He can't afford not to be," I yawned, "we're too hot to be fingered. Not even a stoolie would have the moxie to admit he put us up for the night and I don't think Ben's a rat." I looked over at Larry and saw he had fallen asleep before I finished my comment. His hand and .38 were under the pillow.

"I'll be back in an hour-and-a-half with my load," was Ben's three A.M. wake-up greeting. "Here's two BAR's and some shells. Check 'em over while I'm gone and make your own breakfast in the kitchen. The wife won't get up 'til daylight and she won't get curious when she hears you. Make yourselves at home. See you when I get back."

We checked over the automatic rifles and discovered Ben did indeed have some good artillery.

"Make some coffee, Bill and I'll clean these," was Larry's businesslike reaction to the BAR's.

We heard Ben's truck pull in the yard and went to the back door. It was still dark.

"Gimme a hand to move some of these crates," Ben asked in a low voice. "Get some breakfast? You'll have a long trip. All day."

"We're OK, Ben," I replied and we moved out to help him. After two-thirds of the load was on the ground, Ben stopped.

"That's enough. I'll get some blankets and boards." Ben went into the house.

I looked at the van type truck and whispered to Larry, "Well there it is, kid. Once we're inside, it's up to Ben where we get out."

"Let's go in and get our stuff," was Larry's only comment. "We're part of the load now."

Before Ben moved the first truck-roof-high crate that was to separate us, by six rows of crates from the back, into place, he paused in his work, "Got everything?"

"We're all set, Ben. Like a double bunk in Leavenworth. Pack 'em in," Larry replied.

"Alright, now, listen—Don't panic when you feel the truck stop. I'll be stopping and starting all day. I may even have to open the back door for highway inspectors. Signals won't be worth a damn. You can't tell a horn signal from the real thing and there's no use of my trying to let you know in any way what goes on. If there is any trouble I won't get a chance to do any fancy tapping on the truck body. All I can say is 'come out blasting if any of these three crates in front of you are moved unless I tell you otherwise.' When I unload in Seattle tonight it will be close to midnight at a motel outside town. Don't start blasting then. OK?"

I looked over Ben's shoulder and saw the grey dawn, "OK, Ben. See you tonight in Seattle—I hope."

"All aboard!" quipped Larry.

We slept, tossed, bumped, cursed and jarred our way northward. For the first few hours, we tensed and listened at every stop. Black as a cell in the hole with the lights out at night and stuffy as a fruit market after a long weekend, the gawdamn truck van became almost unbearable. I never wanted to see or smell a tomato again before the trip was half over.

"This is one helluva ride," I groaned to Larry in the middle of the afternoon.

"You want to stop and catch a bus?" was Larry's only comment.

I knew the other kind of a ride available from our pursuers would make this van look like a Santa Fe chair car. I shut up and tried to sleep.

We had been stopped for the longest period of time so far when I heard the van door opening. Larry's hand clutched my arm like the claw of an eagle.

"Listen!" he hissed in my ear.

I heard a crate being pulled out and felt Larry slowly moving one of the BAR's along his side. I could feel my pulse throbbing at both temples. I thought, "Is this the end of our 'plush road'—a gun battle in a truckload of tomatoes with a bankroll that we haven't even had a chance to spend?"

"It checks with the bill of lading. Tomatoes. Want the rest of the crates out?"

"No. I think this one's OK. This is his regular run. Lock'er up and put a seal on it or he'll be stopped at every roadblock between here and Portland to unload and load. These truckers got to make a living and he won't be able to do much with a load of bruised, over-ripe tomatoes." The voice sounded like law.

"Who you looking for, sergeant?" With these words Ben told us it was the law.

"Some tough guys, supposed to be heading this way. Don't pick up any hitchhikers or you'll just be delayed more at roadblocks farther on," replied the voice.

"I never do. Insurance company won't let me," Ben assured whoever was cautioning him.

"OK, Mr. Simpson, here's your papers. Pull out." We learned Ben's alias for the first time. And we learned that luck was still riding in those tomatoes with us.

The shock from that roadblock kept us wide awake for a long time and I realized I was soaked in perspiration in spite of the mountain cold. Long pulls in lower gears told me Ben was getting farther up—and farther away from the heat. Stops became fewer.

I picked up a news report on the transistor set that made the load of tomatoes seem to smell like a load of gardenias: "Las Vegas killers believed to be in Bay area. Notorious underworld fence found slain in alley—former cellmate of two counterfeiter-killers. All exits from San Francisco area sealed off. Arrest of Los Angeles narcotic traffickers reveals planting of one suspect's car near Mexican border to be ruse." The truck was stopping and I had to turn the set off.

"I wonder who got Georgie?" Larry whispered in my ear. The truck had stopped and we both listened. It started again and I pressed my lips to Larry's ear.

"Whoever it was would have preferred to get us." Larry and I pressed our heads close to the transistor to get the tail end of the news.

"Two other former federal prison cellmates of suspects held for questioning—Bernard 'Bobo' Martelli of Los Angeles and Edward Sims of Oakland. . . ." The damn truck was stopping again and I had to turn the transistor off. From the sounds of traffic I knew Ben was in a town.

"We're making a lot of heat wherever we go," I whispered to Larry.

"As Georgie said," he whispered back, "the FBI would peg everyone that was in that eight-man cell with us as soon as they figured us for the caper in Vegas. They're thorough. Maybe our best break so far is that Ben is already on the lam and they have lost track of him. We just got out of L.A. and Frisco in time."

"I think our best plan is to keep moving 'til it costs a dollar to send us a postcard," I remarked for a lack of something better to say.

"You know Vancouver, Bill?"

"I was up there three or four times before I fell."

"Think we can lay up there for a while?"

"Hell, no, Larry. We keep on moving until we're off the continent." I continued, telling Larry about the western Canadian seaport and the chances to get out. He fell asleep and I slept and woke fitfully in the few cramped positions possible between the crates. I watched the hands on my watch creep towards midnight and felt we should soon be getting near Seattle.

Ben made sure to let us know when it was the last stop. We were both wide awake and I could hear the sound of waves and surf. The fresh air from the sea was like pure oxygen after the day and half-a-night in the van full of tomatoes.

"We made it, boys. I'm unloading and we're in the clear," Ben's voice came through the crates.

Larry didn't take any chance on Ben being forced to put us off our guard. As Ben lifted the top crate in front of us to the van floor, Larry had his BAR at his head.

"Put that gawdamn thing down, Larry. We're OK," laughed Ben.

We rubbed our legs and arms to get the circulation back and limped out. We'd have been sitting ducks for any guns. Neither of us could walk for two or three minutes and it was longer before I could completely straighten up. And I could hardly see in the change from complete to semi-darkness.

"Where are we, Ben?" Larry asked.

"Behind a motel. I always stay here and the people know me. They're used to me unloading and shifting parts of loads. We're a few miles north of Seattle. I drove right through. Figured that seal on the back of the van should be used as long as it could. You hear the conversation at the roadblock the other side of Portland?"

"Every horrible word of it, Ben. It shook us," I replied.

"We got a real break there. The road block was at an inspection station and the regular inspector there remembered me and my truck. The driver ahead of me had to unload a whole load of cartons. I had visions of you boys staging another Alamo."

"Let's not press our luck and stand out here," cut in Larry.

"Help me load up. I'm going to deliver this load back in Seattle to keep the trip legitimate and get a receipt for it in case I run into questioning on the way back. You can lay up here in the cabin. I'll be back before the maid makes up the cabins in the morning and will tell her I want to sleep all day and not to bother with it. I'll get back as soon as I can—probably before daybreak. Keep the lights out. If you don't hear me pull in with the truck, I'll knock three times and then twice. And don't stick that BAR in my face, Larry—please. Makes me nervous."

"You carry that stuff inside, Larry, and I'll help Ben finish loading." Larry carried the bags and guns inside the cabin and I worked on with Ben, making as little noise as possible. The truck was well hidden by trees and bushes but the day in that van had left me nervous—and careful. Ben locked the back doors and got in the cab.

"See you, Billy."

"Later, Ben," and I turned to the cabin before he got his lights on.

We were used to the darkness by now, after the trip in the van, but the quietness of the ocean side motel soon put an end to our whispering. I fell asleep in a chair and Larry lay stretched on the bed. We both jumped at the same time when the sound of Ben's knock came at the door. It seemed like a few seconds instead of a few hours. Larry stood back with the BAR in his hand and I peeked through the slit in the curtains to make sure it was Ben before I opened the door for him. He had some papers, a bag of sandwiches and three large bottles of coffee. We talked to daylight without turning on the lights.

"Ben," Larry said in a low voice, "without you we'd both be in a Frisco alley. You read those papers yet?"

"I got a fast look at the first pages in town. You're hot," was Ben's noncommittal reply.

"You read about Georgie and the others?"

"Yes."

"You think there'll be any more heat on you?"

"No more than there's been for the last year. I head back to Frisco tonight and I never saw you. I might need the same kind of help someday myself, Larry. It's a small world." Ben yawned, "I need some shut eye. What's your next move, Larry?"

"First we want to square up with you. Billy and I talked it over while you were in town and we feel you got five G's coming. That sound alright, Ben?"

"Hell, yes. I'd do it for free. You know that, Larry."

"You know this dough may be hot as hell?"

"I know it. And I got a connection for hot dough—in the same town where you got it. I mail it there and lose only twenty cents on the dollar—no questions asked. The faster I get it there the better. Might even take some of the heat off you. I won't take any chances carrying it back to Frisco. I'll mail it from Tacoma."

"No," broke in Larry. "You may think your connection's solid as hell but this dough—if you send it back to Vegas—could kill him and you. And if you mail it from Tacoma, or this part of the country, you finger us. Mail it to yourself in Frisco. Make a trip to Mexico for a load of fruit and get rid of it there. You know any of those gambling joints at Rosarito Beach or Ensenada? Hit them on a Saturday night with the L.A. crowd and you won't have any trouble. OK, Ben?"

"You're right, Larry."

Larry threw the bills on to the bed. "Wish it could be more, Ben. You earned it. But we may need all we got from here on in. Can we get out of here or should we lay up 'til you leave?"

"The people here are used to me sleeping late when I pull in at night. It will look more natural if you stay around and pull out with me late this afternoon—unless you think you should keep on the move." Ben was looking at the papers he had brought back as he spoke and it was obvious that he was becoming more and more aware of the kind of heat he shared.

"Can we get out the back way here, Ben, without passing the office down by the road?" Larry asked.

"Yes, you can cut through the woods and come out on the Bellingham road just over the hill—about a mile, I think."

"What about it, Bill?"

"Let's move out, Larry. The longer that we wait around, the more people are going to get acquainted with our mug shots that the FBI is pouring out by now. And as soon as they decide we're no longer in Frisco they'll send mug shots to papers. Let's keep moving while we can." I walked towards the window and pulled back the curtain. A fog was moving in from the ocean. "See that, Larry? Let's go."

"Better put those BAR's away, Ben. We can't lug them with us," was Larry's farewell observation to Ben Sill as we left the motel and cut into the woods. We came out at a bus stop on the road.

"I'm going to call a cab from that store over there, Bill, and go on alone to Bellingham. You wait for the bus and meet me there. I'll find the bus stop and wait there for you."

Larry was crossing the road before I could protest and when the door of the store closed behind him a bus pulled up. I boarded it, thinking he was right. The heat was probably directed at two men and any two men together would draw the attention of anyone who'd read the papers. I sat down on the left side of the bus so I could watch for a cab pulling by with Larry. I saw him pull by just before the bus reached Bellingham. He was sitting at a lunch counter drinking coffee when I walked in the waiting room. I went to a table over in the corner and ordered some coffee and eggs. No one paid any attention to either of us and I looked around the lunch room and then back at Larry. His clothes looked wrinkled and seedy, making me realize how I looked. I was looking, with interest, at a sign on the wall when I saw Larry walk to the wash room. I followed him.

"Seems cool."

"So far, Larry."

"How do we get across the border, Bill?"

"A little sign on the wall just told me, kid. It's a cinch!"

"You flipping your lid, Bill? What the hell you mean—'a little sign on the wall'?"

"We're going to a dance tonight."

"What the hell you talking about? You going stir bugs on me, Billy?"

"Wait a minute, Larry. Listen to me. There's some kind of a public dance at a golf club north of here and I remember that golf club. Its course sits right on the border—half in this country and half in Canada. It's only a couple miles from White Rock on the Canadian side. We take a cab to the golf club and ease into Canada on the fairways tonight. Today we stay apart here in town. Get a room in a hotel and I'll check in some place else. Buy some haberdashery and fresh clothes and we'll be just a couple more stags heading for the dance tonight. I'll get rid of my bag and you get rid of that brief case. We'll have to spread the dough around in our pockets or improvise a larger money belt some way or another. Two stags on the way to a golf club dance don't pack for the weekend. You buy the idea?"

"If you know what you're talking about, it couldn't be better. Sure you know that golf course?"

"I came across it a few years back with a couple Canadian lamsters who were trying to get into this country. No reason why we can't reverse the process."

"OK, Bill, we'll meet here at nine tonight. Be careful around town today. See you." I waited for a minute or two to let Larry get out and went back to my breakfast.

"Single, with bath, if you have one," I asked the room clerk.

He looked at my wrinkled clothes and asked, "How long will you be staying, sir?"

"Just for the day," while I was laying a double sawbuck on the desk so he could see I wasn't the bum I looked, I replied, "had some car trouble and want to get some fresh clothes and clean up."

He smiled with obvious relief as he gave me my receipt for the room and change for the twenty.

I ran into Larry three times during the day, once on my way into a haberdashery, coming out of a bar and, later in the afternoon, walking along the main street of Bellingham in new clothes—a sports coat and grey flannels—and wearing glasses. He had more gall than a man with gall stones—the last time I saw him, he had a blonde on his arm and was laughing with her.

"Hey, Mike, he called to me," and I had nothing else to do but to cross the street and greet him as nonchalantly as he hailed me.

"Mike Evans—Helen. Come on in and have a drink with us, Mike. Got you a date for the dance tonight, Mike—if you don't mind a blind one—friend of Helen's."

Larry had picked up the dame in some bar and I could only go along with the play. It was an idea for a cover-up at that. I hoped he didn't have any other ideas about the two girls or about laying up here for the night. Playing with the key to my hotel room, I let Larry get a look at it to tip him off to where I was staying. I caught his nod and put it back in my pocket.

"We'll pick you up at the hotel around nine, Mike," Larry promised when I explained that I had some shopping to finish.

"What a cool bastard," I thought as I walked back to the hotel. I took a hot bath and went to bed, leaving a call for seven.

"Who is it?" I called to the knock at the door.

"Just me," came Larry's voice and I opened the door for him.

"Come on in, Casanova. No dame with you?"

"Like Grace and Jean, they're strictly for a front, Bill. Met the broad in a bar and the idea came to me between drinks."

"How do we get rid of them at the dance, Larry."

"We don't."

"Now who's flipping their lid? There'll be no partying at this stage of the game . . ."

"Hold it, Billy. Gimme credit for some brains. These broads are our tickets right into Vancouver. They're both from Canada and are over here shopping. Helen lives on Haro Street in the west end and her girl friend lives just across the border in White Rock. And Betty, that's the one from White Rock, is our answer for the border—her old man is one of the Canadian Immigration officers on duty after midnight at the port of entry. Betty agreed to stay for the dance only on the condition that we would drive her home tonight in Helen's car. That 'condition,' Billy boy, is right up our alley."

"What a break!" and a whistle of joy was the only comment I could make.

"That's not all, kid. I told Helen we would drive her right into Vancouver and come back here in the morning. Feel like dancing now, Bill?"

"It couldn't be better if we had a police escort on both sides of the border, Larry. You're blessed with luck."

He had a bottle and poured a couple drinks while I was shaving.

"One problem, Bill. I never saw a dame yet that could dance all night and not learn a partner was packing a gun. What do we do with these pieces?" Larry was looking at his .38 while he was talking and mine was laying on the bed table.

"Can we leave 'em here in the room and make an excuse to come back here after the dance?" I asked.

"I feel naked without it. Another thing—how do we dance all night with every gawdamn pocket filled with bills. Those broads are going to be half juiced up and the first time one of them snuggles up for some loving they're going to feel either the rod or pockets stuffed with bills." Larry posed a problem that had to be answered.

"Where do we pick 'em up?"

"At that lounge where we met this afternoon—in half-an-hour, Bill. Better come up with an answer."

"Your running this show, Larry, you come up with the answer."

"Gawdamnit, I sure hate to make a move without this piece and leaving it and my bankroll hidden in this hotel room is pushing our luck too far."

I agreed with Larry. The sight of the carton and wrapping paper from the haberdashery gave me an idea—and the answer. "Let's face it, Larry. We can't take off for the night with a couple of partying broads, packing a .38 and pockets filled with bills. We pack the rods and bills inside my soiled clothes; parcel them up in those cartons and check them downstairs at the desk; and pick them up again after the dance. OK?"

"What a pair of bright bastards—all the law and mobs in the country looking for us and we take off for a dance, leaving our guns and bankrolls wrapped up in dirty laundry. But what the hell else is there to do?" and Larry went along with my idea.

It was the longest three hours since the day I'd spent waiting for Larry to show from St. Louis with the queer checks. I couldn't have got drunk if I tried and in spite of Betty's good looks and willingness to dance like she liked it I couldn't get interested. I kept thinking of one thing—that dough and those rods checked back at the hotel. But I went along with the party and played the role of a shy first date.

"Relax, Mikey. You're a good dancer but you dance like you expect the ceiling to fall on you."

"If she only knew!" I thought.

"Where did Helen and Terry go?" I asked Betty, almost forgetting for a moment the name Larry had adopted for the night.

"Probably in the car. Let's see," and Betty took my arm as we headed outside.

We found them necking in the back seat and I thought, "It's a damn good thing he did leave his bankroll and rod at the hotel." We killed the rest of the bottle and I looked at my watch.

"Time to go. You want to drive, Helen, or shall I?"

"We're busy, Mike. You drive." Helen replied from the back seat.

"We have to stop at the hotel, Betty, to leave word that we'll be gone for the night. Mind?"

"I'd even like to stop with you, Mikey, and she dropped her head on my shoulder as I pulled out the driveway and back to Bellingham."

What a perfect setup, Larry picked to get across the border, a couple of hot broads—to front for a couple of 'hot' lamsters, I thought.

"We'll be back in a second," I told the girls as Larry and I got out and went into the hotel.

The night clerk looked up sleepily from the desk and handed the parcel to me in exchange for the receipt tag. Larry and I pocketed the dough in the room and were back in the car before the girls got ideas of coming upstairs. We headed for the Canadian border.

I was surprised and happy to find a fairly heavy stream of traffic on the way to the border—partyers on their way back to Canada and shoppers on their way home. I'd noted quite a few British Columbia licenses on cars parked at the golf club. My pulse quickened as we pulled up at the Canadian Immigration.

"Border, Terry." I warned Larry. Helen straightened her hair and Larry looked ahead.

I didn't know what to anticipate but hoped Betty's old man would be the Immigration officer who questioned us.

"Where's the ownership permit, Helen?" I asked.

"In the glove compartment, Mikey, but you won't need it. We go back and forth all the time and they never bother local people."

I pulled up behind the car ahead and held Betty's warm hand—for luck rather than for passion. I didn't know what the hell to expect as I watched the blue uniformed officer walk over to my side of the car and *stop*.

"Time you were coming home, Bet," smiled the Immigration officer who was obviously Betty's father. "Hello, Helen. You behaving tonight?"

"I always do, Dad!" she quipped to Betty's father.

"You vouch for these boys, Betty?" and before Betty could answer his casual, smiling question, he looked over at me, "You boys from Bellingham?"

"Seattle, I smiled back. We're driving Helen into Vancouver and coming back in the morning."

The Canada Customs officer was talking with Helen about the dance and his only question was directed to the girls, "You bringing in your contraband shopping?" Everyone laughed and we were waved on into Canada. The informality of the border crossing and the protection afforded by the two broads had afforded us a magic carpet out of the country. We couldn't have got a better break if we'd planned it, with control of all the planning, and we had walked into it accidently, thanks to Larry's ability to pick up Helen in the bar and the lucky fate that sent the two broads shopping that day in Bellingham with an eye for some fun. I put my arm around Betty and relaxed for the first time that night.

"You'll have to show me the road, honey. I don't know White Rock."

"Turn left at the next service station, Mikey."

I could hear Larry and Helen laughing in the back seat. The guy was a constant source of amazement to me and I'd known him for over ten years—a wanted killer, partying in the back seat of a strange broad's car in a strange country, making like he didn't have a care in the world. I hoped that broad's hands didn't do too much wandering around his lanky frame and feel things she wasn't feeling for.

"That's my house," Betty warned as we neared a white frame illuminated with a street lamp in front of the lawn.

I kissed her goodnight with a fervor I really meant.

"When will you see me again, Mike?" she asked with what was probably the most sincerely felt question I'd had put to me in a long time.

"The first time I'm back this way, honey," and I meant it even if I knew I'd never be back.

"Bad news, Helen. You'll have to drive," I said when I pulled up at the stop sign at the highway. "Hate to break up what looks like a real romance, kids, but I can't keep my eyes open. Hate to spend the night in one of your Canadian coolers for an accident." I looked at Larry and he got the message. He knew I had no Canadian driver's license and the name he had tagged on me for the night didn't match the forged California one Georgie had provided for me. He got in the front seat with Helen and I curled up in the back not only to sleep but also to keep out of sight of any police cruiser that might give two men in a car with a girl curious looks on the after-midnight streets and highways.

"Wake up, Mike." Larry was shaking me awake in front of Helen's apartment on Haro Street. I'd slept all the way through the city.

"Helen says there's a small hotel in the next block and she knows the manager," Larry explained while she was getting her packages out of the trunk. "Go down and register for both of us and wait for me in the lobby. I'll be there in a few minutes. I'll get Helen to phone from her apartment and explain that we're friends and that will take any suspicion away from us there. OK?"

I said goodnight to Helen and walked down the quiet westend street, taking my time for Helen to phone. I dropped a couple coins in a newspaper box at the corner and picked up a Vancouver Sun.

"Oh, you're one of Helen McTavish's friends," the night clerk smiled as he read my signature on the registration card at the hotel desk. "I have a nice double room for you and your friend."

I thanked him; explained that we would be leaving in the afternoon; and looked at some travel literature on a lobby table while I waited for Larry. The polite night clerk escorted us up the stairs to the second floor room and wished us goodnight.

"Devil's luck, Bill!"

"Hope it lasts, Larry. We've been blessed."

"I was tempted to shack up with that broad for the night until I remembered what I had in my pockets," laughed Larry as he emptied them.

"You and your broads. Forget them for a while, Larry. We're still on the run. We're out of the States but not far enough yet." I was leafing through the paper while I talked in a low voice to Larry. I found what I was looking for but was happy to see it was only covered by a three inch, one column report buried in the back pages.

"They think we're still in Frisco, Larry. Look." I handed him the paper which contained a very brief press association coverage of our flight.

We fell asleep whispering plans for getting off the continent to each other.

The persistent ring of the 'phone brought both of us to life at the same time.

"You leave a call for us?" asked Larry as he reached for the 'phone.

"No."

"Hello," Larry smiled and winked at me. "Just tired, baby." He spoke aside to me, "It's Helen." They quipped back and forth for a while and I heard him tell her we couldn't make it for a breakfast reunion. "Sorry, Helen, we've got to get back to Bellingham. I'll call you the next time I'm in town. Bye now."

"In case those broads pick up a paper and see us looking up from its pages at them, I want them to have the idea that we went back to the States. You got any ideas for today, Bill?"

"First, we'd better check out of here. It's too obvious—two of us checking in together. A routine check of hotels for two strangers together would finger us right away and there's a ready-made trail from the night clerk, to Helen, to Bellingham. I want to get down to the waterfront area today and see what I can find out about getting out of here on a ship. No use thinking of the airlines."

"You know the docks here, Bill?"

"No but I've been in the downtown area and remember a few bars—on Pender and Hastings. I'll try to spot some sailors off ships and make some inquiries."

"About what?"

"About signing on a ship or buying passage. Some of those Jap freighters carry a few passengers."

"Want me to come along, Bill?"

"I don't think so, Larry. Scout around on your own and see what you can pick up. The two of us together are what the law is looking for and the local police and Mounties have our pictures by now. Let's play it like we first did in L.A. and assume they're right behind us—and they may damn well be. You check in one hotel and I'll find another. We better pick up some luggage too. Whadaya think?"

"You're right," and Larry started to leaf through the yellow section of the 'phone book. "Know any of these hotels?" he asked, pointing to the long list of advertisers.

"No, but pick a couple out on East Hastings. They're all small ones there and we'll start from there. We can't hang around this town too long anymore than we can hang around together. Find anything?"

"Here's a couple whose street numbers make them seem close together—the Victory and the Buckingham. Take your pick." He wrote down the names, addresses and 'phone numbers of the two hotels on two slips of paper and I reached for one.

"OK, Larry, I'll be at the Victory. From now on we use the names on our phoney passports. If you can't get me there, in case there are no vacancies, I'll leave a message. You do the same at the Buckingham. Better write it down." I looked at the forged passport, complete with forged visa stamps for half a dozen countries. "You know my name in this passport?"

"Martin, Joe Martin, isn't it?"

"Joseph, if you don't mind. We've had as many names as the original Joseph's coat had colors. What kind of a moniker did Georgie's forgers hang on you?"

"A pansy—'Horace J. Little'— what a handle!" laughed Larry. "You ready to get out of here?"

"I'll walk down to Robson Street and pick up a cab. Check in a couple hours to see if I'm at the Victory and we'll make a meet from there. Don't forget to get some luggage. See you, Larry."

I stopped on Granville Street and bought a bag and some clothes and took another cab to the small hotel. The desk clerk gave me only a casual onceover.

"How long will you be with us, Mr. Martin?"

"Three or four days, I'm waiting to pick up a ship," I explained—and truthfully—while I was signing the card. I paid in advance for three days and turned back to the clerk, "I expect a friend to call later. If I'm not in my room will you tell him to leave a number where I can reach him, please?"

"Yes, be glad to, Mr. Martin."

I changed and shaved. "No use dressing up in this part of the town," I thought, and walked down the stairs to the beverage room wearing a windbreaker over a sweater.

"Beer?" The waiter asked as he was already setting a glass on the table.

"Thanks," I replied, laying a small bill down. I noticed everyone else in the Victory's beverage room was drinking glass beer and wanted to fit in the picture. It was a quiet crowd of early drinkers and I couldn't see any sign of seamen. I finished the beer and walked out the street door.

"Any message?" I asked the clerk.

"Yes, Mr. Martin," and he handed me a slip from the pigeon hole. It was from Larry with a 'phone number. I called him from a pay 'phone in the lobby.

"Buckingham Hotel, good morning." At least I knew he'd checked in.

"Mr. Little, please. Room 8."

"Hello," came Larry's voice—with the sound of laughter and clinking glasses in the background.

"Don't tell me, 'Mr. Little,' let me guess. You're partying?"

"How can you tell?" Larry laughed, "Come on up and join the party, kid—fast," he put in with a lowered voice.

I'd learned to expect anything from Larry by now and new damn well he wasn't partying for just the sake of a party. The Buckingham was only three blocks away and I hurried out and down the street. The door of his room was half open and the party was spreading into the hall and other rooms of the second rate hotel. The Buckingham was less pretentious than the Victory and was closer to a bucket of blood. In the room with Larry were eight or nine partying drinkers, either Aussies or Limeys from their slang.

"Meet my buddy, Joe Martin!" Larry shouted to the revelers.

Responses varied from shouts to handshakes and I had a drink in my hand before I could sit down. The partyers were in assorted stages of drunkenness—from belligerent arguments and re-fighting the war to ribald songs and I noticed Larry's room was only part of the brawl which was going on up and down the hall. He came over and sat on the arm of my chair.

"Crew of a ship."

"I didn't think they were part of a bible pounders' convention, 'Hal,' but how did you get mixed up with them?" I asked.

"It was going on when I checked in and I couldn't think of a better idea than to get mixed up in it. With this crew, we don't stand out. Mingling with these drunks makes us noticeable as part of a crew of drunken sailors. Alone, or together, we stand out for any copper that has our picture in his pocket. And we might even get a chance to ship out with them," Larry explained.

"What ship are they on? Where is it heading for? When does it sail?" I asked impatiently.

"Hell, I don't know. They may be off a barge for all I know. I haven't had time to find out anything yet."

A fight broke out in the far corner of the room and was as quickly stopped by the seamen. In a flat minute the fighters were laughing together and drinking out of the same bottle.

"Larry, we got to get this mob the hell out of your room. Sooner or later they're going to start throwing furniture around and the management will be up with the law. We can't stand a pinch for even a drunken party." One of the seamen came over to us and threw his arm around Larry.

"We're going down to the pub, mates. The gawdamn management won't send up any more ale. Wanna come along?"

We finally got the drunks out of the room and Larry closed the door with a sigh behind him as we followed them downstairs. In the beverage room I picked a table with a group of the more conservative drinkers. Larry went to another table and we became just two more drunks in the crowd.

After two fights, half a dozen beer bottles smashed on the floor and an exchange of snarling arguments with waiters, the manager came in and declared himself, "Get out or I call the police!"

This threat started a real brawl and Larry and I got out with our tablemates while the police were coming in the far door.

"Let's get the hell out of here," I yelled to the three seamen and Larry. We left through a back door and didn't stop running for three blocks when I pulled up gasping at the beverage room entrance to the Victory.

"I'm staying here. Come on in and we'll see if the place is as rough as the Buckingham."

Larry and the other three followed me into the beverage room where the afternoon trade had filled the tables. We found one unoccupied in a far corner and continued the beer party without the brawling of the rest of the crew.

"What happens to those other guys?" Larry asked the oldest of our new friends from the waterfront.

"Depends on what sort of a brawl they get into with the local Bobbies. If it's just a drunk charge, the old man or the shore captain will bail them out. If it turns into a real Pier 6 brawl and they split any heads, they do some time and have to wait for another ship."

I caught Larry's look of interest and knew what was running through his mind. If any of these seamen missed their ship's sailing time, we might be able to ship in their place.

I wanted to talk it over with Larry but he had started a conversation with one of the seamen—who turned out to be a third officer—and wasn't paying any attention to me. They had their heads together and were getting together on something. Other crew members drifted in from the brawl at the Buckingham and were less noisy than before. Three of the seamen had gone to jail and two to a hospital.

"Got your passport, Joe?" Larry asked with his hand stretched across the table. I saw the third officer was already looking at Larry's "Mr. Little" passport. I gave it to Larry who handed it to the mate.

"Your papers are in order and you'd have no trouble landing but you have to get passage from the line's office. The skipper can't book passengers on the dockside. Why not go down to the office now and we can find out if you can sail with us?" The Australian seaman looked at his watch. "It closes at five."

"Let's go," Larry said.

The three of us left in a cab and the mate gave his line's office address to the driver. It was in an office building on Granville and the agent of the line ran it down to us.

"Your papers are alright, gentlemen, but you're American Citizens and you need Internal Revenue receipts from your consulate before I can sell you passage to Hong Kong. We do have cabin space aboard the Maricopa and it would be ideal for you to sail with a crew in which you have friends, but we have regulations which we have to observe meticulously. It's almost five now and I'm afraid the American Consulate will be closed before you could get to it. And the Maricopa sails tonight."

I thought to myself, "We sold the sharpest bunch of cashiers and hotelmen in the US on taking ninety G's worth of counterfeit checks, selling this ship's agent on selling us tickets should be easy."

"Mr. MacGregor, we haven't been in the States for two years. We've been working on a construction job up north. The consulate couldn't provide us with Income Tax receipts if we asked for them. We've been paying our taxes here in Canada," I explained.

"Do you have receipts with you?"

"No, we hadn't planned on sailing right away until we ran into Walt Hagan off the Maricopa." Hagan, the third officer had explained to the agent that we were wartime friends. How Larry talked him into that tale over the afternoon's beer was something I wanted to ask him later.

The seaman came to our rescue, "It's closing time, Mr. MacGregor. Come on and we'll talk it over while we're having an appetizer before supper."

The agent seemed relieved to get out of his office, "Delighted, Walter."

He drove us to the bar in the Georgia and as I looked around I realized we were not dressed for our surroundings. Hagan was in uniform and the agent was in a business suit. Larry and I had on windbreakers and looked a little on the rough side among the cocktail hour trade. I knew we were conspicuous in the Georgia bar.

"Excuse us, Mr. MacGregor and Walt," I said as I nodded to Larry. I had noticed a haberdashery on the way into the Georgia and told Larry about it on our way through the lobby. "We better pick up a couple jackets and shirts and ties if we're going to stay there and we've got to stay with MacGregor until we can induce him to come up with those tickets," I explained. When we returned we wore Harris Tweed jackets, shirts and ties which we had donned right in the store.

"Ah, you look like Vancouverites now," smiled the agent.

"Thank you, Mr. MacGregor," Larry replied, "that's the finest of compliments." Larry turned on his smoothie act while I kept the drinks coming 'til eight o'clock—three solid hours of rum and cokes.

By nine, MacGregor was ready to make out passage tickets and anything else required for boarding the Maricopa as bonafide passengers.

"For old friends we can always stretch a point," he said with an arm around each of us as we lurched into a cab outside the Georgia. I was glad he didn't want to drive. Back at his office we changed from rum to Scotch—after we had the tickets safely in our pockets and MacGregor had 'phoned the dock office. We left him asleep at his desk and piled into another cab with the mate to pick up our bags at the Buckingham and the Victory. Walt fell asleep in the cab.

"I paid him in the last of my old bills," Larry whispered. "They won't bring any heat when he banks them tomorrow. Think there'll be any trouble when he wakes up in the morning and realizes he sold those passages over an evening's drinking?"

"I don't think so," Larry. "He got paid and if he broke any company regulations he won't be in any position to do anything about it."

"I hope you're right, Billy. We'll be unable to do anything about it while on the Maricopa but we'll have one helluva reception when we go ashore in Hong Kong if the law learns we're aboard the Maricopa."

"Wake up, Walt. Heh! Wake up boy." We had to shake the mate awake at the dockside but he came to shaking his own head like a boxer coming out of a knockdown. He looked up at the bow of the black-hulled ocean freighter and spelled out MARICOPA.

"Wonder if the rest of the watch is back aboard?" was his only comment.

He introduced us to the captain and a steward escorted us to our cabin.

"I should probably thank you for getting him back aboard, Mr. Martin," the captain smiled.

"Oh he's not half-bad," I laughed and thought, "you don't realize how gawdamn bad your passengers are, skipper."

The voyage across the Pacific passed without event. We ate with the officers and acted the role we had passed off—or that Larry had originally passed off on the third officer—that we were construction engineers for a company with a job in Hong Kong. Walt Hagan visited us between watches and laughed as he had to ask the events of our first meeting. He wasn't the suspicious type and the open-minded Aussie took us at face value. Larry and I had ample time to talk about plans for the future during the slow freighter's cross-Pacific voyage. After the first day out I couldn't pick up any more news from the States or Canada on the transistor set I'd bought in Frisco. I tired fiddling with it and threw it overboard.

Two days out of Hong Kong, Larry began to grow tense and restless. "I wonder what we'll run into when we *go* ashore, Bill?"

"If these passports and papers stand up we shouldn't have any trouble—providing the law didn't trace us to the Maricopa, Larry."

"That's a helluva provision, Bill."

"Right, but there's not a damn thing we can do about it now. We go ashore and play it by ear. I don't think there's any heat on us. I've watched the captain and the other officers pretty closely and their friendly attitude hasn't changed towards us. And I would have noticed a change in that third mate's attitude if any messages had been sent aboard. The ship's in touch with the shore all the time, I think. If we run into any trouble it will be after we clear the Immigration in Hong Kong."

"You think they've got us on the Interpol network yet, Bill?"

"It's a good bet but if we get ashore in Hong Kong, we cut down the odds against us, Larry." I tried to reassure him as he sat cleaning his .38 and studying it. "Don't let the Interpol boogeyman get to you, Larry. It has no super cops of its own but simply provides a link-up between police forces of the world. It puts our descriptions out on a radio and teletype network and provides information about our records, modus operandi, and what we're wanted for. The Treasury Department's Office of Law Enforcement Coordination is its outlet back in the States and you know damn well the Treasury has a complete dossier on both of us."

"I think we get a break from just that, Billy."

"Why?" I asked and noticed that Larry had perked up just from listening to my amateur explanation of the Interpol.

"The Treasury agents have nailed both of us before and they know we used to lam south of the border. To their knowledge we've never been off the continent and they won't figure us for it this time."

"Hope you're right, Larry. Put that away," I said as I turned to the cabin door. "Come in." It was Walt Hagan, the third mate.

"Any plans for Hong Kong, boys?"

"We have to see our company first," replied Larry. "You got the itch for a party again?"

The mate laughed, "No, I'll be on watch and we don't have much cargo to unload. But leave your address with our office ashore and I'll get in touch with you when we make port again. It's a great town for partying. How long do you expect to be in Hong Kong?" he asked.

"The job should last a year," replied Larry.

We talked for a while about Hong Kong and Walt told us of his home in Queensland. When the Aussie seaman left I felt sure no news had reached the Maricopa of our real identity.

We were up early and Larry and I were looking down on the junks and sampans of crowded Hong harbor when I saw the official-looking boat cruising towards the Maricopa and flying a Union Jack from its stern.

The steward relieved our fears, "'ere comes 'er Majesty's Customs and Immigration, sir."

We watched the officers go to the captain's cabin and I felt the sweat on the palms of my hands when the steward called us. I followed Larry into the cabin where the captain introduced us to the officials. The examination was brief and business like and before the questioning was over I realized there was no heat on us—from these officials. They were satisfied with our papers and I explained to the Customs officer that our trunks were coming by air. He advised where we should claim them in Hong Kong and turned to his business with the captain.

"All the gawdamn worry and sweating for nothing," laughed Larry back in the cabin where we packed to go ashore.

We played the tourist traps at night and shopped in the afternoons for a week. Larry and I had our first argument at the end of the week.

"Why can't we move to a first class hotel? Did we work nine years setting up that caper and commit murder to get away only to live in this gawdamn hovel?" Larry snarled at me when I said "no" to moving. He had picked up some singer and wanted to impress her.

"If you think this is a hovel, let me take you to the border and show you some of the refugees from Commie China and then follow them to what they have to call 'home'. You move into a swank hotel and you'll be in jail in twenty-four hours. You think the heat's off us? You think we're in the clear? If you do, Larry, you're a damn fool—and I mean it."

"We're just another couple tourists here and you can get lost in a crowd in this city in a bat of an eyelash. You're losing your nerve, Billy."

A knock at the door stopped the argument. Larry walked to it and I stepped back behind a screen and pulled out my .38, peeking through the crack to see who knocked at an apartment door when its owners were unknown.

"Excuse me, I am looking for a Mr. Little and a Mr. Martin—I am Chan Lee." It was a tall Cantonese, dressed well in a well tailored western suit.

"I work for Mr. Little," Larry said, "what do you want with him? You can leave a message."

"May I come in?" the Cantonese asked.

Larry opened the door and not only Lee came in but also two other Chinese.

"What the hell is this?" Larry shouted at the three intruders. The two behind Lee had guns in their hands, pointing at Larry. I waited.

"Sit down, Mr. Jennings. Nothing to get excited about." He pushed Larry into a chair and threw an FBI wanted circular on the table beside the chair.

"A small piece of paper which may interest you," the Cantonese smiled, pointing to the flyer. "Or did you think you'd been forgotten? That was a good haul you made in Las Vegas, Mr. Jennings. And where is your partner, Mr. Martin?"

"He's out," Larry answered.

"We can wait, Mr. Jennings. We don't have to hurry."

The Cantonese pulled a Beretta from his pocket and levelled it at Larry and without turning away told the other two Chinese to look around. I had set up the silk screen to keep the breeze and noise from the open French window which faced a gallery-type balcony and I stepped back on it and pressed close to the wall. If one of the searchers stepped out on that balcony he'd die fast or I would drop three stories to the street below.

"Empty," was the report of the searchers when they looked into the bedrooms. One glanced casually behind the screen but didn't look out at me. I stepped back inside.

"What do you bastards want?" Larry growled at Chan Lee.

"Merely to help you and your friend. We're noted for our hospitality here, Mr. Jennings."

"Spell it out, you bastard," Larry barked at him and moved half out of his chair.

"Siddown," one of the Chinese growled back at Larry and smashed the side of his head with a blue automatic.

"Don't get rough with us, Mr. Jennings. We call the plays here."

I wanted to let fly at the Chinese who hit Larry but held back when I saw Lee's Beretta still pointing at Larry. Larry was holding a handkerchief against his head, sopping up the blood.

"Well, what the hell do you want?" Larry repeated.

"What's left of the ninety thousand dollars American you took from the casinos at Las Vegas. In return we offer you your freedom."

"In return you offer me and Bill a grave in Hong Kong harbor or a cell in the prison," mocked Larry. "Let me put a bandage on my head," he asked.

That was my clue and when Lee stepped back I threw a shot at the nearest Chinese. Larry lurched at Lee and grabbed his gun arm. The Beretta went off sending a shot into the ceiling as Larry and Lee fell to the floor. I flattened out and got two slugs into the second Chinese before I had a chance to get to Larry who had a half Nelson on the Cantonese. While Larry held his head I pistol-whipped him to give him a taste of what his oriental hood had given Larry.

"That's enough," gasped Larry, "I want some information from this bastard." Lee sank to the floor. I looked back at the two Chinese gunmen and saw one reaching across the floor for his automatic. I brought my heel down on his wrist and heard the bones crack. Larry scooped up his gun and pocketed it. I frisked him and Lee while Larry went over the other body. They carried a total of six guns and three knives.

"They came prepared," Bill.

"Put a bandage on that cut on your head, Larry, and bring some adhesive tape back here for this bastard. I want him tied up when he comes to."

"Think those shots will bring anybody?" Larry asked while I was taping the Cantonese's wrists and legs.

"Hell no. You could fire off a cannon in this neighborhood and no one would hear it. And if anyone did, they mind their own business. I guess these people have troubles of their own," I replied. Lee groaned and strained against the tape.

"Now *we* call the plays, *Mr.* Lee," Larry growled.

"For a while," observed the cool Cantonese.

"How did you get a line on us?" Larry asked.

The oriental smile infuriated Larry and he kicked the side of the Chinaman's head tearing off part of his ear and knocking him out again.

"You won't get much information out of him that way, Larry," I told him.

"I'll kill the sunuvabich trying." He threw some water from the bathroom sink on Lee's face and started again as soon as he regained consciousness.

"Talk or die—slowly—Lee," was the matter-of-fact proposition Larry made to him. The Cantonese saw the light and started to talk.

"The Hong Kong police do not know you're here. I have a friend who gets me photostats of these wanted circulars and we have more eyes than the police. We find you. Shake you down," Lee explained to Larry, running down his unique extortion racket. His victims, illegally in Hong Kong could not go to the police when the Cantonese shook them down—if he let them live to go anywhere.

"Who else knows about us in Hong Kong?" Larry asked.

Lee only smiled. "If I answer that one, you kill me. That is *my* protection, Mr. Jennings."

Larry slapped him across the mouth, "Talk or I'll kill you anyway," he snarled.

"You kill me, you never learn who follows you, Mr. Jennings."

Larry sent three quick shots into Lee's head. "At least you won't follow me, you bastard," was his only comment as he sat down on a couch and looked up at me. "He asked for it, Bill."

I agreed and didn't say a word.

"What now," Larry asked.

I couldn't resist my opportunity, "Maybe you still want to move into that swank hotel with your night club singer, boy?"

"Wise guy," he smiled.

"We've got only one move left, Larry. To Macao," I answered. "If those phoney visas got us by the Hong Kong Immigration they should get us into Macao. I checked at the Portuguese consulate the other day and my passport is OK, so your own should be too. What do we do with these bodies?"

"Leave them right where they are and head for Macao," Larry shrugged. "Pack up while I wash up and change clothes. My head feels like a morning after."

It was a superficial cut on his temple and a bandage would stop the bleeding. I packed while Larry fixed his head and changed.

From the Hong Kong steamer I looked out at Macao and its whitewashed buildings which, cluttered on the hillsides, presented a disappointing view. Its appearance made me think of a small Mexican seaport rather than the mysterious Portuguese colony it was rumored to be among more well-travelled American thieves I'd met.

The narrow bay was crowded with junks and sampans and the streets were jammed with refugees.

"This town is more Chinese than Hong Kong," Larry observed as we walked along the twisting cobblestone street.

"You're criticizing your 'home town,' Larry. This is the end of the road—like it or not."

"It's sure not plush," was his only comment.

"Exchange it for what's waiting for us back in the States?" I asked. The boys picking up our bags stopped our down-at-the-mouth philosophizing.

We located a house away from the harbor and the tourist traps—away from strangers and pursuers who we know are still pursuing us. But its red-tiled roof and surrounding whitewashed wall is a prison to both of us. Larry haunts the gambling halls and is kicking back loot from the Vegas casinos to the less plush ones in Macao. I've shacked up with a part Portuguese-part Chinese-part nymphomaniac whose charms flare up and die down in heroin nightmares. Larry hits the bottle and calls us a pair of hopheads.

"One of these nights I'll catch the ferry back to Hong Kong," is his intermittent threat. "I've had enough of this gawdamn place."

"One of these days, Larry, they'll catch up with us and we'll hold court on the cobblestones of Macao," is my usual reply. "I get tired too, looking over my shoulder but it's a watching, waiting game. We watch for the law and wait for the Mafia or some other American hood to come gunning. Like you said the day we landed here—'it's sure not plush'."

The Grass Cage
Robert Edmond Alter

January 1964

I am halfway through my third cigarette. I smoked the first two in ten minutes. That was four minutes ago. I can't stall any longer—Haney would consider it 'bad form.' When I finish this smoke we'll go in.

We are standing in a little spread of acacia trees; Haney, the white hunter, Jim Cass, my partner, Billali, Nagool, Bopa, the gun bearers, and Kuku and Hose Nose, the two trackers. Rising on our left is a scrub hill, rising to timber along the ridge. Eastward the plain stretches out for fifteen miles, dotted with little mounds of orchard bush. The far mountain is almost purple because of the distance, but I don't know its name.

And in front of us is the thicket. It is big and it is dense and a man would have to be insane to go in there. Thin reaching reed and tall wavering grass; so tall I can tell from here that it will tower over our heads. We won't be able to see the sky, we'll probably have to crawl, there won't be enough air to breathe, and our visibility will be limited to one yard.

And that damn gut-shot meaner-than-Satan Cape buffalo had to run in there to hide.

It was my fault. It was my shot and I snafu-ed the detail. Haney and Cass had been working along the hill coming south to the acacia stand. I had dropped over the ridge, working down to the swale of tall grass, with Hose Nose and Bopa. Hose Nose was in the lead, and as he approached a giant thorn tree he motioned me down with an urgent demand of his hand.

"*Nyati*" he hissed at me in Swahili.

My mind fumbled off on a frantic memory excursion through the Swahili-English book Haney had given me at the beginning of the safari. Drawing a blank I looked at Bopa. He had my .308 Winchester; I had the Remington. He set the rifle across his knees and hooked his forefingers, put them to his temples and made pop-eyes at me.

Buffalo.

I crawled over to Hose Nose and the thorn tree. He grinned at me and I noticed that his lips trembled. Maybe it was just excitement, anticipation, but it didn't help me any.

"*Doumi sana,*" he whispered. Fine bull.

I nodded and raised my head. .

It wasn't just any old buffalo; it was the African Black Cape.

I don't know why, but when I looked out and saw him standing there sixty yards off—squat, barrel-bodied, bluish-black, nearly hairless, the great black horns curving downward—backward—forward—upward and inward—I suddenly sensed the loss of something I'd always unconsciously held as invulnerable; nothing physical, just the quality man recognizes in himself as his manhood. Cape buffalo—intelligent, quick, powerful; considered by many to be the world's most dangerous game. I wet my lips and glanced at Hose Nose.

When he grinned his upper lip punched under the overhang of that ample snout, looking for a moment as though the teeth meant to snap the nose-ball. *"Piga!"* he hissed. Shoot. Hit. Kill.

I looked back at the Caper, raised the .30-06 Remington and slipped the safety. I rose slowly, bringing the butt to my shoulder. The Cape was barrel-rump on to me but angling leisurely as he browsed muzzle-down in the weed, swinging his starboard into my sights.

And suddenly it was all right again and I had my manhood back. I could feel it burning through me like a double shot of whiskey and I knew I had him cold. One second after I squeezed the trigger the world's most dangerous game would be down and kicking, dying.

I started the slow squeeze. And then those rotten little buffalo birds hit the air and the jig was up. The Caper snorted, swinging his head high, all mad right now and looking for someone to take it out on. He spooked forward and I jerked the trigger.

We all heard the whack of the slug, saw him stumble, but he hitch-kicked, plowing the swale grass like a tank and he was on his way.

"Piga! Piga!" those two damn fools were screeching, and from the north I could hear Cass bellowing something, and through it all the tone but not the sense of Haney's voice shouting instructions, and the Caper swung off his furrowing course and lammed for the thicket, and me losing my control like a homicidal maniac and jerking . . . *Blam! Blam-blam-blam!* and seeing the marsh pools spray up beyond the buffalo as the high powered slugs spanked them, and Bopa and Hose Nose rushing downgrade still screeching, Bopa with my Winchester, me bellowing at him to bring it back, stumbling after them, fumble-fingering shells into the furshlugginer clip, and last the reeds and grass swallowing up the Cape buffalo like Moses in the bulrushes, and then nothing—only eight men standing panting in the short grass under the shadowy spread of acacias.

And all Haney could say was, "Well, we'll have to *go* in and finish him."

It is very warm now, and if you step from under the green shade of the acacias the sun is straight up and it presses down on you until you feel like a rubber ball being squeezed in a prizefighter's hand.

Bopa and Nagool are standing off a little by themselves. They don't look happy. Neither does Haney but he tries to cover it. He takes long hard drags at his cigarette, glances speculatively at the thicket, letting smoke dwindle out his nostrils, then glances at Cass, and then at me. He knows. I think they all do. I can't help it. I've lost it again—for good, I think. I don't want to go in there.

No, God, I really don't.

I could let Haney carry the show alone; let him go in there for the sake of 'good form.' It's what Cass and I are paying him for. I could, if I could find some way of living with myself after that. But there isn't any way, there just isn't. And suddenly I hate Haney, because if he wasn't here I could just turn my back on the thicket and the wounded buffalo and walk off. No, I couldn't either. There are the boys and there is Cass, and I am a coward to the point that I am scared to death of appearing cowardly.

So we'll go in and try to finish the damn gut-shot Cape buffalo.

He's hiding in there somewhere with a gut like red pulp, and every time he breathes the pain rips through him like he'd swallowed barbed wire, and he's waiting with his pig-eyes all bright with hate and he's concentrating his libido on one purpose. Us. He's going to charge when we're right on top of him and we won't see him until it's too late and he's going to use his bone helmet-head as a battering ram and he's going to use his horns to do the things to our guts that I've done to his and it's going to be hell on a pogo stick.

And I saved my money for six years to make this buggy safari: busted my back for six long years to come halfway across the world to die in this lousy, airless, skyless thicket; and I wouldn't marry the girl I loved because at the last moment she might have said No, and what can you say to a pretty young wife who says No? and I'm glad now I didn't marry her because she might have said Yes, and in an hour from now she'd be a widow and I never did carry enough insurance.

So we'll go in and try to finish the damn gut-shot Cape buffalo.

In a minute we will.

I wipe at my mouth. My hand is trembling as if I'd been working a pneumatic drill. Haney is still showing us how to exhale smoke through the nostrils. And Cass is doing everything an embarrassed man can do who wants to speak and not offend, and doing them all wrong.

"Look, Joe—" he starts. "No reason why I shouldn't tag along in there. I mean, we're in this thing together and—"

I shake my head. "No, this is my scene. I botched the damn thing and I've got to put it right. Haney knows that."

Haney drops his cig-butt and places his boot on it carefully. We both watch him do it. Then he speaks to the ground.

"That's right, Mr. Cass. Four of us is too many in there as it is."

"Well, I know, but still—"

"Get off it, will you, Jim?" I say a little sharper than I should.

Now we're all embarrassed and no one says anything. We look at the cig-butt mashed in the dirt.

"Hose Nose will track," Haney says abruptly. "I'll tag him with the Weatherby and you can back me up with Bopa—"

I shake my head. I'm childishly stubborn about my questionable manhood. "No. I'll tag Hose Nose. *You* back me."

Haney says, "Well—" and the word sags into a little silence-pit and sits there stupidly. Then he kicks it aside and gets down to business. "Don't put your sights on his head. That horn-base of his is just like the steel pots we used in the war. Maybe tougher. If he charges it'll be with his neck and head straight out. Whack him right down the snout. Or square in the chest is good too. Then—"

"All right. I've got it. For crysake let's not gab about it all day." I mash out my cigarette and take the Remington from Bopa. All the blue sheen is out of his face, replaced by gray suspense. I wonder what mine looks like.

Cass does a pretty good job on a grin.

"Show the big slob who's boss, Joe."

I let him see that I can make a ghastly grin also.

"Sure. Right down the snout. Be back in a bit."

I look at Haney. "Ready?"

He says, "Let's ramble."

Hose Nose is waiting at the edge of the thicket. He's down on one knee holding his spear like an antenna, inspecting the blood spoor in the grass. He's looking good too, just like a man who has received the word from a somber-eyed doctor: "No, Mr. Hose Nose, I'm afraid you don't have the three-day flu. It's leukemia."

He looks at Haney and then points into the grass. Haney nods.

It's a green wall. It must be ten foot tall and as thick as stacked bricks. But there's a little doorway, a passage where the buffalo lammed for cover. We start in; Hose Nose pushing ahead, rotten egg-stepping; me with the Remington; Haney with the Weatherby; Bopa in the rear with the Springfield he doesn't know how to use.

Here, there, skip a couple of yards, then again the spatterings of blood, still bright in the limpid centers, just starting to congeal at the edges. A fair spoor. No sweat. Should lead us right up face to face with Bingo. Only it's going to be blam-o with the bone-hard head, and hook-o with the giant size horns, and then guts-o all over the lousy grass . . .

Stop it, for God's sake, stop it, I order myself. But why did it have to be a rotten gut-shot? Why couldn't I hit the big slob clean? Why did I have to work and save and not marry for six years just to come all the way over here to fritz-up the furshlugginer shot?

I look at Hose Nose's naked back ahead of me, wobbling slowly from side to side like a deaf-mute without equilibrium, all slick mahogany except for an old blue-ridged scar under the right shoulderblade, where once upon a time he must have been mighty lucky.

I look down at the Remington, feeling its heft and grip in my damp hands, liking the feeling . . . and see that the stupid safety is off. I ease it on, hoping that Haney doesn't notice. Then I ask myself a bright question: Did I reload after I went crazy on the ridge? For a vivid moment everything suspends in me, threatening to drop. But no—no for crysake. Of course I reloaded. Take it easy. Try to take it easy, will you? Sure. I'm all right.

But I'm not. There is no sky overhead. The grass keeps whipping back in my face, powdering me with salty dust. The air is punk. The damn Moses reed is getting thicker, taller. The passageway is becoming a tunnel. The blood spoor is sparse now and other tunnels are criss-crossing us, passages burrowed by other beasts—maybe rhinos. Oh nice! Swell thought, Joe. Keep it up. How about a nice lion? Hey, that's the ticket, Joe-boy! With claws like meathooks and teeth like straight-edge razors.

I want out. I'm bugged bad and I want out. I'm wired for the heeby-jeebies. I glance back at Haney. He looks at me questioningly. *Are you all right?* I nod and look ahead. *Sure* . . . sure, except that the lousy tunnel is closing down. Sure, except that there are so many tributary passages now that Hose Nose has gotten himself lost. He's standing there in waiting bewilderment, blinking around at the green cage.

We all stand, looking, listening. Nothing. Nothing, except that I want a smoke; except that the shoving shoulder of claustrophobia is starting to crowd me. Then Hose Nose picks it up again. He points at a little drying dab of blood and mutters something in Swahili.

But there's a rub. The tunnel has narrowed. It's no longer possible to walk upright. We'll have to continue at a crouch, maybe on hands and knees. I look at Haney, catching a glimmer of Bopa's head beyond his shoulder. The gun bearer's face looks like a pan of old gray dough that's been left out in the rain.

Haney is whispering to me. "If he charges *(why must the man always start out with* 'If he charges?' *He knows damn well the big gut-shot slob is going to charge),* don't worry about Hose Nose. It's his job to get clear, just start pumping at that nose—the Cape's, I mean. If you can't break him down, jump to the side, whack him in the shoulder as he goes by. I'll bop him in the snout. All right?"

I nod looking down at the peaty earth under our boots. Why, I wonder, do men hunt? For the fun? Oh my God! The thrill of danger? Well, buster, there's plenty of that, and anyone who cares to crawl in here and ask for my share can have it.

Haney is trying to un-funk me. He's smiling and it looks as though it must hurt his cheeks like frostbite. "This could be worse," he says. "Wait until next Monday when we go after simba."

There's that damn lion again. Yeah . . . yeah, I'll wait. I can see myself crawling through a blind trap like this shagging a wounded lion. Oh yeah, I'll definitely wait.

So we start on again on the crouch this time, me tagging Hose Nose's rump instead of his back. And it gets worse, and the claustrophobia is sweltering and it is airless and dust-gagging and I know Hose Nose can't see a yard beyond his face and to top it all off he has to drop to his hands and knees to penetrate the thicket and I like a damn fool have to follow him and if something big comes at us now we'll go down like ninepins on a chain reaction to smash-o.

I feel like a skin diver, feel a frightening kinship with the men who fin into the nothingness of underwater to meet the quarry on its own home ground. The hunter may have his high powered rifle, the skin diver his CO2 gun, but the edge is still with the quarry—it was born there. It can breath where there isn't air; it can see where the visibility is void; it can run, jump, cut, or charge where the hunter is hamstrung in the thickets and the skin diver in the water pressure. And perhaps that's why we hunt, because there is something in us—something perversely stupid I'm beginning to think—that craves for a gamble where the odds are on the other fellow's side.

I don't know. I know it's not like Mallory's mountain; we don't do it simply because it's there to be done. It's deeper than that—if anything *can* be deeper than that. I don't know. Whatever it is I've lost it. I want out.

I look back at Haney, his head inches from my beam. He gives a short blank nod, whispers, "It'll widen in a moment."

I look forward at Hose Nose's hunched body, at the green wall shoving in front of him, and I think of Haney, the Bwana M'kubwa. Somewhere I read, or was told, that the average life of a white hunter after he adopts his trade is from six to seven years. And I'm thinking of Haney who is forty if he's a day and who told me himself that he came out here in his early twenties. So he's had a long run of luck. So he's had his share and enough for a couple of other Bwanas as well. So maybe today is the end of his run. Maybe when the sun rose this morning it rose on Haney's day of non-luck.

Something takes off overhead with a wild *flat-a-flat-a-flatter* and I jump as if Haney had pronged my prat with his hunting knife. Hose Nose is cowering before me, his muddy eyes fright-big and angling up and over his shoulder, gawping at the green roof above. Everything about him makes me feel just like hell.

"Wood-pigeons," Haney murmures.

I twist a look at him. "Buffalo birds?" I suggest.

He shrugs. "Goose Hose Nose along," he orders.

We push on, listening very closely now.

The tunnel opens abruptly like a cave-mouth. We file out into a passageway where we can actually stand. Overhead we can even see a few scratchy little traces of turquoise sky. It's much better. I feel a hell of a lot better . . . but if I could just have a cigarette. Hose Nose is contemplating the spoor again. He has three forks to choose from. From where we stand they all appear to run into blind alleys. He says something to himself and points straight ahead.

I start to follow him when my foot snags in a root and for a split-second I'm all over myself to keep from falling and making a smash of noise. But Haney has me under an armpit with his free hand and I lurch to balanced footing. It's nothing. A slight accident and no damage done. But Hose Nose hasn't observed it and it's given him time to work himself some yards ahead of me.

As I look forward I see him stepping through a loose screen of undulating grass. I start after him to catch up . . . and right now we hear the full-chested snort.

I stop dead, Haney slamming into me. There is a rush of something and a scream that magically turns the passageway into a shammering green ball that instantly destroys equilibrium, and there is a clean *whaamp!* of sound and I know death is coming like a flying wedge and out of the green hurtles Hose Nose. He's coming ankles over appetite, as helpless as a black ragbag struck by an open bucket of red paint, and something that must be a black locomotive is thundering right after him, and somebody—has to be Haney—is screaming "*Shoot!* You damn—" and I see the outstretched square head and the slick glistening-like-silver muzzle and the great low-slung bat-ears and the black horns and . . .

Something triggers in me like a spring gun and I hit the reed wall in a blind fury of smashing, plowing, boot-lashing, hand-clawing, head-butting insanity. I dump the trick right in Haney's lap and I'm out of there.

The noise is all rolled into a ball, break it down and it is the smash of the thicket, the bellow of the Cape buffalo, Bopa's scream, and the *car-room!* of Haney's Weatherby. And I don't care. I want to care, should care, but I can't. I've got to get out. The animal instinct has awakened in me, is leading me, dragging me to safety. The unconscious vortex of self-preservation is snatching me out of danger as though I were a ball on a string. It is inexorable.

I run.

If you can call it that! crashing, lunging, hand-pulling along, falling . . . I am on the ground. It is damp, porous, unwholesome with hundreds of little crawling things. I am gasping for my breath, looking around, listening.

The Cape buffalo is snorting somewhere, far off. But there was only the one shot. Then Haney missed . . . and what's become of him? I remember Haney's non-luck day and say, *So I called the shot.* But I can't settle for that, because to man the death of a close friend or loved one is incongruous. We can believe in the death of a stranger, that's easy, but not when it happens to someone we know.

"Haney!" I shout.

There is nothing. Now even the Caper is quiet.

I've got to get out of here. I start crawling, crawl into a tunnel and follow it. What if I run smack into the buffalo? I'm unarmed. I've lost the damn Remington. Never mind about that. Can't be helped. You've got to take your chances and hope for the best. Anyway, you were unarmed even when you had the gun. The man who has a gun and can't use it has no advantage over a man who is unarmed. All right, I was gutless. All right, goddam it. We'll talk about it later. When I get out of here.

If I get out.

Crawly things on me, in everything, everywhere, slip-sliding in my sweat. Bugs. Bugs all over the furshlugginer place; on me, in the grass, around my head, buzzing high-frequency in my ears. Grass and reed—like worming through a ton of barbed wire. No air to breathe. Just bugs. Bugs to breathe. It's enough to drive a man . . .

Something is coming at me, coming down the tunnel my way. I rear back in a panic. Nowhere to turn. Nowhere to run. *My God*—

It is a young hyena, the common striped brown. We meet face to face, the mammal all eyes, ears high and wide open, me with my hands out half-clawed, ready to fight. When he suddenly laughs his fear he is a ventriloquist; it comes from the wrong direction. In a wink he makes his decision: hunkers in on himself, pivots—seemingly turning inside out—shows me his drooping hindquarters and is gone.

I crawl on with the shakes.

In a minute I enter a larger passage, a familiar one. Our boot marks are visible in the soggy earth. This is the way the four of us came to track the Cape buffalo.

For a delicious moment the world is a beautiful place. All I have to do is backtrack to the acacia grove. Then I'll be out of it. Then I'll tell Cass that Haney, Hose Nose and Bopa had their non-luck day; that the buffalo won; that he, Cass, can come to hell in here if he wants, but that I'm through.

That's what I think in the first moment. Then I think of the hyena—the way he turned himself tailover-teeth to escape me. I must have looked that way when I saw the buffalo coming at me. I must have looked like a scared witless animal. That isn't the nicest picture in the world for a man.

And Haney?

I look along our track. Haney's down there somewhere. Dead?

Maybe today's hunter is merely a throwback to the dim ancestor who once left his cave with a club in hand to face a saber-toothed tiger. Maybe we think we owe that ancestor something. Maybe we have an unconscious urge to prove to his memory that in spite of our tranquilized, TV-ed civilization we still have something in us that goes deeper than muscle, bone and blood. Maybe.

But you don't walk out on Haney without knowing whether he's alive or dead. That's one thing you don't do. You may run—run long and hard, but in the end you come back.

All right dammit. So we go back.

I come to the opening where we met the Cape buffalo head-on. It is larger now because the walls have been smashed back all around. Hose Nose is near my feet. He is a dead man. *Kufa.* The Cape's cannon ball head took care of Hose Nose. The Weatherby is lying a few yards beyond. I go and pick it up, eject the expended shell and slide in a new one. Then I see Haney.

He's on his back in the grass, his left leg drawn up and cocked over his outstretched right as though he is preparing to run. But his eyes are closed and there is a ragged rent across his jacket, starting near the stomach and ripping up to his left shoulder. I bend down to him and see that the exposed flesh of his chest is bluish-black. Hooked and hit by the Cape's off horn. But the skin is still in one piece—purple and swollen but no blood.

I take his pulse and feel better. It was not his non-luck day.

I look around. "Bopa?" I say softly.

There is a new passageway opening across the aisle. The Winchester is at the threshold and I can see that it has been trampled.

It is only guesswork, but the conclusion is that with Hose Nose knocked galley west, with me out of the way, the buffalo tried to ram or hook Haney as he fired, clipped him aside and then charged on after Bopa. And Bopa—God love him—must have ran just as I did, must have made his own panic-passage through the reed.

I look down at the Weatherby, feeling its heft and grip in my hands, liking it. Then I start tracking the buffalo.

It is a long way down the passage and it must be working from center outward because the grass is shorter and there is sky overhead, but though I am aware of it I don't dare look up. I ease my way steadily through the trampled, shoved-aside reed, and I seem to be walking down the road that thirty years ago I was born for the express purpose of finding, that I might walk down it and meet someone who will be waiting at the far end for me, and when I meet the someone I will know that the thirty years have been for nothing and that they are finished and that it never really mattered to the scheme of things anyway.

And there is the Cape buffalo.

He is standing in a small grass chamber. His head is down, his eyes blinking with sickness, and I see the scarlet blotch on his underslung belly where I first started this whole damn mess. I don't see Bopa and that is something at least.

I pull in my breath and raise the Weatherby. And the Cape buffalo turns his head and looks at me. Something clicks out of whack inside me and the little monitor of my mind slips into limbo as though edging me into suicide and I stall.

You and me now, Cape, I say to him. *Come and get it.*

And then I'm all right and I know it. Even as his head and neck stretch out and his hoofs get underway, I feel it. And the rifle goes *caa-lam!* But I've jerked the witch. Bone fragments splinter off his head like shrapnel and he's flying at me like the mainspring from a nightmare and I jerk *caa-lam! caa-lam!* and the head and horns are jumping and spitting bone chips, and that glistening-like-black-silver muzzle is reaching right for me, and the two round hate-eyes see me and only me in all this world, and saliva like mercury streams straight back from his muzzle, and the Weatherby goes *caa-lam!* right down his snout as he knocks the barrel flying and his head yanks up and rearward and his bulky body skitters around off course and I leap clear as his snout sprays the air with blood and matter-clots, and he's down, legs kicking, body trying to roll sideways, not making it, head still yanking away from body as if trying to shake loose from the .300 slug that's made mush of his brain, and I step in and lower the rifle and blast his spine and that's all.

Over. I feel weird. I feel like my stomach wants to say goodby to breakfast. I hold onto the rifle hard and let the shakes take care of the rest of me. I . . .

What does it matter? There's nothing to be said. I walk on out of there.

Haney's all right. We have him propped against an acacia tree and Cass has just finished wrapping his chest with everything he could find in the first aid box. He says:

"I'm going back to the wagon and fetch the bottle. This calls for a drink. Right?"

Haney puts a cigarette in his mouth and nods. "Good idea. Better feed Bopa one, too—a short one. He needs it."

Bopa's all right. He'd made his way out of the thicket and had gone to fetch Cass and the others while I was finishing the Cape.

Haney looks at me and smiles. "Well, you got him," he says.

"Yes—finally. The second time."

Haney says nothing. I think he knows but he isn't going to bring it up. I've got to.

"When he charged and I leaped into the reed—I was running. I ran to hell out of there. Pure funk."

Haney looks at the thicket. "Important thing is that you got him," he says. He scrouges into a more comfortable position, but he still doesn't look at me.

"Look—there's no reason why you have to rush into this simba business come Monday. What we encountered today can unnerve a man. I know. And lion hunting isn't child's play. Why don't we reschedule the lions until later? Or, if Cass objects to that, I'll go out with him. You can shook kudu."

He's embarrassing himself trying to make it easy for me.

"Don't get the idea anyone will look down on you if you decide to wait on the lions. Not after what you've been through today."

I say nothing. I think of how the rifle felt in my hands, remember how it felt slamming out shots as that four-legged locomotive charged me. Maybe hunters aren't complex. Give a man a rifle and he simply likes the feel of it. Perhaps we are like Mallory and his mountain after all.

Cass is back with the jug and three tin cups. I take mine, smile at Haney, and give the toast:

"Here's to the three of us come Monday," I say

Also available from Stark House Press:

The Best of *Manhunt*
A Collection of the Best Stories
From *Manhunt* Magazine
Foreword by Lawrence Block
Afterword by Barry N. Malzberg
Edited and Introduction by Jeff Vorzimmer
ISBN: 978-1-944520-68-7 $21.95

The Best of *Manhunt* 2
More of the Best from *Manhunt* Magazine
Foreword by Peter Enfantino
Introduction by Jon Breen
Edited and Introduction by Jeff Vorzimmer
ISBN: 978-1-951473-05-1 $21.95

The *Manhunt* Companion
The complete issue-by-issue compendium
to Manhunt Magazine, January 1953
to April/May 1967, with story and
author indexes.
Edited by Peter Enfantino and Jeff Vorzimmer
ISBN: 978-1-951473-44-0 $19.95